JOHN JAKES'

Sensational Action-Packed New Saga

Twenty Years of Turbulent Growth and Expansion that Bound Two Families and Split a Young Nation

NORTH
AND
SOUTH

"Jakes at his best . . . keep[s] the reader turning pages."
— *Boston Herald American*

"A panoramic, populous . . . lusty trek through the pages of American history . . . thick as a brick with period detail drawn from extensive research. . . . Say it for Jakes that [he] makes the reader care about his characters . . . that he has a firm grip on the intricate connections between private lives and public events. NORTH AND SOUTH is an honest piece of work."

— Jonathan Yardley, *San Francisco Chronicle*

"Jakes has few peers. . . . What [he] can do that history books can't is draw the reader into the mid-1800s, letting us feel the emotions of participants and helping us to understand on a personal level what led Americans to the bloodiest conflict this nation has ever faced. . . . He winds a spell . . . that won't be broken until the last page of the last volume is turned."
— *Detroit Free Press*

"This is historical novel writing at its best."

—*Library Journal*

"A marvelous, lively romp. . . . A superb storyteller, [Jakes] brings a robust excitement to history. . . . The wait for Volume 2 will be unbearable."

—*The Columbus Dispatch*

"The essence of Jakes . . . high on adventure . . . has a sweep as wide as an antebellum lady's skirt. . . . At the very heart of every Jakes saga is a story that throbs to the beat of history." —*The Plain Dealer* (Cleveland)

"[NORTH AND SOUTH has] the story and pacing to keep you turning pages. . . . Jakes has left unfired guns on the mantelpiece. . . . Saga fans will eagerly anticipate the concluding volumes." —*San Diego Union*

BY JOHN JAKES:

Love and War

The Kent Family Chronicles

The Bastard
The Rebels
The Seekers
The Furies
The Titans
The Warriors
The Lawless
The Americans

NORTH AND SOUTH

John Jakes

A Dell • Harcourt Brace Jovanovich Book

Published by
Dell Publishing Co., Inc.
1 Dag Hammarskjold Plaza
New York, New York 10017

and

Harcourt Brace Jovanovich, Inc.
Orlando, Florida 32887

Dell ® TM 681510, Dell Publishing Co., Inc.

ISBN: 0-440-16205-X

Printed in the United States of America

One previous paperback edition

New paperback edition
First printing—November 1985

In memory of
Jonathan Daniels
Islander, Southerner, American, Friend

*Lover and friend hast thou put
far from me, and mine acquaintance
into darkness.*

PSALM 88

PROLOGUE: TWO FORTUNES

1686: *The Charcoal Burner's Boy*

"The lad should take my name," Windom said after supper. "It's long past time."

It was a sore point with him, one he usually raised when he'd been drinking. By the small fire, the boy's mother closed the Bible on her knees.

Bess Windom had been reading to herself as she did every evening. From watching her lips move, the boy could observe her slow progress. When Windom blurted his remark, Bess had been savoring her favorite verse in the fifth chapter of Matthew: "Blessed are they which are persecuted for righteousness' sake: for theirs is the kingdom of heaven."

The boy, Joseph Moffat, sat with his back against a corner of the chimney, whittling a little boat. He was twelve, with his mother's stocky build, broad shoulders, light brown hair, and eyes so pale blue they seemed colorless sometimes.

Windom gave his stepson a sullen look. A spring rain beat on the thatch roof. Beneath Windom's eyes, smudges of charcoal dust showed. Nor had he gotten the dust from under his broken nails. He was an oafish failure, forty now. When he wasn't drunk, he cut wood and smoldered it in twenty-foot-high piles for two weeks, making charcoal for the small furnaces along the river. It was dirty, degrading work; mothers in the neighborhood controlled their errant youngsters with warnings that the charcoal man would get them.

Joseph said nothing, just stared. Windom didn't miss the tap-tap of the boy's index finger on the handle of his knife. The boy had a high temper. Sometimes Windom was terrified of him. Not just now, though. Joseph's silence, a familiar form of defiance, enraged the stepfather.

Finally Joseph spoke. "I like my own name." He returned his gaze to his half-carved coracle.

"By God, you cheeky whelp," Windom cried in a raspy voice, overturning his stool as he lunged toward the youngster.

11

Bess jumped between them. "Let him be, Thad. No true disciple of our Savior would harm a child."

"Who wants to harm who? Look at him!"

Joseph was on his feet and backed against the chimney. The boy's chest rose and fell fast. Unblinking, he held the knife at waist level, ready to slash upward.

Slowly Windom opened his fist, moved away awkwardly, and righted his stool. As always, when fear and resentment of the boy gripped him, it was Bess who suffered. Joseph resumed his seat by the fire, wondering how much longer he could let it go on.

"I'm sick of hearing about your blessed Lord," Windom told his wife. "You're always saying He's going to exalt the poor man. Your first husband was a fool to die for that kind of shit. When your dear Jesus shows up to dirty His hands helping me with the charc, then I'll believe in Him, but not before."

He reached down for the green bottle of gin.

Later that night, Joseph lay tense on his pallet by the wall, listening to Windom abuse his mother with words and fists behind the ragged curtain that concealed their bed. Bess sobbed for a while, and the boy dug his nails into his palms. Presently Bess made different sounds, moans and guttural exclamations. The quarrel had been patched up in typical fashion, the boy thought cynically.

He didn't blame his poor mother for wanting a little peace and security and love. She'd chosen the wrong man, that was all. Long after the hidden bed stopped squeaking, Joseph lay awake, thinking of killing the charcoal burner.

He would never take his stepfather's name. He could be a better man than Windom. His defiance was his way of expressing faith in the possibility of a better life for himself. A life more like that of Andrew Archer, the ironmaster to whom Windom had apprenticed him two years ago.

Sometimes, though, Joseph was seized by dour moods in which he saw his hopes, his faith, as so much foolish daydreaming. What was he but dirt? Dirty of body, dirty of spirit. His clothes were never free of the charcoal dust Windom brought home. And though he didn't understand the crime for which his father had suffered and died in Scotland, he knew it was real, and it tainted him.

"Blessed are they which are persecuted . . ." No wonder it was her favorite verse.

Joseph's father, a long-jawed, unsmiling farmer whom he remembered

12

only dimly, had been an unyielding Covenanter. He had bled to death after many applications of the thumbscrew and the boot, in what Bess called the killing time: the first months of the royal governorship of the Duke of York, the same man who had lately been crowned James II. The duke had sworn to root out the Presbyterians and establish episcopacy in the country long troubled by the quarrels of the deeply committed religious and political antagonists.

Friends had rushed to Robert Moffat's farm to report the owner's gory death in custody and to warn his wife to flee. This she did, with her only son, barely an hour before the arrival of the duke's men, who burned all the buildings on the property. After months of wandering, mother and son reached the hills of south Shropshire. There, as much from weariness as anything else, Bess decided to stop her running.

The wooded uplands south and west of the meandering Severn River seemed suitably rustic and safe. She rented a cottage with the last of the money she had carried out of Scotland. She took menial jobs and in a couple of years met and married Windom. She even pretended to have adopted the official faith, for although Robert Moffat had infused his wife with religious fervor, he hadn't infused her with the courage to continue to resist the authorities after his death. Her faith became one of resignation in the face of misery.

A spineless and worthless faith, the boy soon concluded. He would have none of it. The man he wanted to imitate was strong-minded Archer, who lived in a fine mansion on the hillside above the river and the furnace he owned.

Hadn't old Giles told Joseph that he had the wits and the will to achieve that kind of success? Hadn't he said it often lately?

Joseph believed Giles much of the time. He believed him until he looked at the charcoal dust under his own nails and listened to the other apprentices mocking him with cries of "Dirty Joe, black as an African."

Then he would see his dreams as pretense and laugh at his own stupidity until his pale eyes filled with shameful but unstoppable tears.

Old Giles Hazard, a bachelor, was one of the three most important men at the Archer ironworks. He was in charge of the finery, the charcoal forge in which cast-iron pigs from the furnace were re-melted to drive off an excess of carbon and other elements which made cast iron too brittle for products such as horseshoes, wheel rims, and plow points. Giles Hazard had a gruff voice and a bent for working his men and apprentices like slaves. He had lived within a ten-minute walk of the furnace all his life and had gone to work there at age nine.

He was a short, portly fellow, possessed of immense energy despite his weight. Physically, he might have been a much older version of Joseph. Perhaps that was one reason he treated the boy almost like a son.

Another reason was that Joseph learned quickly. Joseph had come to Giles's attention last summer, about the time he was beginning his second year at Archer's. Giles had been discussing the apprentices with the man in charge of the furnace. The man had bragged about how nimbly Joseph worked his way around the sand trough, where bright molten iron flowed out to many smaller, secondary troughs that resembled piglets suckling on the mother sow. The look of the main and secondary troughs had long ago led to the name "pig iron" for the finished castings.

Giles had seniority at the ironworks and so had no trouble arranging the boy's transfer to the finery. There Giles put him to work handling the long iron bar with which three or four pigs at a time were maneuvered so that the bellows-heated charcoal would melt them uniformly. The boy developed a nice touch, and Giles soon found himself paying a compliment.

"You have a good hand and a natural wit for this trade, Joseph. You have an agreeable disposition, too—except, as I've noticed when the other apprentices rag you about your stepfather's occupation. Take a leaf from the owner's book. He's strong-minded, all right. But he knows it's better to hide it sometimes. He sells his product with smiles and soft words, not by bludgeoning his customers when they resist."

Privately, the older man doubted the boy would listen. The mold of Joseph's life was already formed, and the molten iron of his character was already pouring into it; circumstances and illiterate parents had no doubt condemned the boy to a life of obscurity. Unless, of course, one of his occasional violent outbursts didn't condemn him to death in a brawl first.

Yet, perhaps because Giles was growing older and realized that he had been foolish when he chose a bachelor's life, he continued to encourage Joseph. He taught him not only the trade of ironmaking but its lore.

"Iron rules the world, my boy. It breaks the sod and spans the continents—wins the wars, too." The Archer furnace cast cannonballs for the Navy.

Giles raised his great round cheese of a face to the sky. "Iron came to the earth from, quite literally, only God knows where. Meteor iron has been known since the earliest days."

The boy asked quickly, "What's a meteor, Master Hazard?"

A smile spread over Giles's face. "Shooting star. Surely you've seen 'em."

The boy responded with a thoughtful nod. Giles went on to talk about a great many things that gradually acquired meaning for Joseph as he learned more of the trade. Giles discoursed on the history of iron making. He spoke of the *stückofen* and *flüssofen* that had existed in Germany since the tenth century; of the *hauts fourneaux* that had spread in France in the fifteenth; of the Walloons of Belgium, who had developed the finery remelting process about sixty years ago.

"But all that is just a tick on the great clock of iron. Saint Dunstan worked iron seven hundred years ago. He had a forge in his bedroom at Glastonbury, they say. The Egyptian pharaohs were buried with iron amulets and dagger blades because the metal was so rare and valuable. So potent. I have read of daggers from Babylon and Mesopotamia, long millenniums before Christ."

"I don't read very well—"

"Someone should teach you," Giles grumbled. "Or you should teach yourself."

The boy took that in, then said, "What I meant is, I've never heard that word you used. *Mill*-something."

"Millenniums. A millennium is a thousand years."

"Oh." A blink. Giles was pleased to see the boy was storing the information away.

"A man can learn a great deal by reading, Joseph. Not everything, but a lot. I am speaking of a man who wants to be more than a charcoal burner."

Joseph understood. He nodded with no sign of resentment.

"Can you read at all?" Giles asked.

"Oh, yes." A pause, while the boy looked at Giles. Then he admitted, "Only a little. My mother tried to teach me with the Bible. I like the stories about heroes. Samson. David. But Windom didn't like my mother teaching me, so she stopped."

Giles pondered. "If you'll stay half an hour extra every night, I'll try."

"Windom might not—"

"Lie," Giles cut in. "If he asks why you're late, lie to him. That is, if you mean to make something of yourself. Something other than a charcoal burner."

"Do you think I can, Master Hazard?"

"Do you?"

"Yes."

"Then you will. The race is to the driven, not the swift."

That conversation had taken place the preceding summer. Through the autumn and winter Giles taught the boy. He taught him well, so well that Joseph couldn't help sharing his accomplishments with his mother. One night when Windom was away somewhere, roistering, he showed her a book he had smuggled home, a controversial book titled *Metallum Martis*, by the recently deceased Dud Dudley, bastard son of the fifth Lord Dudley.

Dud Dudley claimed to have smelted iron successfully with mineral coal—or *pit coles*—as Joseph read during his laborious but successful demonstration to Bess.

Her eyes sparkled with admiration. Then the light faded. "Learning is a splendid thing, Joseph. But it can lead to excessive pride. The center of your life must be Jesus."

He disliked hearing that but kept quiet.

"Only two things matter in this life," she went on. "Love of God's son and the love of one person for another. The kind of love I feel for you," she finished, suddenly clutching him against her.

He heard her weeping, felt her shivering. The killing time had whipped out of her all hopes but her hope of heaven, all loyalties but her loyalty to him and to the Savior he was coming to distrust. He was sorry for her, but he meant to live his own life.

They said nothing to Windom about the lessons. But evidently some glimmer of pride displayed itself in Bess's manner, angering her husband. One summer night, not long after the quarrel over Joseph's taking Windom's name, the boy came home to find his mother bloodied and bruised, half conscious on the dirt floor, and Windom gone. She would say nothing about what had happened. She pleaded until Joseph promised not to carry out his threats against his stepfather. But the core of rage was growing steadily within him.

As the Shropshire hills turned gold and red with the coming of another autumn, Joseph's progress grew so pleasing to Giles that he took a bold step.

"I'm going to speak to the ironmaster and ask him to let you spend

16

an hour each week with the tutor who lives in the mansion. Archer's own boys can't keep the fellow busy all the time. I feel sure Archer will permit the tutor to give you a little mathematics, maybe even some Latin.''

"Why should he? I'm nobody."

Old Giles laughed and rumpled Joseph's hair. "He will be happy to gain a loyal and well-educated employee at virtually no cost. That's part of it. The other part is that Archer's a decent man. There are a few in the world."

Joseph didn't really believe him until Giles told him Archer had consented. Excited, the boy forgot his natural caution as he ran home that night. Heavy mist lay on the river and the hills, and he was chilled when he reached the cottage. Windom was there, grimy and half drunk. Joseph, so thrilled at the idea of someone else thinking well of him, ignored his mother's warning looks and blurted the news about the tutor.

Windom didn't care for what he heard. "In Christ's name, why does the young fool need a teacher?" He studied Joseph with scorn that ran through the boy like a sword. "He's ignorant. As ignorant as me."

Bess twisted her apron, confused, not knowing how to escape the trap created by the breathless boy. She walked rapidly to the fire, knocking over the poker in her nervousness. Joseph's eyes were on his stepfather as he said, "Not anymore. Old Giles has been teaching me."

"To do what?"

"To read. To better myself."

Windom snickered, twisting the tip of his little finger back and forth in his nostril. He rubbed his finger on his breeches and laughed. "What a waste. You don't need book learning to work in the finery."

"You do if you want to be rich like Master Archer."

"Oh, you think you'll be rich someday, do you?"

Joseph's lips lost color. "I'll be damned to hell if I'll be as poor and stupid as you."

Windom bellowed and started toward the boy. Bess left off her nervous stirring of the stew kettle hanging on its chain in the hearth. Hands extended, she rushed to her husband. "He didn't mean that, Thad. Be merciful as Jesus taught we shou—"

"Stupid pious bitch, I'll deal with him as I want," Windom shouted. He cuffed her on the side of the head.

17

She staggered, slammed her shoulder hard against the mantel, cried out.

The pain somehow destroyed her allegiance to the Savior. Her eyes flew open wide. She spied the fallen poker, snatched it, and raised it to threaten her husband. It was a pathetic gesture, but Windom chose to see it as one of great menace. He turned on her.

Frightened and angry, Joseph grappled with his stepfather. Windom beat him off. Bess, terrified, fumbled with the poker, unable to get a firm grip on it. Windom easily ripped it from her hand and, while Joseph watched, used it to hit her twice on the temple. She sprawled on her face with a thread of blood running down her cheek.

Joseph stared at her for one moment, then in uncontrolled rage lunged for the poker. Windom threw it against the wall. Joseph ran to the hearth, seized the kettle chain, flung the hot stew over Windom, who screamed and pressed his hands to his scalded eyes.

Joseph's hands were burned but he hardly felt it. He raised the empty kettle and smashed it against Windom's head. When Windom fell, his cries subsiding, Joseph wrapped the chain around his stepfather's neck and pulled until it was half embedded in the flesh. Windom finally stopped kicking and lay still.

Joseph ran out into the mist and vomited. His palms started to burn. He began to realize what he'd done. He wanted to break down and cry, to run away, but he didn't. He forced himself toward the open door. Once inside the cottage again, he saw his mother's back moving slowly. She was alive!

After many attempts, he got her on her feet. She muttered incoherently and laughed occasionally. He put a shawl around her and guided her down the misty lanes to Giles Hazard's cottage, two miles distant. On the way she faltered several times, but his urgent pleas kept her going.

Giles came grumping to the cottage door, a candle illuminating his face. Moments later, he helped Bess to his still-warm truckle bed. He examined her, then stood back, fingering his chin.

"I'll run for a doctor," Joseph said. "Where do I find him?"

Old Giles couldn't conceal his worry. "She's too badly hurt for a doctor to do any good."

The news stunned the boy, bringing tears at last. "That can't be."

"Look at her! She's barely breathing. As for the barber who serves this district, he's illiterate. He can do nothing for her, and he'll only ask questions about the cause of her injuries."

The statement itself was a kind of question; Joseph had only blurted that Windom had hit her. "All we can do is wait," Giles concluded, rubbing an eye.

"And pray to Jesus."

Joseph said it out of desperation. Giles put a kettle on the fire. Joseph sank to his knees by the bed, folded his hands, and prayed with every bit of his being.

There was no sign that the prayer was heard. Bess Windom's breathing grew slower, feebler, although she survived until the river mist floating outside the cottage began to glow with light. Gently, Giles touched Joseph's shoulder, jogged him awake.

"Sit by the fire," Giles said, pulling a coverlet across Bess's battered, peaceful face. "It's all over with her. She's gone to find her Jesus, and nothing else can be done. It's different with you. What happens to you depends on whether you're caught." Giles drew a breath. "Your stepfather's dead, isn't he?"

The boy nodded.

"I thought so. Otherwise you wouldn't have come here. He'd have tended her."

All of Joseph's hurt went into a single cry. "I'm glad I killed him!"

"I'm sure you are. But the fact is you're a murderer. Archer won't employ a murderer, and I can't say I blame him. Still—"

His voice softened; his pretense of sternness had been a failure. "I don't want to see you hanged or quartered, either. What can we do?" He started pacing. "They'll search for Joseph Moffat, won't they? All right, you'll be someone else."

The decision made, Giles inscribed a paper with a statement that the bearer, Joseph Hazard, a nephew, was on an errand of family business. After a moment's hesitation, Giles signed his own name, adding the words *Uncle & Guardian* and several flourishes beneath; the flourishes somehow lent it authenticity.

Giles promised to bury Bess in a Christian manner and insisted the boy could not afford to stay and help. Then, giving him two shillings and some bread tied in a kerchief, instructions about avoiding main roads, and finally a long, fatherly hug, Giles sent a bewildered Joseph Moffat out of the door and into the mist-grayed hills.

On a lonely road in Gloucestershire, something made Joseph pause and look up. The night was flawlessly clear, with thousands of stars

19

alight. Eastward, above the roofline of a dairy barn, he saw a streak of white. Something afire, dropping very fast toward the earth.

Iron. God was sending iron to man, just as Giles had said. The boy could understand why ironmasters were so proud of their calling. It was a trade born and blessed in heaven.

Awed, Joseph watched until the white streak vanished near the horizon. He imagined a huge chunk of star iron smoldering in a fresh crater somewhere. There could be no more potent material in creation. No wonder wars were won, and distances conquered, by machines and equipment of iron.

From that moment, the direction of his life was never in doubt.

Joseph pressed on toward the port of Bristol on the Avon. He was not stopped once, nor required to produce the paper Giles had prepared so carefully. Showed you how much the world valued Thad Windom, didn't it?

Joseph mourned the loss of his mother but felt little regret over having slain his stepfather. He had done what had to be done; vengeance had come as a companion to necessity.

On the journey he found himself thinking strange new thoughts, many of them about religion. He could never subscribe to his dead mother's faith in a gentle, forgiving, and apparently powerless Christ. But he discovered a new sympathy with the Old Testament. Bess had read him many stories about strong, brave men who didn't flinch from bold action. He felt a strengthening kinship with them, and with their God, as he trudged through fields and forests to the great port of western England.

After several false starts, he located a ship's master who soon would be sailing for the New World—a part of the globe in which many Englishmen were finding second chances these days. The man was peg-legged Captain Smollet, his vessel the *Gull of Portsmouth*. The captain's proposition was straightforward.

"You sign a document indenturing yourself to me. In return, I'll provide you with passage and keep while you're aboard. We'll be calling at Bridgetown, Barbados, then going on to the colonies in America. They need skilled workers there. If you know ironworking as well as you claim, I should have no trouble placing you."

The captain peered at Joseph over the rim of the ale pot he was just lifting to his mouth. The boy felt no resentment of the captain's hard bargain; indeed, he rather admired it. A man determined to succeed always had to make difficult choices, he was discovering. So it had been with the heroes of the Old Testament. Abraham. Moses. If he was to be like any man, it would be one of them.

"Well, Hazard, what's your answer?"

"You haven't told me how long I'll be a servant."

Captain Smollet grinned admiringly. "Some are so lathered with excitement—or so guilty over past crimes"—Joseph kept his face absolutely calm, ignoring the probe—"they clean forget to ask till we're on our way down the estuary." He eyed the contents of his drinking pot. "The indenture is seven years."

At first Joseph wanted to shout no. But he didn't. Smollet took his silence for refusal, shrugged, and rose, throwing coins on the soiled table.

Being bound to another man as a slave for seven years wouldn't be easy, Joseph thought. Yet he could use that time wisely and profitably. Educate himself, both generally, as Giles had urged, and in every aspect of his chosen trade. After seven years he would be a free man, in a new land where there was a need for ironmasters, and where no one had ever heard of Thad Windom.

At the inn door, Captain Smollet stopped when he heard, "I'll sign."

Rain was falling that evening when Joseph hurried along a wharf toward the *Gull of Portsmouth*. Light glowed in the windows of the captain's quarters at the stern. How bright and inviting it looked. In that cabin Joseph would shortly make his mark on the articles of indenture.

He smiled, thinking of Smollet. What a rogue. He had asked only a couple of perfunctory questions about Joseph's background. Fearing the offer of indenture might be withdrawn, Joseph had rashly shown the document Giles had provided. Smollet had scanned it and chuckled as he handed it back.

"A family errand. Taking you all the way to the colonies. Fancy that."

Their eyes met. Smollet knew the boy was on the run and didn't care. Joseph admired the captain's ruthless enterprise. He liked him more than ever.

Seven years wasn't so long. Not so long at all.

That thought in mind, he paused at a stair leading down to the water. He descended half way, clung to the slimy wood with one hand, and dipped his other in the salty water once, twice, three times.

21

He did the same with his other hand. If there was any symbolic blood on him, it was gone now. He was making a new beginning.

He examined his dripping fingers by the light of the nearby ship's lanterns. He laughed aloud. Earlier there had been some charcoal dust still embedded beneath his nails. It too was gone.

He whistled as he stepped on to the gangplank. He went aboard Smollet's vessel with rising spirits. About to put himself in bondage for seven years, he faced the prospect with a sharp new sense of personal freedom.

In the New World things were going to be different for Joseph Mof—no, Joseph Hazard. God would make it happen. His God, growing more familiar and companionable by the hour, was a Deity who favored the brave man who didn't shrink from the hard action.

Joseph and his God had become well acquainted during the past few days. They were close now; friends.

1687: *The Aristocrat*

In the late spring of the following year, across the ocean in the royal colony of Carolina, someone else dreamed of making a fortune.

For him the ambition amounted to a lust. He had known what it was like to be rich, powerful, secure. But the security had proved an illusion, and the wealth and power had been swept away like the shining beach sand down by Charles Town when a storm tide attacked it.

Charles de Main was thirty. He and his beautiful wife, Jeanne, had been in the colony two years. Carolina itself had been settled by Europeans for only seventeen years; all of its two or three thousand white citizens were, relatively speaking, newcomers.

Among the colonists was a group of adventurers originally from Barbados. These men had settled in the village of Charles Town and had quickly assumed power under the Lords Proprietors, the English nobles who had started the colony as a financial venture. These same Barbadians had already mantled themselves in superiority.

Charles considered the Barbadians impractical fools. They dreamed of an agricultural paradise where they could grow rich raising silk, sugar, tobacco, cotton. Charles was more realistic. Carolina's coastal lowlands were too wet for conventional farming. Its summers were pestilential; only the very hardy survived in them. Currently the colony's prosperity—such as it was—had three sources: Pelts like those that

22

passed through Charles's trading station. Grazing cattle. And the kind of wealth he was just now engaged in bringing down from the back country at the point of a gun.

Indians destined for slavery.

It could not be said that Charles de Main had come to this land of coastal swamps and back country sand hills because of its physical or commercial attractions. He and Jeanne had fled here from the valley of the Loire, where Charles had been born the fourteenth duke of his line.

In his twentieth year he had married and begun to assume the management of his family's vineyards. For a few years the life of the young couple had been idyllic, except perhaps for the troubling fact that Jeanne produced no children. But then the religious faith traditional in their families for several generations had brought their ruin.

When Louis XIV revoked the Edict of Nantes in 1685, the uneasy truce between French Catholics and Protestants ended. Like all the other fiercely proud Huguenots—for *proud*, some Frenchmen substituted the word *treasonous*—Charles de Main and his wife were threatened by the purges that soon ravaged their homeland. Once the terror began, it became a serious offense to attempt to leave the country. Just like hundreds of other Huguenots, however, the de Mains made plans to do exactly that.

In the village near the great round-towered Château de Main there was a certain lawyer named Emilion who practiced bigotry and thievery behind a pious expression. He knew the profits to be made in England from the sale of the château's rich reds and tart whites. He coveted the de Main vineyards, and to get them he paid a groom to inform upon his master and mistress.

Emilion felt the de Mains might try to flee, and before long the groom saw signs of preparations. One word from him to the proper official was all it took. The night the de Mains left, their coach was no more than half a kilometer from the château when the authorities came galloping up behind it.

Charles put his arm around his frightened wife and whispered words of affection to distract her from thinking of what they would face following their arrest—the inquisition by means of which heretical Protestants were forced to recant. Another Huguenot in the neighborhood, caught while dashing to the coast, had died when the inquisitor's blade slipped and cut off his testicles.

23

The young nobleman and his wife were kept in prison seventeen days. They were questioned with the aid of knives and hot irons. Neither broke; not outwardly, at least, although toward the end Jeanne alternately screamed and wept without stopping.

They would have died in the dungeon at Chalonnes had it not been for Charles's uncle in Paris. He was a clever politician who could change his style of worship as effortlessly as he changed satin robes. He knew a few important men whose Catholic principles did not extend to their purses. Bribes were paid; a certain postern was left unlocked. Charles and Jeanne de Main escaped from Nantes in the bilge of a rickety fishing boat that almost capsized in the furious waters of the Channel.

In London other Huguenot refugees pointed them toward Carolina. The colony's professed religious tolerance made it a likely haven for those of their faith. Months later, depressed by the heat and the arrogance he found after he crossed the ocean, the young nobleman wondered whether the journey—or life itself—was worth the effort. Charles Town was not necessarily lucky for those named Charles. Or so he thought then.

He had simplified his last name to Main to demonstrate that he was making a new start in a new land. Soon his pessimism vanished. In Carolina he was free of many of the rules that had constrained him when he bore a title. He took advantage of that.

He had survived torture—his scarred legs and chest testified to it— and he would survive poverty, too. The greedy little lawyer had stolen his lands and his château, but he would own other land and build another great house. Or his descendants would. Provided Jeanne's body ever yielded him an heir.

Poor Jeanne. Today her gray eyes were as clear and lovely as ever. But a narrow white streak running all the way through her yellow hair betrayed her suffering in prison. So did her sweet-little-girl's smile, and the way she hummed and laughed in response to any serious question. She recognized her husband sometimes, but she thought they were still living in France. Her mind hadn't survived as successfully as her body.

The ruin of Jeanne's mind hadn't dampened her passion. But their couplings produced no children. That and his own advancing age, kept Charles sleepless many a night. At thirty a man was growing old; at forty he could say he had lived a long life.

The effort of establishing his little trading station at a ford on the

24

Cooper River above Charles Town had changed him physically, too. He no longer resembled an aristocrat. He was still tall, and slightly stooped because of his height. But poverty, work, and strain had blurred his good looks.

His smile, once quick and gay, looked false, even cruel, when it appeared, which was seldom. Gone was any trace of a prideful bearing. He slouched on the back of the little marsh pony that labored under his weight. He had become almost a brutish parody of his former self.

Today, in fact, he hardly resembled a white man. His hair, brown as his eyes, hung to the middle of his back, tied with a scrap of red rag. His skin was as brown as that of any of the eight shackled and half-clothed human beings staggering along in a file behind him. Although the spring morning was intensely hot, Charles wore full-length trousers of deerskin and a jerkin of old, cracked leather. In his beaded belt were two loaded pistols and two knives. A musket rested across his knees. A slaver learned to be cautious and a good shot.

This was the fourth expedition Charles had made to the Cherokee towns in the foothills of the mountains. Without the occasional sale of some Indians he would have failed as a trader. The little post by the river simply didn't bring in enough income, even though the Charles Town factors took all the furs he could collect from members of the very same tribes he raided on other occasions.

The seven men and one woman trudging in chains were all in their twenties. Handsome, brown people with wiry limbs and the most beautiful black hair he had ever seen. The girl was especially attractive, he thought. She had a fine bosom. He had earlier noticed that she stared at him frequently. No doubt her large, placid eyes concealed a desire to cut his throat.

Charles rode with his back to the captives because he had an assistant, as heavily armed as he, at the rear of the file. His helper was a hulking half-breed apparently sired by some Spaniard who had wandered up from the Floridas. He was a Yamasee Indian from the northern camps of that tribe. He had come to the trading station a year ago, already knowing a bit of French. He claimed to have no ambition other than to make war on the tribes that were his enemies.

He seemed to like working for Charles. Perhaps that was because there were about thirty different tribes scattered through Carolina, and most of them preyed on all the others; hence for the half-breed, who called himself King Sebastian, vocation and avocation became one.

King Sebastian had a villainous face, and like many other Indians, he enjoyed going about in white men's finery. Today he wore filthy breeches that had once been pink silk, a brocaded bottle-green coat that hung open to show his huge chest running with sweat, and a great frowsy turban ornamented with paste jewels.

King Sebastian relished the work he was doing. Every so often he would jog his pony up beside the captives and jab one or more in the buttocks with his musket. Usually this produced hateful glares, at which times the half-breed liked to chuckle and utter a warning, as he did now: "Careful, little brother, or I will use this fire stick to make you less than a man."

"And you be careful," Charles said in French, having halted his pony to let the column straggle by. The scowls and glares of the captives were unusually ferocious, he noticed. "I'd like to deliver this lot to the vendue table intact, thank you very much."

King Sebastian resented criticism. He took out his anger on the captives, lashing a laggard with a quirt he kept at his belt. Charles reluctantly let it pass.

The vendue table was the local name for the auction block. In this case it was a secret auction block, out in the country above Charles Town. The Indian slave trade had been illegal in the colony for several years, but it was a profitable business and still common.

What made it attractive was the relatively low risk. Charles's prisoners, for example, had been snatched at gunpoint from a melon patch at twilight. The Cherokees were both warriors and farmers. When surprised in their fields in the foothills, they could be captured with relative ease. Of course danger was never completely absent.

Few Indians died on the trek to the coast, whereas large numbers of blacks imported from Africa via Bridgetown died on the long sea passage. Further, one couldn't get into the African trade without owning ships, or at least some capital. All Charles owned was his little outpost, his pony, and his guns.

The heat increased. Clouds of tiny insects bedeviled the procession as it wound through the sand hills. The temperature and the dark smudge of woods on the distant horizon told Charles they were approaching the low-lying coastal plain. Another night plus half a day and they should reach the station, where he reluctantly left Jeanne alone each time he went on an expedition.

He was always on edge during these trips. Today, however, he was more than alert; he was nervous. He noticed the girl watching him again. Was she awaiting an opportune moment when she could signal the men to break away? He dropped back and rode beside King Sebastian the rest of the afternoon.

That night they built a campfire, not for warmth but to keep the insects away. King Sebastian took the first turn on watch.

Charles stretched out with his weapons arranged on his chest and closed his eyes. He began to speculate drowsily about rebuilding his fortune. Somehow he must change direction. He wasn't making any money, only keeping even. Besides, the isolation of the trading station was no good for Jeanne, even in her sorry mental state. She deserved better, and he wanted to give it to her. He loved her deeply.

However, one couldn't avoid practical considerations. If he did manage to rebuild his estate, who would inherit it? His poor wife, to whom he had remained faithful—it was the only point of decency left in his life—was not only mad, she was barren.

He was nearly asleep when a clink of chain roused him. His eyes came open at the moment King Sebastian uttered his shout of warning.

The half-breed had fallen asleep too; that much was evident from his seated position and the frenzied way he struggled to aim his musket. The eight Indians, their ankle and wrist chains stretched to full length between them, were rushing toward their captors in a line. The girl, third from the right, was dragged along. She was the one forced to leap directly over the fire.

Terrified, Charles grabbed one of the pistols off his belly. *Christ Jesus, don't let the powder be damp from the night air*. The pistol didn't fire. He snatched up the other one.

The Cherokee at the left end of the file had armed himself with a stone. He hurled this at King Sebastian, who was trying to get to his knees and aim his musket at the same time. The half-breed dodged; the stone hit his right temple, not much of a blow, but when his musket boomed, the ball went hissing harmlessly into the dark.

The brave near Charles drove his bare foot down toward his captor's throat—and would have smashed it if Charles hadn't rolled onto his left side, raised his right hand, and pulled the trigger. The second pistol fired. The ball went up through the underside of the Indian's chin and lifted part of the top of his head.

That terrible sight broke the revolt, though the fight didn't stop immediately. Charles was forced to shoot a second Indian, and King Sebastian killed another with his musket before the other four dragged the girl and the corpses away. The hair of one of the dead men scraped through the embers, smoked, and caught fire.

Charles was trembling. He was sooty with dirt and powder, and spattered with the blood and brain from the first Indian's head. For supper he had chewed pieces of heavily salted deer meat, which now refused to stay in his stomach.

When he returned from the brush, he found an obviously shaken King Sebastian quirting the braves who were still alive. The half-breed had removed the three dead men from the chain, but he hadn't bothered with the keys to the cuffs. He had used his knife. Somewhere out in the dark, huge black buzzards were already pecking at the corpses.

The half-breed jerked the girl's head up by the hair. "I think the bitch needs punishment, too."

For a moment, gazing down at the sagging bodice of her hide dress, Charles had a clear look at her brown breasts. The sight touched him. Her breasts looked ripe and full of life. Watching King Sebastian warily, she shifted position. The dress fell in place and hid her body.

Charles caught the half-breed's wrist in midair. In the firelight his blood-streaked face resembled a Cherokee brave's painted for war.

"You're the one who needs punishment," Charles said. "You're the one who dozed on watch."

King Sebastian looked as if he might turn on his employer. Charles continued to stare at him. Although the girl didn't understand the tall man's French, she understood his meaning. She didn't dare smile. But there was a flicker of gratitude in her eyes.

A minute passed. Another. The half-breed slapped at a gnat on his neck and looked away. And that settled it.

Except that it didn't. The incident had profoundly shaken Charles. Even after his watch, when King Sebastian again took over, he couldn't fall asleep. The brush with death kept reminding him of his lack of sons. Three brothers had died in infancy. One sister had disappeared over the Pyrenees at the start of the time of trouble. He was the last of his line.

When he finally fell asleep, he had strange dreams in which images of the fertile fields of the Cherokees were mixed with visions of the Indian girl's breasts.

Early the next afternoon they reached the trading station on the Cooper, one of two rivers named for Anthony Ashley Cooper, Earl of Shaftesbury, who was one of the original Proprietors.

Jeanne was safe and well. She and Charles walked for half an hour on the riverbank. He kept his arm around her. She babbled childish things while they watched a white heron perch on one leg in the shallows. She deserved better than this. She deserved a fine house, the protection of servants.

In the morning he made preparations to depart for the coast. He intended to leave around noon, with the Indians and some bundles of pelts he had accumulated to trade. On the trip to the secret vendue table he would, as always, avoid the main trails where he and his human contraband might be seen.

A half hour before his depature, Jeanne came rushing into the post with excited cries. He could make no sense of her warnings, but King Sebastian soon appeared, looking frightened. The half-breed struggled to find the right words in French.

"Who's coming?" Charles interrupted. "Gentlemen? Nabobs? Is that what you're trying to say?"

The frightened Indian nodded and held up one hand with all the fingers extended. "Lot of them." Charles's bowels turned watery.

They rushed the slaves to the outbuilding, which was constructed of palmetto logs and cypress planks. Frantically, Charles chained the four men and the girl in one of the pony stalls while King Sebastian tied rags around their mouths. If the prisoners made any outcry, the slaving operation would be discovered and he'd be lost.

The glaring eyes of his captives told him they hoped it would happen. On Charles's instruction, the half-breed checked all the gags a second time.

To make matters worse, the leader of the party of visitors was a member of the colony's governing council, an elegant Englishman named Moore. He was traveling into what he termed the "demmed pestilential back country" with four Negro servants, one of whom had some skill in surveying. Moore was looking for land for a summer residence away from the fever-ridden coast.

Moore stayed three hours. Charles was in a state of barely concealed nerves the whole time. Once he heard a thump and a rattle of chain from the outbuilding, but Moore, talking at the time, did not.

When one of the servants spied chains and cuffs under his serving counter, Charles had to do some fast talking. "Took them in trade for a gun," he lied. "From a suspicious fellow who claimed he was bound for Virginia. Last autumn, it was—"

Moore didn't give the chains and manacles a second look. With typical arrogance the Englishman occupied himself with a stream of criticism of the weather, the primitive countryside, and the New World in general. By four, when it was slightly cooler, he and his party rode on. Charles poured a heavy drink of warm gin, swallowed it in two gulps, hugged Jeanne, and hurried to the outbuilding.

King Sebastian stood guard at the door. Inside, Charles found the four men directing furious looks at the girl. Her gag had slipped down around her neck. She could have cried out.

She stared at Charles with the same intense gaze, and he at last understood. Perhaps he had understood all along but had been prevented from admitting it by guilt and thoughts of Jeanne. He turned abruptly and hurried out into the steamy sunshine.

Things were growing too dangerous in the Indian slave trade. The conviction stayed with him when he made a belated start next morning. It accompanied him along the swampy trails of the low country, and it was still with him, a hobgoblin riding his shoulder, when he reached the coast.

The clearing was located outside the palisade surrounding Charles Town. The site had been carefully chosen. It was not so close as to be easily detected, not so far as to represent an unduly dangerous trip after dark. It could be reached by riding up the shore of the Cooper River for about ten minutes. In the clearing there gathered half a dozen men Charles silently characterized as Anglican snobs. They were planters from the district, all struggling to find a cash crop whose profits would fulfill their original dreams of Carolina. So far the search had been a failure. The colony was a losing enterprise.

Nevertheless, they persisted in pretending their life was ideal in most respects. They chatted over the latest gossip of the town. They complimented Charles on his offering, though they didn't stand too close to him while doing so. His smell, as well as his lineage, offended them.

Torches driven into the sandy ground shed a smoky light on the vendue table of split palmetto logs. An auctioneer, another eminently respectable gentleman, handled the bidding in return for a small percentage of the total sale. In town Charles had heard the man prate about the evils of Indian slavery. Such talk was common. Most of those present had owned at least one Indian in the past. What they really objected to was not the immorality of enslaving other human beings but possible impairment of trade with the Indians should the tribes ever unite to protest the practice. The white men also feared an Indian uprising.

But that didn't prevent them from showing up tonight. Stinking hypocrites, Charles thought.

One by one the four males were sold. Each brought a successively higher price. Charles stood to one side, his resentment easing as he puffed a clay pipe and contemplated his profit.

He listened to conversations. One man spoke of sending his new purchase to the West Indies for what he termed "seasoning." Breaking the slave's spirit was what he meant. A second gentleman discussed new land grants being made along nearby rivers and creeks.

"Yes, but what's the use of owning land if you can't pay your quitrent and there's no crop that's accepted in lieu of cash?"

"Maybe there is such a crop now," the first man said. He displayed a plump little sack.

The others crowded around, curious. Even Charles drifted up to listen; the auction was stalled while the man with the sack answered a question put to him.

"This is seed. From Madagascar. The same kind of seed that's growing so well in those overwatered gardens in town."

A man pointed, excited. "Is that some of the rice Captain Thurber gave Dr. Woodward last year?" Thurber was captain of a brigantine that had put into Charles Town for repairs; Charles had heard the story of some rice brought ashore.

The man with the sack tucked it safely away in his pocket. "Aye. It thrives in wet ground. Nay—demands it. Many in town are agog over the possibilities. There's a rush for land all at once. And a feeling that a profitable use has been found for these benighted lowlands."

The doubter had another question: "Yes, but what white man could stand to work in swamps and marshes?"

"Not a one, Manigault. It will take men accustomed to intense heat and nearly unbearable conditions." The speaker paused for effect. "Africans. Many more than we have in the colony now, I warrant."

In France, Charles Main had suffered for his religion. But the hypocrisy of schemers like Emilion, and the cruelty inflicted on Jeanne, had all but destroyed the faith that had dragged him into the ordeal in the first place.

His own will, not some supernatural power, had sustained him under the hot irons of the torturers. So, although he still harbored a vague belief in a Supreme Being, his picture of that Being had changed.

31

God was indifferent. He had no benevolent plan for the cosmos or its creatures; very likely He had no plan at all. It therefore behooved a man to rely solely upon himself. It was all right to give God a courteous nod now and then, as you would a doddering uncle. But when it came to shaping the future, a wise man took matters into his own hands.

And yet, in that firelit clearing in the midst of a vast, dense wood that reeked of damp earth and rang with the cries of birds, a curious thing happened to Charles. He felt his old beliefs surge up with unexpected strength. For one intense moment he felt the presence of some outside force that had willed he survive the past couple of years in order to reach this place at this precise instant.

In that instant he set a new course. He wouldn't put a shilling of his earnings back into trade goods for the station. Whatever it cost to consult one of those twisty lawyers, he would pay, in order to learn how he might secure a grant of land down here, closer to the sea. He would investigate what he had just heard about the Madagascar seed. He was, first and foremost, a man who had worked the land. If he could raise grapes, he could raise rice.

But the labor did present a problem. He knew the inhospitable nature of these lowlands. He wouldn't last a month working waist-deep in the water that bore disease, not to mention alligators, on its slow, serpentine tides.

The answer was obvious. A Negro slave. Two, if his earnings would stretch that far.

With the warped logic of someone who knows he is guilty and must find a way to prove otherwise, Charles had always considered himself a man who sold slaves without endorsing the system. Deep in him something recoiled from the whole process. Moreover, he never saw what actually happened to the Indians he caught and sold. Perhaps—the ultimate saving sophistry—kindly owners later freed them.

Now, however, conscience had to abdicate completely. He himself had to own at least one prime African buck. It was a matter of economics. Of opportunity. Of survival.

A man did what he must.

"Gentlemen, gentlemen," exclaimed the auctioneer. "Too much talk diverts us from the choicest offering of the night."

Mounting the table, he raised the hide garment so that the girl's private parts were visible. The men were suddenly attentive.

A man did what he must. That same rule applied to the problem of heirs, Charles realized. If he was to rebuild his fortune in Carolina—and at last he had a glimmer of hope, something he had lacked for years—he had to accept certain realities. He had no intention of leaving his beloved Jeanne. At the same time he could no longer be overly scrupulous about fidelity.

"Gentlemen, who will begin the bidding for this comely tribal maiden? Who will give me a price of—?"

"Stop." With outward thrusts of his hands, Charles parted the group of men ahead of him.

"What's that, Main?" said the auctioneer, while the gentlemen Charles had pushed dusted their sleeves and sneered behind his back. He might be a Protestant, but he was also a churl. What else would you expect of a Frenchman?

Standing as straight as he ever had, Charles stared down the surprised, faintly annoyed auctioneer.

"I've changed my mind. She is not for sale."

Slowly he looked to the girl. The auctioneer let her garment fall. Her large eyes were fixed on Charles. She understood.

He knew better than to try to stay the night at a Charles Town lodging house. Not even the most sordid of them, down near the point of the peninsula where the two rivers met and flowed into the ocean, would welcome a white man with an Indian woman who was obviously not his slave.

Instead he found a secluded glade not far from the palisade. There, despite the risk of snakes and the threat of insects, he spread his blankets, placed his loaded weapons within reach, lay down beside her in the hot, damp dark, and took her.

He knew only rudimentary words of her language, none a term of endearment. Yet she knew his need and was eager for his touch. His mouth on her mouth, his hand on her belly—this was what she had wanted almost from the first. He had seen it in her eyes and failed to comprehend.

Charles was an accomplished lover, tender when necessary. The knowing, courtly ways had not been completely forgotten. Jeanne's plight and her need for consideration had assured that. Yet toward the end the style of his lovemaking changed. A slow, lazy rhythm was replaced by a quicker, more purposeful one. His excitement increased. So did hers. Passive pleasure became frantic response.

Lying on wet, fertile earth, a hundred kinds of life buzzing or crying out around them and scores of stars pricking the black sky, they clasped each other.

That night he planted his seed as methodically as he was to plant the crops that would create the Main fortune.

At that period Charles Town consisted of something less than a hundred rude homes and commercial buildings. Many of the Barbadian men talked of erecting those spacious, breezy houses typical of the islands from which they had come. But it would take a better economy, a thriving future, to bring that about. The town's air of gentility was obviously feigned and not a little shabby.

It didn't seem so to Charles the next morning. The day was bright and clear, the air freshened by a northeast wind off the harbor. He strolled to the wharf with the Indian girl following a step behind. His bearing had changed, touched now with certainty, force.

Charles couldn't help noticing the scornful stares of the gentry who were abroad. To have a liaison with a woman of color, whether brown or black, was acceptable. To flaunt it in public was something else.

The expressions of the gentlemen soon put a new thought in his head. Most Carolinians were infernally snobbish about their pedigrees. If he sired a child known to be half Cherokee, they would never admit him or the child to their circle, regardless of how much money he might accumulate—and never mind that his lineage was as good as theirs.

Swiftly, he began to concoct a scheme. He knew the Indian girl would become pregnant; he would see to it. Once it began to show, he would contrive to keep her in the back country, set her up in a cabin of her own, unseen by anyone except him and perhaps King Sebastian. He would tell her she would be safer that way.

He could then inform Jeanne that he meant to adopt a male child. He never doubted that the Indian girl would deliver a son, just as he never doubted his own ability to withstand and overcome her fury when he took the child away. He was a man, which gave him an advantage; he was white, which gave him another. He could deal with her forcibly, if it came to that. There was little Charles wouldn't do to assure the continuity of his line and the future security of any male who bore his name.

Later, he could pass the child off to outsiders as his sister's orphaned son. The plan excited him, and he couldn't completely conceal the reaction. The girl was walking at his shoulder now. She noticed his sudden hard smile, which just as quickly disappeared.

He saw her questioning look. Gently he touched her arm, gazing at her in a way she took to be reassuring. His fast, noisy breathing slowed. They walked on.

He inquired about arriving ships with Africans for sale. None was expected for three weeks, he learned. The only noteworthy vessel in port was a merchantman out of Bridgetown, a trading vessel carrying a few passengers: *Gull of Portsmouth.*

Charles passed a group of five young men who seemed fascinated by the sights of the little port. He had seen their kind before. Indentured boys. They had a whipped look—all except one stocky young fellow with heavy shoulders, light brown hair, and eyes that glowed like ice in the sunshine. He moved with a certain swagger.

Going in opposite directions, each took brief notice of the other. The bound boy was curious about the man with the primitive clothing, aristocratic bearing, and sprouting beard. The former slaver and would-be slave owner was wondering how someone could voluntarily consign himself to slavery.

A mate leaned over the merchantman's rail.

"Back on board, lads. The tide's flowing. You'll find grander sights to gawk at in Penn's town."

The indentured boys hurried back to the ship, and the tall aristocrat drifted away in the crowd, his Cherokee woman following with adoring eyes. In the cheerful light of the morning, each man had already forgotten the other.

BOOK ONE

ANSWER THE DRUM

*. . . In future wars the Nation must
look to the Academy for the skill
to conduct valor to victory.*

SECRETARY OF WAR JOHN C. CALHOUN
TO SYLVANUS THAYER, SUPERINTENDENT,
U.S. MILITARY ACADEMY
1818

1

"Like some help loading that aboard, young sir?"

The stevedore smiled but there was no friendliness in his eyes, only avarice inspired by the sight of an obvious stranger.

A few moments ago the driver of the Astor House passenger omnibus had thrown the travel-battered trunk down at the head of the pier. Orry had picked it up by the one rope handle still unbroken and had dragged it scarcely three feet before the stevedore stepped between him and the gangway.

It was a brilliant, windless morning in June 1842. Orry was already nervous about the day ahead. The stevedore's fixed smile and hard stare only worsened that state, as did the sight of the stevedore's two associates lounging nearby.

Nerves and cowardice were two different things, though; Orry had no intention of letting the former lead to the latter. He had been warned that New York teemed with all sorts of swindlers, and now it appeared he had finally met one. He took off his tall, stylish beaver hat and mopped his forehead with a linen handkerchief from an inside pocket.

Orry Main was sixteen and stood almost six feet two inches. His slimness accentuated his height and lent him a certain grace when he moved. He had a long, plain face with the good color of someone who spent a lot of time in the sunshine. His nose was narrow and aristocratic, his wavy hair brown. His eyes, brown too, were rather deeply set. Fatigue circles tended to appear under them whenever he slept poorly, as he had last night. The rings of shadow gave his face a melancholy cast. But he was not melancholy by disposition. His smile, which appeared frequently, proved that. He was, however, a deliberate sort. He tended to pause and think before taking any important step.

Impatient, the stevedore put a foot on the trunk. "Lad I asked—"

"I heard you, sir. I can handle the trunk myself."

"Listen to that," one of the other stevedores jeered. "Where you from, country boy?" It was Orry's accent that gave him away; his clothes were far from countrified.

"South Carolina."

His heart was beating fast now. The three were mature men, muscular and rough. But he refused to be backed down. He reached for the rope handle. The first stevedore grabbed his wrist.

"No you don't. Either we put it on the steamer or you travel up to West Point without it."

Orry was stunned by the threat and equally stunned by the ease with which he and his destination had been identified. He needed time to think, time to put himself in a better position to deal with these louts. He shook his wrist to signal that he wanted the stevedore to release him. After a deliberate delay the man did. Orry straightened and used both hands to put his hat back on his head.

Three female passengers, two pretty girls and an older woman, hurried by. They certainly couldn't help him. Then a small man in a uniform stepped off the gangway, an official of the line, Orry suspected. A sharp wave from one of the stevedores and the official came no farther.

"How much to load it?" Orry asked. Somewhere behind him wagon wheels squealed and hooves rang on the cobbles. He heard merry voices, laughter. Other passengers arriving.

"Two dollars."

"That's about eight times more than it should be."

The stevedore grinned. "Could be, sojer boy. But that's the price."

"You don't like it," the second stevedore said, "go complain to the mayor. Go complain to Brother Jonathan." All three laughed. Brother Jonathan was the popular symbol for the nation. A rustic, a Yankee.

Orry was perspiring from tension as well as from the heat. He bent at the waist, again reaching for the trunk. "I refuse to pay you a—"

The first stevedore pushed him. "Then the trunk stays here."

A grave look concealed Orry's fear. "Sir, don't put hands on me again." The words provoked the stevedore to do exactly that. He tried to give Orry a clumsy shake. Orry had planned his point of attack and rammed his right fist into the stevedore's stomach.

The official cried, "Stop that," and started forward. Another stevedore flung him back so hard he nearly pitched off the pier into the water.

The first stevedore grabbed Orry's ears and twisted. Then he kneed Orry's groin. Orry reeled away, falling against someone who had come up behind him, someone who darted around him and charged the three stevedores, fists swinging.

A young man not much older than himself, Orry saw as he lunged back to the fray. A shorter, very stocky chap who punched with great ferocity. Orry jumped in, bloodied a nose, and got his cheek raked by fingernails. Frontier-style fighting had reached the New York docks, it seemed.

The first stevedore tried to jab a thumb in Orry's eye. Before he hit his target, a long gold-knobbed cane came slashing in from the right. The knob whacked the stevedore's forehead. He yelled and staggered.

"Blackguards," a man bellowed. "Where are the authorities?"

"William, don't excite yourself," a woman exclaimed.

The stocky young man jumped on Orry's trunk, poised and ready to continue the fight. Now the official by the gangway was joined by two crewmen from the steamer. The stevedores backed off, calculated the rapidly changing odds, and after some oaths that brought gasps from the two ladies who had just arrived, hurried off the pier and disappeared on the street beyond.

Orry drew a deep breath. The other young man jumped down from the trunk. His fine clothes were hardly ruffled.

"I thank you very much for your assistance sir." Orry's politeness helped hide his nervousness in the presence of Yankees—and patently prosperous ones, at that.

The stocky young man grinned. "We almost had 'em whipped."

Orry smiled too. The newcomer stood just about to his shoulder. Although there was no fat on him, he gave the impression of being very wide of body. His face was shaped like a wide U. He'd lost his hat, and his brown hair, lighter than Orry's, showed several blond streaks bleached by the sun. The young man's pale, ice-colored eyes were saved from severity by a good-humored sparkle. His smile helped, too, although anyone who disliked him no doubt would have called it cocky.

"So we did," Orry replied, perpetuating the lie.

"Nonsense," said a stout, pasty man three or four years older than Orry's benefactor. "Both of you could have been injured or killed."

The stocky lad spoke to Orry. "My brother never does anything more dangerous than trimming his nails."

The woman who had cried out, stout and fortyish, said, "George, don't be saucy to Stanley. He's right. You're far too reckless."

It was a family, then. Orry touched his hat brim. "Whether we won or lost, all of you helped me out of a tight spot. My thanks again."

"I'll give you a hand with that trunk," George said. "You are taking this boat, aren't you?"

"Yes, to the Military Academy."

"Just get your appointment this year?"

Orry nodded. "Two months ago."

"Fancy that," George said, grinning again. "So did I."

He let go of the broken rope handle. Orry's quick jump saved his feet from being crushed by the trunk.

The other young man held out his hand. "Name's George Hazard. I'm from Pennsylvania. A little town you've never heard of—Lehigh Station."

"Orry Main. From Saint George's Parish, South Carolina."

They looked at each other as their hands clasped. Orry had a feeling this pugnacious little Yankee was going to be a friend.

A few steps away George's father was berating the official who had stood by while a fight developed. The official loudly disavowed responsibility for the public pier. The elder Hazard exclaimed, "I've got your name. There'll be an investigation, I promise you that."

Scowling, he returned to his family. His wife soothed him with some murmured words and a pat or two. Then George cleared his throat and, with a mannerly air, made the proper introductions.

William Hazard was a stern, impressive man with a lined face. He looked ten years older than his wife, though in fact he was not. In addition to the parents and their two older sons, there was a sister, Virgilia—oldest of the children, Orry surmised—and a boy of six or seven. His mother called him William; George referred to him as Billy. The boy kept fiddling with his high collar, which brushed the lobes of his ears; all the men, including Orry, wore similar collars. Billy gazed at his brother George with unmistakable admiration.

"Since Stanley's the oldest male, he's going to take over the iron-works," George explained as he and Orry carried the trunk onto the steamer. "There's never been a question of his doing anything else."

"Iron, you said?"

"Yes. Our family's been making it for six generations. The company used to be called Hazard Furnace, but my father changed the name to Hazard Iron."

"My older brother would be fascinated. Anything scientific or mechanical interests him."

"Are you the second son also?" George's father asked, coming aboard with the rest of the family.

"Yes, sir. My brother Cooper refused an Academy appointment,

42

so I took it instead.'' He said nothing more. There was no point in airing family quarrels; no point in telling strangers how Cooper, whom Orry admired, continually disappointed and angered their father with his independent ways.

"Then you're the fortunate one," Hazard Senior declared, leaning on his gold-knobbed stick. "Some say the Academy is a haven for aristocrats, but that's a canard. The true nature of the Academy is this: it's the source of the best scientific education available in America.'' He punctuated each sentence with a kind of verbal period; the man spoke in pronouncements, Orry thought.

The sister stepped forward. She was an unsmiling girl of about twenty. Her squarish face was marred by a few pox marks. Her figure was generous, almost too buxom for her puff-shouldered, narrow-waisted dress of embroidered cambric. Gloves and a flower-trimmed poke completed her costume. Miss Virgilia Hazard said, "Would you be kind enough to repeat your first name, Mr. Main?''

He could certainly understand why she wasn't married. "Orry,'' he said, and spelled it. He explained that his forebears were early settlers of South Carolina and that he was the third member of his family to be called Orry; it was a corruption of Horry, a common Huguenot name pronounced as if the *H* did not exist.

Virgilia's dark eyes challenged him. "Might I ask the nature of your family's business?''

Instantly he felt defensive; he knew what she was after.

"They own a rice plantation, ma'am. Rather large and considered prosperous.'' He realized his description was gratuitous and braggy; he was indeed on the defensive.

"Then I presume you also own slaves?''

No trace of a smile on his face now. "Yes, ma'am, more than a hundred and fifty. You can't grow rice without them.''

"As long as the South perpetuates Negro slavery, Mr. Main, the region will remain backward.''

The mother touched her daughter's arm. "Virgilia, this is neither the time nor the place for such a discussion. Your remark was impolite and un-Christian. You hardly know this young man.''

The sister blinked; it appeared to be the only apology Orry would get.

"Visitors ashore. Visitors ashore, please!'' A bell rang stridently. George bustled around, hugging Billy, his mother, his father. He shook stuffy Stanley's hand and merely said good-bye to Virgilia.

Soon the steamer was backing from its berth. The family waved from the pier. They dropped out of sight as the boat headed upstream. The two travelers stared at each other, realizing they were on their own.

George Hazard, seventeen, felt obliged to apologize to the young man from the South. George didn't understand his older sister, though he suspected she was mad at the world because she hadn't been born a man, with a man's rights and opportunities. Her anger made her a misfit socially; she was too brusque to catch a beau.

The young Pennsylvanian didn't understand his sister's opinions, either. He had never thought much about slavery one way or another. It existed, although many said it should not. He was not about to damn this chap because of it.

The paddles churned the sunlit water. New York's piers and buildings disappeared astern. George glanced sidewise at Orry, who in one way reminded him of Stanley. *Think carefully first, and don't act until you do.* There was, however, a significant difference. Orry had a natural, genuine smile. Stanley's smile was priggish and obviously forced.

George cleared his throat. "My sister was rude to say what she did."

The moment he spoke he saw Orry's shoulders stiffen. But the tone of the statement put the Southerner at ease. Orry asked, "Is she an abolitionist?"

"I don't think so. Not an active one, anyway, although I guess she could be. Hope you don't take her remarks too personally. I expect Virgilia would sass anyone from your part of the country. You're probably the first Southron she's ever run into. We don't see many in Pennsylvania, and I can't say I've ever met one myself."

"You'll meet plenty at the Academy."

"Good. I'm anxious to know what they're really like. I have this picture, you see—"

"What kind of picture?"

"Southerners are people who eat pork and collards, fight with knives, and abuse their niggers."

In spite of the way the description offended him, Orry managed to see the attempt at humor in it. "Each of those things is true about some Southerners, but it's by no means true of all. That's where misunderstandings arise, I reckon." He pondered a moment. "I have a picture of a Yankee, too."

George grinned. "I thought you might. What is it?"

"A Yankee's always ready to invent some new thingamajig or to outwit his neighbor in court. He's a pert sort who wants to sell you jackknives or tinware, but what he likes best is skinning you."

The other burst out laughing. "I've met a couple of Yankees like that."

"My father says Yankees are trying to run the country now."

George couldn't let that pass. "The way Virginia ran it for so many years?"

Orry gripped the varnished rail. "Look here—"

"No, look there." George decided that if they were to be friends the subject should be changed posthaste. He pointed to the stern, where the two young female passengers were giggling under their parasols. The older woman with them had fallen asleep on a bench.

George had made love to two girls back home, thus felt worldly. "Shall we go talk to 'em?"

Orry turned pink and shook his head. "You go if you want. I'm not much for gallanting the belles."

"Don't like to?"

A sheepish admission: "Don't know how."

"Well, you'd better learn or you'll miss half the fun in life." George relaxed against the rail. "Guess I won't talk to them either. I couldn't conduct much of a romance between here and West Point."

He fell silent, giving in at last to the anxiety that had been growing in him ever since he left home. His family would be staying on in the city, his father to transact some business, the others to enjoy the restaurants, museums, and theaters—while he traveled toward an uncertain future. A lonely one, too. Even if he survived the rigorous disciplines of the Academy, it would be two years before he saw Lehigh Station again. Cadets were granted just one leave, between their second and third years.

Of course he had to overcome a lot of obstacles before he became eligible for that little holiday. The academic work was reportedly hard, the deviling of plebes by upperclassmen harder still. The institution was frequently criticized for permitting hazing. The criticism usually came from Democrats who hated the whole concept of the place, as Old Hickory had.

As the steamer moved against the current, the palisades rose on either hand, green with summer leaves. There was no sign of human habitation on the bluffs. The vessel was carrying them into a wilderness. For that reason George welcomed the company of someone else fated to suffer the same uncertainties and, unless he guessed wrong, the same fears of what lay ahead.

2

The steamer proceeded north into the Hudson Highlands. About one in the afternoon it rounded the point that gave the institution its more common name. Orry strained for a glimpse of the cadet monument to the great engineer, Kosciusko, on the bluff above, but foliage hid it.

As the boat maneuvered into the North Dock, the two young men had a breathtaking view of the Hudson gorge stretching north. Ancient glaciers had carved terraced mountainsides and created the peaks with which Orry had familiarized himself through reading. He pointed them out. Mount Taurus behind them on the east shore, Crow-Nest on the west, and, farther upriver, the Shawangunk range.

"Back there where we passed Constitution Island the Americans strung a chain and boom to hamper navigation during the Revolution. Fort Clinton stood up there on the point. It was named for the British general. The ruins of Fort Putnam are over that way."

"Interested in history, are you?" George asked pointedly.

"Yes. Some of the Mains fought in the Revolution. One rode with Marion, the Swamp Fox."

"Well, I suppose some Hazards fought, too. In Pennsylvania we don't keep very close track of those things." Testiness brought on by the heat and by their isolation had crept into George's voice. He recognized that and tried to joke. "But now I understand why you haven't time for girls. You're always reading."

Orry reddened. George held up his hand. "Don't get me wrong. What you said is interesting. But are you always so serious?"

"What's wrong with that? You'd better be serious too, if you want to last through your first summer encampment."

George sobered. "Guess you're right."

The young female passengers waved good-bye as George and Orry left the steamer. The heat was intense now; George doffed his coat.

Two soldiers in uniform waited on the dock. One, rather oafish, leaned against a rickety one-horse cart. He wore a roundabout with brass buttons, trousers, and gloves—all white but not clean. On his head sat a flat round cap decorated with some kind of brass ornament. A big cutlass hung from a heavy belt.

Orry and George were the only arrivals. The crewmen hurled their luggage onto the dock without concern for the contents. While the newcomers gazed about them, the gangway was quickly drawn up. Bells rang, paddles churned, a whistle blast signaled departure.

The smaller of the two soldiers, clad in a somewhat cleaner uniform, clutched the hilt of his cutlass and strode forward. He too wore one of those round caps. He had a wrinkled face and addressed them with a distinct Irish brogue.

"Corporal Owens, United States Army. Provost of the post."

"We are new plebes—" George began.

"No, sir!"

"What's that?"

"You are a thing, sir. To be a plebe you must survive the entrance examinations. Until then both of you are lower than plebes. You are *things*. Remember that and comport yourselves accordingly."

That didn't set well with George. "Everything ranked and pigeon-holed, is that it?"

With a sniff, Owens said, "Precisely, sir. The Academy puts great faith in rankings. Even the branches of the Army are ranked. The engineers are the elite. The acme. That is why cadets with the highest class standing become engineers. The lowest become dragoons. Remember that and comport yourselves accordingly."

What a damn lout, Orry thought. He didn't like Owens. As it turned out, few cadets did.

Owens indicated the cart. "Place your luggage in there, take that path to the top, and report to the adjutant's office." George asked where it was, but Owens ignored him.

The two newcomers trudged up a winding path to the Plain, a flat, treeless field that looked depressingly dusty and hot. Orry was feeling homesick. He tried to overcome that by recalling why he was here. The Academy gave him his best chance to get what he had wanted ever since he was small: a career as a soldier.

If George felt forlorn, he hid it well. While Orry studied the various stone buildings on the far edge of the Plain, George concentrated on a smaller frame structure immediately to their left; more specifically, on several visitors chatting and observing the Plain from the building's shaded veranda.

"Girls," George remarked unnecessarily. "That must be the hotel. Wonder if I can buy cigars there."

48

"Cadets don't smoke. It's a rule."

George shrugged. "I'll get around it."

Orry found the Academy's physical setting impressive, but the buildings themselves had a spartan look; that was the Army way, of course. It certainly gave the lie to critics who said the place pampered those who enrolled. And West Point could hardly be a citadel of indolence if ninety to a hundred young men arrived each June but only forty to fifty of them graduated four years later. Orry and his new friend had a long way to go before they left the place as full-fledged members of the class of 1846.

Admittance to West Point was highly regulated. The minimum age was sixteen, the maximum twenty-one. In any given year there could be enrolled but one cadet from each congressional district. An additional ten cadets held at-large appointments; these generally went to the sons of Army officers who had no fixed residence. There was also one presidential appointment from the District of Columbia.

Scarcely forty years old, the institution had managed to overcome a good deal of opposition from Congress and the public. Its academic excellence was now generally acknowledged, both at home and in Europe, but a fine scholastic reputation wasn't the same thing as public favor. The Academy continually fought charges that it was elitist, a school serving only the sons of the wealthy and well connected. During President Jackson's administration, Congressman David Crockett of Tennessee had introduced a bill that would have dismantled West Point had it passed.

Although the Academy had been established in 1802, it had received little attention or support from Congress or the Cabinet until after the War of 1812. During the war much of America's military leadership had shown itself to be inept. As a consequence a new Academy superintendent had been appointed in 1817. Major Sylvanus Thayer had rapidly upgraded both the military and the academic curriculum. Since Thayer's time West Point had graduated some outstanding officers. Orry had often heard his father mention Robert Lee of the Corps of Engineers. Lee had been a cadet in the late 1820s.

The military skills of the graduates of the past few decades had never been demonstrated to a skeptical population, however. There had been no wars, and without war West Point's claims about the worth of its program couldn't be validated. That skepticism was fueled by the attitude of many of the cadets; few of them planned long Army careers. They sought appointments simply to take advantage of a fine educational opportunity. The present law required just four years of military service after graduation. On the steamer George had told Orry that he intended to serve that length of time, then return to civilian life. No wonder some people said it was a crime to spend public funds on young men who had no intention of repaying the debt with long service.

From clear on the other side of the Plain came shouting. Orry and George quickly saw the source: cadets in uniform bawling orders in the dusty street that ran past the two stone barracks. Other young men in an assortment of civilian outfits stumbled into military formation in response to the hectoring. The haphazard way they lined up marked them as new arrivals.

A drum rattled somewhere, the beats staccato, the pattern distinctive. Closer at hand, a cadet in a splendid uniform walked briskly toward them, bound for the hotel. George held up a hand to catch his attention.

"Excuse me."

The cadet halted, standing rigid and fixing them with hard eyes. "Did you address me, sir?" Rather than speaking, he bellowed.

George managed to keep smiling. "That's right. We're looking for the—"

"If you are a newcomer, sir," the other screamed, "take off your hat, sir." He whipped his eyes to Orry. "You also, sir. Always uncover when you address a superior, sir." To George again. "Now, sir. What did you say to me, sir?"

Intimidated by the shouting and all the *sir*s, George barely managed to ask directions to the adjutant's office.

"That way, sir. I will see you again, sir. Make no mistake about that, sir."

He marched on. George and Orry exchanged dismayed looks. It was their first introduction to the West Point style of address. Neither young man liked it.

The adjutant's clerk was another Irishman, but a genial one this time. He took their appointment papers. A second assistant relieved them of their pocket money and recorded the amount in a ledger. They were then directed to see Cadet Sergeant Stribling in room fourteen of South Barracks.

Near the barracks the two paused by the communal water pump and looked past Superintendent Delafield's grazing cow to groups of young men drilling on the Plain. Orry and George knew they were newcomers because they still wore civilian clothes. The adjutant's clerk had answered Orry's question about uniforms:

50

"You don't get one until you're officially a plebe, m'lad. And you're not a plebe until you pass the entrance examinations."

The marchers on the field executed commands sloppily and stumbled often. This caused their cadet drillmasters to shout all the louder. Soon the newcomers were replaced by members of the cadet battalion, in uniform. Their drill was so smart and synchronized, Orry knew there was hope for the new arrivals.

They found Cadet Stribling turned out in immaculate white trousers and a cadet-gray jacket adorned with black cord herringbones and three rows of bullet-shaped gilt buttons. Stribling abused them verbally, just as the cadet near the hotel had done, then sent them to the post store where they drew supplies: bucket and broom, a tin dipper, a lump of soap, an arithmetic book and slate, and blankets. The blankets were so new they still reeked of sheep's oil. It was the traditional smell of the plebe.

Their room on the third floor of South Barracks was hardly a haven for lovers of luxury: a single window, a few storage shelves, a huge chimney and fireplace dominating one wall. Orry wondered whether the room would hold heat on snowy winter nights. He had seen but one snowfall, and that had lasted just two hours on the ground, but this wasn't South Carolina.

George studied the narrow iron beds with a professional eye. The legs were badly cast, he said. Another drum call, this one different from the first, drifted up to them in the sultry air. George made a face. "That drum seems to signal every activity around here. I feel like a damn slave to it already."

"Do you suppose that's the call to supper?" Orry said with a hopeful look.

"It better be. I'm starved."

But it was not yet mealtime. Downstairs they were ordered to fall in to watch the evening parade. A cadet band struck up a march, and Orry quickly forgot his hunger.

Bayonets on shouldered muskets flashed in the orange light of the sinking sun. The colors and officers' hat plumes danced in the breeze. The marching and the music thrilled Orry, and all at once he felt less homesick, almost happy to be here. West Point was, after all, a kind of fulfillment of a boyhood ambition that still dominated his life.

Orry couldn't remember exactly when he had decided to become a soldier, but he was very much aware of why he thought so highly of the profession. It was glamorous—much more so than the life of

51

a rice planter—and it was important in the universal scheme of things. Many people looked down on military men, yet no one could deny that generals and their armies frequently changed the shape of entire countries and altered the course of history.

Growing up, he had read book after book about commanders who had done just that. Alexander. Hannibal. Jenghiz Khan. Bonaparte, whose apocalyptic shadow had covered Europe less than half a century ago. Out of Orry's reading and his boyhood dreams, which mingled danger and pageantry, nobility and bloodshed, had come his decision about his life's work. He would be thankful forever that his older brother hadn't wanted the appointment.

After the conclusion of the impressive evening ceremony the drum called them again—this time for supper. Cadet Stribling commanded the squad of newcomers who marched to the mess hall in slovenly fashion. In the hall everyone stood until the senior cadet captain gave the command to sit.

The squad was placed at a tottery wooden table reserved for newcomers. At other tables, however, Orry noticed new cadets seated with upperclassmen. He could only assume those *things* had arrived the day before. The first classmen had the best seats at the ends of the tables. Next along the sides came the second classmen, then the yearlings, then the plebes. Finally, at the very center of each side—farthest from the food—were the nervous newcomers Orry was observing. The upperclassmen passed snide comments about them but were slow to pass the bowls of food. Orry was thankful he wasn't at that kind of table tonight.

Someone said the main meal of the day was midday dinner. Hence all they got for supper was standard Army leftovers—beef and boiled potatoes. George and Orry were hungry enough that it made no difference. Besides, there were some positively delicious extras: homemade bread, country butter, rich coffee.

At the conclusion of supper the cadet captain gave the order to rise. Cadets and newcomers marched back to barracks, with fifes supplementing the drum cadence. While George and Orry spread their blankets on their iron beds, George's sullen look asked why they had come to this place of loneliness and regimentation.

Between all-in and tattoo, a couple of upperclassmen stopped by to introduce themselves. One, a six-footer named Barnard Bee, was a South Carolinian, which pleased Orry. George was greeted by a cadet from his home state, Winfield Hancock.

South Barracks housed most of the new arrivals, and that night George and Orry met some of them as well. One was a bright, glib little chap from Philadelphia who introduced himself as George McClellan.

"Real society stuff," George noted after McClellan left. "Everybody in eastern Pennsylvania knows his family. They say he's smart. Maybe a genius. He's only fifteen."

Orry left off examining his image in the small looking glass over the washstand; he had already been ordered to get a haircut.

"Fifteen? How can that be? You're supposed to be sixteen to get in here."

George gave him a cynical look. "Unless you have connections in Washington. My father says there's a lot of political pull employed to get certain men admitted. And to keep 'em here if they can't handle the work or get in a jam."

Two more newcomers stopped in a few minutes later. One, an elegantly dressed Virginian named George Pickett, was of medium height, with a quick smile and dark, glossy hair that hung to his shoulders. Pickett said he had been appointed from the state of Illinois, where he had clerked in his uncle's law office. There had been no Virginia appointments available to him. Pickett seemed even more contemptuous of the rules than the other George; his breezy manner was immediately likable.

The second visitor was also a Virginian, but Pickett's enthusiasm seemed forced when he performed introductions. Perhaps Pickett had struck up an acquaintance with the tall, awkward fellow and now regretted it. There was a marked difference between George Pickett of Fauquier County and the new cadet from Clarksburg. Of course that far western section of the state could hardly be considered an authentic part of the South; it was mountainous and populated with a lot of illiterate rustics—

Of which Tom J. Jackson, as he called himself, was a prime example. His skin was sallow; his long, thin nose looked like the blade of a knife. The intensity of his blue-gray eyes made Orry nervous. Jackson tried hard to be as jolly as Pickett, but his lack of social grace made the short visit uncomfortable for all four young men.

"With that phiz, he should be a preacher, not a soldier," George said as he snuffed out the candle. "Looks to me like he's worrying about something. A bellyache. Cramped bowels, maybe. Well, who cares? He won't last ten days."

Orry almost fell off the bed when someone kicked the door open and a stentorian voice exclaimed:

"And you, sir, will not last a fraction of that time if you don't practice a seemly silence at the appropriate moments. Good night, sir!" The door shut, a thunderclap. Even at a time of rest there was no escaping the system—or the upperclassmen.

The drum called them before daylight. The morning that followed was strange and uneasy. A cadet lieutenant, a Kentuckian, threw all their blankets on the floor and lectured them on the correct way to fold bedding and put the room in shape for inspection. George seethed, but their treatment could have been worse. A newcomer in a nearby room was visited by two cadet noncoms, one of whom introduced the other as the post barber. The trusting newcomer surrendered himself to razor and shears. Next time he was seen, he was bald.

Not all the upperclassmen were dedicated to deviling the new arrivals; some offered help. Cadet Bee volunteered to tutor the roommates in any of the subjects on which they would have to recite during entrance examinations—reading, writing, orthography, simple proportions, decimals, and vulgar fractions.

George thanked Bee but said he thought he could get through all right. Orry gratefully accepted the offer. He had always been a wretched student, with a poor memory; he had no illusions about that.

George didn't feel he had to study. He spent the morning asking questions of some of the less hostile upperclassmen. A couple of things that he discovered pleased him immensely.

He learned that a river man frequently rowed to a nook on the bank below the Plain and there awaited the cadets who had blankets or other contraband to trade. The river man's illegal goods included cakes, pies, whiskey, and—blessed news—cigars. George had been smoking since he was fourteen.

Even more satisfying was the news that young female visitors came and went at Roe's Hotel the year round. Women of all ages seemed to be smitten with a certain malady described with a leer and a wink as "cadet fever." George's four-year exile might not be as grim as he'd feared.

He knew he would find the discipline tiresome but the education offered by the Academy was supposedly very fine, so he would negotiate his way around the rules. His roommate was pleasant enough. Likable, even. Not nearly so clannish as some of the Southrons he observed. In less than twenty-four hours many of them, and many

Yankees as well, had found their fellows and formed their own little groups.

After dinner the drum sounded drill call. George was momentarily content as he joined his squad in the street. The contentment departed when he saw the drillmaster—a plebe who would become a yearling as soon as the first class changed the gray for blue.

This fellow surely weighed more than two hundred pounds. The start of a paunch showed beneath his uniform. He had black hair, sly dark eyes, and a complexion that reddened rather than browned in the sunshine. He appeared to be eighteen or nineteen. George thought of him as a porker, a pachyderm, and disliked him on sight.

"I, gentlemen, am your drillmaster, Cadet Bent. Of the great and sovereign state of Ohio." Bent unexpectedly stepped in front of Orry. "Do you have a comment on that, sir?"

Orry gulped. "No, I don't."

"You will reply with 'No, I don't—sir!' "

George had a sudden feeling that the fat cadet had taken time to discover where his charges had come from and was using the information to bait them. To many Southerners, the word *Ohio* meant just one thing—the state containing Oberlin College, where white and black students defied convention by studying together as equals.

"You gentlemen from down South fancy yourselves superior to we Westerners, do you not, sir?"

Orry's neck reddened. "No, sir, we do not."

"Well, I am pleased you agree with me, sir. Surprised but pleased."

Bent strutted down the squad, passing a couple of obvious bumpkins and choosing George as his next victim. "And you, sir? How do you feel about the West vis-à-vis your section—the East, am I not correct, sir? Which of the three regions is in your view superior?"

George did his best to smile like a perfect idiot. "Why, the East, sir."

"What did you say?"

Bent's bad breath was sickening, but George kept smiling. "The East, sir. Nothing but farmers out West. Present company excepted, naturally, sir."

"Would you make the same remark, sir, if you knew the Bent family had important and highly placed friends in Washington City, sir? Friends whose merest word could affect your standing here?"

Bloated braggart, George thought, grinning. "Yes, I would." Before Bent could scream, he chirruped, "Sir."

"Your name is Mr. Hazard, I believe, sir. Step forward! I shall

55

use you to demonstrate one of the fundamental principles of marching to these gentlemen. Did you hear me, sir? I said step forward!''

George moved quickly. He had failed to heed the order because he'd been stunned by the spiteful light in Bent's eyes. This was not mere deviling; the poor wretch drew pleasure from it. Despite the heat, George shivered.

"Now, sir, I shall demonstrate the principle of which I spoke. It is commonly termed the goose step. Stand on one leg, thus—''

He lifted his right leg but swayed; his weight unbalanced him.

"On the command *front*, the raised leg is flung forward, thus. Front!''

He couldn't lift his leg very high because he was so heavy. Sweating, he held his position with difficulty. Then, shouting "Rear,'' he tried to fling his leg downward and behind him. He nearly fell on his face. Someone snickered. With horror, George realized it came from the rank near Orry.

"You, sir. Our Southern hothouse lily. I believe you were making sport of me—of this military maneuver?''

"Sir,'' Orry began, obviously startled.

"If you had been formally accepted as a plebe, sir, I would place you on report, and you would receive a score of demerits. You know, sir, that if you receive two hundred demerits in a year, you are sent down the Canterberry road''—that was the road to the nearest railroad depot and the familiar term for dismissal—"in disgrace. Even superior academics cannot save you. So curb your levity, sir.''

Awash in self-importance, Bent was enjoying himself. "And, more important, give heed to learning this maneuver. You shall practice it, sir—you and your roommate together. Step forward!''

George and Orry stood side by side. Bent strutted in front of them. In his fiercest hoping-for-corporal bellow, he cried, "On one leg, stand! Ready, begin! Front, rear. Front, rear. Front, rear.''

After a minute George felt pain in his right leg. He was damned if he'd let on. One of the regular officers strolled by, giving Bent an approving nod. Bent's commands grew louder, the cadence faster. Sweat broke out all over George's face. His leg began to throb, especially the thigh.

Two minutes passed. Two more. His ears rang, his eyes blurred. He figured he might last another ten minutes at most. He was in fine shape physically, but utterly unused to this wrenching exercise.

"Front, rear, front, rear!'' Bent's voice was husky with excitement.

Some others in the squad exchanged nervous looks. The fat cadet's obsessive enjoyment was all too evident.

Orry fell first, pitching over and catching himself on palms and one knee. Bent stepped to him quickly, seeming to kick up some dust by accident. The dust struck Orry in the face.

Bent was about to order him to stand and resume the exercise when he noticed that the officer was still watching.

"Back to the ranks, sir," Bent said. He sounded almost regretful. He gave George a scathing look. "You too, sir. Perhaps next time you will not treat a military exercise so frivolously. Perhaps you will not be so pert with a superior."

George's right leg ached horribly. But he made it back to the squad, trying to limp as little as possible. Plebes had their generous share of miseries, he thought, but this spiteful hog, sweating his collar black— he was more than a disciplinarian. He was a sadist.

Bent's sly little eyes sought his again. George returned the look with defiance. He knew he had made an enemy.

The two friends asked questions about Bent. They very quickly got more information than they expected. The Ohioan was a superior student but extremely unpopular. Members of his own class willingly discussed his failings—an unusual, even rare, disloyalty and an indication of Bent's low status.

During Bent's plebe year he had been subjected to an unsual amount of hazing. In the opinion of Hancock and others, he had brought it on himself with his pompous pronouncements about war and his frequent boasts about his family's connections in Washington.

"I would surmise that he's a boor because he's fat," Bee said. "I've known a couple of chubby fellows who were picked on when they were small and as a consequence grew up to be mighty rotten adults. On the other hand, that doesn't explain why Bent's so bloody-minded. His attitude goes way beyond the proper mental set of a soldier. Goes most all the way to queerness," the South Carolinian finished with a tap of his forehead.

Another classmate mentioned Bent's devotion to the Academy's foremost professor, Dennis Mahan, who taught engineering and the science of war. Mahan believed the next great war, whatever its cause and whoever its participants, would be fought on new strategic principles.

One was celerity. The army that could move fastest would gain the advantage. A transportation revolution was under way in America and the rest of the world. Even in this relatively depressed decade railroads were expanding everywhere. Railroads would make celerity more than a classroom theory; they would make it a reality.

Information was Mahan's second new principle. Information from other than the traditional earthbound scouts. The professor loved to speculate about the use of balloons for observation, and about experiments now being conducted with coded messages sent long distances along a wire.

A great many cadets absorbed and pondered Mahan's ideas, George and Orry were told. But few preached them as fanatically as Bent. This was impressed on them when they were unlucky enough to draw Bent as drillmaster a second time. Mahan taught that the great generals, such as Frederick and Napoleon, never fought merely to win a piece of ground but for a far more important objective—to crush utterly all means of enemy resistance. During drill, Bent delivered a queer little lecture in which he referred to this teaching of Mahan's, then stressed the upperclassman's duty to promote military discipline by crushing all resistance among the plebes.

A smile wreathed his sweaty face as he held forth. But his dark little eyes were humorless. Jackson was in the squad and that day became Bent's particular target. Bent reviled the Virginian with the nickname Dunce. He did it not once but half a dozen times.

Back in barracks, Jackson declared that he thought Bent somewhat "tetched." "And not a Christian. Not a Christian at all," he added with his usual fervor.

George shrugged. "If someone slapped you with a first name like Elkanah, maybe you'd be crazy too."

"I don't know much about the Army," Orry put in, "but I know Bent isn't fit to command other men, and he never will be."

"He's just the kind that will make it, though," George said. "Especially if he has those connections he brags about."

It was traditional for the first classmen to fling their hats in the air at their last parade, then harry them around the Plain by kicking them and stabbing them with their bayonets. That was the entire West Point graduation.

Soon after the ceremony, the first classmen left, having willed or sold their uniforms and blankets to friends remaining behind. Each class then moved up, and the Board of Visitors, convened under the command of General Winfield Scott to examine the prospective graduates, now turned its attention to the prospective plebes.

General Scott was the nation's foremost soldier, pompous and obese, but a great hero. His nickname, not always uttered affectionately, was Old Fuss and Feathers. He took up residence at the hotel with his daughters and presided at the entrance examinations, although he dozed through most of them. So did a majority of the regular Army officers who sat on the board. The work of the examinations was done by the professors, who could always be identified by what they wore—not regulation uniforms but dark blue coats and trousers with a military look.

The new cadets had been randomly sorted into small groups, or sections; all academic work at the Academy was done in sections. The examinations were patterned after regular classroom sessions. At West Point students did not passively receive lecture material and months later spew it back to the instructor in a test. Every day, according to a fixed schedule, certain members of each section recited. A blackboard was always used for this demonstration, as it was called.

At the examination George and Orry and the others had to step to a board and demonstrate their facility in all the required subjects. George had done no studying. But the examinations still didn't worry him, and his relaxed manner showed it. He passed with no difficulty.

When Orry's turn came, he found the examination room hotter than the pit, the officers bored—Scott was snoring—and the demonstration work an excruciating embarrassment. He and Jackson were being tested at the same time. It was a guess as to which one sweated more, squirmed more, or got more chalk on his clothes. Was such torture worth it for a cadet's princely pay of fourteen dollars a month? Orry had to keep reminding himself that struggling at the board was the price of becoming a soldier.

At that he was lucky. Twenty young men failed and were sent home. The rest received uniforms; after these few weeks that had seemed endless, they were now officially plebes. Just to run a palm over the sleeve of his swallowtail coat of cadet gray was the greatest thrill Orry had ever experienced.

3

The two-month summer encampment, prescribed by law, began July 1. Except for the new second classmen, who were home on furlough, the entire cadet corps pitched tents on the Plain. Orry was initiated into the mysteries of standing guard and of dealing with upperclassmen who came sneaking around in the dark to see whether they could confuse the new sentinel.

Bent was now a corporal. He placed Orry on report three times for different infractions. Orry thought two of the charges trumped up and one highly exaggerated. George urged him to submit a written excuse for the third offense to Captain Thomas, the commandant of cadets. If the excuse was sufficiently persuasive, the report would be removed. But Orry had heard that Thomas was a stickler for grammar and felicitous phrasing and often kept a cadet in front of him for an hour, while, together, they corrected the written excuse. It sounded too much like blackboard demonstration, so he let all the reports stand and collected the demerits for each.

George seemed to be Bent's favorite target. Somehow he always managed to wind up in the Ohioan's detail. When the plebes policed the encampment, Bent hazed George to exhaustion by making him pick up pebbles and straighten blades of grass the corporal claimed were crooked. George wasn't good at keeping his temper—much to Bent's delight. He collected demerits—skins, the cadets sometimes called them—at a dizzy rate. He soon had three times the number that Orry did.

Despite the cramped tents, bad food, and incessant ragging by a few of the upperclassmen who criticized everything about the plebes from their salutes to their ancestors, the encampment delighted Orry. He relished the infantry and artillery drills that occupied most of the day. The evening parades, watched by visitors from the hotel, were splendid martial demonstrations that made all the travails worthwhile.

A cadet hop was held each week. To make sure there were enough partners for the ladies who attended, the Academy offered its students the services of a German dancing master. George brushed up on the jig and double shuffle and attended every hop if he wasn't on duty. Plebes were permitted to mingle with the female guests, but of course had to defer to upperclassmen at all times. In spite of this, George enjoyed himself immensely and on several occasions strolled down Flirtation Walk with a girl—a deliberate defiance of the rules that placed certain sections of the post off limits to members of his class.

One night after a hop, George crawled into the tent with the smell of cigars on him. He found Orry still awake and urged his friend to join him at next week's dance.

"I'm a terrible dancer." Orry yawned. "I never have enough nerve to hold a girl firmly. I reckon my trouble is that I think of a woman as an object to be admired from a distance, like a statue."

"Stuff and nonsense," George whispered. "Women are meant to be touched and used—like a nice old winter glove. They like it."

"George, I can't believe that. Women don't think the same thoughts as men. They're delicate creatures. Refined."

"They only pretend to be delicate and refined because it sometimes suits their purposes. Believe me, Orry, a woman wants exactly what a man wants. She just isn't allowed to admit it, that's all. You'd better get over that romantic view of the fair sex. If you don't, one of these days some woman will break your heart."

Orry suspected George was right. But he still couldn't bring himself to attend a hop that summer.

At the end of August the furloughed class returned and the corps of cadets moved back to barracks. On that day upperclassmen took advantage of the plebes as beasts of burden, ordering them to carry their gear. Corporal Bent sought out George, who made four trips with staggering loads in ninety-eight-degree heat. At the start of the fifth trip Bent ordered him to run. George got halfway up the stairs in North Barracks, gasped, and passed out.

He bloodied his forehead as he crashed to the landing below. Bent didn't apologize or express sympathy. He placed George on report for damaging an upperclassman's belongings through carelessness. Orry urged that his roommate write an excuse.

George said no. "I'd have to admit I swooned like a girl. I don't want that on my record. But don't worry, I'll get that bastard. If not next week, then next month or next year."

Orry was starting to feel the same way.

The morning gun, the evening gun, the fifes and the drum soon became familiar sounds, even friendly ones. It was the drum Orry liked best. It not only served as a kind of clock; it reminded him of why he was here. It cheered him up whenever he felt the classroom work was too hard—which was almost every time he went to the board.

Plebes received instruction in mathematics during the morning and in French during the afternoon. For the first week sections were organized on a random basis. Then at week's end new cadets were ranked. Orry found himself in the mathematics section second from the bottom. In French he was in the lowest section—among the immortals, as the cadets called them.

Orry's French section recited to Lieutenant Théophile d'Orémieulx, born in France and Gallic from his shrug to his peg-top trousers. He was highly critical of the accents and abilities of his pupils, and his grading showed it.

Class standings were announced once a week at parade. Some cadets rotated in or out of the lowest French section, but Orry remained. This led d'Orémieulx to question him about his background. Orry was prodded to admit that the founder of the Main family had been a Frenchman.

"Then surely your relatives speak the language?"

"No, not anymore, I'm embarrassed to say. My mother can read a little, and my sisters are being tutored in French, but that's all."

"God above," cried the instructor, storming around the room. "How do they expect me to instruct barbarians? I might as well try to teach the M'sieu Attila to paint teacups."

The conversation only seemed to worsen Orry's relationship with the instructor. One day in October, after Orry had given an especially halting recitation, d'Orémieulx blew up:

"Let me tell you something, M'sieu Main. If the M'sieu *Jesu Chri* were to say to me, 'M'sieu d'Orémieulx, will you listen to M'sieu Main speak French or will you go to the hell,' I would say to him 'I will go to the hell, *s'il vous plaît*, M'sieu *Jesu Chri*.' Sit down. *Sit down!*"

Next day, Orry started practicing his French aloud. He did this whenever he was alone in his room. Bent was always snooping around and two days later caught him during one of these recitations. The Ohioan roared into the room, demanding to know what was going on. When Orry explained, Bent scoffed.

"You are entertaining someone in here, sir. Socializing."

Orry reddened. "Sir, I am not. Look for yourself, sir—"

63

But the corporal had already waddled out. He placed Orry on report for attempting to deceive a superior.

Orry wrote an excuse. After an awkward interview with Captain Thomas, he got the report removed. He learned later that Bent had raved and cursed for ten minutes when he heard the news.

The autumn went faster than Orry had expected. Formations, drill, classroom work, and endless study left little time for anything else. The West Point system was founded on filling all a cadet's waking moments. Only on Saturday afternoons were plebes free to do what they wished, and often that time had to be spent walking extra rounds of guard duty to work off demerits.

In bad weather the duty was miserable. Superintendent Delafield, nicknamed Old Dickey, had some strange ways of economizing. One was his refusal to issue overcoats until after the January examinations. Why give a cadet an expensive coat he would carry off with him if he were dismissed? Consequently, in autumn's rain and sleet, new cadets stood guard clad only in thin, incredibly filthy sentinel overcoats that had been in the guardroom, collecting dirt and vermin, for years.

George still didn't study much, but he was always in the first or second sections of mathematics and French. He already had 110 demerits; Orry had 93. Bent was responsible for two-thirds of both totals.

Harassment by the Ohioan slacked off as the January examinations drew near. Orry took to sneaking down to Tom Jackson's room after lights out. They studied together by the glow of banked coals in the fireplace.

Orry regarded Jackson as inherently intelligent, perhaps even brilliant, yet the Virginian had a lot of trouble with lessons and formal classroom routine; each passing mark he obtained required a monumental struggle. Still, he was determined to succeed, and some of the other cadets recognized this extraordinary drive; Jackson had already acquired his cadet nickname, General.

Sometimes, though, Orry thought Jackson was crazy—as when he would sit upright for five minutes at a time so that his internal organs could "hang and arrange themselves properly." He was maniacal on the subject of his own health.

George wrote an occasional letter home; Orry wrote a great many and received an equal number. But letters didn't help as the end of December drew near. Never before had Orry been away from the

64

family plantation at Christmas, and he got quite sentimental over the fact. Showing rare emotion, George admitted that he too would miss home a great deal. Finally, Christmas dawned, and although the chaplain preached an inspiring sermon in the chapel and the mess hall served a fine dinner, the day was a sad and lonely one for most of the cadets.

Soon bitter January weather closed in. Dismal skies lowered spirits as examinations loomed. The Hudson started to freeze, but Orry was hardly aware of it. Even when he stood guard duty in a snowstorm, his mind was on French.

Somehow he survived the inquisition at the blackboard. After the results of the examinations were announced, he whooped and crowed outside his room while less fortunate cadets silently packed their trunks. Sixteen plebes took the Canterberry road. The others took the oath, signed the articles of enlistment—and received a cadet overcoat.

February was only a couple of days old when George made a daring proposal to his roommate. "I'm all out of cigars. And we never really celebrated our brilliant success with the examinations. Let's run it down to Benny's."

Orry looked toward the window. Moonlight touched starry patterns of frost on the glass; the fireplace did little to relieve the night's fierce cold. The Hudson had frozen over almost completely now.

"In this weather? At this hour?" Orry looked dubious. Tattoo and taps would be sounded soon.

George jumped up from his bed; he had been reading a novel. "Of course. We've yet to visit that esteemed landmark. We owe ourselves a celebration. Where's your spirit of adventure?" He was already donning his new overcoat.

Orry's inclination was to say no. But some of George's past remarks about his hesitant nature prodded him to do the opposite. Half an hour after lights out, they sneaked down the iron stairs, eluded the guards, and ran toward the river in the bitter, breathtaking cold.

They scrambled down the path on the side of the bluff and tried to make their way through the snow and frozen underbrush along the shore. They found it hard going. George squinted at the glaring expanse of white to their left.

"It'll be easier if we walk on the ice."

"Think it's thick enough to hold us?"

George's pale eyes reflected the moon sailing high above the Hudson Highlands. "We'll soon find out."

Orry followed his friend, chastising himself for his eternal failure to act boldly. What sort of behavior was that for someone who might be called upon to lead a battlefield charge? He stepped onto the slippery ice and heard a sharp creak.

Ahead, George stopped. "What was that?"

Orry peered at the black mass of the bluff above them. "I thought it came from up there."

"You don't suppose someone's following us?"

Orry looked around. On the moonlit ice they would be completely visible from shore. "It's too late to worry about that."

George agreed. They pressed ahead. Several times the ice creaked and threatened to break beneath them; it really was too thin for safe passage. But there were no signs of pursuit, and very shortly they were peering over a windowsill at the cozy fire burning inside Benny Haven's little drinking establishment on the riverbank. George rubbed his hands together, then blew on them.

"Luck's with us. Not an upperclassman in sight."

In fact Benny Haven had no customers from the post and only two from the village of Buttermilk Falls, located on the bluff above the tavern. Genial, middle-aged Benny had black hair, a big nose, and features reminiscent of an Indian's. He had been selling beer, wine, and ardent spirits for more years than the cadets could remember or the tactical officers cared to acknowledge. He greeted the two arrivals cordially. The townsmen gave them sullen looks.

George ordered three cigars and two pots of beer. The friends sat at a corner table next to a window with a view of the stoop. Should an upperclassman show up, they could cut for the curtained doorway beside the fieldstone chimney. Orry relaxed a little, enjoying the taste of the beer and the smell of hot ham drifting from the kitchen in back. He ordered a plate of ham and some bread.

Benny served the food, then struck up a conversation. As a newcomer Orry was very welcome, Benny said. But Orry's accent identified him as a Southerner. Hence Benny couldn't help asking politely about the Southern clamor for the annexation of Texas. Was it motivated by a desire on the part of politicians to add more slave territory to the Union?

Orry had heard the charge too often to be offended. Besides, his brother Cooper—much to the annoyance of their father—said it was true. Orry took his time framing a reply.

While he was thinking, Benny frowned and looked toward the curtained door. They had all heard a noise in the kitchen. George's face signaled trouble an instant before the curtain was swept aside. A cold red face loomed over a quivering mountain of cloth, a cadet overcoat.

"Well, sir, what have we here? A couple of malefactors, that's evident," said Elkanah Bent with a gloating smile.

Orry's belly hurt. He was sure Bent's arrival was no accident. He recalled the noise they had heard while walking here. How many nights had Bent spied on them, waiting for this kind of opportunity?

Suddenly, George flung his empty beer pot. Bent squealed and dodged to avoid being hit. "Run," George shouted. He went out the door like a ball from a cannon.

Orry ran after him, his only thought a ridiculous one: they hadn't paid their bill.

In one of the deepest patches of snow along the shore, George took a tumble. Orry stopped, ran back, and helped his friend to his feet. He saw Bent lumbering after them while Benny Haven stood in the tavern door, an amused spectator. He didn't act worried about the bill.

"Come on, George," Orry panted as his friend again slipped and floundered in the snow. "This time that son of a bitch will have our heads."

"Not if we beat him back."

"Even if we do, he'll report us, and we can't lie," Orry gasped as they headed up the shore. The Academy's honor code had already been thoroughly drummed into them.

"I guess we can't," George agreed.

Bent's bulk worked against him; the other two cadets were able to run much faster. But the underbrush once again impeded them. Frozen branches slashed at their faces and broke with gunlike sounds when they struck them. Soon George called for a change of direction. He leaped a low thicket and landed on the ice. Orry saw its moonwhitened surface crack and sag.

"Maybe we can bluff him into not putting us on report," George said as he led the way. "He's out after hours, too, don't forget."

Orry didn't answer, just kept running. There was some flaw in George's logic which he couldn't locate.

Footing was treacherous. Every few steps Orry felt the ice give.

He looked back, saw Bent stumbling and lurching in pursuit, a huge, shuddering blot of ink on the pale expanse of the river.

"Another twenty yards and we'll be on the path," George cried, pointing. At that moment a shout went up behind them. George skidded to a stop and squinted.

"Oh, God," he groaned.

Orry lurched against him, turning. Only half of the ink blot was visible above the ice. Hands waved feebly. Frightened outcries drifted to them in the still air.

"He fell through!" Orry exclaimed.

"At his weight, are you surprised? Let's go."

"George, we can't leave him. He might drown."

Bent's cries grew more strident. George grimaced. "I was afraid you'd say that."

"Look here, I don't believe you've suddenly lost your conscience—"

"Just shut up and come on," George said, starting back. His eyes had a furious glint; he didn't need to tell Orry their luck had turned bad.

Then Orry saw Bent sinking. He and George ran even harder than they'd run before.

A second later Bent's head disappeared. His forage cap floated in the water, its stiff visor shining in the moonlight. Just as the two plebes reached the hole in the ice, the Ohioan bobbed into sight again. He groped toward them, splashing and shrieking.

George and Orry tugged and heaved. Rescue was difficult because of the slippery ice. Twice the plebes almost pitched headfirst into the water. But at last they dragged Bent out. He lay retching, a wet, whalelike figure. George knelt beside him.

"Bent? You have to get up and get back to barracks. If you don't, you'll freeze."

"Yes—all right. Help me. Please."

George and Orry stretched Bent's arms over their shoulders so that they could support him. By then the corporal was no longer making coherent sounds, just moaning and gulping air. Because of the water on Bent's clothes, his rescuers were soaked and chilled by the time they brought him to the riverbank. Still keeping silent, he labored up the hillside path. At the top he shook himself, caught his breath, and said:

"I appreciate what you did. It was—a brave act. I had better go this way. You return to your barracks as best you can."

He lumbered into the dark, the squeak of his shoes and the sound of his heavy breathing lingering for a time after he disappeared.

Orry's teeth started to chatter. His hands felt stiff, frozen. How strange Bent's last remark had sounded, how—

He couldn't think of the word he wanted.

George gave voice to his friend's feelings. "He sounded about as sincere as a woman praising spinsterhood. I think we should have let him drown."

Despite his chill, Orry laughed. "Now that it's all over, you've got to admit we had a pretty rotten celebration."

"I'll say." George pulled three broken cigars from under his overcoat. With a rueful grin, he threw them away. "The only consolation is, I never paid for them. Let's get inside before we die of ague."

The following morning, Bent was absent from breakfast. Orry and George presumed he had decided to Wheaton it—a term synonymous with malingering. Surgeon Wheaton, the post's medical officer for nearly twenty years, had a kind, unsuspecting nature. He frequently admitted cadets to the hospital or excused them from duty for feigned illnesses.

George and Orry told only a few close friends about their escapade. Then, later in the day, Pickett brought them some disturbing news.

"I'm afraid that treacherous bag of blubber didn't tell you the whole truth, boys. He had special permission to be off post after tattoo. He requested the permission from one of the tactical officers. Bent said he had information that two plebes were running it to Benny's almost every night, and he meant to catch them."

For dinner the mess hall served Albany beef—the nickname for river sturgeon caught in the Hudson before it froze. The fish didn't set well on Orry's stomach for some reason. Later he wondered if he'd had a premonition.

Before the evening was over, Corporal Bent had placed Cadets Main and Hazard on report.

The Academy honor code was founded on faith in the goodness of a cadet's character. If any cadet stated that a charge was false, his word was accepted without question and the charge was withdrawn. Orry believed in the code. Despite George's cynicism, he did too.

Hence neither denied guilt, although the resulting demerit total brought George dangerously close to dismissal.

To work off some of the demerits, the two friends had to walk a good many extra guard tours. The weather turned stormy. George withstood the outdoor duty with no ill effects, but it was different with Orry. Ever since their river adventure, he had been sneezing and sniffling, and he was feeling weak and dizzy when he started an extra tour on a particularly dark Saturday afternoon.

A blizzard was roaring across the mountains from the northwest. A foot of drifted snow piled up in less than an hour. Then the temperature rose and the result was sleet. Orry was slogging back and forth near the sally port when he realized that despite the cold, he was burning up.

Sweat mingled with melting sleet on his cheeks. His musket seemed to weigh a hundred pounds. He staggered in the snow, then leaned against the barracks wall to rest.

Someone plucked his sleeve. Orry recognized a first classman named Sam Grant, an undistinguished fellow except for his horsemanship, which was outstanding.

"Who sent you out here in this weather?" Grant demanded. "You look green. About ready to faint. You should take yourself to the hospital."

"I'm fine, sir," Orry croaked, attempting to straighten up.

The short, dark-eyed cadet was skeptical. "You're about as fine as my Aunt Bess five minutes before she expired. Shall I find a tactical officer and ask him to see that you're relieved?"

"No, sir, that would be—dereliction of—my duty."

Grant shook his head. "You'll make a fine soldier, Mr. Main. If you don't die of mulishness first."

"You know who I am?"

"Every man in the corps knows about you, and your friend, and that scum from Ohio. It's a pity Corporal Bent's standings are so high. Some of us are trying to remedy that. He's being deviled as furiously as he devils others. I sincerely hope you survive to enjoy that, sir."

With a little smile, Grant tramped off into the storm.

It was about four o'clock, Orry guessed. Dark as midnight. He forced himself to move. He thought he was marching, but actually he was reeling from point to point. Fortunately, most of the officers were indoors, hence didn't witness his awkward performance.

70

Another half hour passed. He began to fear he was desperately ill—mortally ill, maybe—and that his foolish wish to avoid a display of weakness would finish him.

"You're not stepping smartly, sir. Not smartly at all."

Stunned by the voice, Orry turned. He saw Bent's tentlike overcoat looming just this side of the sally port. Bent seemed to float forward, a huge shape in the murk. His eyes shone with glee.

"I heard you were out here, sir. I came to inspect—"

The Ohioan's voice faltered as Orry wrenched the old smoothbore flintlock off his shoulder. Orry was out of his head, beyond fear.

"Why are you pointing that piece at me, sir?"

"Because I'm going to shoot you, Bent. If you don't leave me alone, and my friend too, I'm going to shoot you."

Bent tried to sneer. "That musket is unloaded, sir."

"Is it?" Orry blinked and weaved on his feet. "Then I'll beat you to death with it. They can court-martial me, or even shove me in front of a firing squad, but if you're still here at the end of the next five seconds, you ungrateful bastard, I'm going to kill you."

"By God, we've a madman at West Point."

"Yes, sir. An Ohio madman, who treats plebes like animals. Well, Mr. Bent, sir, this is one plebe who won't be treated that way any longer. Five seconds. One, *sir*, two, *sir* . . ."

Bent huffed, but said nothing. He was intimidated by the wild white specter in front of him. Sleet clung to Orry's cap and eyebrows. His expression almost maniacal, he turned the musket so that he gripped it by the barrel, like a club.

Humiliation and hate flickered on Bent's face. Suddenly, he spun on one heel. He seemed to melt into the storm.

Orry swallowed and shouted, "And you'd better leave us alone from now on."

"*What did you say, sir?*"

The sharp voice turned him the other way. Bundled to the ears, one of the tactical officers came striding toward him. The howl of the wind forced the officer to yell. "Cadet Grant requested that I come out here, sir. He said you were too ill for this duty. Is that true?"

By now Orry had practiced the position of a soldier a thousand times or more. He tried to assume it, not even realizing he had just committed the one unforgivable sin. He had dropped his musket in the snow.

The tactical officer seemed to be tilting back and forth. Orry attempted to stop the motion by blinking his eyes.

"*Is that true, sir?*"

"*No, sir!*" Orry cried, and fell forward against the officer, unconscious.

George came running to the hospital an hour later. Surgeon Wheaton met him in the waiting room.

"Your friend is in extremely serious condition. His fever is dangerously high. We are trying to reduce it, but if it doesn't break within twenty-four hours, his life could be in jeopardy."

George thought of Bent, and the storm outside, and of Orry. "The poor damn fool wants to be a soldier too badly," he said in a bitter voice.

"This place has a way of inspiring that ambition." Wheaton's tone mingled regret and pride. "You look none too well yourself, young man. I prescribe a tot of rum. Come into my office and"—he smiled—"Wheaton it for a few minutes, as the saying goes."

With the surgeon's permission, George kept a vigil at Orry's bedside all night. Pickett joined him for a while. So did Jackson. A first classman named Grant looked in briefly. How Orry knew him, George couldn't imagine.

By morning the hospital was cold and silent. George wriggled on his chair. The others were gone. Orry's face was still as pale as the undyed wool coverlet drawn up beneath his chin. He looked fragile in the flickering glow of the fish-oil lamps. Fragile and very sick.

George gazed at his friend and, to his astonishment, found tears welling in his own eyes. The last time he had cried he was five years old. He had been thrashed by this older brother for daring to play with Stanley's pet frog.

George wasn't surprised that Orry Main's fate could mean so much to him. The two of them had gone through a lot together, in a very short period. Common hopes and hardships had forged a strong bond of affection. West Point apparently had a way of doing that, too.

He stayed in the chair, neither sleeping nor eating, until noon, when Orry's fever broke.

The next afternoon, with February sunshine pouring through the window, Orry looked much better. George visited him before supper call with some good news.

"Bent seems to have gotten tired of deviling us. I passed him when I was coming over here. He looked the other way."

"I'd still like to kill him. God forgive me for saying such a thing, but it's the way I feel."

Orry's quiet savagery disturbed George, but he smiled and tried not to show it. "See here, my friend. You were the one counseling meekness and mercy when he was going down 'neath the icy waves. And I listened to you."

Orry folded his arms. "Almost wish you hadn't."

"It's better to leave him alive and squirming. The upperclassmen are skinning him right and left. That's sweet revenge."

"But he'll blame us. Even if he lets up on us for a while, he won't forget. There's something twisted about him."

"Well, don't fret over it," George said with a shrug. "We have enough to do keeping our demerit total under two hundred. It's a long way until June."

Orry sighed. "I reckon you're right."

But neither believed that merely forgetting about Bent would do away with the threat he posed.

Late in the spring, all the Hazards except Virgilia paid a visit to West Point. George wheedled the necessary permission to join them for Saturday dinner at the hotel. He took his friend along.

William Hazard invited Orry to visit them in Lehigh Station at some time in the future. Orry said he'd enjoy that. He found the family as likable as he remembered—save for Stanley, who talked, or rather bragged, incessantly. Stanley was preening over the fact that he and his father were to dine that night with a family named Kemble, who lived across the river in Cold Spring.

Between bites of a delicious lamb chop, Orry asked, "Are the Kembles relatives of yours?"

Stanley snickered. "No, my boy. They are the proprietors of the West Point Foundry. Who do you think casts most of the ordnance purchased by the Army?"

Stanley's pompous manner made his little brother Billy grimace and silently imitate him. Billy was seated next to Stanley, who didn't see the imitation and thus didn't understand why George guffawed. Billy's antics earned him a thwack on the ear from his father. Mrs. Hazard looked chagrined.

Stiffly, Orry said, "I'm sorry, I never heard of the Kembles."

"Their Saturday-night fetes are famous." Stanley's tone suggested that Orry and his home state somehow existed outside the mainstream of national life.

To Mr. Hazard, Orry said, "They're ironmakers, are they?"

The older man nodded. "With candor and envy, I must admit there are none better in the nation."

"Maybe they could help my brother."

Bored, Stanley forked up a potato. But William Hazard listened politely as Orry explained that in recent letters Cooper had complained about excessive breakage of wrought-iron walking beams and flywheels in the rice mill at Mont Royal.

"That's the name of our plantation. The mill used to be powered by the river tides, but my brother talked my father into trying a steam engine. Father was against the idea. Now he thinks he was right."

"Casting iron is a tricky business," Mr. Hazard said. "Perhaps the Kembles could help your brother. Better still, why not let us try? Have him write me."

"I'll do that, sir. Thank you!"

Orry was always eager to make his older brother think well of him. He wrote Cooper the next day. Cooper's reply began with words of appreciation to Orry. He then said he suspected that the man in Columbia who made the mill parts understood the process even less than he did. Hence he would be grateful for advice and assistance from experts. He was dispatching a letter to Hazard Iron immediately.

June approached. To Orry's surprise, he realized he stood a good chance of surviving his plebe year, although he seemed destined to remain an immortal forever. George continued to stand high in the academic ranking, and without visible effort. Orry envied his friend, but never to the point that jealousy impaired their relationship.

Both friends had managed to keep their demerit total just under two hundred, and when the new group of prospective cadets began to arrive, pressure on the plebes lessened. Orry and George did their share of deviling the newcomers, but there was little meanness in it. Bent had provided too good an object lesson.

It was impossible to avoid the Ohioan completely, of course. But whenever they encountered him, he affected an opaque stare, as if they didn't exist. The friends continued to feel that although Bent had left them alone during their final months as plebes, he certainly hadn't forgotten about them. Nor was it likely that he had forgiven them, either.

About ten days before the start of the summer encampment, Cooper arrived unexpectedly. He had just come from Pennsylvania, where William and Stanley Hazard had examined some of the shattered parts from the Mont Royal mill.

"Your father and brother solved the problem in short order," Cooper reported to George. "As I suspected, that clod in Columbia doesn't know what he's doing. Apparently he doesn't remelt his pig iron at the right temperature. If I can convince him of that, we may have fewer breakdowns. Of course convincing him won't be easy. As far as he's concerned, admitting you can learn something from a Yankee is almost as bad as saying Johnny Calhoun was wrong on nullification."

George was fascinated by Cooper Main, who was twenty-three and taller than his younger brother. He wore fine clothes, which managed to look terribly untidy. He had sunken cheeks and darting dark eyes and was not without a sense of humor, although George found him more inclined to sarcastic smiles than to laughter. Cooper and Orry shared certain obvious family traits, including a slender frame, the brown wavy hair, and the narrow, almost haughty nose. But the older brother lacked the robust color Orry developed whenever he spent even one day in the sunshine; Cooper's thin face and body seemed to have an unhealthy aura, as if he had been born pale, tired, and driven to think too much.

Cooper had decided to make the whirlwind overnight visit not only for the purpose of seeing Orry but to inspect the school that was turning out the nation's smartest soldiers. He remarked that there was nothing in creation unworthy of study, unless perhaps it was family trees in his native state.

During Cooper's short stay at Roe's Hotel, however, his attention seemed to wander repeatedly from the sights he had come to see. Once Orry caught him gazing at the big stone barracks—or perhaps something beyond them—with an almost melancholy look in his eyes.

But just before Cooper left, he put aside his preoccupations and his air of mockery and flashed a big grin at George, saying: "You must pay us a visit, sir. Lots of mighty pretty girls down on the Ashley. Got a couple in our own family. They'll be beauties when they grow up. Didn't see many pretty girls in the Lehigh Valley. 'Course, I spent most of my time staring into fiery furnaces. Your family operates a mighty impressive factory, Mr. Hazard."

"I wish you'd call me George."

"No, call him Stump," Orry put in. "All the cadets get nicknames eventually. We were christened last week."

"Stump, eh?" Cooper shot a glance at his brother. "What's yours?"

"Stick."

That made Cooper laugh. "Parts of the same tree, is that it? Well, Mr. Stump, I want to say I admire the size and scope of your family's enterprise." Again his eyes took on that distant, melancholy look. "I surely do."

Over the bellowings from a calf boat moving down the Hudson, they heard the whistle of the steamer at the North Dock. Cooper grabbed his valise and rushed down the steps of the hotel veranda.

"Come see us, Mr. Stump. Mind that you eat right, Orry. We'll expect you home next summer."

After the visitor hurried out of sight, George said, "Your brother seems like a fine fellow."

Orry frowned. "He is. But there was something wrong. He was making a valiant effort to joke and smile—neither is very easy for him anytime—but he was upset."

"Why?"

"I wish I knew."

4

The river sloop *Eutaw* carried Cooper home from the seacoast. Aboard the sloop were packets of mail and shipments of staples sent up-river to the various plantations by the Charleston factor who served them.

It was a still, sunny morning. The Ashley was placid, glassy. Of all the rice rivers, it was one of the least valuable because the ocean could affect it so drastically. Although the river was fresh here, freak tides or hurricanes sometimes brought the salt of the Atlantic, which killed the rice. But in the opinion of Cooper's father and the other local planters, that risk was offset by the ease of shipping the crop down to Charleston.

The heat of late June baked Cooper's neck and hands as he stood at the rail awaiting his first glimpse of the Main dock. He was often bitterly critical of his state, and of this region in particular. But love of both dwelled deep in his bones. He especially loved the familiar sights of the river, the panorama of pines, live oaks, and occasional palmettos rising on those stretches of shore that remained unclaimed. In the trees, jays and redbirds flashed their colors. At one place a river road skirted the bank. Cooper watched three young blades on fine horses thunder by; racing was a favorite sport in the low country.

Insects nibbled and nagged at his skin. He could almost smell the sickly season coming. At the great house, preparations would be under way for the family's removal to their place at Summerville. From there Cooper's father would ride down to the plantation to inspect on a regular basis, but he would not stay at Mont Royal until the weather cooled again. They had a saying about South Carolina's coastal region, where miasmic fevers killed scores of whites every year: "In the spring a heaven. In the summer a hell. In the fall a hospital."

On the port side the foliage gave way to man-made ramparts—the high main banks. Beyond them lay fields long ago reclaimed from the marshlands by the hard work of Cooper's forebears. The banks themselves were a key part of the operation of the complex agricultural machine that was a rice plantation.

At regular intervals the banks were pierced by rectangular wood culverts called trunks. The trunks had gates at both ends. By means of these gates the water of the river was carefully admitted to, or drained from, the fields where the rice grew. That is, the rice grew if Tillet Main's people did their work properly and on time. It grew if the May birds and the rice birds weren't too numerous. It grew if autumn storms didn't poison the river with salt.

There were all sorts of variables, and endless risks. Many disappointments and few absolute triumphs. The life of a rice planter taught a healthy respect for the elements, and it frequently gave Cooper the feeling that the Mains should be in some less capricious, more modern business.

A hail from the wheel lifted him from his reverie. They had come in sight of the landing, and he hadn't even realized it. All at once he felt strangely sad. *Better keep your mouth shut about the things you saw up North.*

He doubted he could, though.

Soon he was striding up the path through the formal garden that overlooked the river. The air smelled of violets and jasmine, of crab apple and roses. On the second-floor piazza of the great house, his mother, Clarissa Gault Main, was supervising some of the house slaves in the work of closing off the upper rooms. She spied him, ran to the railing, called down with a greeting. Cooper waved and blew her kisses. He loved her very much.

He didn't enter the house but instead circled one end, saying hello to each of the Negroes coming and going around the separate kitchen building. From this spot he could enjoy the pleasing view down the half-mile lane that ran between giant live oaks to the little-used river road. A sultry breeze had sprung up; gray beards of Spanish moss stirred on the trees.

At the head of the lane he saw two little girls. His younger sisters, scrapping as usual; one was chasing the other. Of that rascally Cousin Charles there was no sign.

Mont Royal's business headquarters was another small building beyond the kitchen. Cooper mounted the steps and heard the voice of Rambo, one of the plantation's most experienced drivers.

"They're pipped in South Square, Mr. Main. Landing Square, too." He was referring to fields, each of which had a name.

Tillet Main hedged his bets every year by planting a third of his land during the late season in early June, when the resulting crop would be less likely to be damaged. The driver was telling Cooper's father that the seed in those late-planted areas had put out shoots from beneath the water of the sprout flow. Soon those fields would be drained by means of their trunks, and the long pe iod of dry growth would begin.

"Good news, Rambo. Does Mr. Jones know?"

"He there with me to see it, sir."

"I want you and Mr. Jones to inform all the people who need to be told."

"Yes, sir. Surely will."

Cooper opened the door and said hello to the big gray-haired black man just leaving. Everyone else in the family called the Negroes Tillet's people, *people* being a traditional term that was somehow supposed to soften or obscure the truth. To Cooper it seemed less onerous—though not much—to be honest in one's thinking. He mentally referred to the Negroes by one word only: slaves.

"Thought the Yankees had kidnapped you," Tillet Main said from within the cloud of pipe tobacco hanging over his desk. He quirked the corners of his mouth—which would be all the affection he would display this morning, Cooper suspected.

"I took a day to visit Orry. He's getting along just fine."

"I expect him to get along just fine. I'm more interested in what you found out."

Cooper eased himself into an old rocker beside his father's ledger-littered desk. Tillet was his own bookkeeper and examined every bill pertaining to the operation of Mont Royal. Like other low-country planters, he liked to refer to his holdings as a barony, but he was one baron who personally kept track of every coin he owned.

"I found my suspicions were correct," Cooper said. "There's a scientific reason for the beams and flywheels breaking so often. If enough of the carbon in cast iron isn't oxidized—the carbon and some of the other elements, too—the iron isn't tough enough for machine parts that take a lot of abuse. Now I have to convince that dunce up in Columbia. If I can't, maybe we can order parts from a foundry in Maryland or even Pennsyl—"

"I would rather keep the business in the state," Tillet broke in. "It's easier to put pressure on friends than on strangers."

"All right." Cooper sighed. He had just been issued another parental order. He received dozens every week. Pique prompted him to add, "But I made some friends in Pennsylvania." Tillet ignored the remark.

The head of the Main family was in his forty-eighth year. Already the fringe of hair around his bald head was pure white. Cooper had inherited Tillet's height and his dark eyes. Yet in this last feature there was a distinct difference between father and eldest son. Cooper's eyes were soft, speculative, bitterly humorous sometimes. Tillet's gaze was seldom gentle or merry. It was, rather, direct, unblinking—and occasionally fierce.

Responsible for the behavior and the welfare of scores of human beings, white as well as black, Tillet Main had long ago schooled himself out of a natural shyness. He gave orders as if born to it—which, by virtue of his last name, he was. In summation of his character it could be said that he loved his wife, his children, his land, his church, his Negroes, and his state, and apologized for none of it.

Half the children he had sired hadn't lived past age four. Cooper's mother said that was why Tillet smiled so seldom. But the eldest son suspected there were other reasons. Tillet's position and heritage naturally inclined him to a justifiable touch of arrogance. At the same time, he was the victim of a growing sense of inferiority which he was helpless to control or defeat. It was a malady Cooper recognized in many Southerners these days. His trip had reconfirmed that such a condition was not without good cause.

Tillet studied his son. "You don't sound very happy to be home."

"Oh, I am," Cooper replied, telling the truth. "But I haven't been up North since my last year at Yale. What I saw depressed me pretty thoroughly."

"Exactly what did you see?" Tillet's manner had turned prickly. Cooper knew he should retreat. Stubbornly, he refused.

"Factories, Father. Huge, dirty factories, humming and clanging and fouling the sky like the furnaces of Beelzebub himself. The North's growing at a frightening rate. Machines are taking over. As for people—my God, I've never encountered so many. Comparatively speaking, this is a wilderness."

Tillet relit his pipe and puffed a moment. "You think quantity counts more than quality?"

"No, sir, but—"

"We don't want a lot of foreign nobodies crowding us."

There it was again, that stupid, stiff-necked pride. Cooper snapped, "What was Charles Main except a foreign nobody?"

"He was a duke, a gentleman, and one of the original Huguenot settlers."

"All very fine, sir. But worshiping the past won't build factories or help the South's economy. This is the age of the machine, and we refuse to acknowledge it. We cling to agriculture and our past, while we fall farther and farther out of step. Once the South practically ran this country. No more. Every year we lose respect and influence at the national level. And with reason. We aren't attuned to the times."

He stopped short of citing the familiar proof—the peculiar institution to which the South's prosperity had become shackled as firmly as the slaves themselves were bound to their owners. But he didn't have to go that far to infuriate Tillet. The older man banged the desk.

"Hold your tongue. Southerners don't speak against their homeland. At least loyal Southerners don't. There are enough Yankees doing that."

The son was caught—squeezed—between his own convictions and his eternal inability to change Tillet's mind. They had argued like this before, but never quite so hotly. Cooper found himself shouting: "If you weren't so damn stubborn, like all the rest of the *barons* of this benighted—"

A scream outside brought a temporary end to the quarrel. Father and son ran for the door.

The scream had come from one of the two little girls Cooper had noticed while on his way to the office. Ashton Main and her sister Brett had finished their reading and ciphering lessons a half hour before the sloop docked. Their tutor, a Charleston German named Herr Nagel, had gone off for a late-morning nap, pleased with the younger girl's eagerness to learn but irked by the sauciness of the older one, as well as her boredom with all things intellectual.

Both girls were unmistakably Mains, yet they were different. Only one was ever noticed by visitors—Ashton, who was going on eight and already beautiful. Her hair was much darker than was typical in the family. In certain lights it looked black. In color and sometimes in ferocity her eyes were exactly those of her father.

Brett was two years younger, not homely but less perfectly featured than her sister. She showed signs of growing up to be slender and quite tall, like Tillet and her brothers; she and Ashton were already the same height. It was an inheritance that would prove a handicap when it came time to attract beaux, as Ashton frequently pointed out.

After their lessons, the girls had gone for a stroll along the river. On a branch in a clump of underbrush, beyond the last square where the green shoots of the March planting stood healthy and tall, Brett had discovered an empty bird's nest containing a small, pale egg.

"Ashton, come see," she called.

Ashton approached with a jaunty step that had a touch of swagger. Young as she was, she had a clear awareness of her physical assets as compared to those of her sister. Her sense of superiority showed as she gazed down at the egg.

Brett said, "A green heron left it, I think." She scanned the river with grave eyes. "Bet she'll be back to nest soon."

Ashton noticed her sister's expression, and for a second or so a little smile played on her pink mouth. "Well, she'll be disappointed," she said, bending quickly to scoop the egg from the nest. Then she ran.

Brett pursued her along the bank. "Put that back. You haven't any right to take a mother bird's baby."

"Oh, yes, I have," Ashton said, tossing her hair. That was that.

Brett knew her sister, or thought she did. The situation called for desperate action, but carried out with cleverness. She pretended to be resigned. Soon Ashton was off guard, walking slowly and examining the prize she held on her upraised palm. Brett ran up from behind and snatched the egg.

Ashton chased her around the great house to the lane—the point at which Cooper, on his way to the office, saw them. The pursuit continued for several minutes. Finally, when both girls were out of breath, Ashton seemed overcome by contrition.

"I'm sorry, Brett. You're right and I'm a ninny. We should put it back. Just let me look at it once more, then we will."

Ashton's sweet sincerity lulled the younger girl. She handed the egg to her sister. Ashton's smile changed. "If it isn't mine, it isn't yours either." She closed her fist and crushed the egg.

Brett jumped at her and, being wiry and agile and not very ladylike, easily bore her to the ground. She yanked Ashton's hair and pummeled her until she shrieked. The outcry brought Papa and Cooper from the office. Papa pulled the two of them apart, got widely varying accounts of the incident from each, then turned them over his knee one at a time, and spanked them—all before their mother dashed out of the house in response to the noise.

Brett bawled to protest the injustice. Ashton bawled even louder. Yet while she threw her head back and grimaced and cut up, her eyes were luminous. At first glance the cause seemed to be tears. Closer inspection showed that she was amused. Clarissa, Tillet, and Cooper missed that.

Brett didn't.

*

Roughly three-quarters of a mile from the great house, in a separate little community of the plantation, another fight was taking place about the same time. A black boy and a white boy rolled over and over in the middle of a dusty street, struggling for possession of a bamboo fishing pole.

The street ran between two rows of whitewashed slave cabins. Here, too, carefully separated from the master's residence, stood the plantation sick house, the small church, and, dominating the far end of the street, a five-room residence raised on pillars of tabby. This house belonged to the Mont Royal overseer, Mr. Salem Jones, a New Englander by birth and a martinet by disposition. Jones had been raised in the South by his widowed mother and about eleven years ago had come to Mont Royal with excellent references from another plantation. Tillet still considered him a Yankee, hence an eternal outsider. Jones's good performance on behalf of the Mains helped overcome Tillet's distrust, but nothing could ever dispel it completely.

The two boys were tussling under the casual gaze of little black children and black men too old to work. It was hard to say which of the two was the rowdier or the dirtier. The white boy—seven years old, suntanned, and strong—was Charles Main. Cousin Charles, Clarissa called him, to distinguish him from the Mains in her own family.

Charles was an exceptionally handsome child. But good looks were just about his only inherited assets. He was the son of Tillet's brother, an incompetent lawyer named Huger Main. Together with his wife, Huger had perished on a New York-bound steamer that foundered and sank off Hatteras in 1841. Charles had been staying with his aunt and uncle while his parents vacationed. He was their only child, and he remained with his relatives after the funeral and the burial of a pair of empty caskets.

It was an easy life for Charles, if a lonely one. With the intuition of the young, he suspected Uncle Tillet hadn't thought much of his father, hence didn't think much of him. Charles turned the rejection into a blessing. His aunt and uncle permitted him to go his own way, making no attempt to subject him to the torture of studying with that Dutch tutor. Charles fished a lot and roamed the woods and marshes around the plantation. For friends he had black boys such as Cuffey, with whom he was wrestling for possession of the pole.

Loud voices in one of the slave cottages attracted the attention of the boys and some of the Negroes. Out of the cottage strode a familiar booted figure. Short, bald, and potbellied, with one of the more cherubic faces in the world, Salem Jones found it necessary to emphasize his authority by going everywhere with a quirt in his hand and a thick hickory truncheon in his belt.

The boys stopped fighting. In the process, Charles accidentally broke the pole. As usual, his shirt hung out and dirt streaked his cheeks and chin. Last week's fight with Cuffey's cousin James had cost Charles one of his upper front teeth. He thought the gap gave him a dashing air.

"Jones been tryin' to go at Semiramis," Cuffey whispered. "He been tryin' since his wife died six month ago."

"He was trying a long time before that, only not so's everybody could see," Charles confided. "That's what Uncle Tillet said, anyway."

Salem Jones walked up the street and disappeared in back of his residence. Charles drifted nearer the cottage occupied by Semiramis and her family. The girl was dimly visible beyond the open door. Charles couldn't see much of her, but he could picture her vividly. Semiramis had satiny black skin, gloriously perfect features, and a ripe figure. All the boys on the plantation agreed she was something special.

Looking angry, Jones saddled up his horse and rode rapidly toward the fields. Cuffey offered a prediction. "Priam be in for it tonight. Old Jones don't get what he want from her, he take it out on her brother."

Charles studied the position of the sun. "I was going to the house for dinner. I think I'll hang around till Priam finishes with his task." The family wouldn't miss him anyway.

Soon he was speculating about what might happen. Semiramis's brother Priam was a strong, and strong-willed, Negro. Three generations removed from Angola, he still possessed a great sense of the freedom that he had been denied.

Charles could appreciate Priam's resentment. The boy didn't understand a system that granted some men freedom because they were white and barred other men from it because they were not. He found that kind of system unjust, even barbaric, although he also believed it to be both immutable and universal.

He had several times discussed certain aspects of the slave system with Cuffey. For example, they had both observed that Semiramis had not the least objection to the classical name given her at birth; her fancy name, Cuffey called it. She did not consider it a sly mockery of her status. Priam, on the other hand, understood the mockery very well. He made no secret of hating his name.

"Priam say he won't be Mist' Tillet's man forever," Cuffey had once confided to his friend. "He say it a lot."

Charles knew what was meant. Priam would run away. To what, though? Wasn't slavery practiced everywhere? Cuffey thought not, but could offer no evidence.

Charles loitered around the slave community as the afternoon wore on. He napped for an hour in the cool, dark church and was seated on a cottage stoop, whittling, when the field hands began to stream in with their hoes canted over their shoulders.

Jones had returned to his house an hour ago. He now appeared on the porch, sweat rings staining his shirt and his quirt and his truncheon very much in evidence.

"You, Priam," Jones called with an affable smile. The slave, a full head taller and fifteen years younger than the overseer, stepped out of the file of ambling Negroes. He was barely respectful as he answered:

"Yes, Mist' Jones?"

"Driver tells me you've been slack in your work lately. He says you've complained a lot, too. Shall I give you a task and a half every day?"

Priam shook his head. "I do every lick I'm 'posed to. I don't have to like it, do I?" He glanced at the other slaves, his eyes resentful, even threatening. "Driver never tol' me I wasn't pleasin' him."

Jones swaggered down the steps, but only halfway; going farther would have put the top of his head below the level of Priam's eyes. "Do you honestly think he'd tell you? No. You're too stupid to understand. All you're good for is just what you're doing. Nigger work. Animal's work."

The overseer gigged Priam's stomach with the truncheon, trying to rouse him. "I'm going to keep you busier for a week or so. An extra half task every day."

There were soft gasps from some of the Negroes who were watching. One task, one assigned piece of work, was the customary quota on all but the most repressive plantations. An able man could complete his task well before the sun set and then have time to cultivate his own garden or attend to personal chores.

Priam's jaw set. He knew better than to sass the overseer. But Jones was determined to provoke him. Charles hated the puffed-up little Yankee with his bald skull and whiny nasal voice.

"Got nothing to say about that, nigger?" Jones gigged Priam harder this time. "I could do more than increase your work. I could give you what your insolent stares call for." He shook the quirt at Priam. "Some of this."

The one-sided nature of the quarrel propelled Charles off the stoop like a cannonball. "Mr. Jones, you got a whip and you got a stick, and Priam's got nothing at all. Why don't you treat him fair? Give him one or the other and then pick a fight."

Silence.

The frightened slaves stood motionless. From the river drifted the hoarse bellowing of an alligator. Even Priam lost the murderous look Jones had kindled in his eyes. The dumbfounded overseer gazed down at the boy.

"You taking this nigger's part?"

"I just like to see him treated fair. Everybody says he's a hard worker. My uncle says that."

"He's a nigger. He's expected to work hard. To break his back, if need be. And you're expected to stay up at the great house where you belong. You keep messing around this part of the plantation, I'll start to wonder why. Does something attract you down here? Does something call to you, like to like? A little nigger blood, perhaps?"

It was the sneer, not the insult, that infuriated Charles. He lowered his head and butted Salem Jones in the stomach. Then he punched him twice and ran like the devil.

He hid out down by the river until twilight. Finally, he decided he couldn't stay away from the great house any longer. As he walked slowly through the garden, a hiss from behind a shrub caught his attention.

Cuffey's face shone in the fading light. Grinning, he said the diversion had been successful. After Charles's attack, Jones had been so mad he had lost interest in bullying Priam.

Hungry and tired, Charles drifted on toward the house. Somehow his victory seemed unimportant. It seemed downright disastrous when he found Uncle Tillet waiting for him, a scowl on his face.

"Jones was here an hour ago. Come in the library. I demand to know what you have to say for yourself."

Charles obeyed and followed his uncle. The boy had always loved the sights and sounds of the great house at this hour of the day. The silver pots and bowls, the rosewood and walnut furniture giving back the candle- and lamplight. The crystal chandelier pendants catching the river breeze and jingling. The house servants murmuring and laughing occasionally as they finished their work. He saw and heard none of that tonight.

Charles had always liked Tillet's library, too, with its heavy, masculine furniture and the fascinating and highly realistic mural of ancient Roman ruins that formed part of the wall above the mantel. The shelves held hundreds of fine books in English, Latin, and Greek. Charles had no interest in those, although he admired his uncle for his ability to read all of them. This evening the library seemed unfriendly and forbidding.

Tillet asked Charles to explain his behavior. Haltingly, the boy said that since Jones had a quirt and a stick and Priam had no weapon there had been no question about whose side he would take.

Tillet shook his head as he reached for his pipe. "You have no business taking sides in that kind of dispute. You know Priam's one of my people. He doesn't have the same rights or privileges as a white man."

"But shouldn't he? If someone's going to hurt him, does he have to take it?"

Tillet lit his pipe with quick, jerky motions. His voice dropped, a sign of anger.

"You're very young, Charles. It's easy for you to fall prey to misconceptions—the wrong ideas," he amended when the long word produced a look of bafflement. "I take care of my people. They know that. And Mr. Jones, while a good manager, is in some ways a blasted fool. There is no need for him to strut around with a stick and quirt. We have no troublemaking niggers at Mont Royal—well, I take that back. Priam and one or two others show signs of rebellious temperament. But not all the time, and not to an unforgivable degree. I work hard to maintain a good atmosphere here. My people are happy."

He broke off, awaiting the boy's approval. Charles asked, "How can they be happy when they can't go wherever they want or do whatever they want?"

It seemed a perfectly natural question, but Tillet flew into a rage.

"Don't ask questions about things you don't understand. The system is beneficial to the people. If they weren't here, they'd be living in savagery. Negroes are happiest when their lives are organized and run for them. As for you, young man—"

Tillet's gaze flicked to the door, which he hadn't quite closed when they came in. Someone was out there listening. Tillet didn't appear concerned. He shook the stem of his pipe at the boy.

"If you cause Mr. Jones any more trouble, I'll put you across my knee and give you a tanning. I wish to heaven you'd behave yourself and try to act like a young gentleman—although I realize that's probably an impossible request, given your disposition. Now get out of here."

Charles pivoted on the heel of his boot and ran. He didn't want his uncle to see the tears that had filled his eyes so unexpectedly. He tore the door open and gasped when he saw the looming figure—

It was only Aunt Clarissa. She stretched out a comforting hand.

"Charles—"

His uncle thought him worthless. No doubt she did too. He dodged her hand and ran out of the house into the dark.

Later that night, in the large bedroom on the river side of the second floor, Tillet helped unfasten the lacings of his wife's corset. She breathed a long sigh, walked around several partially packed trunks and valises, and stepped behind a screen to finish her preparations for bed.

Tillet tugged on the linen drawers he wore for sleeping in warm weather. They weren't fashionable, but they were comfortable. The room remained quiet. The stillness upset him. He looked toward the screen.

"Out with it, Clarissa. I'd like a good night's sleep."

She emerged in her nightdress, stroking her unbound gray hair with a brush. Clarissa Main was a small woman with delicate, aristocratic features that somewhat offset a strong peasant look created by her plump face and thick arms. Few people thought her sons resembled her, except in one way: their noses were exactly like hers. Clarissa's ancestors, Huguenots named Gault, had arrived in Carolina two years before Charles de Main—a fact with which she twitted her husband whenever he became overbearing.

"I already apologized for eavesdropping," she said. "How you discipline Cousin Charles is your affair. He's your brother's son."

"You can't abdicate so easily," Tillet replied with gruff sarcasm. "Not when I know you have definite ideas of your own."

"Would you listen if I offered them?" The question was serious, yet free of acrimony. They seldom had arguments, but they had an almost infinite number of what they termed discussions. "I think not. You've already written the boy off as a wastrel and a failure."

Tillet fell back on a catchphrase: "Like father, like son."

"Sometimes. Sometimes not."

"He has dangerous notions. Did you hear some of the questions he asked?"

"Tillet, my dear, Cousin Charles isn't the only one with doubts about the system under which this family has lived for six generations."

"Lived and prospered," he corrected, sitting heavily on the edge of the canopied bed. "As have the Gaults."

"I don't deny it."

"Even my own son harbors the same kind of mad ideas."

His accusing tone kindled her anger. "If this is the start of your standard lecture about Cooper's bookish turn of mind and my responsibility for it, I don't want to hear it. I remind you that Cooper went to Yale—your college—at your insistence. And, yes, I do share some of his doubts about the wisdom of keeping tens of thousands of people enslaved."

He waved. "That's your fear of rebellion. Nothing like that will happen here. This parish isn't Haiti. We have no Veseys at Mont Royal."

He referred to the organizer of an 1822 slave uprising, one Denmark Vesey, a free mulatto of Charleston. The uprising had never taken place; it had been discovered and crushed ahead of time. But the memory of it influenced the behavior and haunted the sleep of most South Carolinians

Tillet's condescending tone infuriated his wife. "Yes, indeed, that is my fear of the black majority. But more than that, it is, believe it or not, the expression of my conscience."

He jumped up. Spots of color appeared in his cheeks, but he withheld an angry retort and quickly got control of his temper. He loved Clarissa, which was why she was the only person in creation able to argue with him—and win.

More mildly, he said, "We're far from the original subject."

"You're right." Her nod and smile signaled a desire to end the quarrel. "I only want to suggest that you might do more than disapprove of the boy. He has a great deal of energy. Perhaps you should try to channel it in a positive way."

"How?"

A small shrug, a sigh. "I don't know. That's always the question on which I founder."

With the lamps extinguished and a cotton sheet drawn over them as protection against the cooling air, he curved his body around hers and rested his arm on her hip, as he did every night. The discussion refused to die—perhaps because, deep down, Tillet felt she was right about Cousin Charles. Like Clarissa, he often racked his brain for a remedy to the problem, and he always failed to find one. Inevitably, he took refuge in hostility.

"Well, I have no time for the herculean task of redeeming that young scoundrel. Did I say herculean? A better word is impossible. Along with every other person of sense in the neighborhood, I'm convinced Charles will come to a bad end."

"If everyone thinks that," Clarissa murmured sadly in the dark, "he will."

To George and Orry, the 1843 encampment proved far more enjoyable than their first one. George was promoted to corporal, which somewhat embarrassed his friend who continued to crave a military career. Nevertheless, Orry shook the new cadet noncom's hand warmly, and together they ran it to Benny's for beer and cigars. They didn't get caught. They were veterans now.

All during camp Orry worried about the third-class academic work. He was no longer a plebe, but that didn't mean he could relax. Not when he faced more French, plus descriptive geometry and instrumental drawing.

George persuaded him to attend the final summer hop. As always, it was held in the Academic Building. Stylishly dressed girls and their mothers converged on the granite and brownstone structure from the hotel and Buttermilk Falls. Orry felt foolish going to such an affair and did so only to put an end to his friend's incessant pleading.

In his full-dress uniform he felt not only hot but comical. There were certain compensations for the suffering, however. Orry loved the sight of the powdered shoulders and flirtatious eyes of the feminine guests, although this emotion was made bittersweet by the realization that none of the girls would ever cast encouraging glances his way.

Elkanah Bent also provided some diversion. He arrived escorting a hatchet-faced girl with a bad complexion. George nudged his friend and smirked. Pickett almost went into convulsions of laughter.

"I can't believe it," Pickett said. "He finally found someone willing to waltz with an elephant."

From across the crowded hall, Bent noticed the attention he was receiving. He gave the friends venomous looks. Undaunted, George continued to grin. "I guess when you're as ugly as that poor creature, even Bent's phiz becomes tolerable."

Ugly or pretty, the girls at the hop made Orry feel cloddish. George was soon dancing with great élan. Orry watched from the sidelines, wanting to ask someone but not sure how to go about it.

After he had stood for an hour, George rescued him. He appeared with a girl on each arm and made it clear he had brought one of them for Orry. Soon George and his girl danced off again. Orry felt as though the earth had opened and he was trying to stand on air. His questions were clumsy, his efforts at repartee ludicrous. But the girl, a plump, agreeable blonde, seemed charmed by his spotless uniform— she kept eyeing his buttons—and therefore willing to overlook his lack of social grace.

She was Miss Draper of Albany. His inability to keep thinking of intelligent remarks—or indeed any at all—drove him at last to dance with her. He trampled her feet. His conversation on the floor consisted of apologies. When he asked whether she'd care to stroll outside, she was almost breathlessly eager.

He had a pass permitting him to be on Flirtation Walk, so he took her there. But the leafy darkness, alive with the sounds of branches rustling—or were they the sounds of silks and satins being disturbed?— only heightened his embarrassment. They sat on a bench in awkward silence.

Unexpectedly, Miss Draper opened her large reticule and brought out a present of some little sugar cakes she had brought from the hotel dining room. Orry tried to nibble one and dropped it. He put the other inside his coat and promptly crushed it. Miss Draper gazed at him with an expectant look for about a minute, then jumped up from the bench.

"Please take me back, sir. It's too chilly out here."

It was, in fact, an exceptionally warm night. Orry escorted Miss Draper back to the dance in agonized silence. In less than thirty seconds she was dancing with another cadet. The evening was a failure and so was he.

"I'll never go to one of those damn things again," he said to George in their room after lights out. "I like being around girls, but I don't know what to do. I especially don't know how to flirt. Miss Draper said good night as if I had some contagious disease."

"My boy, you neglected the *quid pro quo*."

"What do you mean?"

"Didn't Miss Draper offer you a little gift? Some cakes, perhaps?"

"How the devil do you know that?"

"Because I've gotten them too."

"From her?"

"Of course not. Other girls."

"How many other girls?"

"Several. It's part of the game, Orry. In return for the gift, the girl expects a souvenir and a gentleman always obliges. Why do you think I'm constantly cadging spare buttons and sewing them on my coat?''

"I have noticed that you lose a lot of buttons. Do you mean to say Miss Draper wanted me to—?''

"The brave may deserve the fair," George broke in, "but the fair in turn demand West Point buttons. Especially before they give you a squeeze or a kiss. My boy, a button from a cadet uniform is the most sought-after romantic souvenir in the nation.''

"My Lord," Orry breathed softly. "I never suspected. No wonder she was looking daggers. Oh, well, I reckon I'm one of those men the Almighty intended for just one woman.''

"The same way He intended you for just one career? Orry, you're too serious.''

In the dark George's iron bed squeaked as he rolled over to face his roommate. "As long as we're being candid, there's a question that's been bothering me. I must say I think I know the answer.''

"Well?''

"Have you ever been with a woman?''

"See here, that's a personal, not to say ungentlemanly—''

"Confound it, don't give me any of your damned Southern rhetoric. Have you or haven't you?''

Orry very nearly swallowed the answer. "I haven't.''

"We're going to do something about that.''

"Do something? How?''

"You sound as if we're discussing cholera, for God's sake!''

Orry realized his friend's anger was feigned. He chuckled in a nervous way and muttered, "Sorry. Go on.''

"A couple of very accommodating ladies live in the village. A visit to one of them might banish some of your sentimental notions about females. It would certainly help convince you that women won't shatter the first time you glance crookedly—or lustfully—in their direction.''

Through this Orry had been trying to break in, but George refused to permit it:

"No arguments. It won't cost you much, and you'll find the whole thing vastly educational. If you value our friendship, you have to go.''

"I was afraid you'd say something like that.''

Orry hoped his voice didn't reveal his sudden excitement.

*

Orry expected his initiation into sex to be a private matter, with only George and the woman in question knowing about it. Instead, a few nights later, George rounded up four other cadets and all six of them ran it to Buttermilk Falls. The initiation would be about as private as a convention.

The lady they visited seemed ancient to him, though in fact she was not quite thirty-three. She was a buxom brunette, Alice Peet by name. She had gentle eyes, a hard smile, and a face from which work and worry had scrubbed much of the prettiness. George said she was a widow who took in laundry "and other things" to support herself, three youngsters, and a cat. Her husband, a deck hand on a river steamer, had fallen overboard and drowned during a thunderstorm two summers ago.

Alice Peet had sent her children to stay with a friend, so she and the visitors had the house to themselves. House was hardly the word, though; shack would have been more fitting. The place consisted of one large room and a second smaller addition, presumably to be used for the evening's business. A flimsy door divided the two areas.

Orry swallowed a burning mouthful of whiskey Alice Peet had poured. All at once shame and shyness gripped him. He knew he couldn't step beyond that door. Without saying anything, he took himself out to the porch.

Alice Peet's shack was located at the south end of the village, well away from the nearest neighbor. If the place had nothing else, it had a splendid view of the starlit Hudson. Orry sat down and relaxed.

Alice didn't seem to miss her husband much. She laughed and drank and enjoyed herself with the other cadets. The party grew cheerfully rowdy. After an hour or so, Orry figured they had forgotten him, for which he was thankful. Then the front door opened with a bang.

Cadet Stribling lurched out. He had become a good friend now that George and Orry were yearlings.

"Main? Where are you, sir? Madame Pompadour-Peet awaits. And, believe me, I use the word advisedly."

At that point Stribling almost fell off the porch. He caught himself and belched. "My Lord, the creature's insatiable. We'll be here all night. But as long as she doesn't raise the price, who cares? Go on, now. It's your turn."

"Thanks, but I think I'll stay right—"

"Cadet Orry Main sir?" That was George, shouting. "Get in here and do your duty, sir."

After a few more minutes of badgering, he reluctantly went in. The leering cadets rousted him through the main room to the other one and shut the door behind him. He was terrified. Yet to his surprise, he was also living up to his nickname: stiff as a stick against the fly front of his trousers. The fly was a recent innovation in West Point uniforms. It had been introduced despite the opposition of, among others, Old Dickey's wife, who had railed against the moral decay signified by pants with buttons down the front. Lust had been publicly acknowledged. And by the government, too.

Orry had wild fantasies of pressure causing those buttons to burst loose. In the dark the laundress had a pleasantly musky smell, a blend of toilet water, whiskey, and warm flesh. "Over here," she murmured.

He stumbled against the end of the bed, elaborately excused himself. Alice Peet didn't make fun of him. Perhaps she was drunk, but she sounded kind.

"Come, dear. You're Orry, aren't you?"

"That's right. Orry."

"Nice name. Your friend says this is all new to you."

"Well—"

"You don't have to answer. Sit down."

Afire—did he have a fever?—he lowered himself to the edge of the bed. "We'll make it easy and enjoyable for you, dear," the woman said, and touched him in a way so shocking it might have given an older man a fatal seizure.

She was expert. Ten minutes later, Orry gasped involuntarily and no mystery remained.

On the way back to the post he tried to assure George that he'd had a fine time. Secretly, however, Alice Peet's embraces had left him unfulfilled and curiously sad. He might be out of step with the rest of the world, but couplings with near strangers were not for him. The visit to the shack had convinced him again that there would be but one woman in his life. One and only one. He was sure he would know her the instant he met her.

If that made him a romantic fool, so be it.

On a Saturday afternoon in the spring of 1844, George and Orry found themselves with a free hour and no demerits to work off with extra guard tours. They went hiking in the hills above the Academy. That day Orry learned something about the Hazard famiily's involvement with the iron trade. It was not only deep but, in its own way, mystical.

And George shared that involvement—a fact he had concealed until now.

As they were walking, the two cadets happened on a round, shallow crater in the hillside. The crater's diameter was something over two feet. Dirt had run down into the bottom, and the rim was pierced by new shoots of wild grass, suggesting the crater had been hollowed out months or even years before.

Unexpectedly, George looked excited. He knelt by the crater and, with no explanation, dug in the bottom with both hands.

"George, what the devil are you—?"

"Wait! I found something."

From under the loose dirt he produced his discovery—some kind of cinder, conical in shape and measuring about six inches from point to base. But Orry had never seen a cinder that exact shade of dark brown.

"What on earth is that?"

"Nothing earthly," George replied with an odd, almost humorless smile. When Orry's frown signified annoyance with the cryptic answer, George pointed at the cloud-dotted sky. "It came from out there. It's a meteorite. The color shows there's a great deal of iron in it. Star iron, the old-timers at the factory call it." He turned the rough object over and over, studying it with an expression so close to reverence Orry was thunderstruck.

"The ancient Egyptians knew about star iron," George went on softly. "This piece may have traveled millions and millions of miles before it crashed here. My father says the iron trade has had more influence on the course of history than all the politicians and generals since the beginning of time"—he held up the meteorite—"and this is the reason. Iron can destroy anything: families, fortunes, governments, whole countries. It's the most powerful stuff in the universe."

"Oh?" Orry's skeptical glance fell on the Plain below. "You really think it's more powerful than a big army?"

"Without weapons—without this—there *are* no big armies."

He said it with such intensity that Orry shivered. A few moments later they moved on. Soon George was his old self again, chatting and joking. But he still had the meteorite in his hand. Back in barracks, he wrapped it and stored it away like a treasured possession.

One night near the end of May, George ran it for cigars. He pulled up short outside the door of Benny Haven's. Inside, a boisterous crowd was serenading the proprietor with an old and familiar song. Each West Point class tried to add a memorable verse to the song, one that would be passed down to others. Most of the verses were bawdy, but just now the revelers were bellowing a polite one:

"Come, tune your voices, comrades,
And stand up in a row.
For singing sentimentally we're going for to go.
In the Army there's sobriety,
Promotion's very slow,
So we'll sing our reminiscences of Benny Haven's, oh!"

George peeked through the window and frowned. Too many first and second classmen in there, including that damn Bent. He thought about turning around and leaving, but he had been without cigars for several days.

A second peek showed him a couple of yearlings in the group. Most of the cadets were drunk. Spring had that effect. Quickly he planned his tactics. He'd give the upperclassmen no excuse to think he felt guilty. It was mostly a matter of deportment. He put his shoulders back, fixed a cocky smile in place, and went in.

"Benny Haven's, oh! Benny Haven's, oh!
We'll sing our reminiscences of Benny Haven's, oh!"

The upperclassmen turned on him, but their shouted threats were perfunctory and brief. George bought his cigars and was on his way out when Bent lurched to his side and threw an arm across his shoulders.

George's stomach tightened. So did his right hand. But fists weren't necessary. Bent's eyes had a vague, bleary look. He asked George to join him for beer, muttering something about all of them forgetting the past. That didn't lull George for one second, though he agreed to have a drink because it was free and he was thirsty.

Elkanah Bent was tipsy and hence not as pompous as usual. He babbled excitedly about a piece of recent news from Washington. The inventor Morse had sent a message over a wire all the way to Baltimore.

"Don't you understand the significance, Hazard? It's the dawn of the age of improved military information. Exactly what old Mahan predicted! In the next war—"

"What next war?" George interrupted.

97

"How should I know?" Bent spilled beer over his chin and uniform as he drank. "But it will come, sure as the seasons." Some of the dullness left his eyes. "Human beings can't settle their differences any other way. It's the nature of the animal. For the sake of our careers, I say thank God."

Some of the other cadets were listening. One stared at Bent with a disbelieving expression much like that on George's face. The Ohioan paid no attention. His voice took on an unexpected intensity. "When this country fights again, she'll be looking for new leadership." He leaned forward, cheeks glistening, lips moist. "The Army will be seeking an American Bonaparte."

George uttered a nervous laugh. "Well, Mr. Bent, you see a larger canvas than I do. I hope I'm out of the Army before this gigantic war of yours. But if not, I'll have just three objectives. Carry out orders. Do so with reasonable effectiveness. And dodge the bullets."

"Quite right," Bent said with a wave. "A prudent general never exposes himself to fire. The individual soldier is nothing more or less than one of Mr. Whitney's interchangeable parts. Better that fifty thousand such parts should be lost than a brilliant leader."

"Interesting theory," George muttered, rising abruptly. He offered a word of thanks for the drink, but Bent didn't hear. He was too busy snatching at George's sleeve in an attempt to keep his audience.

George pulled away. He was disgusted by the sodden creature and what he had said. He needed fresh air and the sight of something besides Bent's small, crazed eyes.

That same week, Pickett invited George, Orry, and several other friends to a hash. Such affairs were a tradition at West Point. For three days preceding the event, the invited guests filched leftover meat, potatoes, butter and bread from the mess hall. They carried off the food in the traditional way—concealed in forage caps from which the rattan hoop stiffeners had been removed.

On Saturday night, after inspection of quarters, the guests gathered in Pickett's room. Using the donated ingredients, the Virginian prepared the hash in stolen utensils that were the common property of all the cadets in the barracks. A serving of hot hash was given to the nearest sentinel, thus ensuring that the party would be ignored until taps.

It was a happy, carefree occasion. Conversation was lively and wide-ranging. They talked about the Oregon problem; the April treaty providing for the annexation of Texas; the Democratic nominating convention that only the day before had turned from the favorite, Van Buren, and chosen a border man, Polk, who was an avowed expansionist.

Those looking forward to summer leave discussed their plans. Orry was among them. Then George brought up his most recent encounter with Bent.

"When he spoke about an American Bonaparte, I swear he was referring to himself. What's worse, I got a clear impression that he'd cheerfully send a regiment to be butchered if it served his purpose. He wouldn't think twice about it, either. He called soldiers 'interchangeable parts.'"

Pickett reached into the fireplace for the skillet in which he was reheating the last of the hash. "If you'll pardon an execrable pun, gentlemen, the cadet under discussion is hell-bent for glory. God pity anyone who obstructs that advance, intentionally or otherwise."

A slender cadet from Missouri said, "I think you're all taking him too seriously. He's a jackass. A clown."

"If you dismiss him that easily, you're the jackass," George countered.

"Amen," Orry said. "He's dangerous. Maybe even crazy. Stay out of his way."

"And finish the hash," Pickett added.

Orry traveled south by coastal steamer. At his first meal in the dining saloon, he felt self-conscious in his furlough uniform. The coat's long, narrow swallowtails carried an extravagant number of stamped gilt buttons, as did each cuff. The uniform certainly drew attention. All of it was favorable and friendly, except for that of a Connecticut merchant who grumbled about a pampered military aristocracy. The merchant thought a civilian board should be appointed to oversee the Academy.

At Charleston, Orry hired a horse so as to have a slower trip upriver than a boat would provide. He wanted to savor the sights of his homecoming. He'd been away two years and somewhat to his amazement, he had survived an astonishing number of tests of character and intellect. The realization brought a good feeling. This leave would be perfect if only a girl were waiting for him, a special girl to whom he could give the cadet's traditional gift of love—the gold embroidery wreath decorating the black velvet band of his furlough cap. The wreath contained the letters *U.S.M.A.* embroidered in the Old English style.

But there was no such girl. He had begun to resign himself to living his entire life without finding her.

Heavy rain started to fall as he rode out of the city. He stopped to put on his blue furlough coat and pull his cap lower so the bill would keep the water out of his eyes. Even so, he knew he'd be soaked when he reached Mont Royal, where he planned to meet Cooper. From the plantation the two of them would travel on to the family's summer residence.

To the right he glimpsed the rain-dappled river. On his left rose dark thickets of palmetto and oak, with occasional vistas of marsh visible between. The air was heavy with humidity, full of familiar sounds and smells.

He met two Negroes driving a produce cart to Charleston. One pulled out a pass and showed it to him without being asked to do so. No slave could travel anywhere unless he had written authorization from his master. Parish patrols policed the roads and checked passes, although not as thoroughly as some planters would like. The system was years old, intended to prevent gatherings of slaves that could lead to an uprising.

He had been riding about an hour when he heard alarmed voices. He cantered around a bend, then reined in. Ahead he saw a fine lacquered carriage lying on its side to the right of the road.

Then he noticed that a section of the road had been washed away, leaving only about half the regular roadbed and creating a sharp slope. The carriage must have run off the road and crashed down the slope while trying to negotiate the narrowed section. Orry saw broken traces but no sign of a horse.

The white driver stood beside the exposed bottom of the carriage, straining to reach up and open the door by lifting it. The agitated voices were feminine, although Orry could not see the women. He did see half a dozen satchels and trunks littering the roadside. One had burst open, spilling white garments into the gluelike mud. The garments were lavishly decorated with lace, he noted as he rode ahead. The pasengers were not poor.

The driver took note of Orry's uniform. "Sir, are you a constable?"

"No, but I'll be glad to help."

"My arms don't seem long enough to open this door."

"Let me try."

While he was dismounting, he thought he saw something long and thin slither swiftly across the side of the coach and drop out of sight through one of the windows. He had an impression of olive coloring and dark bands.

Orry moved with near-frenzied speed then. As he reached the carriage, he saw that the side onto which it had fallen lay in a marshy pool. His identification of the snake had probably been correct.

"I'll get up there," he told the driver. He climbed via the axle and rear wheel, stepped on the side of the carriage, and looked down into two of the largest, darkest eyes he had ever seen. Even through his carefully concealed tension he observed that the white woman was young, pale-skinned, very lovely. Her companion was a black woman, older.

"We'll have you out soon, ladies."

He crouched and reached for the door handle, trying to be casual about his visual search of the interior. Then he spied it, motionless on the folds of the white girl's skirt, the back of her skirt, which of course she couldn't see.

Orry's cheeks dripped sweat and rain. "Ladies, I beg you to keep control of your nerves while you listen to me." His low, urgent tone got their attention. "Please don't move suddenly or do anything at all until I say so. A snake has gotten into the carriage—"

Their eyes widened. The black woman started to look down, but he whispered, "Don't do that. Stay absolutely still."

They did, and so did he. The snake had just opened its jaws, exposing its fangs and the cottony white interior of its mouth. A drop of moisture fell from Orry's chin; another. The sound of his racing heart seemed thunderous inside his head.

"*Est-ce que le serpent est venimeux?*" the white girl asked. Then she realized she had spoken in French. "Is the snake poisonous?"

Orry kept his voice low. "Very. They don't strike unless they feel threatened. They are easily alarmed, however. That's why I ask you to refrain from any sudden movements and from speaking loudly. If you do that, everything will be fine."

He was lying to them. Or at least exaggerating. Fortunately they couldn't get inside his skin and feel his tightness, his fear.

With a little smile of apology, the girl said, "We don't understand these things, sir. We're city people."

And not from the Carolinas, he knew from listening to her speech. He kept his eye on the water moccasin. The snake had closed its jaws again.

Suddenly the black woman's fear got the better of her. Her shoulders began to shake. She bit her lower lip and tried to hold back tears, but she couldn't.

"Calm her," Orry whispered to the girl. "Do anything to keep her quiet."

Obviously the girl was terrified, but that didn't immobilize her. Slowly, and with great care, she slipped a gloved hand up along the older woman's sleeve. She pressed gently, her voice murmurous.

"*Mère Sally, prière de se taire encore un moment. J'ai peur aussi. Mais si nous pourrons rester tranquilles une minute de plus, nous serons en sécurité. J'en suis sûre.*"

The black woman mastered her fear. She lifted her left hand and touched the girl's pale purple glove—a demonstration of appreciation. But her movement was too abrupt, the rustle of her blouse too loud. Before Orry could shout a warning, the snake jumped.

The girl felt it on her skirt and screamed. Orry's vision swam for one panicky second. He gripped the edge of the window, leaned forward, looked down—

103

The moccasin was gone. It had dropped out through one of the lower windows, frightened away.

Orry felt he'd botched the rescue. The travelers didn't agree. All three thanked him effusively while he inspected the interior of the carriage, laid the door back, and lifted the women to safety.

He assisted the black woman first, then the girl. As she stepped on the side of the coach, he held her waist a moment longer than necessary. He couldn't help it. He was taken with her white-as-cream skin, her dark eyes and glossy black hair, her exquisitely full bosom under a stylish traveling suit. She was about his own age. In all his life he had never seen such a beautiful creature.

"We can never repay you," she said. The lilt of the last word left the sentence unfinished on a note of inquiry.

"Main. Orry Main."

"Are you a soldier?"

"Not yet. I attend the Military Academy at West Point. I'm on my way home on a two-month furlough."

"You live nearby?"

"Yes, our plantation's just up the river."

He climbed down, reached up, and helped her negotiate the wheel and axle. The pressure of her gloved fingers left him aglow with pleasure. Her face was full, and so were her lips. In fact there was a certain deliciously passionate quality about her mouth which only enhanced her unmistakable aura of refinement by contrasting with it. Orry released her with reluctance.

"My name is Madeline Fabray. We are traveling to a plantation named Resolute. Do you know it?"

With difficulty he refrained from frowning. "I do. The LaMotte place. It isn't far."

"We have come all the way from New Orleans, Maum Sally and Villefranche and I. None of us has ever been more than two days' journey from our home. People in New Orleans are fearfully provincial, I'm afraid. Many will tell you there's nothing on the continent worth seeing after you've strolled across the Place d'Armes to the Mississippi."

She was teasing, of course. He reveled in every word. She continued, "In any case, the Carolinas are very new to us. We had hoped to arrive at Resolute by dinner time, but clearly we won't. I must say these roads are pitiable. So many deep holes. Villefranche is a fine driver, but this narrow place proved too difficult. The horses slipped and bolted, the carriage overturned—"

A shrug, broad and expressive. She gave him a wondrous warm smile. "Fortunately a cavalier rode by to rescue us."

Orry turned pink. "You owe more to the snake's state of nerves than you do to me."

"No, Mr. Main, it is you to whom I shall be grateful." Madeline Fabray touched his sleeve impulsively. "Always."

Her eyes remained on his for a moment. Then, coloring noticeably, she withdrew her hand, and a fleeting look of chagrin crossed her face.

Orry didn't understand the reaction. He thought she had wanted to put her hand on his sleeve, but after she'd done it, she had regretted it. He had heard New Orleans women had highly refined manners, but touching a man's arm in gratitude was hardly a cardinal sin. What was wrong?

Of course he didn't dare ask. And even if he had, he suspected she wouldn't have answered. He sensed a shyness in her, a barrier that hid certain of her thoughts and feelings from the world. Behind that barrier lay the answer to the curious little riddle of the glove placed on his sleeve, then withdrawn with a look of surprise and perhaps a touch of shame.

Even with this mystery confronting him, he felt he had learned a good deal about the charming traveler in a very short time. She was intelligent and a gentlewoman, though something told him that didn't mean she lacked emotion. Just the opposite, in fact. These fascinating glimpses of her character attracted him even more profoundly than her beauty. For one dizzying instant he had a sense of two perfectly matched people finding each other.

Romantic ass, he thought a moment later. Villefranche made a polite but pointed remark about getting started. Orry cleared his throat. "There's a crossroads store about a mile ahead. I'll stop and find you a couple of mules and two or three nigras to lend a hand with putting the coach back on the road."

He helped the driver collect and stack the scattered luggage, though he didn't do so with any eagerness. He hated to think of this lovely young woman visiting the owner of Resolute, Justin LaMotte, whom he knew well and disliked.

The LaMottes were an old and aristocratic Huguenot family. The first LaMotte in the Carolinas had arrived more than a year before Charles de Main. Hence Justin, his brother Francis, and the entire clan tended to look down on the Mains, and most everyone else. This was true even though Justin had all but impoverished himself through bad management of his lands and a spendthrift style of life. Many who met him for the first or even the second time thought him exceptionally charming. But Orry knew otherwise.

He wanted to learn as much as he could about the visitor. As he handed another soiled piece of luggage to Villefranche, he said to Madeline:

"From your name, I take it you're French."

She laughed. "Oh, nearly everyone in New Orleans has a French name because those in the majority, particularly the churchmen, kept insisting they couldn't pronounce or remember any other kind. You know the French can be dreadful snobs."

"Indeed I do. Frenchmen settled in the Carolinas, too." A comment about Justin leaped to mind, but he suppressed it. "Where did your family come from, then?"

"On the paternal side, Germany. My great-great-grandfather Faber was one of the earliest arrivals on what's called the German Coast, about twenty-five miles upriver from New Orleans. There are scores of Germans in our part of the world, and in the last hundred years virtually all the names have been changed to sound French. Buchwalter became Bouchvaldre. Kerner became Quernel. I could recite a dozen."

"But your family now lives in the city rather than on this German Coast?"

A touch of strain returned to her face. "There is only my father." She explained that he was a sugar factor, like his father and his grandfather. He had wanted to accompany her on this journey but had been unable. Six months earlier he had been felled by a paralyzing stroke.

Orry brushed dried mud from the last satchel, then prepared to leave. "I hope you have an excellent visit at Resolute, Miss Fabray." He was afraid to say more but knew he must or the moment would be lost. "Perhaps—" He twisted his cap in his fingers. "Perhaps we'll see each other again."

"I would enjoy that, Mr. Main," she answered with a small, grave nod. He was too excited to recognize that she was only being polite.

With a wave he rode off. Elation set him singing all the way to the crossroads store. He didn't understand why a girl as lovely and sophisticated as Madeline Fabray would want to spend a holiday with people as arrogant and empty as the LaMottes. Could there be a blood relationship somewhere? It seemed the only sensible explanation.

Well, he could stomach being polite to Justin if that was the price of calling on his guest. And call on her he would, at the first possible moment. He would have more than a month and a half at home. Ample time to become a young woman's beau. He imagined himself presenting Madeline with the embroidered wreath from his cap, saw the two of them at the end of his furlough exchanging ardent promises to write.

How strangely fate worked. If this dismal rain hadn't washed out part of the road, the chance meeting might never have occurred. But it had—and the result was happiness that was altogether new and wonderful.

Five minutes after he reached Mont Royal, Cooper brought him crashing to earth.

"Fabray, you say? I'm afraid you've wandered down the wrong path, brother. Fabray is the name of the young woman Justin's going to marry."

After a stunned silence, Orry exclaimed, "How can that be? *How?*"

Cooper shrugged. They were in the dining room, a place dreary with shadows now that the rain had started again. Orry's furlough cap lay in a corner where he had flung it joyously after embracing his brother. Cooper was in shirt-sleeves. He had poured two glasses of their father's best claret. Orry hadn't tasted his.

"Haven't a notion," Cooper answered. He put a booted foot on the expensive mahogany table. "I am not exactly a confidant of either Justin or Francis."

"I can't believe that girl would marry Justin. She can't be more than twenty. He must be fifteen or twenty years older. How long has his first wife been dead?"

"Nine years, I think. What difference does it make? The girl's father probably arranged the match. That still happens quite frequently. And the LaMottes do offer a pedigree, even if they did run out of the milk of human kindness years ago."

This was the first time Orry had ever exhibited more than a casual interest in women. He continued to growl and utter lovelorn sounds someone else might have found comical. But Cooper did not. Even though he himself had not as yet been smitten in the same way, hence could not fully grasp the extent of his brother's pain, Cooper had no doubt that it was hellishly real.

He sipped claret and returned to the diagram of the pounding mill he'd been studying when his brother arrived. Orry paced around the table, and then around again, his expression growing more and more agitated. He halted abruptly next to Cooper's chair:

"When is the wedding?"

"This coming Saturday. We're invited as a family, by the way. Reckon you won't be going."

"Saturday! Why so soon?"

"I can only speculate. Justin's mother preferred that the wedding be held in the autumn when it's cooler. But he's old enough to say no to her. I don't know if it's the young lady he's anxious for, or her dowry. If she's as pretty as you say, I can understand the stories I've heard. According to the talk in the neighborhood, Justin's as impatient as one of his own prize stallions—look, don't start that infernal pacing again. She's just a girl."

Orry spun to face him. "She's a lot more than that. I could tell five minutes after we met that she and I would have made a fine—made—"

He didn't know how to finish. Or perhaps he feared mockery if he did. Cooper watched his brother retrieve his cap from the corner and touch its ornamental gold wreath with the tip of his index finger.

Then, without another word, Orry walked out.

Cooper sighed and reached for his brother's untasted claret. Damned if he wasn't feeling sad all at once too.

Next morning the brothers saddled up and rode on to Summerville. When they arrived, Orry made an effort to give each member of the family a warm greeting. But Clarissa knew her children. That evening after supper, she drew Cooper aside.

"Your brother is no actor. Why is he so unhappy? Isn't he glad to be home?"

"I'd say he is. But yesterday he met a young woman on the river road to Charleston. She caught his fancy, and then he discovered she's Justin LaMotte's intended."

"Oh, my. The girl everyone refers to as a Creole?"

"I reckon. Is she?"

"Her name suggests it. My," Clarissa said again. "This poses a problem. In connection with the wedding, I mean. Your father refuses to attend, but courtesy demands that the family be represented. I was hoping you and Orry would go with me."

Cooper understood his father's antipathy for the LaMottes; he shared it. They were shallow, mean-spirited people who worshiped horseflesh

108

and settled inconsequential arguments by resorting to illegal duels. It was consideration for his mother that prompted his answer:

"To be honest, I'd rather not, but I will. We shouldn't force Orry, though."

"Of course you're right," Clarissa said. "Under the circumstances he surely wouldn't want to go."

That night at supper, Orry surprised them by announcing that he would accompany them on Saturday. Cooper considered it foolhardy but said nothing. Tillet ordered Clarissa to take Cousin Charles as well. "The sight of ladies and gentlemen behaving themselves might prove inspirational," he said with sarcasm. Poor Charles was forever being punished in one way or another, Cooper thought.

Saturday brought clear, mild weather with a brisk breeze to drive off the bugs. Departure for Resolute was delayed about an hour because Clarissa was busy. Just before sunrise one of the house girls they had brought from Mont Royal had gone into labor.

Clarissa helped with every confinement on the plantation, and she didn't expect compliments or even recognition for her efforts. She was only carrying out the traditional responsibilities of a woman of her position. One day Ashton and Brett would do the same.

The trip by carriage took an hour and a half. Cousin Charles fidgeted and complained the whole way. Clarissa had dressed him in a fine suit complete with high collar and cravat. By squirming and pulling he managed to wrinkle the outfit thoroughly by the time they reached Resolute.

They arrived forty minutes after the end of the marriage service, which had been held in a tiny separate chapel. Only close relatives had attended. Now the reception was in progress. Guests were chatting and laughing under the oaks and magnolias on the side lawn, where four yellow-and-white-striped pavilions had been erected.

The LaMotte plantation reminded Cooper of some Charleston whore who tried to hide time's ravages under a lot of powder and paint. At first glance the great house looked huge and impressive. Then you noticed planks warping away and extensive evidence of mold. Large pieces of mortar had fallen from the brick pillars supporting the rear piazza—Resolute's great house faced the river at the summit of a low hill—and many of the shutters showed unrepaired storm damage.

Still, the festive crowd didn't seem to mind. Counting family members, guests, and all the slaves required for the occasion, Cooper estimated that three hundred people were present. Fine carriages and buggies were parked on two acres at one side of the front lane. Smoke drifted in the air, evidence that barbecue was being served. Barbecue was a tradition at low country weddings.

An orchestra from Charleston began to play. Cousin Charles ran off. A grim-faced Orry searched for the bride. Cooper hoped the punch would be strong; only intemperance would make the rest of the afternoon bearable.

"There she is," Orry said. "We ought to pay our respects before the line gets any longer." Clarissa and Cooper agreed. They joined the line and presently moved up to greet the rector, the various LaMottes, and the bride and groom.

Justin LaMotte was a handsome, thick-waisted man with a ruddy complexion and silky brown hair that looked as though he treated it with dye. He accepted the congratulations of the Mains with a smile and some charmingly correct phrases of thanks. But his eyes held no warmth.

Cooper was busy studying the bride. She was breathtakingly beautiful. No wonder his brother had taken a hard fall. Justin didn't deserve such a prize. Did the girl know much about the man she had married? Poor creature, he hoped so; it would be a tragedy if she only just now discovered what lay beneath her husband's superficial charm.

Cooper had deliberately gone first in line, so that he might turn back and watch his brother's behavior with Madeline LaMotte, and he hoped there wouldn't be any sort of mawkish display. Orry felt bad enough already; he needed no further embarrassment.

He was the perfect gentleman, however. He held the bride's hand a moment while he leaned forward to give her the ritual peck on the cheek. But as Orry drew back, Cooper saw the young people look at each other. In his eyes—hers, too—Cooper detected sorrow, a swift but stunningly candid acknowledgment of a lost opportunity.

Then, showing a flash of guilt, the bride glanced away. Justin was greeting another guest and missed the little interchange. Thinking of what he had seen in Madeline's eyes a few moments ago, Cooper said to himself, *I hope some woman looks at me that way just once before I die.*

The Mains left the reception line. Cooper wanted to commiserate with his brother but couldn't find the proper words. Anyway, Orry would probably be offended. So, instead, Cooper set out for the punch bowl. On the way he noticed Cousin Charles crawling under one of the trestle tables. The boy was carrying a plate heaped with mutton barbecue and relish. Charles's shirttails already hung out.

Cooper saw that his mother was served, then left her with three matronly ladies, two of them Main cousins, the third a member of the huge Smith family. He consumed four cups of punch in half an hour. It didn't help much. On every side he heard compliments about the bridegroom that made him wince. The guests were being charitable, but Cooper's charity didn't extend to lying.

He soon found himself reeling around the outdoor dance platform with a good-natured matriarch named Aunt Betsy Bull. Cooper loved to polka, but Aunt Betsy spoiled it by saying:

"Don't they make the handsomest couple? She'll be supremely happy. I don't know Justin well, but he has always impressed me as a kind and charming man."

"At a wedding party, all men are angels."

Aunt Betsy tsk-tsked. "How did someone as sweet as your mother raise such a cynical scalawag? I don't think you care for Justin. You'll never get to heaven with that kind of attitude."

I don't want to get to heaven, just back to the punch bowl, Cooper thought as the music stopped. "Thank you for the dance, Aunt Betsy. Excuse me?" He bowed and left.

With a new drink in hand, he lectured himself about letting his feelings show. He didn't give a damn what people thought of him, but he shouldn't and wouldn't embarrass his mother. Not for anything. Still, it was hard to stay neutral about Justin LaMotte. The man pretended to be such a gentleman, but it was a sham. He treated his horses better than he treated his niggers. Abuse and outright cruelty had been staples at Resolute ever since Justin had taken over when his father died.

The previous summer, after Justin had suffered a defeat in a horse race, one of his black grooms had done something to displease him. Justin's rage was all out of proportion to the offense. He had ordered nails pounded into an empty hogshead, then put the offender in the hogshead and rolled it down a hill. The slave's injuries had left him unable to work, useless to anyone else. A month ago he had taken his own life.

Such barbarous punishment was rare in the low country and non-existent at Mont Royal. Cooper considered it a major reason Resolute unfailingly yielded poor crops and year after year slid a little closer to bankruptcy.

Setting aside all moral questions, Cooper found one great practical weakness in the peculiar institution. The very act of holding a man against his will constituted mistreatment. Add physical cruelties to

111

that, and how could you expect the man to work to the limit of his ability? To give everything and then a little more? Cooper had concluded that the significant difference between the economic systems of the North and South was not in industry versus agriculture but in motivation. The free Yankee worked to better himself. The Southern slave worked to keep from being punished. That difference was slowly rotting the South from the inside.

But try telling that to a Justin LaMotte—or a Tillet Main. Feeling dismal, Cooper helped himself to another cup of punch.

Francis LaMotte was three years older than his brother. He excelled in horsemanship, routinely beating Justin and all the other contestants in the medieval tournaments so popular in the low country. Francis thrilled spectators by charging the rows of hanging rings at a dangerous speed, and he inevitably caught the greatest number of rings on the point of his lance. He always rode in the gander-pulling, too, and nine times out of ten he was first to wring the animal's greased neck from horseback.

Francis was a small, sinewy man with a suntanned face and none of his brother's social graces. He looked waspish as he and Justin enjoyed punch, momentarily left alone by the guests. A few feet away, Madeline was chatting with the Episcopal rector.

"I don't know who will win the election in the fall, Father Victor," the brothers heard her say. "But it's obvious the outcome will hinge on the issue of the annexation of Texas."

"Are you aware that one of South Carolina's own played a vital role in bringing the question before the public?"

"You mean Mr. Calhoun, don't you?"

Father Victor nodded. Calhoun was serving as the third secretary of state in the troubled Tyler administration. After receiving his appointment earlier in the year, he had drafted the annexation treaty which the Republic of Texas and the United States had signed in April.

"You're quite right about the prominence of the issue," the rector agreed. "Before the year is out every man in public life will have to declare his position." He didn't need to add that many had already done so. The support of Polk and ex-President Jackson for annexation was well known. So was the opposition of Van Buren and Clay.

"That's as it should be," Madeline replied. "Some are claiming the Texas question goes much deeper than the politicians care to admit. I've heard it said the real issue is expansion of slavery."

112

The rector bristled. "The only ones who say that are agitators, my dear. Unprincipled Yankee agitators."

Out of politeness, Madeline shrugged to admit the possibility, but then she murmured, "I wonder."

Displeased, the rector snapped, "Shall we get some food?"

Madeline realized she had annoyed him. "Of course. Please lead the way."

She gave her husband a smile, which he returned with a rather forced one of his own. After she and the rector strolled off, Francis squinted at his brother. "Your bride has opinions on quite a number of public issues."

Justin chuckled. The sound was deep and mellow.

"You've noticed that have you?"

"She shouldn't speak so freely. Intelligence is desirable in a woman, but only within limits."

"Everything, my dear brother, carries a certain price. The dowry provided by old Fabray is no exception." Justin gazed over the rim of his silver punch cup at the swelling bodice of Madeline's wedding dress. He calculated the angle of the sun with sleepy, half-lidded eyes. In a few more hours he would be the possessor of everything hidden by that pristine satin and lace. He could hardly wait.

How curiously fate worked, he thought. Nearly two years ago he had decided to take a trip to New Orleans, even though he could scarcely afford it. He had gone there to indulge himself at the gambling tables and to attend one of the legendary quadroon balls in the famous hall overlooking Orleans Street. But before he went to the ball or got a look at the nigger beauties, chance put him next to Nicholas Fabray at the bar of a fashionable gambling establishment. Fabray didn't gamble, but he frequented the place because it was one of several where influential men of the city congregated. It soon became evident to the visitor that Fabray must be one of those. He knew everyone, his clothing was elegant and expensive, and he spent money with the ease of someone who didn't have to worry about it. Later, Justin asked questions and learned that all his suppositions were correct.

Two evenings later he ran into Fabray again at the same place. There he made the discovery that the sugar factor had a young unmarried daughter. From that point on, Justin fairly oozed politeness and good humor. Fabray was completely taken in; when Justin wanted to be charming, no one could rival him.

A few references by Justin to his status as a stranger in town prompted Fabray to invite him home for supper. Justin met the daughter, and from the instant he saw her, he was almost dizzy with lust.

He carefully concealed it, of course. He treated Madeline Fabray with the same restrained courtesy he lavished on her father. Before the evening was over, Justin concluded that although his age and experience awed the beautiful creature, she was not afraid of him.

He extended his stay in New Orleans a week, and then another. Fabray seemed pleased to have a gentleman of Justin's caliber pay court to Madeline. And everything Justin learned about the father only heightened his desire to possess the daughter. For one thing, there were no religious problems. The family was German—the original name was Faber—and Protestant. Madeline attended church, although her father did not; he was not interested in his soul, but in making money. Sensing what Justin had in mind, Fabray hinted that he would bestow a good deal of that money on his daughter, as her dowry.

On one occasion Justin inquired about Madeline's mother. He learned little other than that she had died some years earlier. She had been a Creole, which meant she was the New Orleans-born child of European parents—French, most likely, although they could have been Spanish or one of each. Justin, viewing Fabray's small gallery of family portraits, asked whether there were any pictures of the lady, to which Fabray replied with a curious vagueness, "No, not here."

Then and there Justin decided not to pursue the inquiry. Every respectable family, including his own, had a few skeletons hidden away; these usually belonged to wives who ran off with other men or who succumbed to a nervous disorder and had to be locked up until they died. He had heard nothing unfavorable about the late Mrs. Fabray—no one he had questioned had even mentioned her—so he would happily set aside this minor worry in exchange for Madeline's irresistible beauty and the money he so desperately needed to support his style of life.

If Fabray's daughter had any flaw at all, it was her obvious intelligence and her reluctance to conceal the fact that she had opinions about matters that were ordinarily the province of gentlemen. Fabray had seen to it that she received the finest education available to a young woman in New Orleans—that provided by the sisters of Saint Ursula. Fabray had many good friends in the city's Catholic community and was known to be a strong supporter of the worthy causes of the Roman church. He had overcome the initial reluctance of the Ursulines to accept a Protestant pupil by donating heavily to the hospital and orphanage the nuns maintained.

Madeline's forthright nature was no great deterrent to Justin, however. He had methods for dealing with that kind of problem, although he intended to conceal those methods until she was legally his wife.

Before he left the city, he asked for and received Fabray's permission to propose. Madeline listened to his rather long-winded declaration of love, and he became increasingly certain she would say yes at the end. But she said no, although she thanked him several times for flattering her with the proposal.

That night, to relieve his physical and mental frustration, he hired a whore and badly abused her with his fists and cane. After she had crept out of his hotel room, he lay awake in the dark for more than an hour, recalling Madeline's expression at the moment she refused him. She *was* afraid, he concluded. Since she could not possibly be afraid of him—he had been the soul of politeness, after all—it must be the idea of marriage that frightened her. That was a common enough attitude among young girls, and one he could overcome. Her refusal represented a delay, not a defeat.

In the weeks and months that followed, Justin sent the girl long, flowery love letters repeating his proposal. She answered each with an expression of gratitude and another politely phrased rejection. Then, unexpectedly, her father's stroke changed everything.

Justin was not exactly sure why the change had come about. Perhaps Fabray had feared he wouldn't live much longer and had intensified his effort to get his child safely married before he died. In any case, Madeline had reversed herself, and the terms had been arranged. The financial rewards of Justin's long campaign proved highly satisfactory. Beyond that, he would soon have the absolute right to put his hands on Madeline's—

Rudely, Francis jolted him back to the real world. "I tell you, Justin, you may discover that Madeline is entirely too independent for her own good. Or yours. A wife should be discouraged from speaking her mind on political matters—and absolutely forbidden to do so at any public gathering."

"Of course I agree, but I can't achieve a transformation in one day. It will take a little time."

Francis sniffed. "I wonder if you'll ever be able to handle that young woman."

Justin laid a big, well-manicured hand on his brother's shoulder. "Hasn't your experience with blooded animals taught you anything? A spirited woman's no different than a spirited mare. Each can and must be taught who's in charge.'' He sipped from his punch cup, then murmured, "Broken."

"I hope you know what you're talking about." Francis sounded doubtful, but then his knowledge of women was limited to slaves, prostitutes, and his dim-witted, downtrodden spouse. "Creoles are not noted for passive temperaments. All that Latin blood—you took a considerable risk marrying her."

"Nonsense. Madeline may be from New Orleans, but she's also female. Despite their pretensions, women are only slightly more intelligent than horses. She'll give me no—good God, what's that?''

He pivoted, startled by outcries and the crash of a table overturning. "A fight already?"

He rushed off.

A few minutes earlier, Cousin Charles had been seated against the trunk of a live oak, his coat discarded and a second huge plate of barbecue in his lap. A shadow fell across his legs.

He looked up to see a thin, foppish boy and three of his friends. The boy, a couple of years older than Charles, was a member of the Smith clan.

"Here's the creature from Mont Royal," young Smith said as he postured in front of his cronies. He looked down at Charles. "Rather a secluded spot, this. Hiding out?"

Charles stared back, nodded. "That's right."

Smith smiled and fingered his cravat. "Oh? Afraid?"

"Of you? Not much. I just wanted to eat in peace."

"Or is it that you're ashamed of the appearance you present? Cast your optics over him, gentlemen," Smith continued in an exaggerated way. "Marvel at the mussed clothing. Consider the crude haircut. Discern the dirt-stained cheeks. He looks more like white trash than a member of the Main family."

The baiting infuriated Charles, but he didn't let on. He figured he could get Smith's goat if he acted nonchalant. He was right. While Smith's friends made jokes about Charles, Smith himself stopped smiling and said:

"Stand up and face your betters when they address you, boy." He grabbed Charles's left earlobe and gave it a painful tweak.

Charles pitched the plate of barbecue at Smith. Meat and relish splattered the front of Smith's sky-blue waistcoat. Smith's friends began to laugh. He turned on them, cursing. That gave Charles the opportunity to jump up, grab both Smith's ears from behind, and twist them savagely.

Smith squealed. One of his friends said, "See here, you trashy little bastard—" The fellow attempted to grab him, but Charles dodged away. Laughing, he shot around the tree and raced toward the wedding guests. He bet that Smith and his friends wouldn't make a fuss in public. But he didn't bargain on their hot tempers; they charged right after him.

Charles slid on a patch of grass where someone had spilled a drink. He slammed down on his back, the wind knocked out. Smith ran up, took hold of him, and hauled him to his feet.

"Now, you lout, I intend to administer a lesson in deport—"

Charles butted him in the stomach, getting barbecue relish in his hair. The result was worth it. Smith clutched his middle and doubled over. In that position, his whole face was vulnerable. Charles gave him a thumb in the eye.

"Kill him," one of the other boys yelled. Charles wasn't sure that they didn't mean it. He rocketed off in the direction of the food.

Smith's friends raced in pursuit. Dropping to hands and knees, Charles scuttled underneath one of the tables. Fingers closed around his ankle and pulled him backward. He reared up and tipped the table—the crash that attracted the attention of Justin LaMotte, his brother, and many of the guests.

Charles had discovered that Smith knew nothing of frontier-style fighting. He presumed the same was true of the other three. Possessed of that advantage, he began to enjoy himself. He turned abruptly on the boy who had grabbed his ankle. When Justin and Francis arrived, closely followed by Francis's ten-year-old son Forbes, Charles was straddling the boy's chest, merrily pounding his head with bloody knuckles.

"Get him off!" the older boy gasped. "He—doesn't fight—like a gentleman."

"No, sir, I fight to win." Charles raised the boy's head by the ears and bashed it against the hard ground.

"Charles, that is enough."

The voice startled and alarmed him. He was jerked to his feet and whirled around. There stood Orry in his splendid uniform, fire in his eyes. Behind him Charles saw Cooper, Aunt Clarissa, and a sea of guests.

He heard one woman declare, "What a shame. All that intelligence—those good looks—wasted. He'll come to a bad end, that Main boy."

117

Several others agreed. Charles gave the crowd a defiant glare. Orry shook his arm hard, and Aunt Clarissa apologized for the trouble and offered to pay for the damage. Her tone made Charles blush and hang his head at last.

"I believe it might be best if we left now," Aunt Clarissa said.

"Oh, I'm sorry you can't stay longer," Justin said. Charles knew he didn't mean it.

On the way home, Orry started to lecture him. "That was an absolutely disgraceful scene. I don't care how badly you were provoked, you should have held your temper. It's time you began acting like a gentleman."

"I can't," Charles retorted. "I'm not a *gentleman*, I'm an orphan, and one isn't the same as the other. Everybody at Mont Royal makes that pretty clear all the time."

In the boy's angry eyes Cooper detected a flash of hurt. Orry squared his shoulders like a general who had been disobeyed. "You impertinent—"

"Let him alone," Cooper interrupted softly. "He got his punishment when all those people talked about him."

Charles peered at Cooper. He was stunned to find that the thin, studious man knew so much about him. To conceal his embarrassment, he turned to gaze out the window.

Orry blustered and started to argue. Clarissa touched his hand. "Cooper's right. No more discussion until we're home." A few minutes later she tried to slip her arm around Charles's shoulders. He pulled away. She looked across at her oldest son and shook her head.

When they reached Mont Royal, Tillet thrashed Charles in spite of Clarissa's protests. Tillet echoed the sentiments of the woman at the wedding:

"He'll come to a bad end. Do you need any further proof?"

Clarissa could only stare at her husband in silent dismay.

Somewhere in the great house at Resolute, a clock struck two.

The night air was humid and oppressive, heightening Madeline LaMotte's feeling that she was hopelessly trapped. Her fine cotton gown had tangled around her waist, but she didn't dare move to straighten it. Movement might rouse her husband, snoring lightly beside her.

It had been an exhausting day, but worse than that, the last few hours had brought her nothing but shock and pain and disillusionment.

She had expected Justin to be gentle and considerate, not only because he was an older man but because he had behaved that way in New Orleans. Now she knew it had all been a sham, designed to create a false impression for her and for her father.

Three times tonight she had been taught the bitter lesson. Three times Justin had exercised his rights. He had done it roughly, without once asking whether she was agreeable. There was only one small redeeming factor: the revelation of his dishonesty lessened her shame over the deception she had perpetrated on him.

This deception—the slight show of blood the first time—had been arranged with the help of Maum Sally, who knew about such things. The deception was necessary because Madeline had foolishly allowed herself to be seduced at a young age. That one mistake changed the course of her life. But for it, she wouldn't have been forced to ignore her own beliefs about personal honor and resort to deceit on her wedding night. Indeed, she never would have found herself in this frightful situation at all.

Madeline's seduction had occurred in the summer of her fourteenth year. To this day she carried a medallion-bright memory of Gerard, the carefree, good-looking boy who had worked as a cabin steward on one of the big Mississippi steamboats. She had met Gerard by chance one afternoon on the levee. He was seventeen and so jolly and attentive that she was soon ignoring the silent dictates of her conscience and sneaking off to meet him whenever his boat docked in the city—about once every ten days that summer.

Later in August, on a dark, thundery afternoon, she gave in to his pleadings and went with him to a sordid rented room in an alley in the Vieux Carré. Once he had her in a compromising position, he forgot about politeness and used her vigorously, although he was careful not to hurt her.

He failed to turn up for their next prearranged meeting. She took a great risk by going to the gangplank of the steamboat and asking for him. The deckhand to whom she spoke was evasive; he didn't know exactly where Gerard could be found at the moment. Then Madeline chanced to look at one of the upper decks. Behind a round cabin window she glimpsed a dim face. The instant Gerard saw her watching, he stepped back into darkness. She never saw him again.

For days she feared she might bear a child. When that consuming worry passed, she began to feel guilty about what she had done. She had wanted to make love with Gerard, but now that she had and she realized that he'd wanted nothing else from her, passion gave way to remorse and to a fear of all young men and their motives. The events of the summer drove her to try to atone, if that were possible, by means of adherence to new and more rigid standards of behavior she set for herself.

In the next few years she discouraged all young men who wanted to call on her, and in fact she avoided men almost completely until her father brought Justin LaMotte to dinner. The South Carolinian had two things to recommend him—kindly charm and his age. She was positive he was not driven by passions, as Gerard had been. That was one of the reasons she had finally changed her mind about Justin's proposals.

The change actually took place a few days after her father's seizure. One evening by the waxy light of bedside candles, he pleaded with her:

"I don't know how much longer I can live, Madeline. Set my mind at ease. Marry LaMotte. He's a decent and honorable man."

"Yes," she said as the candles wavered, stirred by Fabray's slurred speech. "I think so, too."

Only something as compelling as Nicholas Fabray's plea from his sickbed could have overcome her fear of marriage. But even her regard for her father couldn't banish her sadness at leaving her home, her small circle of friends, and the city she knew and loved. She made the long journey to South Carolina because she wanted to give her father peace of mind and because she trusted Justin LaMotte to be what he seemed.

How wrong she had been. How brutally, idiotically wrong. In terms of what he wanted, Justin was no different from younger men, and in one way he was worse. Gerard, at least, had tried not to hurt her.

She didn't blame her father for what had happened. Yet she believed things might not have reached such a state if she had also had a mother to counsel her. Madeline had never known her mother, whom Nicholas Fabray always described as the finest woman in the world. Evidently she had been an intelligent, sophisticated Creole of great beauty. Fabray said Madeline resembled her strongly, but there was not a single picture to prove or disprove that. Just before his wife's sudden and unexpected death, he had commissioned a miniaturist to paint her portrait. He said it was the second greatest disappointment of his life that he had not made the arrangements sooner.

Dear God, it was all such a frightful tangle, Madeline thought. So full of bitter ironies. How she had argued with Maum Sally about the wedding-night deception! She had said no to it again and again, even though Maum Sally insisted the deception was not only essential but, given prevailing male attitudes on virginity, an act of kindness toward Justin. The deception would ensure a smooth and trouble-free start to the marriage.

How damnably guilty she had felt for giving in—and how pitiable that guilt seemed in the light of her husband's treachery.

Then there was her meeting on the river road with the young military cadet, Orry Main. She had been taken with his gentle good manners and deep, dark eyes. She had wanted to touch him and she had done so, forgetting for a few seconds not only that she was about to be married but that he could not possibly be what he seemed. He was, after all, just about her own age.

Unexpectedly, an image of Orry slipped back into her thoughts as she lay beside her husband. Even at the reception she had felt a brief but powerful attraction to the young cadet. With her mind's eye she studied the imaginary face. Suddenly, guilt attacked her again. No matter what Justin had done to her, he was her husband. Even to think of another man was dishonorable.

Yet Orry's face lingered. To help banish it, she flung her forearm across her eyes, with more noise than she intended. She went rigid. The sound of Justin's breathing had changed. She straightened her arm at her side and tightened both hands into fists.

He was awake.

He started to speak but began coughing. In a faint voice she asked, "Are you all right?" It was concern she didn't feel.

He rolled onto his side, his back toward her. "I will be as soon as I clear this cough with some bourbon."

In the dark he knocked a glass off the bed stand. He blurted words Madeline had heard only a few times in her life, even though she was no stranger to profanity; Papa had strong views and sometimes punctuated them with oaths.

Justin didn't apologize for the filthy language. He drank directly from the bedside decanter. Then he uttered a long sigh and rolled back onto his elbows. The moon was up now; its brilliant light washed over his silky hair and muscular chest. For a man his age, he had very little flab on him.

He grinned at her. "You needn't worry about my health, my dear. It's perfect. Most of the LaMotte men have lived well into their nineties. I'm going to be around to enjoy your favors a good, long time."

She was too upset to say anything. She feared the huskiness in his voice and what it portended. He sounded almost testy when he continued, "I want you to bear me sons, Madeline. My first wife couldn't. Francis once had the nerve to suggest the fault was mine. Nonsense, of course—as we'll soon prove."

He rolled again, coming toward her like some fleshy juggernaut. He swept the sheet off her.

"Justin, if you don't mind, I would first like to get up and use—"

"Later," he said. He pushed the hem of her bed gown up above her stomach and shoved his hand between her thighs, hurting her.

She closed her eyes and dug her nails into her palms as he flung himself on top of her and began to grunt.

Orry went back to the Academy with the embroidered wreath still on his cap. The only person with whom he could discuss the momentous summer was George, who took note of his friend's melancholy state and tried to jolly him out of it.

"What you need, Stick, is a visit with Alice Peet. She'll soon make you forget this Madeline."

Orry gave him a long, level look, slowly shook his head.

"Never."

George was concerned about the fervor Orry put into that word. He hoped his friend wouldn't pine over a married woman for the rest of his life. He clapped an arm across Orry's shoulder and tried to buck him up. It didn't help.

Orry himself saw the need to find some antidote for his misery. He sought it in a herculean effort to lift himself out of the ranks of the immortals. But the second-class curriculum was no easier than those of his first two years. He liked the natural and experimental philosophy course, which included mechanics, optics, astronomy, and even a little about electricity. Yet he couldn't escape from the lowest section, no matter how he tried.

It was the same in advanced drawing. Professor Weir was merciless about Orry's watercolors, referring to them as daubs. George continued to breeze through everything with no apparent effort.

The one distinct improvement over last year was the opportunity to exercise the body as well as the mind. Second classmen took riding instruction from a professor nicknamed Old Hersh. Orry was a good rider, which was probably a blessing. At graduation, cadets were theoretically free to choose the branch of service they wanted to enter. But as a practical matter, the six branches were just as rigidly ranked as the cadets in their academic sections. Only the top graduates got into the engineers or the slightly less desirable topogs. Cadets at the bottom of the academic standings went to the infantry or to the dragoons and mounted rifles. The last two branches were held in such low esteem by the Army high command that all who served in them were permitted to grow mustaches. Orry suspected he would be growing one, and riding a lot.

Elkanah Bent had been chosen a cadet officer during summer camp. He strutted about in his scarlet sash and plumed hat, but the rank did nothing to improve his character. He continued to abuse plebes and yearlings with ruthless glee. One plebe, a lanky Kentuckian named Isham, became a special target because, like Orry and George, he showed defiance when Bent deviled him.

Not long before the national elections, Bent charged Isham with repeatedly losing step during an evening parade. Exhausted and coming down with a fever, Isham confronted Bent outside South Barracks later that night. He asked Bent to withdraw the report since he already had 164 demerits. At the rate he was going, he wouldn't be around to see whether he could pass the first-term examinations.

As the more experienced cadets could have told him, that kind of plea brought out the worst in Cadet Lieutenant Bent. He accused Isham of insolence to an upperclassman—several other cadets overheard that much—then marched the plebe away into the dusk for some "disciplinary drill."

Next morning after reveille, George and Orry learned that Isham was in the hospital. Gradually they pieced the story together. Bent had taken the plebe to the top of the winding path leading down to the North Dock. He then ordered Isham to march up and down the path at quickstep. It was a warm night, exceptional for late October, and heavy with humidity. After forty minutes Isham was reeling.

Bent sat on a boulder halfway down the path, smiling and calling mocking encouragements. Isham refused to beg for quarter, and Bent refused to give any. The plebe lasted about an hour. Then his legs gave out and he pitched sideways, tumbling and crashing down the slope to the bottom. He lay unconscious until a few minutes after midnight. Bent, naturally, had disappeared the moment Isham fell. There were no witnesses.

The plebe staggered to the hospital without his pack. An examination showed him to be suffering from a concussion and three broken ribs. Rumors flew on the Plain. Orry heard from several cadets that Isham would be crippled for life.

But the Kentuckian was strong. He recovered. Only after he was released from the hospital did he tell some fellow plebes what had happened. It was from them that George and Orry learned the truth, although they had guessed much of it, as had many others.

One of the tactical officers heard the story and placed Bent on report for disciplinary excesses. Isham refused to accuse his tormentor, however, so the evidence against the Ohioan remained circumstantial, hearsay. When confronted with the charges, Bent denied them heatedly and at length.

Pickett brought that news down to Gee's Point on a Saturday afternoon. Orry, George, and several friends were taking advantage of the prolonged hot spell and swimming in the river. George's reaction was blunt.

"That bastard. Were the charges dismissed?"

"Of course," Pickett said. "What else could happen after he denied them?"

George reached for his shirt hanging on a branch. "I think we ought to do something to fix Mr. Blubber Bent."

Orry felt the same way, yet, as always, his was the voice of caution.

"Do you think it's our affair, George?"

"It's the affair of the whole corps now. Bent lied to save himself. Do you want a person like him commanding troops? He'd send a company to slaughter, then shift the blame onto someone else without a qualm. It's time we got him out of here for good."

The presidential campaign moved into its last days. Henry Clay, the Whig candidate, had substantially softened his original position on the Texas issue. Now he sounded almost like his opponent. But anti-annexation men continued to warn that bringing Texas into the Union could precipitate America's first war in thirty years. If so, it would be a war that would test West Point programs, and West Point graduates, as they hadn't been tested since the era of Sylvanus Thayer. The issue and the election would be decided on December 4.

George and Orry paid little attention to the political debate. They were preoccupied with their studies and their plot to bring about Bent's downfall. The plot remained little more than a nebulous wish until George made his next visit to Benny Haven's. There he happened to learn that one of Alice Peet's regular customers was Army Lieutenant Casimir de Jong, the tactical officer who had preferred charges against Bent in the Isham affair. Later he reported to Orry:

"Old Jongie calls for his laundry every Wednesday night at ten. They say it takes him at least an hour to complete the transaction. I'll wager he's going to Alice for more than clean shirts and small clothes."

By now Orry was completely in favor of reprisals against the Ohioan.

"Then I would say Jongie's habits dictate our strategy. We should maneuver Bent into the embrace of fair Alice around nine-thirty some Wednesday evening."

George grinned. "I can see you have a brilliant future on the battlefield. However, you should always know your ally as well as you know your enemy."

"What does that mean?"

"Fair Alice may be an agreeable sort, but she's also a camp follower. A mercenary. She won't entertain Bent gratis. Especially not after she gets a look at his belly."

The reality couldn't be escaped. The plot went into suspension for three weeks while various cadet conspirators obtained blankets and cooking utensils. No questions were asked about the way they got them, or where. The contraband went to the river man in exchange for cash.

On the night before the election, George visited Alice with money in hand. Following supper the next evening, the engine of Bent's hoped-for destruction began to roll.

George and Pickett staged an argument in front of witnesses. They quarreled over Polk's support of annexation, George stating the familiar proposition that it had nothing to do with embracing fellow Americans and everything to do with adding more slave territory to the Union.

Pickett turned red. His replies were loud and contentious. Chance witnesses, and even a few who were in on the plot, were convinced he was furious.

Over the next few days it became common knowledge that the two Georges had fallen out. This gave Pickett a chance to cozy up to Bent, a deception his wit and Virginia charm helped him carry off convincingly. The following Wednesday night, as a light snow began to fall, Pickett invited the Ohioan to Benny Haven's for a touch of ardent spirits. Then, en route, Pickett suggested that a visit to Alice Peet would be more stimulating.

George and Orry, the official observers for the corps, trailed the pair through the snow. Shivering at Alice's window, they watched her swing into action. Her theatrical ability couldn't match Pickett's, but that made no difference. By the time she approached Bent, he had hung his cap on the back of his chair, unbuttoned his collar, and downed three drinks. His eyes were already glassy.

Bending close to him, Alice whispered into his ear. The Ohioan wiped a drop of saliva from his lips. Outside the partially opened window, the two friends heard him ask Alice her price. George clutched Orry's forearm; this was the crisis. The plot depended on Bent's believing Alice's statement that she would charge him nothing because she had taken a fancy to him. "That," Pickett had remarked during the formulation of the plan, "is like asking someone to believe the falls of Niagara flow upward."

But Bent was drunk, and far back in the Ohioan's bleary eyes Orry thought he detected the presence of a cringing fat boy wanting to be liked. Bent winked at Pickett across the table. The Virginian rose, grinned, and waved good night.

Pickett came out and closed the door behind him. As he passed the other conspirators, he whispered without turning his head, "I'm relying on you to report everything that happens." Without breaking stride, he went away across the crunchy snow. Through the window George and Orry saw Alice reach for Bent's hand and lead him to the open door to the sleeping area. The bait was taken, the trap ready to close.

At precisely ten, Lieutenant Casimir de Jong came tramping out of the snow, muffled to the eyes and merrily humming "Chester." He went straight to the door of Alice's shack and, after a quick knock, walked in.

The observers heard Alice let out a patently false squeal of fright. She rushed into the main room, smoothing her shift down with one hand and patting her disarrayed hair with the other. From the darkness beyond the doorway came snorting and the sound of rustling bedclothes.

Old Jongie plucked the cadet cap from the back of the chair and studied it a moment. Then he crushed it in his hand and planted himself in front of the doorway. Like all good tactical officers he had long ago learned the technique of the intimidating bellow. He used it now.

"Who is in there? Come out immediately, sir!"

Snuffling and blinking, Bent appeared a moment later. Old Jongie's jaw dropped. "Good God, sir—I cannot believe what I see."

"It isn't what you think," Bent cried. "I came—I only came for my laundry."

"With your pants at half mast and your long underwear gapping? In the name of decency, sir—*cover yourself.*"

Still crouched, Orry and George waddled toward the half-open door of the shack. George was almost unable to contain his laughter. By the light of an oil lamp, Orry saw Bent frantically jerk up his trousers. Alice wrung her hands.

"Oh, Mr. Bent, sir, I got so carried away, I clean forgot the lieutenant calls for his laundry every week at this time. That's the bundle over th—"

She dodged to avoid Bent's fist. "You slut, be quiet."

"That's enough, sir!" de Jong shouted. "Comport yourself like a gentleman while you may."

Bent's face shone as if greased. In the stillness of the nearby woods, a nocturnal animal cracked a twig. The sound was loud as a shot.

"While you may?" Bent whispered. "What do you mean by that?"

"Isn't it obvious, sir? You are on report—for more offenses than I care to enumerate at this moment. But be assured that I will enumerate them. Especially those that are punishable by dismissal."

Bent looked ill. "Sir, this is all a misunderstanding. If you'll give me a chance to explain—"

"The same kind of explanation you provided for Isham's injuries? Lies?" De Jong was a splendid instrument of official wrath; Orry almost felt sorry for the fat first classman.

De Jong spun toward the door. Bent saw his whole career about to vanish with the tactical officer. He grabbed de Jong's shoulder.

"Take your hands off me, you drunken sot," de Jong said in a chillingly quiet voice. "I shall expect you in my office the moment you arrive back on post—and that arrival had better not take any longer than ten minutes, or the view halloo will be heard all the way to New York City."

Grand in his contempt, Lieutenant de Jong marched down the steps and into the falling snow. He never saw the two cadets crouched in the shadows.

Inside the shack, Bent turned on Alice. "You stupid, bungling whore—"

He shoved the rickety table aside. She ran to the stove and snatched a butcher knife from a rack hanging next to it.

"Get out of here. Stump told me you were crazy, but I didn't put stock in that. What an idiot I was—get out. *Get out!*"

The brandished knife flashed. George and Orry exchanged quick, worried looks as Bent stood swaying, stunned.

"Stump? Do you mean Hazard had something to do with this? It was Pickett's idea to come here, and your idea for me to—that is—"

He was unable to continue. His anger was replaced by an expression of such blinding fury, Orry thought he would never again see its like on a human face.

Alice compounded the hurt with a shrill laugh. "My idea? I wouldn't let a pig like you touch me unless I got paid, and paid plenty. Even so, I nearly couldn't do it."

Bent trembled. "I should have seen it. A trick. A plot. All of them against me—that's it, isn't it?"

Alice realized her blunder and tried to rectify it. "No. I didn't mean—"

"Don't lie to me," Bent said. The two cadets outside couldn't see what happened next. Apparently Bent made another threatening move toward the laundress because she began to scream. This time she wasn't playacting.

"Quiet, or you'll wake the whole village!"

That was exactly what Alice intended; she screamed all the louder. Bent came lunging out the door, his hair flying, his eyes full of fright. He ran off with one hand holding up his pants.

George and Orry stared at each other. Neither felt the elation they had anticipated for so long.

Within three days Bent took the Canterberry road.

Most of the cadets said they were happy he had been dismissed. Orry was, certainly. And George. Yet both of them admitted to some feelings of guilt over the way the Ohioan had been entrapped. Gradually the friends put the guilt out of mind. Orry knew his crisis of conscience was at an end when he began to have sensual dreams about Madeline again.

At Christmas everyone was still discussing Polk's victory. Since the President-elect continued to proclaim his intention to annex Texas, Orry wondered whether he would go directly from his graduation, a year from June, to combat against a Mexican army. And would there be a second front in the Northwest as a result of the current dispute with the British over the location of the Oregon border? Thrilling possibilities, but frightening, too.

On the last Saturday night in December, another hash was in progress in Pickett's room when there was a furtive knock. Orry opened the door to find Tom Jackson standing there. Jackson had turned into a superior student, largely through determined effort. If he wasn't exactly likable because of his odd personality, there was yet something about him—a strength, an unspoken ferocity—that inspired respect. He was welcome in the more tolerant cadet groups, such as this one.

"Greetings, General," George called out as Jackson shut the door. "Care for a bite?"

"No, thank you." Jackson tapped his stomach to indicate his concern with his digestion. The lanky Virginian looked even more serious than usual; positively mournful, in fact.

"What's wrong?" Orry asked.

"I am the bearer of unhappy news. Especially for you two," Jackson said with glances at Orry and George. "Apparently Cadet Bent's connections in Washington were not mere products of a boastful imagination. I am reliably informed by the adjutant that Secretary of War Wilkins, as one of his last acts of office, has intervened in the case."

George wiped the edge of his index finger across his upper lip. "Intervened how, Tom?"

"The dismissal was overturned. Mr. Bent will be back among us within a fortnight."

The countermanding of dismissals was nothing new at the Academy. Thanks to the political ties of the families of cadets, it happened often enough to be a major cause of the institution's unpopularity. It was an abuse that even the most conscientious superintendent was powerless to stop, since final authority for West Point rested in Washington.

It took only six days for Bent to reappear, stripped of his former rank. George and Orry expected that revenge of some kind would be forthcoming, but it was not. The two friends avoided Bent as much as they could, but it was impossible to avoid him entirely. When either of them did encounter the Ohioan, his reaction was the same. His jowly face remained composed, stony. George and Orry might have been utter strangers.

"That scares me a devil of a lot more than ranting and raving would," Orry said. "What's he up to?"

"I hear he's boning pretty hard," George said. "Wasted effort, if you ask me. After what he did, he'll be lucky to make the infantry, even with top marks."

As June drew closer, and Bent continued to keep to himself, the overturned dismissal was discussed less frequently, and finally not at all. There were more important things to talk about; it had been a momentous springtime for the nation.

On the first of March, three days before Polk's inauguration, outgoing President Tyler had signed the joint congressional resolution calling for Texas to join the Union as a state. Polk inherited the consequences of that act, the first of them being the reaction of the Mexican government. At the end of the month, the U.S. minister in Mexico City was informed that diplomatic relations were severed.

War fever gripped some sections of the country, notably the South. Orry broke the wafer on a letter from home and found Cooper complaining about Tillet's zeal for a military crusade to protect the new slave state if the Texas legislature approved annexation, as it surely would. Northerners were divided on the question of war. Opposition was strongest around Boston, long the seedbed of abolitionist activity.

Bent and the other first classmen were busy preparing for their final examinations and conferring with the trunk makers and military tailors who always arrived at this time of year. Bent's class, typical of most, would graduate about half of those who had appeared for the first summer encampment. Each departing cadet would become a brevet second lieutenant in his respective branch. A brevet officer didn't receive the full pay to which his rank would otherwise entitle him, so it was the goal of most graduates to escape this provisional status and win promotion to full second during the first year of active duty. George's prediction about Bent came true. The Ohioan was able to do no better than a brevet in the infantry.

Bent finally spoke to George and Orry after the year's final parade. It was sunset, a cool June evening. The softly rounded peaks rose half scarlet, half blue above the Plain where many of the new graduates were receiving the congratulations of beaming mothers, quietly proud fathers, exuberant little brothers and sisters, and feminine admirers not connected with the family. George had noticed that Bent was one of the very few with no relatives present.

The Ohioan looked spruce in the cadet uniform he was wearing for the last time. He had grown generous whiskers, as the first classmen were permitted to do. In an hour or so he would be down on the boat landing, bound for New York and, presumably, the class supper, which was always held in some posh hotel the day after graduation. Leave for Bent and all the other graduates would end on the last day of September.

Orry was puzzled by Bent's smile. Then the Ohioan turned slightly, and fading daylight lit his eyes. Orry saw the hatred then.

"What I have to say to you two gentlemen is brief and to the point." Bent spoke in short, breathy bursts, as if struggling to contain powerful emotion. "You almost kept me from an Army career. That fact will never be far from the center of my thoughts. I will be highly placed one of these days—very highly placed—mark that and count on it. And I will not forget the names of those who put a permanent stain on my record.''

He pivoted away so abruptly that George sidestepped, a nervous reaction. Sunset light reddened Bent's eyes. He lumbered away toward his barracks. His weight made it hard for him to maintain a military bearing.

George was darting stunned looks at his friend, as if to say he couldn't believe the melodramatic recitation he had just heard. Orry hoped to God that his friend wouldn't take it lightly and laugh, because you had to believe the declarations of a madman.

Believe, and be warned.

In summer encampment George advanced to cadet lieutenant. Among the first classmen, Orry was the only one not given a rank.

He remained, as an old joke put it, a high private, which was discouraging because it showed how little his superiors thought of him. Oh, they liked him well enough personally. But as for believing he had any military ability, no.

The first-class courses seemed designed to validate that opinion. While George continued to sail through effortlessly, Orry struggled with the ethics course, which included principles of constitutional law as well as the practice of court-martial. He had an even harder time with the courses in civil and military engineering, which brought him into regular contact with the feared and legendary Professor Mahan.

In his dark blue dress coat, blue trousers, and buff vest, Mahan looked every inch the Academy professor. When a cadet demonstrated before him, he permitted no variance from what he had taught or the way he had taught it. The foolish cadet who dared to disagree, however timidly, was soon humbled by Mahan's celebrated sarcasm—and mentally downgraded to boot. Every cadet was ranked in Mahan's mind. From that judgment, whether it was just or not, there was no appeal.

Yet the cadets liked, even worshiped Mahan. If that hadn't been the case, they would have made fun of his slight speech impediment, which made him sound as if he always had a cold. Instead, the cadets affectionately acknowledged the problem with a nickname—Old Cobben Sense; Mahan was constantly lecturing about the virtues of "cobben sense."

In addition to engineering, Mahan taught military science. In this course he awed his pupils with predictions of a new, apocalyptic kind of war that would be born of the current industrial age. They would all be called on to command in that new kind of war, he said. And perhaps it would take place sooner than any of them anticipated. In July, General Zachary Taylor and fifteen hundred men had been ordered to the Nueces River, which Mexico still insisted was its northern boundary. At Corpus Christi on the Nueces, Taylor took up a position to guard against a possible Mexican attack.

By late autumn Taylor's force had grown to forty-five hundred. On December 29 Texas joined the Union as the twenty-eighth state, still standing by its claim that the peace treaty at the end of its war for independence had established its southern border at the Rio Grande.

Mexico's protests grew increasingly belligerent. The treaty was worthless, and the Republic of Texas was a fraud—nonexistent. How could an illegal political entity annex itself to the United States? The answer was obvious. It could not. If it thought otherwise, there would be dire consequences.

The threatening talk pleased those Americans who believed the nation had an almost divine right to expand its borders. Robert Winthrop, a representative from Massachusetts, encountered a phrase in an obscure journal that seemed to sum up this right in a memorable way. Early in January, Winthrop spoke on the floor of Congress about "manifest destiny," and America had a new rallying cry.

During the winter, attempts at peace negotiations conducted by Minister to Mexico John Slidell failed. Under orders from his superiors in Washington, General Taylor again advanced, this time proceeding south, through the sparsely populated wilderness both Mexico and Texas were claiming, all the way to the Rio Grande. People began to talk of war as a real possibility. "Mr. Polk's war," the President's opponents called it.

In that troubled spring of 1846, George Hazard took a good look around him, blinked, and realized that in four years, while he was busy with cigars, girls, and occasional study, profound changes had taken place. Boys had become young men; young men had become survivors; survivors were about to become brevet officers—in his case, and Orry's, brevet officers with new growths of whiskers.

Orry was going to the infantry, so George put in for it too. Some of the professors and tactical officers disapproved. They said George, with his high marks, could get the artillery, perhaps even the topogs. Orry urged his friend to heed that counsel, but George was adamant.

"I'd rather serve in the infantry with a friend than go flying around on a limber with a lot of strangers. Besides, I still plan to resign at the end of four years. It's immaterial to me where I spend that time, so long as I don't get shot at too often."

If George was not precisely overjoyed at the idea of going to war, Orry, on the other hand, really wanted to confront danger—see the elephant, as the popular phrase had it—on some distant battlefield in Mexico. Sometimes he felt guilty about that desire, but combat experience would be invaluable to a man planning on a military career.

Although Orry's superiors hadn't seen fit to promote him, that hadn't changed his mind about his goal. He would be a soldier no matter what anyone else thought.

Like Orry, most of the other first classmen were thrilled, although nervously so, over the possibility of seeing action. West Point's corps of "pampered aristocrats" might at last have a chance to prove its worth. So might the entire Army, for that matter. A great many citizens were contemptuous of the American soldier, saying he had but one skill—he knew how to raise malingering to a high art.

The question of war was decided before George and Orry graduated. On April 12 the Mexican commander at Matamoros had ordered General Taylor to withdraw. Old Rough and Ready had ignored the warning, and on the last day of the month Mexican soldiers began to cross the Rio Grande. Early in May, at Palo Alto, Taylor's army repulsed an enemy force three times its size and did so again at Resaca de la Palma a few days later. The ball was open. Congress responded to the invasion of American territory by declaring war on the twelfth of May.

The war created a windstorm of controversy. George didn't go so far as some anti-Southern Whigs such as Horace Greeley, the editor of the *New York Tribune*, who called the war a trumped-up land grab and warned that a Southern cabal was pushing the nation into a "fathomless abyss of crime and calamity." George also scoffed at Mexican propaganda about a perverse crusade to expunge Catholicism from North America. After looking forward to four lazy years in the Army, he found the war merely inconvenient and annoying.

The moment George made the decision about his branch of service, he had written his father and asked him to pull a few wires. Now, at last, his orders arrived, posting him to the Eighth Infantry. Orry announced with astonishment that he had been sent to the same regiment. George pretended to be greatly surprised by the coincidence.

In the fine June weather, the graduates accepted the good wishes of their professors and marched in their last parade. George and Orry for the first time donned regular Army blue: the dark blue coat, the light blue trousers with the thin white seam stripe of the infantry.

George's father and his brother Stanley attended the final parade. None of Orry's family had been able to make the trip from South Carolina. Immediately after the parade, the Hazards took a boat for Albany, where they had business. George and Orry were ready to leave about an hour later.

As the steamer pulled away from the dock, Orry stepped to the rail and gazed up at the bluff, visually tracing the path they had climbed for the first time four years ago.

"I'll miss the place. You'll laugh at this, but what I'll miss most is the drum. It gets into your bones after a while."

George didn't laugh, but he shook his head. "You'll miss a drum that divided your life into rigid little compartments?"

"Yes. It lent the days a certain rhythm. A pattern and order you could depend on."

"Well, don't pine away, Mr. Stick. We'll hear plenty of drums in Mexico."

Night was settling as the steamer plowed past Constitution Island. Soon they were moving down the Hudson in darkness. In the city they registered at the American House, and next day saw the sights of New York. On Broadway they happened on a couple of dragoon noncoms and received their first salutes. Orry was excited. "We're soldiers now. Officially."

His friend shrugged, unimpressed. Before George boarded the train for Philadelphia, Orry made him promise to come to Mont Royal toward the end of his leave. They could then travel on to their regiment together. George agreed. In the past four years he had developed a liking for most of the Southerners he had met.

Besides, he had never forgotten Cooper Main's comment about the pretty girls down home.

One of the first things George did when he arrived in Lehigh Station was to unwrap the meteorite he had found in the hills above West Point. In his room he carefully positioned it on a windowsill, where none of the upstairs maids could possibly mistake it for a piece of junk to be thrown out. Then he folded his hands under his chin and contemplated his prize.

Ten minutes passed. Twenty. In the silence, the rough-surfaced, iron-rich fragment seemed to speak to him with a wordless but mighty voice, telling of its power to alter or destroy anything man could build or invent. When he finally rose to leave, a shiver ran down his spine, even though the house was hot this summer afternoon.

George took few things seriously, and fewer still touched his emotions in any significant way. That piece of star iron, the stuff at the heart of the Hazard fortune, was a rare exception. He had no intention of meeting a brave and quickly forgotten death in Mexico; he had important work to do in the years ahead. Let Orry spend his life settling border disputes on battlefields. In the iron trade, George would help change the world in many more ways than that.

He packed and said good-bye to his family in mid-September. Taylor's Army was advancing on Monterrey, Mexico, during an eight-week armistice. George kept track of the Army's position because his regiment was part of Taylor's Second Division, commanded by General Worth. The Eighth had already seen hot fighting and presumably would see more.

On the long train trip to South Carolina, George tried to organize his ideas about Northerners and Southerners. At West Point cadets from both parts of the country had pretty well agreed that the Yankees were better prepared because the North had better schools. The Southerners haughtily amended their agreement by saying that it didn't matter much; it was the bold leader, not the smart one, who usually won the battle.

If quizzed on regional differences, he would have characterized Yankees as practical, restless, curious about the ordinary things of life, and eager to make improvements wherever possible. Southerners, by contrast, struck him as content with life as they knew it. They were, at the same time, given to endless disputation and theorizing, always in the abstract, about such subjects as politics, Negro slavery, and the Constitution, to name just three.

Of course slavery was always discussed as a positive good. Interestingly, George recalled Orry's saying that hadn't always been the case. As a boy he had eavesdropped on the conversation of gentlemen visiting his father. The talk often turned to the peculiar institution, and once he had heard Tillet state that some elements of slavery were abhorrent to God and man. But after the Vesey and Turner rebellions, Orry noted, there was no more of that kind of free discussion at Mont Royal. Tillet said it might tend to encourage another uprising.

George had no strong views on slavery, pro or con. He decided that he wouldn't discuss the subject in South Carolina, and he certainly wouldn't tell the Mains how the other Hazards felt. His mother and father weren't fanatical abolitionists, but they believed slavery to be totally wrong.

Orry met him with a carriage at a tiny woodland way station of the Northeastern Rail Road. During the ride to the plantation, the friends talked animatedly of the war and the months just past. Orry said his family had returned from their summer residence two weeks early, so as to be there when George arrived.

George was fascinated by the lush vegetation of the low country, overwhelmed by the size and beauty of Mont Royal, and taken with Orry's family.

With most of them, anyway. Tillet Main struck him as stern and a mite suspicious of outsiders. Then there was Cousin Charles, a raffishly handsome boy whose chief occupations seemed to be smiling in a sullen way and practicing lunges and feints with a large bowie knife.

Orry's sisters were, of course, far too young for George. Brett, just nine, was pretty and bright but tended to fade into the background when eleven-year-old Ashton was present. The older sister was one of the loveliest little girls George had ever seen. What a beauty she'd be at twenty!

He spent his first full day at Mont Royal touring the fields and learning how a rice plantation operated. Late in the afternoon he was given into the care of Clarissa and her daughters, who took him to a charming summer house at one corner of the garden. When they were all comfortably seated in wicker chairs, two Negro girls served them delicious lemonade and little cakes.

Presently Clarissa excused herself to see to something in the kitchen. Ashton folded her hands in her lap and regarded George with great dark eyes.

"Orry says your nickname is Stump. You don't look like a stump to me." She smiled, her eyes flashing.

George ran an index finger under his tight, hot collar. For once he was at a loss for words. Brett rescued him.

"That's the handsomest uniform I ever have seen—though it's true I haven't seen many."

"Not as handsome as what's in it," Ashton said, and at that George actually blushed. The sisters seemed like miniature women, not children. Ashton's flirtatious nature, rather than being pleasing, made him uncomfortable.

It was her age, he decided. She was too young to act coquettish, yet she did. George was attracted to pretty women, but he tended to avoid beautiful ones. They were too aware of their own good looks, and that awareness often made them moody and difficult. So it would be with Ashton Main, he suspected.

Ashton kept watching him over the rim of her lemonade glass. He was relieved to return to male company when the little party ended.

*

Two evenings later, at the dinner table, Clarissa announced plans for a big picnic at which George was to be introduced to neighbors and relatives.

"If we are lucky, we shall also have the honor of Senator Calhoun's presence. He has been home at Fort Hill for a few weeks. He suffers from a lung disorder which the climate of the Potomac basin only exacerbates. Up-country the air is clear and pure. It affords him some relief, which is the reason—Tillet, why on earth are you making such a face?"

Every head swung toward the end of the table. Outside, far-off thunder rumbled in the still air. Ashton and Brett exchanged anxious looks. This was the season of the hurricanes that came sweeping off the ocean with destructive fury.

"John hardly acts like one of us any longer," Tillet said. An insect landed on his forehead. He swatted at it, then gestured in an annoyed way.

A little Negro boy had been standing motionless in the corner, fly whisk held in front of him like a musket. In response to Tillet's gesture the boy jumped forward and waved the whisk vigorously near Tillet's head, but he knew he was too late. He had displeased his owner. The fear in the boy's eyes told George more about the relationship between master and slave than he might have learned from hours of abolitionist lectures.

"We toast John on every public occasion," Tillet went on. "We put up statues and plaques honoring him as the greatest living resident of the state—possibly the nation. Then he traipses off to Washington and utterly ignores the will of his constituents."

Cooper gave a little snort that clearly angered his father. "Come, sir," Cooper said, "are you suggesting Mr. Calhoun can be considered a South Carolinian only when he agrees with you? His opposition to the war may be unpopular, but it's patently sincere. He certainly supports and reinforces most of your other views."

"Which you do not. Of course, I am not particularly distressed by that fact." The sarcasm made George uncomfortable, and he suspected that deep down Tillet was greatly distressed.

"Good," Cooper retorted with an airy wave of his wineglass. He ignored imploring glances from his mother. "You mustn't worry about what I think. It's the opinion of the rest of the country that you ignore at your peril."

Tillet's hand closed on his napkin. He glanced at George, forced a smile. "My son is a self-proclaimed expert on national affairs. Sometimes I think he'd be more at home living up North."

Rigid in his chair, Cooper said, "Balderdash." His smile was gone. "I despise those damn abolitionists with all their self-righteous breast-beating. But their hypocrisy doesn't blind me to the truth of some of their charges. The moment anyone dares to criticize the way we do things in the South, we all become as defensive as treed porcupines. The Yankees say slavery is wrong, so we claim it's a blessing. They point to scars on nigra backs—"

"You find no scars on anyone at Mont Royal," Tillet interrupted, for George's benefit. Cooper paid no attention.

"—and we respond with windy pronouncements that slaves are happy. No person deprived of liberty is happy, for God's sake!"

"Watch your foul mouth in front of these children," Tillet shouted.

But the younger man was as angry as the older: "Instead of learning from the truth, we avoid it. We're content to be what we've been for a hundred and fifty years—farmers whose crops depend on the sweat of black bondsmen. We ignore men like George's father, even though they're becoming legion up North. George's father manufactures iron with free labor. That iron goes into machines. Machines are creating the future. The Yankees understand what this century's all about, but we only understand the last one. If Senator Calhoun no longer parrots the established wisdom of the state, more power to him. We need a dozen more like him."

There was an uncharacteristic sharpness in Clarissa's voice. "It's rude of you to speak so intemperately in front of our guest."

"Yes, the hell with the truth. Good manners above all." Cooper raised his wineglass in a mock toast. Tillet knocked the glass from his hand.

The black boy with the fly whisk ducked. The glass broke against the wall. Brett shrieked and shrank against her chair, one hand over her eyes. Orry looked at the visitor and shrugged, his smile awkward and apologetic.

Tillet seethed. "You have consumed too much wine, Cooper. You had better retire until you can control yourself."

"Yes, indeed," said Clarissa. Though softly spoken, it was a command.

Cooper did act a mite intoxicated, George thought. The older brother rose, stared at his father, then laughed before hurrying out. Tillet was livid; clearly, mockery enraged the head of Orry's family even more than did heresy.

No one smiled or said much during the rest of the meal. George was depressed. There was a clear rift in the Main household. A rift much like the one his own father said was slowly but inevitably dividing the country.

smell of sun and grass, the trees, the blossoms
and cypress. There was a door that the main house, and
much like the one before it came, and was slowly but surely
closing the window.

Although the picnic fell within the sickly season, it drew a crowd of more than two hundred. Many came from their summer homes, and some all the way from Columbia. This impressed George, but not as much as the late-morning arrival of John Calhoun.

Senator Calhoun and his wife, Floride, drove up the lane in an old but elegant barouche. Friends and the curious hurried to surround the vehicle. George had heard someone say the senator had spent the night in Charleston, attended by his driver and three other Negroes, all house servants, who followed the barouche in a mule-drawn cart.

In the last thirty years of America's national life, no one had played more roles with greater dominance than the tall, hawkish man who stepped quickly down from the barouche and began greeting well-wishers. George couldn't recall all the offices Calhoun had held. He knew secretary of war and Vice-President were two of them.

Early in his career Calhoun had been a fierce partisan of the Federal Union and of the Academy. When others had argued against Sylvanus Thayer's ambitious reform programs, Calhoun had endorsed them, believing America could not be strong without a strong military arm. But of course when Northerners heard Calhoun's name now, most of them thought of one thing—the doctrine of nullification.

The senator had propounded the doctrine in the early 1830s. At issue was a protective tariff unpopular in South Carolina. Calhoun argued that the state had the sovereign right to nullify the tariff—which in effect meant any state could disobey any Federal law it disliked. President Jackson had backed Calhoun down and ended the nullification movement with an implied threat of Federal force.

George was introduced to the Calhouns. He guessed that the senator was in his middle sixties. It was obvious that age and disease had wasted Calhoun's face and tall, strong frame. But echoes of earlier good looks remained in his dramatic crest of gray hair thrown back from his forehead and in his brilliant dark blue eyes.

Calhoun murmured a few complimentary words about West Point, then moved on. George had an impression that the senator was an exhausted, embittered man. His smile looked false, his movements labored.

George soon grew dizzy trying to keep up with all the introductions. He met Mains and Bulls and Smiths, Rhetts and Hugers and Boykins and LaMottes and Ravenels. One member of the Smith family, female and about his own age, seemed as taken with his uniform as he was with her décolletage. They promised to meet in twenty minutes at the punch table.

Herr Nagel, who tutored the Main sisters, was already falling-down drunk. George helped him to a bench. Next he spent an uncomfortable few minutes conversing with Tillet's overseer, a short Yankee named Salem Jones. Jones had a cherubic face but mean eyes, which he kept fixed on a distant section of the lawn. There, some favored house slaves had been given a couple of tables for their own food, which they were permitted to sample while waiting for a summons to perform some chore for the guests. Calhoun's blacks had made straight for the slave gathering, which was growing boisterous. Jones pursed his lips, watching.

The day grew dark with thunderclouds. A light shower sent everyone scurrying. When the rain stopped five minutes later and the guests sorted themselves out again, George couldn't find the Smith girl. He bumped into Orry and noticed his faraway expression.

"Who mesmerized you, Stick? Ah—I see." His appreciative smile faded. "I notice large rings on her hand. One a wedding ring. Is she the one you fell in love with two years ago?"

Softly, Orry said, "She's lovely, isn't she?"

"Lovely is faint praise. I'd say the word is ravishing. So that's Madeline. She looks exhausted." Yet mere tiredness could hardly account for her strange, benumbed expression.

Orry offered the explanation when he said, "She just returned from New Orleans. Her father suffered another stroke, she rushed to his bedside, and a couple of days after she got there, he died. She had to handle all the funeral arrangements herself. It's no wonder that she's worn out."

George was acutely aware of the emotion in his friend's voice. He hadn't heard much about the fabled Madeline during recent months, and he had decided Orry had gotten over the infatuation. He had been wrong.

He studied the girl more closely. Despite the fatigue shadows around her eyes, she was truly one of the most beautiful women he had ever

144

seen. Her mouth was red and full. Her pale skin and black, straight hair created a stunning contrast. He leaned closer to his friend.

"Have I met her husband?"

"Yes. That clod."

Orry inclined his head toward one of the LaMottes. Then George recalled the introduction. Justin, that was the fellow's name. Arrogant sod. So was his brother Francis, who stood nearby with his dowdy wife and handsome young son. The son, in a fine coat and flowing cravat, was preening as much as his father and his uncle. They acted as if they were European royalty, not American farmers.

"How can she possibly get along with that crowd?" he whispered.

"She does very well. Madeline could charm the devil himself. And my mother tells me she's become extremely good at her duties on the plantation. That's unusual because Madeline wasn't trained to birth babies or run a kitchen. I'm sure Justin has no appreciation of her ability. Come on, I'll present you."

The young men started toward her. Madeline saw them and spontaneous joy animated her face. My Lord, George said to himself, she's got a case as bad as his. Then Madeline's lifeless look returned. She reminded George of someone who had just made a horrifying discovery. Something to do with her husband, no doubt, he thought cynically.

Madeline stepped away from Justin. Before Orry could speak to her, however, Calhoun strolled up with Tillet Main at his right hand and several other male guests at his heels. They were hanging on the senator's words.

"Some say the lesson of the nullification affair was this, Tillet. That the doctrine itself was wrong. I disagree. The doctrine is constitutionally correct. Only the way in which we tried to implement it was foolhardy. Foredoomed. One state cannot hope to prevail against the might of the Federal government. But several states—unified and determined—that's another matter."

Tillet cleared his throat. "Are you speaking of secession?"

Calhoun's shrug was quick, almost fierce. "Well, it's a term you hear a good deal in the South these days. I heard it in Charleston just the other evening. A gentleman I respect called secession the only adequate reply to Congressman Wilmot's proviso."

He was referring to an amendment to some Federal legislation that would have appropriated two million dollars to expedite negotiations with Mexico. Wilmot had proposed that slavery be expressly prohibited from territory acquired in any such negotiation. The arguments pro and con had caused a national uproar. The bill had passed the House, but the Senate had beaten it back before recessing in mid-August.

"The gentleman is right," said one of the others. "The proviso is extreme provocation. An insult to the South."

"What else do you expect from a Pennsylvania Democrat?" Tillet asked. "They have a bottomless treasury of righteousness up North."

Calhoun nodded. "Secession talk is in the air for precisely that reason. There may be no other way to redress the grievances of this region."

"I say let's get on with it," Justin LaMotte put in. He walked past his wife, and as he did so he scowled at her. George couldn't imagine the reason, unless it was because she was interested in the discussion—one woman in the midst of a dozen men. The wife of the other LaMotte had crept away.

Tillet said to Justin, "Much as I despise some of those Yankee politicians, I'd hate for us to choose disunion after all the struggles to establish this country."

Calhoun's lips twisted. "The word *choose* puts the wrong color on it. If there is disunion, we shall be driven to it. Flogged to it by those Northerners whose favorite entertainment is sneering at us."

"We'd be better off as a separate nation," Francis LaMotte declared.

"How can you say that, Francis?"

The feminine voice stilled everyone else, turned heads, and set mouths agape. Justin looked as if he wanted to sink into the earth. Orry watched his shock and shame turn to anger.

Madeline seemed oblivious. Once again that odd, stunned expression faded, and her eyes grew lively. Having spoken out, she showed no inclination to stop. She talked to Calhoun.

"I am a Southerner born and bred, Senator. It was years ago that I first heard men speak of seceding from the Union. My father said the idea was pernicious twaddle because it wouldn't work. I've thought about it since, and I agree."

Calhoun's reaction was more polite than those of the other men, who scowled and grumbled. Yet he, too, was obviously put off by a woman intruding into a man's domain. With a faint lift of a gray brow, he said, "Really, madam?"

Madeline managed a disarming smile. "Of course. Just think about the practicalities. What if we were a separate country and the cotton and rice markets went soft. It's happened before. How much sympathy—how much help—would we receive from the other nation up North?

What if a genuinely unfriendly government came to power there? What if they passed laws to prevent us from buying the goods we need for daily living? We depend on the North, Senator. We have no factories of our own. No substantial resources other than—''

''We have our principles,'' Justin interrupted. ''Those are more important than factories.'' He closed a hand on her forearm. George saw her wince. ''But I'm sure the senator isn't interested in feminine opinions.''

Alarmed by the rage in LaMotte's eyes, Calhoun tried to be gracious. ''Oh, I'm always interested in the opinions of my constituents, whoever—''

Justin didn't let him finish. ''Come along, my dear. There is someone waiting to see you.'' His cheeks showed spots of scarlet. His smile looked like the teeth in a skull.

She tugged against his constricting hand. ''Justin, please—''

''Come along.''

He turned her around by pressure on her arm. Francis closed in behind them as they withdrew. George looked anxiously at his friend. For a moment he thought Orry might commit murder. Then Calhoun made a little joke to ease the tension, and the crisis passed.

Justin, meantime, was pushing Madeline toward the far side of the lawn where carriages were parked in long rows. He knew people were watching. He was too angry to care. Francis begged him to calm down. Justin swore at his brother and ordered him to leave. Looking mortified, Francis about-faced and returned to the crowd.

Justin shoved his wife against the big rear wheel of a carriage. The hub jabbed her back. She gasped.

''Let go of me. You have no right to treat—''

''I have every right,'' he said. ''I am your husband. You humiliated me in front of the senator and all my friends.''

She glared at him, color suffusing her face. ''I beg your pardon, Justin. I wasn't aware that disagreement with someone's opinion had become a crime in South Carolina. I wasn't aware that free speech had been abridged by—''

''Don't give me any of that!'' He wrenched her arm, thrust her against the hub again. She cried out softly, then looked at him with loathing.

''You bastard. It's only your damned reputation that matters, not the feelings of those you hurt whenever the whim strikes you. After our wedding night I suspected as much. Now there's no doubt.''

And I could ruin your precious reputation forever. But angry as she was, she knew she could not.

Justin, however, was out of control. Even Madeline's show of resistance—something he found astounding in a female—couldn't do much to brake his temper. He shook her again.

"I'll tell you something else that is not in doubt, my dear. Your position. You are a *wife*. That means you are not entitled to offer opinions on any substantive issue. Women with intellectual pretensions come to a bad end in this part of the world—a lesson your late father should have taught you."

"He taught me there was nothing wrong with a woman's thinking independent—"

"I am not *interested* in your father's *mistakes*. Furthermore, I'm grateful I never had to debate the issue with him. I might have been forced to knock him down."

With a wrench she freed her forearm and drew it against her bosom. "That's all you know how to do, isn't it? Strike those who disagree with you. Bully your way through life!"

"Call it whatever you wish. Just remember this: women and ideas were not meant to mix. The Grimké sisters had to leave this state because they forgot that lesson. Now they're up North preaching nigger freedom and free love, disgracing themselves and their sex. I'll not have any wife of mine behaving that way. You must know your place and stay in it. I also promise you this." He leaned close, his silky brown hair tangled over his forehead. Her defiance drained away, replaced by fear when he looked into her eyes. "If you ever again speak out and embarrass me as you did a little while ago, you'll suffer. Be warned."

He drew himself up and smoothed his hair back into place. Then he returned to the picnic, trying to smile as if nothing had happened. But a change had come into their relationship, and both of them knew it. They had reached down to the hidden places within themselves and revealed things only hinted at before.

"Bastard," Madeline whispered again. How sweet and cruelly fitting it would be to tell Justin what her father had told her just before he died. Tell him every last stunning word.

She leaned against the wheel, struggling to contain her tears. She didn't know which was the worst of it—her humiliation, her rage, or her new certainty that Justin had issued no idle warning.

*

Orry watched the scene in the carriage park from a distance. Seldom had he been so tense and frustrated. He wanted to intervene, rescue Madeline, beat LaMotte senseless. But she was bound to her husband by religious and civil law. She was a *wife*, Justin's property. If Orry followed his instincts, he would only make matters worse for her.

He admired Madeline's bravery when she composed her face and moved back among the people still whispering about her. He silently cursed them for the scornful looks they gave her behind her back. George noticed his agitation. So did Cooper, who had already heard a good deal of gossip about Madeline's dispute with Calhoun.

Both Cooper and George tried to talk with Orry, but he broke away from each of them. Finally, after striding aimlessly for several minutes, he noticed Madeline standing by herself. He cast aside caution and did what his emotions had been driving him to do for the past hour. He walked straight to her side.

"Are you all right?"

"Yes, yes." She wasn't; he could hear the wrath bubbling. "We mustn't be seen talking."

"I love you," he said. His eyes were on the tips of his boots. He felt feverish. "I can't stand to see you treated badly. Meet me tomorrow. Or the next day. Please."

She barely hesitated. "All right. Tomorrow. Where?"

Quickly he gave directions to the first safe spot that came to mind. Just as he finished, she drew in a sharp breath. "Someone's coming."

He whispered a time for the meeting. She whirled away. He hurried in the other direction, his heart pounding from fear and joy.

Nathanael Greene had belonged to John C. Calhoun for most of his adult life. Sixty-three now, he hated the stress of traveling and the necessity of mixing with slaves of inferior station.

Greene's pride had a twofold origin. His master was one of the nation's most eminent men, and Greene served him as a house slave—a position vastly superior to that of common field hands.

Greene had been born in the low country, but he despised its heat, stench, and stretches of insect-infested marsh. He longed for the familiar highlands up at Clemson. For the cool, narrow Calhoun house with its surrounding flower beds and wild orange trees. At Mont Royal he was cranky, and this crankiness tended to bring to the fore a certain meanness of disposition.

He soon grew bored with the company of the house slaves around the buffet tables set up for their use. Greene had certain perquisites and was thoroughly familiar with the limits of his master's tolerance. He took a couple of furtive swigs from a whiskey flask he kept hidden in his fine linen coat. Then he went searching for some sport.

Near the kitchen building he observed a big, strapping field hand lugging stove wood inside. The air near the kitchen felt as hot as the pit. Greene chuckled and waited.

Soon the field hand came out again. Greene beckoned to him. He gave the field hand a peek at the flask under his coat, then said with an innocent grin, "You look mighty thirsty, nigger. Come over into the shade and cool yourself with a nip of the corn."

The field hand was tempted, but held back. "Niggers aren't allowed to drink. You know that."

"Sure I know that. But today's a party day, and Mr. Calhoun, he's looking the other way."

Uneasily, the field hand glanced toward the slaves gathered by the special tables. They were eating and chatting and sipping punch that contained no alcohol. From time to time one of them left to answer a summons from lawn or kitchen, while others returned from like errands.

"I ain't supposed to hang around the house niggers, either," the field hand said. "They get uppity if I do."

"You let me worry 'bout that, nigger. I'm a house nigger for Mr. Calhoun, so if I invite you, it's all right." He steered the field hand toward the group. "What do they call you?"

"Priam."

"Mighty fine name. Have a sip."

Priam was hot and thirsty. That and Nathanael Greene's persuasive manner overcame his caution. Greene walked him up to the others. They recognized Priam, of course, and looked at him scornfully until they grasped Greene's intentions; he was doing a lot of winking and gesturing behind Priam's back.

The scornful looks disappeared. Priam's tense face relaxed. At intervals of three or four minutes, Greene whisked the flask from its hiding place and shielded Priam while the latter drank. It didn't take long for Priam to start chuckling and even laughing out loud. The rest of the slaves, except for two women who didn't approve of the sport, smirked and nudged one another.

" 'Nother drink," Priam said.

"Sure enough," Greene grinned. "Come get it."

He held the flask at arm's length. Priam shambled forward, reaching for it. At the last minute Greene pulled the flask out of the way.

Priam blundered straight into the table. His outstretched hand knocked a dish of butter beans onto the grass.

Greene laughed. "My Lord, you are one clumsy buck."

"He's just a dumb field nigger, that's why," someone else said.

Suspicion pierced Priam's stupor. "Give me that drink," he growled.

Greene waved the flask with a willowy motion. "Right here it is, nigger. All yours, if you can still see it."

Loud laughter.

"You give me that!" This time Priam roared.

"My, ain't he something," said Greene, still waggling the flask. "Givin' orders to his betters."

"Uppity," another slave said with contempt.

Priam blinked and used his palm to swab sweat from his neck. He watched the flask being waved at him in a tantalizing way. Suddenly he leaped forward, trying to seize the flask in a bear hug. Greene danced back. Priam caught nothing but air. The laughter exploded.

Priam lowered his head, turned, and charged the other Negroes with swinging fists. The women screamed. The men scattered.

The tumult brought Tillet and some of the guests on the run. Tillet's temper was short because of the heat and because he couldn't shake the bitter aftereffects of the quarrel with Cooper. It didn't help when he spied Cousin Charles under one of the tables, a rip showing in the knee of his fine breeches. With gleeful enthusiasm, Charles was calling encouragement to both combatants.

Tillet arrived just as Priam again attempted to grab Nathanael Greene. Calhoun's slave darted behind three big house blacks. The senator himself arrived just as Greene recognized Mont Royal's owner and exclaimed:

"That nigger took after me! He's drunk as a coot."

Tillet needed no one to help him see that. "Priam, go to your cabin. I'll deal with you later."

Fear showed on Priam's face. He saw that all the house people would side with Greene, and that made him angry all over again. He stepped up to Tillet and pointed to the fallen flask.

"I took a drink out of that 'cause Mr. Calhoun's nigger gave it to me. He acted friendly, but then he started to call me names."

Tillet was so affronted he could barely speak. "I am not interested in your explanations."

Greene gave a little disbelieving laugh. "What's that nigger saying? Everybody know niggers aren't allowed to drink spirits. He didn't get one drop from me. No, sir," he finished with a soulful look at his owner.

"He's right," said a black woman. "The buck was already drunk when he came sashayin' over here."

Other house slaves nodded and murmured agreement. For a moment Priam couldn't believe his own people would do this to him. He looked as if someone had driven a spear into his side.

Righteous and wrathful, Greene shook a finger at Priam. "Don't you go tellin' any more lies to get me in trouble, nigger."

"No," Tillet said, reaching for his slave's arm. "Don't do that. You're in enough trouble already."

Priam jerked away from Tillet's hand. The watchers gasped, a sound like a great wave breaking. Tillet lowered his eyes and studied his hand, as if he couldn't believe what Priam had done.

Salem Jones appeared then. He slipped up next to his employer, barely able to suppress a smile. Priam stood slightly hunched, his hands fisted and sweat streaming down his cheeks. Orry and George joined the spectators. If Tillet couldn't see that Priam was dangerously out of control, they could.

"We had best leave," Calhoun said. "Nathanael, if you will—"

"No," Tillet said. "It isn't necessary for you to do that, John. The fault is Priam's." Orry recognized signs of an unusual anger building within his father. "You go to your cabin, Priam. Do it now or it will go hard with you."

Priam shook his head. Tillet stiffened as if slapped. "I'll order you one last time," he said.

Again the slave wagged his head from side to side. Tillet's face grew purplish. Hoping to prevent more trouble, Orry started to speak to his father. Before he could, Tillet made a quick, hooking gesture with his left hand. Jones caught the signal. He whisked his hickory truncheon from under his fancy coat, waved several of the house men forward.

"You, Jim. You, Aristotle. Take him."

Priam bellowed and started swinging. The men closed in. Priam retreated three steps and fell backward over a table. Bowls of food crashed to the ground and broke or spilled.

Jones let his two black helpers subdue Priam. Then the overseer leaned forward across the shoulders of Jim and Aristotle and whacked

Priam with the truncheon. He did it several times. On the last blow, Priam sagged to his knees. A line of blood ran from a gash in his forehead. With hate-filled eyes he looked at his master, who had stepped in front of him.

"I told you it would go hard, Priam. I surely do wish you'd listened."

Standing close by his father, Orry said, "Don't you think he's had his punishment?"

Tillet's color was still high. He was breathing hard. "No. Priam disrupted the celebration and embarrassed me in front of my guests. I treat my people well, but I will not tolerate ingratitude or a rebellious spirit. I'm going to make an example of this nigger."

That last word was one Tillet never used in reference to his slaves. It told Orry he had better not try to stop his father from doing whatever he planned.

Priam, too, recognized the master's uncharacteristic rage. He wept silently as he hobbled away in the grip of the other two slaves.

At Resolute, Madeline turned in her bed for the twentieth time. When she had put on her nightgown and blown out the lights an hour ago, she had known sleep would be slow to come. Too much had happened. Too much was yet to happen, if she were brave enough— or foolhardy enough—to let it.

The bedroom windows stood open in the darkness, but no air was moving. Directly underneath her room, someone was padding through the house, securing it for the night. Outside, the barely perceptible stir and hum of night creatures formed a background for the sound of her own breathing.

Justin wasn't in the house, thank heaven. He had ridden off to Charleston with his brother, presumably feeling that she needed time by herself to contemplate the enormity of her sins and the punishment that would be hers if the sinning continued.

Bastard, she thought as her husband's self-righteous face glimmered in her imagination. It was becoming astonishingly easy to call him vile names. How she wished she could do more than that. How she wished she could confront him with the confession her father had made just before his eyes closed for the last time. How she yearned to smile at Justin and say:

"My dear, it is my painful duty to inform you that you are married to a woman with Negro blood."

Justin had deceived her during the courtship, so it was poetic justice

153

that he be told, even if belatedly, that she had deceived him. Of course it was unintentional; she hadn't known or even suspected the truth that her father breathed out through pale lips while she sat at his bedside in the heavily draped room that smelled faintly of candle wax, and sweat, and death.

All his life, Nicholas Fabray had done his best to smooth his daughter's way, and those last moments were no exception. He cushioned the shock as best he could, spoke slowly but eloquently about Madeline's mother: how fine she was, how considerate and loving. Only then did he reveal that his wife, to all outward appearances a white woman, was in fact one-quarter Negro. Madeline was an octoroon.

"Why—" She fisted one trembling hand and pressed it against her knee. "Why are you telling me now?"

"Because you would curse my memory if you ever learned the truth from anyone else." Unspoken was the harsher thought: *Because you are vulnerable to this truth, regardless of my efforts to veil it, unlikely as it is ever to be exposed.*

He and his wife had wanted a better life for Madeline than she would have had if she were acknowledged to be of mixed blood. Fortunate quadroons and octoroons could enjoy the favors of white gentlemen and even be the recipients of some of their wealth. But those boons were always temporary because a woman of mixed blood could never be anything better than a mistress, never anything better than a white man's elegant whore.

Nicholas Fabray had refused to play out that sad little drama so prevalent in New Orleans. He had married the woman he loved, something that took enormous courage. He did not say that, of course. But Madeline understood it and bent over the bed and embraced his frail, half-paralyzed body while tears filled her eyes.

No, Fabray went on, there was nothing to be lost by concealing certain facts about Madeline's background, and everything to be gained. It was not difficult to maintain the deception, he said, because Madeline's mother was almost unknown in the twilight world of the city's quadroons and octoroons. And the dust of time had enhanced concealment. Now Madeline must join the conspiracy of silence and preserve the safety he had so long sought for her.

Finally, he revealed one dominant reason he had wanted his daughter to marry Justin LaMotte. Not only was Justin a kind, decent man— here Madeline averted her head while her mouth convulsed in a sardonic smile—but he also lived far from Louisiana. In South Carolina there would be virtually no chance of her ever being confronted with the truth about her lineage. In New Orleans the possibility, however remote, was present. His voice faltering, Fabray muttered something about a picture of Madeline's mother.

"A picture, Papa? Do you mean a painting?"

"Yes—a painting." His eyes were closed again; speech seemed difficult.

"There's a portrait of her somewhere?"

"Was." The tip of his tongue inched across dry lips. Then he opened his eyes and tried to clarify his answer, but his voice was so weak, his words so vague, she could make little sense of his statements. She got the impression that the painting had disappeared. When and how, he didn't say.

Then the thread of the thought was lost as light convulsions began to shake his wasted body. She held his hand and pressed her other to her own cheek, as if that way she could hold back her grief. She called out and told a passing servant to summon the doctor at once. Ten minutes before he arrived, Nicholas Fabray died.

The shock didn't hit her until the next day, after she had taken care of the last detail of the funeral arrangements. Then she broke down and wept for nearly an hour, stricken by Fabray's death and by the loathsome secret with which he had burdened her. For a brief period she hated him for telling her; in the South, having even one drop of black blood was the same as having skin the color of ebony.

A great many of the city's leading politicians and businessmen, Catholic and Protestant, attended the funeral. They brought their white wives, and when Madeline noticed that, she appreciated the skill with which her father had carried off the deception. The last vestiges of ill feeling left her; she mourned and blessed him at the same time.

Lying in the dark, Madeline wondered how she could have brought herself to say yes to Orry's whispered plea for a secret rendezvous. Her conscience was already torturing her about that, and yet she knew she would go through with this one meeting if she could. Her willingness was a natural reaction to Justin's cruelty. But it was also a clear violation of the code of behavior she had practiced all her life. Even given Justin's character, how could that happen? Many women endured similar mistreatment, or worse, till the day they died. What made the difference in her case?

The answer lay in something that could not be fully reduced to logical explanation. Something in the young cadet's eyes, in his courtly bearing and his shy demeanor, called out to her, spoke to her on a deep and primitive level. That was true despite her fear that, because of his age, he could not possibly be what he seemed.

She laid the back of one hand against her cheek and uttered a small, sad sound. Her life, so carefully and conscientiously put in order by her late father, was growing hopelessly tangled. She was thankful Nicholas Fabray didn't know.

She imagined Orry's face. He *was* young. That was a dire risk, and it was just one of several she intended to accept. Another was the risk she'd take when she left Resolute for the rendezvous. Keeping her hand where it was, she closed her eyes and concentrated on a plan to avert suspicion when she rode away tomorrow. She was still lying in that position when she fell asleep and dreamed of Orry kissing her.

Like Madeline, the slave girl Semiramis was unable to fall asleep easily that night. Jones was going to do something terrible to her brother. Quirt him, most likely. Priam had caused a big fuss at the picnic. After it happened, the Mont Royal slaves talked of nothing else for the rest of the day.

Most of the slaves thought her brother was going to get what he deserved. They said mean things about him because they were jealous of his courage. He was always whispering about the North, about fleeing to freedom. The others called him a boaster. Said he'd never do it, just because they knew he might, and they wouldn't. Of course, he'd never go if his temper got him killed first.

Semiramis wanted to sleep, to forget the beating Priam was going to get. She turned one way, then the other on her thin, sour-smelling pallet of ticking. She couldn't lie still; she was too tense.

Flickering light showed around the edge of the closed door. Torches had been lit in the barnyard behind old Jones's house. The punishment would begin soon. The torches told her, and so did the stillness of the night. Up and down the slave street, no one laughed or spoke.

A furtive knock startled her. She bolted upright.

"Who's that?"

A shadow blotted some of the flickering light. "Cuffey."

"Oh, Lord, no," she called. "Not this evening, boy." She had started pleasuring herself with Cuffey several months ago, although he was quite young; too young, some of the jealous old women said.

156

But they had never seen him without trousers, nor did they know what he could do with his remarkable—

Before she could finish the thought, the boy was inside and kneeling by the pallet.

"I din' come for that. I came 'bout Priam."

"Jones going to whip him."

"Uh-uh. Worse. Jones brought the old mouser down from the great house. They going to cat-haul him."

Stunned silence. Then Semiramis said, "Oh, Jesus, sweet Jesus. It'll kill him." She clutched her stomach.

Her brother had angered Mr. Tillet worse than she had imagined. How Priam must have strutted and fought! She hadn't seen it, only heard about it; she had been working elsewhere at the time. Now she wanted to run to the great house to plead for mercy.

Cuffey dissuaded her. He stayed with her, murmuring empty comforts as they waited for the sound of the first scream.

Torches planted in the ground lit the barnyard brilliantly. Priam lay spread-eagled on his stomach.

Jones had assembled an audience of twenty male slaves because, done properly, this night's work could benefit the plantation for years. It could leave a powerful and lasting impression on any other niggers who might be feeling rebellious. The impression would come not only from Priam's suffering but from his humiliation beforehand. He had been forced to disrobe, kneel, and bow his head while ropes were tied to his ankles and wrists. These ropes, pegged into the sandy soil, kept his limbs extended.

Animal and bird cries rose in the darkness beyond the barnyard. The slave cabins were abnormally quiet. Good, Jones thought. Many others were watching or listening. The lesson would not be lost on them, and the reports of the witnesses would reinforce it.

A big buck named Harmony held a burlap sack at arm's length. The sack jumped and writhed with a life of its own. Jones regarded the sack pleasurably as he took his time donning thickly padded gauntlets. Before this, he had had no occasion to use the gauntlets at Mont Royal, but he had kept them in his trunk, just in case. He was both surprised and delighted that Tillet Main, whom he secretly scorned, was actually able to order a cat-hauling.

Jones strutted past Priam's head to give him a good look at the gauntlets. He then repositioned all three buckets of heavily salted water he planned to dash on Priam's wounds. The buckets of brine were a little touch Jones had added on his own.

He gestured to the burlap sack, then extended his right hand above it.

"All right, Harmony—now."

The nervous slave opened the top of the sack. Jones plunged his gloved hand down. By feel alone he caught and pinioned the tomcat's rear legs. He lifted the furious, squalling animal into the light.

The slaves gulped and stepped back. Jones kept his head half averted, fearing one of the slashing front claws might nick an eye. At last he got a firm two-handed grip on the tom's rear legs.

Breathing hard from excitement, Jones stepped up to Priam's right side, planting one boot next to the slave's hip and the other by his ribs. He fought the tomcat every inch of the way, but the result would be worth the risk. He swung the writhing cat by its back legs, almost the way a gentleman swung a club in the old game of golf. The fore claws struck between Priam's shoulders, cutting and tearing all the way to the base of the spine before Jones jerked the cat up again. He smiled at the blood-daubed paws.

Priam hadn't cried out. But he had nearly bitten through his lower lip, Jones observed. Almost affably, he said, "We're not finished. Not by any means."

George lay sleepless in the guest bedroom on the second floor. He had taken off everything except his cotton underdrawers, but he was still sweltering. His stomach ached. His head hurt.

It hadn't been a pleasant day. The trouble caused by that slave, Priam, had upset and embarrassed Orry. He had become self-conscious with George, speaking only when necessary. The incident had affected George, too. For the first time since his arrival he had been driven to ponder everything he had seen. He thought especially hard about the slaves, and what he read on their faces and in their eyes.

He hated to think ill of people who had treated him so graciously. He hated to think ill of his best friend. But what he had encountered at Mont Royal—well, there was no way to avoid the conclusion. It was deeply disturbing. At last he understood comments at home, especially Virgilia's.

"Oh, my God," he said suddenly, shooting up in bed and twisting toward the windows that opened on the piazza. Far off in the night, someone was screaming.

158

He was sure it was the slave receiving his punishment. The outcries continued intermittently for about five minutes. When they stopped, he lay staring at the ceiling. He doubted that he could go to sleep the rest of the night. He knew the sound of the screaming would stay with him forever.

The screams sent Cooper hurtling downstairs, the hem of his sweaty nightshirt flying around his legs. For weeks he had been feeling that a crisis was brewing in his life, that the status quo had become intolerable. But it needed some major incident to propel him to action.

Tonight he had it. The slaves lived three-quarters of a mile from the great house. When screams carried that far, it said a lot. Too much. He stormed into the library without knocking. "What in hell are they doing to Priam?"

Tillet looked at his son through a choking cloud of pipe smoke. Sweat glistened on his bald head. All the windows were closed. To shut out unpleasant noises?

"I ordered him cat-hauled."

Cooper's face hardened. "My God. That's barbaric."

Tillet leaped up. "I'm not interested in your pious pronouncements."

"What about your own?"

"What are you talking about?"

"The other evening, very smugly, you told Orry's friend that there are no scarred backs at Mont Royal. Would you care to explain Priam's?"

"I don't need to explain it, you sarcastic whelp. Priam is my property, to do with as I please."

The men stood eye to eye. Cooper was suddenly overwhelmed with a sick sensation.

"He's a man. You call him property. This state and the whole damn South will fall to ruin because of that inhuman idea."

"I've heard this lecture before." Tillet waved his pipe. The bowl left a smoke tracery in the stifling air. He turned his back on his son. "Be so good as to leave me alone."

Cooper slammed the door on his way out.

Breakfast next morning was a dismal affair. George asked Orry about Priam's condition. Orry seemed to resent the question and curtly told his friend that the slave was resting in the sick house. A few minutes later Orry said he'd be gone during the late morning and early afternoon. He offered no explanation, nor any apology for leaving his guest alone, and he acted nervous all at once. George wondered why.

Clarissa arrived, striving unsuccessfully to be cheerful. She had obviously slept badly. She picked at her meal in silence, and she looked almost grateful when she had to rush off to mediate a screeching match between Orry's sisters.

Cooper appeared. His hair was uncombed. His shirttail hung out of the waist of his rumpled trousers. He fell into the chair next to George, ignored his food, and several times muttered something in a thick voice. Only once did George make sense of what he heard:

"Can't stay here. Can't stay and help run a place like this. The whole system's not only criminal, it's stupid. Stupid and doomed."

Soon Cooper lurched from the room. Orry raised an eyebrow. "I wonder what the devil's wrong with him?"

It sounded like a rhetorical question, but George answered it. "I smelled wine. I hate to say it about your brother, Stick, but I think he's drunk."

On a direct line, the distance from Mont Royal to Salvation Chapel was no more than two miles. But the tiny, burned-out church was well hidden in the woods and could be reached only by following winding roads through forest and marsh. The ride took almost an hour. As each succeeding road grew narrower and more overgrown, Orry became increasingly sure that Madeline wouldn't be waiting for him. She had probably found his hurriedly whispered directions too vague or, more likely, the trip too difficult for a woman traveling alone.

Salvation Chapel had closed its doors five years ago. When its pastor, a Methodist shouter, fell over dead during a particularly bombastic sermon, another could not be found to replace him. The congregation had never been large anyway: a few marginal rice planters and their families, and some black freedmen who were permitted to worship in the gallery.

The whites drifted away. The Negroes stayed. Soon the church acquired a reputation as a center of illegal assembly, a place where black people were suspected of gathering to discuss forbidden subjects. General emancipation. Rebellion. One night the church was mysteriously burned. The LaMotte brothers were rumored to have had a hand in it. The freedmen never came back. The vegetation closed in.

It was a splendid spot for a secret meeting, surrounded as it was on three sides by woodland. The fourth side afforded a breathtaking view across several miles of marsh. As Orry rode the last quarter of a mile, his emotions were in turmoil. He wasn't overly afraid of Justin LaMotte, but he did fear that he had exposed Madeline to undue risk. He reminded himself that she probably wouldn't be there anyway. But if she were, what did he want her to do? Commit adultery? Much as a part of him shamefully admitted that, his conscience—his concern for Madeline's welfare—told him it was impossible.

These feelings mingled with others churned up by the trouble at Mont Royal. Orry was ashamed to have George see a sample of the cruelty that drove Northerners to condemn the South. Orry's embarrassment made him defensive and even illogically angry with his friend. Thus he was in a state of nerves when he pushed away the last overhanging branches and walked his horse toward Salvation Chapel. The remains of blackened beams and siding had long ago fallen into the wreckage of a tabby foundation. The ruin, and the marsh beyond, lay silent, empty. His face fell.

A horse whickered. Underbrush stirred. Madeline appeared at the edge of the marsh to his left. Screened from him by some trees, she had been gazing at the sunlit vista of reeds and glittering water.

He jumped down, tied his mount, and ran to her. How lovely she looked in her smart riding habit. He grasped her shoulders, leaned forward, then pulled back suddenly, red-faced.

"I didn't even think to ask whether it was dangerous for you to come."

She smiled, shrugged in a self-conscious way. "Not particularly. Not today, at least. I never attract much notice when I go to see the patients in our sick house. That's what a woman is expected to do. I told my house servants that after the visit I wanted to ride by myself for a while. They understand. They know Justin can be insufferable. Besides, he's in Charleston with Francis till tomorrow night. I can't stay here indefinitely, though."

He reached out to clasp her hand. Her smile disappeared; she seemed tense. "I'm very glad you're here," he told her. "Would you think badly of me if I said"—he swallowed—"said that I wanted to kiss you?"

A look of panic flashed over her face, but it was suppressed so swiftly he wondered if he had imagined it. Hastily, he added:

"If the thought upsets you, I withdraw the question."

Her eyes warmed and her mouth softened. The corners lifted in a sweet smile. "You can't; it's too late. Besides"—she returned the pressure of his fingers—"I want you to kiss me. I'm just a little afraid, that's all."

With clumsy hunger he pulled her into his arms. Her mouth was soft and cool. He had never felt a woman's tongue as he felt hers when her lips opened. He was ashamed of his stiffness, but she pressed tightly to him, not seeming to mind.

There was no banter now, just a long, intense moment in which their clinging, their sweet, frantic kissing of eyes and cheeks and earlobes, revealed their emotions, their longings. He had to say it aloud.

"Madeline, I love you. I have from the first."

She laughed with tears in her eyes. Touched his face. Her words came in a torrent:

"Oh, my sweet Orry. My cavalier. I love you too; don't you know that? Like you, I realized it the day we met, and I've tried to deny it ever since." She began covering his face and mouth with kisses again.

Naturally, and without thought, his hand came up to her breast. She shuddered and pressed closer. Then she drew away. She knew, and so did he, what the consequences might be if they let their emotions overwhelm them.

They sat on the tabby foundation, watching white egrets rise from the marsh in beautiful, lifting curves. He put his arm around her. She rested against his side. They sat very still, figures in a domestic portrait.

"Did your husband—" He cleared his throat. "Did he retaliate in any way when you got home?"

"Oh, no. That little humiliation at Mont Royal was quite enough." Orry scowled. "Will you tell me if he ever hurts you physically?"

"He never goes that far. His cruelty's more subtle. And much more devastating. Justin knows countless ways to wound the spirit, I've discovered. He knows how to rob a person of any sense of worth with just a laugh or a look. I don't think the men of this state should fear a rebellion by their slaves. They should fear one by their wives."

He laughed, then touched the sleeve of her riding habit. "He certainly doesn't stint with worldly goods. How much did this cost?"

"Too much. You're right, he isn't stingy with anything except consideration for the feelings of others. Whatever he thinks I need, he buys. He'll permit me to do anything I want so long as I never forget I'm a LaMotte. And a woman.''

"Things would be different if you were married to me. I wish you were.''

"Oh, I do too. So much.''

"I shouldn't have asked you to meet me like this, but''—he looked at her, trying not to show his pain—"I had to tell you once how I felt.''

"Yes.'' Her palm pressed lightly against his cheek. "So did I.'' He kissed her long and passionately.

When they were resting again, a new, embittered note came into her voice. "Justin's beginning to think I'm a failure as a woman.''

"Why?''

"I've borne him no children.''

"Is it because—that is—'' He stopped, blushing.

"It isn't through any lack of effort on his part,'' she said, coloring a little herself. "He's very—vigorous in his attempts at fatherhood.''

Orry's stomach felt as if someone had run a knife through it. He sat motionless. The pain eased, but slowly. Madeline went on, "I dare to be so frank because I've no one with whom I can share these things. The truth is''—she faced him, grave—"I'm convinced it's Justin's fault that I haven't gotten pregnant. I understand his first wife was bar—childless too.''

"That's true,'' Orry said.

"Of course I must never suggest that he's the one responsible.''

"He doesn't permit you to have ideas like that, eh?''

"He doesn't permit me to have any ideas at all.''

For the next hour they spoke of all sorts of things: His friend George. The war that would take the two of them to Mexico and, presumably, combat. Priam's disobedience and punishment, and the resulting uproar in the family. Somehow none of it seemed very real. For a little while no universe existed except this hidden place, no force within it except their love.

At last, though, the sun started down, and the light began to change. Madeline rose. "I must go. I can't come here again, my sweet Orry. Kiss me good-bye.''

They embraced and caressed and spoke their feelings for a few tremulous minutes. Then he helped her mount. As she guided her horse around the ruined foundation, sitting sidesaddle gracefully, she looked back, then reined in.

"When you're back from Mexico, I'm sure we'll see each other occasionally. At parties, weddings. And whenever I look just at you, you'll know exactly how I feel. Oh, Orry, I love you so!"

It was a declaration of joy and a cry of pain. She rode out of sight, and he started homeward twenty minutes later. He almost wished the meeting had never taken place. It had only ripped open a great inner wound that had scarred over once but now would never heal.

10

After supper that night, George and Orry strolled down to the boat landing while George smoked a cigar. Orry hadn't explained his absence, and he was obviously on edge. That and the events of yesterday put George in a testy mood as well.

They sat on a couple of old kegs, watching the Ashley reflect the first evening stars. Suddenly a door banged up at the house. They saw Clarissa rush down the lane leading to the slave community.

"She looks upset," George said.

"I expect Priam's taken a bad turn. Brett told me Mother went to the sick house twice this afternoon."

George let smoke trail from his nose and mouth. "She's very conscientious about caring for your slaves, isn't she?"

"With good reason. They don't know how to care for themselves. They're like children."

"Maybe that's because they're not permitted to be anything else."

"Oh, come on. Let's not debate."

"Debating's for politicians. I was merely expressing an opinion."

"I trust you're finished," Orry snapped.

Orry's tone told George that it would be wise for him to say nothing more. Somehow he couldn't do that. His conscience was deviling him—an unexpected occurrence—and he wouldn't be content or honest if he failed to express what was on his mind. He spoke quietly but with firmness:

"No, not quite. Your family's wonderful, Orry. Gracious. Kind. Very enlightened in many ways. The same can be said of most of your neighbors. The ones I've met, anyway. But slavery, now—well, I agree with your brother. Slavery's like a lump of food that can't be swallowed, no matter how hard you try."

"I thought you never worried about such things."

"I never did. Until yesterday." George tapped ash from his cigar. "What did they do to that slave?"

Orry kept his eyes on the star-flecked river. "I don't know. Whatever it was, it was necessary."

"But that's what I can't swallow. It shouldn't be necessary for one human being to hurt another. If the system makes it necessary or condones it, the system is wrong."

Orry stood, glowering. George was stunned by the sharpness in his friend's voice.

"Let me tell you something about Southerners. Southerners get tired of Yankees self-righteously criticizing everything that goes on down here. Cooper had some tales to tell about the sordid living conditions of workers from the Hazard mill. Is economic slavery any less reprehensible than what you complain about?"

George, too, was on his feet. "Wait a minute. Those mill workers—"

"No, you wait. The North should clean up its own house before it starts pointing fingers. If there are problems in the South, Southerners will solve them."

"Doesn't appear to me that you're solving anything, my friend. And you get damn smug and feisty if anyone suggests you get cracking."

"We get feisty when *Yankees* suggest it. We get angry as hell. The North's been interfering in the affairs of the South for thirty years. If that continues, it can lead to only one thing."

"A separate slaveholding government? Your Southern cronies at West Point were always trotting out that threat. Well, go ahead. Secede!"

"No, I'm not threatening that," Orry countered. "But I do promise trouble, and plenty of it, to any outsider who insists on telling South Carolinians how to think and behave."

"Does the term outsider include me?"

"You're damn right," Orry said, and walked away up the pier.

George considered packing up and leaving that night. But he didn't. He knew Orry was deeply troubled, and he suspected the reason had nothing to do with the subject of their argument. Still, the quarrel disturbed him. It gave him a new and somber insight into the nature of the slave question.

He could understand that casual acquaintances or natural opponents such as politicians might fall out over slavery. But if it could threaten the relationship of good friends, it was a deep and potent issue indeed.

The next few days passed in an atmosphere of tension and forced politeness. The friends didn't patch up their differences until the night before they were scheduled to leave for Charleston. It was Orry who took the initiative after several rounds of drinks.

"Look, we're supposed to be fighting Mexicans, not each other."

"Absolutely right," George responded with vast relief. "I'm sorry I stuck my nose into your affairs."

"I'm sorry I tried to chop it off."

They renewed and repledged their friendship with another drink. But the memory of that quarrel, and its cause, remained with each of them.

A coastal steamer carried them around Florida into the Gulf. The sea was rough. During the first few days, George spent a lot of time hanging over the rail. When the steamer put into New Orleans to reprovision, he was grateful to stagger onto dry land for a few hours.

He and Orry strolled the levee and the old quarter, then drank bitter black coffee in a café. George had bought three papers, and after ordering a second coffee, he caught up on the news. In late September General Taylor had invested and captured Monterrey and was an even greater hero as a consequence. Politicians were saying Taylor would be the next Whig candidate for President, unless his superior, General Scott, also a Whig, had ambitions of his own. In the far West, Americans were rapidly overcoming Spanish California, which the United States had already annexed by proclamation.

Sometimes George found it hard to believe that his country and Mexico were at war; little more than twenty years ago, the Mexican government had invited Yankee colonization of the state of Coahuila y Texas and had granted concessions to the American *empresario* Moses Austin so that he could secure the wanted settlers.

Of course that had taken place in what amounted to the last hours of Spain's long rule in Mexico. The country soon won its independence, and that seemed to be the start of all the trouble. The Constitution of 1824 was repeatedly subverted by revolution. Governments rose and fell with dizzying speed.

The year 1836 brought the short, brutal struggle for Texas independence. Early in March of that year, the Texans defending the Alamo mission were massacred. Little more than a month later, Sam Houston's men won the war and the republic's freedom at San Jacinto. Mexican resentment had simmered ever since.

One name that had been associated with Mexican-American relations for the past two decades was back in the news once again, George discovered. General Antonio López de Santa Anna had voluntarily returned from exile in Cuba with his retinue and his seventeen-year-old wife. Presumably he was about to take command of the Mexican army, and not for the first time.

Tough, wily Santa Anna, now fifty-two, had fought for so many sides and factions, it was almost necessary to consult some kind of printed program to understand his career. He had served Spain as a young army officer, then joined the rebellion against the mother country. He had been, at various times, Mexico's military chief, president, and dictator. He had won the sanguinary victory at the Alamo, then lost at San Jacinto, where he had been ingloriously captured while attempting to escape disguised in a dirty smock and carpet slippers.

At Tampico, defending his country against an attempted Spanish reconquest, the self-styled Napoleon of the West had lost a leg. The leg had subsequently been enshrined and displayed in Mexico City when he was in power, then dragged through the streets by mobs when his fortunes changed. You certainly had to admit the man was a survivor, George said to himself. Santa Anna went with the prevailing winds, and nothing exemplified this better than the current border dispute.

As a defeated general, Santa Anna had personally signed the 1836 peace treaty acknowledging the Rio Grande as the Texas boundary. Now he was declaring that although his name had indeed gone onto the document, he was the only one who had signed; the Mexican government, in other words, had not. Hence, Mexico had every right to repudiate the treaty and fight for the disputed territory—under Santa Anna's command, naturally.

When George tried to discuss some of this with Orry he found his friend uninterested. He wondered about the reason for Orry's long face until he remembered that Madeline LaMotte came from New Orleans. George immediately said he would just as soon go back on board and write a long-delayed letter home.

Orry said he'd be happy to go. His spirits improved the minute they turned their backs on the city.

The steamer plowed on across the Gulf, bound for the mouth of the Rio Grande. A sudden storm, not unusual for the season but this time especially severe, damaged the vessel's port paddle wheel, forcing the captain to anchor off Saint Joseph Island to effect repairs. Lighters took all the military passengers ashore to Corpus Christi. Sometimes known as Kinney's Ranch, the place was a miserable village of about forty shops and houses on the west bank of the Nueces River.

The friends went separate ways for a couple of hours. Orry was fascinated by the flat, sandy terrain of the Texas coast. Strolling the muddy main street, he was amazed to see half a dozen antelope browsing behind the unpainted buildings. He absorbed a shopkeeper's warning about tarantulas and passed it along to George when they met. His friend, however, was interested in other forms of wildlife. But his report was discouraging.

"I've seen exactly one girl. Her face would crack a rock. Maybe I'll have better luck tonight."

"Where?"

"At the social. The local residents are putting it on for all the poor stranded soldiers. I swear, if I don't get to squeeze a feminine waist pretty soon, I'll go berserk."

The social was held in a barn on Colonel Kinney's trading post. Lanterns had been hung and some moth-eaten bunting tacked to the rafters. There was fresh straw on the dirt floor, a fiddler, a trestle table crowded with cakes, pies, and tarts, and a huge bowl of whiskey punch. About eighty officers and noncoms attended, and perhaps half as many townspeople, of which only seven were female. Of these, just one was attractive, and she got most of the attention.

She was worthy of it. She was a slender, stunning redhead in her early twenties. Her skin was white as thick cream and her eyes the bluest George had ever seen. He wasn't daunted by her surprisingly tall height or by the dozen officers already surrounding her.

Some were majors and colonels. They would surely pull rank on him if he tried a direct assault. The enemy had to be outflanked. While the fiddler tuned up, George drifted to the punch bowl, smiling and introducing himself to various townsmen. In five minutes he had made a discovery and formulated a plan.

He strode firmly as he approached a civilian standing in the large open doorway of the barn. George knew he cut a good figure. He had spent half an hour scrubbing travel grime off his light blue trousers and polishing the brass hilt and scabbard decorations of his yard-long infantry officer's sword.

The man he wanted to impress was a ruddy, stub-nosed fellow with short, unruly hair that was more white than red. He wore an old-fashioned suit of black broadcloth. George toasted him with his punch cup.

"A splendid party, sir. You Texans are good hosts."

With a wry smile, the man answered, "In wartime, Lieutenant, patriotism sometimes outweighs prudence."

"I don't understand, sir."

"In Corpus Christi, public opinion of soldiers is about as low as it can get. Zach Taylor's troops camped here on their way to the Rio Grande. That was an experience this town won't forget. Fortunately, Texans know how to protect themselves—and their daughters." He clapped a hand on the immense holstered pistol hanging at his right hip. The barrel was almost a foot long. A Paterson Colt, George thought, perhaps a .36-caliber.

"Oh, do you have a daughter with you tonight?"

The red-faced man gave him an amused look. "I didn't say that, my lad. But you apparently possess the information. Is that why you came over to talk to me?"

George gulped, then laughed. "And I thought I was being subtle. You're right, sir. I knew I didn't stand much of a chance of meeting her with that crowd around her. An introduction from you would give me an advantage."

"You may not be subtle, sir, but you're clever. However, I can't introduce you until I know your name."

"Lieutenant George Hazard, Eighth Infantry."

The stocky man put out his hand. "Patrick Flynn. Born in Cappamore, County Limerick, but I fancy I'm a Texan now. Been here long enough! Arrived the year after Colonel Kinney opened his trading post. Lost my wife that same year, but Constance and I have managed to survive—even though there's hardly enough legal business to keep a flea from starving."

"You're a lawyer? In this town?"

"I occasionally spend a month in San Antonio. That's where I really make my living. They're very disputatious in San Antonio. I did my reading of the law way up in Belfast. Very good training— all the shipping in Belfast Lough created legalistic tangles on every conceivable subject. A series of misadventures brought me to Texas while Sam Houston was struggling to wrest it away from the Mexicans. I settled in Corpus Christi because I thought this would become a port city with plenty of work for lawyers." Smiling wryly again, he added, "Development has failed to keep pace with my hopes." He threw his head back and drained his whiskey punch. "Or my thirst."

"But you must like it here."

"Oh, indeed." Flynn nodded. "There's free air and free space—

and none of the snobbish restraints I encountered as a boy in the old country. Some of the local citizens distrust my Roman faith, which I can't practice since there's no Catholic chapel hereabouts, but that makes us even, since I dislike the prevailing view of slavery."

"I've heard most Texans support it."

"I regret to say that's true. I often remark that a man always works harder for the carrot of personal advancement than he does for the stick of the slave overseer. But that's a truth my neighbors don't care to hear. Most confine themselves to grumbling and cursing, but there are a few hotheads who would like to run me out for daring to say such a thing. They don't because they know I am, shall we say, self-reliant."

He grinned and again touched the handle of his Colt. "But you want to meet Constance."

"Yes, I do. Very much."

"I'll be happy to present you as soon as I rescue her from that pack of dullards—not one of whom displays your imagination. Are you perchance Irish?"

George laughed. "No, sir."

"I shall attempt to overlook the deficiency."

The lawyer strode off. George straightened his collar, saw Orry bearing down and signaled him away. Orry looked around, realized what was happening, and joined several other brevet lieutenants standing near the punch bowl with morose expressions.

Patrick Flynn snatched his daughter out of the group of senior officers. George tried to ignore their hostile looks and fix his attention on the girl. Half annoyed, half amused by the way her father had grasped her wrist and tugged her away, she allowed herself to be brought to George and presented.

"Constance, this is Lieutenant Hazard. He wanted to meet you and knew he stood a better chance if he spoke to me first."

"But how did he know I'd want to meet him, Father?" the girl asked with a tart smile.

George strained to stand as tall as he could. *Lord, I'm still two inches shorter*. He grinned and looked straight into her brilliant blue eyes.

"Give me five minutes, Miss Flynn, and I'll remove all doubt."

Constance laughed. She spied a fiercely mustached major of dragoons stalking them, then took hold of George's hand.

"Dance with me, Lieutenant, or we won't even get that five minutes."

171

He needed no further prompting. The fiddler was scratching out a waltz. George swept Constance past the fuming major and on across the floor. She was soft and sweet-smelling in his arms; so deliciously lovely that he was extremely careful about the way he held her. She noticed:

"Your touch is very light, Lieutenant. Are you afraid I'll shatter?"

"Why, no, you're not brittle, you're exceedingly sof—that is—"

He strangled on the sentence. What the devil was wrong with him? He didn't usually act this way with a girl. He was behaving like Orry, who was watching him from the punch table. Orry had a big, smug grin on his face.

For the remainder of the dance, they exchanged inconsequential remarks. He told her a few things about West Point and about his home in Pennsylvania. She repeated much of the information her father had given him. George's head swam. He simply couldn't select the right words, let alone deliver them with anything approximating charm. Constance, on the other hand, was completely at ease, smiling and chatting without the slightest awkwardness.

He soon discovered that she was not only beautiful but intelligent. "Father sent me away to a young women's academy in San Antonio. He's in favor of education for women. He's really quite liberal for a man of his background. He says that believing in the Holy Trinity should never rule out a healthy interest in the secular."

George smiled, relaxing slightly. "I like your father."

"And he must have taken a liking to you, or he'd never have introduced us. I'm rather glad he did."

"You are? Miss Flynn, that's splendid!"

In a burst of enthusiasm, he swept her into another whirling waltz figure. A moment later she gently tapped his wrist with her ornamental fan. She wanted him to stop dancing. He obliged.

He saw grinning faces all around. Even Orry was covering a smirk. Constance whispered to him, "The music ended several moments ago, Lieutenant Hazard."

"It did? My God. That is—Miss Flynn, I didn't mean to curse in front of—"

"Lieutenant," she broke in, "I'll be the one cursing if you permit me to fall into the hands of that dragoon bearing down on us. Please take me for a stroll."

"With pleasure!"

George gave her his arm, then guided her toward the door of the barn. The major with the mustache pursued, looking more affronted every second. He was only three paces behind them when Patrick Flynn appeared to stumble. Flynn crashed against the major, almost dumping punch on his uniform. The lawyer bathed the officer with so much apologetic blarney he couldn't be angry.

By then George and Constance had slipped through the door into the darkness.

"I'm in love," George said a couple of hours later.

"So that's what it is," Orry said. "I thought it was some sort of nervous condition. I've never seen you look so stupefied over a girl. Or act so tongue-tied, either."

They were trudging along the riverbank toward the white tents and lanterns of the encampment that had been improvised to shelter the men from the steamer. George started as a big jackrabbit leaped across his path. Then, after a distinctly lovelorn sigh, he said, "I think she likes me. But I'm not positive."

"Of course she likes you. She spent most of the evening in your company, didn't she? And she could have had her pick. Not necessarily of men more handsome than you"—Orry's mockery was broad but kindly—"but certainly of men she could look up to."

George called his friend a name and punched his arm. Orry laughed. Again George sighed. "I hope it takes them a week to repair the steamer. She invited me to dinner tomorrow. Boiled Texas beef and potatoes."

"Talking about her cooking already? You do sound as if you've found the love of your life," Orry said quietly.

"By heaven, you may be right. The instant I put my arms around her, I felt—well, something momentous. But there would be problems if it became anything permanent. She's Irish. Catholic, too. Up North that isn't always a welcome combination."

"You're getting serious awfully fast."

"I can't help it. I don't care, either. George Hazard, master of the fair sex, is for once absolutely powerless. That's the strangest part."

"No, it isn't. I understand perfectly."

George knew Orry had said something, but he was too excited to hear the words, or the note of melancholy in his friend's voice.

A distant whistle sounded the last call for the lighter. George shook Patrick Flynn's hand.

"Good-bye, sir. You've been wonderful to a stranger."

"You're no longer a stranger, lad," the lawyer said with a swift glance at his daughter. Constance had put on a light shawl and was fussing with a parasol. Flynn laid his free hand on George's shoulder and pressed gently. "We wish you Godspeed to the battle zone and a safe walk along the pathway of your duty. We want you to come back again."

"Yes, sir, I'll do that."

The words carried more hope than certainty. George had read the papers enough to know that many men had already died in Mexico, not only from enemy fire but from disease. Many others would perish before the war ended. A couple of days ago he hadn't troubled himself about such things. Now, suddenly, in this ridiculous little village on a barren coast, life had become wondrously precious.

He and Constance walked out of the house. George stepped off the plank porch into the mud and raised his hand. She closed her fingers on his, then stepped down beside him and opened the parasol.

It was a dismal autumn day with a hint of winter in the gusty wind. He took charge of the parasol and offered his other arm. She pressed her breast against his sleeve, speaking to him silently that way. It began to drizzle as they hurried toward the pier where the last lighter was loading.

"Will you write to me, George?"

"Regularly. Daily! Will you answer?"

"You know I will. You must come back as soon as you can."

"I promise. I want to show you Pennsylvania. Introduce you to my family."

He knew Constance could charm them and perhaps even overcome the suspicion of Catholics that was so prevalent in the nation. But if by some chance the family didn't welcome her, he would no longer consider himself a Hazard. In just these few days, she had become his universe—and his reason for fearing some random Mexican bullet as he had never feared it before.

"Father's very impressed by what you told him about your family," she said. "He thinks most Texans are fools because they won't admit factories are becoming more important than farms."

"My friend Orry's family won't admit that."

"Southerners can be so narrow-minded sometimes."

No more narrow-minded than Northerners, he thought, recalling an incident in Philadelphia the week he had set off for Mont Royal.

Obscene words and statements had been slathered in red paint all over the walls of a Catholic church. Even his brother Stanley, no admirer of Papists, had been scandalized, though more by the language than by the motivation for the act.

Three senior officers sat in the lighter. All were frowning with impatience. The helmsman signaled for George to hurry. Another gust ripped the parasol out of his hand and sent it sailing into the water, where it bobbed like a lacy boat.

The men in the lighter laughed at him. George didn't care. His mind and heart were filled with Constance: her fiery hair blown loose by the wind, her blue eyes searching deep into his, her cheeks rain-speckled—

No, he realized with a start. That wasn't rain but her tears.

"Constance, I've never said this to any other girl. You may think me rude and forward since we've known each other such a short time. Still, I'm compelled"—he drew a quick breath and plunged—"I love you."

"I'm in love with you, too, George. Kiss me?"

"In public?"

"In public. In private. Anywhere—and forever."

The last word came out as a little cry. She flung her arms around his neck and kissed him ferociously.

He pulled her close, his body rising against her to make the parting all the more intense and sorrowful. Her red hair kept loosening and blowing against his cheeks. He felt unmanly tears on his face—not hers, his own—and didn't give a damn about that, either.

The helmsman shouted, "Last call, Lieutenant. Get aboard or they'll report you for desertion."

Out by a sandbar the steamer sounded its whistle. George tore away and ran down the pier. He jumped into the lighter, falling against an artillery colonel who cursed him roundly. He sat on the middle thwart as the oarsmen strained and the lighter pulled away. Rain pelted him. He realized he had lost his hat. It didn't matter.

Constance Flynn stayed on the pier, her hair completely undone now. It flew over her shoulders and down to her waist like a red banner. "I'll come back," George said softly. The officer seated next to him stared.

He said it again silently, watching the girl's figure diminish along with the town's rude buildings. *I'll come back.*

It was a promise, but it was also a prayer.

Sergeant Jezreel Flicker peered at the empty beach. "Not a sign of a greaser. Mighty funny. We sure ain't made a secret of this here invasion."

Seated next to him in the rocking surfboat, Orry growled, "When are they going to send us in, damn it? If there are sharpshooters behind those dunes, they can pick us off like fish in a barrel."

Flicker's moon face remained imperturbable. He was a regular Army man, a laconic Kentuckian ten years older than Orry. Both of them understood that he was the one who ran the platoon. In response to Orry's nervous outburst he said, "Now, now, Lieutenant. I know you're anxious to see the elephant. But believe me, it ain't that pleasant."

Orry scowled. It was all very well for Sergeant Flicker to sneer at the glory of battle; he had been in the thick of it at Monterrey and elsewhere and survived. But Orry was as yet untested. He had already spent almost six months in Mexico, and the only guns he had heard were those of the damned volunteers who were always getting drunk and blowing their own toes off.

Some of Orry's men were looking bilious; a strong offshore current kept the surfboat in constant motion. Forty feet long, the boat was one of the 150 General Scott had ordered specifically for this assault. Each boat carried an eight-man naval crew and forty to fifty soldiers. Only 65 boats had actually been delivered, and these were strung out in a line just off Collado beach, opposite Sacrificios Island, some two and a half miles below the port city of Vera Cruz. It was here, out of range of the city's defensive artillery, that Scott intended to launch his drive inland to Mexico City.

George and Orry were serving in two different companies of the Eighth Infantry. Both companies were part of the first landing wave, along with other regular infantry and artillery units comprising General Worth's First Brigade. Orry's platoon consisted of Irishmen, Germans, a couple of Hungarians, and six native-born Americans. Even in peacetime, immigrants made up a large percentage of the country's military manpower.

The eight oarsmen struggled to keep the surfboat in its assigned place in the long line of similar craft awaiting the signal to go in. A couple of hours had already been lost because the line was constantly disrupted by the current swirling around Sacrificios. Behind the surfboats lay the troop ships and the rest of the invasion fleet, dozens of vessels of every size from steamers to small gunboats. The yards and tops of the biggest ships were filled with spectators: sailors as well as other soldiers who would go in with later waves. While Navy gunners loaded their cannon with grapeshot, the bands on various vessels competed with one another. Orry could hear "Hail, Columbia" and "Yankee Doodle" above the slap of the waves against the surfboat's hull and the oaths and complaints of the men.

He admitted they had plenty to complain about. They groused about everything from their government-issue shoes—cheaply made and designed to fit either right or left foot—to their India-rubber canteens. One private took a drink, grimaced, and spat over the side.

"No treat to swallow hot water, is it, Novotny?" Sergeant Flicker smirked. "Should have listened to what I told you last week. Rubber heats up. First chance you get, throw that away and fix yourself one of these." He tapped his own canteen, a gourd carried on a thong.

The men groused about being sent ashore burdened with haversacks and greatcoats. And they groused about their weapons. A few units had been issued 1841 percussion rifles, but Orry's men still carried old smoothbores, simply because the high command believed muskets could be more easily maintained by men of limited intelligence. Orry despaired of that kind of thinking. When men knew they were considered worthless, that's how they acted.

It was a mild, cloudless afternoon—perfect weather. Northwestward, the domes and rooftops of Vera Cruz were visible. Straight ahead, the spectacular snowcapped peak of Orizaba jutted up through a light haze some distance behind the beach. But Orry was too preoccupied to notice the scenery. He was reflecting that his view of soldiering had changed since his arrival in Mexico. He still wanted an Army career—that was why he was eager to get into combat—but much of the glamour with which he invested the profession was gone.

First of all, his war duty thus far had not only been frustrating, it had been downright disagreeable. The steamer from Corpus Christi had anchored in the harbor of Brazos Santiago, at the mouth of the Rio Grande. He and George had traveled inland with other troops, and on the second night Orry had been stricken with dysentery—a standard initiation for newcomers, he was informed. Not even his surroundings—the cool, pleasant uplands of the Sierra Madre—could compensate for his misery.

The friends reported to their regiment in Saltillo. They were assigned to replace line officers wounded at Monterrey. Orry's company commander was a lazy complainer named Wilford Place. Captain Place seemed to dislike everyone above or below him, but Orry quickly discovered Place's attitude was typical rather than unusual. In the United States Army, animosity was a way of life.

West Point men scorned officers who hadn't graduated from the Academy. All the regulars hated the undisciplined volunteers, who were prone to burning Mexican houses, stealing Mexican property, and raping Mexican women. Native-born soldiers distrusted the immigrants and vice versa. Even the highest echelons weren't free of antagonism. Since the start of the war, General Worth had been feuding with General Twiggs over who outranked whom. That ludicrous quarrel had created factions within the Army and finally put an end to the friendship of Worth and Zach Taylor, who had known each other since the War of 1812.

Far-off Washington joined in the game of mutual distrust. After whipping the enemy at Monterrey, Taylor had given the Mexicans generous terms. Too generous, some complained; as commanding field general, he had let the beaten army slip away past an armistice line. His detractors said he should have ruthlessly destroyed the Mexican forces and ended the war.

President Polk used this as an excuse to criticize Taylor, whose unpretentious nature and unmistakable courage made him extremely well liked by his men. Taylor's rising popularity with the kingmakers of the Whig party may also have had something to do with Polk's enmity. Polk was, after all, a loyal Democrat.

The President had wanted an independent second front in the south, a direct thrust at the Mexican capital. To achieve this objective, he had no choice but to put a second Whig general in charge—the supreme commander of the Army, Winfield Scott.

For the proposed amphibious landing, Scott took about nine thousand of Taylor's regulars, leaving the latter with an army composed mostly of volunteers. With this Taylor was supposed to face a huge Mexican force rumored to be moving to attack him. The Mexicans were under the command of Santa Anna, the self-styled Napoleon of the West. Less reverent admirers called him the Immortal Three-fourths, because of his wooden leg.

All the strategic maneuvering and professional backbiting had meant

179

but one thing to Orry—no immediate opportunity to go into combat. As part of Worth's command, he and George had marched all the way back to Santiago in early January, there to languish on the beach while the quartermasters coped with delays in the arrival of everything from casks of water to troop transports. To pass the time, Orry wrote long letters to Madeline. As soon as he finished one, he tore it up and started another.

Now, here it was the ninth of March, 1847, and he was bobbing in a surfboat, still unblooded, still seeing action only in his imagination. The waiting was surely worse than the fighting would ever be.

The sudden *crumph* of a cannon hurled him back to reality. Out in the thicket of masts and spars, a puff of smoke was drifting away from the steamer *Massachusetts*. Excitement roughened Orry's voice as he spoke to Sergeant Flicker.

"That's the signal."

"Yes, sir, so I figured." Flicker sounded tense for a change. It reassured Orry to know he wasn't the only one anticipating the prospect of resistance on shore.

A strange, unfamiliar roar brought puzzled looks to the faces of the men in the boat. Private Novotny was first to offer the explanation. "It's from the ships. Tattnall's sailors and cannoneers. They're cheering us on."

The sixty-five surfboats surged toward the beach. Late-afternoon sunshine flashed from the several thousand fixed bayonets. The oarsmen propelled the landing craft between the gunboats of the covering squadron. Caught up in the splendor of the moment, Orry forgot the illness and the boredom, the drudgery and the pettiness of the last few months. This was the high art of war, the glorious side of soldiering.

A naval gig pulled ahead of the other boats. Its oarsmen rowed frantically, obviously intending that the gig should be first on the beach. Standing in the bow, sword drawn, was a man they all recognized: their handsome, white-haired leader, General Worth.

Sergeant Flicker tore off his hat, waved it, and cheered the general. Orry joined in, and so did his men. Soon every soldier in the first wave was screaming himself hoarse.

A half minute before the keel scraped in the sand, Orry unsheathed his own sword. He stood up and was first to leap from the boat, flourishing the sword and shouting, "Here we go, men! All the way to the Halls of Montezuma in Mexico City!"

For that, they cheered him, too.

*

After such a rousing start, the next hour was an anticlimax.

The regiment formed on the colors, then, with bayonets extended, charged to the top of the first dune. The charge quickly ran out of steam because there were no Mexicans lying in wait, not one enemy foot soldier or dragoon visible anywhere. The only foes the Americans met the rest of the afternoon were sand fleas and the rising wind that flung gritty particles of sand into their eyes, noses, and mouths.

For the invasion, Scott had reorganized his men into three large forces. After the first two went ashore—Worth's regulars, then those in General Davey Twiggs's Second Brigade—the volunteers landed. General Patterson was in overall command of this brigade. Within it were units from South Carolina, Tennessee, and Pennsylvania, led by a man named Gideon Pillow who had but one qualification for his recent appointment to the rank of general. Before the war he had been Polk's law partner.

As night approached, the invading army began to extend its line to the northwest. Worth's brigade would hold the right, near the landing site, and it was there that Orry and his platoon went to work digging in. Even in perfect weather it would take several days to unload all the men and matériel necessary to complete the eight-mile siege line. Once the line was in place around Vera Cruz, it was expected that the artillery would begin bombardment. But the city might not fall for a long time. It was heavily fortified, defended by nine forts on the land side and the castle of San Juan de Ulúa in the harbor.

It was after midnight when Orry tottered into the mess tent. He was sodden with sweat and covered with sand and insect bites. He sank down next to George at a badly stained table, peered at what looked like a gobbet of old meat wedged into one of the cracks.

He picked at the dried lump with a fingernail. "Lord, this table's filthy."

Captain Place swabbed his cheeks with a bandanna. "It isn't one of ours. There have been several mix-ups in off-loading equipment. These are surgical tables, last used in Monterrey. Amputations—that sort of thing—"

Orry gagged and wiped his hand on his trousers. Then he heard the raucous laughter. Even Place, not humorous by nature, roared. It was an old Army joke, Orry learned later. That made him feel better. He was no longer a greenhorn; he had finally been accepted.

No one knew, that night or ever, why the Mexican commandant at Vera Cruz hadn't fired so much as one shot at the invaders. But the absence of an enemy made Orry nervous as he went from sentry post to sentry post in his sector about three in the morning. His right hand stayed close to the personal sidearm he had purchased at his own expense, a practice followed by most officers. The gun was a Model 1842, a single-shot percussion smoothbore made by I. N. Johnson and generally considered the best military pistol on the market.

The night was windy, with not a star showing. Orry was midway between two posts when he heard something on his left, the side away from the shore. He caught the sound of furtive voices and movement. His mouth dry, he drew his pistol.

"Who goes there?"

Instantly there was silence except for the wind.

He repeated his challenge, realizing belatedly that from out in the dark he was a clear target; the lantern-lit regimental staff tent was directly behind him. He started to move on quickly. He had taken only two steps when he again heard voices, loud this time, angrily shouting in Spanish.

Three shots rang out. He felt a ball flick his trousers. He dropped to one knee, aimed, and fired. A man screamed. Another cursed. Feet scurried away. Sentries at the nearby posts were shouting challenges.

Pain hit, canceling his brief feeling of triumph. He looked down and to his amazement discovered that a rifle ball had done more than tick against his trousers. It had pierced his calf.

He pacified the sentries and limped to the medical tent, a good half mile, his shoe filling with blood. The orderly on duty saluted. Before Orry could return it, he fainted.

The injury wasn't serious. He was feeling fairly chipper when George visited him late the next day.

"Your first battle wound." George grinned. "Congratulations."

Orry made a face. "I expected my baptism of fire to be a little grander, thanks. Being shot by a skulking guerrilla isn't my idea of heroism. I think I got one of them, though."

"I know you did. Flicker found the body at sunup."

"Soldier or civilian?"

"Soldier. Dressed like a peasant, but his accoutrements were military."

Orry looked less displeased. George crouched beside the cot and lowered his voice.

"Tell me something. When the shooting started, were you scared?"

Orry shook his head. "There wasn't time. But a minute or so afterward, I—" He was silent for a second. "I came to, I guess you could say. I went over every detail I could remember. *Then* I got scared."

The more Orry thought about it, the more convinced he became that he had made an important discovery about the behavior of men at war.

In his tent a few nights later, George hunched closer to a dim lantern and rolled a pencil stub back and forth in his fingers. He was writing another of his long letters to Constance. He sent one about every three days. He loved her so much, he wanted to share as many of his experiences as propriety allowed.

He kept some of his deepest feelings out of the letters, though. His longing to be with her had filled him with a powerful hatred of this war, a reaction that went far beyond the resigned acceptance that had been his attitude before Corpus Christi.

While he was considering what to say next, something tickled the back of his neck. He whipped up his free hand, smacked the tiny insect, grimaced as he wiped his fingers on the edge of the cot. Then he put pencil to paper.

> *Unseen snipers usually fire a few rounds every night, but it has been quiet this evening. I am coming to believe that our true enemy is this land. The wind blows like*

He scratched out the letter *h;* he had started to write *hell.*

> *fury, and as a consequence, the eyes and the skin are constantly savaged by flying sand. Retreating inside a tent minimizes that problem but does not guarantee peace or a good night's sleep, for we Americans are locked in battle with another army which our superior officers neglected to mention. I refer to the army of fleas and wood ticks which infests this coast.*
>
> *Little Mac McClellan, one of my classmates who's down here with the engineers, has devised a novel defense against the infernal creatures. Each night he swabs himself from head to toe with salt pork and, thus odiously "protected," crawls into a canvas bag which he then proceeds to close about his neck with a tight*

drawstring. He says it works splendidly, but I for one am not quite desperate enough to try such an extreme

George bolted up at the sound of a gunshot. Someone cried out. Men began shouting and running. He dropped the letter, hurried outside, and discovered that a nearby sentry had been felled by a sniper's bullet.

The sentry, a private about George's age, lay on his side with the upper half of his face bathed in lantern light. The one eye George could see was open and glaring. The fatal shot had struck the middle of the sentry's back.

A sergeant took charge of disposing of the body. The private had belonged to another company; George didn't know him. Badly shaken, George returned to the tent and picked up the letter. He would say nothing about the killing. He began to write but had to quit almost at once. The face of the dead private kept intruding in his thoughts, along with memories of Orry's close call. It was five minutes later before his hands stopped trembling and he was able to pick up the pencil again.

Gale winds out of the north delayed the unloading of Scott's artillery ammunition, and pack animals. Not a round was fired at Vera Cruz until March 22. That evening the guns opened up for the first time. Scott planned to reduce the city by what he called a ''slow, scientific process'' of shelling.

Orry was soon back on duty. The Mexicans remained hidden as the bombardment continued. The American soldiers were restless and impatient to engage an enemy. They were beset by the climate all day, and now they were kept awake all night by the return fire of Mexican cannon, which could never reach the American lines but which were hellishly noisy nonetheless. Orry was constantly breaking up fights and disciplining his men.

Wherever he and George went, they encountered others from the Academy. About five hundred West Point graduates had been serving in the regular Army at the start of the war, and an equal number had been recalled from civilian life to command volunteer units. Tom Jackson, who seemed to grow more dour and indrawn every day, was in the artillery; Pickett and Bee and Sam Grant were in the infantry. Other Academy men the two friends knew slightly, and some just by reputation: Lee and Pierre Beauregard in the engineers; Joe Johnston and George Meade in the topogs; Dick Ewell and Tom Jackson's roommate, Pleasonton, commanded dragoon units. Robert Anderson, Ambrose Burnside, Powell Hill, and a fanatic abolitionist named Abner Doubleday were artillerymen with Tom. The secure feeling generated by the presence of officers with the same background was one of the few good things about this campaign, George thought.

On March 24, six long-range naval guns supplied by Commodore Matthew Perry joined the siege. That same day, Orry was summoned to brigade headquarters with Captain Place to explain a knifing that had occurred in his platoon. The questioning was perfunctory because everyone at headquarters was in an exultant mood. Scouts kept streaming in to report that the American bombardment was at last inflicting substantial damage on the walls of the city.

"Commodore Perry's cannon saved our skins," Place growled when he and Orry left the tent after the interrogation. "Guess we owe him thanks, even if he did squawk like a mudhen about the Navy's rights." Scott had been forced to let naval gunners operate the six long-range pieces. Orry realized the Army had no corner on officers jealous of their—

"Lieutenant Main. I say—Main!"

"Yes, sir!" Orry automatically brought his hand up to salute, even as he pivoted in response to the voice he couldn't quite place. He froze.

Elkanah Bent returned the salute in a relaxed, almost mocking way. He noted Orry's fatigue cap with a scornful glance. Bent was wearing the more formal, French-inspired *chapeau bras.*

"Thought it was you," Bent said. "I had a report that you had joined us. Your friend, too. Hazard."

Orry took it as a bad sign that the Ohioan remembered George's name. But of course he had promised to remember. Orry tried to act unconcerned.

"You're looking well, Captain."

"Considering all the action I've seen since last year, I feel remarkably fit. I was informed that you were one of our few casualties. A guerrilla ball caught you, did it not?"

"Yes, sir. The night we landed. The wound wasn't serious."

"That's good news." Bent's sly expression said just the opposite. "Well, Lieutenant, I'm confident we shall encounter each other again. When we do, perhaps we can reminisce about our days at West Point."

Captain Place's brows drew together in a frown. He could sense the tension. But Orry was the only one who understood Bent's remark. His spine tightened with apprehension as Bent waddled away, his hand self-consciously placed on the Phrygian helmet pommel of his sword. He was just as fat as ever, and just as poisonous.

"You knew that bastard at the Academy?" Place asked.

Orry nodded. "He was in the class ahead of me. Have you served with him?"

"Never, thank God. But everyone's heard of Captain Bent of the Third Infantry. His regimental commander, Colonel Hitchcock, makes no secret of his contempt for him. He says Bent's afflicted with uncontrollable ambition and is determined to climb upward—on a ladder of bodies, if necessary. Be thankful you no longer have any involvement with him."

But I do, Orry thought as they walked on.

Perry's cannon proved too much for the defenders of Vera Cruz. On March 29, under surrender terms arranged with General Scott's staff, the Mexican garrison struck its colors and marched out through the Merced Gate. Moments later, while American batteries on shore and on shipboard thundered in salute, the Stars and Stripes rose on every flagstaff in the city.

The victory had cost fewer than a hundred American lives. George and Orry were shocked to learn that, back home, politicians and a certain segment of the public were unhappy that casualties had been so light. "They calculate the importance of the victory by the size of the butcher's bill" was the way George put it. "And then they wonder why nobody wants to stay in the Army."

Scott was pleased with the progress of the war. The surrender at Vera Cruz came on top of Taylor's stunning February triumph at Buena Vista. Scott once again reorganized the army for a march on the capital.

On April 8 Twiggs's division started inland. Patterson's division followed the next day. General Worth's men were awaiting orders to move forward in support when word came that Santa Anna, once again elevated to the presidency, had taken a position at Jalapa, on the National Road to Mexico City. On April 11 and 12 units from Twiggs's command clashed with enemy scouts and lancers. Outside Vera Cruz the drums and bugles summoned Worth's command for a forced march to join Twiggs at the village of Plan del Rio.

During the early hours of the march, heat felled dozens of men at the roadside. Close to fainting himself, Orry risked the censure of his superiors by dropping back and propping up a stumbling soldier who had the makings of a fine noncom if the climate, disease, a Mexican ball, or homesickness for Brooklyn didn't overcome him first. After twenty minutes the soldier was able to walk by himself again.

By dusk, four men in Orry's platoon were sick with diarrhea. So were scores of others in the column. The ditches along the road stank and swarmed with green flies. But dysentery wasn't the only malady to be feared. For weeks officers had worried aloud about the coming yellow-fever season. Outbreaks of the disease decimated the low-lying seacoast every year. Scott had wanted to move his men into the highlands before the season began, and the alarm from Twiggs had enabled him to do it. When a corporal complained about marching so far so fast—the distance was slightly less than sixty miles—Orry was quick to say, "As soon as we reach General Twiggs, you'll be a lot better off."

"Better off dodging greaser musket balls? Beggin' the lieutenant's pardon, I don't believe that."

"But it's true. You're much less likely to be felled by a ball than by the *vómito*."

Over the cook fire that night, Orry noticed that the smoke was climbing into clear, haze-free air. Cooler air. They were already above the coastal plain whose sometimes pestilential climate reminded him of home. He pointed out the change to the corporal, but the man remained unconvinced.

Sergeant Flicker arrived. He reported the sentinels posted according to Orry's orders. He squatted by the fire, took out a piece of biscuit, and began picking weevils from it. He observed that the odds now favored a major engagement with the Mexicans; things had been quiet for too long. Then he said:

"By the way, sir. I never had a chance to ask you 'fore this. Did you get close to any of them senioritas in Vera Cruz?"

Orry was astonished at the noncom's cheek. Flicker probably figured his length of service gave him certain privileges when dealing with officers. "No, Sergeant," he answered. "I have a girl back home." It was a convenient if painful lie.

"Oh." Flicker's expression said he didn't understand why one thing excluded the other. "Mighty accommodating, some of them ladies. 'Course, I had the bad luck to visit one of their establishments the night a captain from the Third foot got rough with the girl he'd paid for. She screamed bloody hell, and the head whore almost closed the place."

"The Third, you say? What was the captain's name?"

"Bent."

Quietly: "I've heard of him."

"Sure, who hasn't? Butcher Bent, his men call him. It was a scandal what he did in Monterrey."

"I didn't hear about that."

"You passed through the town last fall, didn't you? Then I 'spect you remember the layout of the fortifications on the east side. The Black Fort on the main approach an' the redoubt named for a tannery a little ways on? Bent was in Garland's column, it headed in past the Black Fort. The fire was pretty fierce. When the column turned, fire from the redoubt damn near blew away the left flank. The men started runnin', figuring to take cover in the streets close by. But those streets wasn't safe either. A greaser pistol or rifle was blazin' away from ever' window and garden gate, seemed like. Things went crazy for a couple of minutes. The only way out was to move to the next streets, where there wasn't so many of the varmints hidin'. That would get Bent an' all the rest out from under the worst of the fire from the forts, too. But Butcher Bent didn't care about savin' anybody. He decided to be a hero and knock out the tannery redoubt. He sent a platoon to storm it."

"Did they take it?"

" 'Course not. It was impossible. Bent lost more'n half the platoon. Afterwards, I heard they found at least two men with bullet holes in their backs."

"You mean they got shot running away from the redoubt?"

"They got shot runnin' away from Captain Bent."

"Godamighty. Why doesn't someone report him?"

"He kisses a lot of backsides, Lieutenant. And some of the idiots in charge of this here army don't give a goddamn about the way a man gets results, just so long as he gets 'em. They do say Bent's got a passel of friends in Washington, too."

Orry could have verified that but he didn't.

"Nobody knows for certain that he shot those men," Flicker went on. "I mean nobody can prove it. I did hear Bent's threatened to court-martial anybody who raises questions about that little operation. That says somethin' to you, don't it?"

Orry nodded. "So his men aren't talking about him?"

"Damn right they aren't. They're too scared. God knows how many he'll send to their deaths before they catch him—or he gets 'lected President, which is prob'ly more likely. Jesus, can't they find us some decent food?" He leaned forward and spat a wiggling weevil into the flames.

Later, Orry located George's company at the roadside. Orry reported what Sergeant Flicker had told him.

"I believe every word," George said. Carefully, he placed a stone on a thin sheet of paper on which he had been writing in pencil. There were eight or ten sheets beneath the partially filled one. Another letter to Texas, Orry presumed.

"I'll tell you this, Stick," George continued. "If the good Lord ever turns against me and arranges for me to be transferred to Bent's command, I think I'll kill myself before reporting for duty. By the way—I just learned that in our batteries at Vera Cruz there were some pieces cast at Cold Spring." And he was off into the enthusiasms of the ironmaster.

Orry had trouble sleeping that night. He was bothered by memories of Flicker's story, and of Bent's eyes.

The evening before Cerro Gordo, George drank a third of a bottle of Mexican wine smuggled in by his company commander, an Academy graduate named Enos Hoctor. George didn't like Captain Hoctor very much. He was too serious, too prone to worry aloud—and at length— over West Point's reputation.

George didn't share Hoctor's concern about the Academy, but he was happy to share his wine. He would have invited Orry to join them, but his friend said he wanted to spend some time rereading Scott's *Infantry Tactics*. Poor Orry, yearning for his first taste of battle. If George never heard an enemy ball whistling by his ear, he'd be perfectly happy.

To continue the march to Mexico City, the Americans had to clear away the enemy fortifications at Cerro Gordo on the National Road. On Telegrafo, a fortified peak some five to six hundred feet high, Mexican batteries were trained on the ravine through which the road ran in a westerly direction from the American camp at Plan del Rio to Cerro Gordo.

Enemy guns were also in place on a second hill, Atalaya. But Captain Robert Lee of the engineers had discovered a mule trail leading around the northern flank to this hill and had reportedly dis-

189

tinguished himself for bravery doing it. Earlier today—it was the seventeenth of April—American sharpshooters had slipped along the trail and in three hot charges had cleared Atalaya. Cannon were now being moved into position to rake Telegrafo.

When the main engagement commenced tomorrow, Twiggs's division had the task of driving through the hills above the highway and outflanking the Mexican defenses. Worth's division, which included George and Orry, had been rushed forward, then held on the National Road in case Twiggs needed reinforcement. In George's view, Orry faced disappointment once again; the division might see no action at all.

After drinking Hoctor's wine, George went to sleep without difficulty. He was up long before sunrise, when an artillery duel commenced. Smoke and a red glow were all he could see from the place where he and his men awaited orders. Then over the ridges came the crackle of gunfire, and drumming and bugle calls, and an occasional protracted cry of pain. George's men stopped their whispering and exchanged silent looks.

George had long ago given up hope of knowing much about the strategy of any battle in which he took part. He was just a lieutenant of the line, a small cog in an immense machine. Besides, all that really mattered to him was doing his job and surviving. Orry was different. He was fascinated by strategy because that was the stock-in-trade of a career officer. George could see his friend farther up the line with his platoon, and he hoped Orry was able to grasp something of the grand plan of the day. It might compensate him for missing combat yet again.

The battle lasted a little more than three hours. At half past nine, drums thudded and bugles blared close at hand, and the men of Worth's division began making the usual nervous jokes as they prepared to march. Their mission, as it turned out, was to rush along the National Road for ten miles, pursuing the beaten Mexican army. Santa Anna had sworn publicly that he would triumph at Cerro Gordo or die. But the Napoleon of the West had often put survival above promises. When defeat loomed, George learned later, Santa Anna had cut a horse from his presidential coach and galloped away into the chaparral.

Corpses already bloating in the sunshine lay along both sides of the National Road. Most were Mexicans, but there were a few American dragoons among them. The stench of dead flesh and emptied intestines made George so sick that he finally vomited in a ditch. He wondered what Orry thought about the glories of war now.

Other debris of the Mexican retreat—dead horses, overturned artillery caissons—littered the approach to the pass of La Joya. Two miles this side of the pass, musketry suddenly exploded from the rocky slope above the north side of the road.

"Take cover!" George shouted, drawing pistol and saber. The command was superfluous; his men were diving to the right and left. All but two went fast enough to avoid bullets.

Crouching below the road, George saw one of the two still moving. He squinted at the white puffs of smoke erupting on the hillside. He swallowed twice, then started climbing up the sloped side of the ditch.

"Get back, Lieutenant," Captain Hoctor shouted from the left. But George was already halfway to the wounded corporal, whom he lifted and carried back to the side of the road while balls from the hillside peppered the ground around him.

He lowered the wounded man into the ditch and jumped after him. An American artillery piece opened up on the hidden snipers. After three rounds of grape, there was no more firing, just cries and moans.

"You exposed yourself needlessly," Hoctor growled at George as litter bearers took the wounded man away. "Your duty is to your men."

"I'm sorry, sir," George retorted. "I believed I was carrying out my duty."

Unfeeling son of a bitch, he thought. *He doesn't care about that soldier—or that I was scared out of my wits.* If West Point was graduating many like Hoctor, it deserved the criticism it received.

That night George commandeered a horse and rode back to the field hospital to check on the corporal. The boy was in good spirits and would recover. On the cot next to his lay a red-bearded sergeant whose midsection was wrapped with brown-spotted bandages. That meant an intestinal or stomach wound, the worst kind. Listening to the man complain to an orderly, George heard Bent's name.

"Excuse me, soldier. Are you talking about Captain Elkanah Bent?"

Instantly wary, the noncom replied in a weak whisper, "Pal of yours, sir?"

"Just the opposite. I despise the bastard."

The sergeant scratched his beard. Surprise and suspicion kept him silent a moment or so. Finally he decided it was safe to continue the conversation about another officer:

191

"How do you know Butcher Bent?"

"We were at West Point together. I saw him damn near kill half a dozen plebes. What were you saying about him? Is he dead?"

"No such luck. Bent cost me the best platoon leader I ever had. He sent Lieutenant Cummins up Telegrafo against a redoubt that a brigade couldn't have taken. Of course Bent stayed to the rear, well protected, just like always. A stray shell from our guns on Atalaya blew the lieutenant and his detail to pieces, and a lot of Mexicans with it. So the Butcher, he led the rest of us up through the smoke and ordered us to spend ten minutes sabering greasers. Dead ones."

"Jesus," George breathed. He could almost see Bent's round, waxy face during the incident; he was sure the captain had been smiling.

In the lamplight, fiery pinpricks showed in the wounded man's eyes. "What was left of Cummins they put in a canvas bag. But you know who'll get the decoration."

"Tell me, Sergeant. If Cummins knew the attack was fool-hardy—"

"'Course he knew. We all did."

"My point is, did he question the order?"

"No. 'Twasn't his place to do that."

"Did anyone question it?"

"The platoon sergeant. He's—he was a crusty old coot. Twenty-year man. Not too impressed by officers—'specially ones from the Academy." A cough; a belated realization. "No offense intended, sir."

"None taken. Go on."

"The sergeant, he spoke right out. He said that sending men against the redoubt was practically murder."

"How did Bent react?"

"He put Sarge in the detail too."

"And still Cummins said nothing?"

"Because he was a good officer! And I 'spose he didn't care to wind up with one of Bent's bullets in his back. At Monterrey—"

"Yes, I heard about Monterrey. Seems to me that if Bent keeps doing things like this, he may get shot himself. By his own men."

Weak as the sergeant's voice was, it had a cold edge when he said, "Not if I get him first."

"Get him? How?"

"The minute I'm on my feet again, I'm goin' to divisional staff and tell the whole story. If there's any justice in this goddamn army, they'll put Butcher Bent on trial and cashier him."

"You mean you're going to charge Bent with a definite act of wrongdoing?"

"I'm sure—" The sergeant coughed a second time; it clearly hurt him a great deal. "Sure as hell going to try."

"But if you're the only one making accusations—"

"I'll get nowhere, that what you mean?" George nodded. "Well, it won't be me alone. I got witnesses from the platoon. Half a dozen, maybe more."

"Are all of them willing to testify?"

"They've all been here, and that's what they told me."

"Any officers in the group?"

"No, sir."

"Too bad. It would add weight to your charges." Only after George said it did he notice the intensity that had come into the sergeant's gaze.

"Yes, it would, sir. Will you help? Will you testify to what you know about Bent? I gather you think he's a bad lot."

"I do, but—"

"He's got to be punished. He's got to be stopped. Help me, sir. Please."

George drew a deep breath. He was almost surprised when he heard his own response:

"All right, I'll do what I can."

Later that night he found Orry with his platoon. He took him aside and described the conversation with the red-bearded sergeant whose name he had learned at the close of the meeting: Lennard Arnesen.

When George finished, Orry shook his head. George bristled. "Don't you believe Arnesen's story?"

"Certainly I believe it. But I have trouble believing you'd involve yourself in something like this."

George squatted and reached up under his right trouser leg to scratch. He discovered a tick and pried it loose. "I have trouble believing it myself. Hazard the self-preservation specialist was ready to turn Arnesen down. But then I thought of all the things that fat bastard did at the Point, and I said to myself, If our men are shot down, it ought to be the Mexicans who are responsible, not our own officers."

"You're beginning to sound like me. Just before you got here I was telling a couple of my noncoms that Pillow should be removed. Did you hear about him bungling his assignment this morning?"

"No."

"He willfully marched into the wrong position on the left. As a result, his troops were exposed to the fire of three enemy batteries, instead of one. Then Pillow started yelling orders so loudly, the Mexicans knew exactly where he was. They opened fire with everything they had."

George uttered a weary obscenity. "What do you expect of a political general? Pillow I can't do anything about. Bent, though—that's different."

"What are you going to do?"

"First, talk to my captain. Tell him I intend to support Arnesen's story. I can't testify to what happened in Arnesen's platoon, but I can sure as hell speak with authority about Bent's character and past history. As the sergeant said—if there's any justice in this army, the divisional staff will listen. Of course"—he looked hard at his friend—"two officers would be more convincing than one."

"I had a feeling you were about to ask me to go with you."

"Will you?"

Without hesitation, Orry said, "Yes." He yawned. "But in the morning."

"I'm shocked," Captain Hoctor said. "No, worse than that. I'm appalled."

George glanced at Orry standing beside him, pleased that his opening statements had produced such a strong reaction. "I'm encouraged to hear you say that, sir," he told Hoctor. "Bent's behavior really is—"

"I was not speaking of Captain Bent's behavior. I was referring to yours. Frankly, I cannot believe that one Academy graduate would impugn the ability, the motives—the fitness—of another. Furthermore, did no one ever tell either of you gentlemen that a commander is *supposed* to send his men against enemy positions, no matter how strongly fortified they are—no matter how impossible the odds?"

For a moment George felt dizzy. "Yes, sir, of course. And on the surface Captain Bent did no more than that. But there are other aspects. Questions of character, of—"

"Of his past actions," Orry put in. "Doesn't the charge have to be judged against those, too?"

Hoctor's look was withering. "I have never read any regulation to that effect, Lieutenant. My point stands. I cannot believe you gentlemen would be parties to such a vicious accusation when the reputation of

194

the Academy—perhaps its very survival—is dependent upon public and congressional opinion of its graduates."

In a strained voice, George said, "Sir, may I respectfully ask what the Academy has to do with any of this? Sergeant Arnesen will swear that Captain Bent all but committed murder. Bent's platoon sergeant questioned the order, and for that Bent sent him to be killed too. The sergeant has witnesses, and they are ready to testify in support of every—"

"You said that already, Lieutenant." The captain's tone was scathing.

"Sorry, sir. I forgot." George tugged at his collar. "But I strongly believe there *is* a case and evidence of guilt. Lieutenant Main and I are willing to offer background information. There's no shortage of it. You must have learned about Monterrey—"

"Of course. Brave officers are always the targets of the less courageous." Hoctor's expression suggested that he was now including George in the latter group.

"I beg your pardon, sir," Orry said. "I think there's a distinction to be made. Let me use Captain Lee of the engineers as an example. I haven't heard a single officer or enlisted man question his courage. He demonstrated bravery at Cerro Gordo through personal action, not by throwing good men into hopeless situations. Bent, on the other hand—"

"That's enough," Hoctor interrupted. "You have made your point, both of you. Let me ask you a question." A note of threat had entered his voice. "Do you really intend to pursue this matter through formal channels?"

George didn't blink. "Yes, sir." Orry gave the same reply.

"I assume, sir," George added, "that when I write my formal report for division, you will receive it and send it along."

The fire in Hoctor's eyes was hot now. His voice was barely audible. "Contrary to the judgment I seem to detect in your words and your manner, Lieutenant, I am not a dishonorable man."

"Sir, I never meant to suggest—"

"Permit me to finish. Of course I would not hold or bury your report. My duty as an officer wouldn't allow it. However, that does not mean I approve of your course of action. I abominate it. If we are now clear on that—get out of here."

Feeling he had won a victory, if a rather dangerous one, George returned to the field hospital that night to inform Sergeant Arnesen.

195

When he reached the foot of the sergeant's bed, he stopped and stared witlessly. A young private with blond fuzz on his cheeks was lying in Arnesen's place.

George's gut began to ache. He pivoted, frantically searched the shadows where men stirred and moaned softly. An orderly came hurrying along with a reeking basin.

"Sergeant Arnesen? He died on the table last night. Most of 'em do when the surgeons get hold of 'em."

The fuzz-cheeked soldier was watching with puzzled, bleary eyes. The orderly rushed on. George could think of only one thing.

He never told me the names of the other witnesses.

Despite apprehensions, George went back to Captain Hoctor to inform him of this latest development and to say that he still intended to prepare his report.

"Have you completely lost your mind, Lieutenant? Every shred of evidence concerning the death of this Lieutenant Cummins is hearsay, and now you can't even produce the source of that! The sergeant is dead, you don't know the identities of his alleged witnesses—drop the matter."

"I could make inquiries. Try to learn the names of—"

"Do that and you'll get no help from me. This has gone far enough. Too far, in my opinion."

The message behind the words was clear. George's report, if he went ahead with it, would be blocked, permanently filed, perhaps even destroyed. Still, conscience drove him to a final effort:

"Sir, Captain Bent is not a stable person. He's committed a wrong, he's dangerous, and he should be removed from—"

Hoctor jumped up. "I will hear no more. Even granting a grain of truth in your assertions, do you seriously believe Bent is the only bad officer—or the worst one—in the Army? Haven't you heard the accusations they're making about that hack Gideon Pillow? Captain Bent is, at very least, an Academy man, and so are we, and your friend Main as well. God knows why the two of you are unable to comprehend the meaning of that bond—or the responsibility it places upon you. But for the sake of your careers, I hope you and Lieutenant Main will reach that understanding very soon. Dismissed."

"Captain Hoctor—"

Scarlet rushed into Hoctor's face. "*Dismissed!*"

Humiliated, George left.

"Well, that's a nasty lesson," Orry said when his friend described the scene. "West Point protects its own. I reckon we should have guessed it from Hoctor's remarks the first time." He sighed. "At least Bent won't know we tried to rob him of his laurels and do him in."

"You think not? I made Hoctor furious. In his eyes we're the dangerous ones. I'll wager Captain Butcher Bent will soon know exactly what we wanted to do. Hell, I bet Hoctor tells him. After all"—George grimaced—"West Point protects its own."

When the realization sank in, Orry was unable to say a word.

Soon after, George again wrote to Constance. The opening paragraphs of the letter said:

> *I have never felt so tired, although I think that is a state induced not merely by lack of sleep but by my revulsion toward this war. Death, injury, filth, eternal fear—an army of incompetents, poltroons, political cronies, and victims—always there are the victims whom the others send to slaughter in their stead—this is the "glory" by which Orry is seduced. When will he discover the "glory" is nothing but a layer of gilt desperately applied to conceal the rot beneath? For his own sake, I hope the enlightenment comes before he commits his life to military service. But sometimes lately, my dearest, I am too tired even to care much about my best friend's fate.*
>
> *What fills my nights and days, sustaining me as nothing else can, is the thought of our being reunited one day, with nothing more fearful ahead of us than the ordinary vicissitudes of a life together. I am not a deeply religious person, but I have found myself praying for that reunion constantly of late. They do say God makes many converts on battlefields, a statement which I am beginning to understand at last.*
>
> *The conditions about which I write have been made all the worse by my recent failure to rectify a criminally unjust situation. I tried to do so, mind you, but*

All at once he glanced back over what he had written. Disgusted, he realized he had been thinking only of himself when he poured out his grim thoughts. If he added to her worries, he deserved to be whipped. He picked up the sheets and crumpled them. It was the one letter penned in Mexico that he never sent.

12

A shell whined in over the highroad to Churubusco. The Mexican gunners in the convent of San Mateo had found the range. So had those on the fortified bridge that carried the road over the Rio Churubusco and on into Mexico City.

Sword in his left hand, pistol in his right, Orry crouched in the marshy cornfield beside the road. He cringed as he awaited the explosion of the shell. The concussion nearly knocked him over.

To his left, a geyser shot up from the wet field, lifting cornstalks and bloody heads and limbs with it. It was mid-afternoon, the twentieth of August. Orry had been in heavy fighting for nearly three hours and had thought himself numb to sights of violent death. The disappearance of an entire squad of men when the shell hit showed him how foolish he'd been. He gagged as the human remains splattered back to earth.

Choking smoke stung his eyes. He could barely discern the spires of the Mexican capital and the snowy summit of Popocatepetl through the murk. He searched for familiar faces but saw none among the milling mobs in the cornfield.

On the highroad he heard hoarse commands; an attempt was being made to re-form Worth's division there. Having overcome and routed the garrison at San Antonio, the division had been racing toward Churubusco when devastating fire from the convent and the bridge drove it off the road into the field.

A stocky figure came lurching out of the smoke, teeth clenched and face barely recognizable under a layer of dirt. Orry laughed in a wild, ragged way and wigwagged his arms.

"George. George, here!"

George staggered toward him. Noncoms and officers ran past, most bound for the road but some going the other way. "I've lost sight of the colors," Orry gasped.

"I've lost all my men," George shouted back. "When the crossfire started, the whole division just seemed to melt. But I saw Captain Smith of the Fifth heading for the road to reorganize—Jesus Christ. *Down!*"

He pushed Orry face forward into the muck. Orry swallowed a mouthful of the foul stuff, but that was better than being ravaged by the charges of canister that blew apart and sent a thousand deadly bits of metal hissing through the corn.

They waited for a lull in the artillery bombardment; then, bent over and running side by side, they started for the highroad. Musket fire from the bridge and the firing platforms in the convent was almost constant. George encountered eight of his men along the way; they were lost, confused, frightened.

With George in the lead, they climbed the embankment near a crossroad where some adobe cottages stood. The walls were pocked by American and Mexican balls, and two rooftops were afire. Everywhere officers were shouting, trying to organize squads or platoons of men, any men available. Orry saw unfamiliar faces and the insignia of units that didn't belong on this part of the battlefield.

He took his cue from the other officers. "Form up, form up in squads!" he shouted, seizing running men and hurling them into a line at the edge of the road. He caught about twenty, but half of them immediately ran toward the rear. George threatened the others with his pistol.

"I'll shoot the next man who bolts."

That held them for about thirty seconds. Then everyone in the little group dove off the road. A shell blew a huge hole in the center.

In the rain of dirt and debris falling afterward, Orry again started to climb the embankment. He found his foot mired in something wet. *I thought all the water was in the cornfield.* He looked down. His foot was planted in the warm red cavity that had been a man's gut. He wrenched backward and gagged again, but there was nothing left to come up.

Someone pushed him from behind. He swore, then realized it was George trying to get him away from the corpse. They regained the road and began re-forming their group. Four had been killed.

Suddenly uniformed men came running from the direction of the fortified bridge. Americans. "We've been repulsed," they screamed, and raced on by.

A figure in the smoke at Orry's left glided toward him. "Perhaps we'd better reconnoiter and find out whether that's true, gentlemen."

Orry's jaw dropped. George was equally stupefied. Dirty, disheveled, greasy with sweat, Elkanah Bent faced them with sword and revolver in either hand. Orry lost his last doubt that the fellow was mad when

200

he saw Bent smiling—*smiling*—in the midst of this hell of musket and artillery fire.

Bent gestured to the little squad huddling nearby. "Lieutenant Main, take those men and bring me a report on the situation at the river." His small eyes flicked to George. "Go with them, Lieutenant Hazard."

"Godamighty, Bent, do you know what you're saying? There's no way a squad can get far enough down that road to see—"

Bent cocked his revolver and pointed it at George. More men ran by, staring. But they didn't stop to ask the reason for the bizarre scene. It looked as if the fat captain might be disciplining a couple of cowardly subordinates.

"Bring me a report or I'll shoot you for disobeying a direct order in action."

Orry's hand clenched on the hilt of his sword. He fought an impulse to run Bent through and let his own life be forfeit. Bent sensed it and swung the revolver to cover him.

George laid a hand on Orry's arm. They both knew Bent meant for them to die. George winked quickly and jerked his head toward the bridge, as if to say, *That way we stand a chance; here we have none.*

With their backs to the fat captain, they stood close together, surveying the highroad. About a quarter of a mile beyond the junction stood two other cottages, apparently deserted.

"Let's advance to those," George whispered. "Once we take cover inside, he won't be able to get at us. Then we can plan our next move."

For an instant Orry was lost to reality. "I'm going to kill him." He repeated it twice in a monotonous voice. George gripped Orry's left arm and applied pressure as hard as he could. In a moment Orry winced, blinked, and collected himself. George shouted the command to advance. Orry shambled forward with the others.

They had taken no more than a dozen steps away from the cottages at the junction when a musket barrel came smashing through an unbroken window in one of the cottages ahead. The door flew open; three more muskets poked out. The muskets boomed, killing two of the surprised soldiers a yard to Orry's left.

George shouted for everyone to go into the ditches again. Two more men fell before they reached the edge of the road. George was suddenly incoherent with rage. He looked back, saw Elkanah Bent gesturing to a major of mounted rifles. God knew how the major and his horse had gotten to this little corner of hell. Feeling just as Orry had earlier, George started for Bent. He had made up his mind. Regardless of the consequences, he was going to murder the swine on the spot.

A scream brought him to a stop. It sounded like Orry, and there was something terrifying about it. George peered through the smoke as the screaming intensified, a crescendo of sound.

It wasn't a cry of pain but of berserk anger. Orry was charging down the center of the road, brandishing his sword as he uttered that wild yell. It unnerved the stunned guerrillas hiding in the cottage. For several moments, none of them shot at the figure rushing toward them. By the time they realized they'd better, Orry was two yards from the door.

The first musket ball missed him. The second sent his forage cap sailing. He reached the door, kicked it wide open, and jumped into the dark interior, still yelling and swinging his sword.

George saw Bent and the mounted rifle officer watching with amazed expressions. Shrieks issued from the cottage. They might be Orry's. George bent low and began to run forward to help his friend.

Three of the men he had assembled clambered up the embankment and followed, their bayonets stirring the smoke ahead of them. In front of George and to the left, a shell hit. He shut his eyes to protect them from flying dirt, cut to the right, and kept running. The shrieking didn't stop; the cottage sounded like a slaughterhouse.

Suddenly two Mexicans in grimy clothing burst through the door. Two others hurled themselves out through a broken window. Orry appeared in the doorway, his sword dripping. He held something in his left hand—some piece of a human being—that he mercifully flung behind him before George could identify it.

The soldiers bayoneted the guerrillas attempting to flee. George raced toward his friend, but before he could say anything, he heard another shell coming in. Very fast, very loud.

He gestured wildly. "Orry, get out of th—"

The shell burst. The cottage flew apart in hundreds of pieces. Dirt and debris mushroomed upward in a roiling cloud. George blinked and choked, conscious of pain in his chest. He was lying on the road and didn't even remember throwing himself down.

The explosion must have done it. But where was his friend? He didn't see Orry anywhere.

He lurched to his feet, looking down the short stretch of road to the new crater where the cottage had been. The last bits of wreckage pattered to earth. The smoke was dispersing. Behind him he heard officers yelling—Bent was one—as they once more tried to organize the men straggling through the cornfield. George's attention fixed on something lying at the crater's edge.

He passed his right hand back and forth in front of his eyes, as if he were shooing a fly. He wanted to deny the evidence of his senses. He couldn't. He began to run.

Next to the crater lay a man's left hand and half of the forearm. The cloth around the forearm was torn and scorched. He found Orry sprawled on the embankment on the left side of the road, bleeding to death.

George's mind blotted out memories of the next four or five minutes. He later concluded that he never could have endured what he saw or done what was necessary if he had stopped to think about it. By shutting the horror out of his mind, he was able to function.

He did remember crouching over Orry and repeating three words—"You can't die"—but he had absolutely no recollection of fixing a tourniquet with material torn from his uniform and twisted tight with the muzzle of his own pistol, stanching the flow from what was left of Orry's arm.

He went staggering to the rear with Orry lying head down over his shoulder. He steadied Orry with his right hand and held the gun in place with his left. He couldn't tell whether Orry was still breathing. He might be trying to save a corpse. He didn't dare think about that. Calling on strength he never knew he had, he quickened his step until he was almost running again.

The major of mounted rifles cantered past, rallying men behind him with flourishes of his saber. Next came Bent, panting but safely surrounded by two noncoms and several privates with fixed bayonets. George gave the captain a murderous look. George's face was blackened, the eyes standing out as comical white circles. If Bent recognized the apparition with the body slung over its shoulder, he gave no sign.

The soldiers disappeared up the road to Mexico City. George kept going in the other direction, the effort filling his eyes with sweat and tears. His chest began to hurt. A couple of minutes later he came upon an ambulance stopped at the roadside.

. The orderly examined Orry quickly. "Help me lift him inside."

On the orderly's instructions, the driver turned the ambulance swiftly and whipped the horses into a run. George was flung back and forth inside. He braced his palms against the walls so that he wouldn't fall on his friend.

"You'll kill him, for Christ's sake!" he protested. "Slow down!"

"Do you want him alive and bruised, or dead?" the orderly shouted. "His only chance is to get to the surgeons. Shut up and hang onto him."

George squeezed his eyes shut, clearing his vision a little. He gazed down at his friend. Orry's head bounced against the filthy blankets spread on the floor of the ambulance. George stripped off his blouse, rolled it into a pillow, and eased it beneath Orry's head. In that moment, with the dust blowing through the ambulance and the sounds of battle ringing outside, he understood how much he loved his friend.

To a God he prayed was listening he said, "Don't let him die." Tears ran down his cheeks.

The field hospital was a bedlam of blood and screaming. The exhausted surgeon turned up the lamps above the red table while an orderly held the gun-barrel tourniquet. After a brief examination, the surgeon gestured to a second orderly.

"Get him ready."

"What are you going to do?" George asked.

"Take the rest of the arm. It's the only way I can save him."

"No," George said with a ferocity that made heads turn six feet away. The surgeon gave him a scathing look.

"Would you like to take over the management of his case?"

George wiped his lips with the back of his hand. "No, of course not, but—if you cut off his arm, it'll kill him."

"Nonsense. He's lost half of it already, and he's still breathing, thanks to your quick action. I perform dozens of amputations every day that there's fighting. Forty or fifty percent of the men survive."

"That isn't what I meant when I said—"

"Well, I've no time for riddles," the surgeon broke in. "Leave the tent, if you please. I'll let you know when we're finished."

Orry woke in unfamiliar surroundings. He saw eight lanterns hanging above him, all glowing. Pain came in great surging waves, but in spite of it he tried to move his arms and found he couldn't. There was a feeling of something wrong, over and above the pain, though what it was he couldn't fathom. Suddenly a man appeared, a paunchy man wearing a stained apron. The man's pudgy hand held a wet red saw. All at once Orry knew where he was and why. He screamed. Unseen hands gripped his shoulders. He twisted his head, saw another man heating a cauterizing iron in a brazier of coals. He screamed again. They poured whiskey into his open mouth to stop him.

Six nights later, George entered the field tent of Orry's company commander. He helped himself to some of Captain Place's whiskey without asking. The valley of Mexico lay silent except for distant bugle calls and the occasional crackle of musketry. The generals had arranged yet another armistice, presumably to discuss peace terms. George didn't know the details and didn't care. Like most other line officers and men in the American army, he thought that whoever had proposed an armistice just when Mexico City was ready to fall ought to be lynched.

"How is he?" The captain's question, as well as George's visit, had become a nightly ritual.

"Still no change. Could go either way."

George tossed down the whiskey. Sometimes, shamefully, he thought it would be better if Orry died.

Place sorted through a pile of reports and orders. He drew out a document which he handed to George, who gazed at it without seeing. "Well," the captain said, "I hope he recovers sufficiently to read that."

"What is it?"

"His promotion. He's no longer a brevet. There's a commendation coming from General Scott, too. For helping to clear the highroad so that the fortified bridge could be stormed and overcome. I presume Captain Hoctor will have the same good tidings for you."

"Full rank," George said in a blank way. "Took less than a year."

"I heard another bit of news that's less satisfying. Captain Bent of the Third Infantry has apparently offered an acceptable explanation for turning up so far from his regular command. He also managed to convince his superiors that he directed the attack on that nest of guerrillas. I'm reliably informed that he's being breveted to major."

George swore and reached for the whiskey. Place was no stranger to soldierly cursing, but George's language embarrassed even him.

One of the surgeons told Orry he would live, but a full day passed before he realized the price of that statement. When he did, he raved and wept for an hour, then turned his face to the tent wall and shut his eyes.

From then on, all he wanted to do was sleep. But even that means of escape was imperfect. Again and again he dreamed of an Army drum standing on a rock in the sunshine, silent. Someone had attacked the drum with a bayonet or saber. There was nothing left of the drumhead but tatters.

It was the sixteenth of September before Orry consented to receive a visitor. Two days earlier, General Scott had ridden into Mexico City as a conqueror. The armistice had failed, there had been hot fighting at several locations, and then the enemy had surrendered.

"Hello, Orry."

George moved an ammunition box next to the cot and sat down. Orry had good color. His beard was thick and luxuriant. But his eyes were dead. He had pulled the soiled sheet over his left shoulder, so that his friend couldn't see the bandaged stump.

At last he said, "Hello, George. I hear we won."

George nodded. "There's a commendation waiting for you. You're a full second lieutenant now. So am I. Our friend Bent, unfortunately, is a brevet major. I'm told we were all great heroes on the road to Churubusco."

He smiled but Orry didn't. Orry stared at the ridgepole of the tent. George twisted his forage cap in his hands. "How do you feel?"

"Oh, I don't know." Orry's voice was so flat, it was impossible to tell what the answer meant. George sat perfectly still, his hat held in both hands. He wanted to tell his friend about some of the sharp fighting that had led to the surrender of Mexico City, but obviously it was the wrong time. Would there ever be a right one?

Somewhere outside an amateur musician started playing a popular tune on a mouth organ. George had always known the tune as "Zip Coon," but some fiddlers were starting to refer to it as "Turkey in the Straw." He wanted to go out and strangle the musician. The song was too zestful, too much of a reminder of the pleasures a man could enjoy if he was whole.

Presently Orry looked at him again. "I reckon I owe you thanks for saving my life. Most of the time I lie here wishing you hadn't."

With a hint of sharpness, George said, "Come on, Stick, don't feel so sorry for yourself. You're alive. Life's precious."

"It is if there's something you care about," Orry agreed. "I've come to understand that I never really had a chance with Madeline. She was lost to me before I met her. But I had a fine chance to have the only career I ever wanted. Now they'll muster me out.''

"But you'll be able to go home."

When George saw the hurt in Orry's eyes he felt like a fool. "To what?" Orry asked.

Anger erupted within George then. He kept it bottled up because he realized he was really angry with himself. He had botched things, failed utterly to raise his friend's spirits. If he couldn't, who could?

He tried one last time. "I'll be back to see you tomorrow. Meanwhile, you rest and collect yourself, and you'll soon be feeling—"

He stopped, scarlet. Thoughtlessly, he had reached down to squeeze Orry's arm. His left arm. He had remembered when his hand was just inches from the sheet.

Orry's dark eyes seemed to say, *You see? I'm not the same as you anymore, so don't pretend I am.* As he turned away he murmured a listless, "Thank you for coming."

George slipped out, whipped. He hoped time would heal his friend's bitterness and melancholy, but he wasn't sure. Orry had been robbed of the two things he wanted most in life. How did a man survive when that happened?

Only the arrival of a letter from Constance kept the day from being a complete disaster.

In the balmy October sunshine, George sat at an outdoor table in a cantina in Mexico City. The cantina faced the magnificent National Palace, where the American flag now flew from all the flagstaffs. With him were Pickett, Tom Jackson, and Sam Grant. The four were together for the first time in months.

Pickett and Grant had several empty beer glasses in front of them, as did George. Jackson had only a single, full glass of wine. Continually fretting about his digestion, he always bought one glass of wine and left it untasted.

The Mexican population had a surprisingly cheerful attitude about the outcome of the war. Civilian shopkeepers and tavern owners had shrugged off the loss and quickly settled down to profiting from the occupation. In the European manner, the government had struck medals commemorating every major battle, whether won or lost. Pickett, who was holding forth about Robert Lee, had gotten hold of a Churubusco medal, which was pinned to his jacket.

"I'm not saying this as a Virginian, though you'll probably think I am. Bob Lee is the best man in the Army. He proved it once and for all in the *pedregal*."

Pickett was speaking of a field of volcanic rock that the Americans had encountered on the approach to Mexico City. It looked impassable, but Lee and Pierre Beauregard had scouted it and said otherwise. Then, during a thunderstorm, Lee had volunteered to recross the *pedregal* to carry important information to Scott. He had ridden over sharp ridges and through treacherous ravines with only lightning flashes to show him the way.

"Agreed," Grant said, and drank some beer. "I don't know of a smarter or more audacious soldier. Thank heaven he's not our enemy."

Generally, members of the Academy-trained officer corps had done well in the six-month campaign. Even Elkanah Bent was being regarded as a hero. Had George accused him of incompetence or attacked him physically, few would have sided with him, and he knew it.

The others at the table were actual proof that West Point was turning out brave and competent officers, George reflected. Grant, for instance, had been among the first to storm Molino del Rey, along with Captain Robert Anderson of the Third Artillery. Later, in the assault on the city proper, Grant had dragged a mountain howitzer up into a belfry overlooking the San Cosme Gate. He had done it on his own initiative. The howitzer's fire had all but wiped out the garrison defending the gate.

Jackson had distinguished himself several times, most notably at the north wall of Chapultepec, where he had single-handedly manned a gun from John Magruder's light battery. As for Pickett, during the same assault an Academy man named Lieutenant Lewis Armistead had fallen wounded while carrying colors up a scaling ladder. A second West Pointer, James Longstreet, had taken up the flag and climbed with it. He, too, was wounded. It was Pickett who finally bore the colors to the top.

George soon began to fidget. The others were lingering over their drinks, and he had two new letters in his pocket. One was from Constance. As the table talk turned to still another subject, he pulled out her letter and opened it. When he finished reading, he laughed and carefully put the letter away, intending to add it to all the others he was saving.

"Who's that from?" Grant inquired. "Your fair colleen?"

George nodded.

"Planning to marry her?"

"I might." He patted the bulge made by the letter. "She still likes me."

"Naturally." Pickett grinned. "You're a flaming hero. We're all flaming heroes this month. For a change even Congress agrees."

The dour Jackson cleared his throat. "Does your young lady practice the Roman faith, George?"

"Yes. Why do you ask?"

"Only to remind you that your career might be impeded if you married a Papist. I've been cognizant of that lately because I—ah— I've been calling on a young woman of this city."

Pickett leaned forward, agog. "You, General? Courting a *señorita?*"

Jackson blushed and stared at his wineglass. "I have that honor, yes. Regrettably, I am afraid marriage is out of the question. God creates all His children equal, but in the eyes of the general staff and the majority of Americans, Catholics are less equal than most."

Grant and Pickett laughed, but George's face remained sober. Loving Constance as much as he did, he tended to brush aside the question of religion. He knew it was a potential problem. He tried not to show that as he said:

"I don't have much of a career to worry about. My hitch is up in less than three years."

"That's long enough for them to make it miserable for you," Grant said.

"Especially the beloved Major Bent," Pickett said.

Bells clanged in the nearby cathedral. A flock of pigeons took wing from the roof of the National Palace. The sunlight had changed to the amber of late afternoon. For George the happy reunion at the cantina table was spoiled.

Well, maybe there would be something cheering in the other letter he had received today. It came from Lehigh Station. While Grant and Pickett ordered one more round, George broke the wax wafer and read the first few lines of his mother's fine hand. He turned pale.

"What's wrong, Stump?"

He looked blankly at Grant. "It's my father. Eight weeks ago he had a seizure at the mill. His heart. He's dead."

Maude Hazard's short letter was followed by a much longer one from Stanley two days later. Stanley begged his younger brother to resign and hurry home. Hazard Iron was too large an enterprise for

209

one man to run, especially now that the firm was putting a new mill in operation. William Hazard had designed that mill, supervised its construction, and had been struggling with an equipment problem the day he died.

Hazard's latest addition was a three-high rolling mill, designed to roll wrought-iron rails of the T configuration. The T was rapidly replacing the inverted U as the standard on American railroads. In his letter Stanley repeated an earlier statement to the effect that their father had been prodded into the expansion by the opening of a competitive mill in Danville, Pennsylvania. Had the decision been his, Stanley wrote, he would have vetoed the idea as too novel and fraught with risk.

"Too novel," George snorted to Orry, who was packing to go home. "Even though Henry Cort has been operating a three-high mill at Fontley, England, for more than twenty years. My fainthearted brother will probably go on crying 'fraught with risk' until the railroad boom's over, the country's covered with tracks from ocean to ocean, and the market's gone."

Orry folded a shirt and placed it in his footlocker. He was becoming adept at doing things with one hand. He had once said that the leather-capped stump hurt a good deal and often kept him from sleeping, but beyond that he never discussed his injury. He seldom smiled these days.

He sat on the edge of his cot to rest a moment. "Have you decided what you're going to do, George?" Since his release from the hospital, Orry never called George by his nickname.

George nodded unhappily. "I'm going to be loyal to my family when they need me. Much as I hate the blasted Army—much as I want to see Constance again—I don't feel good about the decision. I guess it's because I agreed to serve four years, and a promise is a promise. Well, nothing I can do about that. I'm going to write Stanley and tell him I'll come home. Of course, there's no guaranteeing the War Department will release me. Not soon, anyway."

He was in for a surprise on that score. On the day before Orry's departure, another letter from Stanley arrived. Stanley said he had referred George's case to a new friend, Simon Cameron, Democratic senator from Pennsylvania.

"The senator's a prime reason the Democracy stinks to heaven in our state," George told his friend. "He's crooked as a snake with convulsions, and he taints the whole party. Stanley's always mumbling about having political ambitions, but I never dreamed he'd cozy up to someone like Cameron.''

"Does your brother have a talent for politics?''

"In my opinion, Orry, you enter politics when you're incapable of doing honest work. But the answer to your question is no. My brother has never been blessed with an overabundance of brains. Cameron would be interested in Stanley for only one reason: the size of his bank account. Wire pulling in Washington—God above!'' George slapped a fist into a palm. "That makes me as bad as Bent. I'll write Stanley and tell him to stop it immediately.''

Next morning the friends said good-bye. Orry was traveling to the coast in a wagon train carrying wounded and several companies of home-bound volunteers.

It was an awkward moment for both of them. Orry asked George to stop at Mont Royal on his way north. George said he'd try. He wasn't anxious to be a witness to his friend's continuing deterioration. Orry was peaked. He'd lost twenty pounds. There was a beaten look about him as he walked off to find the wagon to which he had been assigned.

George's letter of protest was sent too late. Three weeks after he dispatched it, Captain Hoctor called him in.

"Your orders have just come through, specially processed by Secretary Marcy's office. I didn't know the sons of rich ironmakers qualified as hardship cases.'' The sardonic remark was met by a bleak stare. Hoctor cleared his throat. "In any case, you'll be discharged right here, one week from Friday.''

Afterward, Hoctor tried to understand why that piece of good news had caused the lieutenant to break into a storm of cursing. The captain was glad to be rid of such an obvious troublemaker.

The next wagon train was scheduled to leave the morning after George's discharge became official. By then he had done a lot of thinking. He had been a pusillanimous worm to let Constance Flynn's religion cause him even one moment's hesitation. From Vera Cruz he would travel straight to Corpus Christi by whatever means of transportation was available.

The night before the wagons departed, George got roaring drunk with Pickett and Grant. He was awake an hour before daylight. His stomach ached, his head throbbed, and his mouth tasted brown. An hour later he encountered Major Elkanah Bent for the first time since Churubusco.

George hurried by without saluting; he feared that with the slightest provocation he might commit murder.

Bent called him back. "Why are you out of uniform, Lieutenant?"

"Because I'm out of the Army, Major."

George's temples hurt. He knew he was slipping out of control. He didn't care.

Bent digested the news with a disappointed look. George went on, "Congratulations on your promotion. You earned it at the expense of my friend Orry Main. If it weren't for you, he'd still be a whole man. Everyone thinks you're a damn hero, but we both know what you tried to do on the Churubusco road, *Major*."

"Let go of my arm, you arrogant little—"

George hit him then. He felt the impact all the way to his shoulder. Bent's nose exploded with mucus and blood. George walked away with a slow, firm stride, the Ohioan too stunned—perhaps too frightened—to retaliate.

George's fist felt as if it were broken. He had never known pain to be so satisfying.

13

George arrived in Corpus Christi at the end of October. The air was bracing, cool even at midday. When he stepped from the lighter to the dock, it was just four in the afternoon, but the sun was already sinking. Buildings cast long shadows. The light had the unmistakable look of autumn, brilliant and feeble at the same time.

The scene induced feelings of melancholy. The year was hastening to an end, and so was his time on earth. Mexico had given him an awareness of death unusual in young men; he supposed that was a price you paid for going to war, even if you came out on the winning side. Still, having learned the lesson, he wouldn't be so foolish as to ignore it. That was why he had come straight from Vera Cruz.

There was no one at the dock to meet him. His spirits fell even further. But they lifted suddenly when he heard a cry—"Here I am, George!"—and saw Constance appear around the corner of a building.

She wore one of those newfangled crinoline-stiffened skirts, which swayed back and forth like a ship in a storm as she tried to run. The color of the dress was emerald, very becoming.

"I'm so sorry I'm late. I took extra time getting ready—I wanted to look nice for you—and then I discovered it's impossible to hurry when you're dressed this way. Oh, I wanted to be waiting when your boat docked—"

She was laughing and crying too. He put his valise down. Her hand moved from his arm to his face, as if to test for wholeness, soundness, now that he was back from the war zone.

"I was devastated to hear about your father. I never expected you'd have time to stop here on your way home."

"My father's funeral was weeks ago. A few more days won't matter. I have"—he nearly strangled over the words—"an important question to ask you."

"What is it?" A joyous smile said she knew.

"I think I should speak to your father first."

"He's waiting for us. Minding the lamb roast I cooked for you. But I need a kiss."

She released the front of her stiffened skirt, which she had been holding off the ground, and flung her arms around him. Because of the skirt's bell shape, he had to lean forward from the waist to embrace her. His valise disappeared as her skirt dropped over it. That didn't matter, nor did the expressions of other people on the dock; some were amused, one or two outraged. All he cared about were the words she whispered as they hugged each other.

"Oh, George—how I missed you. I love you so."

While Constance finished setting the table, George took her father for a stroll. The necessary question came as no surprise to the little lawyer.

"I thought the two of you would soon be wanting to marry. She has been preparing for your arrival for days. Did you notice all the issues of *Godey's* near her sewing table? The patterns and other paraphernalia? The poor child's driven me mad with her seams and thimbles—if that isn't love, I don't recognize the beast."

Flynn locked his hands behind his black broadcloth coat. "I've no basic objection to the match. But I have one question, and it's serious."

He halted in the street and turned to face the younger man. "What will you do about the difference in your faiths?"

"I'll have to speak to Constance about her specific wishes, sir. I'll make any accommodation necessary."

"Fair enough. But will your family welcome her?"

"I'm sure of it," George lied.

"Then you may have her."

"Oh, sir, thank—"

"On one condition!" Flynn's upraised finger threw a long, skeletal shadow on the ground. Suddenly he gestured to the treeless horizon. "Marry her in the North. This is too dismal a place for a wedding. Besides, I'd like a trip. I'm sick of listening to people say that Congressman Wilmot is the son of the devil. A change of perspective is in order."

"You'll have it," George promised with a grin. The two of them started back in response to Constance's call to supper.

Later that evening the lovers walked hand in hand to the shore. Constance had donned a long, fur-fringed pelerine, but it was more decorative than functional. George put his arm around her to provide what warmth he could. A chilly breeze blew in across the harbor bar, bending the sea oats growing along the dunes. Stars shimmered in the river. Small white-water crests showed out in the Gulf.

"It gets much colder than this up North," he said. "You'll miss the warm climate, I'm afraid."

"Then you'll just have to work very hard to keep me warm in bed."

He cleared his throat to conceal the embarrassment her teasing produced. She was a forthright girl—it was one of the many qualities he loved—and thus she often said things that would shock more conventional people. Perhaps her frontier upbringing accounted for some of that frankness. He hoped her family would understand.

"Actually," she went on, "I'll be glad to go to a place where you don't have to walk five hundred miles to find an abolitionist. I may involve myself in that work after we're married." They stopped near the top of a dune, both of them looking at the limitless Gulf. "Do you think your family would object?"

He smiled. "Would you stop if they did?"

"No. I don't believe I could do that even for you."

"Good. If you did, you wouldn't be the girl I fell in love with." He bussed her cheek.

"You didn't answer about your family."

"Constance, once we're married, you're my family. Only you, and anyone else who might chance to belong to both of us."

Satisfied, she brought her mouth gently against his, then whispered, "I'll try not to disappoint you there."

"You could never disappoint me in anything. I love you."

He moved behind her and slipped his arms around her waist, standing on her skirt in order to get close. She didn't mind. She leaned against him.

He raised his hands till they rested against the underside of her bosom. He feared she might be angry. Instead, she placed her hands over his, so that he pressed harder.

"This is beautiful," George said presently. "You'll miss it."

"I know I'll miss it sometimes. But I would miss you more." She faced him after some awkward maneuvering made necessary by the skirt. Softly, earnestly, she said, " 'Where thou lodgest, I will lodge. Thy people shall be my people.' The first chapter of the book of Ruth." Again she touched her lips to his. "I read it so often while you were away, I know it by heart."

They laughed quietly, their foreheads touching. Her red hair tossed around them like a gossamer mantle. Walking home, they discussed practical matters, including wedding plans. George said he'd like Orry to stand up with him.

"He will, won't he?"

"I'm not sure," George replied with a frown. "The war robbed him of more than a limb. I'm worried about him. Though I really don't want to, I'm going to stop at Mont Royal on my way home."

14

Several miles below the plantation, George smelled smoke. The late-November sky, already dark, grew darker still. Alarmed, he asked the captain of the river sloop whether one of the buildings might be afire.

The captain gave him a superior look. "Doubt it, sir. They're burning off the stubble, I expect."

The air grew noisy with the caw of unseen birds. The black billows continued to roll over the treetops and the river. Soon George was coughing. And when the sloop docked, Orry was nowhere to be seen, although George had written to say he was coming.

He didn't know whether to blame the postal service or his friend's state of mind. He tramped up the pier, the smoke irritating his eyes and throat. He felt as if he were back in the war zone.

From a three-high stack of rice casks a figure came hurtling down at him. George dodged and caught his breath. He smiled without much humor.

"Scared the daylights out of me, Charles."

"Oh," said the boy who had jumped. "I thought you saw me up there." He offered no apology.

George's heartbeat returned to normal. Cousin Charles went on, "Orry sent me to fetch you. He's working over in Hull Square." He dug some dirt from under a fingernail with his huge bowie knife.

An elderly house servant hobbled toward them along the pier. Charles scowled at the Negro. "Cicero, step lively or I'll carve out your gizzard." Charles lunged with the knife. The old black yelped and leaped away. He missed the edge of the pier and landed in the shallows with a mighty splash. Charles ran to look down at him.

"God above, Cicero—I was only sporting with you."

"How's I to know that?" the old man panted as Charles helped him out of the water. "Sometimes you really take after folks with that wicked thing."

Charles shoved the knife into his belt. "I only take after Smiths and LaMottes, never niggers. Now you get busy and carry Mr. Hazard's bag up to the house."

217

Water dripped from the old man's face and clothes. His brown toes showed through holes in the tips of his squeaking shoes. He picked up George's valise and hurried off, not eager to prolong the encounter with Cousin Charles.

"Come on," the boy said, still amused. He couldn't be more than eleven, but he looked four or five years older. He had shot up several inches since George had seen him last. His shoulders had widened considerably. George wished he looked half as tough, and half as handsome.

Charles led him along the embankments separating the large, square fields. Smoke rose from three fields on the right. In each, slaves were using hoes to drag burning brush through the stubble to set it afire. All the workers were women. Their dresses were tied up at their knees. Bandannas protected their hair. In the distance, seated on a mule on another embankment, George saw Salem Jones. With his quirt and stick, the overseer resembled an equestrian statue.

George took Charles's advice and pressed a kerchief over his mouth. The black women seemed unaffected by the fire-shot smoke. Perhaps they had been forced to inhale it for so many years it no longer bothered them. When the flames advanced too fast, the women ran to the nearest irrigation ditch and jumped to safety. "Fire gonna catch you!" he heard one exclaim. "Better run!"

Hollering and laughing, the others did. It hardly seemed like a game to George. More like a picture of the Inferno. But perhaps the stubble burning brought a welcome excitement into plantation routine.

"Not far now," Charles said, beckoning him on toward fields already burned free of stubble. In these, huge flocks of black birds and wild ducks were noisily attacking the ground. Hunting for unsprouted grains, Charles said in response to George's question. In the growing seasons the Mains fought the birds, but in the burning season they counted on their help.

Loud hammering drew George's attention to the embankment next to the river. There he spied Orry, the only white in a group of six men. Orry was pounding nails into the gate of one of the culverts leading to the river. A nervous Negro positioned each nail and quickly retreated before Orry struck the first blow. He wielded the hammer with great arcing strokes.

Why in God's name would Orry try to do carpentry when he was crippled? George couldn't imagine. Then he realized Orry must be working so furiously precisely because he *was* crippled.

At last Orry finished. He turned to his friend who stood waiting nearby.

"Hello, George. Sorry I didn't meet you. These boys botched the repairs. I had to show them how to do it right." He dropped the hammer, paying no attention to the fact that it narrowly missed a slave's foot.

George was shocked seeing Orry up close. His friend looked older. Gaunt, grim, almost biblical. His unkempt beard hung halfway down his chest. The left sleeve of his filthy white blouse was pinned up at the shoulder.

"How have you been?" George asked as they walked in the direction of the great house.

"Busy." Orry fairly spat the word. "I'm trying to work myself back into the routine of things as fast as I can. Father's too old to do it all himself, and Cooper's leaving. Right after dinner today, as a matter of fact."

George's eyebrows shot up. "Where's he going?"

"Charleston. By mutual agreement with Father. It's a sort of self-exile, I reckon you'd call it. Cooper just can't get along with Father anymore. He has too many radical ideas, and both of them realize it. Cooper offered to move out before the quarrels got any worse."

It was stunning news; no wonder Orry acted upset.

"Will he get a job?"

"There's one waiting for him. A year ago a man owed Father a lot of money and couldn't pay. He signed over his only possession— a little cotton packet company. The assets aren't much: two old side-wheel steamers, a broken-down warehouse, and a dock. Father doesn't give two pins for the whole thing. That's why he didn't fuss when Cooper said he'd take it over and run it. I'm glad to see you, George, but it's a bad time to visit Mont Royal. People have been shouting at each other for days."

You included? George wondered, but kept the question to himself. How haggard and hollow-eyed Orry looked. The sight of his friend in such a state saddened him.

"I had to stop," he explained, noticing that Cousin Charles had departed. He spied the boy down in the nearest field, grinning and patting the bottom of a black woman twice his age. "I'm going to marry Constance. I'd like you to be best man."

"That's wonderful news. Congratulations." Orry didn't shake his friend's hand or even break stride. He put his hand behind him, hunting for his handkerchief in his right rear pocket.

"It's in the other one," George said, reaching for it.

"I can get it." Grim-faced, Orry strained to extend his hand across the small of his back. He caught the tip of the handkerchief and plucked it out.

"Will you stand up with me, Orry?"

"What? Oh, yes, certainly. Provided the work here isn't too heavy. I hope you don't mind eating dinner with my father and Cooper. It probably won't be very pleasant."

Nothing at Mont Royal was pleasant that day. George wished he hadn't come. He made up his mind to leave as soon as possible.

Dinner proved as uncomfortable as Orry had predicted. Tillet, too, looked years older than George remembered. He and Cooper confined themselves to a desultory discussion of several matters relating to the little steamship company. Even an outsider could see Tillet had no interest in the subject. He merely wanted a safe topic for conversation.

Cooper, on the other hand, spoke with enthusiasm about formulating a plan to make the company profitable. "They're shipping more and more cotton out of this state every year. We should get our share of those revenues."

"Well, do what you can," Tillet replied with a shrug. Orry had once said Tillet hated to hear about South Carolina's expanding cotton industry. Somehow he construed it as a threat to rice planters in general, and the Mains in particular. He considered all cotton farmers to be upstarts without pedigrees, even though one of the state's most distinguished citizens, and possibly its richest, Wade Hampton of Millwood, planted cotton.

Cooper heard all of that in the older man's remark, and it irked him. "Count on it, sir," he said with determination. Clarissa sighed and patted his arm. Tillet paid no attention.

Ashton, already showing the first signs of young womanhood, kept staring at George during the meal. The attention made him nervous. Brett elbowed her sister to get her to stop it. Ashton yanked Brett's curls, whereupon Tillet blew up and sent both of them out of the room with Clarissa for a licking.

Brett was gulping, red-eyed, when the others came outside. The carriage had arrived. Ashton stared at her father with hot, hateful eyes. If the child had any feelings, they were all the wrong sort, George thought.

Cousin Charles sat with his back against one of the columns, whittling.

Unexpectedly peevish, Clarissa flicked his ear with her middle finger. "Stand up and say good-bye to your cousin."

Charles looked sullen. "I'm trying to finish this carving."

Orry strode forward. "On your feet." He slipped his hand under Charles's left arm and yanked. He pulled so hard that Charles yelped. Then he glared. Orry glared back without blinking.

George studied Orry's hand. It looked powerful, much thicker through the wrist than he remembered. Had Orry exercised to strengthen it? Apparently.

After Charles muttered a good-bye to Cooper, he put his bowie knife in his belt and rubbed the spot where Orry had held him. He was still rubbing when the carriage pulled away five minutes later.

That night George told the Mains that he would have to depart for Pennsylvania in the morning. Orry said he would accompany his friend to the little woodland way station of the Northeastern line. George slept fitfully and woke at first light. He dressed and left his room. He presumed no one would be awake except the slaves, who would have a pot of coffee ready. To his surprise, he heard loud voices below, voices of masters rather than servants. Tillet was up, and Clarissa, and Orry. Why?

He hurried down the great staircase and found the Mains in the dining room. Outside, the first faint rays of daylight shot over the eastern trees. A mist lay on the lawns, which were white with frost.

"Good morning, George," Clarissa said. He had never seen her with her hair undone—much of it was white—or in anything but proper attire. The dressing gown she wore was old, the colors of its complex embroidery faded by the years.

"Good morning." What did he say next? Why were they gathered? Had someone died during the night?

Tillet slumped in his chair, looking older than ever. A clay mug stood beside his hand. The coffee sent up curls of fragrant steam. Orry let out a long sigh and addressed his friend.

"No point hiding it from you. The whole plantation's in an uproar. Lately we've had nothing but trouble from that buck named Priam— you remember him."

George nodded; how could he forget the screaming that night?

"Well," Orry said, "it appears he's run away."

In the ensuing silence, one of the house girls entered with a plate of biscuits and a pot of wild honey. George recalled the girl from his

221

earlier visit. She was a sunny-tempered creature who joked with everyone. This morning she kept her head down and her eyes averted. Her footsteps hardly made a sound.

When she left, he once again caught the sound of anxious voices, this time through a window that was open a few inches. Out by the kitchen building, the house servants were talking. George heard no laughter. The crime of one slave was apparently the crime of all. But the slaves weren't the only ones who were worried. Here in the dining room, the stink of fear was almost as strong as the smell of the hot biscuits.

"Papa, what's wrong? Why is everyone up?"

The unexpected sound made them start. Brett stood in the hall, grave-faced in her cotton nightdress.

"One of the niggers ran off. We'll catch him. You scoot back to bed."

"Which one was it, Papa? Who ran off?"

Tillet struck the table. "Get back to your room."

Brett fled. George listened to the rhythm of her bare feet on the stairs. Clarissa changed the position of her chair. She folded her arms and stared into the table's brightly polished surface. Orry walked up and down in front of the windows.

The dawn burned away some of the mist outside. Tillet rubbed his palms over his cheeks and eye sockets. George munched a biscuit, finding himself confused. Why were three adults so upset about one man's escape? One man's freedom? Was freedom such an unacceptable idea? Hadn't Tillet Main's ancestors fought against the British for freedom in this very state?

But those were idiotic questions, he soon realized. The Mains had been fighting for freedom for white men, something greatly to be desired. Freedom for a black was altogether different, to be feared not only for its own sake but for its possible consequences. At last George began to understand something of the Southern dilemma. He began to understand the stranglehold that slavery had on those who practiced it. Not one slave could be allowed to escape, for if one succeeded, thousands might try. The Mains and all others like them were prisoners of the very system by which they profited. And they were prisoners of fear. He pitied Orry's family, but for the first time he was scornful of them too.

The sound of a horse brought Tillet to his feet. Salem Jones galloped into sight in the drive. A moment later he strode into the room. The overseer looked exhilarated. He suppressed a smile as he reported.

222

"Still no sign of that buck. Last anyone saw of him was around sunset yesterday. I searched his cottage. I now understand why he's been so troublesome." He shot a quick, accusing glance at Clarissa. Her attention was elsewhere, but Tillet didn't miss the overseer's look.

"What are you talking about?" he said.

Jones reached under his coat. "This. I found it hidden in Priam's pallet." He flung a dirty, dog-eared book on the table. The others crowded around to see it. "I suspect he was reading it before he ran off. I'll wager it gave him ideas. About how bad he was being treated," Jones added with significance.

George said, "I thought slaves weren't taught to read."

"Not usually," Orry said.

"In Priam's case we made an exception," Tillet said, without meeting his wife's eye. "Mrs. Main thought he displayed great potential as a boy. A peaceable disposition, too. She may have been right about the former, but as for the latter—well, I'm not blaming you, Clarissa."

At that point, finally, he looked at her. He was assigning her every bit of the blame.

"I gave you permission to teach Priam to read and cipher," Tillet went on. "It was a calamitous mistake." He turned to George. "Now perhaps you understand why the South must have laws prohibiting education of the Negro. Even the Bible, read with the wrong interpretation, can be a source of rebellious ideas."

Orry picked up the book, which had paper covers. "Who brought this piece of garbage onto the plantation?"

"I don't know," Tillet said. "But you make sure it's burned."

By now George had identified the book. He had seen a copy at home some years ago. On its cover it bore the colophon of the American Anti-Slavery Society of New York and the words *American Slavery As It is*. The Reverend Theodore Weld had published the work in 1839. It was a compendium of excerpts from slave laws, testimony by escaped slaves, and damning quotes from Southern slaveholders attempting to defend the institution and minimize or deny their mistreatment of blacks. George had heard his sister Virgilia say Weld's tract was the most important and influential anti-slavery document yet published in the United States.

Clarissa said, "It's all very well to point fingers, Tillet, but what do you propose to do now?"

Salem Jones spoke first. "I'll question Priam's sister, though it won't do a hoot of good. She's scared. What's worse, she's ignorant.

Even if she wanted to give me a useful answer, she couldn't. If I asked where her brother's gone, all she could say is one word. North. And she'd be telling the truth, I expect. In my humble opinion, we have no choice but to appeal to our neighbors in the district and organize a special mounted patrol to pursue the nigger."

Stiffly, Tillet said, "An armed patrol?"

"Heavily armed, sir. It's regrettable but necessary."

The little monster's going to giggle before this is over, George thought.

Tillet nervously passed his hands across his forehead. "Never in the history of Mont Royal have the Mains resorted to a special mounted patrol. Not one of my people has run off in my lifetime. Not one!" He looked at George with anguish and pleading. Still confused and at the same time angry, George looked away.

Tillet's face hardened. "But you're right, Jones. Evidently the lesson of the cat-hauling was lost on Priam. An example must be made."

"I agree," said Orry with scarcely a trace of reluctance. George stared at his friend, inwardly aghast. Not bothering to conceal his eagerness, Jones strode out.

A couple of hours later, Orry and George rode to the railroad stop. Few words passed between them as Orry led the way along back roads and trails. He had donned a swallowtailed coat, old but obviously of fine quality. His holstered Johnson pistol hung at his right hip.

Mist still floated near the ground, and the orange light of the sun falling through it lent the forest a beautiful, spectral quality. The hoofs of the horses plopped softly on the carpet of pine needles and rotting leaves. George's valise bobbed behind his saddle.

Why was Orry so quiet? He acted angry. But at whom? Priam? His father? Things in general?

Or me?

He wanted to ask about Madeline LaMotte. During the visit her name hadn't come up once. He decided he had better not.

When they were about a half mile from the little way station, the forest echoed with the long wail of a whistle. George booted his horse up beside Orry's.

"Is that my train?"

Orry pulled a heavy gold watch from an inside pocket. He flicked back the lid, then shut it with a click and a shake of his head. "A northbound freight. It passes every morning at this time. It's still five or six miles south of here. Sound carries a long way over the marshes. The passenger local won't be along for twenty minutes yet.''

He rode on. The trail took them out of the trees, around the perimeter of another misty marsh, and back into the woods. Shortly they emerged in a gloomy clearing bisected by a single track running roughly southeast to northwest. At one side of the track stood a weathered cypress shed, open on the side next to the rails.

Orry's judgment of distance had been right. The freight train was close, but not yet visible. The woodland resounded with the clatter of couplings and the shriek of wheels. While George tethered the nervous horses, Orry stepped inside the shed and lifted the lid of a wood box hanging on the wall. From the box he pulled a red flag. He raised the flag on the halyard of a pine pole at one end of the shed.

"There. That will signal the local to stop.'' He crossed the tracks to rejoin his friend just as the freight locomotive rounded a bend to their left. The whistle sounded again, deafening. The engine rattled by, traveling about ten miles an hour. The fireman and the engineer waved. Orry returned the wave laconically. George brushed falling cinders out of his hair.

The locomotive disappeared into the woods on their right. Boxcars and flatcars went shuttling by. Orry started to say something. George was staring past him, startled by the sight of a black man who had burst out of the underbrush and was now running beside the train.

Orry saw his friend's expression and turned. Surprise quickly changed to anger.

"Priam! Stop!''

The slave had seen the white men but apparently hadn't recognized them. He looked terrified. He scrambled up into the open door of a boxcar as Orry ran for his horse. George had never seen his friend move and mount so fast.

Clinging to the floor of the boxcar, Priam made the mistake of looking back. He recognized the bearded face looming above the horse. Wild fright filled Priam's eyes as Orry booted the horse forward. Go on, George found himself shouting silently. Get inside the car, where he can't see to shoot you.

But the sight of his owner apparently threw Priam into confusion. He lay on his belly in the doorway of the boxcar, floundering like a beached fish. His legs hung down outside, his dirty bare feet just

225

clearing the roadbed. Orry galloped past the car, all the way to the edge of the clearing. There he wheeled, his right side nearest the train.

Gasping, Priam raised his right leg and got it into the car. George could only assume the slave was not only scared but exhausted; otherwise he would have clambered inside with no trouble. His left leg still dangled, thrashing the air.

As the boxcar rolled slowly by, Orry reached out and seized Priam's ankle. Priam was dragged backward through the opening. He tried to hold onto one of the doors, but then he shrieked and let go, as if splinters had torn his palms. Orry kneed his horse to the left, still pulling. Priam cleared the train and fell.

He landed on his chest on the shoulder of the roadbed. George could hear the slave's sobs above the rattle of the last cars passing. A brakeman on the caboose platform gaped at the scene in the clearing, then vanished in the trees.

"George, I need your help," Orry called, dismounting and pulling his pistol. George hurried forward. Orry gave him the pistol butt first.

"Keep this pointed at him. Shoot if he moves."

Priam looked up over his shoulder. George could barely stand the sight of the slave's eyes.

"Mist' Orry—please, Mist' Orry—"

"Don't take that tone with me," Orry interrupted, lifting a coil of rope from his saddle. "You knew what you were doing when you ran off. Stand up and put your hands behind your back."

"Mist' Orry," Priam repeated, staggering to his feet. All traces of his former defiance were gone. His escape had rendered him as vulnerable as a little child. There was something shameful and almost obscene in a grown man begging so desperately that tears trickled down his cheeks.

"Keep that gun on him," Orry said without taking his eyes off the runaway. He looped and tied one end of the rope around Priam's wrists. He was as dexterous with one hand as most men were with two. He had taught himself a lot in a short time.

George licked his lips. "What will happen now?"

"I don't know. He'll probably be lamed so he can't run away again. But my father's so angry he may have him killed."

Priam bent his head. "Oh, Jesus. Jesus."

"Stop it, Priam. You knew the penalties before you—"

"Orry, let him go."

George was astonished at the hoarseness of his own voice. He had approached a precipice and impulsively stepped over. This was none of his affair. Yet something in him was constitutionally unable to stand by and see the black man returned to Mont Royal to be crippled, perhaps even executed.

For a moment he felt idiotic. Priam meant nothing to him; his friendship with Orry meant a great deal. Still, he knew he would never be able to live with himself if he kept silent.

"What did you say?" Orry asked, his expression what it might have been if the sun had risen in the west, or the trees had grown bank notes in place of leaves.

"Let him go. Don't be a party to murder."

Orry fought back a furious reply, drew a deep breath. "You're confusing men with slaves. They're not the same th—"

"The hell they aren't! Don't do it." Trembling, George struggled for control. His voice moderated. "If our friendship means anything, grant me this one request."

"That's unfair. You're taking advantage of me."

"Yes, I am. To save his life."

"I can't go back to Mont Royal and tell my father—"

"Why must you say anything?" George cut in. "I won't, and you'll never see Priam again."

"Yes, sir, I be quiet," Priam babbled. "'Fore God, Mist' Orry, I swear that after I'm gone, no one will ever—"

"Shut up, goddamn you."

Orry's shout rang in the stillness. George had never heard his friend invoke the Deity's name in anger.

Orry rubbed his palm over his mouth. He squinted at his friend—angrily—then snatched the pistol out of George's hand. *Christ, he's going to shoot him on the spot.*

Orry's face said he would like to do exactly that. George knew that what he had asked ran counter to everything Orry had been taught, everything he was. Suddenly Orry slashed the air with the pistol, a gesture of rage as well as dismissal.

"Run," he said. "Run before I change my mind."

Priam wasted no time on words. His great, liquid eyes flicked over George's for a second—the only thanks George got. He bolted into the pines at the north side of the clearing.

Orry walked away, then halted, head down. Priam's footfalls faded. From the other direction George heard the whistle of the approaching passenger local.

George took a breath and moved toward his friend. "I know I

shouldn't have asked you to let him go. I know he's your property. But I just couldn't stand by and let—''

He stopped. Orry was still standing with his back turned.

"Well, in any case, thank you."

Orry spun around. He held the pistol so tightly his hand was white as flour. George expected him to shout, but his voice was pitched low.

"Once before, I tried to explain the nature of things in the South. I told you we understand our own problems, our own needs, better than outsiders do. I told you we'd eventually solve those problems— so long as outsiders didn't interfere. I reckon all of that made no impression. Otherwise you wouldn't have asked me to let Priam go. I honored your request because we've been friends a long time. But if you want us to continue to be friends, don't ever ask me to do something like that again.''

George felt a flash of anger, but it was quickly gone. Orry's quiet ferocity impressed him and made the terms of their future relationship absolutely clear.

"Agreed," George said. "I understand your feelings."

"I hope so."

Orry tucked his pistol under his arm and dug into his pocket for his watch. By the time the local came steaming up to the way station, he was calm enough to discuss other subjects.

"I'm sorry your visit fell at a time when everything seemed to go wrong around here." Orry's eyes were less severe now. He held out a verbal olive branch. "Next time you come, it'll be different. Until then, I'm eager to stand up with you when you marry Constance. That is, if you still want me to—''

Relieved, George clasped his friend's shoulder. "Of course. I'll write you with a date and particulars as soon as I have them."

"Good. Safe journey—and say hello to your family."

"I will, Orry. Thank you."

The conductor called for him to board. Soon George was standing on the train platform, waving. Orry waved back, the gun still in his hand. Steam and smoke and the forest closed in. Orry disappeared from sight.

George stowed his valise inside the coach and sat staring out the window at the pines shuttling by. Occasional breaks in the trees revealed vistas of marshland. But the image that stayed with him was something quite different. He kept seeing Priam at the moment he was dragged from the boxcar, the knowledge of his own death showing in his eyes.

Priam had to be punished for wanting liberty, the same liberty Orry enjoyed because he was a white man. George had never considered himself a partisan of the Negro race, but he guessed he was now, especially in the matter of freedom. Why weren't all men entitled to it? Especially in America?

He hoped Orry was right about the South's eventually solving its own problems. If the South did not, the rest of the nation would surely take action. He not only grasped that for the very first time, he also grasped the reason.

15

At Resolute several days later, Madeline stood in the shadows in her dressing room and touched herself. She hurt. Not from physical pain. From loneliness. A lack of love. A growing sense of isolation.

She clasped her hands over her breasts as if she could end the pain that way. She stood a moment with her head back and her eyes closed, but it did no good. Despondent, she walked through the spacious bedroom to the second-floor piazza, where she shivered in the coolness of the dusk. From the kitchen building rose the rich smell of game birds roasting for Saturday dinner. Tomorrow *was* Saturday, wasn't it? The days had little meaning any longer. Each one was like another: a trial.

How she wished Maum Sally were still with her. But the old woman had gone back to New Orleans to attend Madeline's father in his last days. Being Nicholas Fabray's free employee rather than his slave, Sally had chosen not to return to South Carolina after Fabray died. Madeline could certainly understand the decision; a few months of the LaMottes were all Sally could take. She had no patience with anyone who was arrogant or unkind, and Justin and most of his family were both.

Madeline had found one person who might someday take Maum Sally's place. Nancy was a house girl, a beautiful yellow mulatto in her early twenties. She and Madeline got along well and had become confidantes of a sort. Twice Nancy had brought Madeline a verbal message from Mont Royal.

Both times the message was short: "Salvation Chapel," then a day and a time. No names were spoken, and there was no trace of a sly smile in Nancy's eyes when she delivered each message. If anything, her gaze expressed sympathy, understanding.

Madeline never asked how the message passed from the slaves of one plantation to those of another, and she took the discretion of the messengers on faith. What other choice did she have? Her acceptance of Nancy's role as intermediary had built a bridge of trust between the two of them.

Madeline had never answered either message—or gone to the chapel, though she literally ached to go, to be with Orry and hold and kiss him. Now, leaning on the rail of the piazza, she realized she could hear no conversation from the kitchen, even though the slaves were at work there. She wondered about the peculiar silence. Then she heard a sound in the plantation office—the small building in which Justin spent so little time. The sound was the smack of leather on a bare back.

Clearly in the evening stillness there came another sound. A groan. Justin was thrashing one of the bucks. It had happened before.

Repelled yet irresistibly drawn, she slipped downstairs and through the foyer, where an old, dented saber decorated the wall. The sword had belonged to the LaMottes for several generations. Justin said an ancestor had wielded it when he fought beside Gamecock Sumter in the Revolution.

She ran along a path that would bring her to some shrubbery near the office. As she slipped behind the shrubbery there were more blows, more outcries. Then Justin's hoarse voice:

"My brother said for a fact that on the night Main's nigger ran away, someone on this plantation helped him hide out. Who was it, Ezekiel? Tell me."

"Don't know, Mr. LaMotte. Swear to God I don't."

"Liar." Justin struck again. Ezekiel wailed.

Madeline held still, a shadow in deeper shadow. She was alarmed to learn that Justin was asking about the slave Priam. How had Francis LaMotte discovered that someone at Resolute had aided the runaway? Was it certain knowledge or merely a suspicion? How far would Justin's investigation reach? All the way into the house? All the way to Nancy?

Madeline knew she didn't dare linger here. If anyone discovered her, she would be suspect. But there was a small pergola not far from the office, and she could sit inside as if taking the air. On a windless evening such as this, she might with luck hear more of what transpired in the office.

She hid herself in the pergola and was rewarded. During the next three-quarters of an hour, Justin continued to interrogate various slaves, laying a few blows on each. What infuriated Madeline was her husband's interrogation of some of the wenches. He beat them as hard as he beat the men. Over and over he asked the same questions.

"Who did it? Who helped him? Who had sympathy for a runaway nigger? Tell me, Clyta."

Clyta? Madeline sat up as if struck. Her mind had been wandering. There was only one Clyta at Resolute, a single girl of eighteen. Madeline suspected Justin had slept with her a few times. She was carrying a child. Even as she remembered that, she heard Justin hit the girl again. Clyta yelped in pain.

"Who did it?" he shouted. Madeline's nails dug into her palms. The escaped slave had carried the answer to that question until a patrol picked him up a few miles this side of the North Carolina border. Priam had put up a fight and been mortally wounded by a patrolman's pistol. The name of his secret benefactor had died with him.

Madeline was freezing now. Her breath clouded in the air when she exhaled. Justin repeated the question at full voice. Then came another blow and a scream. Madeline dug her fingers deeper, till they cut like tiny knives.

Who did it, Justin? Your wife. It was your wife whom Nancy summoned the night Priam showed up, frightened and hungry. I'm the one who slipped out to help him. You were oblivious. Off with one of your horses or one of your slave sluts—as usual. I'm the one who helped him, you scum. I'm the one with the peculiar sympathy for niggers.

She didn't quite have the courage to rush to the office and say all of it directly to him. She was ashamed of that lack within herself. She fled from the pergola, covering her ears to blot out the sound of Clyta's cries.

Most of the time Justin occupied a separate bedroom, coming to hers only when he felt the urge to rut. She was thankful he let her alone tonight. What she had heard in the pergola left her too upset to sleep. She was filled with a desire to revenge herself on her husband again. Revenge had been part of the reason she had gladly lent assistance when Nancy appealed to her about the runaway hiding in the loft of the sick house.

Presently she calmed down a little, and thoughts of Orry crept into her mind. People said he was a changed man because he had lost his arm in Mexico. They said his frame of mind was dark, embittered. Yet he had twice sent a message asking her to meet him secretly.

Still a creature of her past—still clinging to the remains of the code of right behavior that had once held absolute sway in her life—she had answered neither message. As if Justin deserved that kind of consideration! She slipped her hands downward, trying to suppress what she felt within herself. She couldn't. She would call on Clarissa Main after dinner tomorrow. Justin wouldn't go with her, of course;

the mention of most social amenities started him yawning. When she visited the Main plantation, she would send a message of her own.

Why had she waited this long? Why had she refused to allow herself even a moment's happiness? Her misguided fear of Orry's youth, her own strong conscience, the secret her father had conveyed as he breathed his last—those were the most compelling reasons. None seemed to matter any longer. She prayed Orry wouldn't be so angry over her earlier rebuffs that he refused to answer now.

In the morning, before daylight, she went to the kitchen in her robe. As she had hoped, she found Nancy there, alone, tending the plump turkeys by the light of a lamp trimmed low.

"We're going to Mont Royal this afternoon, Nancy."

"Yes, ma'am."

Madeline was so pleased, so full of anticipation, that she didn't stop to ask herself why Nancy had such a grave, drawn look. "Can you deliver a message there, by the same route the others came to me?"

Nancy's eyes opened a little wider. "A message to the gentleman?"

"That's right. It's to be our secret."

"Yes'm. Surely."

"Nancy, what's wrong?"

The mulatto girl eyed the huge iron stove giving off savory odors. Madeline touched Nancy's thin arm. Her skin was cold.

"Tell me."

"It's Clyta, ma'am. After Mr. Justin beat her last night, she lost her baby."

"Oh, no. Oh, Nancy," Madeline said, taking the girl in her arms to comfort her.

Tears spilled down Madeline's face, but there were none inside her as she thought of her husband. Scum. *Scum.*

Orry rode hatless to Salvation Chapel, even though drab skies hinted of rain. It began to fall during the last half mile. Not a hard rain but a chilling one. Winter rain: the signal that another growing season was over and Charleston's high social season would soon begin.

Nothing could lower Orry's spirits this morning. He ducked beneath the last overhanging branches. The fallen foundation came into sight. Beyond, fog hid most of the marsh. He called Madeline's name. "Here, my darling."

The voice came from his left. As she had the first time, she'd

234

sought shelter under the trees near the perimeter of the marsh. He sprang down and tethered his horse, then hurried to her.

He took hold of her left shoulder. She reached for his other arm, turning red as she realized her thoughtlessness. A sudden grin flashed like a beacon in the dark mass of his beard.

"You'll get used to its not being there. I have, almost."

The smile disappeared as he curved his arm around her. He pulled her to him, wanting to experience every soft contour, yet mindful of his own long-repressed need. She felt him through the layers of her clothing. She moved closer, uttering a small sound deep in her throat.

She rested against his chest. He stroked her hair. "I thought you never wanted to see me again."

"Because I didn't answer those messages? I didn't dare." She drew back. "I shouldn't be here now. I love you too much."

"Then go away with me."

"Where?"

"Anywhere."

There was great relief in being able to say that at last. In response, Madeline smiled and wept at the same time. She stood on tiptoe to kiss him, her palms pressed against his bristly face.

"I'd give my soul to do that. I can't."

"Why not? Surely you don't think all that much of Justin."

"I loathe him. I've only just discovered how much. That's why I called on your mother on Saturday. I couldn't stand being separated from you any longer. I want you to tell me all about Mexico." She was stroking his face now, her fingers lingering at each place she touched. "How you got hurt. How you're getting along—"

"I'd get along much better if we were together."

"Orry, it's impossible."

"Because of Justin."

"Not him personally. Because of what I pledged when I married him. I made a lifetime promise. If I broke it—went away with you— I'd feel guilty forever. Guilt would ruin our lives."

"There's no guilt in meeting me like this?"

"Of course there is. But it's—bearable. I can convince myself that I'm still living up to the letter of the marriage agreement."

Suspicion overcame him. She wasn't being entirely truthful. She had some other reason for saying no. Then he decided he was only imagining that, perhaps to take some of the sting out of the refusal.

She whirled away, walking rapidly to the edge of the marsh. "You probably think I'm a wretched hypocrite."

From behind he touched her hair, lifted it so that he could gently kiss the curve of her neck below her ear. "I think I love you, that's all. I want you with me for the rest of our days."

"I feel the same way, darling. But you have responsibilities, too. No matter what you say, I don't think you could run from them and be happy."

He tried to redirect the conversation, to give them both breathing space. "I'd be happy if my father came to his senses. Did you know he exhibited the body of Priam, the runaway, as an example to our people?"

"No, I didn't." She rubbed her arms, not looking at him. "That's vile."

"Unnecessary, certainly. Our people understood the meaning of Priam's death long before they saw his corpse lying in ice. Sometimes I think my father's already senile. Or maybe the damned abolitionists drive him to it. He's a proud man. He can be defiant."

"It seems to be a local characteristic," she said with a wry smile.

He found it impossible to go on speaking as if they were acquaintances meeting in a parlor. The physical hunger was too strong, almost painful. He faced her, gazing down into her eyes.

"No more talk. What I want is you. Come—please—"

He took her hand and with unmistakable meaning drew her toward a level place where the leaves and pine needles looked dry.

"No, Orry." When she wrenched free, anger brimmed in his eyes.

She flung herself against him, her arms around his chest. "Don't you see we mustn't go that far? Ever? If we do, the guilt will be almost as bad as if we had run away."

Roughly now, he handled her hair, kissed her eyes and the moist, warm corners of her mouth. "You want to make love, you can't deny it." He slipped his arm below her waist, astonished at his own boldness. But fevers were consuming him, and it seemed perfectly natural to pull her hips against his and kiss her again. "You can't."

"No. I ache for you to hold me that way. But we mustn't."

He released her. "I don't understand you."

A strand of glossy black hair had fallen across her forehead. She dashed it back, then smiled again, sadly.

"How can you expect to when I don't completely understand myself? What person ever does? I only know that a small amount of guilt is bearable, but more is not."

Orry's face grew bleak again. The tension he had communicated through their embrace was diminishing. "If we can't live together or love each other properly, what's left?"

"We can—" She drew a breath, facing down his scorn. Her voice strengthened. "We can still meet here occasionally. Talk. Hold each other for a little while. It would make my life endurable, at least."

"It's still infidelity, Madeline."

"But not adultery."

"I thought they meant the same thing."

"Not to me."

"Well, it's a subtle distinction. I doubt it's one outsiders would appreciate."

"I can't help it. Is love ever comprehensible to others?"

He pressed his lips together and, with a sharp shake of his head, strode off toward the marsh, out from under the trees into the light rain. She was proposing an affair but under rules of her own design.

He walked as far as he could, stopping when the ground grew mushy beneath his boots. His long strides left reeds trampled behind him. He turned, rain collecting in his beard. "Those are hard terms. I want you too much. I'm not sure I can stand constant temptation."

"Isn't a little love better than none?"

He almost blurted a no. She walked toward him slowly, the rain ruining her clothes and flattening her hair against her head. Even bedraggled, she was the loveliest woman in creation. He couldn't deny her, even though her terms were nearly as painful as the situation that prompted them.

She stood close to him, gazing into his eyes. "Isn't it, Orry?"

He smiled but without real joy. "Yes."

She let out a small cry and once more crushed against him. He put his arm around her, his smile hollow. "God, I wish you'd been raised a slut instead of a decent woman."

"Sometimes I do too."

The shared laughter eased their unhappiness. They returned to the trees and sat talking for almost an hour. He pointed out that the more often they met the greater became the risk of discovery. She said she willingly accepted that risk. They kissed and embraced again.

Before she started home, they made plans in a few breathless sentences for their next rendezvous. Orry thought he must be mad to agree to such an arrangement. Denial of their mutual hunger brought excruciating physical and mental tension. He knew the tension would grow worse as they continued to meet.

And yet, as he stood by the chapel foundation and watched her ride away, his mood changed. Although the tension remained, in some curious way the self-denial began to enhance and deepen his longing and his love.

16

All the way north, George was haunted by the image of Priam's eyes. He still saw it now, as he sat with his chin in his palm and gazed out the coach window at the Delaware River.

Snow fell in the dreary twilight, melting the moment it struck the ground or the glass. He was worn out from the long trip with its seemingly endless succession of changes from one line to another. A meal in a depot dining room had upset his stomach, and for the last hundred miles he had sweltered because other passengers insisted the conductor keep throwing wood into the stove at the head of the car.

At least he would be in Lehigh Station tomorrow. He planned to stop overnight at the Haverford House, where the Hazards always stayed in Philadelphia. In the morning he would catch the local and, once home, begin the delicate job of preparing his family for his marriage to a Catholic.

The memory of Priam returned. It led to thoughts of his relationship with Orry—and, by extension, Orry's family. George could find something to like about every one of them, even feckless Cousin Charles, but that liking generated a familiar confusion and a good deal of guilt. By a combination of circumstances and choice, the Mains were deeply involved in Negro slavery.

The train slowed, chugging past shanties and dilapidated buildings before it pulled into the station. The roof over the platforms shut out most of the daylight. Instead of snowflakes, sparks from the engine swirled past the window. Passengers rose, gathering their belongings. Their reflections shimmered in the sooty glass. But George saw Priam.

Slavery had to end. His stop in South Carolina had convinced him. The goal wouldn't be easily reached. Too many obstacles stood in the way. Tradition. Pride. Economic dependence on the system. The disproportionately large influence of the small number of families who owned most of the slaves. Even the Bible. Just before George had left the plantation, Tillet had quoted Scripture to justify sending a patrol after Priam. The runaway had clearly disobeyed the charge in the third chapter of Colossians: "Servants, obey in all things your master . . ."

Dismantling the peculiar institution would require flexibility, good will, and, most of all, determination to see it done. George saw none of those things at Mont Royal.

He turned the problem the other way around for a moment, considering his friendship with Orry as something that had to be preserved. There, too, serious difficulties loomed. When he had pleaded for Priam's freedom, Orry's warning had been clear. He mustn't interfere again if he expected the friendship to continue.

Yet how strong was friendship? Could it banish disagreement over a fundamental issue of human liberty—as if the issue and the disagreement didn't exist? Could friendship even survive in an atmosphere of growing sectional tension?

Orry said it would—if the slavery issue was ignored. But old Calhoun, sick and embittered, had indirectly suggested that it could not when he declared that separation was the sole remaining answer.

If a solution was to be found, George believed the burden for finding it rested largely on people such as the Mains. If the South was not solely responsible for creating the problem, the South had preserved it and the South must take steps to solve it. George held the North blameless and free of responsibility in the whole matter. At least that was his opinion as he trudged up the platform with his valise.

Fortunately the Haverford House was able to accommodate him without a reservation. He was signing the ledger when the unctuous clerk began, "I believe we have another guest from—"

"George, is that you?"

The voice behind him overlapped the clerk's. "—your family." He turned, then grinned at the young woman hurrying toward him, diamonds of melted snow shining on her muff and the fur trim of her hat.

"Virgilia. Good Lord. I didn't expect to see you."

She was flushed with excitement, and for a moment her squarish face looked almost pretty. In his absence her waist had grown thicker, he noticed.

"I booked a room because I'm staying in the city tonight," she said in a breathless way.

"By yourself? Whatever for?"

"I'm giving my first address at a public meeting sponsored by the society."

He shook his head. "I'm lost. What society?"

"The anti-slavery society, of course. Oh, George, I'm so nervous—

240

I've spent weeks writing and memorizing the speech." She caught his hands in hers; how cold and hard her fingers felt. Almost like a man's. "I completely forgot you were due back today or tomorrow. You must come and hear me! All the tickets were gone weeks ago, but I'm sure we can squeeze you into a box."

"I'll be happy to come. I'm not going home till morning."

"Oh, that's glorious. Do you want to eat first? I can't, I'm too wrought-up. George, I've finally found a cause to which I can devote all my energy."

"I'm glad to hear that," he said as they walked to the staircase behind the hotel porter who had picked up George's luggage. *You found a cause because you couldn't find a beau.*

Silently he chastised himself for the unkindness. He and Virgilia had never been close, but she was still his sister. He was tired and perhaps a little put off by her enthusiasm.

"It's a very worthy cause, too, though I doubt Orry Main would think so. Honestly, I don't know how you can associate with such people."

"Orry's my friend. Let's leave him out of our discussions, shall we?"

"But that's impossible. He owns Negro slaves."

George held back a harsh retort and thought about begging off for the rest of the evening. Later he wished he had.

The hall held about two thousand people. Every seat was filled. Men and women were standing in the side aisles and at the rear. There were children present and a few well-dressed blacks. Lamps throughout the hall shed a smoky, sulfurous light.

George was squeezed into a chair at the back of the second-tier box at stage right. Three men and three women sat in front of him, all in formal attire. When he introduced himself, their greeting was brief and reserved. He suspected they were members of Philadelphia society.

Although it was quite cold outside—the temperature had plummeted while he was eating dinner—the press of human bodies in heavy clothing made the auditorium hot and put a sheen of sweat on every face. Even before the start of the formal program the audience was in a frenzy, stomping and clapping during the singing of several hymns.

George squinted at the handbill given him when he entered the box. He sighed. The program was divided into nine sections. A long evening.

Loud applause greeted the half-dozen speakers when they appeared from the wings. Virgilia looked poised and calm as she walked to the row of chairs set in front of a vivid red velvet drop. She took the third chair from the left and looked up at her brother. He nodded and smiled. The chairman, a Methodist clergyman, approached the podium and rapped the gavel for order. The program opened with a singing group, the Hutchinson Family of New Hampshire. They were received with loud applause as they took their positions to the right of the podium.

Hutchinson Senior introduced the group as "members of the tribe of Jesse and friends of equal rights." This produced more cheering, clapping, and stomping. The group was apparently well known in anti-slavery circles, though George had never heard of them. He was surprised and a bit dismayed by the fervor of the audience. He hadn't realized Pennsylvania abolitionists could be so emotional. It added to his understanding of the issue responsible for this gathering.

The Hutchinsons sang five songs. A piano and cello accompanied them from the pit. Their last number was a stirring anthem that concluded:

> *"Ho, the car emancipation*
> *Rides majestic through the nation.*
> *Bearing on its train the story—*
> *Liberty, our nation's glory!*
> *Roll it along—roll it along*
> *Through the nation,*
> *Freedom's car—Emancipation!"*

Men and women leaped to their feet, applauding. The enthusiastic audience held the Hutchinsons onstage and kept them bowing for more than three minutes. Virgilia's cheeks looked bright and moist as she smiled up at the box again.

The first address, ten minutes, was delivered by another clergyman, this one from New York City. He explained and endorsed the anti-slavery position of the noted Unitarian divine, William Ellery Channing of Boston. According to Channing, slavery could best be overcome by a direct and continuing appeal to the Christian principles of the slave owners. It was a conclusion not unlike the one George had reached on the train. Tonight he put the theory alongside a mental portrait of Tillet Main and got a shock. He knew Channing's plan would never work.

It wasn't popular with the audience, either. The cleric sat down to just a spattering of applause.

The second speaker received a much bigger hand. He was a tall, grizzled black man introduced as Daniel Phelps, a former slave who had escaped across the Ohio River and now devoted himself to lecturing about his days of bondage in Kentucky. Phelps was an effective orator. His fourteen-minute address, whether true in every detail or not, wrung the last drop of emotion from the audience. His gruesome anecdotes of beatings and torture carried out by his owner brought men to their feet with howls of rage. When Phelps finished, he received a standing ovation.

Virgilia fidgeted with a handkerchief while the chairman introduced her. He put extra emphasis on her last name. Murmurs in the hall showed that some had recognized the name of the well-known family of ironmasters. One of the women in the box turned to give George a quick reappraisal. He felt better, less of a nonentity.

Virgilia continued to display nervousness as she walked to the podium. The poor girl really was too buxom, George thought; unattractive, almost. But perhaps some man would be taken with her intelligence. For her sake, he hoped so.

At first Virgilia spoke hesitantly, offering the audience nothing more than a standard denunciation of slavery. But four or five minutes into her address, the direction of it changed. The audience's nervous foot shuffling stopped, and from the first row to the highest perch in the gallery, every eye was fixed on her.

"I am loath to speak of such things with members of the fair sex and small children present. But it has been said that truth is not and never can be impure. So we must not shrink from examining every facet of the South's peculiar institution, no matter how distasteful— no matter how immoral."

The hall was hushed. The audience sensed that Virgilia was skillfully blending wrath with titillation. The men and women in front of George strained forward to hear. He gazed out across the crowd, unsettled by the sight of so many sweaty faces bearing expressions of righteous zeal. What unsettled him most was his own sister. She gripped the sides of the podium and lost all her hesitancy, and even some of her coherence, as she went on:

"Whatever civility, whatever pretenses of refinement exist in the South—these are built upon a rotten foundation. A foundation which flouts the most fundamental laws of man and God. The South's hateful system of free labor depends upon the perpetuation of its free labor *force*. And where do new laborers come from when older ones drop by the wayside, exhausted by cruel toil or killed by repressive discipline? The new laborers come from those very same plantations. For their true crop is a human crop."

A shiver and a thrilled sigh swept through the hall as the audience realized what she meant. One woman rose in the gallery and dragged her small daughter toward the exit. Many around her scowled and hissed for silence.

"The plantations of the South are nothing less than black breeding farms. Gigantic bordellos, sanctioned, maintained, and perpetuated by a degenerate aristocracy which rides roughshod over the Christian beliefs of the few—the very few—Southern yeomen whose voices cry out in faint futile protest against these crazed satyrs—this godless immorality!"

Degenerate aristocrats? Crazed satyrs? Black breeding farms? George sat dry-mouthed, unable to believe what he was hearing. Virgilia tarred all Southerners with the same brush, but her accusations simply didn't apply to the Mains. Not unless he was an imbecile and had been deliberately hoodwinked at Mont Royal. There were a great many evils in the peculiar institution, but he had seen no evidence of the one Virgilia described.

What horrified him most was the crowd's reaction. They believed every word. They wanted to believe. Like a good actress, Virgilia sensed this eagerness flowing like a current across the footlight candles, and she responded to it. She glided out from behind the podium to let them see more of her. Let them see her righteous frenzy, her flaming glance and trembling hands, clenched white in wrath, which she brought to her breasts.

"The very stones cry out against such wickedness. Every upright human heart proclaims in moral outrage—no. No! *No!*" She flung her head back and struck her bosom each time she uttered the word. A man in the gallery picked up the chant. Soon the whole hall rang with it:

"No! No! NO! NO!"

Gradually the tumult subsided. Virgilia reached to the podium for support. Her breasts rose and fell. Patches of sweat showed on her clothing as she struggled to remember her place in the text. Short of breath, she rushed on to her conclusion, but George paid little attention to the words. He was appalled by her wild statements—and the crowd's instantaneous acceptance of them.

Clearly his sister had found an outlet for long-submerged emotions. There was something indecent about watching her display them before hundreds of observers. Her language was sexual, her style almost orgiastic, as she proclaimed that morality demanded action against black breeding farms:

"They must be burned. Destroyed. Obliterated! And their owners with them!"

He jumped up and left the box, overturning his chair in his haste. He ran down flights of stairs, desperately eager for a breath of cold, pure air. As he reached the main floor, he sensed the auditorium walls shaking from the clapping and foot pounding that greeted the end of the speech. From the rear he looked inside.

The entire audience was on its feet. Onstage, Virgilia stood with her head thrown back. Her exertions had loosened her hair and disarrayed her clothing, but she was unconcerned. Her face shone with a dreamy exaltation, with fulfillment. He turned away, sickened.

Once outside, he gulped air and relished the falling snow. He would have to tell her she had spoken effectively, of course. But he also intended to take issue with her unfounded generalizations.

Her performance deeply offended him, not only on intellectual grounds but on personal ones. It was true that Virgilia was a grown woman in charge of her own life. Nevertheless, to see his sister or any other female display herself so shamelessly made him cringe. No matter what its veneer of propriety, her speech had been an outpouring of sexual passion. It had permitted her to say things no woman—no man, for that matter—would have dared to say in public in another context.

What dismayed him most was his feeling that Virgilia had reveled in the experience—and not solely for the moralistic reasons she proclaimed.

But even if he put aside the personal considerations, the shouts and halloos within the hall continued to upset him. They showed him a dimension of the slavery quarrel whose existence he had never before suspected. No matter how worthy Virgilia's cause, she had somehow twisted it; an appeal for justice was transformed into a sordid, even frightening call for a savage holy war. There were warriors aplenty inside. He could still hear them howling for Southern blood.

On the train he had decided that all the sin lay on the Southern side, the side of the slave owners, and all the destructive pride as well. Tonight had taught him a fearful lesson. He was wrong.

In an hour he had changed his view of Northern abolitionists, for Virgilia had surely taken her cue from other members of the movement. How many of them were more interested in confrontation than in resolution of the problem? How many preached hate instead of common sense? He didn't condone slavery or excuse the Mains because of what he had witnessed tonight. But for the first time he believed there might be some cause for the Mains' resentment—just as they claimed.

Could the friendship of men from different regions, a camaraderie born in shared hardships, endure such terrible pressures? Was there enough good will in humankind and the nation to overcome the kind of mindless passions he had seen unleashed by his sister?

He shivered as wind-driven snow flew at him beneath the marquee of the auditorium. The storm was intensifying, hiding the nearby lights of the town. He began to perceive a future much grimmer than any he had heretofore imagined. He had a brief, dark vision of the country hammered by the slave question until it shattered like brittle cast iron.

Difficult times surely lay ahead. Constance would help sustain him during those times, and he hoped his love would do the same for her. But as for the nation surviving the hammering—finding the flexibility and compassion necessary to resolve the issue—he just didn't know about that.

Until this moment, he supposed, he had lived with illusion or ignorance. Now, huddled against the wall beneath the marquee and unable to light his cigar in the rising wind, he was staring at reality.

It terrified him.

A Lehigh Canal boat carried George on the last stage of his journey. The canal followed the course of the river through the valley, from Mauch Chunk down to Easton. The Grand Valley of the Lehigh had been home to four generations of Hazards. George's great-grandfather had left a job at a forge in the Pine Barrens of New Jersey, then the leading ironworking region of the colonies, to strike out on his own in Pennsylvania.

The valley had no huge natural deposits similar to the bog ore of Jersey. Nor was there as much flux as the Pine Barrens men took from nearby salt bays in the form of clay and oyster shells. But George's great-grandfather did find great stands of timber for conversion to charcoal. He found water power. Most important of all, he found opportunity.

For years his was the only furnace on the river. Ore had to be brought over the mountains in leather bags carried by pack horses, but that didn't deter him. The same transportation system had served furnaces in Jersey for a long time.

Competitors said he was crazy not to move to the Schuylkill River valley, but George's great-grandfather paid no attention and persevered. In the valley of the Lehigh he was his own master, succeeding or failing solely on the basis of his own decisions.

During the Revolution the Hazards threw everything into the war effort and almost went to the wall financially. Luckily the rebels won, and the continuity of the line was not abruptly ended by a hang rope. But unqualified success continued to prove elusive.

Year after year the Hazards were forced to ship their iron down the river to the Delaware in antiquated Durham boats that were forever incurring damage on the rocks of the Lehigh rapids. Then, in 1829, the canal opened. A local man, Josiah White, had developed it principally to ship anthracite coal that had been discovered in the region. But the canal boats brought prosperity to almost every business in the valley, and Hazard Iron was no exception. For a century, products of the ironworks had provided the family with a steady if unremarkable income. Suddenly, thanks to the canal, many more markets were within reach, and in one generation, that of George's father, the Hazards were rich.

George had grown up with the canal. The shouts of the boatmen and the occasional bray of a balky towpath mule were essential parts of his boyhood experience. Now men said the canal era was already passing. It had lasted scarcely thirty years, another dizzying proof of how fast the new, machine-driven world was changing. Evidently William Hazard had believed the predictions about canals. Otherwise he wouldn't have gone into the production of rails.

The boat stopped for half an hour at the expanding town of Bethlehem, which had been settled by members of the Moravian church from Bohemia. A few miles beyond Bethlehem, the skyline of the South Mountains began to take on a familiar aspect. It was a blustery, dark day. All the other passengers stayed below, but George stood on the roof promenade of the main cabin, reveling in the sights of home.

Under racing gray clouds, the low, rounded peaks looked almost black. The mountain laurel that covered them was dormant now. But in the spring, on all the hillsides, there would be pink and white flowers by the thousands. And the blooms would be found in every room of the Hazard house. George's mother had a special, almost religious regard for the mountain laurel. She said the shrub was like the Hazard family. It often took root in rocky, unpromising ground, but it survived and thrived where other plants could not. She had transmitted that special feeling to George, much as his father had passed along his beliefs about the power of iron.

The canal boat proceeded around a long bend, gradually bringing into view the small town of Lehigh Station and, adjacent to it on the upstream side, the sprawl of Hazard Iron.

Nearest the river in the town stood several crowded blocks of poor cottages. This was the section inhabited by the growing population of Irishmen, Welshmen, and Hungarians who migrated up the river to fill the new jobs created by Hazard's expanding product line. More and more cast iron was being used for construction in the large cities. There was a mania for cast-iron pillars and elaborate cast-iron cornices; even complete fronts of buildings were being manufactured. And of course Hazard's now produced rails.

On the hillsides above the workers' hovels rose the larger frame or brick residences of the town's mercantile community, as well as homes belonging to foremen and supervisors at the ironworks. And highest of all, on a huge parcel of ground terraced out of the mountain, there stood the house in which George had been born.

He loved the house because it was home, but he despised its actual appearance. The first part of it had been built a hundred years ago; that section had long ago vanished within various remodelings, each of a different architectural period or style. The house had thirty or forty rooms, but it had no unity, no name, and in his opinion no character.

The dominant features of the Hazard Iron complex were the three furnaces, truncated cones of stone forty feet high. From the top of each, a wooden bridge crossed to the side of the mountain. Two of the furnaces were in operation. George could see the cumbersome movement of the bellows pumping in hot blasts of air and hear the noisy steam engines that powered the bellows. The furnaces spewed smoke, blackening the already murky sky. Charcoal was a dirty fuel and an outdated one.

On the bridge of the third furnace, workmen pushing handcarts crossed from the mountainside. They dumped the contents of the carts down the charging hole, then returned to the other end of the bridge for the next load. Surely some better method of moving ore, fuel, and flux could be devised. A system of steam-driven conveyors, maybe. His brother Stanley would probably want every other furnace in the state to install such a system before he would consider making it a permanent improvement.

The wrought-iron finery looked busy too. George had forgotten how big Hazard's had become—especially with the addition of a good-sized building he hadn't seen before. It adjoined the plate-rolling mill. It was the rail mill, he assumed.

Hazard Iron was a noisy, bustling, unclean operation. Its great slag heaps and charcoal piles disfigured the landscape. The smoke was an abomination, and the heat and din could be infernal. But it became more apparent each day that America was running and growing because of iron and the men who knew how to produce it. The business had gotten into the marrow of George's bones, and it took this homecoming to make him realize it.

How would Constance take to it? Would she be happy here, married to an ironmaster and living in an unfamiliar place? He vowed to do everything possible to make her happy, but how she got along in Lehigh Station was not entirely up to him. That worried him.

He was glad that some business of the anti-slavery society had kept Virgilia in the city so that he could come home alone and slip gradually into his old life, with all its joys. And its sorrows. His father was gone. He felt guilty because, for a little while, overwhelmed by familiar sights, he had actually forgotten his father. He needed to make amends, and say good-bye.

A spectacular sunset lit the marble obelisk with the words WILLIAM HAZARD carved in its base. George uncovered his eyes, gave a last adjustment to the black wreath he had laid, and rose.

He dusted his knees as his mother approached. She had come with him to the graveyard in the hard, bright light of the winter afternoon. But she had remained several yards away while he silently said his farewell.

They walked down a precipitous path toward the waiting carriage. George had been home only a few hours, but Maude Hazard was already bubbling with plans for the wedding.

"It's a tragedy your father couldn't have lived long enough to meet Constance," she said.

"Do you think he would have approved of her?"

Maude sighed, her breath pluming. "Probably not. But we'll make her welcome. I promise."

"Will Stanley make her welcome?" His tone expressed skepticism.

"George"—she faced him—"you already know that some will hate you for the step you've taken. The Irish are a despised lot, though I don't quite understand why. You, however, are obviously very realistic, and I admire that. I admire you for your willingness to face up to the hate you may encounter."

"I hadn't thought of it in those terms, Mother. I love Constance."

"I know, but there is still a great deal of un-Christian hate in the world. Love will somehow defeat it. It will and, if we're all to survive, it must."

He thought of Elkanah Bent, Tillet Main, and his own sister. He could believe in *must*. But *will?* He had great doubts about that.

BOOK TWO

FRIENDS AND ENEMIES

*Human beings may be inconsistent,
but human nature is true to herself.
She has uttered her testimony
against slavery with a shriek ever
since the monster was begotten; and
till it perishes amidst the execrations
of the universe, she will traverse
the world on its track, dealing her
bolts upon its head, and dashing
against it her condemning brand.*

THEODORE DWIGHT WELD,
American Slavery As It Is
1839

17

George was ceremoniously welcomed home with a Christmas party. It gave him a chance to observe all the changes that had taken place in the family in a relatively short time. Some he found quite surprising.

His brother Billy, for example, looked and acted grown-up at twelve. His face had filled out, taking on the broad, sturdy appearance common to adult males of the family—Stanley excepted. Billy's brown hair was darker than George's, his blue eyes less pale and forbidding. He had an appealing smile, but there was no sign of it while he asked sober, intelligent questions about the war. Who was the better general, Taylor or Scott? How did the American and Mexican armies compare? What did George think of Santa Anna?

Billy couldn't be as serious as he seemed, George thought. But then, he recalled being pretty serious about some of the scrapes he'd gotten into when he was Billy's age. Some of them had involved young women. Was Billy similarly entangled? If so, George disapproved.

Then he laughed at himself. He had changed along with the rest of the Hazards.

Virgilia chattered constantly about the anti-slavery movement, which she referred to as her work. She had become not only fanatical about it but self-important. Naturally George didn't say that aloud, but neither did he conceal his anger when he told everyone that Orry would be his best man and Virgilia replied by saying, "Oh, yes— your slave-owner friend. Well, George, be warned. I shan't smile and fawn over someone like that."

It threatened to be a wretched wedding. Virgilia was apparently determined to spoil Orry's visit; and Stanley's new wife made several cool and sarcastic references to Constance Flynn's religion, as well as to the site of the ceremony—the tiny and unprepossessing Catholic chapel down by the canal.

Stanley had married a little more than a year ago, while George was on his way to Mexico. Isabel Truscott Hazard was twenty-eight, two years older than her husband. She came of a family that claimed its founder had been a colleague and friend of William Penn's. Although she had been occupied with a pregnancy during most of her first year in Lehigh Station, her husband's last name and her own ambitious nature had established her as a social leader of the community.

George tried to like Isabel. The effort lasted about five minutes. She was homely as a horse, which wouldn't have mattered if she had been intelligent or gracious. Instead, she openly bragged about never reading anything except social columns.

George could have pitied her, but why bother? She thought of herself as perfect. She also had that opinion of her home, her wardrobe, her taste in furnishings, and her twin sons, born almost nine months to the day after her wedding. She had already informed Stanley that she would bear no more children, having found the entire procedure distasteful.

With great pride, George showed the family a little daguerreotype of Constance. A few minutes later, while a footman served rum punch, Isabel remarked to him, "Miss Flynn is quite lovely."

"Thank you. I agree."

"They say that down South men admire physical beauty without, shall we say, substance. I hope your fiancée isn't so naive as to think the same holds true in this part of the country."

George reddened. Evidently Isabel had decided to condemn Constance because she happened to be beautiful.

Maude Hazard didn't like her daughter-in-law's remark. Stanley noticed the instantaneous frown on his mother's face and scowled at Isabel. That silenced her for the evening, though George was sure it wouldn't shut her up for good.

For Christmas the broad white living-room mantel had been decorated with mountain laurel leaves. So had all the doors and windows. On the mantel stood the family's pride, a massive twenty-four-inch-tall goblet blown in the 1790s by the great John Amelung of Maryland. William's father had bought the goblet in a flush time. On the glass the artisan had engraved a shield and an American eagle with spread wings. A ribbon bearing the words *E pluribus unum* fluttered from the eagle's beak. It seemed fitting that, toward the end of the party, Maude should step to the mantel, near this splendid artifact, and there make a short speech to the gathering.

"Now that George is home for good, we must make a change in the management of Hazard's. From now on, Stanley, you and your brother will have equal responsibility for operation of the furnace and the mill. Your time will come eventually, Billy, don't worry."

Stanley struggled to smile, but he looked as if he were sucking a lemon. Maude went on, "With the family expanding, all of us can't possibly continue to live under one roof, so we must make some adjustments there, too. Henceforward, this house will belong to Stanley and Isabel. I'll stay here with you, and for the time being so will Billy and Virgilia."

Her eyes fixed on George. From the mantel she took a folded document he hadn't noticed before. "One of your father's last wishes was to provide you with a home of your own. So for you and your bride—this. It's a deed to a portion of the land on which we're standing. The plot is a large one, right next door. Your father signed this two days before he was stricken. Build a home for Constance and your children, my dear. With our love and best wishes."

Tears welled in George's eyes as he accepted the deed. Billy started the applause. Stanley and Isabel joined in without enthusiasm. George understood the reason for their behavior. Stanley wasn't the sort to share family leadership with a brother he considered inexperienced and reckless.

Constance and her father came north at the end of March, and the young people were married on a mild day in early April. By then George had already been discharging his new responsibilities for three months.

Growing up, he had done odd jobs throughout Hazard Iron. But now he looked at the operation with a manager's eye, not that of a bored boy who wanted to be elsewhere. He roved through the furnace, the finery, and the mill at all hours, getting to know the men and hoping to demonstrate that they could trust him. He asked questions, then listened with total concentration to the answers. If an answer identified a problem that he could solve, he did so.

Many a night he stayed up until dawn, reading. He dug through past correspondence of the company, struggled with turgid metallurgical manuals and technical pamphlets. His curiosity irked Stanley. George didn't care. What he read was informative—and sometimes infuriating. The material from the files showed that whenever their father had given Stanley responsibilities for a decision, Stanley had chosen the risk-free path. Fortunately William Hazard hadn't delegated too much to his eldest son. Had he done so, George was convinced the business would have stumbled back to the eighteenth century by now.

He did find time to hire a Philadelphia architect to survey his homesite and draw plans for a residence. Italianate villas were the rage. The architect designed one, an asymmetrical L-shape with an elaborate lookout tower rising in the angle. This tower, or belvedere, suggested the name for the showy stone mansion; the architect said *belvedere* meant "beautiful view," and the completed house would certainly offer that. The foundation had just been dug when the Flynns arrived.

Constance quickly grew aware of Isabel's scorn. She smiled and made the best of it. And if Orry felt insulted by Virgilia during the wedding festivities, he kept the reaction hidden. The newlyweds departed for their honeymoon in New York. The family carriage took them past the old trading station that had given the town half its name, but George and Constance never saw the scenery. Inside the carriage they were wrapped in each other's arms. They had one night alone, in Easton—a blissful night—before a messenger summoned George back for what turned out to be the first of many quarrels with his brother.

One of the furnaces had burst from the stress generated by the tremendous forces penned up inside; it was not an unfamiliar kind of accident. Two Hazard workmen had been crushed to death by falling debris. After George completed his inspection, he confronted Stanley in the office.

"Why weren't the wrought-iron bands installed on the stacks? The files say money was appropriated for them."

Stanley looked pale and exhausted. Annoyance edged his voice as he replied, "That was Father's idea, not mine. After he died I canceled the installation. Shipments were off slightly. I felt we couldn't afford it."

"You think we can more easily afford two dead bodies and two families without fathers? I want those bands installed. I'll write the order."

Stanley tried to assume a tone of indignation. "I don't believe you have the authority to write—"

"The hell! Your authority exceeds mine in just one area. You're the only one empowered to sign bank drafts. Those bands are going on. And we're paying a thousand dollars to each of the families."

"George, that is utterly stupid."

"Not if we want to keep good workers. Not if we want to sleep nights. You sign the drafts, Stanley, or I'll collect a hundred men and lay siege to your house until you do."

"Damned upstart," Stanley muttered, but when the two drafts for the families of the dead men were drawn, he signed them.

By the time he told Maude of the plan to go ahead with installation of the protective bands, he made it appear the idea was his.

Zachary Taylor won the presidential election in November 1848. That same month workmen finished Belvedere, and George and a very pregnant Constance moved in. Not long afterward, William Hazard III was born in their canopied bed.

Husband and wife loved the new house. Constance first furnished the nursery, then filled all the other rooms with expensive but comfortable pieces whose function was to be used, not admired. In contrast, Stanley and Isabel maintained their home as if it were a museum.

George discussed every major decision with Constance. She knew nothing of the iron trade—not at first, anyway—but she had a keen, practical mind and learned rapidly. He confessed that he was probably courting failure by acting too quickly, even rashly, on many questions on which he had little except instinct to guide him. But he believed progress could be achieved no other way. She agreed.

Soon the expanding grid of American railroads was consuming all the rails the mill could produce on a twenty-four-hour schedule—and this despite a poor economic climate. But George had to fight his brother at every step, on virtually every important issue.

"For God's sake, Stanley, here we are in the middle of a prime hard coal region, and you seem oblivious. It's been merely a hundred and fifty years since the Darbys started smelting iron with coke in Britain. Is that still too experimental for you?"

Stanley looked as if George were demented. "Charcoal is traditional and eminently satisfactory. Why change?"

"Because the trees won't last forever. Not at the rate we use them."

"We'll use them till they're gone, *then* experiment."

"But charcoal's filthy. If it does this"—he swiped an index finger over Stanley's desk; the fingertip showed black—"what do you suppose it does when we inhale the smoke and dust? I would like your agreement to build an experimental coke-burning—"

"No, I won't pay for it."

"Stanley—"

"No. You've pushed me on everything else, but you will not push me on this."

George also wanted to invest some capital in an effort to duplicate the now-lost process by which the Garrard brothers had produced high-quality crucible steel in Cincinnati in the 1830s. Cyrus McCormick had thought enough of Garrard steel to use it for the blades of his first reapers. But a lowering of import duties during Jackson's administration had permitted an inrush of European steel to meet the small domestic demand, and the infant American steel industry had been wiped out.

Today America produced only about two thousand tons of high-carbon steel each year. As the country expanded, however, George foresaw a growing need and a growing market. The problem was not how to make steel—that had been known for centuries—but how to make it rapidly enough that production was profitable. The old cementation process took almost ten days to yield a minuscule quantity. The Garrards had reportedly found a better way. So George quietly surrendered on the coke issue, saving his resources for the fight that would surely ensue over his proposed investigation of steelmaking.

No doubt egged on by Isabel, Stanley said no to nearly all his younger brother's proposals. That was the case with the one concerning steel. George was in a rage for days, rescued from it only by Constance's announcement that she was carrying their second child.

In the summer of 1849, Stanley and his wife received a visitor from Middletown. The guest stayed overnight. George and Constance were not invited to dine, Virgilia was in Philadelphia, and Maude had taken Billy to New York on a holiday. The privacy seemed planned.

George was unconcerned from a social standpoint, but he was curious about the purpose of the visit. He immediately recognized the tall, dignified man of fifty who alighted from a carriage and disappeared into Stanley's house for the rest of the evening. Simon Cameron was widely known in Pennsylvania and over the years had profitably involved himself in printing, banking, railroad development, and even the operation of an ironworks.

George sensed it was a completely different interest that had brought the visitor to Lehigh Station. Politics, perhaps? Cameron had finished a partial term in the Senate but had subsequently been passed over by the state Democratic caucus when it considered the current full-term appointment made by the state legislature, where the party had a majority. That night as George lay in bed with his hand resting on his wife's stomach, he suddenly formed a connection between Cameron's situation and another fact:

"Good Lord. I wonder if he could be the recipient of those drafts."

"I don't know what you're talking about, dear."

258

"I haven't had time to tell you. I've just discovered that during each of the past three months Stanley's written a draft for five hundred dollars. No name—the drafts are written to cash. Maybe he's trying to help Cameron get back on his feet."

"You mean return to the Senate?"

"Possibly."

"Under the Democratic banner?"

"No, he couldn't do that. He displeased too many people by straying from the party line. Old Jim Buchanan was one he displeased. On the other hand, you don't get rid of Cameron simply by saying no. That only spurs him on. I must find out whether Stanley's handing him money to help him build a new organization."

Gently she kissed his cheek. "All these quarrels with Stanley are making you old too fast."

"What about you and Isabel?"

She turned away with a shrug too exaggerated to be genuine. "She doesn't bother me."

"I wouldn't expect you to say anything else. But I know she does."

"Yes, she does," Constance said, abruptly breaking down. "She's vicious. God forgive me, but I wish the earth would swallow them both."

She huddled against his neck, one hand flung across his chest, and cried.

"Yes, I'm donating to Cameron," Stanley admitted the next morning. He waved a hand in front of his face. "Must you smoke those rotten weeds in here?"

George continued puffing on the Cuban cigar. "Don't change the subject. You're giving away company funds. Money that should be retained in the business. What's worse, you're giving it to a political hack."

"Simon's no hack. He served with distinction."

"Oh, did he? Then why did the Democrats repudiate him for a second term? I must say the repudiation didn't surprise me. Cameron's voting record is a crazy quilt. No one can be certain of where he stands or what party he supports—unless, of course, it's the party of expediency. What's his current affiliation? Know-Nothing?"

Stanley coughed hard to register displeasure with the smoke and to play for a bit of time to find an answer. Outside the window of the little wooden office building, dirty, bedraggled men were filing

259

down the hill—the night shift from the furnace. A train of six connected wagons carrying charcoal creaked in the other direction.

"Simon's building a state organization," Stanley said at last. "He won't forget those who help with the task."

"Stanley, the man's a trimmer! You know the joke they tell about him—his definition of an honest politician: 'Once bought, he stays bought.' You want to associate yourself with someone like that?"

Stanley was unperturbed. "Simon Cameron will be a power in Pennsylvania. In the nation, too. He just had a few temporary setbacks."

"Well, don't help him overcome them with our money. If you continue, I'll be forced to put the matter before Mother. Regrettably, that's the only way I can stop you short of mayhem."

His brother glowered, not finding the sarcasm funny. George intimidated him. Stanley chewed his lip, then muttered, "All right. I'll consider your objection."

"Thank you," George snapped, and walked out.

He knew he had won. He had used a weapon, a threat he had never employed before. He disliked using it; only a fool subjected other men to humiliation. A humiliated man often struck back—and in vicious ways. That risk was increased with someone like Stanley, who was inwardly aware of his own ineptitude.

Still, in this case, George had no other choice.

Constance was right, he thought as he trudged uphill toward the furnaces. The endless battles were wearing him out. This morning, standing in front of his shaving mirror, he had spied several white hairs above his forehead. And he was not yet twenty-five.

When Isabel heard about the latest argument, she erupted.

"Will you let him get away with it, Stanley? When the senator has reestablished himself, he'll certainly remember your generosity. Then you'll get that political appointment we both want. It's our chance to escape from this grubby little village for good."

Stanley sank down in one of the bedroom chairs. He unfastened his cravat with a listless hand. "If I don't agree to stop the donations, George will approach Mother."

She sneered. "The little boy running for help?"

"I don't blame him. While I control the funds, he has no other recourse." Short of turning on me with bare fists, Stanley thought as a thrill of fear chased down his back. George had a temper. He had

260

fought a war and was no stranger to brawling. It wasn't hard to imagine him attacking his own brother. Stanley would not run that risk.

Isabel stormed over to his chair. "Well, by heaven, you'd better not surrender control of the purse to that godless little wretch."

"No, I won't give in on that," Stanley promised. *It's my last bit of authority.*

"And you find some way to keep sending Cameron donations, do you understand?"

"Yes, my love. I will." Stanley let out a pained sigh. "I fear I'm learning to hate my own brother."

"Oh, I don't think you should go that far," she countered. Secretly, she was pleased.

He blushed and stepped behind a screen to remove his shirt. "I know. I don't always mean it. Just sometimes."

"The trouble between you and your brother is that idolater he married." She looked at her reflection in a decorative mirror but saw only the beautiful face of the red-haired chatelaine of Belvedere. "That Papist bitch. It's time to take her down a few pegs."

Stanley poked his head out from behind the screen. "How?"

Isabel's only response was a cold smile.

18

The Moravian Seminary and College for Women was situated on the bank of Monocacy Creek in nearby Bethlehem. Established in 1742, it had the distinction of being the first boarding school for young ladies in the colonies. Virgilia had attended the seminary for two terms but had then been sent home for refusing to obey the rules of the institution.

Late in September each year, ladies in the area conducted a bazaar to raise funds for the school. The affair was held on the lawn outside Colonial Hall. Planning began in the summer. To be asked to chair one of the numerous committees was a sign of social acceptance. Isabel had been a committee head the preceding year.

Constance believed in education for women—as much education as they were equipped to handle, even if it placed them in competition with men. George found the attitude a bit startling but didn't disagree with it. Constance told him she would like to help with the September bazaar; her pregnancy did not yet hamper activity or travel on the rough highland roads. George promised to mention her interest to Stanley but forgot.

Constance waited. She had plenty to occupy her. She tended little William several hours a day, believing that if babies didn't receive sufficient patting and handling when they were tiny, they grew up to be warped, disagreeable adults. More to the truth, she loved caring for the pink, plump little boy.

She had household duties as well. She was a good manager of the servants at Belvedere, mediating their quarrels in a firm, fair way and helping them to accomplish more in less time by showing them how to plan their chores and do them efficiently. They soon came to respect and admire her—and fear her a little, too. She had an Irish temper and displayed it when she saw sloppy work or heard it defended with flippancy or fibs.

Busy as she was, Constance still thought about the bazaar. She finally asked George about the message he had promised to pass along. He whacked his forehead and groaned in such a melodramatic way

263

that she laughed. She said his forgetfulness didn't matter; she would speak to Isabel herself. That required a special arrangement, since the two women seldom saw each other except by accident. That was Isabel's design, Constance thought in occasional moments of pique.

She invited Maude and Isabel to tea. First they discussed her pregnancy. Constance said she felt sure she was carrying a girl this time; she and George had agreed to name her Patricia Flynn Hazard. Hearing that, Isabel pursed her lips and gazed at some distant point.

Constance mentioned her interest in the bazaar. Maude immediately said, "How good of you. I'm sure the ladies would be pleased to have you volunteer. I'll be glad to mention your interest, although I no longer have an active part. I served on my last committee two years ago. I felt it was time for younger women to take the helm."

"I shall mention it, dear," Isabel said to Constance, "at the meeting of the organizing group next Monday."

"Thank you," Constance said, trying to detect insincerity in Isabel's sweet smile. She couldn't.

Isabel brought up her sister-in-law's name at the Monday meeting. "I thought that perhaps she might chair the quilt committee—" she began.

"Perfect choice," one of the other ladies declared.

"But when I mentioned the idea, she refused."

That produced some frowns of displeasure among those seated in the circle. "On what grounds, Isabel?" one inquired.

Another asked, "Is she opposed to female education?"

"I can't say," Isabel answered. "She told me she couldn't participate because the, ah, religious orientation of the seminary violates many of the precepts of her own church, which of course she considers the only true church."

The woman chairing the group spoke up. "Well, that's the last time we need consider her. About anything."

Isabel shook her head. "It's a pity. Constance is a bright person. She has several fine qualities. I've been told Catholics are a queer, bigoted sort, but I never believed it until I became acquainted with her. I'm sure her attitudes are the result of the influence of priests and nuns. How can anyone who lives eternally in a dark cell be quite— well—right? And one does hear the most frightful stories about what goes on in nunneries."

264

Sage nods greeted that statement. It was popular cant in the country just then, and exciting to believe.

Isabel called on Constance the following afternoon. Her face reflected dismay as she said:

"There is no easy way to tell you this, my dear. I tendered your very generous offer, but the ladies of the organizing group declined to receive it. Not because of any personal flaws in yourself, please understand, but it is, after all, a bazaar to raise funds for a religious denomination different from your own."

Constance twisted a lace handkerchief. "You mean they don't want the help of a Catholic."

Isabel sighed. "I'm so sorry. Perhaps next year."

Ever afterward, she knew, she would savor the memory of her sister-in-law's face just then.

While Isabel was calling on Constance, George was running to the rail mill, summoned by a frightened foreman. A quarrel had led to an accident. Stanley always deferred to his brother when such things happened. With a straight face he had said it was because George possessed the common touch. If Isabel had made the remark, George would have been sure it was an insult.

The summer had been exceptionally hot, and the advent of autumn brought no relief. Tempers were frequently frayed in the Hazard family, and George could imagine the tensions that rose in the mill where the heat was infernal.

The rail mill was of the type the trade called Belgian. The long, fast-moving ribbon of red-hot metal was gradually reduced in thickness and shaped to the proper configuration by passing through a series of grooved rollers mounted on stands. Between the stands, burly men called catchers seized the metal with tongs and guided it into the next set of rollers. It was hard, dangerous work, and much of it would be eliminated if anyone could design a mill that passed the metal continuously through the rollers. A mill owner named Serrell in New York had almost done it several years ago, but his design was flawed. George had also attacked the problem, unsuccessfully so far.

George ran as fast as he could. All work had come to a halt in the mill. The iron being fed into the first set of rollers had already cooled, he saw as he neared the scene of the accident. One of the catchers lay on the dirt floor, moaning. George choked when he smelled scorched clothing and burned flesh.

The fallen man was a wiry Slav whose last name George couldn't pronounce. He was a fine worker, unlike his partner at this station, a wide-shouldered hulk named Brovnic.

"We sent for Dr. Hopple," said the foreman.

"Good." George knelt between the injured man and the twisted ribbon of dark, cold iron lying nearby. Evidently the iron had fallen diagonally across the right side of the man's body, burning away his shirt front and deeply searing his chest and bare forearm. The man's charred flesh resembled half-cooked meat. George fought down vomit that rose in his throat. God knew whether the man would ever use the arm again.

George rubbed the back of his hand across his mouth, then asked, "How did it happen?"

"Accident," Brovnic blurted. His jutting jaw threatened anyone who denied it, but the intimidation failed. A sweaty, begrimed worker stepped forward.

"Accident, hell. Brovnic's been bothering Tony's wife. Tony told him to quit it, and—"

Brovnic cursed and lunged. Three men grabbed him and held him back as the speaker pointed to the ribbon of iron. "Brovnic knocked him down with it, then dropped it on him."

"Fucking liar," Brovnic screamed, writhing to get free of his captors. He would have if George hadn't stormed up to him and jabbed a finger into his filthy shirt.

"You've done nothing but cause trouble since the day I hired you, Brovnic. Collect your wages and get off this property. Now."

George's heart was beating fast. Brovnic squinted down at him. "You better not do this—"

George had to tilt his head back to return the other man's stare. "I said leave *right now*."

"I fix you for this," Brovnic promised as he stalked off.

A minute after Isabel left, Constance bowed her head and wept. She stood by a tall window in the parlor. Beyond it spread the panorama of the town, the sultry glitter of the river below. She didn't see any of it. She clutched a drapery as if she feared she'd fall.

The sobs went on and on. She despised herself for crying. She had done it very seldom while growing up in Texas, but here things were different. Sometimes, despite her love for George, she hated Lehigh Station and wanted to flee. Instead, she wept.

She was sure Isabel had engineered the snub. Stanley's wife hated her. There was no other word for it but hate. When George came home, she'd tell him what had happened. She tried never to put her troubles on her husband, but this was too much for her to bear by herself. Isabel had made an issue of her religion, but there were probably other reasons the haughty woman despised her. Isabel was a twisted, unhappy person—and she had the power to wound Constance deeply.

"Ma'am, is there something wrong? I thought I heard—"

The servant girl stopped. She tried to draw back out of the parlor door, which she had opened without Constance's being aware of it. Constance felt more embarrassed for the girl than for herself. She swept tears off her face with both palms.

"I'm sorry for disturbing you, Bridgit. I just wasn't myself for a moment or two. Please don't mention it to anyone. Would you bring little William down if he's awake?"

"Right away, ma'am." Relieved, Bridgit withdrew.

A short time later, with her plump, gurgling son in her arms, Constance felt much better. She was sorry she had allowed Isabel to break her down. Of course she would say nothing to her husband. She would fight her own battles, as she always did. She had chosen to come to this part of the world because she loved George, and she wouldn't let Isabel or a legion of the bigoted, for that matter, defeat her.

She was angry with herself for having let down in front of Isabel, even for an instant. She knew Stanley's wife had seen that her cruel little strategy had succeeded. But it's the last time that shrew will ever have the satisfaction, she thought as she snuggled William on her shoulder.

"We should give some thought to buying a summer residence," Maude said. "The weather the past few months has been perfectly dreadful."

"I agree," said Stanley. "Isabel complains of the heat day and night." Bent over a ledger, George shot him a look as if to say Isabel was always complaining about something.

"We can certainly afford a summer cottage," Stanley went on.

267

"Do you have any thoughts about where we might look for one, Mother?"

"The Atlantic shore would be pleasant."

The little office was stifling. Two hours had passed since Brovnic had stormed away from the mill; Maude had just arrived for her weekly visit. She had begun those visits immediately after her husband died. Prior to that, she had never set foot on the grounds of Hazard Iron.

Stanley had discouraged her interest at first, saying it was unseemly for a woman to involve herself in commerce. When George came home, he soon deduced the real reason for Stanley's disapproval. In just a few months Maude had learned more about matters of manufacturing, inventory, and the flow of cash than her oldest son would know in a lifetime. It was that instinctive expertise that embarrassed Stanley, prodding him to put up an argument about her visits.

The arguments did no good. In her unassuming way, Maude was as tough as the Hazard iron the canal boats carried downriver to market.

Prompted by Maude's remark about the shore, George said, "Orry once told me that a lot of South Carolina planters summer at Newport."

Maude clapped her hands. "Oh, yes. Aquidneck Island. I've heard it's lovely."

Stanley was about to object to the suggestion when the door crashed open. Brovnic loomed in the opening, blowing whiskey fumes ahead of him and brandishing an old horse pistol.

Maude gasped, then held rigidly still. Simultaneously, Stanley flung himself on the floor.

"I told you!" Brovnic shouted, his body swaying, his eyes squinting down the barrel pointed at George. Without hesitation, George whipped the ink pot from his desk and flung the contents in Brovnic's face.

Dripping black liquid, Brovnic bellowed and reeled against the door frame. The pistol discharged, but Brovnic's arm had jerked upward by the time he fired. The ball plowed into the ceiling. By then George had vaulted over the rail that divided the office. He tore the pistol from Brovnic's hand and bashed him on the bridge of the nose. The enraged man groped for him with inky hands. George retreated one pace, then slammed his hobnailed boot into Brovnic's crotch.

Brovnic screamed and windmilled his arms, falling backward out the door and down the steps. Only then did George feel the onset of panic. He clutched the door frame and waved to four passing workmen.

"Grab that drunken idiot. One of you run down to the village and find the constable."

Stanley clambered to his feet. Maude had never moved. She looked at Stanley and said in a mild voice, "You should have helped your brother. He could have been killed."

Stanley reddened, too stunned to speak. For the first time his mother had chosen between her sons. It didn't bode well for the future.

By the time George returned to Belvedere that evening, Constance showed no sign of her earlier unhappiness. George chatted all through supper, obviously still excited by the violence at the mill. He had visited the injured worker at his home near the canal; the man would recover. Dr. Hopple thought his arm could be saved, though whether he would be able to do hard physical labor remained in doubt. If he could not, George would find him an easier job at Hazard's. Brovnic was locked up in the constable's office.

In the house next door, the evening meal was already over. Maude had gone outside to stroll with Billy. Virgilia was in her room. Isabel had paid her ritualized five-minute visit to the twins, Laban and Levi, and had returned to the dining room. Now she and Stanley were alone there. She was just on the point of telling him about her triumphant moment with Constance when he again mentioned the trouble in the office. Since coming home, he had talked of it briefly, then lapsed into morose silence. Maude had conversed in a lively manner but avoided the subject of the shooting.

"Mother looked at me as if I were the worst sort of coward," he said with a forlorn expression. "I can't get over it."

"Stanley, I appreciate that the incident upset you, but I've heard about it. I do wish you'd give me a chance to say—"

He flung his balled napkin in her face. "Shut up, you harpy. Are you so stupid that you can't see what's happening? George is turning Mother against us! Next thing you know, she'll give him control of the money. Then where will you be with your wasteful ways and fancy airs?"

He yelled so loudly the pendants of the chandelier tinkled. Speechless, Isabel gazed at the napkin that had struck her chin and fallen into her empty sherbet dish.

Her first reaction was to turn on her husband, savage him for this absolutely unheard-of display of temper. She quickly had second thoughts. He was only kicking her, so to speak, because his mother had kicked him. And deservedly so. Stanley was a coward. It didn't matter so long as he maintained his authority in the family.

She soon convinced herself that the person who should get the blame for this trouble was George. Pushy, arrogant little George. Today she had triumphed over George's wife, but George had put Stanley in such a state he refused to listen to an account of her victory. Of course she took satisfaction merely from knowing that Constance was feeling miserable.

But even that certainty was called into question a moment later. From the side lawn of Belvedere came the sound of merry voices. Isabel walked to the window and saw George and Constance playing lawn bowls in the late-summer dusk. They were laughing and teasing each other like a pair of children.

Stanley spoke to Isabel. She ignored him. She was staring at Maude, who was seated on the side loggia of George's house, dandling little William on her knee. Young Billy lounged close by. Isabel seethed. Maude never paid that kind of attention to Laban and Levi.

Constance looked happy. *Happy.* Somehow, her strength had undone the day's victory. And it was now grimly clear to Isabel that Constance and her husband were working hard to turn Maude against Stanley.

From that moment, Isabel hated the two of them even more passionately than she had before.

"Another train derailed," Constance said. "Four people killed. That's the third wreck this month." She shook her head and closed the paper.

George continued studying the architectural plans spread on the library table. Without looking up, he said, "The more miles of track that are built, and the more trains that are scheduled, the greater the chances for accidents."

"Surely that's too simple an explanation. I've heard repeatedly that half the accidents—or more—are preventable."

"Well, perhaps. There are human errors in scheduling. Bad materials used on the roadbeds and rolling stock. It would help if all the railroads settled on a uniform gauge, too."

He rose, stretched, then reached down to adjust the position of the object he kept on display on the table, as if it were some priceless antique. It was nothing more than the fragment of iron meteorite that he had found near West Point during his cadet days. He treasured it because he said it summed up the scope and meaning of his work.

She noticed that he moved the meteorite no more than a quarter of an inch. She smiled to herself.

He walked to her chair and planted a kiss on her brow. "As Orry would say, I reckon progress always has its price."

"You haven't had a letter from Orry in quite a while."

"Six weeks." George strolled to the window. Outside, the lights of Lehigh Station blurred behind the first gentle snowfall. "I wrote to invite him to bring all the Mains to Newport next summer."

In October, George and Stanley had visited the island in Narragansett Bay and had purchased a large, rambling house and ten acres of ground on Bath Road, within easy walking distance of a beach. A Providence architect had just submitted plans for extensive modernization of the house; these were the plans George was examining. The architect promised that the remodeling would be complete before the opening of the 1850 summer season.

"And you haven't heard from him since then?"

"No."

"Is anything wrong?"

"If there is, I'm not aware of it."

"Newport is a Northern resort. Do you think he'll accept the invitation?"

"I see no reason why he shouldn't. People from South Carolina still flock to the place in the summertime."

He wasn't being completely honest with his wife. Orry's infrequent letters, superficially pleasant, had a peculiar, bitter undertone. George was sensitive to it because he had known an earlier, more lighthearted Orry Main.

In the letters Orry had several times referred to his "perennial bachelorhood." He only occasionally answered George's guarded inquiries about *M.*, and he sometimes jumped unexpectedly from a bit of innocuous news to what could only be termed a diatribe against anti-slavery forces in the North. He was particularly antagonistic toward the so-called free-soil political groups, which were seeking to ensure that new states or territories would prohibit slavery. He also referred scathingly to the Wilmot Proviso. Apparently the South would hold a grudge over that for a long time.

So, although George very much wanted to see his friend again, a part of him fretted about the eventual reunion.

In mid-December he received word that such a reunion would in fact take place. The news came on a fiercely cold day. That night

George crawled into bed next to his extremely pregnant wife and, as usual, began a drowsy discussion of the day's events.

"There was a letter from Orry."

"At last! Was it cheerful?" Her voice had a breathy quality whose significance he failed to understand immediately.

"Not very. But he said he'd visit us next summer and bring as many of the others as he can persuade."

"That's—splendid," Constance gasped. "But I think—right now—you'd better issue an invitation to Dr. Hopple."

"What? It's time? This minute? My Lord—that's why you sounded so out of breath."

He scrambled out of bed and in his haste stepped into the chamber pot. Fortunately it was empty. But it upset his balance and pitched him onto his back. *"Ow!"*

"Oh, good heavens," she said, struggling to get up. "If you suffer and carry on this way, we'll never be able to have any more children."

At dawn she brought Patricia Flynn Hazard into the world with no great difficulty. George received the news in the library, where he sat smiling sleepily and rubbing his bandaged foot.

Billy, fourteen and growing taller every day, came home from boarding school over the Christmas holidays. He was impressed with his new niece and spent most of his time at Belvedere, even though all his belongings remained at Stanley's.

Billy was feeling adult and independent. He frequently teased his mother with threats of an imminent departure to the California gold fields. Half the nation had succumbed to the fever. Why shouldn't he?

"Because you don't need the money, young man," Maude responded on one occasion at the dinner table.

"Yes, I do. I haven't any of my own." Then, weary of the game, he ran to her chair and hugged her. "I don't really want to pan for gold."

"What do you want?"

"I want to hear about the fight at Churubusco again."

Billy never tired of listening to the story. Telling it inevitably led George into a long, rambling account of his days at West Point. He enjoyed reminiscing by a roaring fire, and it was also a good way to keep his younger brother away from Stanley and Isabel for an extra hour. Stanley had grown sullen since the shooting incident, which had lately resulted in Brovnic's imprisonment in Harrisburg. Isabel was as shrewish as ever. George deemed them bad influences. He was thankful Billy was off at school most of the year.

"Orry sounds like a fine person," Billy said after one of George's monologues about the Academy.

"He is. He's also my best friend. You'll meet him next summer, I hope."

"Does he beat his niggers?"

"Why, I don't think so."

"He owns some, doesn't he?" Billy's disapproval was evident.

George frowned as he reached for the decanter of claret. It seemed there was no avoiding the issue.

"Yes, he owns quite a few."

"Then I've changed my mind. I don't think he's as fine as you say."

George suppressed annoyance. "That's because you're almost fifteen. No one your age ever agrees with adults."

"Oh, yes, we do," Billy shot back so quickly George burst out laughing.

Billy didn't understand the joke. He went ahead doggedly. "I agree with all you say about West Point. It sounds like a wonderful place."

George sipped wine and listened to the comfortable, familiar creaks and murmurs of the house. Families ought to have traditions, and he had just conceived of a splendid one. He didn't want to promote it too directly to a headstrong adolescent, though. That would make it too easy for Billy to say no. He tiptoed around the subject:

"Oh, there were hard times. But you felt much more of a man when you survived them. There were a lot of great times, too. I made some good friends. Tom Jackson—he's teaching at a military college in Virginia. George Pickett. Good friends," he murmured again, gazing back over a short span of years that already seemed much longer. "And there's no question that West Point provides the finest scientific education available in America."

Billy grinned. "I'm more interested in fighting battles."

George thought of the bloodshed at Churubusco and Orry's arm blown away. *Then you don't understand what battle is really like.* His smile fading, he kept the thought to himself. He let Billy make the suggestion, which he did, with some hesitancy, a moment later:

"You know, George, I've been meaning to ask what you thought of my chances—"

273

George concealed his elation. "Your chances for what?"

The boy's eyes showed his admiration for his older brother. "For going through the Academy the way you did."

"Do you think you'd like that?"

"Yes, very much."

"Capital!"

Soldiering was a rough, sometimes damned unattractive trade. In the thick of the war he had found it disgusting and inhuman. He still did. Even so, a man could do no better, in this age and this nation, than to begin his adult life with West Point training. George realized he hadn't always believed that, however. The fact that he now believed it without question was another change in his character that struck him as surprising.

"Of course there's always fierce competition for the appointments," he continued. "But you wouldn't be ready to enter until—let's see— three years from now. You'd be seventeen if you enrolled with the class of 'fifty-six. Ideal. I must see whether there'll be a vacancy from the district. I'll get to work on it immediately."

And he did.

19

By late 1849 people along the Ashley had a saying about Orry Main: every month his beard got a little longer and his conversations a little shorter.

Orry never meant to be curt, just brief. In his head he was constantly sorting and organizing hundreds of details pertaining to the family and the operation of Mont Royal. Most of these details required him to take some action, which in turn had to be planned. Further, every week or so some kind of crisis required his intervention. Hence his time was short. He conserved it when he talked to others.

If neighbors and acquaintances took this to be a sign of a sullen streak—merely one more of those changes wrought by his war injury—that was fine with him. The reaction had a practical benefit. People didn't expect him to chatter about his personal life, nor did they press him about a subject he found infuriating.

That is, no one pressed him except his father.

Tillet was nearly fifty-five now, gout-ridden and prickly-tempered. "Damn it, boy, you're eminently marriageable," he said one night in the library. "Why do you refuse to search for a wife?"

December rain pattered on the windows. Orry sighed and laid down his pen. He had been totting up figures from a ledger, one of several he had fetched from the office. Salem Jones was responsible for keeping the ledgers, something he'd been doing ever since Tillet's health began to break down. In them were recorded the number of barrels in each shipment to Charleston.

After the harvest, Orry had chanced to glance into the ledger for the current year. The neatly inscribed figures somehow didn't jibe with his intuitive feel for the number of rice barrels leaving the plantation. Didn't jibe with a vivid picture of many more barrels piled up on the pier—which needed two pilings replaced, he recalled. He had been meaning to jot a reminder to himself for weeks. He did so now, before turning to his father.

"May I ask what brought up a question I thought we'd settled to everyone's satisfaction?"

"To your mother's, perhaps. Not mine."

From his chair Tillet flourished the pages of Cooper's latest letter. "Your brother is squiring eligible young ladies to all those Christmas parties and balls. Of course, if he ever grew serious about a girl, her father would probably send him packing because of his wild ideas. However, your brother's marital status is of no interest to me. I cite him only as an example of what you should be doing. You—"

Tillet moved slightly, winced, and gripped his outstretched leg. A moment later he finished, "You should be wed and starting a family."

Orry shook his head. "Too busy."

"But surely you feel the need for companionship. A vigorous man of your age always—"

Orry smiled, which gave his father leave to stop. Tillet looked relieved. Orry said, "I take care of that, don't worry."

Tillet smirked. "So I've heard from several gentlemen in the neighborhood. But women of that sort—common women or those tinctured with a drop of nigger blood—they're good for one thing only. You can't marry someone like that."

"I don't intend to. As I've said many times before"—he touched his pinned-up sleeve with his pen—"I no longer consider myself fit to marry. Now I'd like to get back to work. I've found some damned odd discrepancies, going back as far as two and a half years."

Tillet harrumphed, his equivalent of permission. His son had grown a mite gruff when he said he wasn't fit to wed. Tillet had heard the excuse often, and much as he hated to admit it, he believed there was something to it. He knew what people along the Ashley thought of Orry. They thought the war had left him a little queer in the head.

There was ample evidence to support the contention: The way Orry went about his duties at Mont Royal, as though he were driven to prove himself the equal of any uninjured man. His clothes, always too heavy and somber for the climate and mood of the low country. His brusque manner. That damn beard, so long and thick chickadees could nest in it.

Once, out by the entrance to the lane, Tillet had been returning from Charleston in his carriage at the same time Orry was riding away on some errand. Three of the gardeners, scything weeds, had stared at Orry when he cantered by. The slaves had exchanged looks; one had shaken his head, and another had actually shivered. Tillet had seen it and been saddened. His son had become a strange, even frightening figure to others.

Of course the deficiencies had to be kept in perspective. Odd as Orry might be, he pleased Tillet far more than Cooper did. Cooper had jumped right into management of the little shipping line, and he was doing well at it. But he continued to express offensive, not to say downright traitorous, opinions.

Lately there had been a lot written about several resolutions old Henry Clay planned to introduce in the Senate early next year. Clay hoped to prevent a further widening of the rift between the North and the South. The Union, thirty states strong, was delicately balanced. Fifteen states practiced slavery; the other fifteen did not. Clay wanted to throw some bones to each side. He proposed to align the new state of California on the Northern side, with the stipulation that slavery not be permitted there. Southerners would receive a pledge of non-interference with interstate slave traffic, as well as a more effective fugitive slave law.

If Tillet had been required to isolate the foremost cause of his animosity toward the North, he would instantly have named the fugitive slave issue. The fourth article of the Constitution specifically stated that a man had the right to recover any slave who ran away. It also said that laws in force in a state that did not practice slavery had no effect on this right. The Fugitive Slave Act of 1793 had been written to implement the Constitution. And ever since, the high-minded hypocrites up North had sought ways to water down or completely circumvent the law of the land.

Tillet opposed Clay's compromises. So did a great many Southern leaders, including Senator Jeff Davis of Mississippi and Senator John Calhoun. Clay did have the famous and influential Senator Webster on his side. But he was opposed by various abolitionist hatchet men, Senator Seward of New York being perhaps the most extreme. For once Tillet was grateful to that crowd.

Cooper believed the much-debated compromises were reasonable and badly needed. In Tillet's opinion, what was badly needed was a horsewhipping for Cooper.

While those thoughts were passing through Tillet's mind, Orry was recalling his father's remark about people in the neighborhood knowing he carried on with women. He was delighted to hear that. It meant his plan had worked. Over the past year he had taken a succession of mistresses, the latest a mulatto seamstress he had met on a visit to Charleston. He took pains to keep this activity discreet, but not secret.

The women gave him the one thing that Madeline, by the terms of their agreement, could not. But he wouldn't have entered into the affairs just to fulfill that need, although Tillet obviously thought otherwise. Orry took up with various women so that people would notice and would therefore be less likely to connect each occasional unexplained absence from Mont Royal with Madeline's absences from Resolute on the same day. Protecting her from suspicion was almost as important as seeing her regularly.

Pleased that the deception was successful, Orry went back to the ledgers. He had stumbled onto something with a decidedly fishy odor, and he concentrated on it for the next half hour while Tillet dozed into a gleeful dream-fantasy in which a mob stoned Senator Seward.

A sound like a pistol shot jerked Tillet awake; Orry had closed a ledger with a snap. He stood with the book clutched in his hand.

Tillet rubbed his eyes. "What's wrong?"

"Plenty. We've been harboring a thief. He's repaid your trust and kindness with deceit. I never liked the bastard. I'm going to get rid of him right now."

"Who?" Tillet said, still sleepy and confused.

At the door Orry turned. "Jones."

"But—I hired him. You can't just throw him out."

"I beg to differ sir," Orry said in a voice so low and hard that the older man could barely hear it above the sound of the rain. "I'm in charge of this plantation now. You'll agree with my decision when I show you the proof. But even if you don't, Jones is through."

Orry stared at his father. Not angrily, just steadily. The beard, the eyes, the tall, gaunt frame, and the empty sleeve—they had a queer effect on Tillet all at once. He felt he was arguing with a stranger, and a frightening one at that.

"Whatever you say," he murmured. His son gave a crisp little nod and went out.

Orry walked to the overseer's house with the ledgers clutched under his arm and an old cloak belling behind him. Rain collected in his hair and beard. He took long, swift strides and was so intent on his errand that he didn't notice Cousin Charles lounging on the dark porch of one of the slave cabins.

Jones was asleep. Orry roused him with shouts, then confronted him in the kitchen of his immaculate house. The surprise visit had upset the overseer. Sweat shone on his bald head, and there were dark patches of it on his nightshirt. He had brought his quirt and hickory truncheon from the bedroom. Evidently he slept with them.

"It was a simple scheme, wasn't it?" Orry said. He hurled the ledgers onto the kitchen table. A look of panic spread on Jones's face. "In the permanent record of each shipment you put a short total. As many as a dozen barrels less than the number actually loaded on the boat. But our factors pay us for the number of barrels received. Since you kept the books on those transactions too, all you had to do was record a sum that matched the short total in the shipping ledger and pocket the excess. Last time I was in Charleston, I examined the factor's records. They prove that, over and over, the factors paid us more than you showed us receiving."

Jones gulped and pressed his truncheon against his pot belly, as if seized by pain. "You can't prove I'm responsible for the discrepancy."

"Maybe not in a court, though I think I could make a strong case. Until I came home from Mexico, no one handled those records except you and my father, who regrettably grew weak, and a little too trusting. I hardly suppose my father would cheat himself."

"No matter what you say, you still won't be able to prove—"

"Stop prattling about proof. I don't need the verdict of a jury in order to discharge you. It's my decision, and I've made it."

"It's unfair," Jones exclaimed. "I've given everything to this plantation."

Orry's face looked ugly in the lamplight. Points of fire showed in his eyes. "You've taken a lot as well."

"I'm not a young man, Mr. Main. I beg you to give me another chan—"

"No."

"It will take me"—Jones laid the quirt down—"at least a week to gather my belongings."

"You'll vacate this house by daylight. I'll order the drivers to burn anything that's still here in the morning."

"Goddamn you," Jones cried, the shadow of his upraised hickory truncheon flying across the wall and then the ceiling. As he started to hit Orry's forehead, Orry turned sideways, the better to use his right hand. He seized Jones's wrist and held the truncheon above them.

"I'm not one of the slaves, Mr. Jones. If you raise your voice or your hand to me once more, I'll see that you travel downriver on a stretcher."

Shaking, he tore the truncheon from Jones's hand and jammed it under his arm. With a swift, scooping motion he picked up the ledgers and strode toward the door. He barely saw Cousin Charles, who was leaning against one of the foundation's tabby pillars, an excited, almost worshipful expression on his face.

"What's going on?" Charles asked. "Did Jones do something wrong?"

The rain had turned to light mist. Orry walked down from the porch, the thud of his boots muffling his brusque answer. Cousin Charles thought Orry hadn't bothered to reply. The excited look on his face was replaced by one of resentment.

Cousin Charles lay naked beside Semiramis. Her smooth, warm skin radiated the faintly sweaty odor of their recent lovemaking.

In the darkness the girl heard an ominous sound begin. *Thunk, thunk.* Each blow was preceded by a violent movement of Cousin Charles's body. With his bowie knife he was repeatedly stabbing the plank wall to the right of the pallet.

He always fooled with that big knife when he was angry. Surely he wasn't angry with her. They had blended together just fine, as they always did—though, come to think of it, his thrusts had been unusually deep and rough.

Semiramis stretched her arms above her head but experienced no feeling of sleepiness. Charles continued to whack the wall with the knife. It was nearly an hour since he had crept in to tell her he had met Mr. Orry. Now the slave community was buzzing with news that Salem Jones had been ordered to leave. Lamps burned throughout the overseer's fancy house. He was packing right now. From out of the misty dark, Semiramis heard laughter and little snatches of happy conversation. Folks were awake and joyous. For weeks to come the whole place would have a feeling of jubilee.

The news about Jones had had that effect on Semiramis, too. She had been in a splendid, receptive mood by the time the strapping fourteen-year-old mounted her. Charles never failed to satisfy her, but tonight her pleasure had been heightened because of Jones, and because the boy had come back to her again. She had been the first to show him what men and women did together, and no matter how many white girls he fooled with, he always came back. Lately, so she had heard, he had been sniffing around one of the Smith girls. Sue Marie Smith, that was her name. A pretty little thing, but too polite for a cub as lusty as this one.

Thunk. The wall vibrated. She took his free hand and pulled it over on top of her bristly mound. He jerked it back.

"Lord," she said with a small, forced laugh. "Who you so mad at?"

"Orry. He looks through me like I was a window. He doesn't know I'm alive. Or care."

Thunk.

"Mmm. You must hate him 'bout as much as I hate his poppa for showing off my brother like a chicken thief. I guess I was wrong about Mr. Orry."

"What do you mean?"

"I kind of had the idea you liked him."

Cousin Charles snickered. "Would you like somebody who thought you were worthless? Just dirt?"

So many white faces shunted through her mind she couldn't keep track of all of them. "No, sweet boy, I surely wouldn't."

"Then don't expect me to, either."

Thunk. That time he struck so hard the blade hummed.

"I think you were glad to discharge Jones," Madeline said the next time she met Orry at the chapel.

"The devil! I didn't engineer it, you know."

"Don't bristle so, darling. Of course you didn't. But my point stands."

She laid a cool palm against his cheek. "I know you by now. You already have too much work, yet you keep taking on more. Jones could have been let go in a week, or a month. But you were eager to add his work to your own immediately." She kissed him gently. "You look worn out. You're not indestructible, you know."

He felt as if she had shone a great light down into a pit within him, a pit where he hid thoughts and feelings of which he was ashamed. Her perception angered him. But, as always, he could never be angry with her for long. Perhaps—the insight came suddenly—perhaps love existed in its truest, deepest form when one partner saw into the soul of the other and never shrank from what was discovered there.

He managed a weary laugh. "I reckon you've found my secret. Hard work and these visits are the only things that keep me sane."

She looked beyond the smile to the pain in his eyes. She heard the desperate truth of his statement. She held him close, saying nothing.

20

On January 29, 1850, Senator Clay introduced his eight resolutions in Congress.

They had already been hotly argued at Resolute. Two of Justin's uncles, both prosperous tradesmen in Columbia, had been ostracized by the low-country LaMottes because the two had sat at Justin's table and said the South should never be too hidebound to compromise. Especially since the national balance of power continued to swing away from the region; in the House only 90 of 234 members represented slave states.

For days Justin ranted about the heresy his uncles had propounded. Madeline's husband couldn't tolerate opinions that ran counter to traditional thinking, his thinking. It was one of the reasons she often dreamed about running away.

Several things deterred her. She continued to believe that such a course would be dishonorable. More practically, if she fled, she would have to go alone; she couldn't ask Orry to share her disgrace. But that meant she'd never see him again. This way at least she saw him every week or so.

Another reason, nearly as compelling, had emerged gradually over the past couple of years. When Madeline had first arrived at Resolute, she had been a city girl. The intricacies of plantation life were foreign to her. But she was determined to master them. And even though she quickly became disillusioned with her marriage, her determination was undiminished. If anything it increased, for she soon saw that Resolute needed a moderating influence. Someone to work quietly to protect the interests of the blacks wherever possible and to make their unconscionable bondage a bit less harsh.

She conspired with the kitchen help to funnel extra food to the slave community. She took small sums of money from her household accounts and saved them until she had enough to buy better clothing or additional medicines for the sick house. She learned to diagnose common ailments and to treat them with simple traditional remedies, all of which was part of her duty as Justin's wife, and tried to mitigate unusually severe punishments her husband meted out, which was not.

After his quarrels with his uncles, for example, he was itching to find someone to kick—and not just figuratively. He picked on Tom, a fourteen-year-old house boy. The boy had neglected to polish some of the hallway brasswork to Justin's satisfaction.

In response to Justin's questions, the terrified boy offered only mumbled answers. This led Justin to accuse Tom of being uppity. He issued orders that the boy be given twenty blows of the whip. Madeline protested; she always protested his cruelties. As usual, Justin ignored her. He walked away, passing off a snide remark about feminine sensibilities. A few minutes later, Madeline hurried to the slave community to locate the black driver responsible for carrying out the sentence.

It was a delicate business. If she countermanded Justin's order, she would place the driver in jeopardy. All she could do was ask the driver, a huge ebony man named Samuel, to lighten the strokes as much as he could without incurring punishment himself.

"I will, but they's worse I'm to do to the boy," Samuel said. "Mist' Justin told me to pour a bucket on his wounds."

"A bucket of what?"

The humiliated driver looked away.

"Did you hear me, Samuel? What is the bucket to contain?"

"Turp'tine."

"Oh, my God." She pressed her mouth. "That's liable to kill him."

A sorrowing shrug. "Mist' Justin, he was mighty mad. I got to do it."

She laced her hands together at her breast, thinking. "If someone hands you that bucket, Samuel, you're not responsible for what it contains."

He peered at her, starting to understand. "You right, Miz Madeline." He wanted to smile but didn't dare.

"I'll fetch the bucket of turpentine myself. I'll give it to you, and you can then do with it as you must. Just make certain we don't have a crowd of witnesses who might tell my husband what they did or did not smell in that bucket."

"No, ma'am, won't be nobody watchin'. Mist' Justin don't require that."

So Tom was whipped, rather than being whipped and tortured. It wasn't much of a victory for Madeline or the boy. But she knew that if she ran away from Resolute, there would be no victories at all.

*

Much of what Madeline knew about plantation life and a responsible woman's place in it she learned from half a dozen neighbors, the most important being Clarissa Main. Although from different backgrounds, the two women were temperamentally similar. And perhaps Clarissa sensed something of her son's feeling for Justin's wife. At any rate, Clarissa spent hours with Madeline at Mont Royal, patiently teaching.

Among the things Madeline learned was midwifery. Early in February, around ten o'clock on a moonlit night, she was called to the slave community to attend a field wench named Jane. It was Jane's first baby and Madeline's tenth.

Several black women were gathered in Jane's cabin. Madeline knelt and let the pregnant girl clutch her hands as the spasms shook her. Another woman had knelt there first, but Jane had refused her help. Madeline was the trusted one, the mistress. Whatever healing power that conferred, she was glad to share it.

She helped tie Jane's ankles in position, then watched the ancient midwife, Aunt Belle Nin, manipulate her wood forceps. At less complicated deliveries, Madeline was in charge. This time, because of difficulties, she deferred to Aunt Belle, who had been specially summoned. The baby was badly positioned. But Aunt Belle turned it smartly with the forceps and soon brought it popping into the nippy air.

Aunt Belle Nin was a stringy octoroon of sixty-five, perhaps seventy. She lived far back in the marshes, alone, and rode out to help with difficult confinements when she was needed. She took her pay in food, bolts of cloth, and snuff for her cheek. Now she fondled the damp, cocoa-colored newborn as if it were her own.

"He'll do just fine," she said. "I should know. I've survived hell, hurricanes, and husbands. If I can do that, think of what this youngster can do."

Madeline glanced around the mean cabin. It had been years since a coat of whitewash was applied to the walls. She wondered why any woman would bring a child into the world if that child could only spend its life in enforced poverty and servitude. Of late she had begun to have a fuller understanding of what the abolitionists were after and why.

Jane wanted Madeline to hold the baby, which she did, thinking how much she would like Orry to see the child. Later, as she was about to leave, a bent, wrinkled woman with sorrowful eyes made an imploring gesture. Madeline stopped.

"I be the mother of little Tom. The one whipped for being uppity."

"Oh, yes. I hope he's all right."

"He be better. He never be all right. He be marked on his back all his life. Samuel—" She pressed her lips together, briefly fearful. "Samuel tole me what you done. I thank you, Miz Madeline. You a good Christian woman."

Madeline was startled to hear murmurs of agreement. Among those who were behind her, listening, was Aunt Belle Nin. After firing up her clay pipe, Aunt Belle spoke.

"They all say that of you, mistress. I watched you tonight. I think they're right. If ever you have a problem I could help with, you can find me."

"Thank you, Aunt Belle."

Gratified, she hurried back to the great house, where she found Justin examining a book of lithographs of race horses. The slaves might respect her, but he didn't. That was again evident as soon as she told him where she'd been.

"Well," he said, "how charmingly domestic you're becoming. You can deliver nigger babies. What a pity you can't manage to deliver one of your own."

She turned away, appalled and hurt. He sensed that and went on to compound the hurt.

"Perhaps you need special assistance. Should I select one of the bucks and put him at stud? You seem to have an affinity for darkies. You certainly have none for me."

Fury replaced the pain. "Justin, I have made a conscientious effort to be a good wife to you in every respect. You mustn't keep blaming me because I don't get pregnant." *Maybe you should blame yourself.*

He flung one leg over the fragile arm of the Sheraton chair. "Why not? You're never very lively on those occasions when we try to perpetuate this branch of the family. The occasions are getting less and less frequent, although I suppose I bear some responsibility for that. You see, I avoid you by choice. Your fondness for niggers is beginning to bore me. Good night, my love."

He returned to his book.

It had been only a week since she was at Salvation Chapel, but the next morning, desperately unhappy, she paid a visit to Mont Royal so that Nancy could deliver a message to Orry.

*

"Do you think he knows about us?" Orry asked when they met at the chapel the following afternoon. It was a bright, balmy day, not unusual for February in the low country. Orry had discarded his coat and cravat.

Madeline shook her head. "If he did, we wouldn't be wondering. Justin isn't the kind to suffer in silence."

Orry absently tapped a finger against the book he had brought. "Then why is he going out of his way to make you miserable?"

"Because there are no children. That's the current reason, anyway. Justin's one of those poor, wretched people who are always unhappy. But instead of examining his own mind to learn why, he blames some person or cause outside himself—and lashes out. Sometimes I wish he did know about us. Then I could be honest about my feelings. For him and for you."

She had been pacing, but now she stopped. Orry was seated on the tabby foundation, his muddy boots dangling into the brown grass. Madeline crooked her arm around his neck and kissed him.

"I do thank you for coming today. I couldn't stand Resolute one moment longer."

The second kiss was more intense. Then she smoothed her skirt and walked toward the edge of the marsh. As she always did during their meetings, she began to describe incidents of the past few days. The birth of Jane's son. The whipping of Tom. That brought her feelings about slavery to the surface. She usually avoided the topic, knowing how he felt. Today she couldn't.

"I think Southerners would somehow view the system differently if they could see through the slaves' eyes, so to speak." She turned from the sunlit marsh and gazed at him with an earnest expression. "How would you feel watching a man put handcuffs and ankle chains on your mother and turn her over to someone who was going to tell her what to do until the day she died?"

Orry's frown hinted at irritation. "My mother is a white woman. The boy you helped is an African."

"Does that justify the crime? Does it even explain it satisfactorily? Tom may be an African, but can you deny he's also a human being?"

"And I am now a criminal in your eyes?"

For a moment he sounded like Justin, implying she had no right to discuss the subject. She controlled a flare of temper and hurried back to him, trying to answer calmly and without animosity:

287

"I'm not accusing you of anything, my darling. I only want you to see things clearly. You're more reasonable than—" She was about to say "your father" but hastily changed course. "—than most. There is such terrible illogic in the South's attitude about the whole system. You hand a man a new shirt every Christmas but deprive him of his liberty, and you expect him to be grateful. You expect the world to applaud!"

"Madeline, you're talking about a man who is—"

"Inferior." She held up both hands. "I've heard that excuse a thousand times. I simply don't believe it. There are black men on Resolute with better minds than Justin's—they're just not permitted or encouraged to use them. But let that go. Assume for a second that there is some truth in the excuse and whites are, in some inexplicable fashion, superior. How does that justify robbing a man of his freedom? Shouldn't it instead create an obligation to help him succeed because he's less fortunate? Wouldn't that be the Christian response?"

"Damned if I know." Orry rose and slapped the slender book against his thigh. "You get me mightily confused with all this talk."

"I'm sorry."

She wasn't, though. She was pleased. Orry wasn't attempting to deny or refute her arguments. That might mean he was thinking about them. Perhaps she'd never be able to convince him that slavery was wrong, but if she could plant a doubt or two, she would consider it an accomplishment.

He was silent for a time. Then he shrugged. "I'm not smart enough to thread my way through all those arguments. Besides, I thought we were going to read."

He showed her the gold-stamped spine of the book that had arrived on yesterday's boat from Charleston: *The Raven and Other Poems*.

Madeline arranged her skirts and sat beside him. "E. A. Poe. Francis LaMotte's wife mentioned him last week. She read a couple of his fantastic tales and absolutely hated them. She said he belonged in a lunatic asylum."

For the first time that day, Orry laughed. "Typical reaction to a Yankee author. I'm afraid there's no chance of locking him up. He died last year in Baltimore. He was only forty, but a notorious drunkard. There have been some articles about him in the *Southern Literary Messenger*. He was the editor for a while. What's interesting to me is his West Point background."

"Was he a cadet?"

"For one term. The fall of 1830, I think. Apparently he had a brilliant future. He was in the first section of every course. But something went wrong, and he was court-martialed for gross neglect of duty. Just prior to his dismissal, he was spending nearly all his time at Benny Haven's."

"Drinking?"

"I suppose—though the real attraction at Benny's has always been the food. You wouldn't understand how a plate of fried eggs could taste like heaven. You've never dined in the cadet mess hall."

A soft note of reminiscence had come into his voice. His gaze rested somewhere above the marsh. How much he misses it, she thought, and slipped her arm through his. She always sat on his right side so that she wouldn't accidentally call attention to his loss.

"Anyway"—he opened the book—"I'm no judge of poetry, but I do like some of these. They have a strange, marvelous music in them. Shall we start with this one?"

The title of the verse was "Annabel Lee." She began:

"It was many and many a year ago,
    In a kingdom by the sea,
That a maiden there lived whom you may know
    By the name of Annabel Lee."

Her pause at the end of the line was his cue to read.

"And this maiden she lived with no other thought
    Than to love and be loved by me."

By now they were comfortable reading poetry aloud. They had started a couple of months ago, when Orry had surprised her by bringing a book. Some of the poetry wasn't very good, but they enjoyed the ritual, and once again today, responding to the verse, she felt a quiver of desire.

The physical reaction had startled her the first time it happened. Now she looked forward to it with delicious anticipation. The soft alternation of their voices took on a kind of sexual rhythm, as if they were possessing each other, making love to each other, in the only way that was possible. Each of them held the book; the back of her left hand brushed his knuckles. The contact seemed to generate heat all through her. She turned slightly so that she could look at him while they read on.

The anonymous lover in the poem lost his Annabel Lee. They experienced that loss as the stanzas swept on toward a climax. Her voice grew husky.

> "For the moon never beams without bringing me dreams
>   Of the beautiful Annabel Lee—"

Orry's voice quickened the pace.

> "And the stars never rise but I feel the bright eyes
>   Of the beautiful Annabel Lee."

Her eyes flickered back and forth from the page to his face. Under her layers of clothing her breasts ached. Her loins felt molten.

> "And so, all the night-tide, I lie down by the side
>   Of my darling—my darling—"

She stumbled and had to glance down hastily in order to finish the line.

> "My life, and my bride—"

" 'In the sepulcher there by the sea,' " he read. " 'In her tomb by the sounding sea.' "

He closed the book and gripped her hand. They sat in silence, gazing at each other. Then, no longer able to restrain herself, she flung her arms around his neck with a little cry and brought her open mouth to his.

Orry rode home in the early dusk of the February afternoon. He felt as he always did after meeting Madeline. Their time together was never long enough. And reading poetry was no substitute for loving her properly, as God had intended when he designed man and woman.

Today they had gone to the brink, almost surrendered to the hunger overwhelming them. Only extreme restraint, a herculean struggle to master their emotions, had kept them from tumbling into the brown grass beside the chapel foundation. Because they had come so close,

Orry felt more lonely and frustrated than ever as he swung up the lane and turned his horse over to one of the house servants. The slave smiled and greeted him. Orry answered with a curt nod. What was the nigra really thinking? *You hand me a shirt every Christmas and rob me of my liberty and expect me to kiss your hand. I'd sooner break it off.* Damn Madeline for filling his head with doubts and questions about the system he had accepted as moral and proper for most of his life.

He stalked into the library and flung back the draperies to admit the faint rays of the sunset. It was torment to keep seeing her, and torment to think of giving her up. What was he to do?

He poured a heavy drink of whiskey. The last light was going. One by one highlights disappeared from the brasswork of his Army sword scabbard, which hung from a clothes stand he had placed in a corner. His dark blue uniform coat was draped over the stand. Not the coat he was wearing when his arm got blown off, needless to say; this one had both sleeves. The brass buttons, as well as the pommel of his sheathed sword, had a greenish cast, he noticed. Here and there patches of mold speckled the coat.

He sank into his favorite chair, brooding over the mementos. He ought to get rid of them. They were constant reminders of his thwarted ambition. They were slowly going to ruin, just like his own life. They had no purpose, and neither did he. They existed, that was all.

God, if only that day at Churubusco had been different. If only he had visited New Orleans when he was younger and chanced on Madeline there. *If only!* Somewhere there had to be an antidote for the poison of "if only." But what was it?

He stumbled to the cabinet to fill his glass a second time. Upstairs his sisters were quarreling. They always seemed to be these days. They had reached the right age. He shut the windows and sat drinking and listening to the sound of phantom drums. Finally the uniform faded away in the dark.

Clarissa opened the door around eleven and discovered him passed out on the floor. Two servants carried him to his bed.

Although Ashton and Brett had reached adolescence, they still shared a spacious bedroom on the second floor. Ashton, fourteen and already a fully developed, flamboyantly beautiful young woman, constantly complained about the arrangement. Why did she have to surrender her privacy? Why did she have to live with, as she put it, "a twelve-year-old baby who's still flat as a board?"

Tonight the room was exceptionally warm. Ashton, who slept in the bed nearest the window, kept muttering about her discomfort. Kept puffing her pillow noisily, and pressing the back of her wrist to her damp forehead, and sighing.

Finally, drowsy and irritated, her sister said: "Oh, for heaven's sake, hush up and let me sleep."

"I can't. I'm tight as a drum inside."

"Ashton, I don't understand you sometimes."

"Naturally not," her sister huffed. "You're just a baby. Baby white skin and baby white bloomers. You'll probably be like that till you're an old woman."

"Ooo," Brett said, and flung a pillow. Of all the insults Ashton heaped on her, none bothered her more than references to her failure thus far to show a single sign of what some called woman's curse of shame. Once a month Ashton pranced around the room to be sure her sister saw her stained pantalets. This never failed to humiliate Brett, as did her lack of physical development.

Of course she wasn't sure she wanted to grow up. Not if it meant she must roll her eyes and act sugary and coy around every man under thirty. She was positive she didn't want to grow up if it meant cozying up to someone like lawyer Huntoon.

The thought of him gave Brett one of her few opportunities for reprisal. In imitation of her sister's sweetest manner, she said, "I should think you would be blissfully happy tonight. James Huntoon is calling tomorrow—he and all those politicians Papa's been hobnobbing with lately. You fancy Mr. Huntoon, don't you?"

Ashton threw the pillow right back. "I think he's a toad, and you know it. He's an old man. Twenty, nearly. This is how I feel about him."

She stuck out her tongue and retched four times.

Brett hugged the pillow to her stomach, overcome with laughter. In the low country, parents still decided which young men were suitable companions for their daughters. Ashton was old enough to have several beaux, but so far Huntoon was the only one who had received Tillet Main's permission to call.

Brett wanted to continue the teasing, but a noise from outside drew both girls to the window. United by their curiosity, they watched a ghostly figure on horseback gallop up the lane, flash through a patch of moonlight, and disappear in the direction of the stable.

"That was Cousin Charles," Brett said in an awed voice.

"'Course it was," Ashton said. "He must have been off sparking Sue Marie Smith. Either that or one of the nigger wenches." The idea made Brett blush.

Ashton giggled. "If Whitney Smith ever finds out that his cousin Sue Marie is fooling with Charles, there'll be the devil to pay. Sue Marie and Whitney are engaged."

"When are you and Huntoon announcing your engagement?"

Ashton yanked her sister's hair. "When hell freezes!"

Brett threw a grazing punch at Ashton's shoulder, then retreated to her bed. Ashton faced the moonlit window, rubbing her palms back and forth across her stomach and wrinkling her nightgown in what Brett considered a perfectly shameless way.

"I guess Sue Marie can't help herself with Cousin Charles. Or any boy. They say her drawers are as hot as a basket of Fourth of July squibs. I know how she feels," Ashton concluded with a soulful sigh. "You wouldn't, though."

Brett punched her pillow and turned away, more hurt than angry. Ashton eclipsed her in wit, and beauty, and accomplishments. No doubt she always would.

Ashton had more courage, too. She took chances. In that way she was a lot like Cousin Charles. Maybe lawyer Huntoon would tame her down. Brett hoped so. She liked her sister, she supposed, but sometimes Ashton's antics just plain wore her out.

James Huntoon wore round spectacles and an invisible mantle of righteousness. Although he was only six years older than Ashton, he already displayed jowls and the beginning of a paunch. The facial fat spoiled a countenance that was otherwise handsome.

Huntoon's family had been in the state a long time, but it lacked about fifty years of being as old as that of the Mains. The first Huntoon in Carolina, an immigrant who could neither read nor write, had settled in the hills up country. A member of the next generation had discovered that being an ignorant dirt farmer in the midlands was not the path to prominence and had removed to the coast, where sharp dealing and some lucky land acquisitions had generated substantial wealth within two more generations. The Huntoons intermarried with several distinguished families and in this way gradually acquired a pedigree.

Most of the family acreage was gone now, a casualty of the same peril that had ruined the LaMottes—bad management coupled with a too-lavish style of living. James Huntoon's elderly parents subsisted on the charity of relatives. They occupied the family's run-down plantation house, attended by five Negroes too old to find other purchasers. It had been clear to James from very early in life that if he wanted to survive and prosper, he could not live on the land.

Fortunately the Huntoons still possessed an impressive set of friends and acquaintances; in South Carolina the fact that a family had lost its wealth did not necessarily destroy its social standing. Only unacceptable behavior was certain to do that. So James knew all the right people to call on when he set out to make his way in Charleston. He read law in one of the leading firms and had recently established his own practice in the city.

Tillet thought most of the Huntoon clan unworthy of notice; while members of other important families worried about the state's future, the Huntoons nattered about the past and behaved as if the crushing problems of the present didn't exist. But Tillet sensed potential in James, even if the young man did disdain the hard work sometimes demanded of a lawyer. Certainly Huntoon's contacts throughout the state gave him every chance for success.

Huntoon also liked politics and was an effective orator. Philosophically, he was aligned with those who were eager to see the state and the region assert independence in an increasingly hostile world. One such was Robert Barnwell Rhett, the influential editor of the *Charleston Mercury*. Huntoon's mother was related to Rhett by marriage.

Huntoon had first seen Ashton last winter at a theater in Charleston. Clarissa had brought her daughters to town for the social season, and the family had occupied a box for a performance by the noted actor Frederic Stanhope Hill. He routinely included Charleston on his tours, as did most theatrical luminaries.

The moment the young lawyer set eyes on Ashton Main, he was struck by a consuming lust. She was lovely and, though still young, already voluptuous. Huntoon sent a card to Clarissa requesting permission to call whenever the parents deemed their daughter was of suitable age.

Several months and one birthday went by before Clarissa responded with a short, polite letter. Other girls began receiving callers at fourteen, so she and Tillet would not gainsay Ashton. But she put the would-be suitor on notice. "My husband agrees with the low-country maxim which states that a woman's name should appear in the papers twice only—once when she marries and once when she dies. I mention this so as to completely inform you about his attitude toward improper behavior of any kind."

Duly warned, Huntoon initiated his courtship with traditional gifts—flowers first, then kid gloves and French chocolates. He had now progressed to visiting alone with Ashton indoors for short periods. To be alone with her elsewhere—to go riding without a chaperone, for example—was as yet out of the question. Huntoon did his best to bridle his lust. One day, if everything went just right, that splendid body would be his.

He had to admit Ashton frightened him a little. She wasn't outwardly unconventional, yet she possessed a saucy boldness not typical of girls of her age and station. He did admire her regal air, which some called arrogance. He admired Tillet Main's wealth, too.

As for the others in the family, he was unimpressed. Clarissa was a harmless old soul, and Ashton's little sister horridly drab. Huntoon shrank from any contact with Orry—a one-armed ghoul—and as for Cooper Main, who went strutting about Charleston as if he actually had some right to call himself a Southerner, Huntoon believed he should be run out of the state on a rail. The four gentlemen who had accompanied Huntoon to Mont Royal this morning shared that view. One was Rhett of the *Mercury*.

"The convention has been called for June," Huntoon said to their host. "In Nashville. Delegates from all the Southern states will attend for the purpose of appraising Senator Clay's resolutions and determining a common response."

"June, eh?" Tillet scratched his chin. "Won't they vote on the resolutions by then?"

Another of the visitors chuckled. "I wouldn't say it's likely given the present split in the Congress."

Huntoon's lips pursed, an unconscious reaction to the scrutiny he was receiving from Orry, whom Tillet had somehow persuaded to come to this meeting. Orry demonstrated his reluctance by sitting slouched in a corner with his legs crossed, a silent observer.

Why was the damned ghoul watching him? Orry had nothing to say about his sister's beaux. Huntoon concluded that the attention was a product of simple dislike. It was mutual.

"Should this Nashville meeting be held at all?" Tillet questioned. "You told me it isn't an official convention of the party—"

Rhett stood suddenly. The fifty-year-old editor dominated the gathering, as he usually dominated any he attended. "Tillet, my friend, you've been away from public affairs too long."

"Busy making a living, Robert."

The others laughed. Rhett continued, "You know as well as I that for twenty years and more our adversaries have preached a doctrine of animosity toward the South. They have injured our sensibilities with their lies and systematically robbed us with their peculiar tax on Southern agriculture, the tariff. What's more, many of our worst enemies can be found within the ranks of the Democratic party. Hence the party in South Carolina has slowly withdrawn, until it can be said that we are merely in sometime alliance with the national organization rather than active members of it. In no other way can we express our antipathy for the party's views and practices.''

Orry spoke up at last. ''But if we don't like the way the party's doing things, isn't it easier to change that from the inside than from the outside?''

Rhett looked askance. ''Mr. Main, I consider the question unworthy of any man born and raised in this state. In the South, for that matter. One does not compromise with sworn enemies. We have been subjected to Northern aggressions for twenty-five years. To right that situation, wouldn't we be foolish to appeal to the very men who have caused it? We can redress grievances only by following one road: that leading to independence.''

Calhoun was dying, and many said the legislators had already chosen Rhett to replace him in the Senate. Tillet could understand why. He was irked to note that his son looked unimpressed, dubious even.

''Personally,'' Rhett added, ''I too see little need for this Nashville convention, since I find the whole idea of compromise poisonous. But I'll support the convention for the sake of Southern unity.''

''With all due respect to my distinguished relative,'' Huntoon said with one of his waspish little smiles, ''some of the rest of us, although in favor of a self-reliant South, are not quite ready to go along with what you and the *Mercury* are propounding these days.''

With a bleak expression, Orry said, ''Dissolution of the Union.''

''Precisely,'' said Rhett, who reminded Orry of a victorious gamecock just then.

Orry glanced away, unmistakably disapproving. Two of the visitors signaled Huntoon with their eyes, for Tillet was looking skeptical too. Huntoon suppressed lewd thoughts of Ashton, whom he had not yet seen, hastily crossed his legs, and seized control of the conversation.

''We have come here not to discuss that subject, Tillet, but to ask your support for the Nashville convention. To ask for it in a very tangible fashion, in fact. You have recently expressed interest in once again involving yourself in state affairs." A guarded nod from the older man. Huntoon pressed on. "The South Carolina delegation will incur expenses traveling to Tennessee and for meals and lodging while the convention deliberates. We thought—"

That's why they're here, Orry said to himself. Money. He heard no more of the conversation. He had agreed to attend the meeting as a favor to his father. He now regretted the decision.

Tillet was soon won over. He promised to donate five hundred dollars to help underwrite the delegation. Disgusted, Orry continued to stare out the window. Someone knocked. He fairly leaped to answer and gladly excused himself and slipped outside in response to his sister's whispered summons.

"What's wrong, Ashton?"

Brett came rushing up behind her sister. Both girls were wide-eyed with fright.

"It's Cousin Charles," Ashton said. "He's in awful trouble. There's a man here demanding he give satisfaction in a duel."

21

We can't find Cousin Charles anywhere," Brett said as the three of them rushed outdoors. "That's why Ashton interrupted your meeting."

Orry stomped along the piazza toward the visitor waiting beside his horse. "Most ridiculous thing I've ever heard. Cousin Charles has no business fighting duels. He's just a boy."

"I don't think that'll make a mite of difference to the gentleman," Ashton said breathlessly. Orry decided she was right. Icy pride and hostility showed in the exaggerated way the young dandy tipped his out-of-style beaver hat.

"Your servant, Mr. Main. My name is Smith Dawkins."

"I know who you are. State your business."

"Why, sir, I thought these young ladies might have communicated the nature of it. I am here as a representative and kinsman of Mr. Whitney Smith, who last evening came upon Mr. Charles Main of this plantation dallying with his fiancée Miss Sue Marie Smith. The gentlemen exchanged words and Mr. Main struck a blow, whereupon Mr. Smith demanded satisfaction. I am here to make the arrangements. I presume you are authorized to act as Mr. Main's second?"

"I'm authorized to do nothing of the kind. What you're proposing is against the law."

Dawkins fairly dripped contempt. "You know as well as I, sir—the *code duello* is widely practiced despite South Carolina law."

The young whelp was springing a trap, and a damnable one. Cousin Charles couldn't avoid the trap unless he wanted to appear cowardly. Of course, by saving his face and his honor, he might lose his life. That was what made the code so idiotic. If Mr. Smith Dawkins had seen Churubusco, he wouldn't court death so blithely.

The visitor jammed his hat onto his head. "If you could possibly direct me to Mr. Main's second or, barring that, to the gentleman himself—"

Orry sighed and gave up. "I don't know where to find Charles right now. I'll act as second."

"Very good, sir."

"I suppose we'll have to travel all the way to the other side of the Savannah River to avoid prosecution?"

"My party promises absolute discretion and no witnesses other than family members. If you can give a similar assurance, there is no need for the meeting to take place in another state."

Considering the size of the Smith clan, the witnesses could number in the hundreds. Orry let that pass, however. He gave a brusque nod of agreement. "Go on."

They talked for another five minutes, settling on conventional dueling pistols the following Tuesday morning, just after sunrise. The site was to be a clearing known as Six Oaks, two miles up the river.

Pleased, young Dawkins tipped his hat once more and rode away. Orry looked thunderous as he left the porch to find Charles and convey the bad news.

The two girls had watched the scene from behind one of the columns. Ashton started to call to Orry as he left. Brett jerked her sister's arm and put a warning finger to her lips. For once Ashton took someone's advice.

Orry decided to say nothing about the duel to Clarissa and Tillet. His mother would worry, and his father would probably want to watch. Orry hoped to keep the meeting low-key, if possible. More important, he wanted to conclude it without injury to Charles.

At this time of the morning the boy could usually be found loitering near the kitchen where he cadged grits or a slab of fresh cornbread. But none of the kitchen slaves had seen him today. Orry headed for the stable, deciding it would be easier to search on horseback. Distantly, a shot rang out.

He changed direction and walked rapidly down the road to the slave cabins. Behind him, several of the kitchen women speculated about the reason for his furious expression.

Orry flung one leg over the split-rail fence, then the other. On the far side of the field of stubble, Cousin Charles was practicing the measured step of a duelist pacing away from an opponent. From his right hand hung a huge, rusty pistol Orry had never seen before.

Orry stood motionless until Charles took his tenth step and pivoted. The boy swept the pistol up with a wild, jerky motion. As he turned, he saw Orry by the fence, his beard and his pinned-up shirt sleeve flapping in the breeze. Charles's eyes flew wide, but he completed his turn and fired.

The puff of powder smoke drifted away. Orry hurried forward.

"Smith Dawkins was just up at the house," he called. Charles looked wary as Orry came to a halt, glowering. "We made the arrangements for this splendid enterprise of yours. Pistols, next Tuesday. It seems I've become your second."

"I thought you didn't approve of dueling."

"I don't. You and the rest of these country cavaliers haven't the faintest notion of what real fighting's all about."

The boy tried one of those dazzling smiles. "Spoken like a true soldier."

The response was a glare. Charles stopped smiling. "I'm sorry you became involved, Orry. I lost track of the time last night. Didn't leave Sue Marie soon enough. Otherwise this wouldn't have happened."

"But it did. We proceed from there. What do you know about guns?"

"Not much. I reckon I can learn all I need to know, though."

"Not the way you're going about it." Orry aimed a scornful finger at the rusty pistol. "Where'd you get that monstrosity?"

Charles's eyelids drooped. He shrugged. "Doesn't matter."

Stolen, Orry thought in disgust. "Well, the first thing we do is get rid of it." He snatched the weapon and threw it high and far.

"Here!" Charles shouted, reddening. "I have to practice."

"We'll use my Army pistol. Dueling pistols are generally flintlocks, but even with that difference my gun will give you a better approximation of the kind you'll probably use. Something between a sixty- and a seventy-caliber, I expect. One more thing. On a dueling pistol you'll usually find a hair trigger. The way you turned a minute ago—jerking your arm up like a vane on a broken windmill—a dueling pistol would have gone off much too soon. You'd have hit the sky or the trees and left your opponent with all the time he needed to kill you. Steady and smooth is the shooting style you want."

Orry began walking back toward the road. When Charles didn't follow, he turned and waved. "Come on. You're fighting next Tuesday, not next year."

"I thought I would do this on my own—"

The words trailed off, blurred by the breeze blowing through the sunlit field. Charles's expression had grown resentful, defiant almost.

"If you want to get yourself killed through ignorance," Orry shouted back, "you certainly may do it on your own."

White-lipped, Charles blurted, "Why should you want to help me? You don't like me."

"What I don't like, Charles, is your behavior for the last year or so. If that's the same as not liking you, so be it. But I still have a responsibility for your welfare. I can't stand by and let Whitney Smith commit murder. Come with me or not, as you like."

Orry continued on across the field. Charles remained motionless, hands clenched at his sides. Like ice melting, the hostility left his face, replaced by a slow, wondering smile. From the ground he retrieved a rammer, a cracked powder horn, and a bag of shot. Then he ran after Orry.

They practiced three hours a day. Orry swore his sisters to secrecy about the duel. Ashton let the cat out anyway. It happened at the dinner table, and Charles was surprised at how upset Clarissa became. Orry pointed out that he was giving Charles instruction and that the boy stood an excellent chance of coming through with a light wound or none.

Tillet agreed with that prediction, making demeaning comments about the character and nerve of Whitney Smith. He wished his nephew well. Altogether, it was an overwhelming experience for Charles. No one had ever taken such an interest in him before.

"*No!*" was the word Orry uttered most often on the practice field. "You're not taking long enough to aim. I know fear pushes you to haste. But haste will push you straight into a grave."

He grabbed Charles's right arm and shook it. "By God, you'd better remember that. You'll make a fool of me if you get yourself killed."

He spoke the last sentence thoughtlessly, not realizing how ridiculous it was until Charles grinned. "Well," Charles said, "if there's any reason I wouldn't want to be killed, that would be it."

The smile suddenly felt stiff on his lips. Orry was a stern man, a hard taskmaster. By attempting to joke with him, Charles had overstepped. He had been lulled by a change in their relationship these past few days, his resentment of Orry replaced by a kind of brotherly feeling and even an occasional flash of outright affection. Evidently Orry didn't think he was completely worthless, or he would never have devoted so much time to helping him. But now Charles had gone too far. Orry wasn't amused.

Suddenly, though, deep in Orry's matted beard, a glimmer of white appeared. A smile.

"Of course not," he said, finally realizing the foolishness of his remark. "The devil with saving your life. Save my honor. Save my pride. I am, after all, a Southerner."

They laughed together, loudly and long. Then Orry touched the gleaming barrel of the Johnson pistol, so well preserved that not a single speck of rust showed on it.

"We won't accomplish anything cackling like a couple of jays. I'll count ten. You walk, turn, and hit that limb. Try to do it right this time. We've only got two more days."

A cold snap came. Charles and Orry rose at half past four on the morning of the duel, ate a biscuit apiece and drank coffee, then struggled into overcoats. Since Orry had named the site and the hour, the Smith party would supply the weapons.

They went outside where grooms waited in the dark with their horses. Tillet was there, and Clarissa too; the girls hadn't been allowed to come down.

Ribbons of mist floated a foot above the ground. It was a dismal morning. Or perhaps the chill was only in his heart, Orry thought as he mounted and waited for good-byes to be said.

Tillet pumped Charles's hand. Clarissa hugged him. As they walked their mounts down the lane, Orry saw false dawn in the east. Long plumes of mist shot from the nostrils of the horses as they exhaled. Charles cleared his throat.

"Orry?"

"Yes?"

"Whatever happens, I want you to know I appreciate the way you've helped me. I never thought anybody cared a hoot about me."

"All of us care, Charles. You're a Main. Family."

He meant it. He was surprised at the way his attitude toward the boy had undergone a transformation in a remarkably short time. Charles had been an eager pupil, done none of that wisecracking that had caused Orry to look down on him before. Of course Charles's own life was at stake this time. But Orry thought the change in the young man resulted from more than that. Orry had held out his hand, and Charles had grasped it like a true kinsman. What a pity the change had come at this late hour.

The mist rolled around them. Hundreds of stars pierced the paling sky. Charles drew a deep breath.

"Orry?"

"What?"

"I'm scared as hell."

"So am I," Orry said as they turned their horses up the river road.

Daylight was burning off the mist by the time they reached Six Oaks. Orry was annoyed to discover more than twenty men in the Smith party, various male relatives of all ages. At least with that number of spectators there were young men to serve as lookouts along the road and riverbank. Those deputized for the duty protested about missing the action but were quickly overruled.

Orry tethered the horses at the side of the clearing reserved for them. Charles flung off his overcoat, surcoat, waistcoat, and cravat, then rolled up his sleeves. In the shade of a great live oak across the clearing, flawlessly dressed Whitney Smith and others of his clan watched Charles's preparations with obvious contempt.

Whitney's kinsman, Smith Dawkins, strutted toward the Mains with a beautiful rosewood gun case, which he opened for their inspection. The .70-caliber weapons were worthy of the box. Each octagonal barrel was half-stocked in polished walnut and had a little ramrod nestling underneath. The pistols were exquisitely tooled and bore the engraved name of a London gunsmith and a date, 1828.

"Satisfactory?" Dawkins inquired.

"I'll tell you after I inspect them." Orry pulled one of the guns from its bed of persimmon velvet.

There was a light sheen of sweat on Charles's forehead. He paced back and forth while the seconds took care of loading the pistols. They handed one to each duelist, then indicated the agreed-upon starting point. Five minutes would be allowed for final preparations.

Charles looked calm. He betrayed his tension only by repeatedly smoothing his palms across the hair at his temples. Orry badly needed to urinate—tension, he presumed—but he didn't want to leave Charles alone. Especially not with round-faced Whitney Smith and his friend Dawkins smirking and striking poses and whispering jokes about the opponent.

Orry turned his back on them. "I know you're scared, Charles. But remember this. You have a definite advantage. You'll see it if you take a good look at that peacock behind me. Appearances being more important to him than mobility, he's still wearing a heavy coat. Further, he's too stupid to be frightened, and frightened men are careful men. In battle, Whitney's kind tend to fall first."

Charles wanted to answer but could only summon a kind of nervous croak. Orry squeezed his arm. Charles put his hand on top of Orry's and held it a second.

"Thank you," he said.

"Gentlemen, are you ready?" Smith Dawkins called. He sounded impatient.

Orry turned smartly. "Ready."

He walked onto the field, Charles right behind him. The spectators fell silent. A white heron went skating away above the sunlit treetops. At the edge of the clearing, the river flowed golden and peaceful.

Whitney and Charles acknowledged each other with nods; Whitney's was a nod of dismissal, Orry thought. Up close, eruptions on Whitney's skin were quite noticeable. Charles, five years younger, looked far more mature and poised. Whitney's hand trembled as he brought his gun up vertically in front of his face. A good sign—unless Whitney was one of those rare duelists whose aim was actually improved by a bad case of nerves.

Dawkins cleared his throat and addressed the opponents standing back to back with pistols raised. "I shall first pronounce the word *begin*. This is your signal to start pacing off the distance in time to my count. When you have completed the tenth and final pace, you are at liberty to turn and fire at will. Ready? Begin."

Charles moved one way, Whitney the other. Orry's heart began to pound. He drew in a long breath and held it. He and Dawkins quickly retreated to the sidelines. Dawkins stood next to him, counting.

"Three. Four. Five."

Charles took long, confident strides. Sunlight falling through the trees lit his hair. *He has such promise*, Orry thought. *If only there were a way to bring it to fruition. If only he lives long enough for someone to try.*

"Seven. Eight."

Sweat greased Whitney's blotchy face. The trembling had worked its way into his shoulders. Would he shoot or collapse first?

"Nine."

Charles stared straight ahead. Orry saw the tip of his tongue flick up to lick sweat from his lip, the only outward sign of the anxiety that must be twisting his belly. Orry wanted to shout, *"Remember—steady and smooth."*

"Ten."

Whitney's knees buckled, but he stayed upright and managed to pivot. He flung his pistol hand out in front of him with all the violence

305

Orry had criticized in Charles that first time in the field. The roar startled Charles. He blinked so hard Orry thought he was hit. Then, from a tree about four feet behind Charles, a branch came tumbling down.

A damp stain appeared on the front of Whitney's trousers. He executed a clumsy half turn and started to take a step. There were gasps from the spectators and an angry, hissing whisper from Dawkins.

"You must stand, Whitney. Stand!"

He did, but not without a struggle. The humiliating stain widened. He shook so badly the pistol bobbed up and down. Charles slowly extended his arm, took aim, and, with a cool look down the octagonal barrel, fired.

Whitney shrieked like a girl. He twisted to the left and fell, clutching his sleeve. Red showed between his fingers, but Charles had only pinked him. What's more, he had hit the spot at which he had aimed. Orry ran forward, jubilant.

Whitney passed out with Dawkins kneeling at his side. The spectators broke into applause. Drained of tension, Charles was wandering toward the riverbank in an erratic way. Orry caught him.

"You've got to acknowledge that applause. It's for you."

The young man stared at Orry, thunderstruck. Then he looked at the Smith relatives. It was true. They were applauding his marksmanship, his courage, and his generosity in wounding Whitney when he could have killed him. All the characteristics of a true Carolina gentleman, Orry thought, almost dizzy with happiness.

Charles saluted the spectators with his pistol. But he couldn't yet believe what had happened.

"I have to thank you again," Charles said as they rode homeward. Mild sunshine between the trees put bars of light and shadow on the road. Both men found the late-winter day a glorious one on which to be alive.

"You did it yourself, Charles."

"No, sir. Without you, I'd be lying dead back there." He smiled and shook his head. "My Lord, you don't know how it felt to hear those men clapping for me instead of their own kinsman."

"Who unfortunately showed himself a coward. All bluster, no substance. They didn't like that."

"Well, I can't get over it. I never will. I do have one question about—"

He stopped. Orry waited, but Charles said nothing more. Orry pointed ahead to a roadside hovel with a weathered sign hanging crookedly on the front. "Do you know that place? It's a poor excuse for a tavern, but the man does keep a stock of passable whiskey. I think we both deserve a drink. Shall we stop?"

"By all means." Charles grinned and galloped ahead.

The landlord goggled when his visitors ordered ardent spirits at half past seven in the morning. Orry's money quickly curtailed any objections or questions. The hovel smelled, so the two drinkers sat on the front stoop in the sunshine.

Orry swallowed half his whiskey, shivered, and blinked pleasurably. Then he said, "Earlier you started to ask a question."

"Yes. Whenever I got into a fight before, people disapproved. You included. Why was it different this morning? We were doing a hell of a lot more than punching each other. Why didn't anyone object?"

Orry studied Charles, wanting to learn if the young man was having some kind of sarcastic sport. He saw no sign of it. Charles had asked a serious question. An important one, too.

Orry wanted his answer to be right. He thought about it, then tossed off the rest of his liquor and clapped Charles on the shoulder.

"I think I can answer you best back at Mont Royal."

"I don't understand."

But Orry was already swinging up into the saddle. "Come on."

Tillet, Clarissa, and the girls rushed outside the moment they spied the horses in the lane. An inevitable delay followed as the spellbound listeners heard Orry's tale. Tillet offered enthusiastic congratulations, Clarissa sobbed with relief, and the girls jumped up and down and begged to hear Orry describe Charles's cool bravery a second time. All in all it took about an hour. Only then did Orry draw his cousin into the dim library and point to the clothes stand bearing his uniform coat and sword.

"There's your answer."

Charles looked baffled. "I don't know what you mean."

"Consider men who go to war. What do they do?"

"Fight."

"Yes, but more than that, they do so in a manner understood and agreed upon beforehand. Fierce as it may be, there is a code of conduct among honorable men who fight. Those Smiths applauded you not simply because you won but because you observed the rules. Whitney didn't. He tried to step away from your bullet. You saw the reaction. Before this, you never fought by the rules. That's the difference."

Orry lifted the left sleeve of the coat. "The world doesn't necessarily condemn the man who loves a battle. It encourages and rewards some of them. Even a gallant loser may get a share of the glory when the history books are written. I'm not sure it's altogether right to encourage and reward fighting and killing, but that's the way things are. Have I answered you?"

Charles nodded slowly, gazing at the scabbard, the brass buttons, the dark blue coat as if they were imbued with a religious significance. What Orry had just said came as a revelation.

Orry began to rummage in a cabinet. "There's whiskey here. I don't know about you, but I'm still thirsty as sin."

"So am I."

Charles walked around to the other side of the stand, never taking his eyes from the uniform. Orry too was swept up by a revelation. He saw Cousin Charles in a totally new light.

He may not be lost after all. Look at him staring at that uniform. He's fascinated.

Starting that very morning, he took Cousin Charles in hand.

He began with small readjustments. Mild, almost diffident suggestions about appearance. Manners. Regular hours. Nothing too important or demanding at first because he expected rebellion. Instead, he got instantaneous and dramatic compliance. Charles began to show up for every meal, his face and hands scrubbed, his shirttail tucked in, and no bowie knife at his belt.

Three weeks after the duel, Orry offered Charles a couple of books, which he urged him to read. Orry had chosen easy works: light historical romances by William Gilmore Simms, a South Carolinian who was almost as popular as Fenimore Cooper had been in his day. The speed with which Charles finished the novels convinced Orry that the young man was exceptionally intelligent—something Clarissa had said for years. Orry had never believed her.

Next, Orry gave his cousin short lessons in some of the social conventions: courtesies to be accorded to ladies, what constituted proper attire for different kinds of public and family functions. Charles not only paid attention; he began to put some of the principles into action. He was soon treating Ashton and Brett with a new politeness that flabbergasted them. But they enjoyed it because Charles was handsome and carried off the courtly flourishes with hardly a trace of awkwardness.

"The boy's a born cavalier," Orry exclaimed to Madeline at their next meeting. "He puts me to shame. He's graceful, charming—and what's more, it comes naturally to him. Where has he been hiding that side of his character?"

"Under a layer of dirt and resentment, probably," she said with a gentle smile.

"I expect you're right. The transformation's incredible. All it took for him to come into his own was a little affection from his family."

"From you, principally. Even at Resolute they're gossiping about the change. Nancy told me Charles follows you everywhere."

"All day long. Like a puppy! It's embarrassing." But Orry's expression said he really didn't mind the hero worship. "Trouble is, you solve one problem and the solution creates another."

"What now? You've been saying Charles is straightening out—"

"That's exactly what I mean. He is. Before, I was positive he'd wind up dead in some ditch after a brawl or a horse race. Now I'm wracking my brain to figure out what he should do with his life. I must suggest something, and soon."

"You sound like a father."

"Don't joke. It's no small responsibility."

"Of course it isn't. I wasn't joking. I was smiling because you're happy. I've never seen you in such good spirits. You like the responsibility."

He looked at her. "Yes. I do."

After supper every night, if Orry had no work in the office, he and Charles would take a whiskey together in the library. Sometimes Tillet joined them, but if so, he was a silent participant. Silent and amazed. He knew something positive and wholesome had happened in the relationship between his son and his nephew. He didn't want to interfere. He also realized that, in spirit and in fact, Orry was fast becoming the head of the family. Tillet resented that more than a little. Yet it pleased him, too. Cousin Charles was reserved when Tillet was present. When he wasn't, the young man couldn't hear enough about Orry's experiences as a cadet.

"You really liked it at West Point?"

"Well, not completely. But I made several good friends—and I met my best friend there."

"George." When Orry nodded, Charles asked, "Did you want to stay in the Army?"

"Very much. General Scott, however, has this unreasonable prejudice against any officer with just one arm. Maybe it's because he still has two."

Charles smiled. It wasn't much of a jest, but he realized that never before had Orry been able to make light of his injury. It was a remarkable change.

Charles returned his gaze to the uniform on the stand. "I just can't get over the idea that you can fight and get paid for it."

Orry held his breath. Was this the right moment? He seized on it.

"Charles—here's a thought. It's possible that we could secure an Academy appointment for you."

"But—I'm not smart enough."

"Yes, you are. You just don't know enough to pass the entrance examinations. In other words, you have the intelligence but not the facts. Herr Nagel could certainly give you those in the next year or so. You'd have to apply yourself, but I know you can do it if you have the desire."

Stunned by the new future he had glimpsed, Cousin Charles sat a moment before answering.

"Yes, sir, I do."

"First-rate! I'll corner Nagel in the morning."

"What?" the tutor cried when he heard Orry's plan. "Instruct *him?* I should say not, Herr Main. The first time I reprimand him for failing to complete an assignment, he will whip out that gigantic knife and *pfut!*" Nagel's thumb slashed across his throat. "Thus ends my brilliant academic service to this family."

"Charles has changed," Orry assured him. "Give him a chance. I'll pay you a bonus."

On that basis Herr Nagel was happy to gamble. At week's end he came back to his employer with a stunned look.

"You are absolutely right. The transformation is astonishing. He remains stubborn and irritable over some things—chiefly his own unfamiliarity with concepts he should have learned long before this. But he's quick. I believe I can bring him along rapidly, though naturally it will require some, ah, extra effort."

"For which you'll receive extra compensation every week."

"You are too kind," Herr Nagel murmured, bowing. "We shall make a scholar of that one yet."

There was exhilaration in Orry's voice and a sparkle in his eyes. "We just want to make him a West Point cadet. There's going to be

310

a professional soldier in this family."

To himself he added, "After all."

At the end of the first week of April, Orry went to his father. "In two or three years, Charles should be ready to enter the Academy. I've learned there'll be a vacancy at that time. It isn't too early to secure the appointment for him. We might start with a letter to the War Department. We could ask Senator Calhoun to transmit it. Shall I write it, or will you?"

Tillet showed him a copy of the *Mercury*. "Calhoun's dead."

"Good God. When?"

"The last day of March. In Washington."

It shouldn't have come as a great surprise, Orry realized. Calhoun had been failing for a long time, and politically the past month had been one of the stormiest in recent history. Henry Clay's compromise resolutions had come up for Senate debate. Because Calhoun was the South's senior spokesman, his reaction, although predictable, was widely awaited. But he'd been too ill to take the floor. Senator Mason had read his remarks for him. Of course Calhoun denounced the Clay program and warned again that Northern hostility was making secession attractive to Southerners. Over the years Calhoun had moved steadily away from a nationalistic position to one that put the welfare of his section first. Most Southerners agreed that he had been driven to this hardened and parochial stand by the activities of the abolitionists, both in and out of Congress.

Three days after Calhoun's speech was presented, Senator Daniel Webster had risen to plead the opposite view. He had spoken eloquently in favor of the resolutions and of the urgent need to put preservation of the Union above all else. The speech was too full of goodwill and the spirit of compromise for many of Webster's Northern colleagues, who promptly began vilifying him. Tillet, too, called Webster's seventh of March address an abomination—though not for the same reasons the abolitionist senators did.

But at the moment Orry was thinking of Calhoun from another perspective. "The senator was one of the Academy's staunchest friends."

"Once," Tillet snapped. "He was also a friend of the Union. So were we all. Then the Yankees turned on us."

Tillet seemed to suggest the attack had been causeless. Orry thought of Priam but said nothing. The unexpected pang of conscience surprised and troubled him. His father went on:

"It wasn't merely old age and sickness that killed John Calhoun. It was Jackson, Garrison, Seward—that whole damned crowd who opposed him, and us, in everything from nullification to the way we earn our bread. They harried Calhoun like a pack of mad dogs. They exhausted him." Tillet flung the newspaper on the floor. "It won't be forgotten."

Orry remained silent, upset by his father's unforgiving tone.

A few weeks later Tillet had further cause for outrage. A slave who had run away from a plantation near Mont Royal was recaptured in Columbus, Ohio, by a professional slave catcher. The slave catcher had been hired by the owner of the runaway.

Before the man and his prisoner could leave Columbus, abolitionists intervened. They threatened the slave catcher with lynching and took the escaped black into protective custody, saying it was necessary for a court to rule on the legality of the claim. That was a subterfuge; they knew the court had no jurisdiction. But the delay gave them time to spirit the runaway out of jail. A rear door was mysteriously left unlocked. The fugitive was over the border and safe in Canada before most people knew about it. The unsubtle intrigue in Ohio outraged the slave's owner and many of his neighbors. Tillet talked of little else.

Orry, meantime, shared his personal happiness with Madeline. Cousin Charles had settled down to studies with Herr Nagel, and Orry could hardly stop boasting about his protégé's progress.

"We'll have to suspend the lessons for two months this summer, though." It was a clumsy way to introduce another subject that was on his mind, but it had to be done.

"Charles is leaving?"

"Along with the rest of us. I've leased a summer cottage in Newport, near George's place."

"You'll have your reunion at last!"

"Yes."

"Oh, Orry, how exciting." Her response seemed genuine. If she felt disappointment, she hid it well.

"You won't miss me?"

"Don't tease. I'll miss you terribly. Those two months will be the longest of my life."

She threw her arms around his neck and kissed him so passionately that the little volume of Cullen Bryant's poems slipped off her lap unnoticed. After she caught her breath she said, "But I'll survive. That is, I will as long as I know you'll come back to me. I couldn't bear it if you took up with some Yankee girl."

"I'd never do that," Orry replied with that humorless sincerity Madeline found touching sometimes; on other occasions, for no reason she could explain, it infuriated her. He went on, "It's time Charles got a peek at the world beyond the borders of South Carolina. If he goes to the Academy, he'll meet all sorts of people with new and different ideas. That can be a shock. It was to me. He must be prepared."

She touched his face. "You sound more like a father every day."

"Nothing wrong with that, is there?"

"Nothing." She gave his cheek a wifely peck. "It's grand for Charles, but he's not the only one getting benefits from this new relationship—not by any means. You're so much happier. That makes me happy, too."

When she kissed him this time, it was to demonstrate the sincerity of what she had just said. A few moments later, as she was leaning down to retrieve the book, a question occurred to her.

"You say the entire family's going to Rhode Island?"

"Not Cooper, of course."

"That's what I meant. Was the choice to stay home his or your father's?"

Cooper had visited Mont Royal two nights ago. He and Tillet had been unable to stay in the same room without quarreling violently over the Clay resolutions. Orry's smile disappeared.

"Both," he said.

22

Cooper Main loved Charleston.

He loved its narrow, cobbled streets, which reminded many visitors of Europe; the expensive merchandise sold in its shops; the peal of bells from all the white church spires that had weathered salt air and sea gales for so many years. He loved the political rhetoric overheard in the saloon bar of the Charleston Hotel; the clatter of the drays whose drivers were constantly being fined for racing through the streets at dangerous speeds; the glow of the street lamps after one of the two municipal lamplighters, or one of their half-dozen slaves, had passed by. And he loved the house he had bought with some of the first year's profits of the Carolina Shipping Company.

The house was on Tradd Street, right around the corner from the famous old Heyward residence. It was a typical Charleston house, designed for coolness and privacy. Each of its three floors had a piazza, and each piazza ran the length of the building, or about sixty feet. The house was twenty feet deep, the width of a single room, and was situated on the lot so that one long side was flush with the public sidewalk.

Although the house was entered from this side, the opposite one facing the garden was considered the front. Cooper called the garden his second office. Behind a high brick wall he often worked for hours on company matters, surrounded by the seasonal beauties of azaleas and magnolias and the contrasting greens of the crape myrtle and the yucca. He thought it a shame that he lived in such a beautiful house all by himself.

But he didn't think of that often; he was too busy. He had turned his quasi-exile into a triumphant success along with the little cotton packet company. He was now in the process of doubling the company's warehouse space by means of an addition. He never consulted his father about such decisions. Tillet still thought of the Carolina Shipping Company as a burden, a financial risk. That left Cooper free to run it his way.

The company's headquarters, warehouse, and pier were located on

Concord Street, above the U.S. Customs House. The company symbol, appearing on a signboard in front as well as on the ensigns of its two rickety packets, was an oval of ship's line surrounding three shorter pieces of line arranged to represent the letters C.S.C.

Cooper knew Charleston would never be *the* cotton port, as it had once been *the* rice port. Alabama and Mississippi dominated cotton production now. But Charleston still shipped a respectable tonnage, and Cooper wanted an ever bigger share for C.S.C. For that reason, a few months ago he had mortgaged everything and placed an order with the Black Diamond Boat Yard of Brooklyn, New York, for a new packet of modern, indeed advanced, design.

She would be driven by a screw propeller, not side wheels. Below decks, three transverse bulkheads would create four compartments that could be made watertight. In the event the hull was breached on coastal rocks, cargo in the undamaged compartments could be saved.

The bulkheads added substantially to the cost of the packet. But Cooper had already described the innovation to a couple of local cotton factors, and their reaction had been so positive he knew the extra expenditure would give his vessel an edge over its competition—and never mind that packets didn't run aground that often. It was the provision for what might happen that influenced a factor's choice of a ship.

A break in the hull was even less likely because of a second unusual feature—the use of iron instead of wood. Hazard Iron would supply a special run of plate for the hull.

Cooper was proud of the design of the new packet, which was to be christened *Mont Royal*. Before drawing up a list of features and performance specifications and taking them to Brooklyn, he had spent months reading up on naval architecture and filling sketch pads. Black Diamond's president said that if Cooper ever tired of Charleston, they would hire him—and it wasn't entirely a joke.

Cooper had little trouble arranging financing for his project. Although the Charleston bankers didn't care for his political views, they liked his business ideas, his confidence, and his record thus far. He had already increased the volume of C.S.C. by eighty percent and its profits by twenty. He had accomplished it by refurbishing the old packets so that they were more dependable and by offering discounts to factors who placed a large part of their business with him.

In addition to the Concord Street property, C.S.C. now owned another piece of real estate—a twenty-five-acre parcel of land on James Island, across from the peninsula on which the city stood. The parcel had water frontage of one-half mile and was located not far from abandoned Fort Johnson. Cooper had acquired this seemingly worthless land as part of a long-term scheme he had kept secret from everyone. He wasn't afraid of being laughed at; he simply felt that the prudent businessman kept good ideas private until it served his interest to make them public. Now, at twilight on the first Monday in May, he strolled the Battery and gazed at his real estate there beyond the open water. He continued to believe his decision to buy had been right. It might be years before he could put that land to use, but use it he would.

Tucked under his arm he carried the latest edition of the *Mercury*. The paper's extremism repelled him, but it covered city and state matters in adequate fashion. One front-page article told the harrowing story of an old woman suffocated in her bed by two house slaves she had reprimanded. The slaves had disappeared and were still at large; the paper editorialized about the rebellious tendencies of Negroes and how those tendencies were being inflamed by Northern propaganda. Cooper never had any trouble understanding the state's collective nervousness about its large Negro population.

Another article described several new fire laws. Charleston was always enacting fire laws in an effort to stave off another blaze like that which had threatened to raze the city in '38. In the margin beside this article Cooper had jotted a list of things he needed for his trip north tomorrow.

Charleston was approaching a population of twenty-eight thousand people, slightly more than half of them white. In addition to the old aristocracy, there were sizable groups of turbulent Irish, clannish Germans, tradition-minded Jews. The city's spires and rooftops, interspersed with great oaks and palmettos, looked lovely in the dusk. The pleasant prospect, coupled with the bracing salt air, reminded him of a vow he had made to himself months ago. This would be his home for as long as he lived. Or at least until his political views got him run out by a mob.

With a tart smile, he turned from the city to the vista he loved even more—the harbor and the great ocean beyond. Charleston harbor remained one of the Federal government's strongest coastal installations; virtually everywhere you looked there was a fort. Away on his left lay Fort Moultrie on Sullivan's Island. Closer, on a mud flat, he could see Castle Pinckney. Straight ahead rose the bulk of Fort Sumter, and over on James Island the forlorn old buildings of Fort Johnson.

The various forts didn't thrill Cooper at all. What thrilled him day in and day out was the steamship traffic in the harbor. In a relatively short time he had developed a profound love for ships and for the sea that carried them.

The land at his back seemed old, frozen in a pattern fixed centuries before. The land was yesterday, obsolete or nearly so, but the sea with all the restless steam vessels it bore was a modern realm of speed, endless discovery, endless possibility. The sea was tomorrow.

And in some unexpected, almost inexplicable way, Cooper had ceased to be a man of the land and had become a man of the sea. He loved that too.

Cooper rode the train to New York, there spending two weeks at a shabby hotel near the Black Diamond yard. His packet was already under construction; the transverse bulkheads would be finished before the month was out.

He made numerous drawings of the vessel and the construction site, and filled whole booklets of notes before hurrying away with feelings of relief. The twin cities of Brooklyn and New York made Charleston appear drowsy and backward. Their size and their bustling, aggressive citizens intimidated him.

He boarded a train for Pennsylvania. The number of railroads operating out of New York seemed to have increased tenfold since his last visit. By way of contrast, the famous "Best Friend" of Charleston, the first locomotive built for service in America, had made its historic run nearly twenty years ago—December 1830. Three years after that the entire Charleston and Hamburg line went into operation, 136 miles of track running all the way to the head of navigation on the Savannah River. Cooper thought it a sad irony that railroad building was now lagging in the state that had pioneered it. The Yankees were out to become the railroad kings, just as they wanted to be the kings of every other major industry.

When Cooper arrived in Lehigh Station, George took him into the mill and showed him some of the plate destined for the hull of *Mont Royal*. Above the roar George shouted, "A lot of naval architects still scoff at plate for ships. But it's the coming thing."

Cooper yelled a reply, but George didn't hear it. "That British engineer," he went on, "Brunel. He built *Great Britain* out of iron, and she had no trouble with Atlantic crossings. Brunel swears that one day he'll build an iron ship so big that *Great Britain* will look like a speck beside her. So you're in excellent company.''

"I know,'' Cooper called back. *"Mont Royal*'s actually a scaled-down version of Brunel's ship.'' The idea of an adaptation had come to him when he first read a description of *Great Britain*.

George showed his visitor the entire Hazard complex, greatly expanded since Cooper had seen it last. The huge blast furnaces, the finery and plate mill, the new rail-rolling installation—all were running at capacity, George said. The streams of molten iron, which gave off clouds of sparks, blinding light, and hellish heat, intimidated Cooper even more than the cities he had recently quit. In the fire and noise of Hazard's he again saw the growing industrial might of the North.

That power and the teeming crowds in the cities lent a ludicrous quality to the South's posturings about independence. Why didn't the Carolina hotspurs spend a week up here? They would soon see it was the North, and only the North, that provided most of what they used, from structural iron to farm tools; from hairpins for their wives and mistresses to the gunmetal of the very weapons with which some of them proposed to defend their preposterous declarations about a free and separate South.

On the other hand, Tillet Main would never change his ways because of such a visit, Cooper decided. His father didn't want his beliefs muddied by truth. Cooper knew a lot of men exactly like him. He expected the North had its share, too.

He was in poor spirits during supper that night. While spouts of fiery iron jetted across the dark field of his thoughts, he put on a smile he didn't feel. He struggled to keep track of the conversation carried on by George's charming Irish wife and her lively mother-in-law. The Hazard youngsters, William and Patricia, had been fed separately. "They're good children,'' Constance said, "but they can be bumptious. I thought we should dine without the threat of custard flying through the air.''

George's table talk consisted largely of a monologue about the need for a better and cheaper method of producing steel. He explained some of the technical problems with such clarity that Cooper remembered them in detail long afterward. Constance understood her husband's concern and didn't interrupt while he was holding forth. When the meal and the monologue ended, the two men retired to the smoking room. George lit a cigar while Cooper sipped brandy.

"We'll rejoin the ladies in the music room in a little while,'' George said. He didn't sound enthusiastic. "My brother Billy will be coming over from next door. Stanley and his wife, too. Billy's going to the Military Academy. Did Orry tell you that?"

"No. What a splendid surprise. Perhaps there'll be a reunion in a year or two."

"A reunion? What do you mean?"

"Remember Cousin Charles? He's changed a lot since you saw him. He has ambitions to attend West Point too."

George sat forward. "You mean it's possible there could be another Main and another Hazard there together?" They compared dates and found it to be entirely possible.

Smiling, George leaned back in his chair. "Well, that improves the evening." He quickly sobered. "I hope the remainder of it won't be unpleasant for you."

"Why should it be unpleasant?"

"My sister Virgilia is home for a few days. She seldom takes supper with us, but she's here."

"I recall her very well. Handsome girl." Cooper dropped the lie into the conversation gracefully.

"Opinionated, too. Especially on the subject of abolition," George said with a pointed glance at his guest. "In fact she's managed to antagonize most of the residents of Lehigh Station. She takes a nugget of truth and surrounds it with the most outrageous qualifications and conditions. For example, she claims Negro freedom is philosophically related to the principle of free love. Believe in one, and you must believe in the other. Of course that linkage leads to relationships between the races, which to her is perfectly all right."

Cooper swirled his cognac, withholding comment.

"Not even arguing that last question"—George chewed the smoldering stub of his cigar—"I can say this without fear of challenge: by the way she conducts herself, Virgilia stirs up a hell of a lot of animosity among people who would otherwise be sympathetic to some of her views. She upsets the household, too. My mother's patience is tried to its limit. And I can't begin to describe the way Virgilia affects Stanley's wife—oh, but you've not met Isabel, have you? You will this evening. And you'll get to know her this summer."

"Afraid not," Cooper murmured. "My duties will keep me in Charleston." Another lie, but for his benefit this time.

"I'm sorry to hear that. Where the devil was I?"

"Isabel and your sister."

"Oh, yes. Of the two, it's Virgilia I'm worried about. Since she came home, she's already received two vile anonymous letters. Down in the village the other day, someone threw mud at her. There's no telling what will happen to her if she continues to promote her wild ideas. I expect she'll also be joining us tonight. I felt I should warn you."

Cooper crossed his legs and smiled. "I appreciate the concern. She won't bother me."

"I hope not, but don't be too sure."

Cooper found Stanley Hazard as stuffy as ever. Stanley kept dropping names of Pennsylvania politicians into the conversation. He pronounced each one as if he expected Cooper to recognize it and be impressed.

Isabel struck Cooper as a shrew. She had brought her twin sons to the music room. They writhed on her lap and tried to out-howl one another. Constance offered to hold one of them, but Isabel refused—sharply, Cooper thought; the sisters-in-law clearly disliked each other. Stanley finally ordered his wife to take the noisy youngsters out of the room. Everyone was relieved.

Billy talked excitedly about the forthcoming holiday in Newport. He'd completed the program at boarding school and now, guided through occasional visits to Philadelphia for tutoring, continued his studies at home. The boy was unmistakably a Hazard, though he was by no means a twin of George. His hair was darker than George's, his eyes a deeper shade of blue. He had a cheerful face with a blunt chin that gave him an air of rugged dependability. His powerful chest made him look as strong as a tree.

Virgilia arrived. She seized Cooper's hand and shook it, much like a man. Her mother frowned. After a bit of small talk, Virgilia seated herself next to Cooper and bored in.

"Mr. Main, what is the reaction in your part of the South to Senator Clay's proposals?"

Careful, he thought, noting her fiery eye. She wants a rise out of you. Parlor politics seldom led to anything except bad feelings—certainly never to agreement—so he answered with a bland smile:

"About what you'd expect, Miss Hazard. Most people in South Carolina oppose any compromise with—"

"So do I," she broke in. Maude uttered a quiet word of reproof. Cooper was sure Virgilia heard, but she paid no attention. "In matters

321

of human freedom, there is no room for compromise or negotiation. Webster and Clay and that whole gang should be lynched."

Cooper's smile felt stiff. "I think John Calhoun had a similar, if less violent, reaction to those gentlemen and their proposals—though certainly not for the reason you mention."

"Then for once I would agree with the late, unlamented Mr. Calhoun. In other respects he was a traitor."

Having just struck a match, George unthinkingly flung it onto the carpet. "Good God, Virgilia. Mind your manners."

Maude rushed forward to step on the match. "George, see what you've done."

Stanley sniffed and folded his arms. "It's Virgilia's tongue that did it."

"Traitor?" Cooper repeated. "Surely you don't mean that, Miss Hazard."

"There is no other word for someone who advocates disunion in order to protect slavery." She leaned forward, hands fisted on her knees. "Just as there is no other word for a slave owner but whoremaster."

The silence was instantaneous, so complete that the wailing of Isabel's twins carried all the way from the back of the house. Quietly, Cooper said, "If I didn't believe you spoke rashly, I would take that as an insult to my entire family. I won't deny the Mains own slaves, but they run a plantation, not a brothel."

He caught his breath and turned to Maude. "I'm sorry, Mrs. Hazard. I didn't mean to employ vulgar language." It was unnecessary for him to add that anger had prompted it. That was evident.

"Virgilia, you owe our guest an apology," George said.

"I—" She began to twist her handkerchief. Her pitted face turned pink. She dabbed at perspiration on her upper lip. "I only meant to express a personal conviction, Mr. Main. If I offended you, it was unintentional."

But it wasn't. She continued to dab her lip, in that way concealing part of her face. But her eyes gave her away. They fixed on Cooper with a fanatical rage.

"I reacted too strongly myself. I apologize."

He hated to say that, but courtesy demanded he do so. George stepped over the burn in the carpet and practically jerked him up from his chair. "Care to take a stroll?"

The moment they were outside, he exclaimed, "God, I'm sorry

322

she said all those things. I don't know what pleasure she derives from being rude.''

"Don't worry about it.'' Cooper walked across flagstones to the edge of the terraced lawn. To his right the three furnaces stained the night sky red.

"I will worry about it! I don't want Virgilia offending you, and I certainly don't want her offending your family this summer. I'll have a talk with her.'' His determination shaded into puzzlement. "She's my sister, but I'll be hanged if I understand her. Every time she rants about slavery and the South, she puts it in—well, physical terms. Somehow she's gotten the notion that the entire South is one heaving sea of fornication.''

He shot a quick look to see whether Cooper was shocked. Cooper was thinking. People often condemned that which they secretly desired.

"She's gotten too involved in her cause,'' George grumbled. "Sometimes I fear it's affecting her mind.''

I fear you may be right, Cooper thought, but kept it to himself.

That ended the incident. He left in the morning, without seeing Virgilia again. Soon the memory of her wrathful eyes faded a little as he examined his own rather surprising reactions during the exchange. He had been outraged by her statement; outraged as a member of the Main family and, yes, as a Southerner, too.

Cooper considered himself a temperate man. If he could be aroused by a Yankee fanatic, how much more angry would the Southern hotspurs become? And to what sort of violent response would that anger propel them? That was the aspect of last night's display that disturbed him most.

He first saw the girl on deck about an hour after the coastal steamer left New York for Charleston. She was in her twenties and evidently traveling alone. A tall girl with thin arms and legs, a flat bosom, and a long nose. A great deal of curly, dark blonde hair showed beneath her hat. She walked slowly along the rail, then stopped and gazed at the ocean. Her poise and self-assurance suggested familiarity with the world, experience in dealing with it by herself. He stood covertly watching her from a respectful distance.

Her gaze seemed kind and her mouth had a friendly look, as if she smiled a lot and did so naturally. Yet an objective observer would have to say that all the girl's features, taken together, yielded plainness at best, homeliness at worst. Why, then, did he find her so striking? He didn't know, nor did he care about an explanation.

Shortly he noticed another man watching the girl, and less discreetly. The man was fat, middle-aged, and wore a checked suit. Cooper was annoyed and then disappointed when the girl strolled off. If she was aware of the attention of the fat fellow, she gave no sign.

In a moment she was out of sight. Cooper knew he must meet her. But how? A gentleman simply didn't accost a young woman to whom he hadn't been introduced. He was still struggling with the problem when a black steward rang the dinner gong.

In the dining saloon, he was infuriated to see that chance had placed the girl at a table with the man in the checked suit. The man was no gentleman. He crowded his chair closer to hers, ignoring the raised eyebrows of the four other passengers sharing the table. He repeatedly bumped her forearm with his hand as they ate. And several times he leaned over too intimately, offering some witticism that she greeted with a polite smile. She ate rapidly and was the first to leave the table. Moments later, Cooper raced on deck to search for her.

He discovered her at the starboard rail watching the distant dunes on the Jersey shore. I'll do it, and damn the risk, he thought. He cleared his throat and squared his shoulders. Bees swarmed in his stomach. He walked toward her, fully intending to speak. She turned, taking note of him in a friendly way. He stopped, reached for the brim of his hat, then realized he had left the hat in his cabin. His opening remark died in his throat.

He uttered the only greeting he could muster—a kind of grunt— and rushed on by. Idiot. *Idiot.* Now she'd never speak to him, and he couldn't blame her. He had wanted to make a good first impression, somehow conveying to her that he was polite and even shy—qualities he felt she might like, if she were only given the opportunity to notice them. Inexperience had undone him. All she had seen was a fool who didn't say hello, just grunted.

He decided he wouldn't attend the evening entertainment, but at the last minute he changed his mind, joining a crowd of about thirty people in the main saloon. The purser, a cheerful Italian, announced that a special program had been substituted for that originally scheduled. It had been discovered that one of the passengers had musical talent, and she had been persuaded to perform. The purser would accompany her on the piano. He presented Miss Judith Stafford of Boston.

Miss Stafford rose. It was the girl. She had been seated in the first row where Cooper couldn't see her. She was still wearing the same plainly cut black dress he had first observed on deck. He felt sure it was her "good dress." Every woman had one, usually of silk.

He sat enthralled as she announced her first selection, an aria from *Norma*. She sang in a sweet soprano, with phrasing, gestures, and expressions that bespoke professional training. She performed three other selections, all operatic; the last one was a showy, stormy one from Verdi's *Attila*.

With each note, Cooper fell more deeply in love. He got a jolt when he noticed a spectator sidling along the wall toward the front. The chap in checks. Reeling slightly—and not because of rough water. The sea was calm tonight. The fellow's lascivious eyes showed what interested him. It was not Miss Stafford's talent.

The audience responded to her final aria with thunderous applause and demanded more. She conferred with the purser, then delighted the crowd with a lively rendition of "Oh! Susanna," the Negro ballad adopted by the California gold seekers. Again the audience wanted an encore. She sang the ten-year-old favorite, "Woodman, Spare That Tree." Her performance brought tears to the eyes of several in the audience.

But not to the eyes of Mr. Checks, as Cooper had taken to calling him. All that glittered in his repulsive little orbs was lust.

After giving the girl a final ovation, the audience dispersed. The purser thanked her and bustled off, leaving her alone and abruptly aware of Mr. Checks weaving in her direction, a smarmy smile on his face. Cooper found himself propelled toward the pair like a rocket. *He's probably a professional bare-knuckle fighter. If you interfere, he'll pulverize you—and she'll still think you're a clod.*

Despite this pessimistic appraisal, he didn't change course but sped straight to the front of the saloon. Mr. Checks had come to a halt six feet to Miss Stafford's left, blinking witlessly. Cooper seized the girl's elbow.

"That was utterly charming, Miss Stafford. I now claim the reward of that stroll you promised me earlier."

She'll scream for help, he thought. "Here, wait," said Mr. Checks, hurrying toward them and falling headfirst over a large leather chair he had failed to see.

Judith Stafford shone that bright smile on Cooper. "I remember, and I've been looking forward to it."

His heart nearly stopped as she linked her arm with his. She let him guide her outside. The moment they were on deck, she gave his forearm an impulsive squeeze.

"Oh, thank you. That lizard has been eyeing me ever since we left New York." She withdrew her hand. "I don't mean to be forward, but I'm very grateful to you, Mr.—"

She hesitated. Could he believe what he was hearing?

"Cooper Main of Charleston. Are you by chance from South Carolina?"

"I'm from the village of Cheraw, up country. I am going home for a visit. I thank you again for your assistance, Mr. Main. Good evening."

Lose her now and she's lost for good. He seized her hand and once more linked her arm with his.

"Miss Stafford, I demand my reward. That stroll we discussed—oh-oh, there he is. This way."

They sailed past a porthole from which a dejected Mr. Checks was peering. He didn't come on deck or bother them for the rest of the voyage. So much for fears of bare-knuckle prowess.

Judith Stafford laughed at Cooper's audacity. But she held fast to his arm, and they walked briskly toward the stern in the moonlight. He was so happy, if she had told him to jump overboard, he'd have done it. He'd have done it even though he couldn't swim six feet.

They spent most of the following day together. Cooper knew she probably did it because she thought him a safe companion, one whose presence would keep less trustworthy men at a distance. He only hoped companionship could ripen into friendship before they reached Charleston. After a day's shopping there, she planned to travel on to Cheraw by rail and public coach.

She had been born in the foothills of the South Carolina mountains, the only child of a farm couple. Her mother was dead, and her father now lived in Cheraw with a relative; an accident with a plow had crippled him two years ago.

"My father is Welsh and Scotch and a few other things besides," she said as they sat sipping bouillon late in the morning. "Born a Carolina yeoman, and he'll die as one. When he worked his land, he did it all by himself unless he happened to have the help of some neighbors he later repaid in kind. He detests the rice and cotton planters because they can succeed only by using armies of slaves.

326

He also detests them because there are so few of them, yet they have absolute control of the state. As a matter of fact, that control is one of the reasons I moved away five years ago, when I was twenty-one.''

"There are a great many farmers up country who share your father's feeling, aren't there?''

"Thousands. If it were up to them, slavery would be abolished in a minute.''

"To be followed by a black uprising the next minute?''

"Oh, that's just an excuse,'' she said with a toss of her head.

"Well, I hear it often.'' He swallowed and put the truth before her. "My family has planted rice and owned slaves for generations.''

She uttered a little gasp of surprise. "You told me your name, but I never connected it with the Mains of Mont Royal.''

"Because I said I live in Charleston, which I do. I left home myself, year before last. My father and I don't agree on any number of things. One is our peculiar institution.''

"Do you mean to say you oppose it?''

"I do. On practical as well as moral grounds.''

"Then we think alike.''

"I'm glad, Miss Stafford.'' He felt himself blushing.

Her brown eyes lighted with a look he had thus far only dreamed of seeing there. Suddenly every memory of the fiery furnaces of Lehigh Station was gone, and the future looked altogether different.

"Please,'' she said. "Won't you call me Judith?''

Cooper could speak forcefully when he had to, but it always required effort. She had the same shy disposition. Perhaps that was the reason the bond between them was so immediate and so strong.

On the voyage to Charleston, he told her a great deal about himself. She reciprocated. Her father believed in the importance of education and had saved all his life to make hers possible. She had gone north to complete the last two years of her schooling at Miss Deardorf's Female Academy in Concord, Massachusetts, and after graduation had been invited to remain as a teacher of music and literature.

Strictly speaking, then, she wasn't from Boston, but she went into the city as often as possible. She belonged to the Federal Street Church and shared the moderate abolitionist views of its pastor, the Reverend William Ellery Channing.

"A Unitarian, eh?" Cooper grinned. "We're taught to believe most of them have horns."

"Some are much more radical than others. Dr. Emerson, for example. He had the pulpit at Boston's Second Church until his conscience would no longer permit him to administer the Lord's Supper. He's a bit too esoteric for my tastes, although he's unquestionably a man of great moral conviction. He lives in Concord, you know. I see him several times a week. But of course I wouldn't dare speak to him."

She loved the little village where Yankee farmers had first fired at King George's men. Several famous people resided there. Besides Emerson, the writer Hawthorne was perhaps the best known. She also mentioned a radical named Thoreau, a sort of woodland anchorite of whom Cooper had never heard.

They talked of many things: Boston fish chowder and the Transcendental movement. The ubiquitous feminine parasol—Judith had hers, small and fringed—and New England poets. Longfellow. Whittier, the laureate of the abolitionist movement. Young Lowell, just beginning to achieve national prominence.

"I know Lowell's work," Cooper said. "During the Mexican War I read his doggerel purporting to expose the motive for the campaign in 'Californy.' " He quoted: " 'Chaps that make black slaves o' niggers want to make white slaves o' you.' "

For the first time, Judith's glance was disapproving. "You mean to say you don't believe the acquisition of slave territory was the reason for the war?"

"It was one reason, but not the only one. Things are seldom that clear-cut. This country's drifting into serious trouble because of the clamor for simple and immediate solutions to complex problems that will take years to solve—even with total effort on both sides. Gradual, compensated emancipation could free the Negro without wrecking the South's economy. Neither side will hear of it. It's too slow. Too tainted with compromise. Everyone wants quick, pure, destructive answers."

"It's rather hard for me to tell which side you're on."

"There's no handy label for me, I'm afraid. I'm opposed to the slave system, but I'll never condone violence to achieve its overthrow. I believe that trying to preserve the institution by setting up an independent South is ludicrous. We must get along with the Yankees. We don't dare risk a serious quarrel with them—they outnumber us, and we depend on their factories for survival. If we went our own way, that would be the end."

"From what I read, many Southern politicians think otherwise."

"They don't remember the lessons of their Bible," he replied with a faint, bitter smile. " 'The pride of thine heart hath deceived thee.' Jeremiah forty-nine."

"Well, I'm not such a—a gradualist as you," she said after a moment's consideration. "Slavery's an evil that must be rooted out by whatever means are necessary. Reverend Channing tries to appeal to the Christianity of the slave owners, but so far that hasn't worked."

"Nor will it. Down here, money speaks a lot louder than God."

"Doesn't it everywhere? Still, how can we claim to practice liberty in this country if part of the population is in bondage?"

"My father says slavery is a positive good."

"Nothing personal against your father—but despots always proclaim their own benevolence."

He smiled. "I see you've read your Reverend Weld."

"And Garrison, and Douglas. I believe what they all say. The price for emancipation must be paid, no matter how high."

"I can't agree. But perhaps there'll come a time when I do. I find myself more and more out of step with the majority. One of these days I'll probably be run out of Charleston. Before that happens, I'd like to show you my house."

"What? Without a chaperone?" she teased. Her eyes met his. "I'd very much like to see your house, Cooper."

Emboldened by her earnest gaze, he kissed her at the door of her stateroom a few minutes later. She responded with ardor, immediately apologized for her lack of shame, then in a whisper asked him to kiss her again.

It was a magic journey, and by the end they were in love and freely admitting it. As the steamer approached Charleston harbor, they finished a discussion of how soon she might be able to relinquish her duties in Concord, and whether she could be happy back in South Carolina.

The harbor pilot came aboard just at sunset. Cooper and Judith stood at the rail, watching the spires of the city flame in the last light. Never had he met anyone he trusted so completely. Someone to whom he could speak without fear of misunderstanding or scorn.

"My people have always been landsmen, but I've fallen in love with the sea. Maybe because the land is inseparably tied to slavery and its miseries." He faced toward the stern and the Atlantic beyond. "To me that ocean represents a real chance to be free of the old ways. It represents the speed of steam-driven ships. A shrinking world. The future—"

He hesitated, pink for a moment. "Do you find that laughable?"

She shook her head. "Admirable. Realistic, too. But outmoded ideas die hard. That's why we're experiencing such turmoil these days. An outmoded idea's dying, but the people of this state won't accept the fact or the inevitability of it. If they did, it would be so much easier."

Cooper sighed. "Yes, but the resistance is understandable. A man gives up a lot when he gives up his nigras. He surrenders something I've never heard a single slave owner mention, yet it's there, it's fundamental, and it's the one factor that causes and promotes the evil in the system." The harbor wind tossed his hair as he gazed seaward. "Total power. Slavery gives one man total power over another. No human being should have that kind of power. No king, no president— and certainly not my father. The power's destructive. I finally saw that clearly. My father was always a good and humane master, but one day he got angry and ordered one of our slaves cat-hauled. Do you know what that is?"

She shivered. "Yes. I've read of it."

"Well, my father had it done. And because he owned the man— owned him without question—there was nothing to prevent it. Nothing to prevent one human being from behaving like a beast and another from being treated like one. That's why I doubt Reverend Channing's approach will succeed. Total power has a dark appeal to the wicked side in all of us."

Seeing his stark expression, Judith grew bold enough to do something she'd only imagined herself doing heretofore—taking a man's hand in hers, in public.

Gently she closed her fingers on his. She was delighted by the audacious things she'd done on this voyage. When she began the trip in Boston, she'd had no thought of doing any of them. Surely this delicious new freedom was another sign that she had finally found a man she could love all her life.

Cooper, too, had found a partner. A decent, bright woman who was, to him, surpassingly beautiful. A woman who shared his own quirky, iconoclastic turn of mind, and many of his beliefs, and a few of his doubts. With her, if she'd have him, he could weather the stormy times that were surely coming. In the house on Tradd Street, this very night, he would propose.

The decision returned a look of calm to his face. Holding hands and heedless of the stares of some scandalized passengers, Cooper and Judith stood gazing into each other's eyes as Fort Sumter loomed off the bow and slowly fell behind.

23

Tension and quarreling plagued the Hazards that spring. The servants bet small sums on who would be speaking to whom by the time the family left for Newport. Some wagered they wouldn't go at all.

George discovered Stanley had made another donation to Cameron, this time in the amount of two thousand dollars. "You promised to stop that sort of thing!" He punctuated the accusation by pounding the desk so hard a window rattled. Stanley edged to the other side of the office before answering. George was small, but Stanley lived in fear of him. He lived in greater fear of Isabel, however.

"I never meant I'd stop permanently. If you thought that, you misunderstood. Besides, Simon urgently needed—"

"Oh, it's Simon now. Pals! What post are you buying? What's the price?" Stanley reddened. George prowled back and forth like a wild animal. "Our costs rise every day, and you piss our money away on political hacks and private rail cars."

On his own, Stanley had contracted for an eight-wheel passenger car, complete with sitting room, sleeping compartments, and a galley. The unusual car, one of only a handful in the nation, was being rushed to completion in Delaware. Stanley had been pushed into the purchase by his wife, who had repeatedly said she would not ride the public cars to Rhode Island.

"Surely we can discuss this without resorting to vulgarity, George."

"Discuss, hell. It's too late to do anything about the car, but I won't have you giving Cameron another penny."

"While I control the bank account, I'll do as I please. Speak to Mother if you don't like it."

He didn't have the nerve to look at his younger brother as he played that trump. George angrily subsided, as Stanley expected he would. George might threaten to go to Maude, but Stanley had figured out that his pride would never permit him to do it. With a smug smile, Stanley strolled out. The door banged shut, a defiant coda to the conversation.

Swearing, George sat down. He tried to calm himself but failed.

Stanley had him, and they both knew it. He refused to run to Maude, yet the situation as it stood was intolerable. He didn't know what to do. He picked up an inkwell and hurled it against the wall.

"Childish," he grumbled a minute later. But it had made him feel a lot better, even though his problem remained unsolved and the flying ink had ruined his shirt.

Stanley described the argument to Isabel. Naturally George was the villain, Stanley the hero.

She took revenge with a new campaign against her in-laws. With a false smile of concern, she began "wondering"—aloud—about the nature of the religious upbringing little William and Patricia would receive. She dredged up the usual scare tales about sinister Roman priests who exerted an evil influence on parishoners and, by extension, their children. But her special target was George. For several weeks his apparent lack of any faith became a popular topic among the better-class women of Lehigh Station.

No, George didn't worship as a Catholic, Isabel said to them, but neither did he set foot in his own church, the Methodist. Weren't his poor children in danger of growing up godless? People who previously hadn't worried about that question, or George's character, found themselves talking of little else.

Some of the gossip reached Constance, then George. It saddened her and infuriated him. It was no comfort to receive a letter from Orry and learn that there was discord in the Main family, too. Cooper had announced his forthcoming marriage to a Unitarian girl with abolitionist leanings. Tillet could hardly contain his displeasure. Orry hoped the Newport trip would ease the tensions, at least for a little while.

Virgilia left for ten days in Philadelphia, where she was to address another rally. Maude had long ago stopped pleading with her about the need for a chaperone. Virgilia did as she pleased.

Five days later, as packing for 'he Newport trip commenced, one of Isabel's friends called on her. The woman, Grace Truitt, had just returned from Philadelphia. One evening she and her husband had gone to the Chestnut Street Theater to see a revival of *The People's Lawyer*, a perennially popular play featuring one of those Yankee rustics who outwitted supposedly smarter people; the shrewd rustic had been a standard character in American comedy for years.

"Your sister-in-law occupied a box with a handsome escort named Toby Johnson," the visitor said.

"I don't know the gentleman."

"It would be surprising if you did, but everyone in Philadelphia has heard or read about him. Virgilia and Mr. Johnson appeared together at the abolitionist rally." Grace Truitt paused, relishing the next. "On that occasion Mr. Johnson recounted his experiences in North Carolina before his escape."

"Escape? Good heavens, you don't mean he's—African?"

"Brown as a nut," said the other, nodding. "They flaunted themselves at the theater. Kept touching each other and exchanging glances which—well—" The woman dabbed her glistening upper lip. "One could only term them amorous. I hate to bring you such tragic news, but I felt you should know."

Isabel looked sick. "Was there much reaction to their presence at the theater?"

"I should say there was. Several couples left in protest before the curtain rose. At the first interval someone flung a bag of trash into the box. A vulgar action, to be sure; still, Virgilia and her companion sat there bold as brass and ignored it."

Isabel clutched the woman's hand. "Please keep this to yourself, Grace. I'll inform the family at the proper moment, when Virgilia gets home."

"You can depend on my discretion."

But it was an idle promise.

Maude sent a cart and driver down to the village to meet Virgilia's boat. A block from the canal, two loungers saw her riding in the cart with her luggage. One of the men found a stone.

"Don't bring your nigger lover to Lehigh Station!"

He flung the stone with more emotion than accuracy. Virgilia saw it sail harmlessly by. The cart driver gave his passenger a stunned look. She ignored it and glared at the loungers. By evening, when George and his family trooped to Stanley's for supper, the incident had become the talk of both houses.

Before the first course was served, Maude said, "Virgilia, I heard about a nasty incident in the village today. What caused it?"

She shrugged. "My friendship with Toby Johnson, I suppose. I attended the theater with him in Philadelphia. Gossip travels fast. Perhaps some small-minded person from Lehigh Station actually saw me."

It angered Isabel that her revelation had been spoiled. At least she could emphasize the enormity of Virgilia's misdeed:

"In case someone is unaware, Johnson is a Negro."

That wasn't news to George; he and Constance had discussed the incident an hour ago. He chewed furiously on his cigar stub because Virgilia's expression said she was relishing the family's discomfort. He was no longer surprised by such behavior, but it still angered him.

Virgilia's chin lifted defiantly. "Toby Johnson is a fine man, and I shall see him as often as I like."

Billy looked titillated; everyone else was upset. Stanley sputtered, unable to speak coherently. Maude studied her daughter with an air of grieved resignation. George spoke for the group.

"We have no quarrel with your cause, Virgilia. But you carry it too far. I don't say that merely because the man's black—"

Her look withered him. "Of course you do, George. Don't be a hypocrite."

"All right—perhaps his color is part of it. But I expect I could get over that, or reconcile myself to it, if it weren't for your attitude. I don't think you really care for this man."

"How dare you presume to say what I really—?"

"Virgilia, shut up and let me finish. I think what you really want is to draw attention to yourself. Thumb your nose at the world because you believe—mistakenly—that it's harmed you. In the process, you're shaming your mother and dishonoring this family. Certain things just aren't done by decent women, whether the man is black, white, or purple."

Virgilia balled her napkin and tossed it away. "What a dreadful prig you've become." Maude uttered a soft cry and averted her face.

"We're not talking about me but about you and your behavior," George retorted. "We won't put up with it."

She rose and fixed him with cold eyes. "You'll have to, brother dear. I am an adult. Who I sleep with is my affair."

Embarrassed, Constance turned toward Billy. George and Stanley stared at each other, for once united by shock and anger. Isabel drew gulping breaths. Virgilia swept out of the room.

Maude put her hand in front of her face to hide sudden tears.

Next day William broke out in a rash. George and Constance feared measles.

Dr. Hopple said it wasn't measles, but the boy nevertheless developed

336

a fever. Constance stayed up all night to tend him. George stayed up worrying about her and about the mess caused by his sister. He was in a bad mood when the family left the next afternoon in two carriages; a third followed with a small mountain of luggage. At Philadelphia the Hazards would board the private rail car which would take them to a siding near the Newport ferry dock.

George felt nervous about leaving the business for eight weeks. He had prepared pages and pages of instructions for his supervisors and foremen, and he planned on at least one return trip to Lehigh Station during the summer. Still, the family needed him more than Hazard Iron did. Something had to be done to restore peace and keep Virgilia from disrupting it for the next month or so.

Isabel constantly sniped at Virgilia behind her back. The object of this attention acted as if nothing had happened. Virgilia chattered about the passing scenery, the weather—everything but the subject that had precipitated the argument. She was blithely, even arrogantly, cheerful.

During their one-night layover in Philadelphia, she disappeared all night with no explanation. That evening Maude took to her bed before the sun went down. But next morning she seemed better, as if she were determined to accept the situation, deplorable as it was. She went on a shopping trip with toddling William, who was feeling fine again.

They boarded the private car at four in the afternoon.

On each side of the car, five-inch-high gilt letters spelled out *Pride of Hazard*. Above the legend a gilt eagle spread its wings. The interior was equally opulent. Everyone exclaimed over the etched-glass window borders, the gleaming brass fixtures, the wainscoting of rosewood inlay with deep red damask covering the walls above.

Stanley had spared no expense. The upholstery was the finest plush, the washbasins the finest marble. George had to admit the car was beautiful, but he didn't dare ask the final cost. He wanted to be at home, seated and slightly drunk, when he saw the bill.

A Negro chef had been hired for the summer. He was already in the galley, preparing sole for supper. Virgilia conversed with the chef for a good ten minutes. "As if he's her equal," Isabel sneered to Constance behind her hand. "Something must be done."

Constance ignored her. Virgilia emerged from the galley and disappeared into her sleeping compartment with a copy of *The Liberator*.

The boys, William, Laban, and Levi, ran up and down the car, climbing over the furniture, rattling compartment door handles, and creating a cacophony on the pump organ tucked against the bulkhead at one end of the sleeping section. At a quarter to five the car was switched onto the New York fast express, which pulled out a few minutes later.

The family dined on filet of sole and drank expensive French wine while the express rushed north through the dreary New Jersey flatlands. Virgilia was not present; she had taken a tray into her compartment.

"She'll probably invite her dusky friend to Newport," Isabel said in a thickened voice. She had consumed a good deal of claret, disdaining the white wine served to all the others. "We should take action."

George noticed a flare in his wife's eyes. But Constance kept her temper, saying, "Perhaps we should just have patience. If she's involved herself with Johnson merely to assert her independence, it won't last."

Unsatisfied, Isabel whined, "What do we do in the meantime? Suffer humiliation? Social ostracism? I tell you we must take action."

"You keep saying that," Maude snapped. "What do you suggest?"

Isabel opened her mouth, closed it, stood up with nervous movements. "Excuse me, I believe I heard the children."

She rushed off to their compartment. George reached under the fine linen tablecloth, found his wife's hand, and, giving her a resigned look, squeezed it. Then he poured another glass of Chardonnay and drank it in several long gulps.

Around midnight in the New York rail yards, the *Pride of Hazard* was uncoupled from the Philadelphia train and put on another bound for Providence. The car was coupled immediately behind those containing freight and baggage, and just ahead of the public coaches. This placed it at the midpoint of the train.

About that same time, along the Connecticut shore near the hamlet of West Haven, a switchman who had earlier had a big fight with his lady friend resorted to a bottle to drown his anger. He drank so much so fast he forgot to reset a switch after a local headed for New York came off a siding parallel to the main line. The local had backed onto the siding and waited there until a Boston-bound express went by.

The switchman walked unsteadily in the direction of New Haven. Had he been a reliable man and sober, he would have worried about the switch's being out of position. Any train approaching from New York and traveling faster than five miles an hour would shunt onto

338

the siding, which was short, and crash through a barricade at the end. Beyond the barricade lay a wide, dark gully.

Constance wriggled in her husband's arms. There really wasn't room for two, but she hated the discomfort and confinement of her own berth and had moved down to lie with him for a little while.

"Before I become a regular traveler on overnight trains, some genius will have to invent a better sleeping arrangement," she murmured against his neck.

"Cozy, though, isn't it?" The moment he said it there was an abrupt lurch. "Did you notice that? Felt like we switched onto another track."

The driver of the eight-wheel Winans locomotive was terrified. He had seen the position of the switch arm a few seconds too late. The engine had been unexpectedly slewed onto the siding, and even as he pulled the cord to signal for help, he knew the brakemen would be unable to turn their wheels and halt the train in time.

In the spill of light from the oil-fired headlamp, he saw the barricade looming. "Jump, Fred," he screamed at his foreman, who was already stepping off the foot plate into the dark.

So this was how it would end for him, the driver thought. A name in a newspaper account of another accident. So many of them were happening that preachers and politicians said no more railroads should be built.

He yanked the signal cord again. It broke in his hand. By the light of the firebox he saw the frayed end, and that was all he saw. The locomotive burst through the barricade at thirty miles an hour and shot up a slight incline and out over the gully like an immense projectile, dragging the rest of the train behind it.

24

"Constance, get the children. Something's—"

George never finished the unnecessary warning. She knew something was wrong because of the way the car jerked, then began a slow roll onto its left side.

There was a strange sensation of floating. She fought her way up the suddenly inclined floor toward the door separating the compartment from that of the children. The locomotive fell toward the far edge of the gully. Seconds before the shattering crash, she realized the private car and possibly the whole train had left the rails.

She tore the connecting door open. The first thing she saw was the sooty chimney of a lamp she had left burning. The car was all wood and lacquer. They would be roasted to death if they weren't crushed.

It seemed to last forever, that slow, lazy rollover through space. Iron howled as couplings tore apart. The freight car directly ahead landed in the gully, and the Hazard car came crashing down on top of it, roof first. On the rim of the gully the locomotive's boiler burst, the explosion creating a huge cloud of fiery steam and shredded metal. The cloud bloomed upward and outward like some flower from a madman's garden.

Human screams counterpointed the shriek of iron. The Hazard car collapsed onto its inverted roof. The second-class coach immediately behind glanced off the side and sagged into the gully next to the pile of cars on which the Hazards' was resting. Below her, Constance heard injured men cry out in the dark: employees of the line working in the baggage cars had been trapped down at the very bottom.

"William? Patricia? Stay with Mother. Hold onto me. We'll be all right."

The children were sobbing. So were dozens of other passengers, in every car—a whole choir of the terrified trying to be heard above the breaking of wood, the shattering of glass, the swift crackle of flames. Where was George? In her terror she had lost track of him. She thought he had left their compartment through the door leading to the corridor.

The lamps were out in the Hazard car, but there was light. Firelight. She saw it bathing George's face as he reentered their compartment, walking on the ceiling which had become the floor. He rushed to the connecting door.

"Give me one of the children." He held out his arms. Behind him she glimpsed Stanley struggling along the corridor. He was pushing Maude and dragging Isabel, who had a twin in each arm.

Constance passed William to George. Carrying Patricia, she stepped over the high sill created when the car inverted. She dared not listen to the cries or the sounds of the spreading fire. It ate into the wall behind her, its heat scorching.

"Go on, George. I'm all right." With her free hand she lifted the hem of her nightgown so that she wouldn't fall. She began coughing; the smoke was thickening rapidly.

She followed her husband out of the compartment. The corridor was blocked by wreckage in one direction and by Isabel in the other. Isabel had suddenly lost control. She dropped the twins at her feet and surrendered to hysterical screaming.

The smoke reddened as fire consumed the car. The three-year-old twins wept and tore at their mother's legs, hoping she'd notice them. She didn't.

"We've got to get her out of the way," Constance shouted, thrusting Patricia at her husband. He maneuvered William into one arm and with a grunt hefted the girl onto his shoulder. Constance slipped around him, seized Isabel by the shoulders, and shook her. When that did no good, Constance slapped her. Isabel staggered against Stanley, who seized her wrists and dragged her away into the ruddy smoke.

"Laban—Levi," Constance gasped, crouching by the twins as George squeezed past and struggled along the corridor. She had only seconds now; the compartment behind her was aflame. Tongues of fire shot from the doorway. The pudgy-faced twins huddled against her as she fought to keep her nerves from betraying her.

She gave them her hands. "Hold onto me, boys." She led them down the corridor the way George had gone. He had disappeared in the smoke. So had everyone else.

The wooden wall on her right felt blistering. Three feet ahead the wall abruptly split and buckled outward, dissolving in fire. No exit that way. There was a barrier of fire behind her, too.

The windows, then. She kicked one with her bare heel. It shivered but didn't break. She kicked it again. A crash; glass tore her heel and lacerated the sole of her foot.

The air rushing in fanned the flames. What was out there? How far was the ground? Was there only dangerous wreckage below? She couldn't see, but she had no other escape route. She tore a piece of wood from the buckling wall and enlarged the ragged opening by smashing out more glass. She had no recollection of cutting herself, but by the time she finished, her wrists bled from a dozen wounds. She dropped the wood and lifted Laban.

She flung him outward through the opening, and his brother after him. Then she jumped, a moment before the car disappeared in a Niagara of fire that ran toward the sky.

She hit a slope covered with sharp rocks just seven or eight feet below the car. She rolled a short distance, stunned. Above her, the burning wreckage lost its brilliance as her vision dimmed. She gasped for air, powerless to move, close to losing consciousness.

Everywhere, screaming. Drifting smoke. The roar of the fire and the shrill hiss of steam still escaping from some valve in the ruined locomotive.

Hurt and dazed as she was, Constance still managed to separate one sound from the others: the sound of Laban and his brother weeping in fright as they wandered the hillside. They needed someone.

She willed herself back from the darkness that had nearly taken her. She flung red hair off her forehead with red hands and tottered along the sloping side of the gully until finally she reached the twins. She made queer gurgling sounds as she picked them up; it was the closest she could come to laughter.

"Boys, we'll be fine now." She held one under each arm and climbed the slope. The rocks bruised and cut her already bleeding feet. "Just fine. We'll find your mother. We'll find her right away."

If she weren't dead.

Would the little boys remember the shrieks of those victims buried at the bottom of the pile of cars? Would they remember the strident, choking cry of someone trapped in a burning car and roasting alive? She would. God above, she would.

The death toll in the wreck, which the penny press later dubbed the West Haven Catastrophe, was twenty. Fourteen passengers and six employees of the line, including the engineer. None of the casualties turned out to be a Hazard, although the family's Negro chef had died with a broken timber driven like a spear through the bosom of his nightshirt. The center of the train proved to have been the safest spot; all the deaths had occurred at the forward end or in the last two passenger coaches.

One by one Constance found the others. Billy first. Then Maude; she sat on the ground, dazed and unable to rise. George and their children. And Stanley, trying to comfort and quiet Isabel, who alternately sobbed and ranted.

Last of all she spied Virgilia, over on the far side of the wreckage. George's sister had torn up her dress to make bandages. In her undergarments and filthy dirty, she ran up and down hills of teetering rubble like a mountain goat, hunting for survivors and helping to free them. As for the *Pride of Hazard*, it no longer existed.

Constance rubbed her eyes. She saw Stanley kneeling by his sons, examining their bloodied feet.

"How are they?" she asked.

"I don't know. How did their feet get cut so badly?"

Constance didn't answer. She was only able to shake her head. The fool was angry with her. Incredible.

"Who's cut? Are my children hurt? Let me see."

Shrill, but evidently herself again, Isabel rushed past Maude and dropped to her knees beside the twins, who were trying to hold back tears. "Laban—Levi—oh, my poor dears. Look at that blood. Those terrible gashes. What did she do to you?"

She gathered the boys into her arms and peered between them, her eyes brimming with hostility. "Constance, if either of them is permanently injured, I'll never forgive you."

"Permanently—?"

Constance found it so ludicrous she couldn't go on. She threw her head back and laughed, raw, hysterical laughter that brought a scowl to Stanley's face, and George's too. "My God, Isabel," she gasped finally. "Do you have the slightest idea of what you're saying?"

Isabel released the boys and lurched to her feet. Strings of hair fell across her forehead as she stumbled toward her sister-in-law. "I certainly do. Look at them. Look at their feet."

"I'm sorry you don't approve of what I did, Isabel. But then you never do. I was trying to save the twins. No one else was helping them. Certainly not you. You were screaming, hysterical. You had abandoned your children to a horrible fate."

George spoke softly to her. "I don't think you need to say any more."

Constance knew he was asking her to end it there; not demanding that she do so, but asking, so that trouble wouldn't keep piling on trouble. She heard that clearly and understood. Yet it made no difference. Her brush with death had unleashed feelings long suppressed.

With her eyes on Isabel, she said, "Oh, yes, there's a lot that needs saying. You should be horsewhipped for being so ungrateful. I'd do it if you weren't such a pitiable creature—"

"See here—" Stanley began, but Isabel's cry drowned him out: "You Irish bitch!"

She scooped a jagged rock from the ground and ran at Constance. George jumped in front of his wife, tore the rock away from Isabel, and hurled it toward the blazing pyre of the train.

Isabel whipped up her fist to strike him. George seized her forearm in his left hand and gradually but firmly forced her hand down. His voice shook.

"She's right, you're ungrateful. You've done nothing but heap unkindness on Constance ever since she came to Lehigh Station. She's looked the other way—tried to forgive you—and so have I. But this is the end. She saved the twins, and instead of thanking her—"

"George, you've overstepped," Stanley rumbled behind him.

George didn't look at his brother. "Keep out of this. Isabel, I will always insist that my family be civil to you, but that's all. Henceforward I don't want to see you at Belvedere. Don't ever set foot in my house."

"You will not speak to my wife that way," Stanley exclaimed, grabbing George's shoulder. Stanley's impulsive act was a match touched to an emotional fuse. George spun, slammed Stanley's hand away by striking his forearm, then stepped back to set his stance just right.

Stanley was spluttering. Steady on his feet, George ignored the last faint plea of reason and did what he had long dreamed about. With all his might he hit Stanley in the stomach.

Isabel shrieked. Stanley gasped and so did George; he had struck so hard he thought his hand was broken.

"Papa," one of the twins howled, and burst out crying. Stanley attempted to stay on his feet, but the blow had knocked him off balance. His arms windmilling, he staggered backward, then collapsed on his rump. The light of the burning cars made his cheeks glisten red. As he gazed up at his younger brother, a forlorn comprehension crept into his eyes. He struggled for breath. He was paunchy, soft-looking, as he sat there. Old, suddenly. Impotent.

God, I wish I hadn't done that, George thought. But the blow could never be called back. It would exist in memory forever, an embarrassment to him and to all of them. It was odd that he could regret what he'd done and at the same time feel relief and a sense of pride.

He walked forward and held out his hand to his brother. "Let me help you up."

Stanley grasped George's forearm and pulled himself to his feet. He acknowledged the assistance with a flicker of his eyelids, but there was no gratitude in the glance—not that George expected any. There was, however, something else. An emotion George had seen, or at least suspected, before. Now it was unmistakable.

He's afraid of me. He's always been afraid of me.

If George had recognized that fear in the past, he had never recognized the power it gave him; not until now.

Stanley sidled past and reassured Isabel that he was all right. Then he turned to the twin who was crying. He picked the little boy up and comforted him. George and Constance held their children close. Billy went to Maude and stayed with her. No one said much during the next few minutes. A kind of shock had set in. George wasn't sure whether the cause was the wreck or the fight afterward.

Stanley and Isabel avoided looking at George and his family. George's guilt was fading rapidly. An accounting with Stanley was long overdue.

Some twenty minutes later, Virgilia arrived with five men from the hamlet of West Haven. Two of them bore Maude away on a pole-and-canvas litter. By then George had made up his mind to stop regretting his action.

When the sun rose, a couple of hundred railroad workers and volunteers were swarming over the site of the wreck. The Hazards were by then resting in a New Haven hotel. Virgilia decided to go on to Newport. Several servants were already there. The New Haven tradesmen, responding to the emergency and the chance for profit, brought stocks of clothing and fully outfitted the entire Hazard family.

By late morning rail service in both directions was restored. Virgilia's train left at three. Billy volunteered to watch the children while they napped, so George and Constance accompanied Virgilia to the station, then went off to shop for some additional items. When they returned to the hotel, they looked in on Maude, who was still in bed. Two of her ribs had been broken, but apart from some dizziness, she claimed she felt fine.

"That's good news, Mother," George said. "I believe I'll try to find Stanley."

Maude looked at her son without reproof. "Where has he been all morning?"

"I don't know."

"He and Isabel and the children disappeared into their rooms right after breakfast," Constance put in.

Maude sighed. "I'm happy you're going to talk with him."

George stroked his mustache with the tip of his index finger. "Not solely to apologize. Stanley and I have some things to straighten out."

Resigned to it, she murmured, "I understand. I have seen it coming for quite a while. Perhaps this is as good a time as any."

She closed her eyes and rested her hands, one on top of the other, on the clean counterpane. He was glad she understood. It made what he was about to do considerably easier.

He knocked softly at the door of his brother's suite. Isabel answered, informing him coldly that Stanley was downstairs, in the saloon bar. George found him hunched over a large glass of Kentucky whiskey. He ordered one for himself but left it untasted. He made an effort to maintain a temperate tone as he said:

"I am going to assume responsibility for the company bank accounts."

"Oh? You've spoken to Mother?" Stanley asked with weary bitterness.

"I have not. This is solely between the two of us. When we reach Newport, we'll compose a letter to each of the banks we use." His heart was beating fast. "From now on, my signature will be the only one that can authorize expenditures above fifty dollars. There'll be no more private rail cars for a while."

Stanley stared into the mahogany-bordered mirror behind the bar. Above it an antlered stag looked over their heads with glassy disinterest. Abruptly, Stanley laughed.

"I thought something like this was coming. I don't give a damn. I've never liked the iron trade anyway, and you've pushed and pushed to take over the whole thing."

George suppressed anger and continued to speak calmly. "I can give it my full attention. You're developing other interests. I gather you wouldn't be averse to holding political office."

"Eventually," Stanley agreed. "For one thing, it would get me away from Lehigh Station." *And you* was the unspoken conclusion.

George avoided the bait. "Then I'm glad we've reached an understanding. I'm sorry for what I did last night."

He held out his hand. Stanley glanced at it, then curled his fingers around his glass and bent forward, as if to protect it. "If you don't mind, I'd rather drink by myself."

"Whatever you say."

George left the bar.

The others sensed that a change had taken place within the family. Isabel didn't hide her resentment, but Stanley showed occasional flashes of relief. He laughed and joked as he hadn't for years.

They remained in New Haven an extra day, completing and signing depositions about the accident for the railroad's management. The following morning they rather nervously boarded another train for Rhode Island. They had been traveling about an hour when an incident took place that signaled that the transition of leadership was complete, and final.

They were talking about christening their summer place; all such estates in Newport had names. Stanley mentioned that in front of the house there was a broad and beautiful expanse of grass. He suggested the name Fairlawn.

"Very pretty," Maude said. "But what do you think, George?"

George thought the name unimaginative. Then he remembered one of the lessons of West Point. It behooved an officer to show courtesy to a beaten opponent.

"I like it," he said, smiling at his brother.

Disdainful, Isabel said, "Then I suppose that settles it."

It did. Stanley looked boyishly grateful.

25

Fairlawn was a splendid, airy house, three stories high and gleaming with a new coat of white paint. The landscaping had been neglected, however. Weeds choked the flower beds; dead limbs disfigured the trees. And the low brick wall surrounding the property needed mortaring. At George's request, Stanley supervised the masons and gardeners. He appeared to enjoy himself.

The price of the house had included all the furnishings. The women liked very few of the pieces, however, and spent the first couple of days ordering replacements. Constance deferred to Isabel whenever possible. The effort did nothing to moderate Isabel's animosity.

Everyone in the family kept as busy as possible, sensing it would help them forget the wreck. Maude's injuries were the most obvious reminder. Her dizzy spells persisted, and she moved slowly because of the broken ribs. Constance suffered from nightmares, always a recapitulation of her struggle to escape from the burning car. William dreamed of the accident too; he awoke crying and thrashing every night for nearly two weeks.

The Mains arrived on the fifth of July, one day after President Taylor ate too many cucumbers and drank too much cold milk at a patriotic celebration and fell ill. On July 9 he died of *cholera morbus*. Some editorialists said he had really been killed by worry and the pressures of office, particularly those created by sectional antagonism. Millard Fillmore assumed the presidency on July 10.

By then the Mains had settled into their rented house, just a short distance away on Old Beach Road. Both families eased into the abundant pleasures of a Newport summertime. There were pony-cart rides and outings to the beach during the day, lawn games during long evenings sweet with the smell of freshly scythed grass. Newport Beach was close by but crowded; the family preferred a more private bathing area at the south end of the island, within sight of a jutting offshore formation local people called Spouting Rock.

At first Tillet seemed uncomfortable on Yankee soil. Soon, however, he renewed acquaintances with several other families from South

Carolina, including the Izards, and after that he relaxed and enjoyed himself.

Except when he read the news from Washington. Fillmore intended to support Clay's compromise bills, which were now seen as certain to pass, probably before the end of the year. A group of younger congressmen led by Stephen Douglas of Illinois had pledged to break the voting stalemate created by the old guard.

The four young people spent a great deal of time together. Both Ashton and Brett got along well with the stocky, cheerfully pugnacious Billy Hazard, though he was chiefly interested in Ashton. He was fifteen, she one year younger; Brett was a mere child of twelve.

Charles, fourteen, gave the impression of being the most mature of the foursome. His height had something to do with it; he was already a full head taller than Billy. He was handsome and prone to laugh a lot. Charles and Billy were as cordial as could be expected of two boys getting to know each other. Orry and George watched the new friendship with great interest.

George bought a skiff, and one evening after supper, the boys took it down to the beach to experiment. George and Orry went along to keep an eye on the neophyte sailors. Billy had a little experience with small boats, but Charles had none.

George and Orry sat on opposite sides of a big rock. The Atlantic was calm, with just enough breeze for fine sailing close to shore. Orry lifted a handful of sand and let it trickle away. The vacation seemed to be relaxing him. Yet on occasion George still detected a bitter undertone in his friend's speech.

Not tonight, though. Orry smiled as he gazed toward the skiff. "Look at them. Re-chisel a few of the features and that could be the two of us. Stick and Stump the Second."

George nodded and puffed his cigar. "I hope they'll be as good friends at West Point as we were, even if they will be a year apart. Charles is a devilishly handsome fellow, isn't he? Almost the perfect picture of the dashing Southern gentleman."

Orry chuckled. "Who'd have believed our salt crow would turn into a hawk? He cleaned up right well, as the saying goes."

"Your father says you deserve the credit."

Orry shrugged. "Charles loves to scrap. When he found there were ways to do it without being tossed in jail or having everyone furious with him, it was a most impressive lesson. He's learned it well."

"And a lot of other things. I always thought I was pretty good with the ladies, but I can't bow and kiss a woman's hand as gracefully as he does. The first evening you came to Fairlawn, he fussed over my mother till she blushed like a girl."

Rowdy shouts rang across the water, then a gleeful whoop and a splash. Billy dumped Charles off the skiff.

Orry and George jumped up. Charles quickly clambered back onto the little boat. He pointed at something on the horizon—something nonexistent—and when Billy turned to look, grabbed Billy's belt and shirt and threw him in. Soaked, the two boys sat laughing in the skiff a few moments later.

"I'm proud of the way he's turning out," Orry admitted as he took his place on the rock again. "I had my share of regrets when I came home from Mexico. Charles has helped me banish some of them."

"The change showed in your letters. It was welcome."

"And this has been a welcome vacation. Well, in most respects. I still hate the stench of those weeds you smoke."

George laughed. Orry stretched his right arm high above his head and yawned. The sunset flung their long, attenuated shadows across the beach. The wind picked up. Snaky veils of sand blew past them.

George found it a melancholy sight. It reminded him of how quickly time was slipping away. Even time seemingly recaptured in the forms of those two laughing youngsters was an illusion, one that his own mind created as an antidote for the way things really were. A futile antidote; neither time nor change could ever be stopped. Of late, the realization lent life a bittersweet quality.

Still, this was a good moment, the kind of calm, complete moment he found rare these days.

Orry felt it too. His mood grew mellow. "I'll tell you how much I'm enjoying myself. So much, I'm even beginning to feel charitable toward my older brother."

"How is Cooper?"

"Happy. Married to that free-thinking Unitarian. A good marriage. Father can't quite accept it. Of course he's delighted to accept all the profits Cooper is generating from the packet line. Did I write you about our new vessel? She'll be off the ways in a month. Cooper's already talking about investing in more. He wants to get to Britain to study their methods of shipbuilding."

George cleared his throat and finally asked the question that had been on his mind since Orry's arrival.

"Is there any news of Madeline?"

Orry turned toward his friend, away from the sun. His eyes were sunken in patches of shadow. "No news, and no change."

"Do you still see her?"

"As often as I can. It's a bad bargain, but better than none."

The sand veils whispered past their feet. The beach was growing dark. George rose and signaled the boys. Billy and Charles beached the skiff, unstepped the mast, and raised it to their shoulders. "You'll make a sailor yet," Billy said as they followed their elders toward the dirt road leading home.

Charles grinned. "A sailor but never a Yankee, I hope."

"What's wrong with Yankees?"

"Mr. Hazard, sir, I'll be happy to tell you—if you have the rest of the night free."

"Not to listen to tall tales and made-up stories." The banter irked Billy somehow. "Let's discuss something we can agree on."

"Girls?"

"Girls," Billy said emphatically, his good humor restored. He was thinking about a particular girl named Ashton.

Ahead, slow-moving shadows in the purpling dusk, George smiled at the sound of the young voices. Orry smiled too. Stick and Stump the Second.

The mellow mood disintegrated as soon as they arrived at Fairlawn. The ladies had gathered on the side porch with pitchers of iced lemonade—and without Virgilia at first. Now she was present; she had joined them after drinking a quantity of claret. George and the others found her in the midst of a sermonette on revisions to the fugitive-slave law of 1793, revisions that the Congress was currently debating.

"The whole business is nothing but a scheme to appease the South," she declared, slurring more than a few words.

"Dear me," Clarissa sighed. "I feel so lost in discussions of such issues."

"Then I would inform myself if I were you, Mrs. Main."

Virgilia's tone irked the other women in her family. Among the Mains it was Ashton who reacted most visibly. Seated in a cane rocker with an untasted glass of lemonade in her hand, she glared at Virgilia, who paid no attention.

"Very simply, the revisions will remove fugitive slave cases from state jurisdiction. From now on all such cases will be handled by the

Federal government. That would lead you to believe that the decisions would probably benefit the runaways, wouldn't it?"

"Yes, that would be my assumption," Clarissa said.

"You would be wrong. The true purpose of the revisions is to circumvent strong liberty laws, such as the one in Vermont. The revisions favor the slave catchers and the slave owners. All it will take to establish proof of ownership is an affidavit, which can easily be forged. Further, a runaway slave won't be permitted to say a word on his own behalf. It's a put-up job and a shameful one. Why Washington keeps truckling to the South I'll never know."

Maude had remained silent as long as she could. Now, firmly, she said to her daughter:

"It's rather impolite of you to lecture when this is a social occasion. If you've finished, perhaps you'd like to excuse yourself. You sound tired."

Isabel laughed. "Oh, let's tell the truth. The poor child's had too much to drink."

"Isabel—" Maude began, but before she could say more, Ashton jumped up, thrust out her chin, and rushed to Virgilia.

"If you don't like Southerners, why did you invite us here?"

Clarissa rose. "Ashton, that's enough." She turned to the men, who had been standing silently. "I'm glad you're back, Orry. Will you escort us home, please? So nice to have been with you," she finished, extending her hand to Maude. The visit ended hastily on a note of embarrassment.

After the Mains left, George cornered his sister on the lawn, where she had gone to avoid the family's wrath. "Will you kindly tell me why you continue to bait our guests?" he demanded.

"Why shouldn't I say what I think?"

"If I truly believed you were doing that, you'd hear no complaints from me. But your candor goes far beyond mere discusssion or even conviction. You try to insult people. Wound them. And you do it to my very good friends."

"They are not *my* friends. They represent a way of life that's despicable and utterly wrong. I wouldn't care if the earth opened and swallowed the lot of them."

"By God, you're the rudest, most inconsiderate—"

He was talking to the lightning bugs; Virgilia had turned and rushed to the house.

It took three cigars and a long tramp along Newport's deserted

353

roads for George to regain a measure of calm. What was the use of arguing with her? She was incorrigible. *Lord, what will the rest of the summer be like?*

Fortunately, two days later a letter from an abolitionist colleague summoned Virgilia to Boston. She packed and left for the ferry with scarcely a word to anyone. Maude acted relieved. Though George didn't show it, he was too.

Ultimately the strongest reaction his sister generated within him was pity. She struck out viciously at too many people. Someday one of them would strike back. It might even be a Yankee. Northerners were hardly as virtuous as Virgilia liked to pretend.

What of her future, then? What had she to look forward to? Unhappiness? Without a doubt. Tragedy? Yes, that was very possible, he admitted with a feeling of sadness.

"Tarnation. What's this we got?"

"Another one of the summer bunch, from the looks of him."

"I ain't speakin' of him, Oral. Look at that fancy pole and creel."

Unseen, Billy heard the low voices and held still. He was high in the tree he had climbed to reach the good apples. Down below, the four townies had appeared through a break in the hedge bordering the orchard. Three of the townies were white, one black.

Billy and Charles had hiked north of town, fished the bay unsuccessfully for two hours, and detoured into the orchard on their way home. Now they were in for trouble. Most townies hated the hordes of visitors who infested the island every summer. These four were no exception.

Billy was crouched in a fork created by two upper limbs of the tree. His left leg was bent, his heel jammed tight against the underside of his thigh. The muscles of that leg already hurt like the devil. The townies hadn't seen him. They were concentrating on the expensive fishing gear lying in the grass next to Charles, who sat with his back against the tree. His chin rested on his shirt. His eyes were closed.

"If you like it, help yourself," said the boy addressed as Oral; he was the Negro. "He won't fuss. He's sleepin.' "

Charles's eyes flew open. One of the townies yelped. Charles used the distraction to draw his right leg up in an inverted V so that his boot was within reach. The boot in which he hid the bowie knife.

"Afraid you're wrong on both counts," he said with a broad smile. Billy gazed down at the top of Charles's head, at long hair ruffled

354

by the wind. He didn't miss the casual way Charles laid his right hand on his knee, a few inches above his boot top.

"Damn if he don't sound like a Southron," a towheaded townie said. He nudged the black. "Bet he's one of them boys that whups your kinfolk down in Georgia."

"Yeah, I bet he is," Oral said. His eyes were ugly. "We're takin' them fishing things."

Still smiling, Charles clasped his right hand lightly around the upper part of his calf. "It would be a serious mistake to do that, boys."

"Oh, yes?" Oral sneered. "It's four on one." He bent at the waist, reaching for Charles's big wicker creel. Suddenly the towhead spotted the other rod leaning against the trunk.

"Lookit, Oral. They's two poles. Why would he have two?"

Oral was so eager to claim Charles's things he ignored the anxious note in his friend's voice. The other two townies began to look around the orchard in a puzzled way. Slowly and silently, Billy straightened his left leg, never taking his eyes from Charles's right hand. When Charles grabbed for the top of his boot and rolled, Billy jumped.

"Jesus Almighty," Towhead screamed, a second before Billy's heavy walking boots struck his shoulders.

Bone cracked. Towhead went tumbling backward into the hedge. Crouching, Charles moved his right hand slowly. Oral watched the point of Charles's knife trace a circle in the air. The black youth began to perspire.

"Now, sir," Charles said to Oral. "Is it all Southerners you dislike? Or just Southerners who can't abide thieves?"

By then Billy had gained his feet. For a few moments he had lost track of the other two townies. He found them suddenly, as shadows that leaped across the grass. The townies came racing at Charles from the rear, each swinging a piece of tree limb snatched from the ground.

"Behind you!" Billy yelled.

Charles started to pivot. The nearest townie bashed the side of his head. The limb was rotten and flew into half a dozen pieces. But the blow dazed Charles, knocking him against Oral, who plucked the bowie knife out of his hand with no effort. Oral's eyes slitted down. He smirked, sidestepped, grabbed the back of Charles's collar, and with his other hand stabbed the bowie toward Charles's face.

Terrified, Billy launched himself through the air. He hit Oral's legs. The knife missed Charles's cheek by half an inch.

Billy grappled Oral to the ground. Charles seized the nearest weapon,

355

his fishing pole, and flicked the line at the other two townies who were charging again. Towhead brandished a sharp rock.

The flying fishhook struck a roll of flesh at the nape of Towhead's neck. Charles pulled back on the pole with a snap of his wrist while braking the line with his thumb. The hook buried itself. Towhead shrieked.

Billy, meantime, was rolling back and forth while Oral knelt on his chest. Oral was tough, strong, and determined to cut him. Billy slammed his head to the right an instant before the knife speared the ground close to his left ear.

"You white fucker," Oral breathed. He pushed his knee into Billy's groin.

Billy's lower body exploded with pain. The pain slowed his responses. He knew he'd never be able to dodge the next slash. Oral raised the knife slowly, almost like some pagan priest with a sacrificial offering.

Sunlight flared on the big blade. Then suddenly the knife disappeared from Oral's hand. His mouth flew open. He fell sideways into the grass, writhing. Charles gracefully plucked out the knife which he had driven into the back of Oral's right thigh.

Even breathing hard, Charles seemed calm, perfectly in control, as he gave the townies a big, cold grin. "Boys, you better run before we kill you. And if you should see my friend or me on the streets of Newport, turn and go the other way or this'll be just a sampler."

He put his right boot up on a stump and rested his elbows on his knee. The uninjured townie dragged Oral toward the hedge, leaving red swaths in the grass.

Billy used his own knife to cut the fishing line. The other two townies slunk away. The one with the hook still in him, Towhead, looked back once with awe from the break in the hedge.

Charles waved the bowie so that it flashed in the sun. "*Get!*"

Towhead vanished.

Only then did Billy exhale. Shoulders sagging, he sprawled in the grass. "Why in the hell did they pick a fight?"

"'Cause I had a pole and creel they wanted. 'Cause they didn't like my speech or place of origin—" He shrugged. "There's just no accounting for human cussedness, I've found. Anyway, we got through it. I'd say we make a pretty good pair of fighters. Many thanks for your timely assistance, Mr. Hazard."

Billy's smile was less assured than that of his companion. "Think nothing of it, Mr. Main. I just wish I had your style. I was scared to death."

"Think I wasn't? My guts felt like a pan of water."

"You surely didn't show it."

"Good. If you don't show the other party how you feel, it gets 'em fidgety, so they make mistakes. Orry taught me that."

"Maybe I should take a few lessons," Billy said as they gathered their things.

"But you'd have to explain why you wanted them." Charles's grin was fading. "Personally, I'd like to keep quiet about this little mess. Orry and Aunt Clarissa and Uncle Tillet think I've gotten over this kind of scrapping. I'd just as soon preserve the illusion." He stuck out his hand. "Bargain?"

"Sure."

Billy clasped the offered hand to seal the bond of secrecy. For the first time, he felt Charles Main was his friend.

As it turned out, however, the fight didn't remain a secret.

A couple of days later, Ashton and her sister went to the beach to wade in the surf. Charles and Billy were offshore in the skiff. Presently the wind died. They beached the boat. Charles lay down to nap.

Ashton was some distance away, resting in a wicker chair under a large striped parasol. She wore a summer frock of light lilac material which the sea breeze pressed against her maturing breasts. The effect was so provocative that Billy had to look the other way.

He thought of Ashton almost constantly. In his fantasies she was always nude. The summer seemed to encourage such visions. Here they were, two young men and two young girls, unchaperoned, sharing the same bit of beach.

Billy didn't consider that circumstance accidental. Pesty Brett followed him everywhere. She had probably teased and wheedled her sister into accompanying her to the beach. Alas, Ashton had no interest in Billy. Most of the time she behaved as if he didn't exist.

He knelt and began building a castle. He dripped watery sand from his clenched fist to form spires. He had been at it ten minutes when a shadow fell across the intricate towers and ramparts. There stood Brett, twisting one of her pigtails back and forth.

"Hello, Billy."

"Oh, hello."

She was pretty enough, he supposed, though it was impossible to overlook her freckles which the summer sun had a way of darkening.

Because she was so young, she was flat as a board in front. But those weren't the only things about her that bothered him.

"I heard you were fighting," she said.

His hand jerked and toppled a spire. "Who told you that?"

"Yesterday I went to the store for some licorice. I heard a boy telling about two bullies who attacked him the other day."

"Did you know the boy?"

Brett shook her head.

"What did he look like?"

"He had yellow hair. Pale, almost white. There was a dirty bandage on the back of his neck." She touched the approximate position at which Charles had sunk the hook into Towhead.

"Go on."

"I stood looking at the candy jars till he finished his story. He said the bullies were summer people. When he described them, I decided he was talking about you and Charles."

Billy glanced past her. Ashton was still resting, paying no attention. Damn.

"You must be mistaken, Brett."

"For heaven's sake, don't bite my head off! It was you, all right." She stared at him in an earnest way. It annoyed him and made him uneasy. "You'll get hurt if you hang around Cousin Charles," she went on. "I know he's handsome and fun, but he's too fond of fighting. He's a bad influence."

Billy scowled. "Are you always so damn free with your opinions?"

"You shouldn't swear, either."

He jumped up and kicked the castle apart. "If I want your advice, I'll ask. Meantime, don't say anything bad about Charles. He's my friend."

Bewildered, she watched him storm away, kicking more sand. "I was only trying to help you. I just wanted to tell you honestly—"

The sentence died unfinished. She twisted her pigtail so hard it hurt. Billy misunderstood her every word and action. He didn't realize her pursuit of him was adoration, her warnings expressions of concern. Just like all other boys, he was unable to deal with a girl who spoke her true mind.

Oh, she knew she was often too tart with him, but that was the result of being nervous. Of feeling a longing and lacking the experience to express it. Why couldn't he look beyond the words and into her eyes, her soul? Discover what it was that she thought about every moment of the day and wept over every night? Why couldn't he *see*?

She watched him slow down as he approached the big striped parasol. She knew the answer to all her desperate questions. Billy couldn't see her because of Ashton.

Ashton was expert at handling any boy. She dimpled and lowered her lashes in that coy way of hers, and the boy melted. She always agreed with the boy's opinion, and if she truly wanted something from him, she got it so sweetly and skillfully he never suspected he had been manipulated.

She had one other, immense advantage. She was older, already a woman.

Angry at Billy, but more angry at herself, Brett spun and marched up the beach in the other direction. She raised a palm and pressed it against her hatefully flat bosom. She pressed hard, until there was pain.

Oh, Billy, Billy, she thought. You'll never see what I really am. Or how much I love you.

Ashton had awakened while Billy was still talking to her sister. She knew Brett worshiped Billy, but she had never seen the younger girl speak to him so directly or with such obvious emotion. Even from a distance, the imploring look on Brett's face was evident.

Hopeless little ninny, Ashton thought. Brett had no idea of the meaning of the word *love*. Ashton did, three times over. But on none of those occasions had her lover been that slug Huntoon.

The first time had been terrifying, the second less so. Neither time had she derived any physical satisfaction from her partner, a young man from the Smith family who was about her own age and plainly inexperienced. Not that experience mattered; her fright coupled with her curiosity kept her tense and unresponsive.

She felt sure her failure to feel anything was the boy's fault. She had heard whispered remarks from girls in her set who were just a bit older, and every such remark hinted at the intense delight of lovemaking. The third time proved the other girls were right; the experience was a revelation.

It had happened one dark, wet day in Charleston. Just as twilight was settling and a thundershower ending, Ashton had slipped off by herself. The streets were virtually deserted.

The man she chanced to encounter was a sailor, rough-spoken and a good fifteen years older. They walked awhile. Then, with great anticipation, yet great trepidation too, she agreed to accompany him to a dingy riverfront inn. She was mindful that she could still be recognized—undone—at any moment. Yet she was so overcome with wicked excitement that turning back was out of the question.

A block from the inn, the rain began again, soaking her bonnet. She stopped to remove it and examine her reflection in the window of a seamy shop.

The merchandise displayed in the window was junk, even including the plated locket and chain on which her eye fell. The sailor was impatient, and in an instant she decided to test the level of that impatience. She indicated the locket and chain, and with sweet, circuitous language made clear that the trinkets were the price of her favors. The sailor shot into the shop with scarcely a hesitation. Thus Ashton discovered the power of the sexual appetite to motivate a man.

Having learned such a valuable lesson, it was then an added pleasure to disrobe for the sailor in his sordid rented room and to find herself hardly frightened at all but rather damp and trembling with expectancy as he undid his trousers and showed his machine. It was immense; a spasm shook her at the sight of it. Before long, alternately groaning and blaspheming, she was stunned by a succession of spasms, each more violent than the one before.

No one had adequately prepared her for such pleasure. Not only was this act of great practical use, it was something to be enjoyed—voraciously. The two lessons together were almost more than she could bear. She soon threw the locket and chain away, but she was happy for days.

Because of this background of experience, Ashton pitied her skinny, naive little sister. Yet now she suddenly found herself jealous of Brett, too. Ashton didn't care a fig for Billy Hazard. But she expected every young man who met her to worship her and no one else. Even though she didn't consider Brett a serious rival, rivalry of any kind had already become unacceptable to her; rivalry from her sister was unthinkable. So when Billy came tramping back up the shore, kicking sand every which way, Ashton was alert and smiling her sweetest smile.

She called his name and waved. In seconds he was on his knees beside her. "I thought you were resting," he said.

"Resting for very long is boring. We've had so little chance to become acquainted. Won't you sit and chat?"

"Yes. Surely. Of course!"

His pliability amused her. But he *was* rather good-looking, in a burly, bullish way. Perhaps she would do more than just keep him away from Brett.

A week later, on the skiff. Charles said to Billy. "Noticed you strolling with cousin Ashton again last night. Saw you heading down Beach Road. Can't imagine what you find so fascinating there—unless it's an absence of human habitation."

Billy laughed. "Habitation. That's a real five-dollar word."

Charles leaned over the transom and drifted a hand in the water. "Last year I'd never even heard of it. But you can't be an ignoramus and attend the Academy." He grinned. "You surely did a smooth job of changing the subject. Tell you one thing about Ashton. I never thought she'd take a fancy to a Yankee."

They came about as lightning forked in the belly of some thunderclouds far out at sea. The chance remark about Yankees led them into a conversation about the issues their elders discussed frequently. The start of the exchange was friendly enough, but both boys were soon speaking with the intensity typical of their age.

"The thing is," Charles said, "the rights of a state are supreme."

"Over those of the Union?"

"Absolutely. The Union was created by the consent of the separate states. Any state can withdraw that consent whenever it wishes."

"No, Charles, it's a legal contract. And unless there's a specific part of the contract—"

"Clause."

"All right, clause. Unless there's a clause that describes a method for voiding the contract—"

"Now who's using fancy words?"

"Let me finish," Billy said with a scowl. "A contract can't be broken legally unless the contract provides for it. In the case of the Union, it doesn't."

"You sound like a regular Philadelphia lawyer. We're not talking about an agreement between a couple of peddlers. It's a compact between government and the governed. It's altogether different. I maintain that any state has the right to withdraw at any time."

The sail began to flap. As Billy corrected their course, he growled, "That would lead to chaos."

"No, sir—just to an end of a Union grown tyrannical. There's another dandy word for your collection."

He fairly spat the remark into the wind; Billy couldn't recall seeing his friend so tense or humorless. He tried to lighten things by smiling and saying:

"George told me that you Southerners love argument. He's surely right."

"It's liberty Southerners love," Charles retorted. "And they love it too much to see it whittled away to nothing."

Offshore, thunder resounded like cannon fire. Billy's lips compressed and lost color. Charles's taunt had abruptly made him angry.

"You're speaking of the liberty of white men, of course."

Billy knew he had overstepped. Yet he was damned if he'd back off. Charles glared and started to reply. Then he noticed white combers beginning to break about a mile off their bow. While they argued, the dark clouds had blown in on a rising nor'east wind.

"Storm coming," Charles muttered. "We'd better head for shore."

"I agree."

They were curt with each other the rest of the day. Neither apologized, but neither continued the unresolved argument. They simply let it fade as it would. Gradually, good feelings returned. But in those moments when Billy's mind was free of visions of Ashton, he recalled the scene and was amazed at how close he and Charles had come to shouting at one another. A couple of years ago he had laughed whenever members of his family got into windy disputes about national issues. Now he found himself pondering the same issues and taking sides.

But he'd better not do it if he meant to keep Charles as a friend. From then on he carefully refrained from making any remark that might spark controversy. Charles showed a similar restraint.

Still, a definite change had taken place in their relationship. They had both become aware of a force that could destroy their new-found friendship, and although they pretended to forget it, they couldn't. It was always there, threatening, like that distant storm the afternoon they had quarreled.

Ashton led him behind a rock that perched on the shore like a seven-foot brown egg. She leaned back against the rock, safely sheltered from accidental observation. Billy squeezed his legs together and hoped she didn't notice the reason.

The sea rolled gray under a gray afternoon sky. Gulls shrilled and dove for fish. The day was tinged with the melancholy of summer's end.

"I hate the thought of leaving tomorrow," she said.

Billy braced his palms on the rock on either side of her head, as if to hold her there forever. Cool air raised bumps on his bare arms. "I'll write once a week," he promised.

"Oh, that's wonderful."

"Will you write me?"

Her red mouth glistened as she smiled. Her brows puckered slightly. "I'll surely try. But I'll be fearfully busy this fall."

How skillfully she did that. Gave something, yet withheld something too. She withheld just enough to keep him from feeling satisfied or comfortable. She did it with little things, and with her whole self as well. Sometimes he hated her for it. Then he gazed into her dark eyes and didn't care about anything except possessing her, on whatever terms she demanded.

"Will you be back here next summer?" he asked.

"I hope so. This has been so delightful."

His face fell. "Is that all—delightful?"

She gazed past his bare wrist to the ocean. "It would be forward of me to say more. Perhaps you wouldn't think me too unladylike if I showed you how I feel."

She rose on her toes and kissed him on the mouth. Then her tongue squirmed between his lips. Billy's mind reeled. He had only heard about girls who kissed that way.

He groped for her waist and dragged her against him so she'd feel him through her layers of clothing. She did, and uttered a soft little moan. A moan of pleasure, he thought.

How experienced was she? Partly to find out—but only partly— he slid his hand upward from her waist. The moment he touched her breast, she broke the embrace. She dashed down to the water, laughing and patting her hair.

He chased her, fearful that he had made her angry. But that wasn't the case.

"Billy," she gasped, her eyes on the sea, "we mustn't do that sort of thing. You have a power to make me forget what's proper."

He was flattered but confused. He didn't believe her. She knew exactly what she was doing; she always knew. It was part of the terrifying fascination she held for him. The disbelief didn't trouble him long, though. He was too caught up in the memory of their embrace.

So was Ashton; annoyingly so. She had manipulated Billy until the moment they embraced. Then he had crushed against her and utterly destroyed her control. For a moment or two she had actually felt she was falling in love. It must never happen. She, and not the man, always had to be the one in charge.

She seemed powerless to translate the warning into action. As they started home, she twined her fingers with his and pressed his hand against her skirt. She leaned her head to the side so that her temple touched his shoulder. Then she started murmuring like a lovesick fool:

"I'll insist that Orry bring us back next summer. I do so want to see you again, my dear. I don't think I've ever wanted anything more."

26

Cooper went to the pier to welcome the family home. He planned to extend Judith's invitation to a family reunion at the Tradd Street house as soon as they'd recovered from traveling. He was in a fine mood. The unexpected arrival of James Huntoon spoiled it.

With the young lawyer was a tall, princely black man of about thirty. Cooper recognized him as one of the few slaves still owned by the Huntoon family. His name was Grady. He was a second-generation Ibo whose father had been brought illegally from Benin around 1810, two years after Congress outlawed the importation of blacks. Very likely Grady's father had arrived via Havana and some deserted cove on the Florida coast. Even today Cooper heard occasional rumors of a secret slave trade operating along that route.

Ibos had never been popular as slaves because of a marked tendency to run away. The Huntoons had ensured that if Grady ever chose to run, he could be identified easily. Long ago, his four upper front teeth had been pulled. It was a common means of marking human property.

Grady gave Cooper a polite greeting, much more polite than Huntoon's. "I brought Grady to help with your sister's luggage," the lawyer explained. He gestured at some poorly dressed black men nearby. "Those nigger porters are worthless. I've seen them deliberately drop a valise because they know the owner is white but powerless to punish a freed man."

Cooper held his tongue. What in the world did Ashton see in this fool?

Some problem held the incoming steamer offshore an extra thirty minutes. Huntoon began damning the compromise bills. Cooper didn't want to debate, but the lawyer annoyed him so badly he was soon in the thick of it. They argued over a state's right to secede, an argument being heard all over the country these days.

Neither man won. The only result was bad feeling on both sides. Huntoon wished that he had the physical strength—and the courage—to give Cooper the thrashing he deserved. But the lawyer's only combative skills were verbal, and he knew it. He had to be content with getting in the last word.

"It's no wonder you don't have a friend left in the ruling class of this state."

The steamer warped to the pier. From the rail Clarissa and Brett called down and waved.

Cooper lifted an eyebrow and said to Huntoon, "Do we have a ruling class in South Carolina? I was under the impression that we did away with that sort of thing in the Revolution. What's the next idea that will experience a rebirth? The divine right of plantation owners?"

His cool sarcasm enraged the lawyer. But Cooper got an unexpected comeuppance, with his entire family watching.

As he walked toward the gangway that Negro stevedores were lifting into place, he spied a familiar figure approaching on the crowded pier: Huntoon's relative, Robert Rhett of the *Mercury*. With him was a visitor who had been pointed out to Cooper on the street yesterday, a Georgia politician named Bob Toombs—another strong defender of Southern rights.

Toombs and Rhett strolled arm in arm. When they saw Cooper, their smiles disappeared. Cooper said hello. Neither man replied. They swept by and went straight to Huntoon, shook his hand, and greeted him loudly so that Cooper would be sure to hear.

Ashton watched Rhett and the other man cut her brother. She had been dreading the return to Charleston because it meant Huntoon would be pestering her again. Sure enough, there he was, the poor slug. He had even brought his handsome nigger with the missing teeth.

How soft Huntoon looked in comparison to Billy Hazard. How weak, with the sunlight flashing on his spectacles. And yet, she couldn't fail to be impressed by the warm greeting Rhett gave the young lawyer.

Her father pointed to Rhett's companion. "That's Bob Toombs of Georgia." He sounded impressed. She must find out about the stranger. Lately she had begun to ponder the significance of being a Main from South Carolina. The significance of being wealthy, prominent—powerful, and a friend of the powerful. The distinction became clearer and more important when she saw what it was like to be devoid of power and dismissed because of it, as her own brother had been dismissed a moment ago.

Power had always been the key to Ashton's relationship with Brett. Ashton knew very well that she had a deep, only partially understood need to be the person in charge. Now, abruptly, she saw her need in relation to the wider world. There, too, she wanted to be the one who gave the orders, and she wanted to be recognized as such.

What came over her there at the rail was not merely a realization of this new goal but an awareness that her behavior had better be more calculated if she was to reach it. Huntoon had important connections. She must react to that fact, no matter how she felt about him personally. Billy was the summer, but Huntoon was the future.

So when the Mains left the steamer, she contrived to take her father's arm because she knew he'd go straight to Rhett and the others. He did. When she reached Huntoon, she greeted him with a bold kiss on the cheek.

"James! I've missed you so."

"You have? That's marvelous."

It's a lie, too. But she merely thought that.

She was pleased with herself for showing all of them where her interest and her loyalty lay. Let Brett run to Cooper and hug him, as she was doing now. Brett made no difference; she'd never amount to a row of beans anyway. Ashton waved casually at her brother from a distance.

At Belvedere one evening in early October, Constance said to George, "Dear, do you recall that shed at the back of the factory property?"

He pushed aside the sheet on which he had been writing. He was developing a plan for quick expansion of the rail mill. In September the Federal government had for the first time granted public lands to railroads, to stimulate construction of new routes. George paid a sizable monthly retainer to a Washington lawyer whose duties included alerting his client to decisions affecting the iron trade. When reporting on the grants, the lawyer had also predicted that many similar ones would eventually be made throughout the West and South. To George that signaled a boom market in rails for the next ten, possibly twenty years.

He realized Constance had been quiet a long time before she asked the question. Something important was on her mind.

The parlor and the house were still. A gilt clock ticked. After ten already. He rose and stretched. "The shed where we formerly stored tools," he said with a nod. "What about it?"

"Would you be willing to let me use it?"

"You? Whatever for?"

She didn't give a direct answer. "I wouldn't use it often. But I would want you to know what might happen there."

"Good Lord, I've never heard such mystery. What's going on?"

He was smiling, but she was frowning, as if worried about his reaction. She hurried to him.

"Let me show you. Come with me."

"Where ?"

"To the shed."

"Right now?"

"Yes. Please."

Curiosity and the seriousness of her expression led to quick consent. A few minutes later they were climbing a sloping road at the back of the factory property. The air was cold, the sky cloudless. The shed stood out clearly in the starlight.

George stopped suddenly, pointing. A gleam of yellow showed between pieces of siding that didn't quite meet.

"Someone's in there."

"Yes, I know." She took his hand. "It's perfectly safe. Come on."

"You know?" he queried, pulled along. "Will you kindly explain what this is all—"

"Mr. Belzer?" she whispered at the shed door. "It's Constance. You must move the lantern. It can be seen from outside."

The light in the gap faded. Belzer was a storekeeper from the village, a Quaker. What in God's name was he doing here? The door opened, and George saw the frail, nervous merchant. Beyond him, wrapped in old blankets, he spied a second figure, one whose appearance shocked him and explained everything.

The young man wrapped in the blanket was probably not yet twenty, but fright and emaciation made him look twice that. He had amber-brown skin.

"We didn't have any other place to conceal him," Belzer said to George. "He came to my house early this morning. But it's no longer safe for me to keep—travelers. Too many know of my involvement. This afternoon hiding the boy became imperative. An agent of the new district commissioner arrived in Lehigh Station."

Belzer referred to the Federal fugitive-slave commissioner. President Fillmore had signed the bill on September 18, and the machinery for enforcement was rapidly being put in place.

The runaway sniffled, then sneezed twice. George turned to his wife, still feeling stunned. "How long have you been involved in this work?"

"Mr. Belzer approached me in the spring. I've been helping ever since."

"Why didn't you say something?"

"Don't be angry, George. I wasn't sure how you'd react."

"You know my feelings about slavery. But evading or obstructing the new law is a serious offense. If you're caught, you could go to prison."

Constance indicated the shivering boy. "And where will he go if he's caught? Right back to North Carolina. Back to God knows what brutal punishment."

"Why did you decide to involve yourself?"

"Because the slave owners now have all the advantages. The Federal commissioners are supposed to judge cases impartially. Yet the new law pays them ten dollars for every slave they return, and five for each one they don't. Impartial? It's a farce."

"It was a compromise," George replied.

Belzer sounded almost antagonistic as he said, "You may call it whatever you like, Mr. Hazard, but the new law remains an offense to God and the conscience of this land. Constance, I'm sorry if I caused trouble between you and your husband. I believe we misjudged him. I will try to locate another place for Abner."

Stung, George blurted, "Wait." The others looked at him. "I didn't say no, did I?"

Hope replaced anger in his wife's eyes. She ran to him. "All we need are some staples and extra blankets, a padlock for the door, and one or two 'no trespassing' signs to warn people away. If I spend money for anything beyond that, I'll tell you. Otherwise, you needn't worry about what goes on here."

"Not worry about an underground railroad station on my own property? I disagree." He gnawed his lower lip. "Why on earth do you want to use this particular place?"

Belzer answered. "It's isolated, and it can be approached through the woods farther up the hill. The—ah—passengers can arrive and leave for Canada virtually undetected."

For perhaps fifteen seconds George stared at the sniffling, under-nourished runaway. He knew he had no choice.

"All right, but I must impose some conditions for everyone's protection and—"

He didn't have a chance to finish. Constance flung her arms around him and began kissing him while Belzer murmured reassurances to Abner, who grinned and then doubled over in a fit of sneezing.

George was proud of what Constance had done. They took Maude into their confidence. All three agreed that no one else in the family should be told about the station. Stanley and Isabel would object because Stanley wanted no involvement with controversy. Lately he was spending only two or three days a week at home. The rest of the time he was courting new friends in Harrisburg or Philadelphia.

A power struggle had developed within the state Democratic party. It pitted Stanley's friend Cameron against the acknowledged head of the party, Buck Buchanan of Lancaster. After serving as Polk's secretary of state, Buchanan had wanted the 1848 presidential nomination. He blamed Cameron's machinations for his failure to get it. The men were now disavowing each other publicly. Stanley had cast his lot with Cameron, which George thought foolish.

But who could be sure in a period in which party loyalties, and the parties themselves, seemed to change overnight? Recently a new political entity had emerged, the Free Soil party. This militant group was a coalition of anti-cotton Whigs, former members of the Liberty party, and some Barn Burners, the name given to hard-line, anti-slavery Democrats. In George's opinion the Free Soilers seemed dedicated to throwing out the baby with the bath water. They said that if the price of national expansion was acceptance of slavery in new territories, they would stand foursquare against creation of those territories. Virgilia attended every Free Soil caucus within the state; every one, that is, at which women were permitted in the gallery. She wrote lengthy memorials demanding that women be allowed to sit on the main floor as participants.

She was another from whom the three conspirators wanted to conceal the existence of the underground railroad station. She would approve of it, of course, but she might also talk too freely. There were many men working at Hazard's who remained anti-Negro, and violently so. Freed blacks would threaten such men by competing for their jobs. George wished that kind of hatred didn't exist at the ironworks, but he also knew no government could legislate it out of existence because it was rooted in fear; illogical. Nor could it be quickly overcome with appeals to conscience. It would take a generation or so and plenty of education to do away with such attitudes permanently.

"I don't imagine it would be wise to tell your Southern friends, either," Constance said.

George frowned. "You say that as if there's something not quite decent about them. I assumed they were your friends, too."

"Oh, of course," she said hastily. "It's just that I'm not as close to the Mains as you are. If I had to choose between pleasing Orry and helping Joel Belzer, my choice might not be to your liking."

She wasn't trying to bait or annoy him, he realized; she was speaking honestly. Still, the words rankled within him. Maude noted the fact and examined her hands.

"Why say something like that?" George snapped. "You won't have to make that kind of choice, ever."

But he wasn't sure of the statement, and that uncertainty, with its grim implications, was the real cause of his concern, his irritability.

27

"Pettiauger," Charles said. He held up the object he had been carving. With the tip of his bowie he indicated a long groove he had been deepening in the wood. "It's a Carolina river dugout. Down in Louisiana I think it's called a pirogue."

Four-year-old Laban Hazard sat at Charles's feet on the front steps of Fairlawn. The boy worshiped Charles and had been waiting an entire year to see him. The Mains had arrived in Newport that morning.

Laban's twin brother appeared at the corner of the house, rolling a hoop. He pointed to the boat. "That for Laban?"

Charles nodded.

Levi looked sour. "I want one."

Charles chuckled. Levi seemed to have inherited his mother's disposition. "All right," Charles said. "As soon as I finish this one."

Levi stuck out his lower lip and shook his head. "Make mine first."

Charles pointed the knife at him. "You mind your manners, Mr. Yankee, or I'll stick you on a spit and cook you for supper."

He said it jokingly, but Levi screamed and fled. Laban laughed and leaned against his idol's knee. Billy emerged from the house.

"Froggy going a-courting so soon?" Charles asked. "The girls won't even be unpacked."

Billy ignored him and fussed with his cravat. Charles whistled.

"Me oh my, look at that jacket. I don't recall you dressing up so fancy last summer. It surely must be love—"

Billy grinned. "Go to hell. Laban, don't tell your father I cussed in front of you."

And away he went. Halfway down the lawn he broke into a run. He vaulted the brick wall, startling the masons who were once again repairing the mortar.

Young womanhood had touched Brett Main that spring. Will he notice? she wondered as she examined her mirrored image and tried to force her small breasts to greater prominence by tugging her dress and undergarments downward from the waist.

Behind her, Ashton exclaimed in delight:

"Oh, mercy. He's here already! I can hear him talking to Orry."

She went down the staircase with the speed and display of a Fourth of July rocket. Brett was only a few steps behind her. It made no difference. By the time Brett was halfway down the stairs, Orry had left the foyer, and Billy and Ashton were racing out of the house without so much as a glance in her direction.

She walked the rest of the way to the bottom. From behind, a hand touched her shoulder. She squealed and jumped.

"Papa!"

"I thought you'd be resting, missy."

Tillet noticed a tear on his daughter's cheek. With a little groan and a pop of knee joints, he sat on the lowest step and drew her down beside him. He put his arms around her.

"Why so unhappy?"

"It's that Billy Hazard. He's the most stuck-up person I've ever met. I wanted to say hello, but he wouldn't even look at me."

"Don't be too hard on the lad. He's got a case for your sister. I think it's mutual."

"She always gets anything she wants! She'll get him too, won't she?"

"Oh, I don't know. They're both mighty young for any discussions of matri—missy, come back. I didn't mean to upset you."

But she had already bolted upstairs, her wail of misery echoing behind her.

Billy and Ashton went straight to the rock where they had kissed last summer. The instant Ashton felt Billy's arms around her and the sweet, shy pressure of his lips, practical considerations melted away.

What a lot of time she'd wasted on all those deep plans made last year after she had looked down from the rail of the steamer and seen Mr. Bob Rhett snub her brother. The plans and the pathetic Huntoon were now completely forgotten. She'd marry Billy and no one else.

That could fit into her larger scheme, though. The Hazards might be Yankees, but they were rich and prominent. She must let Billy know about her ambitions. But not right this minute. All she wanted to do now was savor her surrender to love and to him.

She squeezed him hard, so he'd be sure to feel her breasts. "I

374

never thought I could miss anyone so much. I just died waiting weeks for each of your letters."

"I'm a bad writer. For every one I sent, I tore up ten."

"You can make up for it now, sweet. Kiss me, and don't you dare stop till I'm ready to faint."

He obliged with enthusiasm.

A mantle of false peace enfolded the two families and the nation in that summer of 1851. Most Americans were exhausted from the war and the wrangling over the slave issue. Even if the Compromise of 1850 had achieved no permanent solutions, people were prepared to act as if it had. Some loud voices on both sides continued to proclaim that little had been changed and nothing solved; a cancer hidden by bandages remained a cancer. But the James Huntoons and Virgilia Hazards had trouble promoting their militant views during those warm, gentle months. The majority of Americans wanted a respite, at least for a season or two.

Cooper and Judith had been married on the first of June 1850, and nature had quickly interfered with Cooper's plan to visit Britain. Exactly nine months after the wedding, Judith delivered Judah Tillet Main—or J.T., as his proud grandfather called him from the moment he first heard of his arrival. In late July 1851, the parents, the baby, and a wet nurse traveled to Newport to spend ten days with the Mains.

A few hours after the group arrived, Tillet seated himself in a rocker on the porch of the rented house. Cooper sat down next to him. Tillet gazed proudly at his grandson, who was resting in a blanket in Cooper's arms. Judith was out on the lawn, playing ninepins with George, Billy, and Ashton. Their shadows were long in the twilight.

Tillet cleared his throat. "Your wife is a fine woman."

Cooper was overwhelmed. Never before had his father paid her a compliment. "Thank you, sir. I agree." He folded a corner of the blanket to protect the top of his son's head from the breeze.

Tillet leaned back and laced his fingers over his paunch. It grew larger every year. How old he looks, Cooper thought. What is he now? Fifty-five? No, fifty-six. It shows in the wrinkles in his skin. It shows in his eyes. He knows it's nearly over for him. For the first time in a long while, Cooper felt an outpouring of love for his father. Love without reservation or qualification.

But Tillet had a qualification, which he stated a moment later. "I can praise Judith without agreeing with everything she says. I don't, you know. Still—families shouldn't fight amongst themselves.''

"I agree, sir." *But it's damn hard to achieve that ideal in these times.*

"You've done well with the company," his father continued. "In fact your record is outstanding. *Mont Royal*'s a beautiful thing—yes, I know, a resounding commercial success as well."

"We could use three more like her, to handle all the business we're being offered. I'm looking into it. And something else. I've been asked to design and build ships for others. I'm looking into that, too."

Tillet scratched his chin. "Do you think it's wise to expand so rapidly?"

"Yes, sir, I do. I think we stand to make a larger and more dependable income from ship construction than from carrying cotton."

"Is all of this just conversation or is there substance to it?"

"If you're asking whether I have firm commitments, I do. One from a shipping line in Savannah, another from a Baltimore company. Some points are still being negotiated, but each firm definitely wants a vessel like *Mont Royal*—if I can provide them. I surely intend to try."

He leaned forward enthusiastically. "I envision a day, maybe as little as five years from now, when Main steamers will be shuttling up and down the East Coast and to Europe under the flags of a dozen companies. The cotton market may shrink eventually, but I'm convinced the demand for cargo space and fast delivery of all sorts of goods will only grow during our lifetimes."

"During mine, perhaps. Long-term, I wouldn't venture a guess. The Yankee politicians are unpredictable. Greedy and tricky as—ah, but let's not get onto that and spoil everything. I am frankly awed by the reputation you've established with just one vessel."

"*Mont Royal* incorporates a great many innovations. Two small ones are mine. I patented them."

"Why couldn't these other cargo lines get a ship by going directly to that yard in Brooklyn?"

"They could, but they want something more. They want me to supervise the planning and construction. Quite by accident, I've become a Southern expert on shipbuilding. There aren't many." Cooper smiled then. "You know the definition of an expert, don't you? Someone from out of town."

Tillet laughed. The noise roused his grandson, who started to cry.

Cooper caressed the delicate, warm cheek until the baby was quiet again.

"Don't be overly modest about your accomplishments," Tillet told his son. "You've worked hard in Charleston—I've heard that from any number of sources—and you're still at it. Just look at the reading you brought along on your vacation. Naval architecture, metallurgy—books I can barely lift, let alone understand."

Cooper shrugged, but he was basking in the sudden and unexpected praise. "As part of that learning process, we're finally going to Britain in November."

"My grandson too?"

"Yes, all of us. The doctor said Judah could travel with the wet nurse. Brunel's granted me an interview. Imagine spending an hour with that man. His talent—the breadth of his imagination—incredible. He and his father built the tunnel under the Thames River, did you know that?"

"No, but why does anyone need a tunnel under a river? What's wrong with ferryboats? Or bridges? For that matter, why does anyone need faster ships? I remember something the Duke of Wellington said about railroads in Europe. He said they would only promote social unrest by enabling the lower classes to move about. I feel that way about all the newfangled things coming along these days. Too revolutionary!"

"The precise word, Father. We *are* in the middle of a revolution—a peaceful revolution of industry and invention."

"We should stop it for a while."

"It can't be done. Nor can you go backward. The only possible direction is forward."

"Don't sound as if you enjoy it so much!" Then Tillet sighed. "Ah, well—let's not get into that, either. You're certainly entitled to a trip. But you've earned more than that, and I've been meaning to say something to you." Again he cleared his throat. "I've instructed the family lawyers to prepare documents changing the ownership structure of C.S.C. Henceforward you will control fifty-one percent of the company stock—and receive an equivalent percentage of the profits, free and clear. I have read every report you've sent me. At the rate you're generating income, under the new arrangement you'll soon be a very wealthy man. Self-made. That, too, is a distinction."

After a long moment, Cooper overcame his surprise enough to say,

"I don't know how to thank you. For your show of faith. Or for your generosity."

Tillet waved. "You're my son. You gave your firstborn my name. That's thanks enough. Families shouldn't fight."

He said it a little more poignantly this time. A plea? A warning? I hope that's not it, Cooper thought. I hope he isn't trying to ensure my silence or agreement with his views. I love him, but I can't be bought.

Then he wondered if he was being ungrateful. He wanted to ask Tillet exactly what he meant by the remark about families fighting, but he was unwilling to disturb the tranquillity of the evening. Like the tranquillity of the nation, it was fragile. It would not last.

Both families embraced the summer happily. A relaxed and mellow mood prevailed, a mood that everyone worked to maintain. Even Constance and Isabel had short conversations occasionally.

Talk of national issues was banned by mutual agreement—violated only once. Virgilia, her constraint overcome one evening by too much wine, denounced the latest public pronouncements of William Yancey, the Georgia-born lawyer and former congressman who had become the spiritual heir to Calhoun's most extreme views. The South still held a grudge against Senator Seward of New York. Seward had defended the Wilmot Proviso by saying it fulfilled a law higher than the Constitution, God's law, which would one day prevail against slavery. Yancey verbally lashed the senator from a lecture platform. When Virgilia read of it, she called Yancey a lot of names, including whoremonger. Before long she was substituting the South for Yancey. Orry exploded:

"What a marvelous storehouse of righteousness you've built here in the North, Virgilia. All the sin is below the Mason and Dixon Line—and never mind that I just read about Iowa's posting harsh penalties for any free Negro who dares set foot in the state. All the hypocrisy is down South, too—never mind that California, which your politicians worked so diligently to drag into the Union as a free state, is sending pro-slavery men to the Senate. You never admit to things like that. You ignore them and just keep spouting invective!"

He threw his napkin aside and left the table. Ten minutes later George cornered his sister and yelled at her until she promised to apologize. With great reluctance, she did.

*

Except for that one lapse, the warm, euphoric days remained peaceful. Brett delighted everyone with her piano rendition of Foster's new song, "Old Folks at Home." George proved to be an unbeatable ninepins champion. There was a lively front-porch discussion of the current effort by some preachers to ban Mr. Hawthorne's racy novel *The Scarlet Letter*. One cleric called its publication "the brokerage of lust."

Isabel and Tillet agreed that such trash should be proscribed by law. George replied that anyone who made such a statement didn't understand free speech. Clarissa said timidly that although the novel did sound salacious, she believed George might be right in principle. "Woman," Tillet roared, "you don't know what you're talking about." Fortunately, further argument was forestalled by the appearance of Ashton, Billy, and Cousin Charles on the lawn of the Mains' house.

The young people were bound for the beach. They went there almost every evening, with Charles the token chaperone. That amused Orry. Charles had reformed, but it was still a bit like hiring the devil to do missionary work.

George watched the young people stroll out of sight in the moonlight. Then he said to Orry, "I get the impression that your sister has set her cap for Billy."

"George, not so fast," Constance exclaimed, not entirely teasing. "Next summer Billy goes to the Academy. For four years."

"Nevertheless," Orry put in, "I think George is right."

He didn't bother to say that he doubted there would ever be a match. Ashton was too mercurial. Of course, like Charles, she could change. With that possibility in mind, he added, "You ought to bring Billy to South Carolina."

"Yes, we'd love to have you—all of you," Clarissa said. Seated apart from them at the end of the porch, Virgilia looked skeptical.

"I'd love to see Mont Royal," Constance said.

Orry leaned forward. "Why not this fall? October's one of our loveliest months. Cooper would be happy to show you Charleston, then you could come upriver for a long visit."

"All right, we'll do it," George said after Constance squeezed his hand to encourage him.

A moment later he had second thoughts. Virgilia was watching and listening with great interest. If they took her along, the Mains would probably come to regret their offer of hospitality.

*

Charles leaned back against the damp rock, moonlight splashing his closed eyelids as he imagined naked thighs in various pleasing shades of pink and brown. One pair of thighs belonged to a plump and cooperative girl named Cynthia Lackey. Charles had met her during the first week of the summer, when he had gone to buy some hard candy in her father's general store.

Away to his left he heard laughter. He opened his eyes and saw two figures emerging from the shadow of the bluff. Two figures that looked more like one. Arms around each other's waist, they crossed the brilliantly lit sand.

"Watch out, there's our chaperone," Billy said. Ashton giggled. The single inky shape divided. Charles blinked away the last of his erotic visions. That didn't relieve the tension in his groin. It was time to call on Cynthia again.

Ashton smoothed her hair. Billy tucked in the tail of his shirt. Charles felt sorry for his friend. He had no specific information about Ashton's experience, but he had suspicions. At minimum, she would be an expert tease, goading a suitor until he acquired a glassy-eyed look of frustration. Billy looked that way right now, Charles noticed.

On the way home, Ashton discussed plans for the following evening. Some clam digging first. Then a driftwood fire on the beach, and—

"I'm afraid we can't do that tomorrow night," Charles broke in. "Billy and I have a long-standing engagement at the other end of the island."

Dumbfounded, Billy said, "We do? I don't remember—" Charles elbowed him to silence.

Ashton pouted, then grew almost nastily insistent. Charles smiled and held firm. After Billy had seen Ashton to the door of the house on Beach Road, he came charging around to the side porch, where Charles sat in the moonlight, one long leg resting on the porch rail.

"What the devil is this fictitious engagement at the other end of the island?"

"My boy, it isn't the least bit fictitious. I'm going to introduce you to Miss Cynthia Lackey and her sister Sophie. I have it on good authority that Sophie's just as eager as Cynthia to please the boys and be pleased in turn. Have you ever had a girl before?"

"Of course."

"How many?"

Under Charles's steady stare, Billy wilted. "All right. I haven't."

"That's what I thought. We'll make it a summer to remember."

380

He clapped his friend on the shoulder. "Besides, I know cousin Ashton's reputation for coquetry. I've left the two of you alone so much, I expect you need the relief of an evening with Miss Sophie."

The following night they drove a pony cart to the Lackey place, a small farm in the open countryside. They drove back to Newport at two in the morning, with Billy thanking his friend and saying it was now a memorable summer indeed.

"But I want to see the South," Virgilia said to George. "And they invited me."

"They invited you because politeness required it, that's all!" They had been back in Lehigh Station two days. This was their fourth argument about the trip. "They don't want you down there insulting them and sneering at their way of life every waking moment," George went on. "You'd probably parade this around Mont Royal." He snatched up the broad satin ribbon she had brought into the study. She would be wearing the ribbon on Saturday when she marched in a Free Soil parade in Harrisburg. The ribbon bore the slogan of the party: *Free soil—free speech—free labor—and free men*. "Inviting you to come with us would be like carrying a torch into a dry forest, Virgilia. I'd be a fool to say yes."

"What if I promise that I'll be on my very best behavior? I feel it's important for me to see the South firsthand. If you'll take me, I'll be good as gold. Not a word about free soil or anything else the Mains might find offensive."

He peered at her through smoke curling from his cigar. "You mean that? You'd be polite the entire time?"

"Yes. I promise. I'll swear it on a Bible, if you want."

He managed to smile. "That won't be necessary." He shaped his mouth into an O and blew out a thin rod of smoke while weighing the risks. Then:

"All right. But at the first slip, I'll send you home."

She flung her arms around him and squealed her thanks. It had been a long time since she'd behaved in such a girlish way. For a moment he felt he had a sister again.

When Virgilia went to bed that night, she was too excited to go to sleep. But at last she did. She dreamed of black men's bodies.

28

The Hazard party consisted of eight: Maude, George and Constance, the children, their nurse, and Billy and Virgilia. All but Billy were seasick on the stormy trip to Charleston. They rested a few days at Cooper's house and improved rapidly.

After supper the second evening, Judith entertained them by playing the piano. Then she gathered the guests around her and they had a grand time for almost an hour, singing hymns and popular songs in a rousing way. Everyone took part except Virgilia, who excused herself and went to her room.

Mont Royal happened to be in port, loading cotton for New York. Cooper took them through the vessel, pointing out every detail from the sleek clipper bow to the advanced-design propeller. The visitors didn't understand the engineering innovations as well as their host did, hence couldn't be quite as enthusiastic, but all of them could appreciate the vessel's exterior design. She was lean, graceful—unmistakably modern.

Next Cooper took them over to James Island, to the acreage he had bought earlier. "What I'm proposing to put here, using my profits from C.S.C. to do it, is a shipyard. A yard to build commercial vessels. A yard that will be the best on the East Coast."

"You're starting to sound like a Yankee," said George. They both laughed.

Cooper and Judith showed them the sights of Charleston, including the marble marker at Calhoun's grave in St. Philip's churchyard. Then Cooper proposed to take any interested adults to a rally being sponsored by an organization calling itself the Charleston Southern Rights Coalition.

"Is that a political party?" George asked.

"Nobody's sure," Cooper answered. "Not yet, anyway. The traditional parties are disappearing faster than I can keep track of. 'Whig' and 'Democrat' have become virtually meaningless labels down here."

"What has replaced the regular parties?" Virgilia wanted to know.

"Groups that fall into two camps. In one camp you have the Unionists, men such as Bob Toombs of Georgia who love the South but can't quite swallow the secession pill. In the other camp are the Southern rights crowd: Yancey, Rhett, Ashton's friend Huntoon—he's one of the speakers at the rally, incidentally. You probably won't like anything you hear"—the gently pointed statement brought a prim and humorless smile to Virgilia's mouth—"but it will give you a flavor of current thought in Charleston."

Only George and his sister accepted the invitation. George feared Virgilia might make a scene despite her promises—perhaps even disrupt one of the speeches by shouting insults from the box in which they were seated. But she seemed uninterested in the oratory, preoccupied. While Huntoon was at the rostrum, proclaiming the need for "a great slaveholding republic from the Potomac to the tropic latitudes," she whispered that she needed fresh air and left.

She rushed down the dim staircase to the foyer. Sure enough, he was there, loitering with the other coachmen outside the main doors. He was a strikingly handsome black man wearing heavy velvet livery. She had noticed him earlier, as he was opening a carriage door for his master—Huntoon, she realized suddenly.

Virgilia's breasts felt tight and heavy as she walked to and fro, waving her lace handkerchief in front of her face to indicate why she had left the hall. Sweat glistened in the down on her upper lip. She could hardly keep her eyes off the Negro.

Huntoon's voice rolled through the open doors behind her. "Our institution must follow the American flag, wheresoever it goes. For our system to contract, or even fail to expand at a steady pace, would be tantamount to defeat. We shall not permit it to happen."

Wild applause and cheering interrupted him at that point. Boots stomped and shook the floor. The sound poured out of the hall and engulfed her, somehow heightening her feelings of desire. Over the shoulder of another coachman she tried to catch the tall Negro's eye.

He noticed her but didn't dare show cordiality toward a white woman, lest he be punished for his boldness. She understood. With one long glance she tried to convey that understanding, and something else. His eyes flickered with surprise. Then, looking past the other coachman's shoulder, he smiled. She caught her breath. Four of his front teeth were missing. He was one of those poor wretches whose owners identified them in that inhuman way.

His dark, shiny eyes dropped to her breasts for a second. She thought she might faint. He understood! Another coachman took note of his stare and turned to see its object. At the sight of Virgilia's white skin, the coachman looked at his tall companion with shock and disbelief.

"Here you are." George came hurrying out to her. "You left so quickly I was worried. Are you ill?"

"No, it was just too hot in there. I feel better now." She slipped her arm through his and led him inside.

She couldn't get the tall Negro out of her mind. On the way back to Tradd Street she asked whether there was any special significance if a slave had several teeth missing. "I saw a man like that outside the hall."

George tensed while Cooper explained the probable reason for extraction of the teeth. Virgilia reacted as if it were new information, but no outburst followed. Then Cooper said, "The chap you saw must be Huntoon's man, Grady. Tall fellow? Handsome?"

"I honestly didn't notice," Virgilia lied, pressing her legs together beneath her skirts. She had the information she wanted.

Grady. She savored the name as she drifted to sleep that night. A sultry breeze blew from the fragrant garden. The sweet odors and the dampness of the night heightened her hunger until she ached.

"Grady," she whispered in the dark. She knew she would never see him again, but she wished there were some way it could be otherwise.

Cooler weather arrived at Mont Royal just when the Hazards did. October's sharp, slanting light lent a melancholy beauty to the days, but it was beauty of which Billy was unaware. He hardly saw anything, or anyone, except Ashton.

He spent every free hour with her. On horseback she took him around the plantation, though he suspected she was improvising much of what she said about it. He sensed that she had little understanding of, or interest in, the way rice was planted or harvested.

The slave community fascinated Billy in a grim, almost morbid fashion. The Negroes returned his stare with sad, hopeless eyes. He heard laughter, but not much. For the first time he had some understanding of why Virgilia, Constance, and the rest of the family opposed the peculiar institution.

In the past his attitude had been largely a reflection of theirs: correct, but lacking any passion. The ride down the dirt street between the rows of mean cottages changed that. If slaves were carefree and happy, as Southerners claimed, he saw damned little evidence. He grew angry. Here was an obvious wrong. The conviction was like a splinter in his foot, not really severe enough to interfere with anything, yet a constant source of discomfort.

There was a similar splinter produced by his relationship with Ashton. At first he couldn't identify the reason he felt uneasy in her presence. She still excited him. This was true even though some of the mystery of sex was gone, thanks to tumbling with that Newport girl in her father's hayloft; after the initial embarrassment of removing his pants, Billy had enjoyed his hour with Sophie.

Physically, Ashton remained one of the most perfect creatures he had ever seen. And if not exactly intelligent, she was gifted with an innate cleverness and a glib tongue. What troubled him, he concluded toward the end of his first week at Mont Royal, was a certain quality in the way she kissed, or touched his face, or looked at him. It was *adult;* there was no other word. Yet she had only turned fifteen this year.

Orry arranged a Saturday-night picnic in honor of the visitors. As the breezy twilight was deepening, cousins and neighbors began to arrive. One guest was a handsome woman named Mrs. LaMotte, whom Orry seemed to treat with great politeness. She spent almost no time with her husband; he was off with some of the men and, to judge from their muted voices and raucous laughter, telling dirty stories.

When darkness fell, torches planted in holders in the ground lit the side lawn and kept the insects away. Billy and Ashton left the picnic site and slipped down to the river, hand in hand.

"It's so grand to have you here," she said as they walked to the end of the pier and stood gazing at the black water ruffled by the wind. "Will you stay long?"

"George says another week or so."

"That makes me very happy. But sad, too."

"Sad? Why?"

"When I'm close to you—"

She turned to face him. The distant torches put small, hard reflections in her eyes. Guests passed back and forth in front of the smoky lights, wraithlike.

"Go on," he said.

"When we're close, I must constantly fight my own feelings. I want to be even closer." She brought her bodice, her mouth, then her whole body against him. He felt her lips move as she murmured, "Much closer than is altogether proper."

386

He started to kiss her but abruptly felt something below his waist. God above! She was reaching down to grasp him through his pants and underdrawers. He couldn't have been more astonished if the earth had opened under his feet.

She moaned his name, closed her hand tight, and kissed him ferociously. He quickly overcame his own surprise and reticence, and returned the kiss. Her left arm crooked around his neck while her right hand kept squeezing, squeezing. The play of mouths and hands rapidly reached an embarrassing conclusion. She felt him go rigid in her arms.

She jumped back, palms pressed to her lips. "My heavens, did I cause—?"

He was utterly humiliated, unable to speak. He turned away toward the river.

"Billy, I'm so sorry. I couldn't help myself, dear."

"It's all right," he mumbled.

Five minutes later, Brett and Charles came strolling across the lawn, searching for them. Billy had to face people whether he was ready or not. Fortunately his trousers were wool, in a busy checked pattern, so if anyone was so rude as to ask what had happened, he'd lie and say he'd spilled a cup of punch.

They rejoined the others. There were no questions. But Ashton's behavior had left a vivid impression. She was too accomplished. Those were the words that repeated in his thoughts half the night and for days afterward. For someone so young, she was *too accomplished*.

How had it happened? When he considered the possibilities, an overpowering jealousy gripped him. He wanted to know how she had learned all she knew. And yet he didn't. He knew the relationship had begun to wither. He was sad about it, yet a little relieved somehow.

A spell of gray, muggy weather settled in. Small annoyances began to spring up between Billy and Ashton. She didn't understand something he said, even though he repeated it twice. A pebble in his boot kept him from walking as fast as she would have liked. Small annoyances, angering them, spoiling things.

The end came on a hot, still Saturday. They were unable to find anything to do that didn't bore them. Finally they went strolling along the high bank separating the river from the fields. After ten minutes Ashton sat down, heedless of dirt on her skirt. He sat next to her, and she said bluntly:

"Are you anxious to go to the Academy next year?"

"Yes."

"I think a man can find better things to do."

He frowned. "Why should you worry about that? You're not a man."

She looked at him. Not with hostility, exactly, but neither did she show the warmth he'd seen in her eyes during the summer.

"No, but I'll marry one," she said.

"And you already know what you expect of him, is that it?"

"I know what I expect for myself. I know what I want, and he must give it to me."

The tenor of the conversation was growing steadily more unfriendly; did she sense his withdrawal? He didn't want to fight with her, though. He smiled in hopes of relieving the tension. He poised an invisible pencil over the tablet of his palm.

"Might we have the list for purposes of reference, Miss Main?"

"Don't joke, Billy. I'm fifteen. In another five years my life will be nearly half over. So will yours."

It sobered him. "True."

"If you go through life without a plan, you wind up with nothing. I intend to marry a man with money. At least enough so that I know he isn't after mine. But more important than that, he must be someone. A congressman. A governor. I wouldn't mind if he were President. It's time we had another Southern President."

"Old Zach Taylor came from Louisiana."

"Pooh. He was more Yankee than you are. Anyway—I want to be the wife of a man who's powerful and important."

The rest of it, unspoken, was still unpleasantly clear. The man she married would be driven to achieve her goals if he didn't possess those same goals himself. With a flash of her dark eyes, she finished:

"Of course a soldier can become famous and important. Look at General Scott. Or that New Hampshire Yankee they're mentioning for President—what's his name?"

"Pierce. General Franklin Pierce."

"Yes." Her smile was taunting. "Will you be that sort of soldier?"

It was all over. He knew it. "No," he said.

She wasn't prepared for such a positive, final answer. Her smile grew coy. She leaned to him, letting her bosom brush his arm as a reminder of what she could give a man.

"Bet you could be if you wanted."

"I don't have the ambition." He rose and slapped dirt off the seat of his pants. "Shall we go back? Looks like it might rain."

They returned to the great house in silence. Hers was bewildered and sullen, but his was invested with an unexpected new peace. She had offered herself and informed him of the price. She was too deep, and too dangerous, for him. He had stepped back from the brink and was relieved.

A rising wind stripped leaves from the water oaks near the house. The leaves whirled around the young people as they came upon Orry supervising half a dozen slaves who were nailing shutters closed.

"Cooper just sent one of his men on horseback from Charleston," Orry said. "Incoming ships are reporting gale winds a hundred miles offshore. I've got riders out warning the other plantations. We may be in for a hurricane."

Ashton picked up her skirt and dashed into the house. Orry watched her, then scratched his beard. "Looks like we've already got one closer to home."

Billy's smile was perfunctory. "Have you seen Charles?"

In the morning Ashton was all smiles again. She swept into the dining room and sat down next to Billy, who was finishing the last of several slabs of smoke-cured ham. She patted his hand.

"What shall we do today?"

He pushed his chair back. "Charles is taking me deer hunting with bows and arrows. I'll see you tonight."

After he walked out, a knot of pain formed in her stomach. She regretted what she'd said to him while they sat by the river. She had done it largely as a test, curious to discover what he was made of and how far she might bend him. Not that it really mattered; she was in love with Billy. He could remain a lieutenant all his life and she'd still love him. For him she'd gladly throw away her dreams, her ambition—everything.

But she had a feeling it no longer made any difference.

Squinting, Billy leaned forward over the neck of his horse. Visibility was cut to a few feet by the pouring rain. Trees creaked. Limbs snapped off and sailed away. Although it could hardly be later than mid-afternoon, the sky had turned an eerie dark gray.

"There's the house," Charles shouted from up ahead. Billy could see nothing but the tail of his friend's horse switching back and forth. Without Charles as a guide, he'd have been lost. He ached from riding in the buffeting wind. Charles yelled something else, but a deafening cracking obscured it. Billy looked up just as a huge live-oak limb sheared off and dropped toward him. He booted the horse forward. Small branches whipped his face, but the heaviest part of the limb missed horse and rider.

The horse pranced in panic. A hand reached out of the murk to stroke the animal and calm it. As the effects of the scare passed, Charles asked:

"You all right?"

Billy gulped and nodded.

Five more minutes and they were in the stable. The other horses fretted and kicked the sides of their stalls. Billy and Charles surrendered their mounts to the frightened grooms and laid their bows and quivers on a hay bale. They were two very wet, tired, and unlucky hunters. They had sighted only one buck all day. Charles had given Billy first chance at it. Billy's arrow flew wide, and the buck fled. Charles slashed the tail of Billy's shirt in half—the traditional sign of a novice who had missed his shot.

Billy was disgruntled by his failure but not exactly surprised. All day long he had been distracted by thoughts of Ashton. He saw her more realistically now, without the distortions his own emotions had created. She was still a beautiful girl, desirable in many ways, but she wasn't for him. He felt fortunate to have made the discovery before he became more deeply involved.

"Lucky the crop's harvested," Charles shouted as they ran for the house. "Sometimes the storm tide drives salt water this far up the river, and it poisons the fields."

"I thought the big storms arrived in August or September."

"Usually, but they can come later, too. The season lasts through November."

They reached the house. Gasping with relief, they ran inside and pulled up short at the sight of a tense family group in the downstairs hall. "Well, at least you two are safe," George said in a strained voice.

Billy pushed wet hair off his forehead. "What's wrong?"

Orry answered. "Your sister insisted on going riding late this morning. I sent one of my people with her. They haven't come back."

Billy was aware of Brett by the staircase. She watched him with anxious eyes as he said to Orry, "Shall we saddle up again and look for them?"

"I asked the same question," George said. "Orry discourages it."

"For good reason." Orry sounded testy, as if hurt by George's implied criticism. "Virgilia could be riding on any of a dozen trails and back roads. I wouldn't know where to begin to search. And with the storm this bad already, we could pass within ten yards of her and never see her. But I'll go if you want, George."

"No, not if it's foolhardy. I didn't mean to be sharp about it."

"Cuffey's a reliable boy," Orry told the others. "He'll find shelter for them. I'm sure they'll be all right."

Somewhere overhead, the wind ripped a shutter off the house, then blew through one of the rooms, toppling furniture and shattering glass. With exclamations of alarm, Clarissa rushed upstairs. Maude followed, then three of the house girls. Brett rushed to Charles. Ashton wasn't present, Billy realized belatedly.

"I'm thankful both of you are back," Brett said. She touched her cousin's arm but looked at Billy.

He blinked, noticing her—really noticing—for the first time. He was surprised and pleased by her display of concern.

Tillet suggested the hunters come with him and warm themselves with a cup of whiskey. Charles agreed enthusiastically. Billy trailed after him. As he passed Brett, his eyes lingered on hers a moment. She was young but pretty. Her face had a gentleness that Ashton's lacked. He found her extremely appealing.

Maybe he'd been paying attention to the wrong girl.

"Miss, we better turn for home," Cuffey said about an hour after their departure from Mont Royal.

"No, this is exciting," Virgilia said above the moan of the wind.

Cuffey made a face. But he was ahead of her, straddling an old mule, and she couldn't see his reaction.

Virgilia rode sidesaddle. She had asked the young Negro to show her scenic places near the river, and he was leading her to one such area now, following a woodland trail that was little more than a narrow, muddy rut. The heavy growth of trees held back most of the failing light, but rain reached the two riders—an indication of how fiercely the wind blew.

Virgilia was more than a little frightened. She had never experienced a hurricane before. At the same time, the ferocity of the oncoming storm excited her in a way that was completely unexpected. Under her riding habit, she began to feel tense and damp. Her steel stays hurt.

"Cuffey, you haven't answered the question I asked you sometime ago."

"I be worried about the storm, miss. I don't 'member the question."

Liar, she thought, more in pity than anger. Somewhere behind them, a tree uprooted with a great cracking and a thrashing of underbrush. When the tree fell, the ground shook.

"Can you wait here a minute, miss? I better go back an' see if the trail's still clear."

He kicked his mule with bare heels and rode past her, giving her a nervous glance. He was a handsome boy, just about the age of Cousin Charles. He was intelligent, too—but doing his best to hide it. He was frightened of the questions with which she had bombarded him the past half hour. The Mains had cowed him into denying and concealing the powers of his God-given mind. That was one more reason she hated the family and the whole accursed slavocracy.

To come to South Carolina and get a firsthand look at the system, she had been forced to feign friendliness and to suppress her convictions, emotions, and desires. She wasn't entirely successful. Today, when that damned high-handed Orry Main had tried to discourage her from taking this ride, she had politely defied him. She had done it on principle and also because she wanted to talk privately with a slave. On his own ground, so to speak. So far the conversation had been one-sided.

Cuffey came back, whacking his mule with a stick. He appeared apprehensive about returning to her company. No, she realized, something besides that was bothering him.

"Miss, that tree opened up a whole nest of copperheads when it fell. They swarmin' all over the trail. Big storm—it scares 'em. Makes 'em mean. Can't take a chance on goin' back that way. Got to ride the long way 'round. It be about an hour longer that way."

"I'm not worried. You're an excellent guide."

Smiling, she leaned over to pat his hand. He pulled away as if he had touched fire. Then he jogged the mule into motion. "Can't do nothin' but go ahead to the river road now," he mumbled.

"Since it will take a while to get home, you might as well answer my question. I want to know if you understand the meaning of the word *freedom*."

The sound of rain filled the silence. Seconds became half a minute. "Cuffey?" she prompted.

"Think so," he said without looking back.

"Do you have any comprehension of what your life would be like if you were free?"

"Compre-what, miss?"

"Do you have any idea of how it would feel to be free?"

"No, miss, I don' never think about that. I'm happy here."

"Look at me and say that."

He neither turned nor spoke.

"Cuffey, I could give you money if you wanted to run away."

Hearing that, he wheeled the mule while his eyes darted about wildly, trying to pierce the intensifying rain.

The poor creature feared that someone might be listening in the middle of the forest. Damn them for destroying his spirit. Damn every one of the Mains—every Southerner—and damn her brother George as well. He was turning into a regular doughface—a Yankee with sympathy for the South. She'd give anything to punish the lot of them.

Cuffey stared at her with big, pleading eyes. "Wouldn't ever run away, miss. Mist' Tillet and Mist' Orry treat me good. I'm a happy nigger."

How sadly desperate he sounded. She gave a curt little wave. "All right. Let's go on. It's raining hard."

The trail grew dark as it twisted through the deep woods. What had been merely a rain became a downpour that soaked her riding clothes. She saw two deer go bounding westward. The underbrush came alive with whisperings and slitherings as the animal population ran ahead of the advancing storm.

Virgilia's anger rose like the groaning wind. She had dissembled, given false promises, in order to persuade George to bring her south. Now she didn't know whether she could endure the rest of the trip without denouncing those who had crippled Cuffey's spirit and castrated his courage. She wanted to strike them, hurt them—

"What you doin' out here, nigger?"

Startled, Virgilia realized Cuffey had reached the edge of the forest. He was shouting at someone she couldn't see. Quickly she rode up beside him. As she did so, she caught sight of a fine carriage with its rear wheels mired to the hubs in a gumbo of mud.

The carriage driver was still perched on his high seat. Rain beating on his bare poll, he flaunted the handwritten card hanging around his neck on a piece of twine. "Don't yell at me, nigger. I got my travel pass."

Virgilia sat absolutely still. The driver's face was contorted, as if that would somehow keep the rain off. His grimace showed his teeth. Four upper ones were missing.

Less hostile, Cuffey said, "Didn't rec'nize you, Grady. What happened?"

"What the hell's it look like? Old Mrs. Huntoon, she wanted me to drive the carriage back to Charleston so Mr. Jim could use it. I told her the storm would muddy the roads too badly, but she wouldn't listen."

Virgilia heard resentment, even a suppressed fury, in that last statement. Grady's owners hadn't robbed him of his manhood.

Cuffey noticed the other slave staring at Virgilia with great interest. When Cuffey spoke, his voice held a note of warning. "This lady's a visitor at Mont Royal. We come up the trail yonder, but it's swarmin' with snakes. Got to take the long way home."

"Better not try it now," Grady advised. "Least, the lady better not. Storm's too fierce. Put her inside the carriage and I'll stand watch. You ride lickety-split to Mont Royal and tell them she's all right."

Cuffey gnawed his lip. "I think you should go."

"You know the way better'n I do. You go!"

Cuffey looked miserable. He was clearly afraid of being punished if something happened to the visitor. Grady was older and stronger, and Cuffey was intimidated. But he didn't yield until Virgilia spoke above the wail of wind and rush of rain.

"Yes, Cuffey, go. They'll be worried. I'll be safe with this man."

"All right," he said. "But you watch her good, Grady. I be back with some of the gen'emen quick as I can."

He rode out of sight. When the last muddy plop of the mule's hoofs died behind the storm noise, Grady climbed down from the driver's seat. His eyes never left Virgilia as he walked around to the carriage door.

"Don't know if you want to shelter in here, miss. Might be wet and muddy."

"Yes. Especially if the door won't close properly." With her face and her eyes, she tried to show him that he needn't be afraid.

He studied her a moment longer, then clamped both hands on the lower edge of the window in the upper part of the door. He gave the door a sharp pull. When he let go, the door fell into the mud, connected only by the leather hinge on the bottom. The two upper hinges had been ripped apart.

He pointed. "Sure won't close now. Water'll be over the sill soon."

"What"—she swallowed—"what if Cuffey remembers the door wasn't broken when he arrived?"

"He's too worried to remember. But if he does, he won't say anything. I'll make sure."

She was almost faint with excitement. "Where can we go?"

"About a half mile down the road there's an abandoned pounding mill. I should be standing guard when they show up, but I don't expect that will be for several hours." He gave her a last long look, then picked up the bridle of her horse and started walking along the road.

"My name's Grady."

"Yes. I know."

That made him glance back and smile.

Cobwebs and the smell of mold filled the old mill. But the roof was solid, and the place offered excellent protection from the weather.

Virgilia felt as nervous as a schoolgirl dancing her first quadrille. For her that was an unusual reaction. Grady caused it because he was so rough-looking, yet so kingly. She found him kingly despite his muddy hands and feet and ragged clothing.

With a cynical light in his eye, he asked, "Why do you want to do this?"

"Grady, Grady"—she ran her palm up along his thick, wet forearm—"don't look at me that way. I'm your friend."

"There isn't a white man or white woman who's the friend of a nigger. Not in South Carolina."

"Up North it's different."

"Do you come from there?"

"Yes. Northern people hate slavery. I hate it. I belong to organizations that help escaped slaves start new lives. As free men."

"I thought about going north once or twice. Wasn't sure the risk was worth it."

She seized his arm with both hands, her fingers kneading deep into his flesh. "Believe me, it is."

"You just want to help me, that's all?"

"No," she whispered. "You know that isn't all."

He grinned. "But I'm still asking why. Never been with a nigger before?"

"Don't flatter yourself."

That flare of temper produced a rumbling laugh in response. "Well, you're not the prettiest woman I ever laid eyes on—"

She bit her lip and accepted the insult offered with a smile. He was showing who had the upper hand.

"—but your eyes are just about the warmest." He rubbed his knuckles lightly up and down her cheek. Up and down. "Sure would like to see the rest of you."

A moment later, drowning in her own heat, Virgilia stepped out of her pantalets. Using both hands, she raised the front of her skirt and petticoats. Grady's smile faded.

"My, my. Guess I didn't speak too kindly a minute ago. You're pretty enough."

"No, I'm not. It doesn't matter."

"But I got to tell you the truth, Miss Virgilia. I've never been with any white woman before."

"Then come here," she said, giving her skirt a little flounce.

She lost track of time then, taking him into her again, and again, and again, while the hurricane blew.

A dawn, pink and still, followed the night of wind and rain. Almost as soon as it was light, Orry came riding to the abandoned mill together with George, Billy, and Cuffey. They found Grady on guard outside.

"We've been searching for hours," Orry barked. "Why didn't you stay with the carriage?"

Scrambling to his feet, Grady answered respectfully. "Sir, I surely meant to do that. Just like I tole this here nigger of yours. But the carriage door was broke an' mud an' water come in. It weren't a fit, dry place for a white lady to shelter. I 'membered this old mill, and we reached it 'fore the blow got too bad. I knowed you'd have some trouble findin' us, but I knowed you'd come along this here road an' see me, or I'd see you. I stayed awake out here the whole night long. The lady is fine inside. Hungry, I 'spect, but otherwise jes' fine."

Inwardly, he was chuckling. He always slurred his words when addressing any white man. It made them think they were dealing with another dumb, guileless darky. The deception worked perfectly; it usually did.

Virgilia appeared, pretending great relief. She complimented Grady on his politeness and loyalty throughout the long night. George looked relieved as she went back inside to collect her wet shoes and stockings— the only articles she had removed for sleeping, she said.

*

The worst destruction had occurred along the coast. As the hurricane roared up the Ashley, its force was already diminishing. When it whipped over Mont Royal, it uprooted trees to render roads impassable. But the plantation, and those nearby, sustained nothing more serious than roof damage and some staining of furniture when rain blew in through shattered windows. The tidal surge had not been strong enough to drive salt water this far upriver. All in all, the Mains could give thanks that they had again been spared the full wrath of one of the great storms.

On Wednesday of the last week of the Hazards' visit, Virgilia announced that she was taking the river sloop down to Charleston in order to do some shopping. She wanted one of the house girls to accompany her, if Mrs. Main would permit it. Clarissa naturally said yes.

Maude questioned her daughter about the trip. Couldn't she shop when they went to Charleston to catch the steamer? No, Virgilia replied with a smile, that would be impossible. Maude would see the reason when she returned.

Virgilia's behavior was puzzling, her mother thought. But then Virgilia's behavior had been unusual during the entire visit. She had behaved herself. Ah, but perhaps she was going to Charleston to buy gifts for the Mains. Maude planned to send hers after she returned to Lehigh Station. If her daughter felt a need to express appreciation sooner than that, Maude had no intention of hindering her. The change in Virgilia was too welcome to be interfered with.

Slipping away from her slave chaperone wasn't as easy as her desire had led her to suppose. Virgilia had to wait until the girl dozed off on her pallet, and that took longer than she had anticipated. Finally she crept from the hotel room and down the stairs.

A lone white woman hurrying along Meeting Street drew stares from some late-hour idlers, but they were people she would never see again. She had her newfound passion to help banish fears of discovery. In an alley near the Dock Street Theater she came upon Grady crouching in the darkness of a doorway. During their time at the mill they had worked out the day for the meeting, the hour, and the place. The instant she arrived, he snapped at her.

"You're late."

"I couldn't help it. Did you have trouble sneaking out of the house?"

"No, I never have trouble with that, but the curfew for niggers rang a half hour ago. The pass I'm carrying is six weeks old. Should have figured out a way we could meet in the daylight."

"If we met in the daylight, we couldn't do this." She put her arms around him and kissed him fiercely. "We might have been forced to wait months till I could arrange stops on the underground railroad. We decided it should be now. We decided it together, remember?"

"Yes," he admitted.

She kissed him again, then opened her reticule. "Here. This is all the money I have. This slip of paper has an address in Philadelphia. A safe house run by Friends. Quakers," she amended when she realized he didn't understand the other term.

He fingered the paper, sheepish. "I can't read this. Can't read anything."

"Oh, my God. I never thought of that."

"But I can always find the North Star on a clear night."

"Of course! Anytime you're lost, ask at a church for directions. Churches aren't universally safe for runaways, but I can't think of any better place—or one that's easier to recognize. Now about food. Can you cipher?"

He shook his head.

"Then if you buy food, you may be cheated since you don't know about money. Worse than that, it could arouse suspicion. Stealing may be a lot less risky. You must decide."

He heard the anxiety in her voice, patted her gently. "I'll get there, don't you worry. I've got good reason to get there now."

Another long, intense embrace. She pressed her cheek against his clean work shirt. "Many more reasons than one, Grady. Up North I'll teach you to read and figure. We'll buy you a fine new set of teeth. You'll be the handsomest man in creation."

She drew back, gazing at him in the weak light filtering from the end of the alley. "Oh, I do care for you so."

It surprised her to realize that. Why had it happened? Because of her desire to spite the Mains and their kind? Because she wanted to prove total dedication to the cause? It was both of those things, but it was more.

After an uneasy chuckle, he whispered, "Sometimes I get the feeling we'll both burn in hell for this."

How bleak he sounded beneath the laughter. She tried to jolly him out of it. "White man's hell, or black?"

"Oh, white. I hear that's a lot nicer. But in either place you end up the same way."

"We won't. We'll have a happy, useful life together."

And just let George or any of them try to stop us.

A shadow leaped up at the end of the alley. A bull's-eye lantern flashed.

"Who is that?"

A fierce whisper: "Run, Grady!" He fled into the dark.

She counted ten, her heart beating frantically as the shadow enlarged. She flung the handbag to the far side of the alley, then called, "Watchman? Down here. A boy snatched my reticule, and I chased him."

She had given Grady all her money; the story would work. The portly watchman reached her, puffing as he shone the lantern in her eyes.

"A nigger?"

"No, he was white. About fifteen, I'd say. With a small gold ring in the lobe of his left ear. I'll wager he's a cabin boy off one of the steamers. Please shine your light over there—I believe I see something."

A moment later she showed him the inside of the reticule.

"Every dollar gone. I was a fool to step out of the hotel for some air. I thought Charleston was safe for white women after the retreat drum cleared the slaves off the streets."

Her skillful performance completely fooled the watchman. There were no skeptical questions, and he personally escorted her back to the hotel.

Two days later, Grady's owner showed up at Mont Royal.

29

When the visitor was announced, Orry and the others were gathered around the dining-room table where Virgilia had piled the presents for the family. Thus far only Tillet had opened his gift—an expensive silk cravat.

Orry pushed his chair back. "Excuse me, I'll see what he wants."

"I can't imagine," Tillet said. "Do you suppose it has something to do with Grady's running off?"

"How could it?" Clarissa countered. Then she noticed her husband staring at Virgilia, who had taken the seat at the head of the table without invitation. Virgilia's lips were pursed in a curious way. A smug way, Clarissa called it in the privacy of her thoughts. George noticed, too, and frowned.

Orry strode to the foyer. "James—good morning."

He extended his hand to clasp Huntoon's, which as usual felt flabby. It was also unexpectedly damp. The weather was cool but the visitor was perspiring heavily; sweat streaked the lenses of his spectacles. As he wiped them on the lapel of his coat and jammed them back on his nose, Orry wondered how Ashton could tolerate such a slug.

"What brings you here?" Orry asked.

"Not a social matter, I assure you. Are you aware that one of my slaves has decamped?"

"Yes. Grady. The news reached us. I'm sorry about it."

"I find it more than somewhat coincidental that a nigger who has never before displayed the slightest sign of dissatisfaction suddenly elects to run away while you are entertaining visitors from the North."

Orry stiffened. "James, you're not suggesting—"

"I am suggesting nothing," the other broke in. "I am stating it outright."

Through the open doorway he had spied the Mains and their guests in the dining room. He had spoken loudly so that they would hear. In response, a chair scraped. Orry recognized the heavy thump of his father's boots.

Huntoon continued, "I'm convinced that someone encouraged Grady to run away. Further, I think the responsible party is staying in this house.''

Tillet's shadow fell across the pale wedge of sunshine cast by the fanlight. The others followed him out of the dining room. Huntoon glowered.

''Orry, it is widely apprehended that one of your Northern visitors is engaged in the work of encouraging rebellion among the nigras of the South. On the night of the storm Grady guarded, or purported to guard, this selfsame visitor.'' Huntoon strode past him. ''I put it to you directly, Miss Hazard. Did you help my slave escape?''

Orry seized Huntoon's arm. ''Just a minute, James. You can't come in here and speak to my guests like a prosecutor. I realize you've suffered a financial loss, but that's no excuse for—''

''Let her answer,'' Huntoon snapped.

The others were facing him in a rough semicircle. Ashton watched Virgilia with unconcealed hostility. Billy was equally upset, but with Huntoon. Tillet looked unhappy, Clarissa baffled, George dismayed. And George's sister—

A stone seemed to fall and strike the bottom of Orry's belly. Virgilia had her chin in the air and defiance on her face.

Orry collected his wits and said, ''No, James. Not until you favor us with a reason.''

Huntoon's pink cheeks indicated his rising temper. ''Reason for what?''

''For your suspicion. It's hard to believe that a surmise—a mere guess—brought you here, of all possible places, to look for a culprit.''

With the quickness of a cat pouncing, Huntoon said, ''Ah, but I'm not guessing. First, as previously stated, Miss Hazard spent an entire night in the company of my nigger—something to which no Southern white woman would admit, of course, but that's beside the point. I expect she filled Grady's head with disloyal thoughts—''

''Virgilia, do you realize what this man's saying?'' George broke in.

Her smile never wavered. ''Perfectly.''

''Tell him it isn't true, for God's sake.''

''Why should I? Why should I dignify his rantings?''

Orry's stomach ached all the more. She hadn't said she was guiltless. George realized that too. He looked ill.

''Now,'' Huntoon went on, self-consciously fingering his lapels, ''here is further evidence. On the night Grady fled from Charleston,

402

carrying an old pass I inadvertently neglected to destroy, I am reliably informed that Miss Hazard was in the city.'' That was true. Orry had forgotten.

Huntoon's voice grew louder. "Her only companion was a nigger girl from this plantation. A girl with the limited intelligence typical of her race, a girl easily deceived. I am further informed that this girl awoke sometime after nine on the night in question and that she discovered Miss Hazard absent from their hotel room. What do you suppose she was doing abroad at that hour of the night if not abetting the escape of my slave?''

Huntoon stormed forward. "Why don't you answer that, Miss Hazard?''

"Yes, do,'' Ashton said. "It's time you repaid our hospitality with the truth.''

Tillet reached for his daughter. "Step back here and keep out of this.'' But she had already slipped past his outstretched hand. She linked her arm with Huntoon's, clearly his partisan.

Orry stared at his sister, finally understanding how Huntoon had happened to come to Mont Royal. Ashton had summoned him, her suspicion fortified by a couple of scraps of information. He was shocked by that kind of behavior, but not surprised. Ashton's dislike of Virgilia had been evident for a long time.

Orry was experiencing some of the same dislike. Virgilia's expression remained smug, even arrogant. He cleared his throat. "It might be helpful if you'd respond to what James just said, Virgilia.''

"Respond? How?''

It was George who erupted. "By denying it.''

"Why should I do that?''

"Goddamn it, Virgilia, stop smiling.'' George paid no attention to his wife's sharp intake of breath. "Don't ruin everything. Deny it!''

"I will not.'' She stamped on the floor. "I refuse to be hectored and intimidated by this man when his own hands are unclean. How dare he prate about guilt when he keeps human beings as chattels?''

With a touch of desperation, Constance said, "No one wants to compromise your principles. But be reasonable. Don't repay the kindness of the Mains with hostility and bad manners.''

"I'm sorry, Constance, but I am following the dictates of my conscience.''

She's as crazy as Huntoon, Orry thought. The lawyer thrust his jowlly face close to Virgilia's.

403

"You did it, didn't you? That's why you won't deny it."

Her sweet smile returned. "You will never know, Mr. Huntoon."

"What else did you give my nigger? Your favors? Did you rut with him to demonstrate your egalitarian spirit? I'd expect that of an abolitionist whore."

Billy and his sister had never been close. But the last word, forbidden in polite conversation, was too much for him. With a yell, he lunged for Huntoon.

Ashton screamed and tried to push Billy away. He was too strong. But Huntoon jerked backward, so instead of catching him by the throat, Billy only managed to rip his glasses off. They clacked on the floor and glittered in the wedge of sunshine. George powdered both lenses when he jumped in to seize Billy's arm.

"Stop it. Get hold of yourself! Leave him alone!"

"He can't call Virgilia names," Billy panted.

George stepped in front of his brother and raised his left arm like a barrier. Tillet snatched Huntoon's ruined spectacles off the floor and held them out by one earpiece.

"Please leave, James," he said. "Now."

Huntoon waved the bent spectacles at Virgilia. "She conspired to rob me of my property. That young ruffian assaulted me. I demand satisfaction. My second will call."

"There'll be no dueling," Orry said. Cousin Charles, who had been standing silently at the back of the group, looked disappointed.

Billy pushed against his brother's arm. "Why not? I want to fight him. I'll kill the custard-faced son of a bitch."

Huntoon swallowed audibly. Ashton gave Billy a surprised, almost admiring look, then whirled and began urging her suitor toward the door. He blustered and fumed, but in a few moments he was inside his carriage. The wide-eyed driver whipped up the team.

Dust clouded through the open front door, the motes distinct in the sunbeams from the fanlight. Orry didn't let embarrassment stand in the way of what had to be said to the Hazards:

"When Huntoon's accusations get out, they'll arouse strong feelings in the neighborhood. It might be wise if you left for Charleston today."

"We'll be ready in an hour," George said.

He shoved Billy toward the stairs. Virgilia glided after her brothers, still maintaining that queenly arrogance. What disturbed Orry most was his friend's reaction to the warning. George seemed angered by it, angry at him. Orry shook his head, swore under his breath, and went outside for some air.

*

Calmer, George went searching for his friend forty-five minutes later. He found Orry occupying a wicker chair at one end of the downstairs piazza. The family carriage stood in the drive. House men were lashing trunks and valises to the brass guardrails on top.

Orry sat with one boot resting on a second chair and his right hand shielding his eyes. Somehow the pose suggested defeat. George twisted the brim of his hat in his hands.

"Before we left Pennsylvania, Virgilia promised that she would do nothing to antagonize you and your family. Obviously she broke that promise. Perhaps she intended to from the beginning. The point is, I don't know what to do about it. I spoke to her just now, and she isn't the least contrite. Seems rather proud of the whole business, in fact. I consider that unforgivable."

"So do I."

The blunt statement produced a shamefaced look from George. Orry rose abruptly, the air of defeat vanishing. "See here. I know you had nothing to do with it. Grady will no doubt be caught before he gets very far. I'm sorry it happened, but it's over, and there's nothing more to be done."

"Except keep my sister out of South Carolina in the future."

"Yes, that would be a good idea."

Still uncomfortable, George and Orry stared at each other. Gradually, then, the past and the friendship it had created overcame mutual awkwardness.

George spoke for both when he said: "These are angry times. The anger deepens every day. We keep bumping into hard questions that seemingly have no answers. But I don't want those questions to drive a wedge between our families."

Orry sighed. "Nor do I. And I really don't hold you responsible for your sister's behavior." Yet a small, festering part of him did.

"Will you bring your family to Newport next summer? I'll arrange to send Virgilia somewhere else."

Orry hesitated before replying. "All things being equal—yes, I'll try."

"Good!"

The friends embraced. George clapped his hat onto his head. "We'd better go before Huntoon rides up the lane with a posse carrying lynch ropes."

"We don't do that sort of thing down here!"

"Orry, calm down. I was only joking."

405

Orry reddened. "I'm sorry. Guess I'm a little too sensitive. That seems to be the nature of the Southern temperament these days."

Maude and Constance emerged from the house, followed by the nurse with the children. "All ready?" George asked his wife.

"Not quite," she said. "We can't find Billy."

At that moment Billy was walking rapidly along the breezeway connecting the great house with the kitchen building. One of the housemaids had told him Brett was helping with the day's baking.

"Billy?" For an instant he thought the voice was the one he wanted to hear. Then he realized the speaker was Ashton. She came rushing from a corner of the great house. "I've been searching for you everywhere."

She dropped the hooped skirt she had lifted in order to run. She scrutinized him. "All dressed for traveling. My, how handsome you look."

"I'm sorry we have to leave under these circumstances." He stumbled over the words, monumentally uncomfortable in her presence. "I know Virgilia betrayed your trust, but I still couldn't let your friend call her names."

He expected Ashton to challenge that, but she didn't. Instead, she surprised him by nodding. "I lost my temper, too. I shouldn't have— I really can't explain why I did. I don't care a snap for old James Huntoon."

Relaxing slightly, Billy managed a smile. "Then you're a good actress." But of course he'd figured that out long ago. "I wish your brother and George had let me meet Huntoon. I'm a pretty fair pistol shot."

"Oh, James is too yellow to go through with a duel. He's all brag and bluster—just like most of those politicians he runs with. You're different—"

She fingered his wrist below the velvet trim of his cuff. "Brave. I admire bravery in a gentleman. Bravery and strength—"

The tip of her index finger slid back and forth through the fine hairs on his wrist. She wanted him, and with her eyes, the tilt of her chin, the caressing movement of her finger, she tried to tell him so. Tried to draw him back to her. Tried and failed.

"I appreciate the sentiment, Ashton. But I must go now. There's something I must do in the kitchen."

"Oh, are you hungry?" she asked with a brittle smile. "They say growing boys are always hungry." She emphasized *boys*.

The insult made him redden. "Please excuse me." He turned and hurried off along the breezeway. He was through with her. If she had harbored the slightest doubt before, the quick good-bye had done away with it. Her eyes filled with tears she struggled to hold back and could not.

Billy felt something of a fool, dashing away from one sister in pursuit of another. But he was determined to find Brett. How would she react? Angrily? Or with scorn? He believed it would be one or the other. Yet he rushed straight ahead, into the heat and clamor of the kitchen, which was crowded with black servants and awash with the odors of biscuits baking and thick slabs of red ham frying on the immense claw-footed stove. Kettles of soup stock simmered on the hearth. Occasional puffs of wind down the chimney sent acrid wood smoke billowing across the room. Through one such cloud he saw Brett kneading dough.

"Yes, sir, what can I do for you?" asked a buxom cook with a cocked eye; she clearly resented a stranger's entering her domain.

"I'd like to speak with Miss Main."

Brett glanced up, saw him, and grew flustered. She used her apron to scrub at the flour on her cheeks. As she hurried around the big plank chopping table, the cooks and helpers exchanged cautious glances of amusement.

"I wanted a chance to say good-bye to you," Billy told her.

She lifted strands of loose hair from her forehead and smoothed them back. "I thought you'd be saying good-bye to Ashton."

"She's Mr. Huntoon's friend." The smoke made him cough. Brett took his hand impulsively.

"Let's go outdoors. It's hot as Hades in here." Her use of the word Hades suggested she was either bold or nervous. Billy guessed the latter.

Outside, the fall breeze was cooling. The redness slowly left Brett's face. "I must be a sight. I didn't expect anyone to come looking for me."

"I had to see you before I left. Virgilia ruined this visit, but I don't want that to spoil the friendship of our families. Not when we're just getting to know each other."

"Are we? That is—"

She wanted to die on the spot. Mortified by what she perceived as a total lack of feminine grace, she could barely speak two words coherently. How ugly she must look to him, all daubed with flour and flecked with yeast dough. But what she had told him was true; she was completely unprepared for this encounter. She had dreamed of his noticing her—but not, dear God, when she was sweating in the kitchen.

"I hope we are—will—" Billy too got lost in his own embarrassment. He gave up and just laughed, and that broke the tension for both of them.

"No one blames you for what your sister did," Brett said.

He studied her eyes. How pretty they were. How free of guile. She wasn't as flamboyantly attractive as Ashton, and she never would be. Yet she did possess beauty, he thought; beauty of a simpler, more substantial sort, compounded in part of the shy gentleness of her gaze and the kindness of her smile. It was a beauty that time could never erode, as it could her sister's. It ran like a rich, pure vein, all the way to the center of Brett's being.

Or so his romantic eye told him.

"It's kind of you to say that, Brett. Virgilia made an awful mess. But all the rest of us want your family to come back to Newport next summer. What I wondered—"

The rear door of the great house opened. Out poked the bonneted head of the nurse.

"Master Billy? We've been searching for you. We're ready to go."

"Coming."

The door closed. He abandoned caution. "If Orry does come to Newport, will you be with him?"

"I hope so."

"Meantime—though I'm not much with words—could I send you a short letter now and then?"

"I wish you would."

The smile on her face kindled joy in his soul. Dare he kiss her? Instead of yielding to impulse and giving her a regular kiss, he bent from the waist, seized her hand, and pressed his lips to it, like some lovelorn nobleman. Then he ran like the devil—chiefly to hide his beet-colored face. Brett clasped her hands at her bosom and gazed after him, her face shining with happiness. After a long moment she turned toward the house.

The angle of the sunlight at that moment created glittering reflections in every window. It was impossible to see whether anyone was watching. Ashton didn't know that, however. Fearing discovery by her sister, she quickly stepped back from the upper window from which she had observed the entire, sickening encounter between her sister and Billy Hazard.

Brett was soon gone from her line of vision, but Ashton continued to stand motionless with her gaze fixed on the window. Pale sunlight fell through the lace curtain, casting a pattern like a spider's web onto her face. Only the compressed line of her mouth and the slitted look of her eyes revealed her fury.

"Papa, what did the man with the whiskers want?"

Little William Hazard asked the question while leaning against his father's legs. Patricia sat on George's lap, her arms around his neck and her cheek pressed drowsily to his. Both youngsters wore flannel nightgowns.

Belvedere smelled sweet with the greens of the Christmas season. The scent here in the parlor was augmented by the tang of apple wood burning in the fireplace and by the not unpleasant scent of soap on the children.

"He wanted me to be a soldier again," George answered.

William grew excited. "Are you going to be a soldier?"

"No. Once is enough. Off to bed, both of you."

He kissed each child soundly and patted their bottoms to speed them along. Constance was waiting for them in the hall. She blew George a kiss, then raised her index fingers to her forehead and bleated like a billy goat. The children squealed and ran. They loved the nightly game of pursuit. Sometimes Constance was an elephant, sometimes a lion, sometimes a frog. Her invention delighted them. George wasn't surprised. She thoroughly pleased and delighted him, too.

This evening, despite his time with the children, George felt out of sorts. The visitor had come representing the adjutant general of the Pennsylvania militia. He had begun by saying the militia needed qualified officers in order to expand and prepare for the war that was a certainty within the next few years.

"What war?" George wanted to know.

"The war to silence the treasonous utterances being heard in the South. The war to guarantee personal liberty throughout the nation's new territories." Thus the caller revealed himself an advocate of free soil. He went on to explain that if George joined the state militia, he was virtually certain of being elected to a captaincy. "My contacts in Lehigh Station tell me you're a popular man. I'm sure that would overcome the handicap of a West Point background."

He said it so condescendingly that George nearly threw him out into the snow. Memories of the Mexican War were fading. The public was reverting to its old suspicion of the military—and its dislike of the institution that trained professional officers.

The visitor was stubborn. George had to decline to join the militia three times. The third time, growing annoyed, he said he would hate to see slavery ended by any means except a peaceful one.

George had disliked the discipline of soldiering and hoped he never again would have to put up with it. His dislike was even stronger for the visitor and his sneering intimation that George somehow lacked patriotism because he didn't care to kill other Americans. At that point George became rude. The man left in a huff.

The visit brought back the nagging questions George had thought about so often. How could the South's peculiar institution be dismantled if force were rejected as a means? He didn't know. No one knew. In most discussions that might lead to an answer, passion usually supplanted reason. The quarrel was too deep-rooted, too old. It was as old as the Missouri Compromise line of 1820. As old as the first boatload of black men brought to the continent.

He remembered the letter he had been meaning to write for several days. Perhaps he hadn't written it because he disliked withholding some of the truth. Yet he knew that was necessary. He passed the gaily decorated Christmas tree, nine feet high. The sight failed to cheer him. He sat with pen in hand for about ten minutes before he put down the first lines.

My dear Orry—
Perhaps it will help ease the memories of last autumn if I report that my sister has moved away, at my request. Virgilia's behavior in her various abolitionist groups became too outrageous to be borne.

He told no more than that. He said nothing about Grady's having reached Philadelphia safely; nothing about Virgilia's going everywhere with the escaped slave. She had ordered new artificial teeth for him, teeth to replace those removed by his former masters. The matter of the teeth had provoked her final quarrel with George.

She had asked him for a loan to pay for the new teeth. He had agreed—provided she accept one condition: she must stop flaunting herself on Grady's arm. The fight that followed was brief, loud, and bitter. It ended with his ordering her to leave Lehigh Station. For once Stanley endorsed his brother's decision.

Virgilia and her lover were now living in Philadelphia. In squalor, George presumed. A few landlords with decent quarters to rent might be willing to give them to a man and woman who weren't married, but that would never be the case if the woman was white and the man was black.

Grady had thus far been secretive about his past; as far as most people knew, he was Pennsylvania-born. But his background couldn't be kept completely quiet for long, especially when Virgilia was pulled by conflicting desires to protect her lover and to use him to forward her cause. So there had been one or two requests for public speeches, which Grady had declined. Speeches were reported in newspapers, and Northern newspapers might be read by Southern slave catchers in the employ of James Huntoon.

The runaway had, however, addressed a private meeting of Philadelphia abolitionists, one of whom was a business acquaintance of George's. Appalled, the man reported to George that Grady had called for the overthrow of slavery by "rebellion, arson, terror, or any other effective means." George suspected Virgilia had written most or all of the speech. God knew what insane plots against established order she and Grady were hatching.

Sometimes George wished he didn't care about his sister. But family loyalty never quite deserted him—nor did the memory of something his mother had once said: "Love will somehow defeat hate. It will, and if we're all to survive, it must."

That was why he said nothing about Grady in the letter. The news might reach Huntoon and cause him to send a slave catcher to Philadelphia.

What a hypocrite you are, George thought. He didn't give a damn about Virgilia's relationship with the former slave, yet he was protecting it, protecting a Negro fugitive right along with his own sister. Some compulsion drove him to it. At the same time, his behavior left him with a bad feeling, a feeling of betraying his friend.

God, how he hated this turmoil. Like the nation, he was slowly being torn apart.

411

30

That winter Brett acquired another beau, though not entirely by her own choice.

Some sportive strain in Francis LaMotte's family had produced a son much taller than his father and much better-looking than either parent. Forbes LaMotte had grown into a strapping six-footer with fair hair, a swaggering walk, and a disposition that inclined to indolence except when there were drinks to be downed, horses to be raced, or pretty girls to be pursued. Francis had hoped to see his son graduate from The Citadel, the state's own version of West Point that had been established in 1842. But after one term at the Charleston military school, Forbes had been dismissed for academic deficiency.

Weary of low-class sluts too easily bedded, and not interested in Ashton Main, who secretly frightened him, Forbes took notice of Brett. In 1852 Brett would reach her fourteenth birthday. She was continuing to mature rapidly, filling out and gaining the poise that frequently accompanied young womanhood. With that poise went an awareness of her own powers of attraction.

Forbes rode to Mont Royal to ask permission to call on her. Normally he would have made the request of Tillet, but the health of the patriarch of the Main family had lately begun to suffer. He had trouble breathing and was bedridden much of the time. Orry had taken over virtually all family responsibilities.

Neighborhood gossip had revealed to Forbes that Brett received an occasional letter from that Pennsylvania boy who had visited the plantation last fall. Forbes didn't consider Billy Hazard a threat. He was far away, and in the long run his temperament would never blend with that of a girl bred in the South. If Billy ever did turn into a serious rival, Forbes, who was bigger, would just bash him and scare him off.

Orry found Forbes less objectionable than some of the LaMottes but still didn't like him very much. Nevertheless, he said yes to Forbes's request. Permission to call was a far cry from permission to marry. Besides, he didn't expect his sister to pay a great deal of attention to the courtship gifts Forbes immediately began to send or to be cordial when Forbes visited in person.

Brett surprised her brother. She had her reasons.

Even if she hadn't known Billy, she would never have considered Forbes a serious suitor. Like most of the other LaMottes, he thought his own opinions were holy writ, and he angered easily when someone disagreed with any of them. When sober and in a good mood, however, he could be charming.

Brett couldn't judge the seriousness of Billy's intentions. There was always a long interval between his brief, awkwardly phrased letters, and she recognized the possibility that he might all at once take up with some Northern girl. By seeing Forbes now and then she hoped to cushion herself against possible disappointment; she liked Billy more than she cared to admit.

Forbes was five years older than Brett and three years younger than that pale toad Huntoon. There was no resemblance between the two suitors—Ashton's beau was a dog on a leash, but Forbes was his own man, which Brett rather enjoyed.

Fending off Forbes was a constant challenge. "Stop that" was what she said most often. Never harshly, but always firmly. She had said it again just now as he leaned over her shoulder while she played the pianoforte. Instead of turning the page of her sheet music, he reached down and gently grasped her breast.

"I said stop that, Forbes," she repeated when he didn't let go. She took her fan from the music rack and slapped his thumb. "Why do you insist on treating me like one of those Charleston trollops you fool with?"

He grinned. "Because you're ten times as pretty as any of them, and I want you ten times as bad."

"*Want* is a word for husbands and only for husbands," she said with a smile.

"My. Pretty racy talk for a girl of your tender years."

But he relished it. Apparently she did too, for she teased him right back:

"If you're so concerned about my tender years, why is your hand always groping every which way like I'm some old hen?"

"Can't help myself," he said, sidling to the end of the pianoforte, where he could rest on his elbow and gaze down at her. His unexpectedly serious expression made her squirm. "You know I'm crazy about you, Brett. You and I are going to be married one of these days."

414

"Don't count on it," she replied, jumping up. "Why, you won't even bring me the presents I ask for."

"Now listen, blast it—I don't know anybody who sells the *National Era* in Charleston. And if somebody did, I wouldn't be caught dead buying an abolitionist rag."

"But Forbes—all the papers and periodicals are discussing Mrs. Stowe's serial. I want to read part of it." Even Orry had expressed interest in the new novel.

"Read," Forbes parroted with a contemptuous wave. "Girls aren't supposed to read. Oh, I guess *Godey's* is safe enough, and some of Mr. Timrod's verse is harmless. But if God had wanted women educated, he'd have let them go to places like Harvard. They can't get in, so I guess that tells you."

"That's an idiotic statement. Idiotic and backward."

"The devil it is. Uncle Justin suffers something fierce because Aunt Maddie reads so much. You should see some of the trash she orders from New York. Sends him into a perfect rage."

"Your whole family's good at raging when you don't like something. Good night, Forbes," she said with finality, and swept out of the room.

Thunderstruck, he gaped at the empty doorway. "Brett? Wait, damn it. I didn't mean—"

No use. Her footsteps were already fading on the stairs.

He whacked his right fist into his left palm, then glanced up to see Ashton in the hall with Huntoon. The couple had been in the library for the last hour, occupied with a book of pencil mazes.

Ashton's beau had few chances to score a point against someone as physical as Forbes. This opportunity was too good to resist.

"Cussing, friend? Tsk, tsk. That's no way to court a young lady. Most especially, it's no way to court her family. What you should do—" Huntoon gulped and swallowed the rest of his advice as Forbes stormed toward him:

"You make any more comments, I'll punch that pig bladder you call your face." He grabbed Huntoon's shirt ruffle. "There'll be blood all over your nice clothes. I 'spect the sight of it would make you faint."

He jerked, tearing the ruffle. Then he picked up his hat, stick, and gloves and stomped out into the mild February night. "Nigger, fetch my horse!"

The bellow made Ashton shiver with disgust. "He's nothing but an animal."

"Absolutely," Huntoon agreed, fingering the torn ruffle. "I don't know how your sister tolerates him."

Ashton glanced at Huntoon's glistening cheeks and suppressed a shudder of loathing. Smiling sweetly, she took his arm.

"She has no ambition. She chases one worthless boy after another."

Including the one I still want.

Forbes and Brett soon patched up their quarrel. It was largely Brett's doing. She decided that nothing Forbes said should be taken seriously.

Huntoon visited Mont Royal at least twice a week that winter. Somehow, the attention never made Ashton happy. Someone else was on her mind. One afternoon she raced her sister to the wicker basket that held the day's mail. She beat her and snatched up a wax-sealed letter. "Why, here's another one from Billy! That's two this month. He's getting ever so much better."

Brett reached for the letter. It was impossible to miss the jealousy in her sister's eyes. "Ashton, that's mine."

The older girl laughed and raised the letter over her head. "What'll you give me for it?"

"If you keep teasing me, I'll give you a black eye."

"My. We're sounding more and more like Mr. LaMotte all the time." She flung the letter on the floor. "Does Billy know about him?"

Brett's voice trembled. "You go to the devil."

The older girl was stunned. Ashton had never heard her sister use any word that even approached profanity. Perhaps she'd gone too far. She couldn't help it. She was miserable, and Huntoon's visits only exacerbated the feeling. He always tried to draw her into some secluded corner and paw her. On those occasions when she chose to resist, he responded with a hurt whine:

"Why do you treat me this way, Ashton?"

"Because we aren't married yet. Just because you and Orry agreed on a dowry and I said I'd become your wife in due time, that doesn't give you any right to take liberties."

Her whimsical behavior was a continuing source of puzzlement to him. Frequently, she seemed to enjoy his advances, although she never permitted them to go too far. On other occasions she rejected them with an almost prudish fervor—which was mightily confusing when he thought of the old rumors linking her with a male member of the Smith family.

"Sometimes it gives me the right," he complained.

"Well, not just now. I don't feel like arguing about it, either."

Huntoon's face mottled. "Is that the way you intend to act after we're married?"

"You'll just have to wait and see."

Then she realized she had angered him. In her eagerness to keep him aware of who had the upper hand in the relationship, she had gone too far. She gave him a hasty kiss. "Calm down, James. You know I want to marry you. And after I do, you're going to have a most distinguished career."

"According to plans which you have already mapped out."

Now he went too far. White and rigid, she drew away. "My dear, you sound peevish. If you've changed your mind about the things we discussed—"

There she stopped. It was precisely the right strategy. He seized her hand, panicking.

"No, no. I haven't changed my mind about anything. I want you to have a role in mapping our future. I'm not like those bullheaded LaMottes. I believe a man's wife should be his partner. Especially if the man intends to enter public life."

"I'm happy you plan on doing that, James. You already have important friends. You'll make many more. The LaMottes will spend their lives rattling dice and racing horses, and they'll die forgotten. But not Mr. and Mrs. James Huntoon of South Carolina!"

He laughed, though somewhat nervously. "Ashton, you're just wonderful. I'll wager that if I wanted to do so—if I weren't the architect of my own destiny—I could place myself entirely in your hands, let you make every decision, and my success would still be assured."

Still? Did the fatuous creature believe he could rise in spectacular fashion by himself? He might achieve some minor fame, but without her he would never be truly eminent. He would learn that soon enough.

"You're right, my dear." She gave him a warm smile. Then she kissed him, opening her mouth after their lips touched.

He had come too near the truth for comfort. She'd marry him, but it would be a marriage conducted entirely on her terms. The poor fool suspected that and had already surrendered himself. But if he dwelled on the surrender too much, it could sour things.

Thank heaven she knew how to divert him. While they kissed, she laid her palm against the inside of his trouser leg, then began to move it in a small, languorous circle.

*

417

Spring approached. One March evening, Orry retired to the library with a letter from Billy which he read three times. Even after the third reading, he was not certain of his reaction.

He sat staring into space, the letter dangling from his hand. Shadows lengthened. The stand with his uniform and sword stood in the corner farthest from his chair, barely visible. Just before dark he heard a horse in the lane. Moments later Charles bounded in, his fawn breeches and fine linen shirt sweat-stained. He was grinning.

"Where have you been?" Orry asked, though he could guess.

"Riding Minx on the river road."

"Racing her, you mean. Did you win?"

Charles flopped in a deep chair and kicked a leg over the arm. "Yes, sir. I beat Forbes, and Clinch Smith, too. Minx left both their animals half a mile behind. I won twenty dollars."

He displayed a couple of gold pieces. Clinking them in his hand, he leaped up. "I'm starved. You ought to light a lamp. This room's dark as a cave."

The advice was probably useless, Charles thought. When Orry fell into one of his moods, he sometimes sat for hours in the pitch-black library. The house men usually discovered him in his chair at sunrise, snoring. There were always an empty glass and a whiskey jug somewhere close by.

Orry had never completely recovered from his war injury; Charles and everyone else at Mont Royal understood that. But perhaps memories of Mexico and its aftermath weren't to blame tonight. Perhaps there was another reason for Orry's melancholy state. It dangled in his long, thin fingers.

Charles pointed to the letter. "Is that bad news of some sort?"

"I don't think so. It's from Billy." Orry extended his hand, an invitation for Charles to take the sheet of paper.

Puzzled by Orry's words, Charles lit a lamp and read the brief, stilted letter from his friend. Before traveling to the Military Academy in June, Billy wanted to return to Mont Royal and, in accordance with custom, formally request permission to pay court to Brett.

"This is wonderful," Charles exclaimed at the end. He sobered abruptly. "Would there be any problem about Billy coming here — with the Huntoons, I mean?"

"No. I've long since paid them thirteen hundred and fifty dollars for Grady, just to forestall trouble."

Charles let out a low whistle and sank back into his chair. "I had no idea."

A shrug. "I felt somewhat responsible for their loss, and I wanted George to be able to pay other visits to Mont Royal without a fuss. No one knows about the payment except the Huntoons and my father. Keep it to yourself."

"Of course."

"The replacement cost of a prime buck goes up every year," Orry continued. "Francis LaMotte predicts it'll be two thousand dollars by the end of the decade. Last week the *Mercury* printed an editorial saying the African slave trade should be legalized again. I've seen several articles demanding the same thing—well, never mind. We were speaking of Billy."

Charles waved the letter. "Does Brett know about this?"

"Not yet."

"You'll tell Billy he may come, won't you? And you will give him permission to court her?"

"I'm not sure of the answer to either question. Billy's a fine young man, but he plans to be an Army officer."

"So do I. I'll be going to West Point a year from this summer, remember? Good Lord, Orry—you arranged it. You encouraged me!"

"I know, I know," Orry said quickly. "And I'm glad you're going. On the other hand, since we had our first discussions about the Academy, the situation in the country has changed. For the worse. In the event of trouble, I presume your first loyalty would be to your home state. Billy, however, is a Yankee."

Softly: "Do you believe there's trouble coming?"

"Sometimes, yes. I just don't know what kind. Or how far it might go."

"But why should it make any difference? The Hazards and the Mains are good friends in spite of what Virgilia did. In spite of everything. If you didn't believe that—want that—you wouldn't have paid off the Huntoons."

"I suppose you're right. At the same time, I wouldn't want to send Brett down a road that would lead to unhappiness."

Charles's manner grew frosty then. "I should think it was her choice."

"It's mine, too. Now that my father can barely manage to get out of bed, I'm the head of this family."

They argued for another ten minutes, with Charles citing all the reasons Orry had to grant Billy's request. In truth, they were Orry's reasons as well. He was playing the devil's advocate tonight. He thought he must.

On the other hand, perhaps he was being unduly pessimistic. Although there were indeed many reasons for anticipating sectional strife, there were others that argued for a different outcome. Southerners still played a vital role in the life of the nation. General Scott, a Virginian, remained the commanding general, and Orry had read recently that Robert Lee, already a good possibility to succeed Scott, would very likely be the next West Point superintendent. In the Army's officer corps, most of the outstanding men hailed from the South.

Cooper claimed he saw signs of a new interest in industrialization throughout the region. True enough, slave-grown cotton was still king; annual production was measured in the billions of pounds. But owners of Southern railways were busily expanding and improving their lines. *Mont Royal* had more offers of cargo than she could handle. Cooper had returned from Britain with new enthusiasm for the future of Southern commerce in general, and his packet line in particular. Perhaps the new ways would gradually replace the old, and men of good will would push the Rhetts and Huntoons aside, and resolve differences—

Somehow, though, Orry remained unpersuaded.

"Orry?"

He looked up from his reverie. "What?"

"You will say yes to both questions, won't you? You'll let Billy visit, and give him permission to court her?"

"I'll give Brett this letter and think about it. That's the best I can do for the time being."

Disappointed, Charles stalked out.

"He forbade me to read the novel," Madeline exclaimed. "He snatched it out of my hands and ordered it burned—as if I were a child!"

She walked toward the edge of the marsh. Orry remained seated on the tabby foundation, tapping the book he had brought to the rendezvous. The book contained a strange new kind of verse by a Northern newspaperman named Whitman. Cooper was lavish in his praise of the rambling poems, claiming they captured the rhythm of the machine age. Orry found them hard going, although the rhythm was certainly there. To him it was the hammer of a drum.

"I'll ask George to ship me a copy," Orry said. "Though why you want to read rabble-rousing trash is beyond me."

She whirled to him. "Don't start talking like Justin, for heaven's sake. Mrs. Stowe's novel is the success of the hour."

She was right about that. George had written that his entire family had read the sentimental story of slaves and slaveholders, first in serial form and again in its regular two-volume edition, just recently published. Despite all the attention the novel was receiving, however, Orry was frankly not interested in *Life Among the Lowly*, as Mrs. Stowe's book was subtitled. He witnessed life among the lowly every day and needed no enumeration of its severities. They nagged on his conscience a good deal of late.

So in reply to Madeline's remark, he growled, "It isn't the success of the hour in this part of the country. A more appropriate term would be scandal."

She could easily have taken offense. She didn't because she knew he'd been fretting over the content of Billy Hazard's letter, which he had discussed with her at great length. She put her arm around his waist and kissed him just above the tangle of his beard.

"All you South Carolina men are such hotspurs. I keep forgetting—to my everlasting regret."

"What does that mean?"

"It means that when Justin discovered my copy of *Uncle Tom's Cabin* last week, the consequences were extremely unpleasant."

"He flew into a rage—"

"He was nearly incoherent for half an hour. But that's not the worst. The discovery took place a little while before supper. Francis happened to be dining with us that night. The book prompted Justin and his brother to spend most of the meal shouting about the need for a free and independent South."

"I'm sorry you have to put up with that sort of thing."

She studied her hands. "I didn't. I said it was fine sentiment for a stump speech but as a practical idea it was ridiculous. I knew speaking out was a mistake, but with those two I just can't hold my tongue sometimes. Justin, however, is determined that I will come to understand my place—which does not include expressing an opinion about any subject more weighty than the latest—" A catch in her throat interrupted the sentence. The memory was placing her under an extraordinary strain, he realized. In a faint voice, she finished: "The latest decorative stitch."

He laid the Whitman aside and clasped her hand. "When you spoke up, how did Justin take it?"

"Very badly. He locked me in my room for a day and a night. He had Nancy take away all my books and deliver my meals. Nancy was the only person I saw during the entire time. I even had to pass the chamber pot out to her—"

Madeline bowed her head and covered her eyes. "My God, it was humiliating."

"That bastard. I ought to kill him."

Quickly she rubbed the tears from her cheeks. "I don't mean to cause trouble by telling you. It's just that there's no one else."

"I'd be more angry if you didn't tell me." He went striding through the weeds, scattering clinging raindrops that had fallen earlier in the day. "I'd like to kidnap you out of that damned place. Resolute isn't a home; it's a prison."

"That's true. It's becoming harder and harder to tolerate Justin or my position. Once I had fine notions about honor and the sanctity of the marriage vow." Her mouth wrenched, a ghastly attempt at a smile. "Justin's turned every one of them into a joke."

"Leave him. I'll go to him for you. I'll tell him—"

"No, Orry. It's too late. Too many people at Resolute depend on me now. I can't do a great deal to make things better, but I know they would be infinitely worse if I were gone. The only reason I'm able to bear the whole dismal business is you." She hurried to him, her skirts rustling in the wet weeds. "Just you."

She held his waist and looked at him, a film of tears in her eyes. Then, out of a desperate need for affection and simple comfort, she hugged him ferociously. Kissed him again, again.

He buried his face in her hair, savoring its black sweetness. As always, his body betrayed him. She felt him wanting her and hugged him harder to show she wanted him too. The tension created by their self-denial was always excruciating. Today it approached the unbearable.

She unlaced her bodice. Pushed her undergarments down. Pulled his mouth tight against her while she threw her head back. She closed her eyes and reveled in the feel of him kissing her breasts.

They had never gone this far. They only refrained from the final act by desperate strength of will.

"Orry, we mustn't." Her voice was hoarse.

"No."

But he didn't know how much longer he could stand the strain of loving her, wanting her, and denying that want.

*

A couple of days later, after supper, Orry and Charles went to the piazza to sip whiskey. Haze hid the sinking sun, lending its light a pale rose cast. Orry sat watching pink reflections down on the river while Charles leafed through a *Mercury*. Lately he was spending a few minutes with the paper every day, another sign he was maturing, and in Orry's estimation a good one.

Ever since the meeting with Madeline, Orry had felt a renewed physical frustration. He was ready for another overnight visit with a homely but ardent widow with whom he had an understanding. He still hadn't decided how he would answer Billy. Nor could he decide now.

Charles closed the paper. "Have you read this yet?"

Orry shook his head.

"Huntoon gave another speech."

"Where this time?"

"Atlanta. What is popular sov—? Here, you pronounce it for me."

Orry leaned over to see the word Charles was indicating with his thumb. "Sovereignty. Senator Douglas coined the term. It means that once a new territory is organized, the people living there have the right to decide whether to allow or prohibit slavery."

"Huntoon says that's unacceptable, just like the free-soil doctrine. I don't know what that is, either."

"The free-soil doctrine states that Congress has a moral duty to prohibit slavery in new territories. The will of the people doesn't matter. I can imagine the speech James made." Orry spread his fingers and pressed the tips against his shirt, like an orator. He spoke pompously. "I stand with the great Calhoun. Slavery must follow the flag. It is the sacred responsibility of Congress to protect all property taken into a territory—"

At that point he stopped his mimicry. "Property means slaves. That's the only territorial doctrine most of our neighbors find acceptable."

"How do you feel?"

Orry pondered a moment. "I believe I side with Douglas. So does George, I think."

"Well, I've been trying to learn about some of these things. I reckon I'd better—I'll be meeting people from all over the country when I go to West Point."

"The question of the territories may come to a boil sooner than that. Some say as soon as we elect a new President this fall. The country out West is filling up fast. Loyalties are going to be severely tested. Family loyalties and others," he finished with a pointed look at Charles.

The younger man stretched his legs and studied the river, where only a few wavery touches of pink remained. "You keep worrying about that. It's the reason you haven't written Billy, isn't it?"

Orry frowned. "How do you know I haven't?"

"If you had, Brett wouldn't act so glum all the time. I reckon it isn't respectful of me to go into this, but I get the idea you mean to turn Billy down strictly for one reason: he's a Yankee. That's just like—" He swallowed. He had reached the hard part. "Just like Huntoon. Or Virgilia Hazard. They sweep every person on the other side into the same bin."

Orry was indeed irked by Charles's presuming to judge him, but the reaction lasted no more than a few seconds. Reason prevailed. Reason and strong emotion—for if Billy courted his sister, that might strengthen the bonds between the two families. Virgilia had come close to destroying those bonds.

A smile showed in the thicket of Orry's beard. "You're turning into a shrewd young man, Charles. I'm glad to see that." A deep breath. "I'll compose a letter to Billy tonight. A letter he'll be happy to receive. You might want to hunt up Brett and tell her."

Charles whooped, pumped Orry's hand, and ran into the house.

Orry did write the letter that night. He told Billy he'd be welcome at Mont Royal and invited him to bring all the Hazards with him. Except Virgilia, he thought, knowing he didn't need to put that down. He promised that if the family came, he'd arrange a party or ball to compensate for the unhappy ending of the previous visit.

He felt good about the letter. It was a small step but a positive one. If Northern and Southern friends didn't keep peace among themselves, how could the men they sent to Washington be expected to do it?

31

The Hazards accepted Orry's invitation. They arrived on Wednesday of the third week in May. Maude was not with them. She had sprained an ankle working in her garden and couldn't travel.

A ball was to be held at Mont Royal on Saturday. Invitations had gone to the entire neighborhood. "Although given the origins of your visitors, Justin would prefer to stay home," Madeline had told Orry at their meeting the preceding week.

He kissed the curve of her throat. "Let him. You come, though."

"Wouldn't that be a heavenly arrangement? I'm afraid we won't be so lucky. Justin will be present. He's afraid of unfavorable comment if he refuses an invitation from the Mains. But don't count on him being pleasant."

On the first night of the visit, the men and women gathered separately after supper. Over whiskey and cigars, George said, "Coming through Virginia and North Carolina on the train, I heard only two topics discussed: Mrs. Stowe's novel"—Tillet made a hacking noise to show his contempt—"and secession."

"The idea is blowing through this state like a storm wind," Orry said. "It happens every few years."

"But it seems more intense now," Cousin Charles put in.

Cooper swirled his whiskey in his glass. He and his wife and little Judah had arrived about five o'clock. "A storm wind indeed. It'll be our house, none other, that blows down. Some Southerners understand. Alexander Stephens, for one. But most of the fools are entranced by the sound of their own rhetoric. They don't realize that the Union can't be broken up as casually as you draw a breath of air. Too much is at stake, economically and emotionally, for the Federal government to allow it. In Charleston I hear people speaking of peaceful secession. I just laugh. It's a contradiction in terms."

"You are certainly the expert on the whole matter," Tillet said with thick sarcasm. Cooper chose to study the contents of his glass. His father went on, "Separation by peaceful means would be the ideal, but if it's impossible—as you claim—the alternative is separation won by force of arms. Some verities endure, Cooper. Death is preferable to tyranny.''

Unblinking, Cooper again looked at his father and said in a mild voice, ''Yes, sir. That's what the nigras are telling you every time they run away.''

Tillet rose. ''Excuse me. I thought this was a social occasion.'' He left the room with a slow, halting step and slammed the door behind him.

George looked sheepish. ''I'm sorry. I provoked that.''

Billy protested. So did Orry: ''Are we now at the point where we can't even disagree as reasonable men?''

Cooper laughed in a humorless way. ''In this household we reached that point years ago. I keep deluding myself with the hope that things may change. They never do.''

He held out his glass to Orry, who saw the pain lurking behind his brother's wry smile.

''Pour me another, please,'' Cooper said. ''Fill it up.''

Constance clapped her hands. ''Judith, that's splendid news.''

The others echoed the sentiment, except for Ashton, who sat eyeing the ceiling in a bored way. The ladies had gathered in the music room with sherry; Brett had been permitted only strong tea. As one of the house girls cleared away the empty glasses, Clarissa asked, ''When do you expect your confinement, my dear?''

''As best we can calculate, in about six and a half months,'' Judith said. ''The doctor's already banned extensive travel. Cooper sides with him. Your son's really very conservative in some ways,'' she added with a smile. ''He'll be going to Britain by himself this summer, I regret to say.''

''To Britain again?'' Brett exclaimed. ''The two of you just got back.''

''Very nearly,'' Judith agreed. ''But as you know, Cooper's quite taken with the ideas of Mr. Brunel, the famous engineer. They got along splendidly the first time, and Brunel has invited him to return for an extended visit. Cooper has this wonderful dream of building—''

They heard someone grumbling and cursing outside. Clarissa hurried to the door and looked out. Tillet's angry voice gradually faded away upstairs.

"Oh, my," she said as she took her seat again. "It's my husband. I'll wager there was another political discussion."

"Politics spoil everything these days," Judith said with a sigh.

Clarissa's mouth grew firm. "I do not intend for it to spoil your visit. And most particularly I don't intend for it to spoil the ball. It's going to be a happy occasion which all of us can remember as such. The men won't see to it; therefore we must."

The others agreed. Ashton was forced to join in to maintain appearances. But a ball in honor of Billy Hazard and his family, and, by extension, in honor of Brett—that kind of celebration filled her with rage. Out of the rage sprang a desire to strike back at all those who had done her injury.

"Oh, oh. Push it in."

"Ashton, I"—he was gasping as hard as she was—"don't want to hurt you."

"Damn you, Forbes, push it in. All the way. Oh. Yes."

The last word slurred into a groan. Faintly, above the roaring in her ears, Ashton heard carriages arriving and the orchestra tuning. Forbes and his family had been among the first guests. Lying in wait for him, Ashton had immediately whisked him to this dark and remote corner of the stable.

She had been wild with the urge to take a man. And not simply any man but the one Brett was intending to discard. Nor was that the only reason she had been ready to pounce the minute Forbes showed up. It had reached her ears that he was a magnificent male specimen. He didn't disappoint her in that regard. She felt as if she had a cannon inside her.

They stood facing each other, she with her back against the side of an empty stall. How she had gotten her skirts hoisted and everything else out of the way she couldn't remember. The frantic rhythm of the coupling repeatedly slammed her against the stall. Her left leg felt as if it would collapse at any moment. Her right one was crooked over Forbes's hip, her heel against his backside.

They reached a climax in which she had to bite her lower lip to muffle her own cries. She scratched the nape of his neck with both hands, drawing blood. Some moments later he displayed a redspeckled handkerchief. "How the devil am I going to explain this?"

His trousers still hung at his ankles, but Ashton was already busy putting her various garments back in place. "You'll think of something.

dear. Could it be the skeeters? They're bad tonight. Two of them bit me a while ago."

"Sure, that's it, bad skeeter bites." He dabbed his neck again, then chuckled, half admiringly, half in awe. "I tell you, Ashton, you're something."

"You mean you're not sorry you came out here?"

"Not on your life. That was—well, I've got to be straight about it. Nearly the best ever."

She pouted. "Is that all? Nearly?"

He laughed. "You're a damn conceited wench, too." He fondled her bosom affectionately. "All right. The best."

"Thank you, Forbes. But keep your hands off my dress, please. You'll get me all mussed again."

Busily, she straightened petticoats and patted lace gone limp in the heat. She could have made the same statement he did. Never had she felt so aroused beforehand or so satisfied afterward. He was rough, he had hurt her, but she had relished every moment.

She didn't dare tell him, though. It would swell his head. Better to keep him dangling. She hummed.

Finally he blurted: "Will you let me see you again? Like this, I mean?"

"Not tonight. I must be sweet for all those Yankees."

"Of course not tonight. I meant from now on till you marry Jim Huntoon."

She glided to him, her hoops swaying to and fro. "Forbes, you must understand something. My relationship with Mr. James Huntoon is what you might call business. This is pleasure. As long as people are discreet, there's no reason pleasure can't go on and on, indefinitely."

"You mean even after you and Huntoon—?"

"Why not? 'Less, of course, you get to drinking like you do sometimes and blab and embarrass me. Let me hear of that happening just once, and you'll never see me again."

"I swear I'll never open my mouth. You can ask anything of me, Ashton—I'll do it. Oh, my God—aren't you something?"

She let him kiss her once more before they left the stable by separate routes. She was pleased with her accomplishments thus far this evening. Forbes had helped relieve some of the awful strain that had been building up within her lately. Just as important, he had put himself completely in her hands. She felt as if she had become the owner of a new slave.

A little smile sat on her rouged lips as she hurried up the lawn toward the great house aglow with lights. She had a hunch Mr. Forbes LaMotte was going to be a very valuable ally.

Candles in branched holders shone in every window that night; Chinese lanterns bedecked the lawns. The house couldn't contain all the guests who had arrived by carriage and horseback. They spilled outdoors, spread among the trees, strolled into the shadows in couples or small groups.

The entire downstairs had been cleared of all furniture except chairs. The dining room was reserved for dancing, the music provided by Von Grabow's Orchestra from Charleston. Orry had chartered *Eutaw* to bring all fourteen musicians and their instruments to the plantation. At midnight, given favorable breezes, the river sloop would take guests on a cruise, with supper served aboard.

On the piazza facing the river, trestle tables had been erected for the food and drink. Slave boys with whisks kept the insects off the platters of ham, lamb and beef barbecue, broiled chicken, oysters, shrimp, ocean crabs. Two hundred pounds of ham had been purchased for the affair and similar quantities of everything else. French champagne flowed as well as imported French and German wines—there were forty cases of each.

The guests had attired themselves to match the elegance of the occasion. The air was fragrant with the scents of powdered shoulders and perfumed décolletage. Macassar oil dressed the hair of many of the gentlemen, glistening brightly beneath the paper lanterns. Before an hour had passed, Orry could close his eyes, listen to the party, and know it was a huge success. The laughter and conversation were loud enough to be heard in Columbia, he fancied.

It was a warm evening. His coat, waistcoat, and cravat were making him uncomfortable. And the temperature seemed to be rising—or perhaps that was the effect of the champagne. He carried a glass as he circulated; when it was empty some black hand was always close by to fill it, whether he would or no.

Orry's discomfort was minor compared with his pleasure. To him the party represented everything that was fine and gracious about his home state. The dazzling lights, the food and wine and music, all generated an aura of good feeling. It was a magic occasion. He saw that demonstrated again and again.

Tillet and George told stories and laughed uproariously together—

as if the argument about secession had never taken place. Orry saw them refill their glasses and stroll away arm in arm.

Constance came staggering off the dance-floor, red-faced, out of breath, and giggling. One of the Smith boys had invited her to polka and overcame her initial hesitancy with an outpouring of charm. Many ladies and gentlemen named Smith had come to the ball, though none were close relatives of Mr. Whitney Smith, who was absent.

Constance had danced fast and hard, earning a compliment from her partner and an embrace from Clarissa, who said, "You dance just like a Southern girl. Sure you wouldn't like to move down here?"

"It's such a splendid party—so many nice people—I might be persuaded, Clarissa."

Orry drifted back outside. He leaned against a white pillar, sipping champagne and smiling at everyone. He felt slightly bleary but wonderful. Not everyone shared his euphoria. Cooper was still rankling over his father's behavior last night. It showed in the owlish look on his face as he stood drinking by himself.

Orry wandered up to him and amiably punched his shoulder, slopping some champagne on Cooper's sleeve in the process.

"Come on, enjoy yourself for once. You have to admit it's a damn fine party."

"Fine," Cooper agreed, without much sincerity. "It would be splendid if people always felt this charitable toward Yankees."

Orry blinked. "Well, if you like the party, why don't you smile?"

"Unfortunately, I keep thinking of what it costs to make it all possible. Not everyone here is having a fine time, you'll notice."

With a slow, stately motion of his glass, he led Orry's eye to a man struggling along the piazza with sweat drenching his face and two heavy cases of wine balanced on his shoulders. The man was a house slave, sixty-eight years old.

Furious, Orry turned and left.

From that moment, Orry's mood soured. Everything he saw and heard contributed to a mounting displeasure tinged with melancholy.

One of the Bull boys pulled down a rope holding half a dozen paper lanterns, one of which caught fire and almost ignited Aunt Betsy Bull's hoop skirt. She scolded her young relative, urging him to locate a horse trough and soak his head till he sobered up. His smile faded, as if the scolding had sunk in.

But it wasn't a contrite heart that altered his expression. It was too much liquor in an upset stomach. Standing right in front of Aunt

Betsy, the boy vomited. Several spectators fled in dismay; one turned pale, swayed, almost swooned. Things were beginning to go wrong with a vengeance, Orry concluded.

A little while later, in the crowded house, he encountered Justin LaMotte. Justin had one gleaming boot planted on the cane seat of a chair that otherwise would have provided a resting place for someone. Every other chair was occupied.

"—frankly don't care who the parties nominate," Justin was saying. "Yancey was right. Traditional party loyalty has become a foul, feculent disease. Vote the Whig ticket and you're voting for a party which is an invalid, if not a corpse. Vote for the Democrats and you're siding with a political organization that no longer represents the interests of this region. I for one lean toward the American party. No immigrants. No popery. I'm sure they'll soon add 'no abolition' to that platform."

Orry stared at Justin's boot, his meaning unmistakable. Justin gave his host a faintly defiant look and kept his foot on the chair as he pontificated. Orry walked away in disgust.

Ten minutes later he was leaning against the dining-room wall, watching George waltz with Madeline. George had earlier announced his intention of doing that. He appeared to be enjoying it.

Orry spilled champagne on his shirt when he raised his glass. He realized he was drunk. He didn't care. It was a quarter after eleven, and the party was roaring along under its own power. If he fell down unconscious, it would make no difference.

He had no intention of falling down, however. Not while he could stand and behold Madeline. How beautiful she was, turning gracefully beneath the chandelier with his best friend. Her bosom was white as milk against the emerald silk of her gown. The color suited her dark hair and eyes.

George waltzed expertly and with dash. Not surprising, Orry thought, taking another drink; George had the proper number of limbs for it.

How he wished he were a whole man. Able to ask Madeline to dance with him to the beautiful music. Able to stop hiding the love that filled him so full of thoughts of her and longing for her that he hurt. His lips compressed to a slit. His dark eyes, reflecting the myriad lights, reflected his anger, too. He held out his glass without looking. A black hand holding a bottle was there to fill it, just as he expected.

"She's a charming partner," George said when he brought Madeline to Orry at the conclusion of the dance. "Utterly charming. But I see

431

Constance hunting for me. You'll excuse me, Orry? Your servant, Mrs. LaMotte.''

And away he went, leaving Madeline flushed and nervous at Orry's side.

"I see why you like him," she said. "He's kind and intelligent and amusing." She opened her lace fan and began to cool herself with it. "It's a glorious evening. What a pity it rushes by so fast.''

He let his gaze sink deep into her eyes; drunk, he didn't care whether anyone noticed.

"Everything's rushing too fast, Madeline. The months. The time we have left—''

She snapped her fan shut so quickly one of the ribs broke. She closed her eyes and silently spoke one urgent word.

Don't.

Then, startling him, she stepped backward, animated as a child's marionette. "Yes, time does pass swiftly, doesn't it? We all grow old before we know it." Why the hell was she speaking so loudly? "Do you know what Francis's boy Forbes calls me now? Aunt Maddie." She laughed, but he could tell she wanted to cry.

"There you are, my dear.''

They turned at the sound of the voice; it belonged to Justin. "Someone told me you were dancing with a Yankee," he continued as he came up behind Orry. "I trust none of it rubbed off.''

Justin's expression was an unpleasant blend of boredom and smirking humor, and his remark had been a deliberate insult directed against Orry's guest. Though Orry was angry, he could do nothing. Justin's smile made the remark a joke, and any man who took it as something more would be considered boorish.

Justin crooked his left arm to form a V. "Shall we sample some of our host's fine food, my dear?''

"You go ahead, Justin. I've already had ample—''

"I insist." He seized her right hand and forced her to take hold of his arm. Humiliation brought a rush of color to her cheeks. As Justin led her away, Madeline managed to give Orry a quick, covert glance of longing. He felt the same longing, nearly unbearable. *This can't go on without some kind of change. Without some break in the stalemate.*

It might not happen at once or even soon, but a rush of intuition told him that it was inevitable. It *would* happen. Would the outcome favor them or destroy them?

The emotional pressure suddenly became too great. He wheeled around, stepped forward, and crushed his champagne glass into the wall. Dozens of tiny tinkling pieces struck the floor.

His frustration diminished a little. Why the devil had he done that? Drunkenness? Fortunately no one appeared to have been watching. He raised his hand. A small cut leaked blood down over his knuckles to his wrist.

Waltzing, Billy and Brett whirled past Orry. They didn't notice him or his cut hand or his bleak expression. Under the flashing pendants of the chandelier, surrounded by the wavering flames of lamps and candles, they were lost in emotion and each other. Billy wished the surging music would go on and on, and the night too.

"The camellias arrived just before I came downstairs," Brett said. He let out a relieved sigh. This was the first time she had mentioned the courtship gift. "There were so many of them," she added. "The arrangement must have cost a fortune."

"I guess the Hazards can afford it."

Instantly, he felt foolish. The remark was pompous. Lord, how she muddled him with the sparkle of her eyes, the tilt of her head, the wry but not unkind set of her lips. George had once told him that many West Point cadets claimed to be "anti-romance" because romance addled your mind, and that in turn interfered with academic work. Billy could understand that attitude, but it was far too late for him to develop it within himself. Besides, he didn't want to.

"In any case," she said, "the flowers are truly lovely—and so is the thought that sent them."

"Thank you. Some girls might not be kind enough to say so."

"I can't believe that."

"It's true. That's why you're different. You don't flirt or keep someone guessing. You speak your mind. It's one of the things I love"—he swallowed the word, turning red—"like about you."

"At one time I had the impression you didn't like it at all."

He grinned. "We'd better not start a discussion of my past mistakes. There are so many, we'll have no time to discuss anything else."

"Oh, you don't make many mistakes. Not serious ones, anyway."

"Indeed I do." At the edge of his vision, Ashton's pale face blurred by. She was standing with Huntoon but watching him. "Occasionally, though, I do something right. Such as asking Orry for permission to call on you. I only wish I could do it more often than once a year."

"But I'm glad you asked, and I'm glad he said yes." She squeezed his hand. "I'll write you a lot of letters. And perhaps Orry will bring me to West Point for a visit. It's still a popular resort, isn't it?"

"So I'm told. Guess you won't be too lonesome here, though. That LaMotte fellow will be paying court to you—"

"Not anymore. Forbes is handsome, but he acts—well—too old. He won't be calling again," she finished emphatically.

"Does he know?"

"Yes, I told him a few minutes ago. I thought I should, since you sent the camellias and—" Her face grew as pink as his had been a few moments earlier. "Billy, don't look at me so hard. I just turn to water inside. I'm a ninny to be so forward and say this, but I can't help myself—" She pressed her cheek to his for an instant, whispering, "I've cared for you such a very long time. I thought you'd never notice me."

He drew back and gazed into her eyes again. This time he had no difficulty choosing his words or saying them.

"I'll never notice anyone else. Ever."

A half-empty glass dangling from one hand, Forbes LaMotte watched Billy and Brett dancing. The sight of their lovesick faces disgusted and infuriated him. He didn't notice Ashton slipping up to his side. When she linked her arm with his, he started.

"Forbes, my sweet, you look mad as an old bear."

"That's how I feel." He studied the crowd behind her. "Where's Huntoon?"

"I sent him away for a while. I wanted to speak with you"

"Fine. I'm sick of watching those two."

He turned his back on the dance floor and led her through the press. She was deliciously skillful at smiling and nodding to others in a gay, simple-minded way, all the while carrying on a whispered conversation:

"What's wrong? I thought you were enjoying yourself."

"I was. Then your dear sister informed me that she'd prefer it if I didn't call on her again."

"Did she, now? And how do you feel about that?"

"I'm damn insulted."

"Can't say I blame you."

"Don't get me wrong, Ashton. Brett doesn't have the only—I mean to say, she isn't the only female in creation."

Smiling, she gave his arm a squeeze. "I know what you meant to say, you wicked boy. You found another one tonight, didn't you?"

434

He gave her a quick, salacious grin. "Certainly did. Still, a man has to think about choosing a wife, too. I figured Brett would be a fine one. I don't take kindly to being dismissed."

"How do you suppose I feel about being dropped flat by Mr. Hazard?"

"Same way I do, I reckon. Is that what you wanted to talk about?"

"Exactly. Here's the punch bowl. Get me a cup, if you please."

He jumped to it. He emptied his own glass and refilled it before they strolled outside. He consumed the champagne in gulps, then stepped to the edge of the piazza and flung the glass into a clump of azaleas. Sometimes Ashton found him revolting. But he would suit her purposes, physical and otherwise.

They left the piazza and moved down the lawn. "Frankly, Forbes, I'm not surprised by what you told me. I had some inkling that Brett would speak to you this evening."

"How so?"

"She mentioned it while we were dressing. She was chattering like a magpie. All excited about seeing Billy—"

"Christ," he growled. "I surely can't understand why Orry would permit a Yankee to court his sister."

"Oh, he's infatuated with that whole clan."

"If Brett wants a soldier, what the hell's wrong with a fellow from The Citadel? And how in hell can Hazard court her from some Army post a thousand miles away?"

"Forbes, don't keep cursing. You'll attract attention. It will serve our purpose much better if people don't notice us together—now, or in the future."

"Our purpose," Forbes repeated. "What's that?"

"Why, getting even with Billy and Brett."

He halted, faced her, then threw his head back and laughed.

"God, you are priceless. A genuine, brass-bound bitch."

She struck his chin with her fan. The blow was light, yet it stung him—as she intended. Although she was still smiling, her eyes were venomous.

"I take that as a compliment. But if you curse again or raise your voice, you will never get so much as one more peek at what you crave."

"All right, all right—I'm sorry."

"That's better."

They resumed their walk in the direction of the river. Festooned

435

with lanterns, *Eutaw* had just put out to midstream for the supper cruise. Two fiddlers on board sent gay music over the black water.

"Now," Ashton said in a cheerful tone, "let's continue our chat. I am correct in assuming that you'd like a taste of revenge?"

"You're godda—that is—yes. I would." He shivered. She was a scary creature.

"Splendid. I want to be certain. We shall be secret allies. I'll probably marry James one of these days, but a wife and an ally are two different things. And in my alliance with you, there's an extra dash of spice—"

Using her closed fan, she lightly caressed the back of his hand. "Or there can be if you behave yourself."

Another shudder ran down his back. "I understand. But you're not drunk, are you?"

She wrenched away. "What the devil do you mean by that?"

"You're talking about doing something to hurt your own sister."

"That's right." Her smile returned. "I hate her."

He turned pale. "Jesus." He couldn't help the utterance. "All right—I had to get it straight."

He felt he should run away from her. Then he thought of what had transpired in the stable. He again offered his arm. "Mind telling me how we're going to"—he swallowed—"to do what we're talking about?"

"I can't because I don't know yet. We'll have to shape our plan to the circumstances, but we'll know the right moment when it comes along. We mustn't rush into anything. We must smile and wait, and then one day when Billy Hazard and my sister least expect it, we'll repay them."

Despite his misgivings, Forbes smiled. It was a slightly bleary smile, which she nevertheless found charming.

"Indeed we will," he said. He pointed up the lawn to the glitter of the great house. "May I have a dance to seal that bargain?"

"You may, Mr. LaMotte. Lead on."

32

On the first of June, 1852, Billy stepped onto the North Dock at West Point. A hot gray haze lay on the river and the mountains. He strained for a glimpse of the Academy, but it was hidden by the steep bluff rising behind the dock. How had his brother felt on the day he arrived? As nervous as this? As excited?

Billy was determined to do well during the next four years. He wanted to go into the engineers, and that meant earning top marks. With application and a touch of luck, he knew he could get them. He had already started to prepare. He had been boning hard throughout the trip and before. What filled most of the space in his big carpetbag were books—secondhand copies of *Bourdon's Algebra, Legendre's Geometry and Trigonometry, Descriptive Geometry*—all adapted and expanded from original sources by Professor Davies of the Military Academy.

"Sir, don't stand there and gape. You are the only newcomer on the steamer? Very well, sir. Put your valise in that cart, sir."

The voice and the brogue belonged to a wrinkled and rather ferocious-looking little man in a soiled Army uniform. He swaggered away with one hand on the hilt of his cutlass. The man was far from the ideal picture of a soldier, yet he impressed Billy and gave him a sense of the tradition of this place. Billy felt proud to be standing where his brother had stood ten years ago. The Academy had acquired a bad reputation during Jackson's time, but George said that was fading, and West Point was taking its place among the world's leading military schools: Woolwich and Sandhurst in Britain, St. Cyr and L'Ecole Polytechnique in Paris. Old Thayer had used the French polytechnic school as his model when reshaping the West Point curriculum.

"Sir, I shall not ask you again to step lively. I am Sergeant Owens, provost of the post, and I remind you that you are now on a military reservation. Comport yourself accordingly!"

"Yes, sir," Billy said, and hurried after him.

Captain Elkanah Bent sat picking at his lower lip with the nail of his index finger. Sweat dripped from his chin onto the open file before him. Although every window in the old-fashioned brick house was wide open, the obese officer was roasting.

The house was one of two that stood at the west edge of President's Park. In another eight months a new man would be moving into the residence at the center of the wooded park. The Democrats had nominated Franklin Pierce of New Hampshire, on the forty-ninth ballot. When Pierce had been appointed a general in the Mexican War, he had promptly been dismissed as one more politician who craved military rank. But he had proved to be a surprisingly able commander, and many professional officers favored his election.

The Whigs, on the other hand, had chosen the Commanding General himself. Old Fuss and Feathers had wanted the nomination in 1848 but had been forced to wait another four years. This time he had gotten it on the fifty-third ballot, after President Fillmore had been denied the nomination by his own party—if it was possible to call the Whigs a viable party any longer. That was the obstacle facing General Scott. He was about to charge into the political lists on a dying horse.

Ah, well. However it came out, the country would have a President with military experience. Perhaps that kind of man would understand that the government's chief mission was to prepare for war against the traitors gaining control in the South.

Bent had been at the War Department slightly less than four weeks. He already hated the capital, as he had known he would when he accepted the transfer. Washington was a permanently unfinished city, Southern in style and viewpoint, and plagued by flies and open sewers and many other undesirable features. He loathed all the free Negroes who flaunted themselves in public, as if they were the equals of white men. He loathed the civilian bureaucrats—pismires who ran to and fro in a futile attempt to prove they had some purpose.

Despite all the drawbacks of the town, transfer to Washington was a good step and one long overdue. Staff duty was important professional experience. For the past thirty-four months Bent had been stuck in a line post at Carlisle Barracks. This new assignment might be a turning point in a career in which advancement had been far too slow, even for peacetime. He knew whom to blame for that.

The adjutant general's office handled all personnel records for the Army. Soon after arriving, Bent had reviewed the list of next year's confirmed appointments to the Military Academy. On the list he discovered the name of Charles Main of South Carolina. Some in-

438

vestigation disclosed that this Charles Main was the nephew of a certain former officer of Bent's acquaintance.

Then, just today, an official pouch had brought the revised final list of June entrants, already in camp, as well as a list of the Seps, who wouldn't arrive until the start of the fall term. A name leaped out from the June roster. William Hazard II, Lehigh Station, Pennsylvania.

It could only be someone from the same family.

Bent could barely contain his delight. He had lost track of Orry Main and George Hazard. The pressures of his own career had contributed to that. Also, both had left the Army and placed themselves beyond his reach, so to speak.

But he had never abandoned a desire to revenge himself on Main and Hazard. Thanks to them and the doubts they had planted about him, he hadn't advanced as far or as fast as he should have. For that and other reasons, he had an abiding hatred of both men. Now, through members of their families, he just might have another chance at them.

A small, fuzzy caterpillar appeared at the far edge of Bent's desk and worked its way toward the file he had just closed. Out of habit, Bent began to think of his old adversaries by their Academy nicknames. Had Stick and Stump forgotten the promise he made to them? If they had, so much the better. Secrecy and surprise were valuable for all campaigns, military or personal.

"Captain Bent?" The voice of the adjutant general sounded from the inner office. "Please come in here a moment."

"Right away, sir."

Elkanah Bent heaved himself out of his chair. He took a step, halted, reached to the center of his desk, and pressed his thumb down on the caterpillar. When the creature was dead and brushed away, Bent lumbered to answer the summons.

BOOK THREE

"THE CORDS
THAT BIND
ARE BREAKING
ONE BY ONE"

*If they break up, in God's name let
the Union go . . . I love the
Union as I love my wife. But if my
wife should ask and insist upon a
separation, she should have it,
though it broke my heart.*

JOHN QUINCY ADAMS,
On Burr's rumored secession conspiracy
1801

33

George Hazard claimed to have no special feeling for West Point. Yet he had talked about the place often and at length with his younger brother, so by the time Billy arrived at the Military Academy he knew a good deal about it.

George had warned him about "Thayer's men and Thayer's system." The heart of the system was the belief that personal accomplishment could be measured in absolute terms and expressed by a numerical ranking. The system, and the men who implemented it, still ruled West Point.

But there had been changes in the six years since George's graduation. The most visible ones were architectural. The old North and South Barracks had been razed, and a new cadet barracks with 176 rooms had been built at the staggering cost of $186,000. Corniced with red sandstone, the building reminded Billy of pictures of English castles. Its large hall above the central sally port provided the cadet debating society with a permanent home, and in the basement an Army pensioner had opened a refreshment shop that sold cookies, candy, and pickles. A central hot-water system heated the barracks. There were none of those grates of which George spoke so fondly. No grates meant no cooking after hours. A disappointment; Billy had been looking forward to his first hash.

East of the barracks and directly south of the Chapel, a new stone mess hall was under construction. The Observatory and Library were still there, however. The classroom building, too.

To provide practical demonstrations and perhaps a little inspiration, a company of engineers had been stationed on the post since the end of the Mexican War. They could be identified by their dark blue single-breasted tailcoats with black velvet collars and cuffs, and by the official insignia of their branch, the turreted castle. Billy hoped to wear the same insignia one day.

He knew he would have to study hard during the next four years. But he found his preparation for the June entrance tests to have been wasted effort. To pass the math section, he needed only to solve one easy blackboard problem and orally answer three equally simple questions. No wonder some civilians called the entrance requirements ludicrous.

Cadets now were summoned by the bugle instead of the drum. But the mess hall served the same old food, and he hadn't been in his assigned room ten minutes before a third classman swaggered in, identified himself as Cadet Caleb Slocum, and demanded that he assume the position of the soldier.

He did so as best he could. The third classman, an emaciated fellow with straight black hair and bad skin, criticized him, then said in a drawling voice:

"Tell me something about yourself, sir. Is your father a Democrat?"

Billy answered pleasantly. "I think that will depend on the person the party nominates this month."

"Sir, I asked you a question requiring a simple yes or no response. You have instead chosen to deliver a lecture on politics." The third classman lowered his voice from a shout to a purr. "May I infer from your answer that your father is a politician, sir?"

Billy gulped and fought his anger. "No. Sir. He's an ironmaster."

"Sir," roared the other, "I asked you straightforwardly whether your father was or was not a politician, and in reply you regale me with a discourse on manufacturing. Stand in that corner, facing it, for fifteen minutes. I shall be back to check on you. Meantime, ponder this. Continue to be garrulous and headstrong, and your career at this institution will be short and unpleasant. Now, sir. Into the corner!"

Red-faced, Billy obeyed. If he had been like his brother, he would have punched the arrogant cadet and worried about the consequences later. But he was a more deliberate sort, and for that reason George said he would probably make an outstanding engineer. Moreover, his trusting nature made him an easy victim. He stood for nearly an hour before a second classman looked in, took pity on him, and ordered him to stand at ease, because Slocum had no intention of coming back.

Slocum. Billy rubbed his aching leg and noted the name.

"Better get used to that kind of deviling, sir," said the second classman. "You're going to be a plebe for a good long time."

"Yes sir," Billy muttered as the other left. Some things at West Point didn't change, and never would.

Still wearing civilian clothes, Billy and the other plebes marched to the Plain for summer camp behind the uniformed battalion, just as

George and Orry had. The plebes staggered through the dust carrying the gear of the upperclassmen, and bloodied their knuckles and lost their tempers trying to drive tent pegs into the hard ground.

That first day in camp, Billy was exposed to another change taking place at the Academy. It was a change less marked than many of the others, but no less important. Some said later that it was the most important change of all because it was so destructive.

Each tent held three men, their blankets, a rack for the muskets they would eventually be issued, and a battered, green-painted locker. The locker had three compartments, one for each cadet's linen. It also served as the tent's only seat. When Billy walked in, followed by a thin, pale plebe with a bewildered air, the third occupant of the tent was sitting on the locker, polishing his expensive Wellington boots with a kerchief.

He glanced up. "Good evening to you. McAleer's the name. Dillard McAleer." He extended his hand.

Billy shook it, trying to identify the boy's accent. It was Southern, but a little harder and more nasal than the speech of South Carolina.

"I'm Billy Hazard. From Pennsylvania. This is Fred Pratt, from Milwaukee."

"Frank Pratt," said the tall boy. He sounded apologetic.

"Well, well. Two Yankees." Dillard McAleer grinned.

McAleer had pale blue eyes and blond curls that fell over his pink forehead. Billy had seen him before, when the newcomers had been sized and divided into four squads, one of which was attached to each cadet company. Billy and McAleer were of medium height, hence had been put in a squad attached to one of the interior companies. Frank Pratt, who remained meekly by the tent entrance, stood almost six feet. He had been assigned to a flank company squad.

"You boys plan to gang up on me?" McAleer asked. Something about him struck faint chords of memory. What was it? McAleer was still smiling, but there was a detectable seriousness in the question. Billy thought it a bad omen.

He heard noises outside—footfalls, and someone whispering. The skulkers were on the side of the tent away from the sun, so no shadows fell across the canvas. Billy countered McAleer's question with another:

"Why should we do that? We're all suffering through this together."

"I don't aim to suffer," McAleer declared. "First Yankee son of a bitch that fools with me, I'll push his nose out the back of his head."

Billy scratched his chin. "Where are you from, McAleer?"

"Little place in Kentucky, name of Pine Vale. My daddy farms there." He stared at Billy. "Him and the four niggers he owns."

The cadet clearly expected a reaction. He remained seated on the locker, his cheerfully truculent expression telling them he could and would deal with any criticisms they might offer. Billy hadn't expected to confront sectional hostility at West Point. He had been naive, and the realization gave him a jolt. But he certainly didn't intend to get into any arguments over slavery.

Still, as tent mates, the three of them were equals, and McAleer had to understand that. Billy gestured. "I'd like to stow my linen. Mind moving out of the way?"

"Why, yes, I do." McAleer stood up slowly, like a snake uncoiling. Though he was stocky, he had a natural grace that heightened his girlish look. But when he brushed the tips of his fingers over his palms, as if preparing for a fight, Billy saw that his hands were callused.

McAleer's grin widened again. "Reckon that if you want into this here locker, you'll have to displace me."

Frank Pratt uttered a small, pathetic groan. Now Billy knew why Dillard McAleer seemed familiar. He acted like some of the young men Billy had met at Mont Royal. Arrogant, almost desperately pugnacious. Maybe it was a standard defense against Yankees.

Billy gave the Kentuckian a level stare. "McAleer, I've no quarrel with you. We have to live in this canvas hell hole for sixty days, and we need to get along. As far as I'm concerned, getting along doesn't depend on who we are or where we hail from, but it surely does depend on how we treat each other. Now I didn't ask anything unusual, just to get into that locker, which is one-third mine. But if I have to displace you, as you call it, I guess I can."

The firmness of the statement impressed McAleer. He waved. "Hell, Hazard, I was only having a little fun." With a deep bow, he stood aside. "All yours. Yours too, Fred."

"Frank."

"Oh, sure. Frank."

Billy relaxed and turned toward the entrance where he had piled his belongings. Suddenly:

"All together, boys—pull!"

Billy recognized Slocum's voice an instant before the lurkers yanked all the tent pegs out of the ground. Down came the poles and the canvas.

McAleer cursed and thrashed. When the three plebes extricated themselves, Billy had to hold the Kentuckian to prevent him from going after the laughing upperclassmen.

George said that as plebes he and Orry had been plagued by one upperclassman who took a special dislike to them. It was the same with Billy. Caleb Slocum of Arkansas constantly sought him out in order to hive him for real and imaginary infractions. Billy's nights were soon haunted by dreams of Slocum's homely, blotchy face—and of triumphant moments in which he saw himself killing Slocum in a variety of ways.

He endured the harassment because he knew he must if he wanted to reach his goal. He liked to think about the future while he was standing guard; the routine consisted of two hours pacing your post, then four hours of rest, then another two hours on duty, for a total of twenty-four hours. To pass the time, Billy sent his imagination shooting ahead to a bright day when he had won his commission in the engineers and could support a wife. There was no longer any doubt in his mind as to who that wife would be. He only hoped Brett would want him as much as he wanted her.

A week before the end of summer camp, Dillard McAleer got into an argument with a couple of Northern plebes. They quarreled over the free-soil question. A fight developed. McAleer held his own until a foulmouthed first classman intervened, a New Yorker named Phil Sheridan who had a reputation as quite a brawler himself. This time he was serving as officer of the day and came down on the side of discipline.

Sheridan tried to stop the fight. His interference only infuriated McAleer all the more. The Kentuckian tore a limb from a nearby tree and ran at Sheridan, ready to club him. Fortunately other cadets leaped in and separated the two, but it took about five minutes to completely subdue McAleer.

Next day, Superintendent Henry Brewerton called McAleer to his office. No one knew what was said behind the superintendent's closed door, but by late afternoon McAleer was packing.

"Boys," he said with a cocky grin, "I hate to leave you both, but the supe made the choice pretty damn clear. Take the Canterberry road or face formal charges. Well, if I had to get thrown out of this abolitionist hog wallow, I'm glad I went out in style."

447

If McAleer had regrets, he hid them well. Billy thought it ironic that the Kentuckian accused the Academy of abolitionist leanings. Most of the country perceived it as tinged with pro-slavery sentiment.

Ever eager to please, Frank Pratt said, "Yes, you surely did that, Dillard." Billy concealed how he felt; the fury and the senselessness of the fight had disgusted him.

Frank went on in his high-pitched voice, "You tackled those two plebes and Sheridan like they were little boys."

McAleer shrugged. " 'Course. Gentlemen always fight better than rabble, and that's what Yankees are—rabble. Mongrels. Most Yankees," he amended hastily for the benefit of his tent mates. Billy had already heard the same opinion expressed by other cadets from the South. Maybe it was a pose to compensate for feelings of inferiority.

Whatever the reason for the attitude, the resulting fights were setting a bad precedent. He vividly recalled McAleer's savage expression as he ran at Sheridan with the tree limb.

McAleer shook hands. "Been a grand lark, boys."

"Yes," Billy said, not really meaning it. "Take care of yourself, Dillard."

"Sure will. Don't worry about me."

With a wave, he left. The memory of the tree limb and his hate-wracked face remained.

Billy continued to find evidence of the schism over slavery. Although cadets were assigned to companies according to height, he observed that a couple of the companies consisted mostly of Southerners or those who sympathized with them, and that in these companies some cadets were noticeably taller than others. Obviously some connivance on the part of the cadet adjutant was involved. What kind, he couldn't discover.

On the first of September a new superintendent arrived. Like Brewerton, Robert Lee was a member of the engineers, but his reputation was much superior to that of the superintendent he relieved. Lee was generally acknowledged to be America's finest soldier; it was said that Winfield Scott practically worshiped him. Lee did face one unique problem at the Academy: his oldest son, Custis, was a member of the class of '54. There were a great many snide jokes about favoritism.

Billy first saw the new superintendent up close at a Sunday chapel, which all cadets were required to attend—something else that hadn't changed since George's day. Lee was nearly six feet tall, with brown eyes, heavy brows, and a face that radiated strength of character.

448

Gray streaks showed in his black hair, but there were none in his mustache, whose tips trailed out half an inch on either side of his mouth. Billy guessed him to be in his middle forties.

The chaplain delivered one of his sleep-inducing sermons, this one on a very popular religious topic—the coming of the millennium. He offered a prayer for the new superintendent. Then, at the chaplain's invitation, Colonel Lee stepped from his pew and delivered a brief exhortation to the assembled cadets and faculty.

Although quarrels might rage outside the confines of the post, he said, those seated before him had a solemn duty to rise above such quarrels. Quoting the young king in Shakespeare's *Henry V*, he termed the cadets a band of brothers. He urged each listener to think of the corps in that fashion and to remember that West Point men owed allegiance to no section but only to the nation they had sworn to defend.

"What do you think of him?" Frank Pratt asked in that tentative way of his. Billy had drawn the Wisconsin boy as a roommate. They were hastily straightening their quarters before dinner call.

"He certainly fits the picture of the ideal soldier," Billy said. "I just hope he can keep peace around here."

"Band of brothers," Frank murmured. "I can't get that phrase out of my head. That's what we are, isn't it?"

"What we're supposed to be anyway." In Billy's mind an image flickered—McAleer's face as he attacked Sheridan.

A peremptory knock at the door was followed by the familiar inquiry, "All right?"

"All right," Billy replied. Frank repeated the same words, so that the inspecting cadet officer would know he was in the room too.

Rather than continuing on, the inspecting officer stepped in. James E. B. Stuart was a gregarious, immensely popular second classman from Virginia with a reputation for fighting that almost matched Sheridan's. Someone had nicknamed him Beauty precisely because he wasn't one.

Affecting sternness, Stuart said, "Sirs, you'd better watch your step now that Virginia has one of her own in charge of this institution." With a quick glance over his shoulder, he lowered his voice. "Came to warn you. One of the drummer boys smuggled a batch of thirty-rod onto the post. Slocum bought some. He's drunk and mentioning both of you by name"—Frank Pratt paled—"so avoid him if you can."

"We will, sir," Billy said. "Thank you."

"Don't want you thinking ill of every Southerner you meet," Stuart said, and disappeared.

Pensive, Billy stared at the autumn sunlight spilling through the room's leaded window. *Don't want you thinking ill of every Southerner.* Even in small turns of conversation, reminders of the widening chasm were inescapable.

Frank broke the silence. "What did we do to Slocum?"

"Nothing."

"Then why is he down on us?"

"We're plebes and he's a yearling. He's from a Southern state and we're Yankees. How should I know why he's down on us, Frank? I guess there's always someone in this world who hates you."

Frank gnawed his lip, speculating on some dour future. He wasn't a coward, Billy had discovered, just pessimistic and easily startled. Once he got over that skittishness, he might make a good officer.

"Well," Frank said finally, "I have a feeling that one of these days Slocum's really going to nail our hides to the doorpost."

"I agree. Best thing we can do is take Beauty's advice and avoid him."

But he felt that an encounter with Slocum was inevitable. So be it. When it happened, he would stand up to the Arkansas cadet, and to hell with the cost.

He wanted to reassure Frank that they could handle Slocum. Before he could, the bugle sounded. Doors crashed open; cadets rushed noisily to the stairs and down to the barracks street, there to fall in for the march to the mess hall. On the stairs Frank stumbled, fell, and tore the left knee of his trousers. Out in the sunshine, Slocum spied the rent and placed Frank on report.

Billy started to say something but checked himself. Slocum smirked and proceeded to place him on report for "insolent bearing and expression."

No doubt about it, there'd be a reckoning one day.

34

Beset by sleeplessness and thoughts of Madeline, Orry picked up George's letter again.

The writing was blurred. He moved the paper a few inches away and the date, December 16, grew legible. So did the rest. He had first noticed the problem with his vision earlier this fall. Like so many other things, it depressed him.

The letter was a mixture of cheer and cynicism. George had visited Billy at West Point earlier in December. Billy was doing well, albeit the same could not be said for the superintendent. Lee disliked the part of his job that required him to discipline the cadets. He wanted them all to behave well out of a desire to do so, without the threat of demerits or dismissal. "Unfortunately," George wrote, "the world is not peopled with Marble Models—although it would be a distinctly better place if it were."

Lee had greeted George warmly, as an old war comrade, although in truth they had met only a couple of times in Mexico, George said. The superintendent confided that his biggest problem was the sectionalism threatening to divide the cadet corps.

On a pleasanter note, he had observed that Billy was in the top section in every class and would no doubt pass his January examinations easily. A born engineer, Lee told the visitor. Mahan already had his eye on Billy.

The letter closed with some comments about the President-elect. Quite a few in the North were already accusing Franklin Pierce of being a doughface. Of the many names being mentioned in connection with the Cabinet, one of the most prominent was that of Senator Jefferson Davis.

Davis of the Mississippi Rifles, Orry recalled with a faint smile. Colonel Davis and his red-shirted volunteers had fought valiantly at Buena Vista. If he became secretary of war, the Military Academy would have a true friend in Wash—

The crash downstairs brought him leaping out of bed. Before he was halfway to the bedroom door, his stiff kneecaps were hurting.

God, he was falling apart. Age and the dampness of the low-country winter were accelerating the process.

"Orry? What was that noise?" his mother called from behind her door.

"I'm on my way to find out. I'm sure it's nothing serious. Go back to bed."

He meant to say it gently, but fear roughened his voice for some reason. At the bottom of the staircase he saw black faces floating in the halos of hand-held candles. He clutched the banister and hurried down. The effort intensified the pain in his joints.

"Let me pass."

The slaves fell back. Cousin Charles came racing down the stairs behind him. Orry opened the library door.

The first thing he saw, bright on the polished floor, was the river of spilled whiskey. Tillet's glass lay in pieces. The sound Orry had heard was his father's chair overturning.

Orry rushed forward, too stunned for grief. Tillet lay on his side in a stiff pose. His eyes and mouth were open, as if something had surprised him.

Seizure, Orry thought. "Papa? Can you hear me?"

He didn't know why he said that. Shock, he later decided. Even as he heard Clarissa's fretful voice from the second floor, he knew he had asked the question of a dead man.

They buried Tillet in the small plantation cemetery on the second of January. A big crowd of slaves watched from outside the black iron fence. During the prayer before the lowering of the coffin, it began to drizzle. On the other side of the grave, Ashton stood next to Huntoon, in defiance of the custom that required all members of the family to mourn together. The coffin was let down into the ground with great care.

Clarissa didn't cry, merely stared into space. She hadn't wept since the night of Tillet's death. After the burial Orry spoke to her. She acted as if she didn't hear. Again he asked if she was feeling all right. She replied with an incomprehensible murmur. Nor did her face give any clue. Altogether, he couldn't remember a sadder day at Mont Royal.

After the family left the enclosure, the slaves slipped in to surround the grave and pay respects with a few soft words of prayer, or a hummed phrase of a hymn, or merely a bowed head. Cooper fell in

452

step beside his brother. He marveled that the Negroes could feel kindly toward their owner. But then, he thought, human beings of all colors had never been famous for logical or consistent behavior.

Judith and Brett were walking with Clarissa. Cooper fondly watched his wife for a moment. In mid-December she had presented him with a daughter, Marie-Louise. The infant was at the great house, in the care of the maids.

Cooper noticed his brother's slumping shoulders and dour face. He tried to think of something to take Orry's mind off their father's passing.

"Before I left Charleston, I heard some news about Davis."

"What is it?"

"You know that last month he refused to confer with Pierce in Washington—"

"Yes."

"They say he's relented. He may go to the inaugural after all. It would be a fine thing for the South if he became a member of the Cabinet. He's an honest man. A sensible one, too, for the most part."

Orry shrugged. "His presence wouldn't make a whit of difference, Cooper."

"I refuse to believe that one man can't make a difference. If you take that position, what's the use of going on?"

His brother ignored the question. "Washington's one huge madhouse these days—and the worst lunatics are the ones the American people elect to represent them in Congress. I can't think of a less respectable deliberative body, unless it's our own state legislature."

"If you don't like the drift of things in South Carolina, change them. Stand for election and go to Columbia yourself."

Orry stopped, turned, gazed at his brother to see if he had heard correctly. "Are you saying I should enter politics?"

"Why not? Wade Hampton did." The wealthy and well-respected up-country planter had just been elected to a seat in the legislature. Cooper went on, "You have the necessary time and money. And your last name makes you eminently electable around here. You haven't alienated half the population the way I have. You and Hampton are a lot alike. You could be another voice of reason and moderation in the rhetorical storm up in the capital. There are precious few."

Orry was tempted, but only briefly. "I think I'd sooner be a pimp than a pol. It's more respectable."

Cooper didn't smile. "Have you ever read Edmund Burke?"

453

"No. Why?"

"I've been studying all his speeches and papers that I can locate. Burke was a staunch friend of the colonies and a man of radiant good sense. He once wrote in a letter that just one thing is necessary for the triumph of wicked men, and that's for good men to do nothing."

Resentful of what that implied about him, Orry started to retort. A cry from Brett prevented it.

"It's Mother," Cooper exclaimed. Clarissa sagged into Judith's arms, sobbing loudly. Orry was thankful she was letting her misery pour out at last.

His relief changed to anxiety an hour later when he heard his mother still crying in her room. He summoned the doctor, who gave her laudanum to calm her, then said to the assembled family:

"Bereavement is never easy to bear, but it's particularly hard for a woman who has always been an inseparable part of her husband's life. Clarissa is a strong person, however. She'll soon be herself again."

In that, he was wrong.

Orry noticed the first change within a week. When Clarissa smiled and chatted, she seemed to look through him rather than at him. Servants would put a question to her about a household matter, she would promise to answer as soon as she took care of some other, unnamed task, and then she would walk away and not return.

She developed a new passion, one that was common enough in South Carolina but had never been pursued at Mont Royal. She began to research and draw a family tree.

A green line represented her mother's family, the Bretts. A red line stood for the paternal line, which culminated in her father, Ashton Gault. Other colors were used for the Mains, so that the entire tree, which filled a large piece of parchment, resembled a rainbow-hued spiderweb.

Clarissa spread the parchment on a table by the window in her room. She spent hours working on it, so that it quickly became smudged and virtually unreadable. Yet she kept working. Every plantation duty to which she had once attended so diligently she now ignored.

Orry said nothing. He understood that Tillet's death had pushed his mother into some far country of the mind. If sojourning there soothed her grief, well and good. He would take up the slack as best he could.

But there were areas in which he was unskilled or simply ignorant. The plantation began to run roughly, like a clock that was always twenty minutes slow no matter how often it was adjusted.

"Straight, damn it—straight! What's the matter with all of you?"

It was a bright blue February morning. Orry was supervising preparation of the fields for March sowing. He had yelled at the trackers, experienced Negroes, mostly older, who were stringing guide ropes in parallel lines eleven inches apart. At the moment the trackers were working on the far side of the square. They turned to stare at their owner in a bewildered way; their lines looked straight.

Equally puzzled by the outburst were the trenchers, younger men and women who followed the lines and dug the seed trenches with hoes. Orry had shouted so loudly even some male slaves shoveling out the irrigation ditches at the edge of the square looked up. All the stares told Orry he was in error.

He closed his eyes and rubbed the lids with his fingertips. He had been up most of the night, fretting about his mother and then composing a letter to George to tell him the Mains would no longer summer in Newport. The reason he cited was Clarissa's condition; the truth was never mentioned. Last summer Orry had felt an unmistakable hostility on the part of some citizens of the little resort town. Putting up with Yankee unfriendliness was not his idea of a vacation.

"Orry, the lines are perfectly straight."

Brett's voice brought his eyes open abruptly. He turned and saw her a short way down the embankment. Her cheeks shone. She was breathing hard. Evidently she had come running up behind him just as he reprimanded the slaves.

He squinted over his shoulder. What she said was true. Fatigue or some trick of his mind had caused a misjudgment. The slaves had all resumed working, knowing they were right and he was wrong.

Brett walked to him, touched his hand. "You stayed up too late again." He shrugged. She went on, "I just broke up a noisy muss in the kitchen. Dilly boxed Sue's ears because Sue forgot to order more curing salt. Sue swore she told you we needed it."

Memory rushed back. "Oh, God—that's right. I am the one who forgot. Last week I was just about to put curing salt on the factor's list when I was called to look at Semiramis's baby with the measles."

455

"The crisis has passed. The baby will be all right."

"No thanks to me. I didn't know what the devil to do with a six-month-old infant. Anyway, how do you know so much about it?"

She tried to say it kindly. "They sent for me right after you left. I couldn't do much for the child other than wrap him up to keep him warm. But Semiramis was wild with worry, so I held her hand and talked to her awhile. That quieted her, and the baby got some rest—which is exactly what was needed most."

"I had no idea what was needed. I felt like a helpless fool."

"Don't blame yourself, Orry. Mama carried a lot of the burden of this place. More than you men ever realized." That was as close as she came to teasing him, and it was just a brief, gentle sally accompanied by a smile. She touched his hand again. "Let me help you run the plantation. I can do it."

"But you're just—"

"A little girl? Why, you sound just like Ashton."

From a whole quiver of arrows she had chosen precisely the right one to pierce and destroy his resistance. He burst out laughing. Then he said, "You're right, I had no idea how much Mama took care of. I'll bet Father didn't either. I'll be glad to have your help. Thankful for it! Take over wherever you see a need. If anyone questions you, tell them you're acting on my authority. Tell them to speak to me—what's wrong?"

"If the slaves must check every important order with you, it's pointless for me to do the work. What's more, I won't. I must have equal authority, and everyone must know it."

"All right. You win." His admiration was tinged with awe. "You're a wonder. And only fifteen this year—"

"Age has nothing to do with it. Some girls learn to be women at twelve. I mean they learn everything, not just how to be pert and flirtatious." The jab at Ashton wasn't lost on Orry. "Some never learn at all. I'll be hanged if I'll be one of those."

With an affectionate smile, he said, "Don't worry, you couldn't be." He felt no less tired but a lot better. "Well, I guess we should arrange to get some curing salt."

"Cuffey's already on his way to Charleston with the cart. I wrote his pass myself."

Again he laughed, then slipped his arm around her. "I have a feeling things are going to be a lot better on this plantation."

"I know they are," she said. In the field a couple of the trackers exchanged looks, and then relieved smiles.

Ashton paced back and forth in front of the bedroom hearth. Brett was bent over the desk. Outside, ice-covered tree limbs clashed and tinkled. The wind howled along the river.

Another series of sneezes exploded from the guest bedroom. Ashton grimaced. Huntoon had brought her home from Charleston right before the storm hit and had promptly gone to bed with raging influenza.

"I do wish he'd stop that dreadful sneezing," she exclaimed. Brett glanced up from one of the plantation ledgers, struck by the venom in her sister's voice. How could anyone be so enraged by illness?

But Ashton wasn't infuriated by that so much as by some other things. She already missed the lights and gaiety of Charleston. Huntoon had squired her to the season's most prestigious social event, the great ball sponsored by the Saint Cecilia Society. Back here on the Ashley, she felt caged.

Her little sister, however, seemed perfectly content to spend her time with shopping lists and ledgers. In the past few weeks Brett had started acting as if she were mistress of the plantation. What was even more galling, the niggers treated her as if she were.

"When I'm finished here, I'll mix up a batch of Mama's hot lemon toddy," Brett said. "It might clear his head some."

"Quite the little physician, aren't we?"

Again Brett looked at her sister, but this time her expression was more stern. "There's no call to be snide. I just do what I can."

"Every chance you get, seems like. I heard you were down in the cabins again today."

"Hattie developed a bad boil. I lanced and dressed it. What of it?"

"I really don't know why you waste your time on such trashy business."

Brett snapped the ledger shut. She pushed her chair back, rose, and kicked her skirt to one side.

"Somebody ought to remind you that all that trashy business, as you call it, keeps Mont Royal running in the black. It pays for those bolts of brocade you bought for your Saint Cecilia gown."

Ashton's mocking laugh was a defense. She had chosen to reach her goals by manipulating others while pretending to play the traditional feminine role. Brett, by contrast, was asserting her independence,

457

Ashton envied that. At the same time, it made her hate her sister all the more.

She hid the hatred with a shrug and a pirouette toward the door. "Calm down. I don't give a hoot if you bury yourself in this place. But remember one thing. Those who mean to rise in the world don't waste time on the problems of niggers and white trash. They court the important people."

"I expect they do, but I'm not trying to rise, as you put it. I'm just trying to help Orry."

Smug little bitch, Ashton thought. She wanted to use nails on her sister's eyes. Injure her, make her weep for mercy. Instead, she smiled and said gaily, "Well, you go right to it, and I'll tend to James. Oh, but I am curious about one thing. You're so busy doctoring and ciphering, when will you have time to answer those letters from your cadet? He's liable to forget you."

"I'll always have time for Billy, don't you worry."

The quiet words pushed Ashton close to the point of explosion. She was diverted by the sound of another gargantuan sneeze from Huntoon. She rushed into the hall, nearly colliding with Cousin Charles, who was on his way downstairs. A moment after she stepped back, she too sneezed.

"Say, Ashton, where'd you get that cold?" Charles grinned and hooked a thumb toward the guest room. "Did he give you anything else in Charleston?"

"Go to the pits of hell, you foul-minded scum!"

"What's the matter? Getting too uppity for a joke?"

The slam of a door was his answer.

Inside the guest room, Huntoon stared at Ashton while listening to a storm of the vilest profanity he had ever heard.

In the spring following the inauguration, President Pierce toured the North with members of his Cabinet. Lavish banquets were held in several major cities. George and Stanley attended the one in Philadelphia.

Pierce was a handsome, affable man. Stanley was so overwhelmed to be in his presence he practically fawned. George was more interested in the new secretary of war, Jefferson Davis.

Davis carried himself like a soldier. He was in his mid-forties and still slim, although his fair hair showed a generous amount of gray. He had high cheekbones and deeply set blue-gray eyes. George had heard that one eye was blind but didn't know which. Nor was it apparent.

During the reception that preceded the dinner, George had a chance to hear some of the secretary's views. Davis began with a topic that seemed to be his chief reason for accompanying the President—promotion of a transcontinental railroad.

"I am a strict constructionist," the new secretary told George and half a dozen others gathered around him. "I believe the Constitution prohibits the Federal government from making internal improvements in the separate states. So you might logically ask—"

"How is it possible to justify government aid for a railroad?"

Davis smiled politely at the man who had interrupted. "I couldn't have said it better, sir." Everyone laughed. "I justify it as a matter of national defense," he went on. "If not linked to the rest of the country, the Pacific coast territories could all too easily be snatched away by some foreign aggressor. Further, a transcontinental line—running through the South, preferably"—a couple of his listeners bristled at that; the secretary appeared not to notice—"will help us defend our frontiers by making it easier to move men rapidly to threatened areas. At present, the Army numbers only about ten thousand officers and men. Between here and California there are an estimated four hundred thousand Indians, forty thousand of them considered hostile. That danger demands new responses."

"What might those be, Mr. Secretary?" George asked.

"For one, more men in the Army. At minimum, two new regiments. Mounted regiments that can travel a long distance in a short time. The Indians don't fear our foot troops. They have a name for them. 'Walk-a-heap.' It is a term of contempt."

George had heard that Davis was more soldier than politician; he was beginning to believe it. The man impressed him.

"Many things about our military establishment are badly out of date," the secretary continued. "Our tactics, for example. To remedy that, I plan to send an officer to study the tactics of the French army. If the Crimea explodes, as appears likely, we'll also have a rare opportunity to observe European armies in the field. Further, improvements need to be made at our Military Academy."

"That interests me, sir," George said. "My brother is currently a plebe, and I graduated in the class of 'forty-six."

"Yes, Mr. Hazard, I'm aware of both facts. In my opinion, the West Point curriculum must be expanded"—nothing new there: the idea of a five-year course of study had been afloat for several years—"with more emphasis given to mounted tactics. I want to build a new riding hall. Enlarge the stables—"

Another listener broke in, "They say you might also build a second military academy in the South, Mr. Secretary."

Davis whirled on the speaker, sharp for the first time. "Sir, that is a false and pernicious rumor. A second military academy may have been proposed by others, but never by me. Such an institution would only promote sectionalism, and sectionalism is the last thing we need in this country at present. When John Calhoun spoke against the Clay compromise, he said that the cords binding the states together were breaking one by one. He believed disunion was inevitable. I do not. One of the bulwarks of my faith stands in the Hudson Highlands. If any institution promotes a national point of view, it is West Point. I for one intend to keep it that way."

In spite of automatic suspicion of any politician from the deep South, George found himself joining the others in a round of applause. Still, Davis's attitude represented the ideal rather than the reality. Billy had recently written to say that strong Northern and Southern cliques existed at West Point and that sectional tensions were increasing. Charles Main would be enrolling at the Academy in June. Would the tensions interfere with the friendship he and Billy had formed? George hoped not.

When the applause subsided, George said, "Good for you, Mr. Secretary. There are too many extremists on both sides these days. We need more voices like yours."

He lifted his glass. "To the Academy."

Davis raised his own glass in response. "And the Union," he said.

35

Charles traveled north while Russia mobilized for war against Turkey and her allies on the other side of the world. The prospective cadet arrived at West Point wearing a wide-brimmed planter's hat and an old coat of rust-colored velvet. His hair hung to his shoulders, and his bowie knife was tucked in his boot.

Billy and his friend and classmate, a jolly Virginian named Fitzhugh Lee, leaned out a window in the second floor of the barracks and watched Charles come trudging along the street below. They had been expecting him all afternoon. Presumably Charles had already turned in his appointment papers and signed the adjutant's register and circumstances ledger. In the latter he had no doubt listed Orry's financial status as "affluent" rather than "moderate." Having deposited his cash with the treasurer, Charles was now coming to find his room.

"My Lord," Fitz Lee said in amazement. "Just look at all that hair."

Billy nodded. "I knew he had plenty, but I didn't expect that much." A gleeful look crept into his eye. Friendship hadn't prevented him from organizing a reception for Charles.

"He's shaggy as a bison." The moment Fitz spoke, something clicked in Billy's mind. Charles didn't know it, but he had just received his Academy nickname. Billy was still searching for his.

Charles sensed someone watching and started to glance up. Billy pulled back hastily, dragging Fitz with him.

"Don't let him see you. Is the room ready?"

"Far as I know," Fitz said with a grin of unabashed wickedness. The young Virginian was the superintendent's nephew, but Billy felt sure that wouldn't save him from eventual dismissal. Fitz Lee habitually broke the rules, and did so with relish. "Beauty went up awhile ago to lay out his tools and slip into one of those smocks we stitched together. I'll fetch mine. You keep the victim here till I come back."

"All right, but hurry. We don't have much time before parade." Billy leaned out the window, waved. "Hey, Charles. Hello!"

Charles blinked, then returned the wave with enthusiasm. "Damn, it's you! How are you, Billy?"

"Anxious to see you. Come on up."

Again he retreated from the window and discovered Fitz still lingering at the door. "What's wrong?"

"I forgot to tell you that Slocum invited himself to the party. You know Beauty—he's so blasted cordial, he tells everybody everything."

Billy scowled. "Well, Slocum had better not give the game away. Tell him I said he's to keep his mouth shut."

"Do you want me to say it that—ah—directly?"

"Yes. I'm not his plebe whipping boy any longer."

"Right you are." Fitz grinned and hurried out.

Moments later Charles bounded up the stairs, the swallowtails of his coat flapping. He and Billy whooped and embraced like long-lost brothers. Then Charles flung his hat and valise on one of the beds and pushed his long hair off his damp forehead.

"Godamighty, Billy, you look fine in that uniform. But I forgot that the North got so blasted hot."

"It'll get hotter for you before the summer's over—even if the temperature dips. You're going to be a plebe, remember? And I think I can make cadet corporal in camp."

Charles frowned. "Does that mean we can't be friends for a year?"

"We can be friends. We just can't show it too much, or—"

"Cadet Main?"

The bellow from the hall sent Charles into a crouch. Billy had to grip his friend's arm to keep him from pulling his knife.

Charles scowled at the stranger in the doorway. It was Fitz Lee, wearing a thigh-length smock of coarse gray cloth. "Who the hell are you?" Charles demanded.

Fitz matched his truculence. "Don't raise your voice to me, sir! I am Mr. Fitz, one of the post barbers. It is the duty of Mr. Jeb and myself to attend to the tonsure of all incoming cadets."

"The ton-what?"

"Your hair, sir. It is decidedly in need of attention. Should you refuse to cooperate, I shall be forced to report you to the superintendent." Hands raised, Charles said, "No, wait. Billy, do they always do this when you get here?"

"Absolutely," Billy answered with a straight face. "Mr. Fitz and Mr. Jeb gave me a trim the first hour I was on the post."

"Damn if they look old enough to be barbers."

"Oh, when they took care of me they were still apprentices."

"Well—all right."

Still suspicious, Charles nevertheless followed Fitz out the door and up the stairs to the trunk room, which had been cleaned and prepared for the occasion. Billy brought up the rear, barely able to suppress eruptions of giggling.

The trunk room felt like an inferno. Windowless, it was illuminated by a pair of oil lamps that added to the heat. On a cheap table lay a silver-framed mirror, combs, brushes, shears, and a razor. Next to a rickety chair stood Beauty Stuart. He wore a smock and radiated authority.

"Sit down, sir. Quickly, quickly! This cadet is waiting for a trim as soon as we finish with you."

He pointed to Caleb Slocum, who was lounging by the wall. Billy and the Arkansas cadet exchanged nods but neither smiled. As soon as the first classmen had donned Army uniforms and departed, Slocum would be going home on leave. None too soon to suit Billy.

Charles sat down. With great panache, Stuart motioned and snapped his fingers. "Mr. Fitz? The cloth, if you please."

Fitz Lee produced a filthy, tattered sheet which he proceeded to fasten around Charles's neck. "That's a damn dirty sheet," Charles complained. "Looks like a whole flock of people bled on it. What kind of tonsorial parlor is—?"

"Quiet, sir, I cannot concentrate when you babble," Stuart said, giving his customer a fierce look. He clicked the shears several times, then attacked Charles's hair above his left ear. Billy tried to judge the time by sounds from downstairs. They had only until four o'clock.

"The mirror, if you please, Mr. Fitz."

The assistant barber jumped forward, tilting the glass this way and that in response to Stuart's exaggerated gestures. How could Charles not see it was all a sham? Yet no newcomer ever did; fear and unfamiliar surroundings made it work perfectly, year after year.

Presently Stuart cocked his head to the side, folded his right hand under his chin, and rested his right elbow on his left palm, studying his artistic creation. The entire left side of Charles's head had been clipped to a length of half an inch, while to the right of a perfect dividing line across the top of his head the hair was as long and full as ever, untouched. Billy faced the wall and bit his lower lip while tears ran from his eyes.

"Half done," Stuart announced. "Now for the other—"

Out on the Plain the bugle pealed. Perfect timing. Mr. Jeb dropped

463

the shears. Mr. Fitz threw the mirror on the table, and Billy and Slocum cut for the door. "Wait," Charles cried. "What's going on?"

Stuart ripped off the smock. "We must assemble. Come along, sir."

"We'll finish the trim another time," Fitz shouted from the landing below.

"Another time?" Bellowing, Charles pursued his tormentors. From the door of the trunk room he gave Billy a withering look—the look of a man betrayed—which Billy could barely see through his mirthful tears. "What other time?" Charles screamed. "How in hell am I going to explain the way I look?"

"I don't know, sir," Fitz caroled as he ran away down the stairs. "But explain it you shall—for I'm sure all the officers will be curious about it."

"A damn trick!" Charles howled. He yanked his knife out of his boot and flung it.

Slocum had lagged behind. The bowie flashed past his ear and buried in a beam on the landing below. While the knife hummed, Charles launched into a profane tirade against West Point men and West Point perfidy.

When questioned, Charles would say only that he alone was responsible for his haircut. He stuck to the story despite threats from the tactical officers and some upperclassmen. His silence earned him the respect of most of the leaders of the cadet corps, including Beauty Stuart.

Charles soon came to idolize Stuart. This was true even though the two seemingly had little in common. Charles was handsome whereas Stuart was most decidedly the opposite: his stocky trunk contrasted oddly with his unusually long arms. What he lacked in appearance, however, he more than made up for with dash and charm. His blue eyes almost always brimmed with good humor. And he had an amazing record of success with young ladies who stayed at the hotel.

Stuart's romantic prowess was not the only reason for Charles's admiration. To him, the Virginian represented all the good qualities of Southerners. Courage. A high sense of personal honor. A zest for life. The ability to smile when trouble engulfed you; smile and endure.

Stuart was also passionately loyal to his friends. Early in Charles's plebe year, Fitz Lee got drunk and was unlucky enough to be caught. He faced court-martial. Stuart organized Fitz's classmates, who presented the superintendent with a pledge that, as a class, they would never be guilty of a similar offense.

By tradition, such a pledge from an entire class resulted in cancellation of charges against the offender. Colonel Lee could not otherwise have intervened in his nephew's case. On the day after his receipt of the pledge, the superintendent was seen smiling frequently. He was probably pleased that his nephew had escaped dismissal, but no doubt more pleased that a band of brothers had lived up to its name.

Charles had no trouble with the military aspect of Academy training. Scholastically it was a different story. The fourth-class course in English grammar and geography was relatively simple, if boring. But in spite of the excellent preparation from Herr Nagel, the algebra course was an absolute mystery. Charles immediately joined the immortals and remained in their ranks through the January examinations, which he barely passed. Things got no better when he began his study of French in the second term.

"Why the devil do soldiers have to know French?" he asked Billy on one of the rare occasions when they could talk without being hampered by class rank. It was a Saturday afternoon during a February thaw. They had gone hiking in the hills above Fort Putnam. To the north they could see chunks of ice floating in the gray river. The air had the dry, astringent smell of winter. Occasional whiffs of wood smoke rose from the chimneys of the brick faculty houses below. Billy broke a twig in his mittened hands and tossed both halves away.

"Because, Mr. Bison, a lot of important military and scientific treatises are written in French. You might need to translate one someday."

"Not me. I'm going into the dragoons and chase Indians." He squinted at his friend. "You sure that's the reason?"

"Why would I lie to you?"

"Because I'm a plebe, and you're very good with buncombe. You proved that when you set me up for the haircut."

"You'd better go back to your dictionary. *Buncombe* means lies and smooth talk from a politician."

"Don't tell me what it's supposed to be; I already know—and you're an expert at dispensing it." With obvious delight, he rolled the word out again. "Buncombe. Mr. Buncombe, that's you—" Sudden inspiration. Charles pointed like a prosecutor. "No. Bunk. Old Bunk. From now on."

Billy snorted and complained, but secretly he was pleased. He had been embarrassed by his lack of a nickname. It seemed fitting that his best friend had finally bestowed it.

Toward the end of May 1854, the Senate passed the Kansas-Nebraska Bill. Senator Douglas had introduced it in January, once again heating up the simmering slavery controversy.

The bill organized two new territories. Douglas called it an expression of popular sovereignty. Anti-slavery men called it a betrayal, a repeal of the old Missouri Compromise that prohibited slavery north of 36 degrees 30 minutes of latitude. Secretary Davis reportedly influenced President Pierce to sign the bill. The anti-slavery forces said a new political party was obviously needed to combat sinister combinations at work in Washington.

Orry wrote Charles to say that judging from the rhetoric on both sides, Clay's compromise of four years ago was in ruins. And Charles, without knowing or caring much about national issues, found himself on the defensive because of them. Upperclassmen occasionally put him on report for a glare or a swallowed retort, calling his behavior Southern insolence. Southerners such as Slocum reacted against that sort of thing by cruel hazing of Northern plebes. Lee continued to exhort the cadets to be a band of brothers, but Charles saw the corps quietly separating into two hostile camps.

Of course there were gradations of behavior within each camp. Slocum represented one end of the Southern spectrum, Beauty Stuart the other—when he was on his good behavior with his temper unruffled, that is. Stuart claimed he patterned himself after the Marble Model, the superintendent, but he was too fond of assignations on Flirtation Walk for the resemblance to be perfect. Charles took Stuart as one of his exemplars and Billy as another, because Billy kept himself aloof from political arguments and concentrated on good marks, which he seemed to achieve with little effort.

Still, given his upbringing and the nature of the times, Charles sometimes found it hard to keep his temper. While standing at attention during a reveille roll call in the spring, he was singled out for harassment by an obnoxious cadet sergeant from Vermont. The Yankee pulled three buttons off his uniform on the pretext of inspecting them.

"No wonder you never look trig, sir," the Yankee snarled. "You don't have your niggers to do for you."

466

Under his breath, Charles said, "I polish my own brass. And fight my own fights."

The Vermont cadet thrust his jaw forward. The sunrise flecked his eyes with points of light.

"*What did you say, sir?*"

"I said—" Suddenly Charles recalled his demerit total. It stood at 190 with two weeks of the plebe year still remaining. "Nothing, sir."

The cadet sergeant strutted on, looking smug. Perhaps he was relieved, too. Charles had established a reputation as an expert with knives and bare knuckles.

He hated to cave in under a Yankee's insults. He did it only because he owed Orry a decent showing at the Academy, and the debt meant more to him than real or fancied insults to his honor.

For the moment, anyway.

Curiously, it was one of his own who first prodded Charles to think seriously about slavery. The culprit was Caleb Slocum, who had now advanced to cadet sergeant.

The Arkansas cadet had an excellent academic record. He was in the first section in most of his subjects. Billy said he got to the top by stealing examination questions ahead of time, and by various other forms of cheating. Although cheating wasn't condoned by the officers and professors, it never received the attention given to other breaches of discipline such as drinking.

Thus Billy had one more reason to despise Slocum. He told Charles he intended to thrash the Arkansas cadet one of these days.

Slocum was a master at tormenting plebes. He hung out at Benny Haven's—the proprietor was still alive, immortal, it seemed—and there learned about certain kinds of hazing that had been tried in the past and abandoned as too nasty.

They were not too nasty for Slocum. His targets remained the plebes from Northern states. When Charles observed the absolute power Slocum had over them, it struck him that the same power relationship existed back home between white master and black slave. The relationship had been present all along, of course; he had just never appreciated its potential for abuse and outright cruelty.

He felt disloyal about questioning the South even slightly. But he couldn't help it. Ideas different from his own bombarded him every day. Like the nation, the Academy was in ferment. One proof could be seen in the Dialectic Society. Cadets organized fewer debates on

467

so-called soft topics. "Ought females to receive a first-class education?" They reasoned—argued, sometimes shouted—over hard issues. "Has a state the right to secede from the Union?" "Has Congress an obligation to protect the property of territorial settlers?"

Privately, Charles began to consider different aspects of the peculiar institution: the justice of it, the long-term practicality. He had trouble admitting the system was wholly wrong—he was a Southerner, after all—but with so many people opposed to it, there was surely something amiss. In terms of the animosity it produced, slavery seemed more of a burden to the South than a benefit. Sometimes Charles was almost ready to agree with that Illinois stump speaker and politician, Lincoln, who said gradual emancipation was the only answer.

Although his inner turmoil persisted, he was determined to avoid fights that were in any way related to the issue. On the night of June 1, that resolve was destroyed.

At half-past nine, Charles gathered up soap and towel and tramped downstairs to the barracks washroom. Since it was late, he hoped to have the place to himself. Cadets were required to bathe once a week but could not do so more often without special permission from Colonel Lee.

Oil lamps shed a dim light in the basement corridor; rumor said Secretary Davis hoped to install a gaslight system soon. Charles hurried past the entrance to the refreshment shop, not wanting to be noticed or hived. He was tired and sore from marching. He longed to lean back in the tub and drowse in warm water for ten or fifteen minutes before taps.

He started to whistle softly as he approached the double door of the washroom. Suddenly he stopped and listened. He frowned. On the other side of the doors he heard voices. Two were low-pitched, the other slightly louder—

Pleading.

He jerked the door open. Startled, Caleb Slocum and a skinny classmate from Louisiana spun toward him. Slocum had an open jar in one hand. From it, mingling with the smells of soap and dampness, rose the pungent odor of spirits of turpentine.

The Louisiana cadet was holding a third young man face down in an empty tub. The youth peered at Charles, his dark eyes big and moist and scared. Charles recognized him as a newcomer who had arrived only today.

468

"Get out, sir," Slocum said to Charles. "This disciplinary matter is none of your affair."

"Disciplinary matter? Come on, boys. That fellow just got here this afternoon. He's entitled to one or two mistakes."

"This Yankee insulted us," the Louisiana cadet snarled.

"I did not," the youth in the tub protested. "They grabbed hold of me and dragged me down here and—"

"You shut up," Louisiana said, seizing the newcomer's neck and squeezing until he winced.

Slocum stepped forward to block Charles's view. His blotchy face darkened as he said: "I'll tell you just once more, sir. Leave."

Slowly Charles shook his head. The water pipes running to the tubs radiated heat. He wiped his sweating palm on his shirt bosom and said, "Not till I see what you're fixing to do to him." He suspected he knew.

Quickly he stepped to one side, then darted forward before Slocum could react. The victim was naked. He looked scrawny and pathetic with his bare buttocks elevated slightly. Between his legs Charles saw the cord around his testicles. It was tied so tightly his balls were already swollen.

Charles licked the roof of his mouth, which was dry all at once. This was one of the little stunts tried a few times in the past and abandoned. Charles had walked in just before the conclusion—the pouring of turpentine into the victim's anus.

Bile and anger thickened his voice. "That isn't fit treatment for a dog. Let him up."

Slocum couldn't permit a plebe to bully him. "Main, I'm warning you—"

The door opened. Charles spun, saw Frank Pratt with a towel draped over his arm. Frank registered surprise as he took in the scene. He gulped and looked bilious. Charles spoke softly but with authority.

"Get Old Bunk. I want him to see what Slocum's up to this time."

Frank ran out and slammed the door. Slocum deposited the turpentine jar on the slippery floor, then began to massage his knuckles with the palm of his left hand. "Apparently there's just one kind of order you understand, sir. Very well, I shall provide it."

Charles almost snickered at the posturing. He didn't because these two were upperclassmen, and cornered to boot. That made them dangerous.

The Louisiana cadet released the youth in the tub, who flopped on his chest and uttered a feeble cry. Slocum continued the melodramatic massaging of his hand. His companion grabbed his arm.

"Don't fool with him, Slocum. You know his reputation. He's within ten skins of dismissal—if we put him on report, we can get rid of him."

The idea appealed to the Arkansas cadet, who really didn't want to fight anyone as big and as formidable as Charles. Slocum continued to rub his hand, saying to no one in particular, "Damn fool ought to be on our side anyway. We're all from the same part of the—"

The door opened. Frank and Billy walked in. Billy slammed the door. His opinion of what he saw was expressed in an explosive, "Jesus Christ! You"—he pointed to the cowering boy—"put your clothes on and get to your room."

"Y-yes, sir." The newcomer groped over the side of the tub but couldn't reach his clothes. Charles kicked them closer. Slocum was glaring at Billy.

"Don't come in here issuing orders, sir. Remember that I'm your superior—"

Billy cut him off. "The hell you are. You think West Point's your plantation and every plebe a nigger you can mistreat. You're nothing but Southern shit."

"Come on, Bunk," Charles exclaimed. "There's no call for that kind of talk."

But his friend was furious. "If you're on his side, say so."

"Goddamn you—"

Charles's shout reverberated in the damp room. His fist was raised and shooting forward before he realized it. He just managed to pull the punch.

Billy had already retreated a step and was raising his hands to block the blow. He looked almost as astonished as Charles felt.

What Charles had done, or almost done, was profoundly upsetting to him. He had been ready to brawl over a few words that he had interpreted not as an individual but as a Southerner. He had behaved exactly like Whitney Smith and his crowd. He was stunned to discover that the vein of pride existed within him and ran deep.

He wiped his palm across his mouth. "Bunk, I'm sorry."

"All right." Billy sounded none too friendly.

"Slocum is the one we should—"

"I said all right."

Billy's furious gaze locked with his friend's for a second. Then his anger cooled. He tilted his head toward the door.

"Everybody out—except you, Slocum. Your brand of discipline isn't popular around here. It's time someone demonstrated that."

Worried, Frank Pratt said, "Billy, you'll have half the corps down on you if you do this."

"I don't think so. But I'll take that chance. Out."

"I'll stand watch outside," Charles said. "Nobody will bother you."

Charles had made a gesture the corps would understand. A Northerner dealing with Slocum while a Southerner acted as lookout would establish that Slocum's behavior, and not his birthplace was the cause of the fight.

"Hurry," Charles said to the newcomer, who was struggling into his ruffled shirt. "Put your shoes on outside."

The youth left, followed by Frank Pratt. Charles looked at the Louisiana cadet. "Guess I'll have to drag you out."

"No—no!" Louisiana fled, moving sideways like a crab until he was in the hall. There, he turned and ran.

Charles gazed down the gloomy, lamp-lit corridor, empty save for Frank Pratt crouching by the stairs and staring upward apprehensively. The pensioner who operated the refreshment shop came out, locked the door, noticed Charles and Frank, then walked upstairs without a word.

Charles leaned back against the double door, still shaken by what had happened. Far away the bugler sounded the first notes of taps. He heard a weak cry of fright in the washroom just before the first sound of a fist striking.

Billy came out ten minutes later. Blood spattered his blouse, and bruises showed on the backs of his hands. Otherwise he was unmarked.

No, that wasn't entirely correct, Charles realized. A certain uneasiness showed in Billy's eyes. Charles asked, "Can he walk?"

"Yes, but he won't feel like it for a little while." Again his eyes met those of his friend and slid away. "I enjoyed that too much."

From the stairs Frank Pratt motioned for them to hurry. They would all be given demerits if the inspecting officer called "All right?" outside their doors and received no reply.

Well, Charles didn't care. He was thinking of Billy's remark a

471

moment ago. Was Billy concerned that he had enjoyed mistreating Slocum because Slocum was a Southerner?

They reached Frank, who asked anxiously, "What's going to happen when Slocum talks about this?"

As they started climbing the stairway, Billy said, "I tried to impress on him that he'd better not. I think he understands that if our little session gets on the record in any official way, the one thing I'll do before I'm dismissed is visit him again—and his Louisiana chum, too."

"Of course," Frank went on, "you could take the offense and formally charge him with mistreating that new fellow—"

Billy shook his head. "If I did that, Slocum would be a hero, and I'd be just another vindictive Yankee. There's friction enough in this place already. I think we should let matters stand."

He sounded less than happy, though, and that finally prompted Charles to offer his friend the assurance that, by tone of voice, he had asked for some moments ago:

"You said you enjoyed it too much, but I don't believe you. Whatever you did, Slocum had it coming."

Billy gave Charles a grateful glance. Neither said anything more as they trudged up the shadowy staircase. Charles began to feel despondent about himself, and about Billy too. It couldn't be denied that both of them had caught the infection from which the whole country was suffering. Then and there, he made up his mind that it mustn't get any worse.

Slocum explained his injuries as the results of a fall down the stairs. The Louisiana cadet didn't dispute him. The vicious hazing stopped.

Despite this, the incident quickly became known and thought of as a sectional fight. Hearing only that one cadet had thrashed another, some Northerners and Westerners took Billy's side and cut Slocum. Some Southerners cut Billy. Charles drew the silent treatment from both camps, a response so insulting, yet at the same time so ludicrous, all he could do was laugh.

A week later Fitz Lee informed Charles that the Louisiana cadet was spreading his own version of the incident. He was telling friends that casual criticism of the Kansas-Nebraska bill by Slocum, and his statement that a code of Southern rights must be written in Congress

472

to protect property in the new territories, had provoked Billy's brutal attack.

And why had the Louisiana cadet kept this from his friends until now? To prevent the officers from hearing of the incident, he said. He had been thinking solely of the welfare of the corps, and the truth of the matter had just slipped out.

"Oh, it just slipped out, did it?" Charles growled. "It just slipped out on two or three different occasions?"

"Or more," Fitz replied with a sour smile.

Charles lost his temper. He said he was going to pull Louisiana out of formation at evening parade and pound his lies down his throat. Billy and Fitz talked him out of it.

Gradually, interest in the fight waned. The cadets began speaking to Billy and Charles again, while generally ignoring Slocum—exactly the state of affairs that had existed before the trouble.

But the quarrel had left some bad memories, and they piled up with others like them.

Soon the first classmen left. The graduates included Stuart, the superintendent's son, and a Maine boy named Ollie O. Howard from whom Charles bought a good used blanket. Billy, meantime, was packing to go home on leave.

Everyone at the Academy was talking about the changes to be instituted in the fall. For almost a decade the Academic Board had been recommending a five-year curriculum, and Secretary Davis had finally secured its adoption. Half of the incoming plebes would be put into the new program, while the other half would follow the old four-year course—the last class to do so. The plebes were being divided in this fashion so that there would never be a year without a graduating class.

The five-year curriculum was designed to correct what many considered an overemphasis on mathematics, science, and engineering. New course work in English, history, elocution, and Spanish was to be introduced.

"Why the devil do I need another language?" Charles complained. "I have enough trouble with French."

"The war added a lot of new territory—in which there are a lot of people who speak Spanish. That's the excuse I heard, anyway." Billy shut his valise, stretched, and walked to the window.

"In the dragoons," Charles said, "they don't converse with greasers, they just shoot 'em."

Billy gave him a wry look. "I don't think Mexicans would find that very funny." Charles's shrug acknowledged that his friend was right, but Billy didn't see it; he had put both hands on the sill and was gazing at a familiar figure limping across the Plain. By chance the cadet noticed Billy in the window and looked away.

"Slocum," Billy said soberly.

Charles joined him. "He's walking better."

The Arkansas cadet limped out of sight. Charles turned from the window. For days he had been tormented by guilt. Until September this would be his last chance to say something about it.

"I feel rotten about that night. Not over Slocum. Over what I almost did to you."

Billy's deprecating wave gave Charles a feeling of immense relief. "I was just as much to blame," Billy said. "I think it was a fortunate lesson for both of us. Let the rest of the corps shout epithets and brawl if they want. We shouldn't, and we won't."

"Right you are." Charles was glad to have Billy's assurance, but he felt it was more hope than certainty.

Silence for a moment. Charles plucked a piece of stable straw off his trousers. The urge to confide was powerful.

"Let me tell you something else. Most of the time I hate being a Southerner around here. It means being second-rate in academic work—no, don't deny it. You Yankee boys always outshine us. We get by on toughness and nerve."

"Even if that were true, which I don't believe, those aren't bad qualities for a soldier."

Charles ignored the compliment. "Being a Southerner here means feeling inferior. Ashamed of where you come from. Mad because the rest of the corps acts so righteous"—his chin lifted—"which of course it damn well isn't."

"I guess smugness is a Yankee disease, Bison."

A smile softened the defiance in Charles's eyes. "I reckon no one except another Southerner could understand what I just said. Really understand it. But I thank you for listening." He held out his hand. "Friends?"

"Absolutely. Always." Their handclasp was firm, strong.

A whistle sounded from the North Dock. Billy grabbed his valise and bolted for the door. "When you write Brett, tell her I miss her."

474

"Tell her yourself." Charles's eyes sparkled. "I believe she'll be up here to visit soon after you get back."

Billy's mouth dropped open. "If you're joking—"

"I wouldn't joke with you. Not after the way you made hog slops out of Slocum." From the shelf Charles took his copy of Lévizac's French grammar. He opened it and removed a folded letter. "I got this from Brett only this morning. She said to surprise you at a"— he located the word in the letter—"propitious moment. Do you understand that?"

"You bet I do." Billy did a jig with his valise. Two cadets passing outside laughed. "Who's to chaperone her while she's here?"

"Orry. He's bringing Ashton, too. If he didn't, she'd throw a fit."

Even that news couldn't mar Billy's happiness. He sang and whooped all the way down the stairs, and Charles watched him race across the Plain in a most unsoldierly manner, throwing giddy salutes at a couple of professors.

Charles felt fine for all of half an hour. Then he heard four cadets in the next room arguing loudly about Kansas. An explanation, a handshake—such things might alleviate tensions between friends, but they'd never solve the problems plaguing the land. Not when some Southerners wouldn't even admit problems existed.

Hell, he thought. What an infernal mess.

Superintendent Lee and the younger officer strolled along the west edge of the Plain in leisurely fashion. A large crowd of hotel guests, including some children, had turned out to watch the exhibition of horsemanship, which the younger officer had ordered moved outdoors because of the intense heat in the riding hall. It was a Saturday afternoon in July; the surrounding hillsides shimmered in haze.

The heat didn't seem to inhibit the applause of the audience, or the enthusiasm with which the cadets performed. Some demonstrated the correct way to saddle and bridle a horse, and to mount and dismount. Others rode at different gaits or jumped their horses over a series of hay bales. A select group of first classmen charged straw dummies at the gallop. They thrust at the dummies with regulation dragoon sabers, curved swords over a yard long, as they rode by.

All this was watched critically by the younger officer, whose dress cap bore an orange pom-pom as well as an emblem—sheathed crossed sabers with the number 2 in the upper angle. Lieutenant Hawes of the Second Dragoons taught equitation. A year ago he had voluntarily begun a needed course of instruction in cavalry tactics—something the Academy had never before provided.

Because of the presence of spectators, Hawes had ordered his pupils to don their gray merino firemen's shirts, which were worn outside regulation gray kersey trousers but looked neat since the shirttails were trimmed square.

"Impressive," Lee said above the sound of thudding hoofs. "You have done a fine job, Lieutenant."

"Thank you, sir." Hawes pointed out a dark-haired, good-looking rider who handled his sorrel mare skillfully, almost appearing to float her over the hay bales. "There's the best horseman in the cadet corps. He shouldn't even be demonstrating with the others. He's only in the third class. But all this year he's been coming to the riding hall every free hour. When he starts equitation work in the fall, there isn't much I'll be able to teach him. I like to let him ride with the older boys because he keeps them on their mettle."

The cadet under discussion jumped another bale, coming down on his regulation Grimsley saddle with a natural grace. Lee watched the cadet's dark hair streaming behind him, studied his profile, thought a moment.

"South Carolina boy, isn't he?"

"That's right, sir. His name's Main."

"Ah, yes. Had a cousin here about ten years ago. The boy cuts a fine figure."

Lieutenant Hawes nodded enthusiastically. "He's the same sort as Stuart—only better-looking."

They both laughed. Then Hawes added, "I don't doubt he'll be posted to the dragoons or mounted rifles after graduation."

"Or perhaps to one of those new regiments of cavalry the secretary wants."

"Main's marks won't permit him a choice of branches," Hawes observed. "But in military studies he's exceptional. He seems delighted by the idea that a man can fight and be paid for it."

"That delight will pass when he sees his first battlefield."

"Yes, sir. In any case, I hope he manages to graduate. He's a scrapper. Again like Stuart."

"Then he'll be an asset wherever he goes."

Hawes didn't say anything. But he agreed, and he knew why he was able to endure the torture of instructing hundreds of inept boys

476

who would never be able to ride anything more frisky than a camp chair. He endured it in the hope of finding one outstanding pupil. This year it had happened.

Both officers watched Charles jump the last bale with a huge smile on his face. For a moment, horse and rider seemed to hang in the sultry sky, centaurlike.

36

Orry and his sisters arrived at the hotel on a Friday in September. They were in time for the evening parade. When Brett saw Billy, she clapped her hands in delight. He wore new chevrons.

He had been appointed company first sergeant, she later found out. He had just missed being named to the highest rank in the second class, sergeant major. He had saved the news as a surprise.

Ashton noticed her sister's pleased expression. Animosity boiled up within her—as well as an unexpected reaction to the sight of Billy Hazard. The surge of longing disgusted her. She suppressed it by force of will. He had abandoned her, and he would pay.

But she didn't want him on guard against her, now or in the future. Her face, bathed in sunshine, remained composed and sweetly smiling. A moment later she realized that two gentlemen from the hotel were watching her. That made her feel much better. Her drab little sister didn't get so much as a smidgen of attention. Not that kind, anyway.

Billy Hazard wasn't the only man on earth. Right in front of her, marching and counter-marching in precise formation, there were several hundred of them. Surely a few would be willing to help her enjoy this vacation—probably her last fling. James was pressing her for a wedding date.

She watched the trim, strong legs of the marching cadets. The tip of her tongue ran across her upper lip. Her loins felt warm and moist. She knew she was going to have a wonderful time at West Point.

For Orry, the parade was a highly emotional experience. It was good to hear the drumming again, mingled with the bugles and the fifes. The flags flying against the backdrop of hillsides splashed with the first yellow and crimson of autumn brought vivid memories and thoughts of loss. And when he spied Charles marching among the taller cadets in a flank company, he felt intense pride.

Next day, Billy invited Orry and the girls to observe his fencing class. Ashton said she had a headache and remained on the porch of the hotel. Brett and her brother spent an hour seated on a hard bench.

watching Billy and a dozen other cadets working out with various pieces of fencing equipment: hickory broadswords for the beginners, foils, or, in the case of Billy and his opponent, practice sabers.

The sword master, de Jaman, hovered near the visitors. Billy confused his opponent with a composed attack of feints, beats, and binds. "That young chap, he has a natural talent for this sport," the Frenchman said with the enthusiasm of a doting parent. "But, then, cadets who excel at scholarship usually do. Swordplay is above all cerebral."

"True," Orry said, recalling that he hadn't been very good at it.

Billy's match ended with a simple lunge that drove the protective button of his saber straight into the target on his opponent's padded vest. After the hit, he saluted his opponent, jerked off his mask, and turned to grin at Brett. She was on her feet, applauding.

Orry smiled broadly. Then he noticed the face of the opponent. A pronounced purplish half-circle showed beneath the boy's right eye. "How did he get that bruise?" Orry asked when Billy joined them.

Billy forced a smile. "I understand he had a discussion with one of his roommates."

"What kind of discussion?" Brett wanted to know.

"Something to do with Senator Douglas, I believe. My opponent's from Alabama, you see—" He let the sentence trail off.

Disturbed, Orry said, "Does much of that sort of thing happen here?"

"Oh, no, very little," Billy answered too quickly. His eyes met Orry's. Each saw that the other recognized the lie.

That evening Orry hiked off to Buttermilk Falls for what he termed his first legal visit to Benny Haven's. With Orry's permission, Billy took Brett to Flirtation Walk.

Shadowy couples glided by on the darkening path. Through the leaves of the overhanging trees, the last sunlight illuminated clouds high in the eastern sky. Below, on the river, the firefly lights of the Albany night boat moved slowly by.

Brett had put on her prettiest lace *canezou* and lace mittens—not much in vogue up North, she had been noticing. Billy thought her the loveliest creature he had ever seen:

"*Mademoiselle, vous êtes absolument ravissante.*"

She laughed and took hold of his arm. "That must be a compliment. It sounds too pretty to be anything else. What does it mean?"

They had paused beside one of the benches set into a nook along the path. Nervously, he took her mittened hands in his.

"It means I finally found a practical use for all those hours and hours of French."

She laughed again. Put at ease, he bent forward and planted a gentle kiss on her lips.

"It means I think you're beautiful."

The kiss flustered her, even though it was what she had been craving. She couldn't think of a thing to say. She feared that if she used the word *love* in any way, he might laugh. Out of desperation, she rose on tiptoe, slipped her arm around his neck and kissed him again, fiercely this time. They sank down on the bench, holding hands in the dark.

"Lord, I'm glad you're here, Brett. I thought this moment would never arrive. I thought my leave would never end."

"Surely you enjoyed going home."

"Oh, yes, in a way. I was glad to see Lehigh Station again, but not nearly as glad as I thought I'd be. Everyone was there but the one person who matters most. The days dragged, and by the end I couldn't wait to pack and go. George understood, but my mother didn't. I think my boredom hurt her feelings. I was sorry about that. I tried to conceal how I felt, but I—I couldn't stop missing you."

After a moment's silence, she murmured, "I've been missing you, too, Billy." He clasped her hands more tightly between his. "You can't imagine how lonesome I was all year. I lived for the days that brought a new letter from you. I don't see how you ever have time to be lonesome here. The schedule you keep is just ferocious. I've very much enjoyed meeting your friends, but I saw some of them give me queer looks the first time I said something."

"They were charmed by your accent."

"Charmed, or disgusted?" A couple of cadets—Yankees, she presumed—had cast decidedly unfriendly glances her way.

He didn't reply. He was aware of the rudeness, even outright hostility, some of the Northern boys directed at the occasional female visitor from the South. The difference in his background and Brett's presented some practical problems for the future, problems he didn't want to face but could not indefinitely ignore.

This wasn't the time to discuss them, though. He shifted his sword belt out of the way and reached into his pocket. From it he pulled the scrap of black velvet snipped from his furlough cap. He twisted it in his fingers as he explained the tradition connected with it, concluding:

"But I couldn't give it to my best girl when I went home this summer. She was in South Carolina."

He pressed the velvet band into her palm. She touched the wreath of gold embroidery, whispered, "Thank you."

"I hope"—he swallowed—"I hope you'll be my best girl always."

"I want to be, Billy. Forever."

A cadet and a companion passing in the dark overheard that. Being acquaintances and not lovers, they laughed in a cynical way. Billy and Brett didn't hear. They were sitting with their arms around each other, kissing.

Presently they strolled back to the top of the bluff. Billy had never experienced such a perfect night or such a certainty that the future would be equally perfect.

Figures loomed in the dark—a cadet lieutenant with a girl on his arm. The cadet, from Michigan, had never been particularly friendly. Now, as he and his companion went on toward Flirtation Walk, he spoke so that Brett would hear.

"That's the one. Do you suppose a Southern girl with a Yankee beau gives lessons in the mistreatment of niggers? You know, just in case he marries into the family?"

The girl tittered. Billy started after them. Brett pulled him back. "Don't. It isn't worth it."

The couple passed out of sight. Billy fumed, then offered his own apology for the cadet lieutenant's behavior. Brett assured him she had seen worse. But the earlier mood was shattered. The insulting remark reminded him that if he married her, each of them would face the wrath of bigots in their own part of the country.

Of course his brother George had dealt with that kind of hatred when he brought Constance from Texas. He had dealt with it and overcome it. If one Hazard could do it, so could he.

"Law, what is this smelly old place?" Ashton whispered as the Yankee first classman again attempted to insert the key in the lock. The darkness made it difficult.

"Delafield's Pepperbox," the cadet said in a slurry voice. He had obviously drunk a lot before spiriting her out of the hotel, but she didn't mind. He would probably give her a better time because of it. He was a rather thick-witted sort, but very big through the shoulders. She presumed the bigness was duplicated elsewhere.

"It's the ordnance laboratory," he went on, finally getting the door open. Odors of pitch, paste, and brimstone assailed her. "First classmen

482

get to work down here. We mix up powder, take Congreve rockets apart—''

''How did you get a key?''

''Bought it from a cadet who graduated last June. Aren't you coming in? I thought you said you wanted to—''

He wasn't sufficiently drunk to be able to finish the sentence.

''I did say that, but I didn't know you'd bring me to someplace that smelled this bad.''

She hesitated in the doorway. Above her, one of the building's castellated turrets hid some of the autumn stars. The building was secluded below the northern rim of the Plain.

From the dark interior, the hard-breathing cadet tugged her hand. ''Come in and I'll give you a souvenir. Every girl who stays at the hotel wants a West Point souvenir.''

He lurched to her, leaned against the door frame, and fingered one of the gilt buttons on his coat. She had inspected them closely before. They said *Cadet* at the top, *U.S.M.A.* at the bottom, and had an eagle and shield in the center.

Still she hesitated. The stink of the laboratory was overpowering. But so was the need that had been rising in her for weeks.

''You mean that if I come in there with you, you'll give me a button?''

He flicked a nail against one of them. ''Just take your pick.''

''Well—all right.'' A slow smile. ''But those weren't the buttons I had in mind,'' she added as she put her hand below his waist.

Later, in the dark, he whispered, ''How do you feel?''

''Like I didn't get nearly enough, sweet.''

An audible gulp. ''I have a couple of friends. I could fetch them. They'd be mighty grateful. By the time I get back, I'll be ready to go to the well once more myself.''

Ashton lay resting, her forearm across her eyes.

''Fetch them, dear. Fetch as many as you like, but don't keep me waiting too long. Just be sure every boy you bring is willing to present me with a souvenir.''

''I tell you I saw it,'' said a New Jersey cadet whom Billy knew fairly well. It was three days after the Mains had left for New York. With his index finger, the cadet marked a two-inch width of space

483

in the air. "A cardboard box about this big. Inside she had a button from everyone she entertained."

"How many buttons?"

"Seven."

Billy stared, obviously nonplussed. "In an hour and a half?"

"Or a little less."

"Were any of them from her part of the country?"

"Not a one. Appears that some Yankees can get over a prejudice against Southrons mighty fast."

"Seven. I can't believe it. When Bison hears, he'll start issuing challenges right and left."

"Defending fair womanhood—that sort of thing?"

"Sure," Billy said. "She's his cousin."

The other cadet blurted, "Look, no one forced her. Fact is, I'd say it was the other way 'round. Anyway—I don't think Bison will find out."

"Why not?"

"The lady claimed she'd be back for another visit inside of six months, but she said if any of the seven mentioned her name in the meantime—her name or anything else about the evening—she'd hear of it and there'd be hell to pay."

"What kind of hell? Did she get specific?"

"No. And maybe nobody believed her, but they're sure acting like they did. Guess it's because they'd all like to see her again," he added with a smile that was smug, yet curiously nervous, too. "Or maybe 'cause they don't want a close view of Main's bowie knife."

Billy suspected Ashton had gulled the seven cadets. He knew of no plans for the sisters to return. Then he realized he had failed to see the obvious—which was right in front of him in the other cadet's smirk.

"Wait a minute. If everyone's keeping quiet, how do you know all this?"

The smile widened, lewd now, but the undercurrent of nervousness remained. "I was number seven in line. Here's the best part: she didn't want coat buttons from all of us who—ah—took advantage of her generosity."

Billy felt queasy. "What did she want?"

"Fly buttons."

He turned pale. All he could say was, "Why are you telling me?"

"Friendly gesture." That rang false, but Billy kept quiet. "Besides,

484

I saw you sparking the other sister and figured you'd like to know. You drew the better of the pair—from an honorable gentleman's standpoint, anyway." He winked. Billy barely saw that and didn't respond in an amused fashion.

"Godamighty. Seven fly buttons. We've got to keep it from Bison."

The cadet's smile was gone. "That's the real reason I came to see you, Hazard. I meant what I said about Bison and that hideout knife of his. Not many men scare me, but he does. He scares all seven of us. There'll be no bragging, no talk at all. Count on that."

Later, after the initial shock passed and Billy was again alone, he realized the cadet was right about one thing: he'd been incredibly lucky to escape a liaison with Brett's sister. He didn't know what to call her, but there was certainly something wrong with her. He was thankful that she was no longer interested in him. During the entire visit she had barely spoken to him, and had acted as if he didn't exist. She had forgotten about him, thank the Lord.

37

Virgilia pulled the tattered shawl over her shoulders and pinned it. Then she resumed stirring the cornmeal gruel on the small iron stove. One of the stove's legs was gone, replaced by a stack of broken bricks.

A November storm was piling a cosmetic layer of white on the tin roofs of nearby hovels. Snow filled the ruts in the lane of frozen mud outside the door. Cutting wind rattled the oiled-paper windows and brought snowflakes through gaps in the wall near a tacked-up engraving of Frederick Douglass.

Grady sat at a rickety table. His faded blue flannel shirt was buttoned at the throat. He had lost about thirty pounds and no longer looked fit. When he smiled—not often these days—he showed perfect upper teeth, hand-cut and wired in place. Only a slight yellow cast betrayed their artificiality.

Opposite Grady was a visitor—a slim, fastidious Negro with light brown skin, curly gray hair, and an intense quality in his brown eyes. The man's name was Lemuel Tubbs. He had displayed a pronounced limp when he walked in.

The cup of thin coffee Virgilia had set before Tubbs was untasted. He didn't enjoy visiting the slums in the midst of a blizzard, but duty required it. He was speaking earnestly to Grady.

"An account of your experiences would lend authenticity to our next public meeting and increase its impact. Nothing is more powerful in persuading the public of the evils of slavery than the narratives of those who have endured it."

"A public meeting, you say." Grady thought aloud. "I don't know, Mr. Tubbs. There's still the problem of South Carolina slave catchers reading about it."

"I appreciate the concern," Tubbs replied in a sympathetic way. "Only you can make the decision, of course."

He hesitated before raising a difficult final point. "If the decision should be affirmative, however, we would impose one restriction. We want the strongest possible condemnation of slavery, but there should be no appeals for violent uprisings in the South. That sort of talk alarms and alienates some whites whom we desperately need for the furtherance of our cause. To be blunt, it scares them out of donating money."

"So you water down the truth?" Virgilia asked. "You prostitute yourself and your organization for a few pieces of silver?"

A frown chased across the visitor's face; for the first time his eyes betrayed a hint of anger. "I would hardly put it in those terms, Miss Hazard." She still went by that name in anti-slavery circles, preferring it to Mrs. Grady.

The truth was, the leaders of the movement in Philadelphia were sharply divided on the question of accepting help from Virgilia and her lover, because their extreme opinions tended to create problems. As a matter of fact, so did their mere presence. Part of the leadership wanted nothing whatever to do with them; the other faction, of which Tubbs was the foremost representative, was willing to use Grady provided he would submit himself to a measure of control. Reluctantly, Tubbs decided he'd better emphasize that again.

"In dealing with power blocs, certain compromises are always necessary if you hope to achieve—"

"Mr. Tubbs," Grady interrupted, "I think you'd better leave. We aren't interested in making an appearance under your terms."

Tubbs labored to control his voice and his temper. "I wish you wouldn't be so hasty. Perhaps you'll reconsider if I add this. I believe you can be very useful to the cause of abolition—but not everyone in our society shares that view. It took a long time to persuade some of our members to agree to tender this invitation." A glance at Virgilia. "I doubt it will be repeated."

"Grady doesn't want to speak to milksops and whores," Virgilia said with a toss of her head. Her hair was uncombed, dull, dirty. "Our brand of abolitionism is Mr. Garrison's."

"Burning the Constitution? That's what you favor?" Tubbs shook his head. On Independence Day, Garrison had caused a national uproar by touching a match to a copy of the Constitution at a rally near Boston. Virgilia obviously thought he had done the right thing.

"Why not? The Constitution is precisely what Garrison called it: a covenant with death and an agreement with hell."

"Such statements only alienate the people we need most—" Tubbs began.

Virgilia sneered. "Oh, come, Mr. Tubbs. What kind of attitude is that—if you really believe in the cause?"

Again his eyes flashed. "Perhaps I demonstrate my belief in a different way than yours, Miss Hazard."

"By refusing to take risks? By dressing so splendidly and hobnobbing with bigoted white people? By refusing to sacrifice your own personal comfort and—"

He exploded then, striking the table. "Don't prate at me about risks or sacrifice. I grew up as a slave in Maryland, and when I was fourteen I ran away. I took my younger brother with me. We were caught. Sent to slavebreakers. They left me this"—he slapped his bad leg—"but they did worse to him. He's had a deranged mind ever since."

Grady was contemptuous. "And you don't care about paying them back?"

"Of course I care! Once, nothing else mattered. Then I escaped to Philadelphia, and in a year or two, when the furor and fear of pursuit abated, I began to think. I've become less interested in revenge for myself than in liberty for others. It's the system I hate most—the *system* I want to abolish."

"I say let it end by violence!" Virgilia exclaimed.

"No. Any movement in that direction will only guarantee the prolongation of slavery, and all the repressions that go with it—"

Tubbs faltered, noting their hostility. He rose, carefully placed his stovepipe hat on his gray head. "I'm afraid I'm wasting my breath."

She laughed at him. "Indeed you are."

Tubbs pressed his lips together but said nothing. He turned and limped toward the door. Virgilia called in a nasty voice, "Be sure to close it on your way out."

There was no reply; the door shut softly but firmly.

Grady had been sitting very straight in his chair. All at once his shoulders slumped. "Not that closing the door will do a blessed bit of good." He shuddered, partly from cold, partly from despair. "Throw some more wood in."

"There isn't any more wood—and only enough money to get me to Lehigh Station." She wasn't angry, just stating facts. She spooned gruel into a tin bowl and set it in front of him. "I'll have to go home again."

Grady peered into the bowl, grimaced, and pushed it away. "I don't like for you to do that. I hate to have you beg."

"I never beg. I tell them what I need, and I get it. Why shouldn't I? They have enough. They squander more in a single day than all the people here in niggertown spend in a year." She stood behind him, trying to warm him by kneading his neck with her fingers. "Soldiers at war don't expect to live in luxury."

"Tubbs doesn't think we're at war."

"Eunuchs like Tubbs have been too comfortable, too long. They've forgotten. We'll win the war without them. The jubilee will come, Grady. I know it."

Listless and unconvinced, he reached for her hand while she stared into space. Snow continued to blow in through cracks in the wall, settling on the blankets that served as their bed. In a corner, where there was an even larger crack, the snow had already formed a fluffy loaf on a big pile of rags. Grady picked rags to keep them alive. When there were no rags, he stole. When even that method failed, Virgilia went back to Lehigh Station for a few days.

"I can't feel any heat from the stove," she said. "We'd better crawl under the blankets for a while."

"Sometimes I feel so bad for getting you into this kind of life—"

"Hush, Grady." Her cold fingers pressed his mouth. "I chose it. We're soldiers, you and I. We're going to help Captain Weston bring the jubilee."

Grady's look reproved her. "You aren't supposed to say his name out loud, Virgilia."

She laughed, angering him with her white woman's superiority. "Surely you're not taken in by that nonsense? All those code names and cipher books? Dozens of people know the true identity of the man who calls himself Captain Weston. Hundreds know about his activities, and millions more will know in a few months. After we've helped him free your people down South, we'll deal with mine up here. We'll deal with every white man and woman who opposed us actively or by indifference. Starting, I think, with my brother Stanley and that bitch he married."

Her smile and her whispered words scared Grady so badly he forgot his anger.

"I don't mind going home for clothing or food," she assured him as they settled themselves under the cold blankets, which smelled of dirt and wood smoke. "But I wish you'd let me take you along someti—"

"No." It was the one point on which he never bent. "You know what people would do to us if we showed up together in that little town."

"Oh, yes, I know," she sighed, pushing herself against him. "I hate them for it. God, how I hate them, my darling. We'll repay them, too. We—oh."

What she felt startled her. Even in the cold he wanted her. Soon they were fighting off their mutual misery in the only way they knew.

The fringe of the winter storm passed over Lehigh Station, dusting the ground and the rooftops with white. It was still snowing intermittently when Virgilia arrived on the night boat. Next year she would be able to make these trips in a heated railway coach with no concern about whether the river had frozen. The Lehigh Road had announced plans to extend service to Bethlehem and on up the valley.

Much as she hated her family, she understood that it was only their tolerance that made it possible for her to survive in Philadelphia. Specifically, the tolerance of her brother George and his wife, who let her stay a night or so at Belvedere and permitted her to steal away with a burlap bag full of cast-off clothing or a valise loaded with tins and paper-wrapped packages of food. Despite her steady drift into the mental set of a revolutionary, a certain practicality remained in Virgilia's makeup. She really knew better than to bring Grady to Lehigh Station, and she tried to time her arrivals so that darkness concealed them. Certain bigoted citizens of the village might actually attempt to harm her if they saw her. She knew who they were and had marked them for elimination at the proper time.

Clad only in thin woolen gloves and a coat too light for the season, she struggled up the hill in blowing snow. By the time she reached Belvedere, the snow had turned her hair white. A buggy and blanketed horse stood at the hitching post. She let herself in—George allowed that—and heard voices from the parlor: Constance, George, and another she recognized as the local Roman Catholic priest.

"What is a Christian response to the Kansas issue?" the priest was asking. "That is the question which plagues me these days. I feel obliged to discuss the matter with each of my parishioners, so I will know their—"

He stopped, noticing Virgilia in the doorway. George looked at her with surprise, Constance with some dismay.

"Good evening, George. Constance. Father Donnelly."

"We weren't expecting you—" George began. They never knew when she would arrive; he made the same remark each time. Lately she had begun to find him tiresome.

An insincere smile acknowledged his statement. Then she said to

491

the priest. "There is no Christian response to the situation in Kansas. It is so-called Christians who have enslaved the Negroes. Any man who dares to bring a slave over a territorial border invites—demands— the only response which is possible. A bullet. If I were out there, I'd be the first to pull a trigger."

She made the statement in such a reasonable way that the elderly priest was speechless.

George wasn't. Livid but controlled, he said, "You'd better go upstairs and get out of those wet clothes."

She stared at him for a moment. "Of course. Good evening, Father."

After the priest left, George paced up and down, fuming. "I don't know why we tolerate Virgilia. Sometimes I think we're fools."

Constance shook her head. "You don't want to treat her the way Stanley does. She's still your sister."

He stared down at the little puddle of melted snow left by Virgilia's shoes. "I find it increasingly hard to remember that."

"But we must," she said.

Later that night, George woke in bed to find Constance stirring in the dark.

"What's wrong? Are you sick again?"

The explanation came to mind because she had been weak for a month or so. She had lost a child spontaneously about sixty days after realizing she was once more pregnant. It was the third time it had happened in as many years, and each loss seemed to produce physical aftereffects that lasted longer than previous ones: dizziness, sweats, and nausea in the night. George was worried not only about his wife's health but about her state of mind, since the doctor hinted that she might never carry another child to full term.

"I'm fine," she said. "I must get dressed and leave for an hour. There's another shipment due."

"That's right. I forgot."

"You go back to sleep."

He was already putting his feet on the chilly floor. "I'll do no such thing. The weather's miserable. You can't walk all the way to the shed. Let me put on some clothes, and I'll bring the buggy to the front door."

They sparred another minute or so, she telling him he needn't go out into the cold with her and he insisting. Both knew he would have his way. The truth was, Constance was happy he wanted to accompany her. She felt weak and on the verge of a severe chill. She hated the thought of venturing into the winter night alone, though she would have done it.

George was glad to go for another reason, too. He could see and perhaps speak with the new arrival. More than all the orators, editorialists, and divines put together, the passengers traveling the underground railroad helped to shape his thinking about the issue dividing the country. He snapped his galluses over his shoulders and patted her arm.

"I'm going. No more argument."

Twenty minutes later, he drove the creaking buggy up to the shed at the rear of the mill property. A lantern glimmered inside. He helped Constance climb down with the valise she had brought from the house. Impulsively, she kissed him. Her lips and his cheek were icy, stiff as parchment. Yet the kiss was warming.

She hurried to the door and gave the signal: two knocks, a pause, then two more. George crunched through the brilliantly lit snow and felt it spill over the tops of his shoes and soak his stockings. The storm had passed. The moon hung in the clear sky like a fine china plate.

Belzer, the merchant, opened the door cautiously. He started when he saw a second figure.

"It's only me," George said.

"Oh, yes. Come in, come in."

The passenger was seated at a table with a square of jerky beef in his hands. He was a muscular, reddish-brown man whose cheekbones suggested some Indian blood. He was about thirty-five but all his curly hair was white. George could imagine why.

"This is Kee," Belzer said, as proud as if he were introducing a member of his own family. "He comes to us all the way from Alabama. His name is short for Cherokee. His maternal grandmother belonged to the tribe."

"Well, Kee, I'm glad you're here," Constance said. She set the valise beside the table. "There are boots in here and two extra shirts. Do you have a winter coat?"

"Yes'm." The runaway had a resonant bass voice. He seemed nervous in their presence.

"They gave him one at the station near Wheeling," Belzer said.

"Good," Constance said. "Most times Canada is even colder than Pennsylvania. But once you're there, you'll have no more worries about slave catchers."

"I want to work," Kee told them. "I be good cook."

"I gather that's what he did most of his life," Belzer said.

George was only partly aware of the conversation, so fascinated was he with the former slave's posture and mannerisms. Kee's head seemed to sit low between his shoulders, as if held in a perpetual cringe. Even here, in free territory, his dark eyes showed fear and distrust. He kept darting glances at the door, as if he expected someone to crash through at any moment.

"—worked for a particularly strict, vicious master," Belzer was saying. "Kee, show them what you showed me, will you please?"

The runaway laid the untasted jerky aside. He stood up, unbuttoned his shirt, and slipped it to his waist. Constance choked softly and gripped her husband's arm. George was equally sickened by the sight of so much scar tissue. It ran from Kee's shoulder blades to the small of his back; some of it looked as if a nest of snakes had petrified just beneath the skin.

Belzer's mild eyes showed fury. "Some of it was done with a whip, some with heated irons. When did it happen the first time, Kee?"

"When I be nine. I took berries from master's garden." He cupped his fingers to illustrate a small handful. "This many berries."

George shook his head. He knew why his own beliefs had become rock-hard in recent months.

Later, back in bed in Belvedere, George held Constance in his arms to warm them both. "Every time I encounter a man like Kee, I wonder why we've tolerated slavery this long."

He couldn't see the admiration in her eyes as she replied, "George, do you realize how much you've changed? You wouldn't have said such a thing when I first met you."

"Maybe not. But I know how I feel now. We've got to put a stop to slavery. Preferably with the consent and cooperation of the people who perpetuate the system. But if they refuse to listen to reason, then without it."

"What if it came to a choice between abolition and your friendship with Orry? He is one of those perpetuating the system, after all."

"I know. I hope it never comes to a choice like that."

"But if it did, what would happen? I'm not trying to press you, but I've been anxious to know for a long time. I understand how much you like and respect Orry—"

Despite the pain of it, his conscience would permit but one answer. "I'd sacrifice friendship before I sacrificed what I believe."

She hugged him. Clinging to him, she soon fell asleep.

He lay awake a good while longer, seeing snaky scar tissue and dark eyes constantly darting toward a doorway. And after he drifted off, he dreamed of a black man screaming while someone seared him with an iron.

If members of the Southern planter class represented one extreme that George disliked, his own sister represented another. During her two-day visit at Belvedere they argued about popular sovereignty, the fugitive laws, indeed almost every facet of the slavery issue. Virgilia's position on all of them left no room for compromise.

"I would solve the whole problem with a single stroke," she said as she sat at the supper table with George and Constance. Fearing the conversation would drift into acrimony—it usually did—Constance had already sent the children off to play. "One day's work in the South, and it would all be over. That's my dream, anyway." Virgilia added with a smile that made George shiver.

She pressed her fork into her third wedge of pound cake, took a bite, then poured on more hot rum sauce from the silver server. She looked at her brother calmly. "You can shudder and grimace all you want, George. You can prate about scruples and mercy until you turn blue, but the day's coming."

"Virgilia, that's rot. A slave revolution can't possibly succeed."

"Of course it can—properly financed and organized. One glorious night of fire and justice. Iniquity washed away in a great river of blood."

He was so appalled he almost dropped his demitasse. He and Constance stared at each other, then at their visitor. She was gazing at the ceiling—or at some apocalyptic scene beyond.

George wanted to shout at her. Instead he tried to make light of her remarks.

"You should try writing stage melodramas."

She looked at him suddenly. "Joke all you want. It's coming."

Unintimidated by the chilling stare, Constance said, "You realize, of course, that it is fear of revolution by the black majority that prevents many Southerners from even discussing gradual, compensated emancipation?"

"Compensated emancipation is a pernicious idea. As Mr. Garrison says, it's the same as paying a thief to surrender stolen property."

"Nevertheless, what Southerners see in the wake of emancipation

495

are freed slaves coming after them with rocks and pitchforks. Your inflammatory speculations don't help the situation."

Virgilia shoved her dessert plate away. "It's more than speculation, I promise you."

"So you've said. Repeatedly," George said in a brusque way. "While we're on the subject, let me be blunt about something. You ought to sever your connection with Captain Weston."

Her eyes flew wide. For once her voice was faint. "What do you know about Captain Weston?"

"I know he exists. I know Weston is merely a *nom de guerre*, and that he's as much of an extremist as the worst Southern hotspur."

She managed scorn. "Have you hired spies to watch me?"

"Don't be an idiot. I have business contacts all over the state, and I know many of the legislators in Harrisburg. All of them hear things. One thing they hear is that Captain Weston is actively fomenting black revolt down South. He's stirring up tremendous animosity, even among people who would otherwise oppose slavery. You'd better stay away from him, or you'll suffer the consequences."

"If there are consequences, as you call them, I shall be proud to bear them."

His mind floundered. What was he to do with her? He tried another tack. "I wouldn't be so quick to say that. There are also plenty of men in Pennsylvania who hate abolitionists. Violent men."

"Is that what success and money do to you, George? Rob you of principle and replace it with cowardice?" Like an affronted queen, she rose and left the room.

Constance pressed her palms against her eyes. "I can't stand her any longer. What an obsessed, wretched creature she is!"

He reached out to take her hand and calm her, but his gaze remained fixed on the door through which Virgilia had vanished.

"It goes beyond obsession," he said softly. "Sometimes I don't think she's sane."

Eyes open and bulging, discolored tongue jutting between clenched teeth, the man hung from a rafter. From the angle of his head, it was clear the noose had snapped his neck.

Below the slowly turning, rigor-stiffened form, half a dozen men spoke in low voices. Two held smoking torches. Behind them stood long crates bearing painted inscriptions: GEOR. AL. MISS. One of the crates had been torn open with a crowbar. It contained new carbines.

Mortally terrified, Grady saw all this through a crack in the barn door. He had been sent from Philadelphia to the outskirts of Lancaster with a coded dispatch, two pages long. The man to whom he was to deliver the dispatch was hanging in the barn. Thank the Lord he had heard the voices as he crept through the feedlot and stopped in time.

He started to sneak away again. A sow suckling piglets honked loudly as he passed her pen. The noise brought an armed man to the barn door.

"Stop, you!"

Grady broke into a run. A shot whined over his head.

"Catch that nigger. He saw us."

Grady ran as he had never run in all his life. Now and then he risked a look back. The men were pursuing on horseback. Behind them, the bright red barn was bathed in the sullen light of a December sundown. All at once flames licked from the hayloft, then began to swallow the huge, gaudy hex sign painted on the building. They had fired the place.

Their shots fell short but drove him on. He scrambled wildly over a stone stile, lost his balance, and smashed his mouth hard as he fell. Blood dripped, but he paid little attention, panting as he plunged into thick woods. He finally eluded the horsemen by lying in cold water under a creek bank for half an hour. Only then did he realize the price he had paid for his life. As he touched his upper lip, tears brimmed in his eyes.

Next morning he staggered into the hovel in Philadelphia. There he permitted himself to break down at last. His thoughts tumbled out.

"Captain Weston's dead. I saw him hanging. They burned him, too, right along with his barn. They almost got me. I ran and fell. The wires came loose. I lost my teeth. Goddamn it, I lost my teeth." Tears rolled down his cheeks as he slumped in Virgilia's arms.

"Now, now." She held him, stroking his head. "Don't cry. Captain Weston wasn't much of a leader. He talked too much. Too many people knew about him. Someday another man will come along, a better one. Then the revolution will succeed."

"Yes, but—I lost my new teeth, goddamn it."

She cradled his head on her breasts and didn't answer. She was gazing past him, smiling faintly as she imagined white blood flowing.

38

Ashton turned the key, then tested the door to be certain it was locked. She rushed across her bedroom, pulled the shutters in, and latched them. She tried to counsel herself against panic, but with little success.

She took off her clothes, layer after layer, flinging the garments every which way. Naked, she stepped in front of the pier glass and scrutinized her reflection.

Could anyone tell? No, not yet. Her stomach remained smooth and flat. But it wouldn't stay that way long. About ninety days had passed since the trip to West Point. Her recklessness had caught up with her.

It couldn't have happened at a worse time. About a month ago, sick of Huntoon's constant importuning, she had given in and agreed to marry him in the spring. At that time she had already missed one flow. She told herself it was because of some slight female problem that would clear up, and not the consequence of the enjoyable night in the powder laboratory.

But the problem didn't clear up. And Huntoon spoke with Orry; a date in March was chosen. Now she was trapped.

"Godamighty, what am I going to do?" she asked the dark-haired girl staring at her from the glass.

Orry. She'd go to Orry. He'd be kind and understanding. She managed to convince herself of that for all of five minutes, while she dressed and touched up her hair with comb and pins. Then she realized she was a ninny. When she thought about it seriously, she knew her brother would never agree to do what she wanted.

Brett, then? She ruled that out instantly. She was damned if she'd give her sister the satisfaction of knowing she was in a fix. Besides, Brett was much too cozy with Orry these days. Chasing him everywhere, conferring with him over this and that, as if she were the mistress of Mont Royal—presumptuous little bitch. If Ashton confessed to her, Brett would run straight to their brother and snitch.

A dreadful pinpoint headache began in the center of her forehead. She unlocked the bedroom door and walked slowly down the hall. At the bottom of the staircase she thought she felt a quiver in her middle. Frantically, she pressed her fingers against her skirt, searching for signs of growth.

She felt nothing. Must be gas. Lately every part of her had been upset.

Brett appeared from the back of the house, a letter in her hand. "Billy's studying chemistry. He says Professor Bailey is just wonderful. He shows them how chemistry applies to all sorts of things, like the manufacture of guncotton, and the heliograph—"

"Think I give a hang about Billy's affairs?" Ashton cried, dashing past her.

"Ashton, what in the world is the matter with you late—?"

The slammed front door chopped off the rest.

Terrified and half blinded by the low-slanting December sunlight, Ashton went running down to the Ashley. She nearly pitched off the end of the pier before she realized where she was. For a while she gazed at the light-flecked river and toyed with the idea of suicide.

But a gritty inner streak rebelled. James Huntoon might be a soft, silly slug, but he traveled in important political circles, and he was becoming more influential all the time. She didn't intend to throw away her marriage, or the opportunity it presented, by drowning herself like some simpering heroine in a Simms novel.

What to do, then? Where to turn? By behaving as she had, she had courted this kind of trouble, and although she had known she might be tripped up, she had never prepared for it in any practical way. Well, there was no help to be found at Mont Royal. All the nigger women hated and distrusted her. It was mutual. Nor did she consider her poor mother as a possible source of assistance. All Clarissa did was drift through the house with a fey smile, or sit for hours rubbing out lines she had inscribed the day before on the family tree.

"Damn," Ashton said to a great blue jay grouching at her from a wild palm. "There isn't a single person in the whole state of South Carolina who's smart enough or trustworthy enough to—"

Abruptly, a face floated into her thoughts. She could help, if anyone could. At least she might know to whom Ashton could turn. Everyone said her niggers just worshiped her. Moreover, they trusted her implicitly.

But how would she feel about the solution Ashton was determined to achieve? Some women thought that sort of thing a sin.

Only way to find out is to ask, she said to herself. What choice did she have unless she was willing to suffer utter ruin? Which she most definitely was not.

Surprisingly, the more she thought about her inspiration, the better she felt. She slept soundly and looked clear-eyed and rested when she came downstairs next morning, fancily dressed and carrying her gloves and parasol.

Immediately after she called for the carriage, Orry appeared from around the corner of the house. His right sleeve was rolled up, and there was a hammer in his hand.

"My, aren't you pretty today," he said, tucking the hammer in his belt.

"I declare, Orry—you must think I'm some old chore woman who never fixes herself up. That's Brett, not me."

He fingered his long beard and let the remark pass. "Going calling?"

"Yes, sir, over to Resolute. It's been way too long since I paid my respects to Madeline."

A wrinkled black footman opened the door. "Mistress Madeline? In the music room. If you'll please wait here, I'll announce you, Miss Ashton."

He marched away with a stately stride. Another door opened. Justin poked his head out.

"Who's that? Oh, Ashton. Good morning. Haven't seen you over this way in an age."

"Yes, indeed, it's been too long." Ashton smiled. "You look wrought up, Justin."

"Why not?" He strolled toward her, holding up a copy of the *Mercury*. "More of those infernal Republican groups are forming up North, and they all want the same damn thing—repeal of the fugitive-slave laws and the Kansas-Nebraska bill."

Ashton sighed. "Isn't that just terrible? Orry said there was one better piece of news, though. He told me that out in Kansas they elected a pro-slavery delegate to the Congress." She was never completely sure of such things: "Didn't they?"

"'Deed they did. But a lot of good men had to ride over the border from Missouri to ensure that the election would come out the right way. I hope to heaven this new party withers on the vine. It's clearly nothing more than a combination of Yankee fanatics out to do us dirt."

Slapping the paper against his palm, he left. Ashton was grateful. She was nervous. She fished a bit of crisp lace from her reticule and

501

dabbed her upper lip dry. The footman returned to conduct her to the music room.

Madeline rose to greet her, smoothing her skirts and smiling. It was a polite smile, but that was all; the two women had never been more than acquaintances. Ashton's eyes flicked to the little book Madeline had laid on the table: *Walden, or Life in the Woods*. She'd never heard of it. People said Madeline read a lot of trashy Northern books.

"This is an unexpected pleasure, Ashton. You're looking fit."

"So—so are you." After that hesitation, she gained control of herself, resolving to do the best job of acting she had ever done.

"May I ring for some refreshments?"

"No, thank you. I came here to talk very seriously to you. No one else can help me." With an exaggerated glance over her shoulder, she added, "Is it all right if I shut the door to keep our conversation private?"

Madeline's dark brows lifted. "Of course. Is someone in your family sick? Is it Orry?"

Ashton rushed to the door and closed it. She might have noticed the way Madeline mentioned her brother with a catch in her voice, but she was too preoccupied with her own performance.

"No, they're all fine. I'm the one in need of assistance. I won't mince words, Madeline. I don't know of another soul I can trust to advise me. I certainly can't go to my family. You see, a few months ago, I—" This time the pause was deliberate, designed for a poignant effect. "I committed an indiscretion. And now I'm, as they say, in trouble."

"I see."

Mercifully, Madeline's tone held no condemnation. She gestured to a chair with a pale hand. "Please, sit down."

"Thank you. It's such a strain bearing the secret all by myself. I'm just about out of my wits—" Tears sprang to her eyes almost the second she willed it. Why not? She was desperate. Everything had to work perfectly, or she was finished. There would be no second chance here.

"I can understand," Madeline murmured.

"You know so many people in the neighborhood—they all think so well of you—that's why I knew I could speak. Beg your help—"

"I gather you don't want to have the child?"

"I can't! I'm to marry James in the spring. The date's already set. I love him, Madeline—"

Did the lie sound believable? Under her skirts her knees were shaking. She pressed them together.

"But God forgive me—" She sighed a little too much on that, she thought. She cast her eyes down to her lap. "The child is not his."

"I won't ask whose it is. But I'd be less than honest if I didn't say this about the solution you're seeking: morally, I disapprove of it."

Now, Ashton thought in a panic. Now! Don't hold back. She leaned forward from the waist, her sobs so artful they almost felt real to her.

"Oh, I was afraid you might. So many women do. I appreciate that you have your convictions. I freely admit I've been sinful. But must I lose James and see my entire life destroyed because of one stupid mistake? Can't you at least give me a name? I know there are people in the low country who help girls in trouble. I'll never reveal the source of the information. Just tell me where to turn." She laced her hands together, as if in prayer. "Please, Madeline."

Madeline studied her guest. Gradually, the sight of Ashton's reddened eyes overcame her suspicions. She glided to the younger woman with a rustle of skirts, slipped her arm around Ashton's shoulder, and said as Ashton clasped her hand:

"Calm yourself. I'll help you. I can't pretend to believe it's right. But then, as you say, neither is it right for your life to be wrecked because of a few moments of uncontrollable emotion. We all have those," she added. Then, thoughtfully: "I know of a woman who lives back in the marshes. She said I could call on her if I ever needed help. It wouldn't be safe for you to go to her alone. You'd need a companion."

Ashton's upturned face had grown bright with hope. Madeline took a long breath, as if she were about to dive into a deep pool—which was almost the way she felt, not really wanting to involve herself in the problems of this shallow, prideful girl who turned to her only because she was desperate. Yet Ashton was a human being and in need of help. It was Madeline's misfortune always to be swayed by those considerations.

"I'll go with you," she said suddenly. "It will take me a few days to make arrangements and obtain directions. I've never visited Aunt Belle before."

"Oh, thank you. Oh, Madeline, you're the most wonderful, compassionate—"

"Not so loud, please," Madeline cut in, though not harshly. "I'll have to confide in my servant, Nancy, but beyond that only you and

503

I must know. We don't want anything to hurt your reputation or cause trouble for you."

Nor do I want any trouble out of this, she said to herself in the wake of some nervous thoughts of Justin.

The preparations were intricate. First, contact had to be made with the midwife. Nancy handled that. Then a date had to be chosen, and Ashton informed by means of a sealed note smuggled to Mont Royal by the one man Nancy could trust, a big tea-colored slave named Pete with whom she had been living for over a year.

Several days before the appointed date, Madeline told Justin that she wanted to travel to Charleston to do some shopping. He muttered his consent, scarcely paying attention when she said she'd be gone overnight. He did insist that she take a male slave with her, and Nancy, too. She had expected that stipulation.

The night before the fictitious Charleston trip, she slept very little. Justin lurched into her room around eleven; he and Francis had been sitting downstairs for the last two hours, drinking and cursing the anti-slavery agitators in Kansas. He approached her bed without a word. He flung her nightdress above her waist, put his hands around her ankles and pulled her legs apart. Ten minutes later, still having said nothing, he left.

She hated his crude lovemaking. But at least when he visited her this way, he returned to his own room afterward and left her in peace the rest of the night. Now there was no chance of his detecting her nervousness.

In the morning—a sunny, pleasant day, exactly two weeks before Christmas—Nancy packed Madeline's valise. At noon Pete brought the chaise around, its hood in place to protect them from the elements. During the past hour the sun had disappeared, and the weather looked threatening. Madeline didn't want to travel the back roads in a storm, but it was too late to make other arrangements.

Once out of sight of Resolute, she took the reins from Nancy. Pete trotted along at the left side of the chaise. In this fashion they proceeded to a deserted crossroads where Ashton was waiting in her buggy. She looked pale and anxious.

Pete took Ashton's buggy and drove away into the pines. He had a friend nearby, a freedman, and would stay with the man's family overnight, meeting the women at the crossroads about the same time tomorrow. Ashton spent a few moments chattering about her excuse for being away from Mont Royal; it also involved staying with a friend, a nonexistent one. Madeline heard Ashton's voice, but few of the words registered.

The three women crowded into the chaise, Ashton in the middle. It was evident to Madeline that Orry's sister didn't like squeezing against a Negress, but she'd just have to put up with it.

Madeline tugged the reins and the chaise got under way. She glanced apprehensively at the swift-moving slate clouds. She was feeling more and more nervous about this expedition. One thing was in their favor, however—the remote location of Aunt Belle Nin's cabin. It lay far back in the marshes above Resolute, accessible only by dirt roads that seldom saw any traffic. Madeline believed they had an excellent chance of reaching Aunt Belle's without encountering another soul and certainly no one who would recognize them.

When they were about halfway to their destination, the sky grew black and the rain came, along with a high wind and pellets of hail. The road, here running beside a murky marsh, quickly turned to gumbo. Madeline stopped the chaise.

The hail and rain let up after ten minutes, and the wind moderated. Madeline flicked the reins over the back of the horse and they started on, only to founder within fifty yards when the left wheel sank into a muddy rut.

"Everyone out," Madeline ordered.

She and Nancy put their shoulders against the wheel. They freed it while Ashton stood by and watched. Just as the wheel pulled out of the mud, Madeline heard a sound that made her heart freeze. A horseman was approaching from up the road.

"Get down. Hide over there!" she said to Ashton, who was confused by the order. Surely Madeline wasn't telling her to ruin her fine dress by squatting in the wet, dirty weeds?

"Blast you, girl, hurry!" Madeline pushed her. None too soon, either. The rider galloped into sight, slowing when he spied the carriage.

There was something familiar about the man's sturdy form and wide-brimmed black hat. Madeline's stomach spasmed. She recognized him. Would he know her?

"Miz Madeline, what on earth are you doing this far from Resolute on such a bad day?" said Watt Smith, a middle-aged man who frequently raced his horses against those of her husband.

"Just an errand, Mr. Smith."

"Out here? Don't nobody live out here but a few ignorant niggers. Sure you ain't lost?"

Madeline shook her head. Smith looked unconvinced. He glanced at Nancy in an unfriendly way. "Ain't safe for white women to be on the roads, what with half the nigger population always mutterin' about revolt. Would you like me to ride along with you?"

"No, thank you, we'll be perfectly all right. Good day."

Rebuffed and mightily puzzled, Smith scowled, touched his hat brim, and cantered off.

Madeline waited about five minutes, then called Ashton from her hiding place. Her heart was racing. She feared the whole plot would now come to light somehow.

Well, the damage was done. They might as well go ahead.

Inside the ramshackle cabin, Ashton was moaning, though as yet nothing had happened. Madeline sat on the small porch in Aunt Belle's rocker, exhausted by the strain of the afternoon.

The stringy old octoroon woman listened to the outcries of her patient and puffed her clay pipe. "Soon as it's over and she's resting, we'll fix pallets for you and Nancy inside."

"That'll be fine, Aunt Belle. Thank you."

"I want you to know"—she pointed at Madeline with the stem of her pipe—"I'm helping her strictly because it was you who asked. That girl mistreats her people."

"I know she does. She and I have never been close, but I felt I had to help her. She didn't know where to turn."

"Don't make a habit of riskin' your skin over her kind. She's a mean, spoiled crybaby, not fit to kiss your hem."

Madeline smiled in a weary way. Aunt Belle went inside. The door closed.

The sight of the midwife sent Ashton into another fit of fearful moaning. The old woman exclaimed, "Nancy, grab that bottle of corn and pour some down her throat. And you, missy—you shut your mouth and lie still, or I'll send you back up the road to have your bastard whether you want it or not."

Ashton's complaints subsided. Madeline slumped in the chair, trying to relax. She couldn't. She kept remembering the suspicious eyes of Watt Smith.

As they drove back to the crossroads next day, Ashton swooned several times. Madeline felt the girl was putting on because she thought she should. Pete met them with the other buggy. They saw Ashton into it, then started home. Ashton had barely remembered to offer a feeble smile and a halfhearted word of thanks.

Yesterday's storm had strewn the roads with branches and palmetto fronds. Madeline found the grounds of Resolute equally littered. She must get a crew to work to clean up the debris. But not today. Tomorrow would be plenty of—

"Miz Madeline!" Nancy's urgent whisper jerked her out of her tired reverie. She looked up and saw Justin stride from the house. His face looked thunderous.

"I heard you were searching for Charleston upriver," he said. "Did you forget where it was?"

Panic and confusion churned in her. Watt Smith must have ridden by to say he had seen her on a remote road where no respectable white woman belonged. Any conscientious man would have done the same thing. She had almost expected it of Smith and yet had hidden the fact from herself.

"Justin—"

The word trailed off. She was too stunned and weary to think up a lie.

Nancy and Pete shot terrified glances at each other. Justin strode to the chaise, grabbed Madeline's arm, and dragged her out. She quailed, unable to believe he could smile at a time like this. He was enjoying her entrapment.

"Where have you been?" He jerked her wrist, hurting her. "Fitting me with a set of horns?"

"Justin, for God's sake, you mustn't say such things in front of— *oh!*"

Tears sprang to her eyes; he had pulled her arm again, hard. He thrust his face close to hers.

"Have you been whoring behind my back? We'll soon find out." He hauled her into the house.

"I'll ask you once again. Where were you?"

"Don't do this, Justin. I wasn't betraying you, as you call it. I'd never do such a thing. I gave you my pledge the day we married."

She retreated in front of him as she spoke. He followed her across the bedroom, his manure-flecked boots thumping softly, steadily. A small tripod stand bearing a vase stood in his path. He picked up the tripod and threw it over his shoulder. The stand clattered. The vase broke.

507

"Then where were you?"

"On a—a private errand. Woman's business." Desperately frightened, she didn't know what else to say.

"I must have a better answer than that." His hand shot out, clamping on her wrist again. "A truthful answer."

"Let go of me. Stop hurting me or I'll scream the house down."

Unexpectedly, he was amused. He released her and stepped back. "Go ahead. No one will pay any attention, except maybe that nigger slut you're so thick with. I'm going to take care of her, too, don't you worry."

A new, sharper fear drove through Madeline then. Though she was frightened, she knew she could hold out against his questions almost indefinitely. But if poor Nancy were dragged into it—

"You needn't look so alarmed, my dear." His tone was pleasant, conversational. "I won't injure you physically. I'd never leave so much as the smallest mark on you. It would be bad for appearances. Besides, you're a lady, or you're supposed to be. Whippings and similar methods of persuasion are for niggers. I'll try them on your wench tonight. On the buck, too. Meantime, I shall continue to ask you politely for an answer."

In spite of herself, she began to cry. She hated the weakness that brought on the tears. That weakness sprang from tension, exhaustion, and fear. Somehow she couldn't control it.

"I gave you an answer, Justin. I didn't betray you. I never would."

A long, aggrieved sigh. "My dear, that isn't acceptable. I shall have to leave you in this room until you come to your senses."

"Leave me—?"

Belatedly, understanding widened her eyes. Like an animal fleeing for its life, she ran past him toward the door. She almost reached it. Her fingers stretched to within inches of the polished brass knob. Then his hand swooped in. He seized her wrist and flung her back across the room. She cried out, struck the bed, and sprawled.

"You have deeply offended me with your lies and disobedience. This time I shall not limit your confinement to a day and a night. Good-bye, my dear."

"*Justin!*"

She wrenched the knob back and forth and managed to open the door half an inch. But he was stronger; he pulled it shut from the other side. She sank down in a heap at the sound of the lock shooting home.

Once outside, Justin stopped smiling and allowed his true emotion, rage, to show itself. What he had just decreed as punishment—imprisonment for at least a week—was a mere palliative. Madeline had defied him for years with her books and her unfeminine opinions. This latest escapade was merely the culmination of her revolt. A revolt fostered by his tolerance—

His weakness.

That situation would change, he vowed to himself as he stormed downstairs. He began screaming at the house men to fetch Nancy and Pete. They couldn't be found.

An hour later, he realized they had run off. His wild rage grew wilder. He dispatched a boy to Francis's house with instructions that a patrol be organized immediately. A patrol that would shoot the fugitives on sight.

They were glimpsed only once, two days later, crossing the Savannah River on a ferry. Somehow they had obtained forged passes. No one questioned their right to travel, and no one in the neighborhood of Resolute ever saw them again.

How long had she been locked up? Three days? No, four, she thought.

There was no way to find out what had happened to Nancy and Pete. She feared they had been tortured or killed. Light-headed, she was barely able to recall why she was worried about them. She slept during the day and roamed her room—her cage—at night. Outside the shuttered windows on the piazza, a man stood guard around the clock. Once a day, about sunrise, two house blacks came to the door. One kept watch while the other slid her day's allotment of food inside. It consisted of three half slices of coarse brown bread. With them was a shallow bowl of water. During the few seconds the door was open, the slaves gave her swift, sorrowing looks, but they dared not say anything aloud.

She was permitted no water for washing. Each day she used a little from the shallow bowl. Even so, she soon began to smell. On the third day, while she slept, someone slipped in and emptied her brimming slops jar. By then her quarters had acquired the odor of a barn.

What did it matter? As each hour went by, she was less aware of her surroundings. Strange ringings in her ears distracted her. Strange lights, purple or fiery white, danced in the corners of the room—

Or were they in her head?

"Orry. Orry, why didn't you come sooner?"

She saw him standing by the door, holding out his right hand while his eyes grieved. Thankfully, she rushed toward him. The instant she touched his hand, he vanished.

She started to cry. Some small, calm voice in the well of her soul said, *How ashamed your father would be if he saw this.*

She didn't care. She was sick, spent, terrified. Her sobs soon changed to screaming.

"A nourishing meal—that's what she needs."

"Yes, Doctor," Justin said in a solicitous tone, "but we've tried all week to persuade her to eat. She refuses."

Justin and the physician looked at each other, their expressions the picture of sympathy and concern. Only their eyes communicated their true feelings.

Madeline saw that but failed to grasp its significance. She was semiconscious, lying in bed with her dark hair tangled on her shoulders and her eyes huge, childlike. Her face was the color of flour.

"Oh, I'm not surprised," the doctor said with a sagacious nod. "That is a frequent symptom of nervous prostration." He was a rotund, elegantly dressed man whose cheeks had the glossy look of success. His name was Lonzo Sapp.

"Fortunately," he continued, "modern medicine can prescribe a treatment which is usually successful. Bed rest. Plenty of hot tea, then food when she feels better. I also want you to give her a generous dose of a special celery tonic once a day."

"Celery tonic," Justin repeated. "Is it your own formulation?"

Dr. Sapp nodded. "The base is wine vinegar, but the therapeutic ingredient is pulped celery."

The physician leaned over the bed and brushed a lock of hair from Madeline's brow. Her skin glistened in the light of the candles in a branched holder at the bedside. Smoothing and patting the hair above her brow, he resembled a kind father as he said, "If you can hear me, Mrs. LaMotte, I want you to know that you can soon be yourself again. Do you want that?"

Her thick, dry tongue inched over her cracked lower lip. She made no sound, staring at the doctor with tortured eyes that she closed briefly to signify assent.

"Then you must follow my regimen to the letter. It was your husband who summoned me from Charleston. He's deeply worried about you. I have reassured him, but recovery is in your hands alone. Will you do everything I ask?''

"Y-yes."

Justin bent and planted a gentle kiss on her cheek. He felt much better, having found a remedy for the rebelliousness that had plagued their marriage. The remedy was also a way of repaying her for cuckolding him. He was positive she had done so last week and might have been doing so for years. She certainly went off by herself often enough.

By locking her up and starving her, he had broken all her defenses except one. Had that fallen, she would have confessed freely, would have told him where she had gone and with whom.

At first his failure to gain that information had driven him wild with anger. Then, seeing that she would ultimately defeat him, he turned her silence around and transformed it into a benefit. If he learned the name of her lover, he would probably be humiliated. Suppose it was some white trash tradesman or mechanic. Some nigger. Ignorance was preferable. Or so he said to himself on one level of his mind. On another, he conceived a new and permanent hatred of his wife.

But no sign of it showed as he straightened up beside the bed. Before coming in he had doused himself liberally with a cinnamonny skin tonic; she and the room smelled abominable. That could end now. He strode to the shutters and flung them back.

Cool night air gusted in, stirring the candles. Her eyes shone with gratitude. "She'll be herself when she regains her strength," Sapp assured him as they left. "It's weakness which causes her disorientation."

The doctor closed the bedroom door, glanced up and down the hall, and continued in a low voice, "After a week, she should be accustomed to the tonic. Not suspicious of it. You can then substitute the formulation we discussed."

"The one containing the laudanum."

"A small dose only. Nothing harmful, you understand. Just enough to keep her calm and agreeable."

They strolled toward the head of the stairs. Dr. Sapp continued, "Should we wish to discontinue the tonic, there are other ways for her to receive the medication. Tinctured opium is a dark, sweetish liquid, but it can be baked into cookies, or employed to baste certain meats, or mixed with wine vinegar and poured over greens. What I'm saying is, the treatment is eminently flexible. Of course, if you've read de Quincey, you know there will be symptoms. Fatigue. Constipation. Possibly signs of premature aging. The symptoms are easily attributable to other causes, however. The stress and strain of daily living," he said with a shrug. "She need never know that she's receiving laudanum."

"That is good news," Justin declared with the fervency of a man who had stayed up all night and at last saw a prospect of rest. A sad smile settled on his face. "I've been so worried about her."

"Naturally."

"I want to do everything possible to soothe her nerves and restore her peace of mind."

"An admirable goal."

"So she won't embarrass herself—or the family."

"I quite understand," murmured Dr. Sapp, his smile as thin as that of his host.

"One more question, Doctor. How long can the treatment be continued?"

"Why, if you're happy with the results—a year. Two years. Indefinitely."

Again the two men looked at each other, their unblinking stares communicating a perfect understanding. Chatting like old friends, they continued downstairs.

39

Late in March 1855, Ashton's marriage to James Huntoon was celebrated at Mont Royal. Orry thought it a dismal affair. Clarissa smiled at the bride but didn't know who she was.

Ashton staged a nasty scene right after the ceremony. Up to that point, Huntoon had steadfastly refused to consider a wedding trip to New York, which was the only place Ashton wanted to go. She found no inconsistency in despising all Yankees while adoring their restaurants and theaters. To the very last minute, Huntoon insisted they were going to Charleston. Ashton threw a piece of cake at him, and pouted, and the sweating bridegroom quickly changed his mind, fearing that if he didn't it would be weeks before he enjoyed his wife's favors. By the time the carriage pulled away, Ashton was in a good mood again.

On top of all that, Cooper naturally outraged most of the male guests with his opinions. He repeatedly asked why neither abolitionists nor planters would give a moment's consideration to the proposal Emerson had made to the New York Anti-Slavery Society in February. Emerson's carefully worked-out scheme for gradual emancipation called for payments to slaveholders that would eventually total two hundred million dollars—small enough price for ending a national shame and preserving peace, he argued.

"Both sides jeered," Cooper said. "Well, I can think of one explanation. The instant you do away with the reason for protest, the protesters are out of business."

"Are you saying the fight for Southern rights is being made by cynical men?" a listener demanded.

"Some are sincere. But others want the abolitionists to continue to act in an extreme way. Only then can the South justify disruption of the Union, or a separate government—which of course is madness."

They thought Cooper the mad one and a menace. Once he had been considered little more than a harmless nuisance, but that had changed. It had changed as a result of his continuing interest in Edmund Burke and Burke's political wisdom. Cooper had taken that English statesman's warning about apathy to heart, and he began to involve himself in the affairs of the Democratic party in Charleston.

He gained entrée to the party by a simple expedient. He donated several large sums for its work, so large that the leaders couldn't afford to ignore him. Also, he was not the only man in the state expressing unpopular opinions about the way the South was going. Although there were not many who spoke out, there were enough for his presence at party meetings to be tolerated, if not welcomed.

He began to travel, to meet and confer with other moderate Democrats. In Virginia he was introduced to a man very much to his taste—a tall, blunt-jawed politician named Henry Wise who had ambitions to be governor. Wise was an outspoken defender of slavery, but he also believed that those who wanted to redress Southern grievances any way except within the framework of the Union were schemers—or idiots.

"Of course I understand why they do it," Wise said. "They want to regain the power that has passed from the South to the North and West. Maybe they don't even admit that to themselves. Hell, maybe they believe their own silly pronouncements. But they're dangerous men, Cooper. They're organized, active, vocal—and a threat to the entire South."

Cooper smiled that wry, sad smile of his. "'When bad men combine, the good must associate, else they will fall one by one, an unpitied sacrifice.'"

"Sage advice."

"As it was when Burke first wrote it back in 1770. Trouble is, it's been forgotten."

"Not forgotten. The fire eaters would just prefer not to listen to it. The fire eaters on both sides." Wise paused and studied the visitor. "I've heard about you, Cooper. You've been a pariah down in your home state for a long time. I'm glad you hied yourself back into the Democratic camp. We can use more like you—assuming that it isn't already too late."

Evidence said that it might be. Each side continued to defy the other.

Massachusetts passed a tough personal liberty law to protect all people, including blacks. The law was a reaction to the Burns affair the previous year. A fugitive slave, one Anthony Burns, had been detained at the Boston courthouse, where an abolitionist mob had attempted to rescue him and failed. Federal and state authorities had then cooperated to return Burns to his owner in the South.

In Kansas, meanwhile, a pro-slavery legislature had been elected with the help of so-called border ruffians from Missouri. They had streamed into the territory with rifles and pistols and had swung the outcome by means of intimidation and fraud. The fraudulently elected legislators had then passed laws establishing stiff penalties for anti-slavery agitation.

Month after month, both sides pushed bigger chips, and more of them, into the violent game. Missouri sent hordes of night riders over the border. The Northeast sent crates of weapons to arm the free-soil men. The crates were labeled as containing Bibles. This prompted Cooper to remark to some Democrats at a caucus in Columbia, "Even God has been recruited. In fact, each side is claiming He's with them. Do you suppose He runs back and forth on alternate days? He must get mighty frazzled."

No one was amused.

One afternoon at the C.S.C. dock, Cooper struck up a conversation with the dock foreman, a second-generation Charlestonian named Gerd Hochwalt. The foreman could be hard on malingerers, but personally he was a mild man with a generous disposition and strong religious beliefs. He had a wife, eleven children, and a house at the outskirts of town barely big enough to contain them.

Cooper and Hochwalt were soon discussing the recent anti-slavery convention at Big Springs, Kansas. Those in attendance had drawn up a plan for the territory to seek admission as a free state. They had also repudiated the laws enacted by the fraudulently chosen legislature sitting at Shawnee Mission. A particularly fiery *Mercury* editorial had condemned the action at Big Springs. Hochwalt praised the editorial.

"I read it," Cooper said. "I found it nothing but the same old rhetoric." As they talked, both men kept an eye on the lines of black stevedores filing aboard *Mont Royal* with bales marked for a Liverpool cotton factor. On this and every other trip the ship was loaded to capacity. And for each current customer, Cooper had three waiting. The packet line was showing a monthly profit of sixty to seventy percent. Even Orry had begun to take notice of the success.

Hochwalt yelled a reprimand to one of the stevedores who had stumbled and slowed up the loading. Then he wiped his perspiring neck with a blue kerchief and said, "The sentiments expressed by Mr. Rhett may be getting a bit shopworn, Mr. Main, but I believe in them."

"How can you, Gerd? He was calling for a separate government again."

"And why not, sir? For as long as I can remember, Northern people have scorned and insulted us. They think we're dirt, every last one of us. A nation of brothel keepers! Isn't that the term? Yet I have never owned a slave, or favored the institution, at any time in my life. The Northern abuse outrages me. If they don't stop it, then by heaven we should go our own way."

Emotionally, Cooper could understand Hochwalt's feeling. Rationally, it was incomprehensible.

"You honestly don't think men like Bob Rhett and James Huntoon and Mr. Yancey from Alabama are marching us along a path to a cliff?"

Hochwalt pondered. "No, sir. But even if they are, I'm inclined to go with them."

"For God's sake, man—why?"

The foreman peered at Cooper as if he were callow, not very bright.

"South Carolina is my home. Those men speak up for it. No one else does, Mr. Main."

"I tell you, Orry, when Hochwalt said that, a chill came over me. My foreman is no wild-eyed revolutionary. He's a solid, respectable Dutchman. If he and decent men like him are listening to the fire eaters, we've drifted farther than I ever suspected."

Cooper made that statement a few nights later. Orry had ridden to Charleston to go over the books of the shipping company. He and Cooper had devoted most of the day to the work, and at the end Orry had declared himself pleased, even offering his brother a rare word of congratulations. Now the two of them were seated in comfortable chairs of white-painted wicker, looking out on the garden at Tradd Street. Little Judah, a chunky boy, was rolling a ball to the baby, Marie-Louise, who sat spraddle-legged on the thick Bermuda grass.

"Well," Orry replied, "I try to pay as little attention as possible to that kind of thing. I've enough to think about."

But you don't find it very satisfying, Cooper said to himself as he noted the melancholy look in his brother's eyes. Orry slouched in his chair, long legs stretched in front of him. He watched the children play in the gathering shadows. Was there envy in his expression?

In a moment Orry returned to the subject of the company. "I'm thankful the vessels are full every trip. The rice market in southern Europe is still depressed. Every month it falls a little more. You were wise to insist we diversify."

Saying that, he sounded no different from the way he always did. Yet Cooper knew something was wrong. But he couldn't identify the problem or the cause. He was about to ask Orry to do so when Judith came out of the house carrying a small parcel.

"A boy from the Colony Bookshop delivered this for you, Orry."

"Oh—the book I asked for this morning. The shopkeeper was out of stock but expected a dozen copies by mid-afternoon." He quickly unwrapped the parcel. When Judith saw the gold stamping, she clapped her hands in surprise.

"*Leaves of Grass*. That's the book of verse Reverend Entwhistle preached against last Sunday. I read all about his sermon in the paper. He said the book was the work of a man who had abandoned reason and order, and it was filthy to boot."

Cooper said, "The fellow's receiving just as much hellfire from clerics up North—what's his name?" He turned the book in his brother's hand. "Whitman. Since when have you found time or a liking for modern poetry?"

Under his beard, Orry turned pink. "I bought it as a gift."

"For someone at Mont Royal?"

"No, an acquaintance."

Cooper didn't press, but if he had, he wondered whether he might have discovered the reason for Orry's bleak mood.

"Supper is nearly ready," Judith said. "Rachel's been picking blue crabs since early morning." Rachel was the buxom free black woman employed as a cook. "I invited Ashton and James to join us, but they had another obligation. We seldom see them. Close as they are, they've never been here for a meal, I regret to say. Each time I ask, they're busy."

The Huntoons had moved into a fine, airy house on East Battery, a few doors below Atlantic. From there it was a short walk along Water and Church to Tradd Street. Orry had ridden past Ashton's house on horseback, but he was curiously reluctant to call on his sister.

"They have a flock of new friends," Cooper explained. "Most of 'em are members of Bob Rhett's crowd. I can't pretend it feels good to be shunned by one's own blood relation, but I expect it's for the best that they don't visit or dine with us. James and I are so far apart politically, we'd probably be arranging a duel by the end of the soup course."

Looking more cheerful, he clapped his hands. "Children," he called, "it's almost time to eat. Come sit on your father's lap."

Unable to stop thinking of Madeline, Orry gazed at the book, rewrapped it, and carefully slid it into his pocket.

During supper, Cooper tried several times to introduce the subject of an expansion plan that was much on his mind lately. The plan was unconventional. It would require nerve and much more capital than the Mains could handily scrape together. He was thinking of George Hazard as a potential partner, but he never got to mention that. Orry repeatedly turned aside all discussion of business. In fact, he hardly said twenty words while at the table. That night, in bed with Judith, Cooper remarked that he hadn't seen his brother in such a strange, sad mood since the months right after his return from Mexico.

Huntoon's law practice was growing. So was his reputation. Ashton helped that growth. She gave parties, receptions, dinners; she cultivated local leaders and their ugly, overbearing wives, never letting any of them know how much she loathed them or how cynically she was using them.

Huntoon worked long hours to prepare a definitive speech on the developing national crisis. One evening in late summer, at the house on East Battery, he delivered a condensed version to an audience of about thirty guests. The guests included editor Rhett and the gentleman recognized as perhaps the foremost advocate of separation, William Yancey of Alabama. A mild, even innocuous-looking man, Yancey was a splendid platform orator. Some were calling him the Prince of Fire Eaters. Ashton dreamed of promoting him to king, so that her husband could assume the other title.

Holding his silver-rimmed spectacles in one hand as a prop, Huntoon did his best to demonstrate his worthiness. The guests listened attentively as he launched into his conclusion, which Ashton knew by heart.

"The Union is like a great fortress, ladies and gentlemen. Half of it has already passed into the hands of barbarian invaders. Loyalists still hold the other half, which they have defended without stint for generations. Now that part of the fortress is being threatened. And I for one will apply the torch to the magazine and blow the whole place to bits before I will surrender one more inch to the barbarians!"

Ashton led the applause, which was loud and enthusiastic. While house slaves offered punch from silver trays, Yancey approached Huntoon.

"That kind of extreme action may very well be necessary, James. And afterward a new fortress will have to be constructed on the rubble of the old. The task will require loyal workers—and able leaders."

His expression said he considered Huntoon one of the latter. Or at least a candidate. Huntoon preened.

Ashton had little understanding of the issues the men debated endlessly. She honestly didn't give a hang about Southern rights and wasn't even sure what they were once you got beyond the fundamental God-given right to hold property in the form of niggers. What excited her about all the talk was the way it stirred others. In that reaction she sensed an opportunity to create and hold power. Her husband had convinced her there would someday be a separate Southern government. She meant to be one of its great ladies.

"James, that was simply wonderful," she exclaimed as she took his arm. "I declare, I don't believe I've ever heard you speak so well." She was conniving for more applause, and it worked. There was another round from guests nearby. Yancey joined in, adding a "Hear, hear!"

"Thank you, my dear." Huntoon's look of gratitude bordered on the pathetic. Ashton seldom complimented him in private, and often told him that he was an inadequate lover.

Tonight, however, the presence of notables and the success of the performance generated an unexpected sexual excitement within her. She could hardly wait to see all the guests to the door, rush upstairs, throw off her clothes, and drag her husband down beside her.

Blinking and sweating, he labored hard. Afterward, he whispered, "Was that all right?"

"Just fine," she lied. He was doing so well in his role of fire eater, she didn't want to discourage him. But he never moved her with his clumsy caresses, and in fact frequently repelled her. She consoled herself by thinking that everything, including being a great lady, had its price.

She decided that she needed to make another trip home, however. Soon.

Ashton's lover had found a new spot for their assignations: the ruins of a country church called Salvation Chapel. What a deliciously wicked thrill to hoist her skirts and let Forbes have her right out in the sunshine, on top of the tabby foundation.

Nearby, his tethered horse whinnied and pawed the ground. In the distance she could hear the boom of muskets as the bird minders in some planter's field tried to scare the September rice birds away from the ripening grain. The sounds of the horse and the guns increased her excitement; she was limp with satisfaction afterward.

"I worry about plantin' a baby," Forbes said, his handsome and sweaty face only inches above hers.

Ashton licked the corner of her mouth. "Seems to me the risk just adds a dash of spice."

She really didn't think there was much chance of a pregnancy. Huntoon was at her all the time, and she had thus far failed to conceive. She suspected some damage had been done by Aunt Belle Nin's solution to her earlier problem. That might turn out to be a convenience, although the thought of being barren saddened her sometimes.

"It will until a youngster pops out who looks like me instead of your husband," Forbes said.

"You let me fret about James. Your job's right here."

With that, she pulled him down into an embrace. The far-off explosions of the guns had excited her again.

She went home with her buttocks scraped red by the tabby, but it was worth it. Forbes was a fine lover, attentive and enthusiastic when he was with her but content to do without her until he was summoned again. Vanity prevented Ashton from asking where Forbes practiced his considerable skills when she was absent. If there were others, they obviously couldn't compare to her; Forbes came running at her every call.

On the return trip to Mont Royal—Forbes accompanied her to within a mile of the plantation—they had another of their obsessive discussions of various ways they might injure Billy Hazard. Forbes was always fascinated by Ashton's inventive imagination, not least because it was so centered on power, sexual adventure, and revenge.

"Saw that you entertained Mr. Yancey a few days ago," Orry remarked at supper that night.

Ashton had been quite proud of the half column that the *Mercury* had devoted to the gathering. "'Deed we did," she answered. "He had some peppery things to say about the Yankees. So did James.

520

'Course''—she turned to Brett, who was seated opposite her—''we make exceptions for friends of the family.''

''I was wondering about that,'' Brett said, not smiling.

''Surely we do. Billy's special.'' Ashton's smile was sweet and flawlessly sincere. Inside, her feelings were so intense, venomous, her stomach hurt. ''Has he said anything about a wedding date?''

Orry answered the question. ''No. He doesn't even graduate until next June. What's a second lieutenant earn these days? A thousand dollars a year? A family can't live on that. I'd say it's much too soon to discuss marriage.''

Brett's eyes flashed as she looked at her brother. ''We haven't.''

But they would one of these days, Ashton felt. That might be the ideal moment to strike; just when they were happiest.

After supper, Ashton walked to the family burying ground. A strong, steady wind had come up. Her hair whipped around her head like a dark flag. She knelt at the foot of Tillet's grave, the only place she ever felt ashamed of her behavior with men. She spoke softly but with great emotion.

''Things are going splendidly for James, Papa. I wish you could be here to see. I know you wanted another son instead of a daughter, but I'll make you proud of me, just like I've promised before. I'll be a famous lady. They'll know my name all over the South. They'll beg me for favors. And James too. I swear that to you, Papa. I swear.''

When Ashton left the house, Orry went up to his mother's room to visit for a little while. Clarissa was polite and cheerful, but she didn't recognize him. On her work table lay her third version of the family tree. The first two had been erased so hard, so often, that they had fallen to pieces.

Walking downstairs again, he thought about Billy and Brett. He was glad they weren't interested in marrying the moment Billy left West Point. He didn't know how he'd react if Billy asked for his sister's hand right now. All he could see in the future was turmoil.

He let himself into the library and blew out the one lamp already burning. He threw the shutters back and inhaled the cool evening air. It smelled of autumn and the river. His gaze drifted lazily about the room, settling on the shadowed corner. He stared at his uniform. He reminded himself that he had a crop to harvest. He had no interest in it.

What had happened to Madeline?

That was the question savaging him these days. She had become a recluse. She seldom left Resolute, and when she did, she was always in the company of her husband. Orry had passed the LaMotte carriage on the river road a few weeks ago. He had waved at the passengers— almost too enthusiastically, he feared. He needn't have worried. Madeline's response was exactly like her husband's: a fixed smile, a steady stare, a hand barely lifted in greeting as the carriage rattled on down the road and out of sight.

From a bookshelf he took *Leaves of Grass*, still in its brown paper wrapping. He'd had no opportunity to present it to Madeline. She no longer called on Clarissa or responded to his pleas for a meeting. Three times during the summer he had waited at Salvation Chapel, hoping she would appear in response to one of the notes he had sent covertly to Resolute. She never did.

The last time he waited, he found broken branches and trampled grass, suggesting that other lovers had discovered the ruined church. He didn't go back. In desperation he asked one of his house slaves to try to learn whether his notes might have been intercepted. Nancy had run away months ago, so the whole system of communication could have broken down. But apparently it hadn't, at least not the way he feared. Within a few days the slave reported, "I heard trom Resolute, Mr. Orry. She gets the notes, all right. Girl name Cassiopeia takes 'em to her."

"Does Mrs. LaMotte read them?"

"Far as I can find out, she does. But then she tears 'em up or throws 'em in the fireplace."

Recalling that, Orry struck out with the book. He accidentally hit the uniform stand and sent it toppling. The crash brought Brett and two house girls. Without opening the door, he shouted that he was all right.

A thought occurred to him, renewing his hope. On Saturday there was to be a tournament near the Six Oaks. It was possible that Madeline would attend with Justin. Orry usually avoided such affairs, but he would go to this one. He might have a chance to speak with her, discover what was wrong.

Saturday's weather was close, showery, with rumbles of thunder. A large and enthusiastic crowd gathered for the tourney, but Orry had no interest in watching the young men who had christened themselves Sir Gawain or Sir Kay. As they rode recklessly at the hanging rings and tried to capture them on their lances, he roamed the crowd searching for the LaMottes.

He finally spied Justin conversing boisterously with his brother and several other men. Encouraged, he kept moving, looking for Madeline. He caught sight of her from the spot where Cousin Charles had stood and waited for Whitney Smith to fire at him. She was seated on a log, watching light rain stipple the river.

He approached, noticing that the log had dirtied her skirt. She must have heard his footsteps, but she didn't turn. Feeling awkward, adolescent—fearful—he cleared his throat.

"Madeline?"

She rose slowly. He stepped back when he saw her face. It was white, the pallor of sickness. She had lost weight; ten or fifteen pounds at least. The loss gave her cheeks a sunken look. She seemed to struggle to focus her eyes on him.

"Orry. How pleasant to see you."

She smiled, but it was the same perfunctory smile he had glimpsed when he encountered the carriage. He could barely stand the sight of her eyes. They had always been so lively and warm. Now—

"Madeline, what's wrong? Why haven't you answered my messages?" Though there was no one else close, he was whispering.

A troubled look flickered across her face. She glanced past his shoulder. Then her eyes met his again. He thought he saw pain there, and an appeal for help. He strode toward her.

"I can see something's wrong. You've got to tell me—"

"Madeline?" Justin's voice jerked him up short. "Please come join us, my dear. We'll be leaving soon."

Orry turned, trying to keep his movement casual, belying the tension within him. Madeline's husband had called from the other side of the dueling field. To allay possible suspicion, Orry tipped his hat in formal greeting, which Justin acknowledged in the same way. Orry kept his smile broad and rigid, as if he were only exchanging pleasantries with a neighbor's wife.

In reality he was whispering: "I must talk to you alone at least once."

She looked at him again. Longingly, he thought. But she sighed and said, "No, I'm sorry, it's just too difficult."

With a slow, almost languorous step, she walked away to rejoin her husband. Orry was fuming; he wanted to seize Justin by the throat and shake him until the man told him what was wrong. Clearly

Madeline wouldn't. She acted listless, dazed—as if she were in the grip of a fever.

But it was the memory of her eyes that tortured him as he rode homeward. They held a strange, submissive look, devoid of hope; lifeless, almost. They were the eyes of a beaten animal.

40

About to don the yellow facings and brass castle insignia of the Corps of Engineers, Billy Hazard could examine his world and declare it a fine place.

The fears of the New Jersey cadet whom Ashton had entertained had never been realized. The silence of the seven had evidently kept any rumor from reaching Charles. One of the group had grumbled to Billy that Ashton must have lied about a second visit—something he could have told them from the beginning. But after that, the incident was gradually forgotten under the continual pressure of military drill and academic work.

Billy's view of the world tended to be shaped by events in his daily life and not by what was happening elsewhere. Had he looked outward, beyond the Academy and his thoughts of Brett, he would have seen turmoil.

Bloody warfare continued in the Crimea. One of his brother's classmates, George McClellan, had been sent there to observe by Secretary Davis. Other kinds of violence boded ill for America. Men fought each other in Kansas—and in the halls of Congress. During a speech about Kansas, Senator Sumner of Massachusetts had mingled his political rhetoric with an unwarranted personal attack on Senator Andrew Butler of South Carolina. On the twenty-second of May, Congressman Preston Brooks of South Carolina strode into the Senate chamber with a gold-knobbed cane, which he proceeded to employ to demonstrate what he thought of the speech, and Sumner.

Sumner soon cried for mercy as blood dripped onto his desk. Brooks kept hitting him until the cane broke. Incredibly, other senators looked on without interfering. One of the bystanders was Douglas, whose legislation had created the very issue Sumner had addressed.

A few weeks later, Brett wrote Billy a letter saying Brooks was being feted all over South Carolina. Ashton and her husband had entertained him at their home and presented to him a cane inscribed with words of admiration. The cane was one of dozens Brooks received. The letter continued:

When James and Ashton were here last week, Orry remarked that Sumner might not recover for a year or more. James raised one eyebrow and said, "So quickly? What a pity." I hate these times, Billy. They seem to call forth the very worst in men.

Not even those sentiments could discourage Billy just then. He was only days from leaving the Academy, and he had done well there, particularly in his first-class year. Mahan had publicly praised his work in the military and civil engineering course. Billy could differentiate between *Pinus mitis* and *Pinus strobus*, write an essay on argillaceous and calcareous stones as construction materials, or recite the formula for grubstone mortar in his sleep. He would graduate sixth in overall standings in the class of 1856.

George, Constance, Maude, even Stanley and Isabel were coming to West Point for the event; George and Isabel could manage to speak to each other when the occasion required it. The conversation was always cool and formal, however; the ban on visiting between the two houses was still in force. Billy had heard Constance say it was a shame to hold grudges considering life was so short, to which George replied that precisely because it was short, anything that prevented him from wasting part of it in Isabel's company was a godsend.

Charles congratulated Billy on his class ranking while relieving him of blankets and personal cadet effects. Charles had never competed academically with his friend; he remained steadfastly a member of the Immortals, bound for the mounted service, exactly what he wanted. Prospects for advancement in the cavalry—in all branches, in fact—had greatly improved since Davis had pushed through an expansion of the Army a year ago. Two new regiments of infantry had been authorized, and two of cavalry. Superintendent Lee had already been transferred to the new mounted regiment commanded by Albert Sidney Johnston, another Academy graduate. Charles hoped to join one of the new units next year.

Billy already knew his first posting as a brevet second lieutenant. After his graduation leave he would report to Fort Hamilton in New York harbor, there to work on coastal fortifications and harbor improvements.

Traveling home with the family, Billy got his first ride on the Lehigh line, which now served the upper reaches of the valley, including Lehigh Station. When the Hazards left the train, the baggage master complimented George on his brother's appearance.

"You're right, he does make a good soldier. He's dashing enough to make me miss the Army. Almost," George added with a smile.

"I wish Brett could have come up for June week," Billy said.

George studied the tip of his cigar. "Do the two of you have plans to discuss?"

"Not yet, but I expect we will. I need to talk to someone about that."

"Will an older brother do?"

"I was hoping you'd offer."

"Tonight, then," George said, taking note of Billy's serious expression.

After supper Billy went upstairs to put on mufti. George kissed the children and hurried to his desk, where he eagerly opened a letter that had arrived during his absence; it bore a mailing address in Eddyville, Kentucky.

Some months before, he had heard about a Pittsburgh man, William Kelly, who operated a furnace and finery in Eddyville. Kelly claimed to have found a fast, efficient way to burn silicon, phosphorus, and other elements out of pig iron, thereby sharply reducing its carbon content. What Kelly termed his pneumatic process produced a very acceptable soft steel, he said.

Beset by creditors and jeered at by competitors who called his process "air-boiling," Kelly continued to perfect the heart of the process, his converter, at a secret location in the Kentucky woods. George had written to propose that he travel to Eddyville and inspect the converter. He had also said that if he liked what he saw, he would finance Kelly's work in return for a partial interest.

George's face fell when he read the reply. True enough, Kelly could use the money to stave off his creditors. But he didn't want to show his converter to anyone until he was satisfied with the design and had applied for a patent. The man's suspicion was well founded. Some in the iron trade would say or do almost anything to learn the details of a successful process, then cheerfully pirate it if it was unprotected. Still, Kelly's answer left George disappointed, and it was in this frame of mind that he went to the front porch to meet his brother.

Billy was not there yet. George sank into a rocker. Down on the near shore of the river, a freight train was traveling up the valley, shooting puffs of smoke from its stack. The smoke turned scarlet in the sundown, then quickly dispersed.

Amazing, all the changes he had seen in thirty-one years. He had grown up with the canal boats, and now they were gone. Trains and the rails that carried them were the symbols of the new age.

Railroads were playing a role in affairs in Washington, too. Slavery, and the ultimate fate of Kansas and Nebraska, were inextricably bound up with a forthcoming decision on a route for a transcontinental line. Secretary Davis wanted a southern route, through slaveholding states. Senator Douglas favored a northern route, with one terminus in Chicago. It was no secret that Douglas had speculated in Western land. His enemies openly accused him of introducing the Kansas-Nebraska bill to stimulate settlement, which would in turn attract railroad development and increase the value of his holdings.

No motives were pure anymore, George thought as he watched the sinking sun burnish the low peaks beyond the river. No man seemed capable of dealing with all the problems and passions of a world grown complex and cynical. There were no statesmen, only politicians.

Or did he merely think that because he was getting old? At thirty-one, he had already lived three-fourths of an average lifetime. The knowledge weighed on his mind. He mused that a man's hopes, dreams, time upon the earth, disappeared almost as quickly as those puffs of smoke from the freight locomotive.

He heard Billy's tread on the stair and pulled himself together. His younger brother looked to him for advice—wisdom—never realizing that older people were almost as uncertain of everything as Billy was, if not more. George did his best to hide the fact. He was rocking and contentedly puffing a cigar when Billy appeared.

"Shall we take a walk up the hill?" George asked.

Billy nodded. They left the porch, strolled toward the rear of the house, and soon passed the stable and woodshed, reaching an open, level area where mountain laurel grew from crevices in the rock. Above, on the slope, more laurel had taken root and flourished. Hundreds of white blossoms moved in the evening wind, and there was a faint sound of pointed leaves clashing.

George started toward the summit, considerably higher than the loftiest point of Belvedere. The path was difficult to find, but he remembered its starting point and was soon laboring upward with the laurel blowing and tossing around his legs. The climb winded him, but not Billy.

528

On the rounded summit, a few stunted laurel bushes survived. They reminded George of his mother's mystical feeling for the hardy shrub and the way she equated it with family and with love.

Below, the panorama of the houses, the town, and the ironworks spread in perfect clarity. Billy admired the view for a moment, then reached into his pocket and handed his brother something in a cheap white-metal frame.

"I've been meaning to show you this."

George tilted the photograph to catch the last light. "Good Lord. That's you and Charles. Neither of you looks sober."

Billy grinned and returned the photograph to his pocket. "We posed for it right after a trip to Benny's," he said.

"When did photography reach West Point?"

"They started class pictures a year ago. Charles and I wanted one of the two of us."

George gave a kind of grudging laugh, then shook his head. "Cooper Main's right. We live in a miraculous age."

Billy lost his relaxed air. "I wish a few miracles would drift down to South Carolina. I don't think Orry wants me to marry Brett."

"Is that what you wanted to talk about?" When Billy nodded, he went on, "Have you spoken to Orry or written him about your intentions?"

"No, and I won't for a year or so. Not until I'm positive I can support a wife."

What a careful, deliberate sort he is, George thought. He'd make a fine engineer.

Billy continued: "Brett's dropped a few hints to him, though. We both get the feeling he doesn't favor the match. I guess he doesn't like me."

"That's not it at all. You and Brett come from different backgrounds, from parts of the country growing more hostile to each other every hour. I'll bet Orry's worried about the sort of future you two would have. I admit I share that worry."

"Then what can I do?"

"Follow the same advice Mother gave me when people said I shouldn't marry a Catholic and bring her to Lehigh Station. She told me to heed my own feelings, not the bigotry or the misguided opinions of others. She said love would always win out over hatred. She said it had to, if human beings were to survive. Orry doesn't hate you, but he may be doubtful of your prospects." A flickering smile. "Stand fast, Lieutenant. Don't surrender your position, and in the end I expect Orry will give in.''

"What if it takes a while?''

"What if it does? Do you want Brett or not?'' Suddenly George leaned forward. He snapped off a sprig of laurel and held it up in the faint light. "You know Mother's feeling for this plant. She says it's one of the few things that outlasts its natural enemies and endures.'' He handed Billy the sprig of white and green. "Take a lesson from that. Let your feelings for Brett be stronger than all the doubts of others. You must outlast Orry. When you feel hope ebbing away, think of the laurel growing up here in the sun and storm. Hanging on. It's the best advice I can offer you.''

Billy studied the leaves and the blossom for a moment. He wanted to smile but somehow could not. His voice was heavy with emotion.

"Thank you. I'll take it.'' He put the sprig in his pocket.

All the light had left the sky. Stars by the thousand spread overhead. Presently, laughing and chatting companionably, the brothers started down the path. They disappeared in the darkness on the slope, where the laurel still tossed with a sound like that of a murmuring sea.

Old political loyalties continued to crumble away that autumn. Buck Buchanan finally got the chance to run for President on the Democratic ticket. Cameron, although still at odds with his old colleague, felt it might damage his carefully built machine if he joined the Republicans, as so many in the North and West were doing. So during the fall of 1856, he politicked under the banner of something called the Union party, while listening privately to proposals for an alliance. Republicans such as David Wilmot said they would support Cameron for a Senate seat if he threw in with them. Stanley worked loyally for Boss Cameron without knowing what the man stood for, other than what Stanley perceived as Cameron's own self-interest.

In South Carolina, Huntoon continued to proclaim his views from public platforms. He feared the rising power of the Republicans but was nearly as disenchanted with Buchanan, who purported to champion noninterference with slavery in the states and yet endorsed the Douglas doctrine in the territories. How could the South survive under either party? Huntoon asked in his speeches. It could not; secession was the only answer. Huntoon closed every address by raising his arm dramatically and offering a toast.

"To the sword! The arbiter of national disputes. The sooner it is unsheathed to maintain Southern rights, the better!"

The toast always produced loud applause and was widely quoted in the South Carolina press. The *Mercury* christened him Young Hotspur. Ashton was thrilled and deemed it a significant advance in her husband's career. A man could tell that he had achieved fame when the public began referring to him as Old This or Young That.

Up North, Hazard's had recently been facing increased competition from the British iron industry. George placed the blame on the Democrats and their low-tariff politics and for this reason joined the Republican party. His decision had nothing to do with the party's harder line on slavery, although he endorsed that. He voted for the Republican candidate, Frémont, who lost to Buchanan by about five hundred thousand votes. That was a very strong showing for a new party in its first presidential race.

A few days after the election, Cooper showed up at Mont Royal with an engineering drawing tucked under his arm. When he unrolled it, Orry saw a plan and elevation for a cargo vessel. A decorative ribbon at the bottom enclosed the words *Star of Carolina*.

"How big is that ship?" Orry asked in amazement.

"Five hundred and fifty feet, stem to stern. That's only a little smaller than the vessel my friend Brunel is building to carry coal and passengers out to Trincomalee in Ceylon. Her name's *Leviathan*. She's under construction on the Isle of Dogs in the Thames River right now. I'm leaving in two weeks with the family to take a look at her."

Orry tugged his beard in a reflective way. "You may be in need of another holiday in Britain, but I'm not sure the Mains need another ship." He tapped the drawing. "You don't really intend to build this monster—?"

"I surely do. I propose to establish the Main Shipyard in Charleston, expressly for the purpose of launching the *Star of Carolina* as an American flag carrier."

Orry finished pouring two glasses of whiskey and handed one to his brother. "Is this why you've been holding the acreage on James Island?"

Cooper smiled. "Precisely."

Orry tossed down half his whiskey, then said with some sarcasm, "I'm glad you have faith that this family can prosper while everyone else is going under. Unemployment's rising—George says he fears a depression, maybe even another panic—but you want to build a cargo ship."

"The biggest in America." Cooper nodded. His manner was cool and sure. He had learned how to deal with opposition from any source, including his family.

"She'll soon pay for herself, too," he went on. "Carrying cotton or anything else you can think of. I know there are hard times coming. But they don't last forever, and we must look beyond them. Consider the state of the domestic shipping industry for a minute. The clippers have no flexibility. They were built for one purpose—speed. Be the fastest to the gold fields and don't worry about cargo capacity, that was the prevailing attitude. Now there's no more gold, and no one's building clippers any longer. Those still in service are obsolete. They can't carry cargoes of the size our farmers and manufacturers are prepared to ship. I tell you, Orry, as a maritime nation we're far behind. America's oceangoing steam tonnage amounts to ninety thousand tons. Britain's is almost six times that. A vacuum exists, and the *Star of Carolina* can sail right into it. One more thing: the shipyard will benefit Charleston and the state too. We need industries that don't depend on slavery."

Laughing—how could he not in the face of such breathless enthusiasm?—Orry held up his hand. "All right, I'm convinced."

"You are?"

"Maybe not completely, but sufficiently to ask how much this beauty will cost."

That dulled the sparkle in Cooper's eyes. "I'll have more reliable figures when I come home from England. Right now I can only base my projections on those of Brunel. The Eastern Steam Navigation Company estimates *Leviathan* will cost—in dollars—four million."

While Orry recovered, Cooper took a breath. "Or more."

"Are you out of your mind, Cooper? Even with everything mortgaged, we could barely raise half that."

Quietly. "I'm thinking of approaching George about the other half."

"With the iron trade sliding into a depression? You have lost your senses."

"George is a good businessman—like you. I think he'll see the long-term opportunity, not merely the short-term risks."

The challenge was clear. Orry would either go along with the project or put himself in the camp of reactionaries such as Stanley. In truth, Orry thought his brother's idea visionary, exciting, and not as foolish as his own initial reaction might have suggested. He wasn't ready to give instant approval, however.

"I need figures. Realistic projections of cargo capacity, cost, future income. I won't speak to a single banker until I have them."

That was good enough for Cooper. Glowing, he said, "They'll be ready two weeks after I return. Maybe even sooner. They built small ships in Charleston at one time. A reborn industry could be the salvation of this part of the state."

"Not to mention the ruination of the Mains," Orry said. But he smiled.

Cooper and his family landed at Bristol, there transferring to the Great Western Railway that I. K. Brunel had laid out and brought to completion in 1841. The train left from a platform beneath the vast hammer-beam roof of Temple Meads Station, a structure that Brunel had planned. It traveled 120 miles on broad-gauge track, passing over the brick arches of Brunel's Maidenhead Bridge, considered an engineering masterpiece, and arrived at the new Paddington Station, which had been officially opened by the Prince Consort two years earlier; Brunel had designed every detail of the station, as well as the Paddington Hotel that adjoined it. Since Brunel served on the hotel's board of directors, Cooper had decided to stay there. He discovered that his reservation had been changed from a small suite to a much larger one, at no increase in cost.

Isambard Kingdom Brunel was now in his fiftieth year, a restless, imaginative man who delighted in wearing a stovepipe hat and dangling a cigar from one corner of his mouth. Not all his ideas were good. His choice of broad-gauge track for the G.W.R. was much criticized; carriages from intersecting lines could not be switched onto it. But for sheer soaring size of visions, he had no peer. Cooper saw that again when the little engineer took him to the Thames shipyard of his partner, Scott Russell.

Because of *Leviathan*, the Millwall yard had become Europe's premier tourist attraction. All around the construction site, the marshy fields of the Isle of Dogs had blossomed with coffee stalls and souvenir shops constructed of canvas and cheap lumber. Every conceivable kind of trinket was offered for sale: Miniature models of the finished ship. Lithographic views. *Leviathan* ABCs for the children. Right now—a weekday with bad weather—the shops were not doing much business.

Fifty-four feet high, *Leviathan*'s double hull reared against the rainy sky. The inner and outer hulls were three feet apart and heavily braced. The ship would have six masts, five funnels, and two sets of engines, one for her paddle wheels and one for her immense screw. She was positioned so that she could slide sideways into the Thames, her great length prohibiting launching in the regular manner.

"We hope to have her afloat within a year, provided I can finish my plan for the slipways and rekindle a spirit of cooperation with Mr. Russell. It has become evident that his original cost estimates for the hull and paddle engines were frivolous and irresponsible."

Brunel chewed his unlit cigar. Despite evident disenchantment with his partner, his pride was unmistakable when he swept his gaze along the huge keel plate. Using his cigar as a pointer, he indicated the

534

section of the outer hull already finished with plates of inch-thick iron.

"My great babe will take thirty thousand of those plates before she's done. And three million rivets. At peak times we have two hundred basher gangs hammering in the rivets."

Cooper pulled off his old beaver hat, the better to see the iron monster above him. Rain splashed his face. "I want to build one like her, only smaller, in Charleston. I copied *Great Britain* once—"

"Handsomely. I saw drawings. But surely what you just said is facetious, Cooper. You've always struck me as an intelligent chap and one who likes his comforts. Surely you don't want to surrender your friends, your family, your health, and all your money to such a venture."

"I know there are risks, enormous ones. But I feel compelled to go ahead. I want to build her for more than selfish reasons. I think she can help the South, at a time when the South very much needs it."

"I am aware of the South's increasing isolation in commerce and politics," Brunel said with a bob of his head. "Anti-slavery societies are quite active in this country, you know. Well, if you are serious, I'll show you my drawings and specifications, share as much information as I can. I suppose I needn't tell you that many find my design suspect. My babe is the first ship in history to be built without ribs. They say she'll hog, arch up in the center, break apart—"

"I'll take your opinion rather than those of your critics."

The engineer smiled. He seemed to lose some of his own negative feelings as he described the great four-cylinder screw engines he had subcontracted to James Watt's company. "Then there's the paddle shaft. Forty tons. The single largest forging ever attempted by man—"

He talked with mounting enthusiasm as they walked on through the drizzle. Flocks of crows were perching on the deserted souvenir stalls. A section of canvas flapped. Shipyard workers on scaffolds hailed Brunel, but he missed most of the greetings; he was speaking too rapidly. So rapidly that Cooper could barely keep up with the writing of notes.

Cooper took his family out to a plain little churchyard in Beaconsfield. The children didn't understand why he stood silent, with his head bowed, at the grave of a man named Burke. But even four-year-old

535

Marie-Louise dimly grasped that the place meant something special to her father.

The children were much more interested in the Thames River tunnel, the monumental nineteen-year project Brunel had finished after the death of his father, who had done the original engineering work. Brunel had already shown the Mains a model of his Great Shield, a huge, compartmentalized iron work-face in which thirty-six laborers had stood with pick and hammer removing the soil of the riverbed a little at a time.

The family entered the pedestrian tunnel from the Wapping side of the river. It was a cool, eerie place, and Judith was somewhat put off by the sight of so many derelicts sitting or sleeping against the walls. But Cooper, with Marie-Louise held in his left arm and Judah hanging onto his right hand, saw only the grandeur of the concept. His eyes shone.

"If free men can do this, why on earth does anyone keep slaves?"

The whisper brought a shiver to Judith's spine. Cooper looked as if he had glimpsed the face of God. She slipped her hand around his right arm and squeezed, loving him more than she ever had.

Next day, Cooper and Brunel planned to go over rough cost estimates for *Leviathan*. Without warning, Cooper postponed the appointment and went chasing off in a new direction, on behalf of George Hazard.

What started the chase was a four-word headline in the *Mail*.

The issue was weeks old. It had been picked up from a railway-station bench and used to wrap the cores of some apples the children had eaten on the return trip from Beaconsfield. Cooper found the remains of the apples and the paper on a table in the foyer of their hotel suite. He was about to toss everything away when a headline caught his eye:

BESSEMER SEEKS AMERICAN PATENT.

A student of inventors and inventions, Cooper recognized the name at once. Henry Bessemer was a successful inventor best known for developing a method to put the proper spin on projectiles fired from a smoothbore gun. He had done the work during the Crimean War, with the aid and encouragement of Emperor Napoleon III of France.

What was he attempting to patent in America? Two short paragraphs supplied the answer. "Good Lord, fancy that!" Cooper exclaimed. He was already beginning to sound somewhat British.

Judith appeared from the parlor. "Is anything wrong?"

"Quite the contrary. Have a look. Chap named Bessemer claims to have invented a fast way to convert pig iron to steel. He's going after an American patent. I wonder if George knows. I must look into this for him."

And so he did, canceling his appointment in order to do it. Most of his investigation consisted of searching through old newspapers. He also sent several notes to Bessemer requesting an interview. The inventor never answered.

"Not surprising," Brunel told him several days later. "Bessemer claims he was pressured into revealing the existence of his process too soon."

"How did he reveal it?"

"He read a long wheeze of a paper before the Association for the Advancement of Science. *The Times* reprinted it *in toto*."

"When?"

"Sometime in August, I recall."

"I didn't look back quite that far."

Cooper wrote another note to the inventor; Brunel wrote as well. That turned the trick, but Bessemer's reply said Cooper could have no more than ten minutes of his time.

Brunel's genius lay in conceptual thinking, ideas that could not be patented and that he was glad to share. Henry Bessemer's inventions were different, each a specific device or process and hence to be protected—or stolen. Cooper found Bessemer a suspicious, defensive man.

"The announcement was premature. It brought down a wild pack of wolves. They're fighting with me and among themselves for a share of my discovery. The steelmakers of Sheffield are deriding me, as of course they must. It currently takes them a fortnight to obtain a small crucible of cast steel from pig iron. If I can make five tons of steel in a half hour, they're finished."

"What can you tell me about your process, Mr. Bessemer?"

"Nothing. I have said all I am going to say to the public or to you. Good day, Mr. Main."

Cooper already knew one reason for Bessemer's hostility. There were problems with his process. Again digging through old newspapers, Cooper located the *Times* article and learned more about the nature of the controversy surrounding the inventor. He copied out everything that might interest his friend in Lehigh Station.

Bessemer had been led to his discovery while working with Napoleon III's armaments expert, Minié, on the problem of projectile spin. An intensely curious man, he had been drawn into other aspects of ordnance, including a study of possible substitutes for the fragile cast iron currently used to make cannon. What resulted from this line of inquiry was Bessemer's process to manufacture quality steel in quantity and the necessary machinery—an egg-shaped converter, a hydraulic apparatus for operating it from a safe distance, and what he called his blowing engine for sending an oxygen-rich blast of air over the pig iron.

In theory the process was astoundingly simple. But that was the case with many revolutionary inventions. One month after making his sensational revelations, Bessemer was licensing his process to various firms for thousands of pounds. A month later the press was branding him a charlatan. "A brilliant meteor which flitted across the metallurgical horizon, only to vanish in total darkness."

By the time Cooper arrived in England, the public furor had died down. Bessemer still had faith in his process and was pursuing his American patent, but English ironmasters were after his head. Those who had paid to use his process declared it a failure and a hoax. The steel was unsatisfactory. Frantic to find the reason, Bessemer was now committed to nonstop laboratory work. The reason for the failure seemed to lie in the high phosphorus content of all the ore mined in Britain. Unwittingly, the inventor had used Swedish ore in his experiments, an ore virtually free of phosphorus.

Brunel told Cooper that even this discovery did not solve Bessemer's problem. However, there were persistent reports that an anonymous steelmaker from Wales had found a way to make the process work and was planning to patent his own method. No wonder Bessemer felt threatened and angry. He had rocketed to prominence, then fallen, all within three months.

Still, Cooper was impressed with the man and believed that he was onto something. What persuaded Cooper were the frequent public statements of the Sheffield manufacturers—they continued to denounce Bessemer and the theoretical base of his process. Anytime an idea was opposed that vehemently, there was usually something to it.

He continued to clip old papers, building up a thick file and sup-

42

"What's the name of this mysterious fellow who is Bessemer's savior?" Stanley Hazard asked.

The question carried not only skepticism but a sneer. To be sure, the sneer was faint—this was, presumably, an occasion governed by politeness—but it was there. Cooper despised Stanley's narrow mind almost as much as he despised his smug face, whose resemblance to an overflowing bowl of gruel grew more pronounced every year.

Recalling the larger purpose of his visit helped Cooper curb his anger. "I don't know, Stanley. His finery is in Wales, but beyond that, nothing is said." He pushed the thick file across the table. "All I could learn is in here."

Suddenly he pressed his hand to his lips and coughed. George was excited by Cooper's news. He showed it by smoking faster than usual, quick, nervous puffs of the cigar clenched in his teeth. When Cooper's fit of coughing continued, George waved his hand through the layers of blue smoke, stirring and dispersing them a little.

"Sorry, Cooper." He strode to the window and raised it. Cool night air flowed into the small private dining room of the hotel.

In New York, Cooper had put Judith and the children on a steamer to Charleston, then come straight on to Lehigh Station. He had arrived in the middle of the night and secured a room at the Station House. The hotel was located a block from the depot. It had been built soon after the railroad came through. It was small, but modern in every respect. Each guest room had a bathtub in a smaller room adjoining, and the entire place was lit by gas mantles.

After a good breakfast, Cooper had sent a note up the hill, informing George of his arrival and inviting him to bring his brother to supper that evening. Cooper really didn't want to present his ship design to Stanley, but felt he must. George was in charge of all direct spending by Hazard Iron, but the ship would be a different sort of expense, an investment, and one so large George probably wouldn't dare authorize it without consulting his brother. Better to have Stanley on their side than working against them.

George was still riffling through the notes and press clippings. "You know, this sounds remarkably like Kelly's process."

Cooper forked a last morsel of rabbit pie from the deep dish in front of him. "Who's Kelly?"

George told him about the Kentucky ironmaker. "But if Bessemer has already applied for an American patent—"

"Did I forget to tell you?" Cooper interrupted. "He got it before I left London."

"Then Kelly may be out of luck. In any case"—George's cigar had gone out; he struck a match and puffed—"I'm going to book passage at once. I can send Constance off to see the French cathedrals while I look into this."

Stanley began, "I think you're a fool to risk—"

"Risk what? My time? The price of a trip? Good Lord, Stanley, unless you want to stand still in business, risk is inevitable. Why can't you ever understand that? Suppose Hazard's could obtain an American license for Bessemer's process. Think of all we'd stand to gain by being first in the market."

"Gain—or lose," Stanley countered. "Is it not a fact that this process is still producing steel of unacceptable quality?"

Unexpectedly infuriated, George pounded the table. "What difference does it make to you, goddamn it? I'll pay for the whole trip out of personal funds."

Stanley leaned back and smiled. "Yes, I would be much happier if you did that."

George pressed his lips together, drew a long breath, then addressed the visitor. "I'd like to see Bessemer personally. Perhaps he'll be less suspicious of me since I'm in the iron trade."

A thin smile from Cooper. "Not likely. Practically the whole of the British metalworking industry is laughing at him."

"What do you suppose they know that we don't?" Stanley asked with a sigh. He stood up.

George drew the cigar from his mouth and peered at his brother through a squiggle of smoke. "Stanley, I know it's been years since you practiced good manners, but try to remember how you behaved before you took up with politicians. Cooper did us a great favor by coming here. We owe him the courtesy of listening to whatever he cares to say. There *was* something else, wasn't there?"

"Yes," Cooper said. Disgusted, Stanley sat down.

With a sinking feeling, Cooper reached for his valise. He hated to

542

present his drawing of the *Star of Carolina* in this atmosphere of skepticism and hostility.

He moved dishes and silver, then unrolled the drawing, which by now had become smudged and dog-eared. Slowly, earnestly, he began to speak. He started with the specifics of his design. He enthusiastically described the great steamer's capacity and cargo flexibility. Finally he revealed his plan to build the vessel in Charleston. He concluded by saying:

"Our family has capital to put into the project, but not enough for a venture of this magnitude. If the Hazards came in as partners, we could proceed, and I think both families would stand an excellent chance of making a profit. Perhaps a very large one."

Stanley's quizzical eyes skimmed the drawing again. "What do the banks say about this?"

"I haven't approached any banks. I wanted to give you first chance." To George: "Of course there are risks—"

Stanley snickered and under his breath said something snide. George heard the word *understatement*. He shot his brother a dark look. Stanley sat back with folded arms and half-lidded eyes.

George said: "You've already explained those. More than adequately, in my opinion. But I'm not qualified to evaluate this sort of proposal. I know nothing about ship construction."

"All I know is what I've learned from personal study," Cooper responded. "I intend to bring the best New England shipwrights and naval architects to Charleston—"

He talked for another ten minutes. He might have saved his breath. Arms still folded, Stanley announced:

"I'm opposed. I wouldn't put a half-dime into it."

Cooper's face fell. George toyed with the corner of the drawing. Then he sat up, squared his shoulders, and said to the visitor:

"How much do you need?"

"To start? Something around two million."

The older brother snorted and got to his feet again. George glared. "For Christ's sake, shut up, Stanley. I'm sorry I invited you. This will be my money. I'll mortgage my assets or, if I can't, liquidate them. No one will trifle with your precious income."

Stanley was taken aback. "Where did you get assets worth two million?"

"I'm not sure they are, quite. I'll have to ask the bankers. But I have plenty of money you don't know about. I made it while you

543

were busy ingratiating yourself with Boss Cameron. Each to his own,'' he finished with a shrug that sent Stanley back to his chair, speechless with humiliation.

George extended his hand to Cooper. "We're partners, then. At least we'll explore the feasibility of a partnership. It will take me a week or so to learn whether I can in fact raise the money."

"You're reckless,'' Stanley exploded. "You've always been reckless.'' He leaned toward Cooper. "Just how many years will it take to design and launch this great vessel of yours? Five? Ten?''

"Three. She can be in service by 1860.''

"Fine,'' Stanley sneered. "Then you can make it the flagship of the navy of your new Southern nation. The one all those traitors in your state keep prophesying.''

He reached for his hat, stick, and overcoat. George said, "His friend Cameron is flirting with Republicanism. Stanley's trying on the party rhetoric for size.''

This drew another hateful look from Stanley. He pointed his stick at the drawing. "That thing is a joke. You'll all come to ruin, mark my word.''

He marched out. George sighed. "He didn't even thank you for supper. If he weren't my brother, I'd wring his neck.''

Cooper grinned, holding up the rolled drawing.

"Never mind. We're launched without him.''

Within two weeks, George pledged one million nine hundred thousand dollars of capital to build the *Star of Carolina*.

A draft for fifty thousand, matched by a similar amount from the Mains, would pay for the initial steps. These included a survey and plan of the James Island acreage, clearing of the land, and a deposit in an escrow account representing three years' salary for a man Cooper had traveled north to steal from the Black Diamond firm. The man's name was Levitt Van Roon; he was one of the country's top naval architects. Cooper soon had Van Roon moved to Charleston with his family. He then sent Van Roon to England to visit the Millwall Yard and confer with Brunel.

Articles incorporating the Carolina Marine Company had to be prepared, along with the partnership agreement between the Mains and George Hazard. For this work Cooper went to Ashton's husband; Huntoon was expensive but expert. Cooper approved the twenty-seven-page partnership document and gave it to Orry, who forwarded it to George.

Several weeks later Orry said to his brother: "George tore up the agreement."

"Oh, Lord. Is he pulling out?"

"No, nothing like that. He doesn't think a contract's necessary. He said the two of you shook hands."

"And on that basis he'll trust me with nearly two million dollars?"

Orry nodded, amused by his brother's reaction. For his part, Cooper understood more graphically than ever before why Orry had such great respect and affection for the stocky little man from Pennsylvania.

In the spring of 1857, Billy finished his short tour at Fort Hamilton. There he had assisted the senior officer in charge of repairs on the twenty-three-gun terreplein and, additionally, undertaken a project assigned to him alone.

It wasn't much of a project: the restoration of two floors and a ceiling in the magazines at Battery Morton, whose guns guarded the Narrows. But he had worked out all the calculations himself, done the drawings, and hired and supervised six civilian workers, all of whom were at least ten years older, and frequently quarrelsome. They didn't give a damn about his engineering training, but after he broke up a fight and held his own against the bully of the group in two minutes of brutal, clumsy punching, he had their respect.

Billy liked the color and bustle of New York. Being a Yankee, he was at home there. Yet he felt that his heart now lay in the South. He hoped his next posting would take him in that direction. To Cockspur Island in the Savannah River, for instance. Or—even better—to the fortifications in Charleston harbor. To his regret, the Army's mysterious bureaucracy chose to move him halfway across the country, to follow in the footsteps of a giant.

Not quite twenty years earlier, the man still considered the Army's foremost soldier and Scott's likely successor had been sent to St. Louis with one clerk and orders instructing him to do something about a problem on the Mississippi River. The river was silting up along the west bank and slowly ruining navigation near the St. Louis waterfront.

Robert Lee of the Corps of Engineers had decided the solution lay in long dikes. He built these at the upstream and downstream ends of Bloody Island, a long, cottonwood-covered shoal on the Illinois side. Two and a half years of his life were devoted to this and other river improvements in the vicinity. When he was finished, the well-planned dikes diverted the current so that it scoured out accumulated sand and satisfactorily deepened the steamboat channel on the city side.

Lee's work earned him the gratitude of the St. Louis business community, and then his heroism in the Mexican War turned him into something of a legend. Now Brevet Lieutenant Hazard, again with one clerk, was being posted to St. Louis to effect repairs on the dikes—a job considerably easier than Lee's had been, but no less lonely.

Billy wrote Brett that he felt he was being banished to the remote frontier. One good thing could be said: he was still banking part of his pay each month. The marriage fund, they called it in their frequent and highly sentimental correspondence. Brett promised to visit him in St. Louis, provided she could persuade Orry to chaperone her.

Despite the 1855 expansion program which had created four new regiments, the U.S. Army was still small. Hence it was not at all unlikely for a young officer to be posted to a place where the Marble Model had served—or even to be assigned to his command, which turned out to be the case with Charles.

Charles graduated third from the bottom of the class of 1857. He ordered uniforms with yellow facings, pinned on the insignia of the mounted service, and went home on furlough. He had been ordered to duty with the Second Cavalry in Texas. The Second was one of the new regiments. There were so many Southerners from West Point in it that the unit was called Jeff Davis's Own. The term was not always complimentary.

When Ashton heard of the assignment, her reaction was similar to Billy's: "Why, that's the end of the earth. Nothing there but dust, niggers, and red savages."

"Nonsense, Ashton. There are Texans, Spaniards—and the best mounted regiment in the Army. Bob Lee's in command now. He moved up when Albert Johnston was reassigned. Lee has written friends at the Academy, and he says Texas is beautiful. He keeps a garden and a pet rattlesnake. I think I'll do the same."

"I always knew you were crazy," she said with a shudder.

43

A steamer from New Orleans delivered Charles to Indianola on the Texas Gulf coast. From there he traveled by stagecoach up to San Antonio, the headquarters of the regiment and the Department of Texas, which Lee was also commanding temporarily.

Texas was a new experience for Charles, a new kind of landscape. Neither mountainous like the Hudson Highlands nor overgrown and dank like some sections of the low country, but flat or gently rolling, open to the burning sun and scouring winds, subject to brutal summer heat and miserable winter chill. Something in him responded instantly to the space and the freedom. The land produced a feeling that here a man could live to the full, unhampered by the traditions and trivial rules that forced behavior into a rigid pattern in more settled parts of the country.

Charles had been happy to leave the East and all the sectional hostility there. In March the Supreme Court had decided the case of Dred Scott, the slave who had sued for his liberty on the grounds that he had become a free man the moment his owner took him into free territory. Charles didn't understand all the complexities of the case, but the heart of the majority opinion written by Chief Justice Taney was a judgment that Scott had no right to sue because slaves were not citizens, not legal persons in the constitutional sense. Hence they could not seek justice in American courts. The decision had enraged people on both sides of the issue and provoked a score of nasty fights at West Point during the spring.

Charles doubted that he would completely escape such quarrels out here, but maybe they would be fewer. Frontier or not, Texas still belonged to the slaveholding South.

San Antonio spread beside the river of the same name. The city was an odd but delightful blend of three cultures that first became evident to Charles in the architecture. As the stagecoach bumped through the outskirts, he saw neat single-story homes of square-cut white limestone, each with its small painted sign identifying the owner.

German names, mostly. Later, on narrow Commerce Street, he sauntered past shops with signs in German as well as in English. The American colony lived nearby, in solid brick residences two or three stories high, with picket fences surrounding them.

And, of course, there were the adobe houses, distinctively square and flat-roofed. All in all, he liked the look of the town as much as he liked the look of the state. The people seemed friendly, acting as if they believed life had treated them well and given them reason to be confident about the future. Charles saw a good many raffish plainsmen, heavily armed, and he was particularly charmed by the dark-skinned Spanish girls.

Before reporting to Lee, he took pains to brush the dust from his pale blue trousers and tight-fitting dark blue jacket. He polished the brass eagle ornament and plumped up the two black ostrich plumes on his Hardee hat—the cavalry's version of a precedent-breaking full-brimmed hat of gray felt introduced in the Army in 1855. The left brim of the Hardee hat was turned up and held by the claws of the metal eagle.

After Charles handed his papers to Lee's aide, a cheerful Pole named Lieutenant Radziminski, he was received by the regimental commander. Lee ordered him to stand at ease, then invited him to sit. September sunlight flooded the white-painted room. The open windows admitted dry, bracing air.

Lee was punctilious, yet cordial. "It's good to see you again, Lieutenant. You look fit. The Academy agreed with you, then."

"Yes, sir. I liked it—though I confess I wasn't much good in the classroom."

"Out here, other qualities are just as important as scholarship. The ability to ride well and endure hardship. The ability to lead men of varying backgrounds." He turned toward a large lacquered map of Texas hanging behind him. All the posts in the department were identified by pins with small ribbons on them. "Where you are being sent, the troops are composed chiefly of Alabama and Ohio men. Of course we have our quota of recent immigrants throughout the regiment. By the way—"

Having failed to satisfy Charles's curiosity and name his destination, Lee faced forward again. "My nephew is serving with the Second."

"Yes, sir, I know."

"You and Fitz were friends—"

"Good friends. I'm looking forward to seeing him."

548

Lee nodded, thought a moment. "For your information, General Twiggs will soon be arriving to assume command of the department. Major George Thomas will take over the regiment and transfer its headquarters back to Fort Mason. I'm returning to Virginia."

Charles tried to hide his disappointment. "A new assignment, sir?"

Gravely, Lee shook his head. "My wife's father passed away. I must take a leave to attend to some family matters."

"My condolences, sir. I'm sorry to hear you're leaving."

"Thank you, Lieutenant. I plan to return as soon as practicable. Meanwhile, you'll find Major Thomas a very capable commandant. He graduated in the class of 1840."

It was said as if to stamp Thomas with a mark of approval. Charles was learning that the mark united those officers who had gone through the Academy and separated them from those who had not.

Lee relaxed, grew more conversational. "Our work here is confined to just a few tasks, but each is important. Guarding the mail coaches and emigrant trains. Scouting. And of course suppressing an occasional Indian outbreak. The threat of Indian trouble isn't as constant as our playwrights and novelists would have gullible Easterners believe. But neither is it imaginary. I think you'll find the duty both interesting and challenging."

"I know I will, Colonel. I already like Texas very much. There's a feeling of freedom here."

"We'll see how you like it after you've lived through a norther," Lee replied with a smile. "But I understand what you're saying. Last year I read a book by a chap named Thoreau. One line stuck in my mind. 'There are none happy in the world but beings who enjoy freely a vast horizon.' That certainly applies to the frontier. Perhaps it also explains why there is so much turmoil and disputation in our country. Ah, but I haven't mentioned your post, have I?"

He stood up, faced the map, and indicated one of the ribbons pinned almost due north of San Antonio at what looked to be a distance of about 250 miles.

"Camp Cooper. On the Clear Fork of the Brazos. It's two miles upstream of the Penateka Comanche agency and reservation. Your troop commander is also a West Point man recently transferred from Washington back to line duty here. His name is Captain Bent."

Charles drew equipment and a fine horse, a roan, for the trip to Camp Cooper. He would ride north with the departmental paymaster and his party. On the night before his departure, he was on his way to find supper when he encountered Colonel Lee and Major George Thomas on the street. Lee asked him where he was going, and when he answered, the colonel said that he and Thomas were on their way to dine at the Plaza Hotel, and why didn't he join them? Lee again made reference to the Academy background the three of them shared, and that overcame Charles's hesitation. He thanked the senior officers for the invitation and fell in step beside them.

Hot, humid weather had produced a new crop of flies and mosquitoes—overnight, it seemed. In the hotel dining room, little black boys with palm fans stood by the tables to shoo the insects away. A touch of home, Charles thought with a twinge of conscience. Though he remained a loyal Southerner, four years at West Point had exposed him to new ideas and changed some of his thinking. He had begun to feel that the South's economy was built on a rotten foundation, one that could not help but collapse eventually—if it were not swept away by outside forces first.

Lee and Thomas chatted in a convivial way about a variety of things. The Indian problem. Major Bill Hardee's new infantry tactics, which were replacing those authored by General Scott. A horse race won by another South Carolinian in the regiment, Captain Nathan Evans of Marion. He commanded Company H and still went by his West Point nickname, Shanks.

The talk turned to the weather. "Texas brings out the mettle of our military Shadrachs and Abednigos," Lee said. "Wait till you patrol in this kind of heat for twenty or thirty days at a stretch."

"While trying to find ten thieving Comanches in a thousand square miles," Thomas added. Heavier than Lee and more reticent, the major was forty or so. His quiet demeanor suggested a strong will, as did the occasional flash of his silvery blue eyes. Like the commandant, he was a Virginian.

"If most of the Comanches are cared for on reservations, why do they steal?" Charles asked.

Lee answered the question in a roundabout way. "We've tried to turn the southern Comanches into farmers, but I don't believe they're temperamentally suited for it—and beyond that, for the last year or so, the weather's been against us. Nothing but drought. So their crops have failed, which means they have no money. Yet, like all human beings, they have wants. Tobacco, knives, strouding. Certain unscrupulous traders are willing to deal with them and supply those things. The traders are Choctaws, mostly, down from Indian Territory. A few are Comancheros from New Mexico.''

Still puzzled, Charles said, ''But if the Comanches don't have cash crops, what do they trade?''

''Horses.''

''Stolen horses,'' Thomas clarified. ''Colonel Lee's predecessor believed in what he called rigorous hostility toward the Indians. Patrol, pursue, punish—that was the strategic concept. Lately, however, Washington has followed a somewhat more passive policy. We are under orders to stand pat until there's an outbreak, until the Comanches descend on some white settler unfortunate enough to have a few horses in a pole corral. Then we rush into action, praying to God we aren't too late to prevent the settler's murder.''

Lee studied his plate of venison steak in a pensive way. ''You can't entirely blame the Comanches. We took their lands for settlement. Then we drove off the game they depend on for survival. If they have nothing, and steal, we're partly responsible.''

''Don't let Governor Houston hear you say that,'' Thomas declared with a humorless smile.

But Charles could only think of the excitement of it. A mounted chase, a charge with sabers swinging. *Patrol, pursue, punish.* He was glad he'd been posted to the Second instead of some stodgy regiment in a safe part of the country.

Three times a year the paymaster brought the departmental payroll from New Orleans in the form of coin. Six times annually he set out on a circuit of the Texas forts, carrying the payroll in a padlocked chest. He traveled in a mule-drawn ambulance accompanied by a provision wagon and six mounted men commanded by a sergeant.

The mounted men were dragoons in orange-faced uniforms. Riding with them, Charles felt himself the object of the veteran's unspoken contempt for the greenhorn. The dragoon uniforms and gear were weathered, whereas his were obviously brand-new.

The dragoons were America's original mounted service. Now they were being superseded by the cavalry; light cavalry, really. Like the other new mounted regiment, the Second had no heavily armored men, as European cavalry did. Further, the Second was supposed to fight on horseback, not merely ride to a battlefield and then dismount. The dragoons felt threatened by this new style of mounted warfare, of which Secretary Davis obviously approved. Their resentment showed. Except for military courtesies, they ignored Charles during the journey.

At Fort Mason he had a joyful and alcoholic reunion with Fitz Lee, who was as cheerful and carefree as ever and just as scornful of authority. He and Charles discussed most of the West Point men in the regiment: Shanks Evans of South Carolina; Earl Van Dorn from Mississippi; Kirby Smith of Florida; John Hood of Kentucky; Alabama's Bill Hardee, whose name had been given to the new-style hat while he was serving with the Second Dragoons. No wonder critics accused Davis of creating an elite regiment staffed with Southern gentlemen.

Just before the pay train moved out, Fitz said to his friend, "Watch out for that troop commander of yours. He hasn't been out here long, but his reputation's already bad."

"Incompetent?"

"Not that so much. Devious. Not to be trusted. Be careful."

Charles pondered the warning as he rode in the dust raised by the provision wagon, occasionally patting and murmuring to the roan he had named Palm in celebration of his home state.

A hot southwest wind flung grit against the back of his neck. Then, within a period of ten minutes, the wind shifted almost 180 degrees, the sky filled with boiling black clouds, the temperature plummeted, and a norther came tearing at him with torrential rain and hail so large that one piece gashed his cheek and drew blood.

In an hour the sun shone again. Ahead, the now-muddy road wound on across low hills toward a horizon rapidly clearing of clouds. As the caravan moved from a vale of glistening pecan trees to a stand of post oaks, a frightened cottontail rabbit bounded in front of the roan. Deep in the oaks, Charles heard larks singing.

His old, brash smile returned. His uniform was soaked, but he didn't mind. The violent, changeable weather appealed to his sense of adventure. He liked Texas better and better every minute.

From a bluff above the Clear Fork, the paymaster's party descended to a pleasant green valley that stretched northward until its floor became lost in the noon haze. Charles had seldom seen a lovelier place. Somehow, the twisted mesquite trees and stunted prickly pear contributed to its fierce beauty.

But the valley's verdant look was a trick of distance and perspective. Near the meandering river, heat-withered leaves on huge elm trees were barely stirring in the sultry breeze. The caravan passed melon and pea fields that had a parched look. Here and there an Indian stood in a dusty furrow watching the soldiers with sad eyes or sullen ones.

Beyond the drought-stricken fields, Charles saw his first Indian settlement—about two hundred animal-hide teepees decorated with yellow and red designs and symbols. The village generated an overwhelming impression of poverty.

Columns of smoke rose from cook fires. The odor of broiling meat mingled with the smell of human waste. Children laughed and played, emaciated dogs barked and ran every which way, and half a dozen young men added to the dust and din by riding bareback through the settlement. They were careful not to come close to the column, Charles noticed.

Two more miles and he'd be able to dismount. He was sweating and his thighs were sore despite the protection of the regulation saddle piece that reinforced the inside of his trousers. When he finally saw Camp Cooper, it looked like paradise, even though it was simply an assortment of fourteen primitive buildings made of stone, logs, clapboard, jacal, or combinations of two or more of them.

The post was laid out as a rambling reversed L. In front of the flagstaff on the parade ground, a platoon of foot soldiers was listlessly practicing the manual of arms. Charles recalled that two companies of the First Infantry were posted here, in addition to a squadron from the Second Cavalry.

The paymaster's detail passed a little bakehouse with a clapboard roof. Two sweaty, bare-chested bakers stood in the shadow of a wall, never moving except to raise and lower their pipes in greeting. As the smell of hot bread gave way to that of manure, the dragoon sergeant rode up to Charles.

"The stables are there, sir. Those two log buildings."

Charles returned the salute and trotted ahead. He turned into the nearest building, which was open at each end and empty except for the horses. A moment later, a long-striding, lanky man came through the far entrance.

The man wore bleached cord pants and a flannel shirt decorated with small wood pickets. A sheath knife hung on his left hip, and on the other a Holster Pistol—the cavalry nickname for Colt's 1848 Army Model revolver. Charles owned a similar gun, a six-shot .44 with beautiful walnut grips and a brass trigger guard. He had also paid for a couple of optional extras: a detachable shoulder stock with a sling ring and a cylinder with a decorative engraving of dragoons in combat with Indians. A cavalryman's revolver was a prized and highly personal possession.

The man scrutinized Charles. He was about forty and had a long, pleasant face partly hidden by a red beard the sun had bleached to copper. In the lobes of both ears he wore brass rings, pirate style. Some civilian attached to the Indian agency, Charles presumed. Or maybe the fellow was the post sutler. Charles dismounted and addressed him brusquely.

"Direct me to the adjutant's office, if you please."

The man pointed the way. For some unfathomable reason his eyes were simmering all at once.

"Where can I find Captain Bent?"

"In his quarters nursing a bad case of dysentery."

Tired and irritable, Charles slapped Palm's rein against his pants leg. "Then who's in charge of K Company?"

"I am, sir." The man's eyes froze him. "First Lieutenant Lafayette O'Dell."

"First—?"

"Stand at attention, sir!"

The shout, so reminiscent of thousands at West Point, automatically drove Charles into the correct braced position. He saluted, his face turning red.

O'Dell took his time returning the salute. He eyed Charles with what the latter took to be hostility. "My apologies to the lieutenant," Charles began. "I'm—"

"The new second," the other broke in. "Been expecting you. Academy man?"

"Yes, sir. I graduated in June."

"Well, the captain's also an Academy man. It's a regular damn club in this regiment. I'm afraid I'm not a member. I'm a plain Ohio farm boy who graduated from plow horses to cavalry nags. The captain isn't very keen on line duty, especially out here. But I like it just fine. If you want the respect of the men, you'd better like it too."

"I will, sir." Charles all but swallowed his words, the same way he was struggling to swallow his embarrassment and anger.

"Let me tell you one more thing about serving in Texas. You'd better learn to dress for it. That fancy coat isn't practical for long patrols, and neither is that sword you're wearing. The hostiles don't sit and wait for a saber charge. By the time you draw that pig sticker, they'll swarm all over you and lift your hair. The captain doesn't like those facts of life either, but he has to put up with them."

Charles lost the battle to keep his temper. His eyes were fiery as he whispered, "Thank you for the advice. Sir."

Suddenly, O'Dell's stern look disappeared. He chuckled and sauntered forward.

"That's better. For a minute I thought they'd sent us a second with no gumption. Let me help you unsaddle that horse. Then you can report and present your compliments to Captain Bent—provided he isn't squatting on his china pot. Don't laugh. The water does that to every newcomer."

Grinning, Lieutenant O'Dell held out his callused hand.

"Welcome to the north part of Texas or the south part of hell, I'm not sure which."

Charles was thankful the first lieutenant wasn't as truculent as he had seemed at first. Like all other troops, Company K had only three officers, and Charles could imagine the problems if they disliked one another. It was already clear that the troop commander was unpopular.

By the time Palm was stabled, rubbed down, and fed, Charles knew a good deal about O'Dell. He had been born and raised near Dayton, Ohio, and at fourteen had lied about his age in order to enlist. His current rank was a brevet; being a second lieutenant at forty was just about what an officer who lacked West Point training could expect.

O'Dell accompanied Charles to a spot near a drab building constructed of jacal—upright poles chinked with clay mortar. He pointed out the captain's quarters, a door at the end from which the paint was peeling. Just then another troop cantered in, its red and white swallow tail guidon snapping. Only three of the troopers wore regulation uniforms; the rest looked much like O'Dell. Charles remarked that no one had prepared him for Camp Cooper's relaxed style of dress.

"What you want," O'Dell said, "is anything that suits the weather and keeps you free to move fast. Find it, steal it—and don't let the captain talk you out of it."

"Thank you, sir. I'll take your advice." He almost expected there'd be more, and there was.

"I'd go see the captain right away if I were you. I sort of compare it to slopping pigs. The sooner you get it over with, the sooner you can go back to things that are more pleasant."

An hour later, having presented his orders and located his own tiny room, Charles knocked on the door O'Dell had indicated. A gruff voice bade him come in.

The troop commander's quarters consisted of a single large room.

Half of the far wall was nothing more than an open window with a canvas blind rolled up at the top.

If O'Dell didn't quite resemble the typical mental picture of a cavalryman, Captain Bent resembled it even less. He was a soft, whalelike man about Orry's age. He had restless little eyes and skin that had turned pink and blistered, rather than browning in the Texas sun. Charles's immediate reaction was negative.

Instead of a uniform, Bent wore a quilted dressing gown over a singlet that showed between the open lapels. The quilted material of the gown was sweated through under the arms and down the back.

"I have been here four months" Bent complained as soon as Charles presented his compliments. "I should be over this damnable malady. But it keeps recurring." The captain gestured at a footlocker piled with books. "You may sit down if you wish."

"Thank you sir, but I'd prefer to stand. I've been in the saddle a long time today."

"Suit yourself."

The sight of the books intimidated Charles—as did the odd look in Bent's black eyes. The captain took the only chair, uttering a long sigh. "I regret that you find me in such straits."

"The first lieutenant prepared me, sir. I'm sorry that you're—"

"Ah, you've met O'Dell," the other interrupted. "We're both from Ohio, but we have nothing else in common. Sets a fine example, doesn't he? Sloppiest officer I've ever seen. What's worse, all the men ape him. Major Thomas informed me that if I was too strict about dress regulations, I'd have a mutiny on my hands. Captain Van Dorn seconded the opinion. I was virtually ordered to condone an unmilitary appearance. Imagine!"

The outburst had a snarling quality. Bent's eyes were ringed with fatigue circles, like charcoal smears above the blistered pink of his cheeks. Charles cleared his throat.

"In any case, sir, I'm sorry you're ill."

"In this godforsaken place, even illness is a diversion."

Desperate to break the tension, Charles forced a pleasantry. "If dysentery's a diversion, I've been told that I'll probably be diverted."

Unsmiling, Bent said, "Pray you get nothing worse. Some newcomers contract stomach ulcers. Some never recover."

He lumbered to the open side of the room and gazed out, swabbing his sweaty throat with a kerchief. "We have all sorts of charming entertainments at Camp Cooper—named, incidentally, for the adjutant general with whom I served before I had the misfortune to come to this sinkhole." He pivoted to face Charles. "How do you find Texas?"

"So far, I like it."

"You must be mad. No, you're Southern, aren't you? Amounts to the same thing—" Bent blinked. "Here, don't bristle so. I was merely making a little jest."

"Yes, sir." The reply had a forced, strained sound, but Charles couldn't help it.

Bent returned to his chair and sank down with another exhausted sigh. "As you may have surmised, I didn't request this duty, and I loathe it. I am not by inclination a line officer. My forte is military theory." A gesture at the books. "Are you interested in that?"

A little color was slowly returning to Charles's face. "At the Academy I found the subject difficult, sir."

"Perhaps some private study would be useful and enjoyable for both of us."

Bent's darting eyes swept over Charles's face, making him nervous again. Courtesy demanded an answer, but he refused to say more than, "Yes, sir, perhaps."

"Heaven knows there's a need for intellectual stimulation on this post. Duty at Camp Cooper consists of nearly equal parts of bad food, wretched weather, occasional forays against ignorant Indians, and pursuit of deserters driven away by loneliness or the lure of gold. The choices for leisure activity are even less attractive. The main ones are drinking and wagering on cockfights. If your temperament inclines you to cohabit with squaws, the French pox is also available."

The captain licked his lips. Charles had the eerie feeling that, in a curious and convoluted way, Bent was asking whether he liked women. With care, he said:

"I doubt I'll have much time for that, sir."

"Good." Bent's gaze slid to the lower part of Charles's face. The younger officer found this visual inventory distinctly unsettling. "Gentlemen always have other means of relieving the tedium."

He sighed once more. "I suppose we are expected to endure the boredom and hardship without complaint. We're career officers and the frontier must be defended. I accepted this post only because turning it down might have been held against me later. I should imagine Colonel Lee felt the same way, given his background."

What a presumptuous peacock, Charles said to himself. Rather than funny, he found it vaguely frightening that Bent compared himself to the Army's foremost officer. The captain cleared his throat.

557

"I thank you for the courtesy of your call, Lieutenant. I believe I should rest now. Oh, by the way. Are you aware that K Company was recruited in and around Cincinnati? A majority of the men are Ohioans. We shall try not to hold it against you that you happen to come from a less enlightened region."

On the point of saying something foolhardy, Charles fought the impulse. Bent was deliberately baiting him, as a test of how well he held his temper—or failed. What word had Fitz Lee used? Devious. It was well chosen.

"Just another little jest, Lieutenant Main. You'll find I'm fond of them. There is but one kind of factionalism in this troop. It is the kind which occurs naturally in the Army. You may put the needs and wishes of your men first or, alternatively, those of your commander. I needn't tell you which choice will better serve your career and your future. Dismissed."

Charles saluted and left. The moment he stepped into the sunshine and closed the door, he shivered. Bent's warning had been unmistakable. If he became the captain's toady, he'd have an easy time of it, but if he allied himself with the men—and, by inference, with O'Dell—he'd suffer.

He recalled his favorable impression of O'Dell and asked himself whether Bent had issued his warning from strength or from weakness. The latter, Charles suspected. The captain probably feared his first lieutenant.

Well, it didn't matter. Charles already knew where he stood, and it was not with the fat misfit who lived behind the peeling door.

Handsome young man, that cousin of Orry Main's, Elkanah Bent thought after the door closed. Almost too attractive. His good looks could divert Bent from the objective. Still, there might be a way to blend pleasure and vengeance. One never knew.

With a groan he rushed behind a cheap paper screen that concealed one corner of the room. He emerged ten minutes later, thinking of how much he hated Texas. Since arriving at Camp Cooper he had lost over twenty pounds. His spine and thighs constantly hurt from all the damned horseback riding, although with the weight loss he was getting better at it. Now, once again, intestinal pain was added to his woes.

And yet—today had been auspicious. His plan was working.

Being ordered to Texas had come as a shocking surprise. He could have called on his contacts to help him get the orders changed, but he didn't. He knew that if he appeared reluctant to accept the assignment, it might create an unfavorable impression in the minds of certain of his superiors. That, he definitely did not want at this stage in his lagging career.

Still, the orders upset him so badly that he left his desk in the War Department and went on a three-day binge. Twice during it he awakened to find sluts in his bed; one was colored. A third time he was surprised to discover a snoring Potomac bargeman—a boy, really—whom he dimly remembered paying. Bent had long ago discovered strong drives within himself. They almost matched the strength of his ambition. He preferred the companionship of women, but he could take pleasure from almost any flesh that offered itself.

Once he had forced himself to accept the idea of going to Texas, he had set to work to make the tour rewarding in another way. The West Point graduation roll revealed that Brevet Lieutenant Main was scheduled to join the mounted service. Since the adjutant general's office handled personnel matters for the entire Army, it was not difficult for Bent to arrange Charles Main's posting to the Second Cavalry.

Bent's hatred of Orry Main and George Hazard had never diminished. And if he couldn't strike directly at the two men who had hurt his career, he would be satisfied to take revenge on their relatives—starting with the young officer now under his command.

He would await the opportune moment.

44

As Bent had said, about three-quarters of the enlisted men of Company K hailed from Ohio. The rest were recent immigrants. German, Hungarian, Irish—a typical mix for almost any unit in the Army.

The troopers treated O'Dell differently from Charles and the captain. All three officers were obeyed, but the first lieutenant had the respect and even the friendship of his men. Charles determined to win that same kind of respect, Friendship could take care of itself.

During his fourth week on the post he discovered one of his men missing from morning formation. He found the fellow, a recent immigrant named Halloran, drunk as a tick in the stables. He ordered Private Halloran to go to his bunk and sleep it off. Halloran swore and pulled a knife.

Charles dodged the clumsy slash, disarmed Halloran, and flung him into the watering trough outside. Halloran climbed right out and charged. Charles hit him four times—twice more than was probably necessary, but the trooper had a wild look in his eye. Charles then personally hauled the semiconscious man to the guardhouse.

An hour later he sought out the troop first sergeant, a stub-nosed eighteen-year veteran of the mounted Army, Zachariah Breedlove.

"How is Halloran?" Charles asked.

"Dr. Gaenslen said he has a broken rib—sir." The slight pause before the flnal word was typical of Breedlove's professional insolence. He was older and much more experienced than most of the officers, and he never wanted them to forget it.

Charles rubbed his chin. "Guess I shouldn't have hit him so hard. I thought he was out of control."

"Well, sir—with all due respect—you're dealing with soldiers here, not nigger slaves."

"Thank you for explaining that," Charles replied in an icy way. He walked off.

Later when he calmed down, he realized the significance of the incident. First Sergeant Breedlove, and no doubt most of the other men, distrusted him because he was a Southerner. He might never be able to win their trust.

The thought discouraged him, but he was not about to give up.

Every morning the bugler sounded reveille at five before six. For a change Charles didn't mind getting up early. The Texas autumn was beautiful and cool, the dawn skies the clearest and purest blue he had ever seen. It seemed to him that he had never tasted anything as delicious as the cook's standard morning fare—hot Dutch-oven biscuits, beefsteak, stewed apples and peaches, and the familiar Army coffee.

Mounted drill and practicing the manual of the saber and the carbine took up a good deal of the troop's time. So did grooming the horses. To promote the Second as a crack unit, Davis had decreed that each company should have mounts of one color. Company K had nothing but roans, Van Dorn's company of Alabama men nothing but grays—hence the name Mobile Grays. The men in Company K soon noticed Charles's fine horsemanship, and it even drew some laconic words of approval from O'Dell. The first lieutenant offered his compliment in front of all the enlisted men—a small but important step forward, Charles thought.

Occasionally an alarm from some settler out in the countryside sent a detachment on a forced ride, but Indian marauders were seldom found. Horses owned by settlers continued to disappear, however. And the Delaware trackers employed by the Army regularly found signs indicating the presence of raiding Yamparikas—northern Comanches—who were continuing to slip down from Indian Territory.

Boredom remained the main enemy at the post. Charles dug and hoed a garden he intended to plant next spring. He bought a pair of scraggly hens and built a small house for them. And he finally, reluctantly, sat down to compose the letter he felt he owed Orry after all this time. He started by attempting some description of the Texas landscape, but he knew his words and his literary skills were inadequate. The first few paragraphs took so much thought and struggle that he brought the letter to a hasty close by promising to describe Camp Cooper and his odd company commander the next time he wrote.

Because he couldn't stand to live like a monk, he slept with Indian girls occasionally. He found them lively and affectionate, and he didn't catch the pox. And of course, because it was an expected part

562

of military life, he participated in the chief sport of the officers—argument.

They argued about everything. One favorite topic, good for hours, was the flat Grimsley saddle adopted ten years earlier. Albert Sidney Johnston had liked it, but most of the officers sided with Van Dorn, who insisted the design was responsible for too many sore-backed horses.

They argued about weapons. Generally, Colt repeaters and Sharps carbines were considered best, although such views didn't make a particle of difference, since the government's theory of ordnance seemed to be that the Army should use whatever old weapons happened to be stockpiled in Federal warehouses. Hence most of Company K was equipped with 1833-model Hall smoothbore carbines, and never mind that European and American arms experts agreed on the superiority of a rifled barrel. There were even some musketoons in the troop. Old single-shot horse pistols were used for holster weapons. Charles felt fortunate to possess a ten-year-old Colt.

There were arguments about food, drink, women. About the motives of Indians and the character of Colonel Lee. About the purpose and execution of Colonel Johnston's campaign against the Mormons and their so-called State of Deseret. The hottest differences of opinion were always generated by political issues, such as the pro-Southern constitution adopted at Lecompton, Kansas.

The Lecompton constitution offered Kansas voters a choice between a limited form of slavery and the unrestricted practice of it. President Buchanan supported it. Senator Douglas damned it, and most of the Northerners on the post agreed with the Little Giant. Charles kept out of the disputes, but his restraint did not really work to his benefit. Everyone assumed he was on the pro-slavery side.

Arguments on any subject frequently ended with a pronouncement by Captain Bent which soured whatever friendly spirit had prevailed until then and left the other officers moodily staring at plate or coffee cup. Now and then Charles caught Bent watching him with more than routine interest. He couldn't account for the attention, and it bothered him.

In a chilly rain, the column returned from maneuvers in the northern reaches of the valley. It was the second of December 1857.

Taking O'Dell's suggestion, Charles had soon abandoned regulation uniforms for field duty. Today he wore a slouch hat pulled far down over his bearded face, trousers of buffalo calf leather, and a deerskin coat. Around the coat collar hung a bear-claw necklace.

Mud flew as Bent rode up next to him. The captain's glance usually registered disapproval of Charles's clothing. This time, however, he chose to smile.

"A fire will feel good, eh, Charles?"

The first-name familiarity was unusual and made him nervous. "Yes, sir, very good."

"After you tend to your mount and put on fresh clothes, why not drop into my quarters for a toddy? I'd like to show you my edition of Jomini's *Summary of the Art of War*. You're familiar with the baron's concepts, are you not?"

"Of course, sir. We heard a lot about them from Old Cobben Sense." In fact, some of Professor Mahan's critics had said he devoted too much of his course on the science of war to the ideas of the Swiss military theorist.

"I'll expect you, then. We'll have a splendid discussion."

Squinting against the rain, Charles got a clear look at Bent's wet face. Something in the captain's eyes put him off. He knew he must be polite, but he refused to go further.

"It's a very kind offer, sir, but I think I'm coming down with grippe." It was true; he felt feverish after riding for hours in this bad weather.

"Later, then. Next week—"

"Sir—" He knew he ought not to say the next, but he was damned if he'd encourage the captain's quest for friendship. "If it's all the same, I prefer to be excused. I'm not much for theory."

Bent lost his look of smarmy good cheer. "Very well, Lieutenant. You have made yourself clear."

He kicked his horse and rode to the head of the column. A bolt of lightning ripped downward to the horizon. Charles shivered as Lafayette O'Dell dropped back beside him.

"What did he want?"

Charles explained.

"Did you turn him down?"

"Flat. He didn't like it much."

O'Dell leaned on his saddle pommel, from which hung a pair of expensive closed holsters. Charles had a similar pair on his saddle, although he had paid extra for leopard-skin flaps. One holster held his Colt, the other an extra horseshoe, some nails, a small brush, and a currycomb.

564

"You're smart not to hang out with the captain," O'Dell said. "I guess I should tell you about him."

"Tell me what?"

"That he has what are politely referred to as appetites. Strong ones."

"Don't we all?"

"No, not the same kind—at least I don't think so. The captain pretends to hate the Indians, but that doesn't extend to squaws. From what I hear at the agency, he'll sleep with any woman who's available. If he can't get his hands on a woman, a boy will do—or even an Army private too dumb and scared to refuse him. We've got a couple of those on the post, in case you hadn't noticed."

"No, I hadn't." Charles spat out a swear word.

"The captain hates to be turned down by anyone. I expect you're in for a rough spell."

Suddenly O'Dell's head jerked up. A startled look fleeted over his face. Neither lieutenant had realized that Bent had pulled his horse to the side of the muddy trail and was sitting there, watching them, as rain dripped from the bill of his forage cap and soaked his knee-length talma. Seconds later, Bent stood in his stirrups and called, "Trot—*march!*"

The road was much too rough for it, but Charles understood the reason for the order. Because of his refusal, everyone would suffer.

A day later, riding on the road from Camp Cooper to the Comanche Reserve, as the agency and reservation were officially called, Charles came upon an ox-drawn carreta with one of its huge wooden wheels half buried in mud. An old Indian, his fine features worn by time and toil, was vainly trying to free the cart by pushing the wheel. Without a second thought, Charles dismounted.

"Here, let me help." Not certain how much English, if any, the Indian understood, Charles used broad gestures to illustrate his words. "Lay that whip on the ox a couple of times while I push."

Moments later, with a great lurch that spilled half a dozen melons from the pile in the cart, the wheel was free. Just as Charles started for his horse, he heard riders behind him. He saw the captain, Sergeant Breedlove, and six troopers. Bent and the others reined in.

"What the devil are you doing, Lieutenant?" Bent demanded.

"Helping this man push his cart out of the mud." Resentment edged his answer; it was quite evident what he had been doing.

Sergeant Breedlove glanced at Charles with something close to sympathy. Bent said, "Don't you recognize that fellow? Katumse is chief of the reservation Indians. We do not give aid and comfort to the enemy."

With that he rode on; the rest followed. Charles recalled O'Dell's prediction. Bent's reprimand and the look in his eyes were harbingers of things to come.

From then on the captain found fault with nearly everything Charles did. He criticized him in front of the entire troop and assigned him extra duties. Charles held his temper with great difficulty, assuming that if he obeyed each order and refused to show a trace of emotion, the harassment would eventually stop.

It didn't. It grew worse. In January, riding in from patrol, he found the captain waiting in the stable. Bent stepped up to Palm, slipped his index finger beneath the single band of blue woolen webbing, and tugged.

"This girth is entirely too tight."

Charles was tired, cold, and consequently not inclined to patience. "Sir, it's perfectly all right."

A small, pursed smile. "What's this? Insubordination? That can't be allowed. Before you go to your quarters, I want you to unsaddle your mount, then saddle him again. Do that—let's see—ten times."

"Damn it, sir, what's the purpose of—?"

Charles bit off the blurted question. He knew what the purpose was, but he didn't dare confront his superior with it.

The outburst pleased the captain. "More insolence? Do it fifteen times. I shall send one of the noncoms to observe and report when you're finished. Sergeant Breedlove, I think." Bent was not insensitive to relationships within Company K. Breedlove was known to think poorly of the troop's second lieutenant.

Shortly the first sergeant arrived in the freezing stable where Charles had just lit two lanterns. For the first time Breedlove looked at him with a flicker of compassion.

"Sure sorry to have to do this, Lieutenant."

"Keep your mouth shut and we'll both get out of here sooner," Charles retorted.

Breedlove found a nail keg, turned it on its end, and sat down. His face no longer showed sympathy. Charles worked with angry motions, his breath pluming every time he exhaled. When he finished over two hours later—he had been slowed by exhaustion toward the end—his

arms and shoulders throbbed. Leaving the stable, he stumbled and fell.
Sergeant Breedlove didn't offer to help him up.

"The Butterfield coach is four hours overdue," Bent said above
the howl of the wind.

A fire of fragrant mesquite wood sizzled in the stone hearth of the
small day room. O'Dell stood in front of the fire, warming his hands.
Although he was indoors, he wore his fur coat, the kind of shaggy
garment that caused the Comanches to call the cavalrymen buffalo
soldiers.

The first lieutenant needed that coat. The fire produced almost no
warmth. The room felt like an icehouse. How cold was it outside?
Ten below? During this kind of late-winter storm, the temperature
sometimes dipped even lower than that.

Bent was on his feet now. His small eyes, pricked by the light of
several oil lamps, grew thoughtful as he studied the map tacked to
the jacal wall. The recently opened stagecoach line connected Fort
Smith with El Paso and California. Part of the route lay along the
military road that ran southwest from Camp Cooper. The coach was
lost somewhere out there.

"I expect they just stopped till the storm blows over," O'Dell said.

"That's the logical assumption, naturally. But we mustn't permit
that to lull us into complacence. What if there was a wreck? What if
passengers are hurt? In need of assistance? We must send a search
party. I have already spoken with the commandant, and he's in agreement."

"Sir, that's a norther outside! The wind's going sixty miles an
hour. Ice is already an inch thick on everything. We should at least
wait until morning before—"

Bent interrupted: "The commandant left the timing entirely to my
discretion. The detachment will leave within the hour." He avoided
O'Dell's eyes as he went on, "Ten men, I think. With extra rations
and whiskey. Put Lieutenant Main in command."

O'Dell was so stunned he couldn't bring himself to send a noncom
to waken Charles. He went in person, taking ten minutes just to fight
through the storm to the barracks. Shivering in his long underwear,
Charles sat up, a bewildered expression on his face.

"Tonight? God above, Lafe, is he crazy?"

"I'd say so. But of course circumstances protect him. The coach is way late, and it's remotely possible that the passengers do need help.''

''More likely they're holed up. Or dead. I think the son of a bitch means to kill me.''

''Just because you turned him down that time?'' O'Dell sounded skeptical.

''I know it's senseless, but what else could it be?''

Charles flung off the layers of blankets and hides under which he had been trying to keep warm. ''I don't know why he wants me out of the way so badly, but I sure as hell won't give him the satisfaction. I won't let him squander the lives of good men, either. I'll come back and bring the whole detachment with me, don't you worry.''

He sounded more confident than he felt. He put on every hickory shirt and pair of cord pants he owned, while the Texas norther screamed outside like someone gone mad.

The eleven mounted soldiers left Camp Cooper at one in the morning. The wind-driven sleet had coated everything. But it wasn't deep, as snow would have been, so they were able to keep to the wagon road. The footing was extremely treacherous, however. They traveled no more than a mile in four hours. By then Sergeant Breedlove was calling Bent every name he knew and, when he ran out of those, invented some.

Charles had wrapped a long wool scarf around his ears and the lower part of his face. He might as well have worn gauze. His face felt like a block of wood. He could barely move his lips to issue orders.

The men cursed and complained, but they kept on. They followed in single file behind him, recognizing that he was riding on the point, taking the brunt of the wind and risking himself by being first to cross the treacherous ground.

At daybreak the wind abruptly shifted to the southwest. Then it moderated. Rips appeared in the clouds, with the glow of sunrise showing through. Half an hour later, as they picked their way across a landscape that still resembled glass, Breedlove croaked, ''Look, sir. Down the road.''

A slender column of smoke rose to the clearing sky. ''I'll wager it's the coach,'' Charles said in an equally hoarse voice. ''They're probably tearing it apart and burning it to keep warm. Looks like it's about a mile away.''

A mile and a half, as it turned out. It took them more than three hours to reach the source of the smoke. The coach lay on its side with its two near wheels and doors missing. Part of the door had not yet been consumed by the nearby fire. Just as the detachment came close enough to discern that, Breedlove's roan slipped and lamed the left forefoot.

The other troopers saw to the survivors of the accident—the coach driver, guard, and three male passengers who were nearly comatose. Charles heard the driver mumbling about the vehicle's overturning on glare ice. Nearby lay the frozen corpses of three of the horses; the other three had galloped into the storm to die.

Charles watched Breedlove finish his examination of the injured roan. Reluctantly, he offered the sergeant his revolver.

"Shoot him. I'll do it if you can't."

The sergeant couldn't stand to look at his fallen mount any longer. "How will I get back to camp?"

"The same way as the passengers. Riding behind someone else. I'll take you."

"Lieutenant, I know—I know you prize Palm as much as I prize Old Randy. Any horse that carries a double load very far in this kind of weather will be wore out long before we reach camp. As good as dead. You carry me and you'll have to shoot Palm, too. I'll ride with one of the men."

"Goddamn it, don't argue. A man's more important than a horse. You'll ride with me."

They sounded like shrill children. Two troopers helped the glassy-eyed coach guard toward one of the horses. Breedlove stared at the revolver, then at his fallen mount. He shook his head.

"I can't. If you'll do it for me, I'll be in your debt forever."

"Turn the other way."

Breedlove did, squinting into the flare of the morning sun on the fields of ice. Charles raised the gun and prayed the mechanism wasn't frozen; to prolong this would be torture for the sergeant. Slowly he squeezed the trigger. The revolver bucked. The echo boomed away into space, followed by Old Randy's startled bellow of pain. Chunks of flesh were blown from the other side of the roan's head. They landed on the ice, smoking.

Sergeant Breedlove covered his face with his hands and cried.

Half a mile this side of the post, Palm sank down, unable to go farther. Heartbroken, Charles put two bullets into the horse. Then he and Breedlove walked the rest of the way with blood oozing inside their boots. The post physician told Charles he had come close to losing three toes from frostbite.

He slept eighteen hours. Shortly after he woke, Breedlove paid a call and offered a nervous apology.

"I sure had you figured wrong, Lieutenant. I am one hundred percent sorry for that. You showed plenty of sand when it counted. I've never seen that in any of the Southrons in this regiment."

"Not in Colonel Lee or Van Dorn?"

"No."

"Well, believe me, it's there, in just about the same measure as in other men. Yankees, for example," Charles added with a wry smile. "Maybe you never looked for it, Sergeant."

"Yes," Breedlove mumbled, shamefaced. "Something to that, all right."

That night Charles wrote a letter to Orry, a letter long overdue. His accumulated anger could be heard in the harsh, rasping sound of his pen on the paper. After the salutation, he came directly to the point.

> *I am fortunate to be alive to send this to you, for reasons I shall shortly describe. I know you will find it startling, but know that I am being truthful when I say I am now almost certain that my company commander wishes to see me come to harm because of fancied slights and incidents of insubordination which exist more in his own mind than in fact. Orry, I have somehow become mixed up with a d——d lunatic, and since he is about your age and an Academy man, I hasten to ask whether perchance you know him.*

Charles paused to stab his quill into the ink pot again. The shimmering flame of his desk lamp shifted shadows back and forth on his bleak face. His eyes revealed his confusion and his wrath as he added the next:

> *His name is Elkanah Bent.*

45

Bent's plan had failed. Disastrously. Not only had Charles Main survived the rescue trip in weather that could have left him dead or maimed for life, he and his detachment had been cited in General Orders from headquarters of the Department of Texas. The citation spoke of "performance of a humanitarian mission in the face of extreme natural hazards," and it became part of each man's permanent record. The commandant had hosted a banquet for the detachment and toasted Main's bravery.

Privately, the commandant called Bent's judgment and courage into question.

"When I put you in charge of the emergency, Captain, I never imagined for a moment that you would send men out before the storm showed signs of abating. I further note that you did not lead the detachment, choosing to remain here while permitting Lieutenant Main to absorb the brunt of the danger. I won't make an issue of those lapses for one reason only. Thanks to Main, all turned out well and no lives were lost. The angels were on your side. This time."

The criticism burned. Bent immediately ceased his harassment of Orry Main's cousin, and in fact went out of his way to praise him—always when others were listening. But it was hard to do. As a result of the ride in the storm, the first sergeant was now Charles's staunch partisan, as were most of the enlisted men. With O'Dell also supporting Charles, Bent was completely isolated. He held Charles responsible. No longer was Charles just a convenient representative of the Mains. Bent now hated him personally.

He had learned one lesson, however. Never again would he send his second lieutenant into jeopardy while remaining behind. He'd go along and find some way to dispatch Charles personally, perhaps in the thick of a skirmish. He had used that technique successfully in the past.

But the passing weeks denied him an opportunity. The Texas frontier remained quiet. Soon a new worry was gnawing at Bent. It began when he first noticed a subtle but unmistakable change in Charles's behavior. Charles continued to be courteous to his company commander—courteous almost to a fault—but he had abandoned even the slightest pretense of cordiality.

Bent realized Charles had identified him as an enemy. The question was, had Charles done anything about it? Had he, for example, mentioned Bent's name in a letter to Orry Main? And was it possible that Orry had already warned his cousin to be on guard? Delivery of mail to most of the Texas forts was slow, with service frequently interrupted for weeks or even months by bad weather in the Gulf, by the activities of hostile Indians, or simply by slipshod handling of mail sacks. Still, by now Orry could have informed Charles of the reason for Bent's animosity.

Bent knew he dare not dismiss that potential danger. But as for abandoning his plans—never. Nothing but the saving of his own skin, his own reputation, came before revenge against the Mains and the Hazards. He need only wait and, at the appropriate moment, strike. Warnings from Orry Main would hardly help the young lieutenant survive an attack carried out at an unexpected moment.

As the days dragged on and a clear chance still failed to present itself, Bent's frustration mounted. Occasional Indian raids were reported to Camp Cooper, but the Second fired no shots in anger because no detachment could ever catch the marauders. Closer at hand, Katumse was saying his people had been treated so dishonorably on the reservation that the tribe's only possible response was war, unremitting and without mercy. But the chief never did more than threaten.

In the East the war of words over slavery raged on. Senator Douglas thundered that the Lecompton constitution violated squatter sovereignty. Senator Hammond of South Carolina retorted that the Little Giant's opinion was of no consequence; Southerners no longer needed the approval of, or alliance with, the North. "Cotton is king!" Hammond declared.

In Illinois a lawyer and former congressman named Lincoln prepared to challenge Douglas for his Senate seat. Addressing the Republican state convention in Springfield, Lincoln attacked slavery, but not those who owned slaves, and sounded a warning with words from the twelfth chapter of Matthew: "A house divided against itself cannot stand."

In a month-old paper, Bent read the quotation over and over. He took it not as a cautionary remark but as a statement of the inevitable. Secession first, then war. Often he closed his eyes and envisioned himself as a triumphant general on a corpse-littered battlefield. The

572

mangled bodies were merely so much stage decoration; he was the actor everyone watched and admired.

From the first of May until mid-June, Camp Cooper received no general mail delivery, only official dispatches delivered by courier. Finally two bulging sacks arrived with some supply wagons. One sack, months old, had mistakenly been sent to Fort Leavenworth and only then forwarded to Texas. In each sack there was a letter from Orry. Charles eagerly tore them open, only to discover the first had been written in January; the second around the first of March, two weeks before Bent had sent the rescue expedition into the storm. Hence, neither had anything to say in response to the question about the commander of Company K.

Bent's chance to strike at Charles came in August, in the midst of another drought. A frightened farmer rode into the post on a mule. The commandant summoned Bent, saying to him:

"It's the Lantzman farm. Two miles beyond Phantom Hill."

Phantom Hill was an abandoned fort whose smoke-scarred chimneys were landmarks. "I live close by the Lantzman place," the white-haired farmer explained. "They seen Penateka Comanches in the neighborhood, so they holed up and sent me for help."

"Penatekas, you say." Bent frowned. "Reservation Indians?"

"It's more likely they belong to Sanaco's band," said the commandant. Sanaco was another chief, Katumse's rival. He had refused to settle on the reserve and had scorned Katumse for doing so.

"Have the Indians harmed anyone?" Bent asked.

The farmer shook his head. "Lantzman reckoned they wanted to sport awhile—maybe a day or two—'fore they drove off his horses."

"I fail to understand why the whole family didn't get out."

"Lantzman's oldest son, he's crippled. Sickly. Can't ride too good. Lantzman's a stubborn coot, too. Figures he and his boys can hold off a half-dozen hostiles till help arrives. 'Sides, he knows that if the family lights out, the Injuns are liable to burn the place just for meanness."

The commandant put the matter in Bent's hands. After the stagecoach fiasco, Bent wanted to appear competent as well as prudent. He feigned deep thought for ten seconds, only then saying:

"Half a dozen. You're sure Lantzman saw no more than that?"

"I'm sure, Cap'n."

plementing it with his own notes. He intended to take the file to George the moment he was back in America.

"After all," he said to Judith as they traveled to Southampton for the voyage home, "if I'm going to ask him for a couple of millions to build my ship, I'd better do him a favor first."

Bent had no reason to doubt the statement. Marauding bands of Comanches were seldom large; this one sounded typical. He pondered again, then said, "I'll take twenty men, including both lieutenants and our tracker, Doss."

The commandant looked dubious. "Are you positive you don't want the entire troop?"

Panic clogged Bent's throat momentarily. His judgment was once more suspect. He brazened ahead.

"Twenty-four against six should be a safe margin, sir. Especially when they're men like mine."

The touch of braggadocio pleased his superior. Bent left quickly, excited and not a little fearful at the thought of taking the field against hostiles. He was not eager to do it. But leading a detachment against a band of Comanches, albeit a small one, would look good on his record. It might even offset the blemish left by the coach incident.

He sent his orderly to find O'Dell and Main. He described the situation at Lantzman's and ordered them to have twenty men ready with field gear and two days' rations in one hour. A provision wagon would follow at a slower pace.

Both lieutenants saluted and hurried toward the door. Just as Charles left, he gave the captain a quick glance. God, how Bent loathed his swaggering manner, the beard that made him resemble a hairy animal, his relationship with the men—everything about him. But if he were lucky, Main would soon go to his grave. In his room Bent opened his footlocker and took out his spanking new Allen and Wheelock Army Model .44. He laid the blued octagonal barrel in his palm and caressed it as he thought of his second lieutenant's face. Unless the Comanches had melted away by the time the detachment reached Lantzman's, there would surely be a chance for a well-placed but seemingly stray shot.

Bent shivered with expectation.

The double column sped southwest along the wagon road. The countryside was parched. No rain had fallen for three weeks. Charles realized an electrical storm could ignite a dangerous fire and, if they were unlucky, force them to detour for miles.

Such pessimistic thoughts were unusual for him, but he had a bad feeling about this expedition. The weather contributed. So did the absence of First Sergeant Breedlove, who had left on furlough a week

574

ago. Charles's new roan was unfamiliar and somewhat skittish. But the chief cause of his uneasiness rode at the head of the column.

Captain Bent was the only member of the detachment correctly uniformed in yellow-trimmed fatigue jacket, regulation light blue trousers, and flat kepi-style forage cap. The others wore clothing better suited to the climate and terrain. Charles's shirt of blue flannel was the lightest one he owned. His pants were white and, for the moment, still fairly clean. At his belt hung his Colt and his bowie. A saddle scabbard carried his two-year-old Harpers Ferry rifled musket. A slouch hat protected his eyes from the sun.

Charles doubted Bent had the ability to lead this kind of expedition. Indian fighting was new to the Army. During Professor Mahan's entire course he had devoted only one hour to a discussion of it. But it was more than Bent's inexperience that generated the feeling of distrust. Charles felt Bent had within him a streak of evil, perhaps madness, and for God knew what inexplicable reason, it was directed against him.

The terrain was monotonous. Low, seared hills. Ravines. Creeks dried to a trickle by the drought. Haze dulled the sun and turned it to a defined disk in the sky. A sultry wind blew.

Doss located Indian signs several times. Small parties, he said. The tracks were a day or two old. It made Charles uneasy to think that the emptiness of the countryside might be deceptive.

After a late-afternoon stop to rest the horses, they pushed on. Bent hoped to reach the vicinity of Lantzman's by sundown. Charles was already hot and saddle-weary, but he recognized that speed was necessary. So did most of the other men. This was not an exercise but a relief mission; there was little griping.

O'Dell rode alongside Charles for a while. At one point he said, "This is damn dull, isn't it? If I'd brought my book, I could read awhile."

"What are you reading?"

"That little work by Mr. Helper."

The first lieutenant was good-naturedly trying to get a rise out of him. Charles had heard of *The Impending Crisis of the South—How to Meet It,* but had not yet seen a copy. He did know that Hinton Helper's book was a jeremiad against the peculiar institution, which the author claimed had ruined the South by making it dependent on the North for all its manufactured goods. What was remarkable was that the author hailed from North Carolina.

"I swear, Charles, that man hates the black race damn near as much as he hates slavery. The book does raise some mighty interesting questions, though. Such as why you Southern boys refuse to give up your slaves."

"These days the answer's simple. The spinning mills in England and France are expanding like blazes. That means cotton planters can ship their crops to Europe and get rich overnight. Nobody's going to kill a golden goose."

"You think that's the reason? I wonder."

"What else could it be?"

"Oh, maybe keeping the niggers in their place. Slavery does that nice and comfortably. I'll bet deep down you Southerners are scared of the nigger. He's dark and different. People don't like anything too different. I don't. I'll bet it isn't only money that makes you hang onto the system but the sheer fact of black and white."

"But if you had your way, you'd free all the slaves?"

"Yes indeed."

"What would you do with them?"

"Why, just what a lot of those Republicans propose."

"Black Republicans, they call 'em down home."

"Whatever. I'd deport the niggers. Resettle them in Liberia or Central America. Lord knows they ought to be free, but we don't want 'em here."

Charles threw his head back and laughed. "You're right, Lafe. It's black and white, sure enough. With you, too."

Lieutenant O'Dell didn't exactly like hearing that. He scowled. Charles had grown accustomed to the unconscious hypocrisy of Yankees, which usually turned into anger when it was exposed.

O'Dell had touched a nerve, though. In the South as in other parts of the country no one really knew how to abolish slavery without creating an economic and social calamity. If he could judge by O'Dell's comments, it was a problem haunting a great many people on both sides of—

"Column—halt!"

Ahead, across the mesquite flat, Charles saw ruined adobe chimneys jutting into the red evening light. He and O'Dell trotted forward. Bent summoned the round-faced Delaware tracker. A few moments later O'Dell and the scout cantered to the ruins of Phantom Hill and over the crest of a rise beyond.

The men dismounted, broke out canteens, talked quietly. Charles had nothing to say to Bent, who abruptly rode off about fifty yards and heaved himself down from his saddle. Charles swallowed warm water from his iron-hooped barrel canteen and watched the captain. The lonely commander, he thought. Yet mockery couldn't banish his nagging fear of Bent—a dread made worse because its origin continued to escape understanding. Reasons that came to mind seemed too trivial or too unbelievable.

"There they come."

A corporal's exclamation turned Charles toward the hilltop. Doss and Lafe O'Dell slipped down from the crest, walking their horses so as not to raise dust. The scouts went straight to Bent. From their expressions Charles knew they were not bringing an encouraging report. Charles and the enlisted men drifted within earshot. All heard Doss say:

"Plenty more Panateka now. Sanaco's braves. Some of Chief Buffalo Hump's, too. Bad."

Bent's cheeks were sweat-speckled. "How many are there?"

O'Dell said, "I counted close to forty."

"Forty!" The captain almost staggered. "Describe—" He swallowed. "Describe the situation."

O'Dell plucked out his sheath knife, hunkered, and drew a large U in the dust. "That's the bend in the creek. The hostiles are here." The tip of his knife touched the ground outside the bowed bottom of the U. Within the U he traced a rectangle and an adjoining square. He touched the rectangle. "This is the Lantzman house." He touched the square. "Their corral."

He added two smaller squares near the side of the house facing the corral. "A couple of boys are laid up behind hay bales here and here. They have muskets. The farmer's sons, I would imagine. They're protecting about a dozen horses."

"What's behind the house?" Charles wanted to know.

O'Dell scratched three parallel lines within the open end of the U. "A flat. Rows of corn so sun-scorched it won't amount to anything this year. The corn is low enough and thin enough that a couple of guns can keep anyone from sneaking up on that side."

Bent breathed noisily. "What are the Indians doing now?"

Eyes lit with points of red from the sunset, O'Dell stood up slowly. "Eating supper. Drinking. Letting their victims stew a little longer."

"Forty," the captain said again. He shook his head. "Too many. We may have to turn back."

"Turn back?" Charles exploded. To show what he thought of the idea, O'Dell hawked and blew a big glob of spit between the toes of his dusty boots.

Hastily, Bent raised one hand. "Only until we can call up reinforcements."

Frowns and grumbling from the troopers told the captain he had said the wrong thing. In quick looks passing between the men he read their judgment:

Coward.

He held the other officers responsible for that reaction. Their expressions had encouraged it. Main had encouraged it, goddamn him. And he didn't let up:

"Summoning reinforcements would take another full day at least. By then the Lantzmans could be burned out and scalped."

Bent's chin jutted. "What would you propose, Lieutenant?"

"That we get the family out of there."

"That means going in."

"Yes, it does. Doss, is there a way?"

The breeze stirred the fringing of the Delaware's hide shirt. He pointed. "Two miles. Maybe three. A cut through the hills. Can circle, come in through the corn. Take most of the night, but by then Comanche should be drunk asleep. Some will be watching the corn. Maybe they asleep too."

Charles wiped damp palms on his dirty white pants. Distantly on the wind he heard chanting and the faint *tub-tub* of a hand drum.

Don't push the captain too hard, he said to himself. Bent might balk, order a retreat, and doom the farmer and his family to die as soon as the whims of the Comanches prompted a charge.

Keeping his voice free of emotion, Charles said: "I'll volunteer to lead some men to the farm, Captain. We should go tonight, in case the Comanches decide to attack at daylight."

Bent struggled to sound as calm as his subordinate. "You're right, of course. What I said was never meant to be my final word. I was merely examining the alternatives aloud."

He watched the others from the corner of his eye. They weren't convinced. But what could they do? Quavering inwardly, he finished, "We'll send two men for reinforcements. The rest will start in as soon as it's dark."

"All of us?" Charles countered.

For an instant Bent's eyes revealed his rage. *I swear I'll see him dead before the night's over.*

578

"All," he said.

"Good," said O'Dell, shoving his knife back into the sheath at last. The troopers looked tense but pleased. Doss, too. Over the sun-reddened hills drifted the wailing and yipping of the Comanches.

46

The stunted corn rustled from the passing of the horsemen. The corn was worthless for cover. The tallest stalks reached only haunch-high on Charles's roan. He had suggested that they dismount to advance, thus taking advantage of what little protection the field did afford. Bent had vetoed that.

"Need I remind you that the new cavalry is supposed to fight from horseback, Lieutenant?"

Charles didn't think consistency was worth the risk of casualties, but he kept his mouth shut. He reckoned it to be four or a little after. The moon had set. Directly above, the stars were visible, but around the horizon they were hidden by a haze. It lent an eerie quality to the cornfield and to the line of men riding through it at a walk.

The mounted men formed a big, slow-moving half-circle, each rider separated from the next by an interval of about four feet. Bent held the center, with his orderly bugler directly behind him. Charles was about halfway down the line on the right flank. O'Dell rode at the same position on the left.

Because they were walking their horses, each man was able to carry a revolver in one hand, a carbine or musketoon in the other. Only Bent varied the pattern. He held his Allen and Wheelock six-shot in his right hand, his saber in his left. The sword felt awkward there, but at least he was correctly equipped.

Bent had sipped only a little water during the long ride around the Comanche flank. Even so, his bladder was painfully full. No doubt that was fear working on him. Fear of the hostiles. Fear of death. Fear that he'd again tarnish his record by bad judgment. He was sure that every other member of the detachment wanted him to fail, and that Main wanted it most of all.

Slowly, so as not to attract attention, Bent looked to the right. He located his second lieutenant in the misty half-light. An owl hooted. Bent gripped his revolver tightly and prayed that at the right moment his bullet would find its target.

*

Charles squinted. How far to the log farmhouse? About a quarter of a mile or a little more. No lights showed, but Lantzman and his family were surely on guard in the darkness.

Would they start firing indiscriminately the moment they saw horsemen in the corn? Bent ought to be alert to that possibility and order a bugle call to signal the presence of soldiers. Did he have enough sense?

The feeling of dread continued to plague Charles. He shoved his Colt into the saddle holster and, with his carbine resting in the angle of his left elbow, reached up with his right hand to try to squash a mosquito. He slapped his ear twice. Each time the whining faded, only to resume. With a curse he again drew his revolver.

A horse whickered on the far side of the farmhouse. The roofline blotted the dim campfire on the slope on the other side of the creek. Not a sound came from the Comanche camp. If they meant to launch a dawn attack, they had not yet begun to prepare.

Suddenly a black scarecrow figure rose in the corn ten yards out from the house. Charles had a blurred impression of long hair and a long-barreled weapon flung up to firing position. One of the troopers shouted a warning. The Indian's musket squirted fire and roared.

Between Charles and the center, a trooper pitched from his saddle. Other Comanche sentinels, five or six of them, popped up suddenly and began firing. Charles braced his carbine against his hip and pulled the trigger. The angle was wrong, the shot too high. He scabbarded the carbine and laid his Colt across his left elbow, steadying the roan with his knees.

He aimed for the nearest Comanche as horses shied and yelling broke out along the line. He squeezed off his shot. The Comanche sank from sight.

Inside the farmhouse a man was bellowing an alarm. There were other outcries across the creek. Then more musket fire. A shot from a loophole in the house felled a soldier. Why in the name of God didn't the captain sound a call before Lantzman's family killed them all?

Bent was trying. For the third time he cried, "Orderly bugler—sound trot march!"

The orderly swayed in the saddle as if he had imbibed too heavily. Furious, Bent sheathed his sword, switched gun hands, and brought his prancing roan under control. He reached out to seize the bugler's hickory shirt. His hand closed on sticky cloth.

Without thinking, he pushed the enlisted man, who fell off the far side of his horse with his head tilting back. In the faint light, Bent saw that a musket ball had pierced the bugler's right eye.

Two or three Indians remained between the soldiers and the farmhouse. Bent heard balls whizzing and hissing to the right and left as he leaped to the ground. Confused and frightened, all he could think of was the necessity for a bugle call.

"Close up. Close up and advance!"

Whose voice was that? he wondered as he stumbled to the body of his orderly and seized the bugle. Main, that's who it was. Afterward they'd say he was the one who showed initiative. Damn him. *Damn him.*

The bloody bugle in hand, he regained his saddle and saw Charles speeding by from right to left. Bent flung the bugle away, snatched his revolver from the holster, and quickly surveyed his surroundings.

No one was close; no one was watching. The line was falling apart, each trooper firing, defending himself as best he could. Bent aimed the revolver at Charles's retreating back. Pressed his lips together. Slowly exerted pressure on the trigger—

An Indian ball nicked his roan on the left flank. The horse bellowed and bucked. Bent's revolver boomed, barely heard in the gunfire. Charles rode on, untouched.

Infuriated, Bent was ready to try another shot, caution abandoned now. A thrashing in the corn caught his attention. He whipped his head around. Not eight feet away there was a horseman.

"O'Dell! I didn't see you—" Terrified, Bent felt his bladder let go.

"What in hell are you doing, sir? Why did you shoot at one of your own men?"

The quiet accusation had an unexpected effect. It restored Bent's calm, made him realize the extent of the danger into which his hate had pushed him. No words could save him at this point. He answered O'Dell by raising the Allen and Wheelock to firing position.

O'Dell's mouth opened, but he had no time to cry out. Bent's shot destroyed most of O'Dell's face and flung him sideways. His left boot tore free of the stirrup, but not his right. The roan cantered away with O'Dell hanging head down. His skull was quickly beaten to pieces by the hard ground.

Fighting panic, Bent looked around hurriedly. No one had seen the shooting. It was still too dark, with powder smoke and mist further hampering visibility. Bent holstered his gun and again drew his saber. With the blade at tierce point, he screamed the order for his men to advance at a trot.

Charles had already taken care of issuing that order. Three troopers closed on the last Indian sentinel and dropped him with well-placed shots. One man sabered the Comanche's throat for good measure.

Charles rode to within twenty feet of the farmhouse, risking himself so that the Lantzmans would be sure to hear his shout:

"This is the Second Cavalry. Hold your fire."

Silence settled. Smoke drifted away in the mist. Bent trotted forward. "Dismount. *Dismount!*"

Gradually the troopers obeyed. Panting, Bent dropped to the ground in the midst of milling horses. He hoped the dark would help hide his damp trousers.

"Good work, men. We carried the day."

"We lost three men," Charles said, still in the saddle. Bent wished he could raise the revolver and blow Charles's head off. But reckless action had nearly undone him once; it must not happen again.

"No, wait," Charles exclaimed. "Where's O'Dell?"

He called the officer's name twice, loudly. Then Bent spoke. "No use, Lieutenant. One of the savages got him. I saw him fall. His horse dragged him off."

Bent's heartbeat thundered in his ears. If anyone was to challenge his lie, it would happen now—*now*—

"God," Charles said softly, climbing down. No one else uttered a word.

Bent exhaled. He was safe. He squared his shoulders. "I regret the loss as much as you, but we must consolidate our gains and plan our next move. We'll want pickets along this side of the house, Lieutenant. Take care of it while I see to those inside."

He pivoted, one hand resting on his saber hilt. He felt exactly like a conquering general as he strode toward the log house, calling, "Lantzman?"

Charles detailed four troopers to bring in the dead; it hadn't occurred to Bent, apparently.

He watched one member of the detail spread tarpaulins close to the farmhouse wall. Dawn light filled the eastern sky now. The mist was dissipating. Inside, Bent could be heard making pronouncements to people who spoke much more softly than the captain; Charles detected at least one feminine voice. Bent's tone of authority angered him. The man might do passably well as a staff officer, but as a line commander he was an incompetent. He had botched the advance to the farm. In anticipation of sentinels, they should have approached in double file, to present a narrower target. Or, better still, on foot, as Charles had suggested.

The captain's refusal had cost them four dead. A fifth trooper was out of action with a ball in his foot. Add to that the two men dispatched to Camp Cooper, and their effective strength was reduced to seventeen. Against thirty or more Comanches still left.

Two of the detail appeared, dragging something in an indigo saddle blanket. "We found everyone but Lieutenant O'Dell, sir. There's no sign of him."

Charles nodded in an absent way. He looked to the hills beyond the pitiful fields. The man who had befriended him was lost out there with no one to mourn him. Charles's eyes filled with tears. Then shock settled in. His legs shook. He had to lean against the log wall to keep from falling. The men in the detail looked elsewhere until the worst of it passed.

Suddenly, there was an outburst of yelling from the creek side of the house. Charles hurried to the corner and peered around. Over in the Comanche camp, the braves were milling their horses, brandishing lances, whooping. Most of them were young men, their glossy hair parted in the center and braided in long queues. Some had accentuated the part by streaking it with white or yellow clay. Faces were painted red, with white or yellow eyelids. One warrior had drawn huge black fangs all around his mouth.

A wagon creaked down the hillside toward the noisy Indians. The sight of it hit Charles like a hammer. It was the provision wagon that had been following the soldiers, but now it was being driven by three braves. The left side of the wagon's canvas top was splotched by a huge bloodstain.

Troopers crowded up behind Charles, whispering and pointing at the wagon. "The red fuckers," one man growled. "What d'you suppose they did with our boys?"

Charles said, "I'd rather not know."

He headed for the back door of the farmhouse. The death of Lafayette O'Dell placed an unwanted responsibility on him. To make matters worse, the captain refused to admit that he was in over his head. If any of Bent's ideas were questioned, he would surely fly into a rage.

Charles would just have to accept that fact—that added problem—and deal with it as best he could.

Thank God no decisions were required immediately. All they had to do was dig in and await the reinforcements.

The last hour had changed Charles's ideas about the nature of war. War was not a gay martial parade on the Plain with the ranks perfectly aligned, every bit of brass polished, and the flags flying while the drums beat cadence. War was disorder, dirt, death. It was nerve-shredding fright.

His legs still felt shaky as he entered the farmhouse. The interior consisted of a long, flat-roofed room with alcoves for sleeping, plus another housing an iron stove. The place reeked of powder smoke and something far worse. He saw flies walking on two bodies covered to the neck by blankets. One, an older, gray-haired man, he presumed to be Lantzman. The other was the farmer's oldest son, Karl, the one whose leg injury had prevented the family from fleeing. He presumed both men had died outside.

Four members of the family remained. Mrs. Lantzman was a worn little woman with moles on her chin. Two blond sons in their late teens moved slowly, like sleepwalkers. Their eyes were glassy. The fourth survivor, a girl, seemed less affected by the siege, perhaps because she was younger.

She was about twelve, Charles guessed. Her sweet face reflected her youth, but she had already developed a woman's figure. As Charles stood silently, he saw Bent's eyes shift and linger on the full bosom within the tight, stained bodice of the girl's kersey dress.

The girl was unaware of the attention. She was busy pulling round shot from a leather pouch hung from her shoulder. Her long gun leaned against her other hip. An Augustin musket, Charles noticed; Austrian jaeger battalions carried them, and the quartermaster of the Army, Joe Johnston, imported a good many.

Close to tears, Mrs. Lantzman said, ''How can we stay here, Captain? We have no more food. My husband died trying to reach the creek to bring back water.''

''We have rations to share. Water, too.'' Bent sounded smooth and confident. ''I'll have my men dig in around the house''—Charles had crossed the room and now put his eye to a loophole on the creek side. His right hand clenched—''while we await the reinforcements. With no bad weather to hamper them, they should arrive before the end of the day.''

Without turning, Charles said, "I think not, Captain.''

"What's that?''

"You'd better see this. A half-dozen braves just rode in. Look at the ones with lances.''

Bent waddled to the loophole and squinted. His face drained of color. Four of the new arrivals held their lances high and shook them. On the points of two, trophies were impaled.

The heads of the two soldiers sent to Camp Cooper.

Charles thought the captain would go to pieces. Bent paced, muttered to himself, several times turned to blurt some thought but never did. There was a wild, vacant glint in his eye. The dazed Lantzman boys knew something was amiss. Even the girl stared at the captain fearfully.

Every second was precious now. Charles cleared his throat. "Sir—''

Bent whirled, shouting, "What is it?''

"I'd like permission to send scouts back through the cornfield. That's our only avenue of retreat.''

The captain gave a limp wave and sank onto a stool. "Go ahead.'' He stared into space as Charles hurried out.

Charles was back in twenty minutes, looking grim. "They've already moved men into the gullies behind the field. At least fifteen, Corporal Ostrander said. We're cut off. Surrounded.''

Why hadn't they left before this? Charles asked himself in a silent burst of fury. But of course he couldn't hold Bent responsible for their failure to do so; they had all anticipated the eventual arrival of a relief column. Evidently the two dead troopers had run into one of those small bands whose signs Doss had discovered. Charles had a feeling the entire expedition was cursed.

Bent swiped a hand across his perspiring face. "Surrounded? Then we must dig in and wait for help.''

"From where?'' Charles exclaimed.

"I don't know! Someone will come—'' The sentence trailed off.

"But Captain,'' the girl said, "is there enough food?''

Mrs. Lantzman shook her head. "Hush, Martha. Don't question the soldiers. They know best.''

"Yes. Exactly right,'' Bent said with another of those vague looks.

He was foundering again. Charles couldn't permit it to continue. "Just a minute," he said.

Bent's head jerked around, his moist eyes brimming with resentment. Charles spoke to the others rather than to his superior: "We have to recognize that we're in a bad situation. We're outnumbered, and no one from Camp Cooper will be coming to relieve us. The Comanches can build up their forces and attack at their pleasure. I don't believe any of us wants to sit here and wait to be killed. Or taken prisoner," he added with a glance at Martha. Mrs. Lantzman understood his meaning.

"What do you propose we do?" Bent snarled.

"Hold on till dark, then attempt to break out. I've thought of a way to distract—"

Bent jumped up, overturning the stool and screaming his answer. "No."

As the cry died away, a strange feeling swept over Charles. He felt as though he had just decided to leap into a chasm—which, in a way, he had. But what other choice did he have? Bent was out of control, incapable of dealing with the situation.

"I'm sorry, sir, but escape is the only way."

The captain's face reddened again. He grabbed a small puncheon table, hurled it aside, and stormed toward Charles. "Are you disputing me? Questioning my authority?"

"If you mean to stay here, Captain, I guess I am."

"Lieutenant"—Bent took a deep breath in an effort to control himself, but his voice still shook—"you will say nothing more. That is a direct order. Go outside until I send for you."

Charles hated matters to come to this—a test of authority, of wills. The two of them should be pulling together to save the others. But how did you convince a lunatic of that? he asked himself wearily.

"I'll go, sir," he said, "but I can't obey the rest of the order. If we stay here, we're finished."

Bent looked at him a moment, then said quietly, "Lieutenant Main, you will obey my order or face court-martial."

"Captain, we're leaving."

Bent grabbed Charles's collar and twisted. "Goddamn it, I'll see that you're cashiered!"

Charles deliberately removed Bent's hand. He wanted to hit the fat officer; only with great effort did he restrain himself. His voice dropped low. "If we get back alive, you're welcome to try."

He glanced at Mrs. Lantzman, her two sons, and finally at the girl, who stood holding her Austrian musket in both hands. "We'll leave as soon as it's dark. I'll take anyone who wants to go. If you do, you'd better bury those bodies. We can't take them."

Mrs. Lantzman knelt beside her husband's corpse, shooed the flies off, and began to straighten the blanket. Suddenly she burst into tears. Charles looked away.

The resolute expression on Martha's face showed she had already made up her mind. Charles turned to the captain and said, "I'll make the same offer to the men. No one will be forced to go."

Bent whispered, "Get out of my sight."

Doubled over, Charles ran toward the edge of the cornfield a few minutes later. From the ravines on the far side, a shot boomed. The ball hissed through the tassels above him. Kneeling, he tore off a couple of leaves and rolled them between his palms.

Dry as powder. Now if he could persuade Mrs. Lantzman to turn her horses loose—the Comanches would get them anyway—they might have a chance, although not much of one.

47

Westward, only a thin rind of sun showed above the foothills. The light was rapidly fading from the land and sky. In his mind Charles had gone over the escape plan and the signals involved half a dozen times.

An hour ago, following his instructions, troopers had built a cook fire halfway between the house and the field, where the Indians would be sure to see it. Inside, Mrs. Lantzman and her daughter had wrapped rags around the ends of cottonwood branches and soaked the rags in lamp oil. The Lantzman boys had saddled horses for the family and were now in position behind the hay bales on the far side of the building, prepared to make the dangerous dash to the corral.

Corporal Ostrander slipped through the shadows to Charles's side. "Sir, everything's ready."

"All right, it's time. We—"

He stopped as Ostrander's startled eyes focused somewhere beyond him. Charles turned. From the farmhouse door Bent spoke.

"I'm going."

The captain had been the sole holdout. Charles tried to extend an olive branch by replying in a mild tone. "Fine, sir."

It did no good. "I'm going principally for the satisfaction of seeing you thrown out of the Army in disgrace."

Charles's gaze hardened. "Whatever you say, sir. But I must respectfully remind you that I have temporarily assumed command."

Did the captain's eyes twinkle then? Charles's spine crawled. Bent almost smiled as he drew on the fringed gauntlets he favored.

"You have made me quite aware of that, Lieutenant. All day I have watched you busily undermining my authority and turning the men against me. Enjoy the command. It's your last."

He stared at Charles without blinking. Across the creek the besiegers whooped and thumped their hide drum.

Martha Lantzman appeared with the unlit torches. Holding them down close to the ground so as not to draw the attention of the sentinels beyond the field, she passed them one by one to Ostrander. He in turn gave them to men pretending to lounge at the cook fire. In the darkness at either end of the house, horses whickered; the rest of the troopers were in the saddle and were holding the mounts of the men responsible for lighting the torches.

"Find your horses," he said to Mrs. Lantzman and her daughter. They hurried away. He looked pointedly at the captain, who incredibly seemed to laugh, then followed after them.

Charles turned and studied the cornfield, wondering whether he—all of them—might die out there. Unexpectedly, like a river current in spring flood, a powerful will to live surged in him. Reckoning that the situation was almost hopeless anyway, he realized he had precious little to lose. He therefore could, and should, act boldly. The dirty bearded mask of his face cracked open and his teeth shone as he forced a smile.

Some of the men saw, and they too began to smile. Charles realized he had discovered one of the secrets of being a good officer in a tight spot. Perhaps he'd live to put it to use again.

He looked at each of the others to show the moment had come. Then he thrust his revolver up over his head and fired.

At the sound of the shot, all activity stopped in the Comanche camp. Then Charles heard a commotion among the horses in the corral and quickly thereafter one of the Lantzman boys yelling, "Hah!"

The horses galloped out. Some of them splashed into the creek, just before the first Comanche shot rang out. The Indians had no clear targets, but they obviously knew something was afoot.

Charles fired twice more. In response to the signal, the troopers plunged the torches into the embers. The rags ignited with soft explosions. Each man dashed to a prearranged place on the right or left and there set fire to the corn, the plan being to leave a fifty-foot-wide lane in the center. Charles counted on the lack of wind to help keep that lane open long enough for them to escape.

He sprinted to his horse and mounted. Flames were already shooting up above the dry stalks; the field was burning faster than he'd anticipated. He rode to the entrance of the lane, reined to one side, and slashed downward with his revolver as he shouted:

"Column of twos, trot march, ho!"

A line of men rode from each corner of the house, quickly forming the double column. Charles had put the most experienced riders in front and the Lantzmans at the most protected position, in the center.

By twos the men and horses pounded into the lane. The spreading fire already threatened the entrance. The fainter sound of splashing water told Charles the Comanches were crossing the creek. "Hurry, damn it!" he yelled to the men who had handled the torches. They mounted and trotted into the lane. Charles felt the heat of the fire on his back. Bent's horse shied, but he forced it ahead, following the double column.

Flames leaped from both sides of the lane and interlaced across it. A painted Indian rode into sight at one corner of the house. Charles squeezed off a shot and dropped him. Then, applying spurs, he drove his roan through the fire. He bent low over his mount's neck. Ahead, fire had narrowed the lane to a width of ten feet. Bent was some twenty yards in front of him, and beyond the captain Charles could see little except the bobbing forms of his men, silhouettes against the brightness.

A lick of flame touched Bent's sleeve. Smoke curled from the fabric. The captain yelped and slapped the fire out. His horse carried him from the burning field into the dark, where Ostrander was supposed to hold the column together and lead it forward at a gallop. Charles hoped the corporal was still alive.

Smoke billowed around him now. The fire consumed the corn with a roar. The lane was nearly closed directly ahead. Charles bent so low he thought his ribs might crack. He whispered encouragement to the roan as the flame barrier loomed.

The roan leaped as fearlessly as the best Academy jumper. Light blinded Charles. Heat scorched his cheeks. Then they were through into cool air and darkness.

The roan came down surely, but hard. Charles was almost unseated. He held on and a second later a nightmare face—yellow-clayed cheeks, white eyes—came rushing at him from the right.

A Comanche sentinel, on foot. The Indian hacked downward with his trade hatchet, striking for Charles's thigh. Charles applied spurs and the roan sprang on. The hatchet missed Charles but buried in the animal's flank, cutting clear through the massive muscle and severing an artery. The roan bellowed and reared. Charles tumbled off.

As he fell he managed to shove his revolver against the Comanche's chest and pull the trigger. The explosion blew the Indian backward into the burning corn. In seconds he was afire from head to foot.

Charles lay pinned by the heaving, bellowing horse. He dragged his leg free, then put his last two shots into the dying roan's head.

The corn crackled as it burned. Charles looked around but saw no sign of his men. Panic set in. He began running after the others. Recalling that the last rider in the column was the captain, he shouted, "Bent! Bent, help me!"

He staggered on. Had the captain heard him? Had anyone?

He turned to observe the fire. It had spread, building into a high wall of light half a mile wide. As he watched, the flames swallowed one edge of Lantzman's field and swept to the prairie grass beyond, igniting it instantly.

A humorless smile jerked the corners of his grimy mouth. He had counted on the fire to block the charge of the Comanches who came across the creek. Beyond the flames he could hear them milling and shouting angrily. The sentinels on this side had represented the smaller, more acceptable risk. He had slain one of them, but there must be others—

"*Lieutenant, look out!*"

The voice belonged to a trooper who had heard his cry for help and doubled back. Turning toward the dim figure of the mounted man, Charles let out a gasp. Another Comanche came loping at him from the darkness with a lance.

Charles pivoted to present his right side, then raised and parried with his empty gun. The barrel diverted the thrust just enough to prevent a fatal injury. The iron lance head tore through his sleeve into his shoulder.

The Indian's run had carried him to within a foot of Charles, who now pulled his knife with his left hand. The painted mouth contorted; the Indian couldn't pull back quickly enough. Charles rammed the knife to the hilt into his stomach, then yanked it out.

The Comanche lurched sideways. Rage overcoming his agony, he tried a final thrust with the lance. Charles jumped away and waited for the Indian to fall. After an endless moment, he did.

Reaction set in then. Nausea, trembling, blurred vision. Charles couldn't identify the soldier who had heard his hail, ridden back, and shouted a warning. "Bent?" He shielded his eyes with his forearm but still couldn't see.

"No, sir, it's Private Tannen. Captain Bent rode on ahead."

After he heard me call for help.

"Climb up, sir," said the private. "We're going to make it—all of us."

They followed the fleeing column. Charles held the private's waist and rode with his eyes closed, his silence blended of shock and relief.

594

*

The Comanches pursued them through the darkness for nearly an hour, but never came within musket range. Soon their fading cries signaled their weariness of the profitless sport. They melted away into the summer night—probably heading back to round up the Lantzman horses.

After another hour of hard riding, the column stopped to rest. Miraculously, the only injuries were a couple of flesh wounds similar to the one Charles had suffered. Despite their losses the Lantzmans were jubilant, and so were the troopers, who laughed and talked boisterously. Several congratulated Charles on the success of his daring plan.

After Charles ordered scouts out, a trooper offered him a swig of lightning whiskey. Charles didn't say a word about the impropriety of that or inquire about the source of the stuff. He drank gratefully, then poured some of the raw spirits on his gashed shoulder. With Mrs. Lantzman's help he bound the wound with a kerchief. Through all of this, Bent kept aloof.

Soon Charles felt considerably better. He was tired but in possession of his faculties again. He re-formed the column, and they covered the next two miles at a walk. This brought them to an ideal campsite in a ravine whose open end was easily guarded.

Bedrolls were broken out for the first time since they had left Camp Cooper. Mesquite wood gathered by foragers was lit to keep off insects and the night's chill. Charles squatted by one of several small fires, gnawing on a square of hardtack. He had seldom tasted anything as delicious.

A misshapen shadow stretched across the fire suddenly. He glanced up, drew in a sharp breath. Bent's expression was controlled, masklike. He had again assumed command, which Charles did not contest. He had no desire to embarrass the captain any further. He had said nothing to the men about Bent's near hysteria inside the farmhouse and in fact had taken pains to create the impression that it was the captain who had placed him in charge of the escape effort.

"I want to commend you on your behavior during the escape, Lieutenant. You displayed exceptional courage."

"Thank you, sir."

Charles wondered about the reason for the unexpected compliment. He could find none until he noticed five troopers relaxing at the next fire. A moment ago they had been discussing the action at Lantzman's.

Now they were quiet, listening. Bent had been speaking so that they would be sure to hear.

The captain glanced at the listeners and began walking in the other direction. He motioned Charles to his side. Reluctantly, Charles followed.

"At the farm," Bent resumed, "perhaps both of us were undone by anger. When danger threatens, no man can be expected to think clearly at all times."

I would say that you could expect that of a good leader, Charles thought, but remained silent. There was no point in provoking Bent just now; in his clumsy way, he seemed to be trying to establish a truce.

They left the perimeter of the firelight, walking in silence. For the first time Charles smelled whiskey. That Bent carried a secret supply didn't surprise him.

When they were safely away from the five listeners, Bent stopped and faced him.

"Of course, the success of the action doesn't expunge your guilt. You disobeyed a direct order."

Charles felt his bile rise. Now he understood the captain's scheme. Bent wanted some of the men to hear him compliment his subordinate, as a normal commander would. That dispensed with, he was now delivering his real message in private. Bent's voice hardened.

"Charges must and will be filed against you."

Charles sensed, then clearly grasped, what Bent had earlier realized. The angry exchange with the captain and his near breakdown had been witnessed only by the Lantzmans. They would not be called to testify at a court-martial unless Charles insisted on it; and if they were called, the prosecutor could easily demolish their qualifications as witnesses, noting first that they were civilians, with no comprehension of military matters. He could then point out that grief over the loss of two loved ones made their judgment and their statements even more suspect.

Charles saw the trap closing. He would have no support for what he had done, no one to state that temporarily relieving Bent had been imperative. Dismally, he realized he himself had helped set the trap. Trying to spare his superior, he had said nothing to any of the men about the captain's behavior. Bent could exaggerate and color his testimony any way he chose. Finally there was the matter of rank. A court would tend to believe the word of an experienced captain over that of a brevet second lieutenant.

Firelight brushed Bent's profile as he turned away. He allowed himself a little smile.

"I think you, not I, will be the chief casualty of this expedition. Good evening, Lieutenant."

Sleepless and tense, Charles lay with his head on his saddle. The fire had gone out. The cold of the night stiffened his bones. His bandaged shoulder throbbed.

How stupid of him to think even for a moment that Bent wanted to make peace. Charles was the target of an unfounded hate so deep and so venomous it defied explanation, except in one way. Bent was a madman. He had suspected it before, but the harrowing events involving the Lantzmans had placed the matter beyond all doubt.

He shuddered, then plopped his hat over his eyes to block out the starlight. It didn't help. He lay awake for hours, hearing the captain's voice, seeing the captain's face.

48

Bent planned to cover the distance to Camp Cooper in a single day's ride, but around three in the afternoon the younger Lantzman boy came down with acute stomach cramps. His mother pleaded with the captain to stop for a while so that the boy could rest. A few minutes became an hour. By then a thunderstorm was muttering in the north. Bent ordered a lean-to built for the civilians, deciding that, since no danger threatened, they would camp for the night and go the rest of the way tomorrow. The men grumbled about the decision. Bent paid no attention; he was sore from riding, and he welcomed the chance to reassert his authority.

Wind whipped the grass, and dust and debris blew through the air for half an hour. But no rain fell. The storm passed by, leaving the troopers more disgruntled than ever. They could have pushed on, been in their bunks before taps.

Camp had been pitched in a level area beside a dry creek bed. A few cottonwoods lined the bank, and among these Bent had put down his blanket and built his fire. Normally any other officers would have shared the fire, but Charles knew better than to approach.

The lean-to stood on open ground about twenty feet from the cottonwood grove where Bent sat drinking, hidden by shadows as the night deepened. After two long drinks from his flask, he felt more relaxed. He savored the smell of firewood, the sounds of insects and of the men conversing softly. He drank again. His mind drifted into colorful visions of Alexander, the Mongol Khans, Bonaparte.

He had already excused his own behavior at the farm, placing the blame on other factors: A shortage of men. The unfortunate killing of the troopers sent for reinforcements. The hostility of his lieutenants.

Well, he'd eliminated one of the traitorous officers, and he'd soon get rid of the other. He imagined the effect on Orry Main when he heard that his relative had been cashiered.

Chuckling, Bent again raised the flask. The sound of voices at the Lantzman lean-to attracted his attention. He remained motionless in the concealment of the trees, watching.

*

"Why do I have to lie there when I can't sleep, Mama? Let me walk a little while."

Carrying the long Augustin musket, Mrs. Lantzman followed her daughter out of the lean-to. "All right, but don't go far. And take this."

"I don't need it," Martha retorted. "There's no more danger. The Delaware scout said so."

Cross-legged beside the dying fire, her older brother laughed and flung his arms wide. "With all these soldiers around, Martha wants to be defenseless."

"Take it back!" She fisted her hand.

"Walk if you must, but let's have no more of that kind of talk," Mrs. Lantzman said, unsmiling. She planted the stock of the musket on the ground and watched her full-bosomed daughter walk through the rustling grass. She let Martha go three steps before she softly called:

"Not that way. You'll disturb the captain."

"Oh, that's right. I forgot."

The girl changed direction, moving toward the perimeter of the cottonwoods rather than straight into them. She was grateful for her mother's warning. She didn't like the captain, with his coarse, fat face and his small eyes that watched her so closely. She knew the reason he watched her. She was old enough to be vaguely titillated by it, yet still young enough to be frightened.

Her new course took her past another small fire. There, the lieutenant—dashing, good-looking—sat with his shirt off. He was struggling to tie a clean bandage around a nasty cut in his shoulder. Martha paused to help him with the knot. He thanked her in that courtly Southern way of his. Thrilled, she went on.

Charles reclined on his elbows and kept track of her, almost like a watchful parent, until she faded into the darkness.

Elkanah Bent lay with his hand between his thighs, surprised at his sudden strong reaction. The Lantzman girl, whom he had been watching from the concealment of the cottonwoods, was a mere child.

Ah, but not above the waist, he thought, licking his lips.

It had been a long while since he had slept with a woman or even touched one. Naturally no officer dared lay a hand on one so young. But he still had an urge to speak to her. With luck, maybe he could even contrive to touch her.

The mere existence of that impulse proved things were once again moving in his favor. He lifted the flask, shook it, then drank until it was empty. Still quite timid, he lurched to his feet and slipped through the grove, away from the light of the campfires.

Following her mother's instructions, Martha didn't walk far, only to the creek bank on the other side of the cottonwoods. She was surprised at how much she could see by the light of the rising moon. She folded her arms across her breasts, tilted her head back, and sighed with contentment.

The night breeze soothed her, stirred a pleasant rustling in the grass. Softly, she began to hum "Old Folks at Home." Then all at once she heard a noise in the grove. She whirled.

"Is someone there?"

"Only Captain Bent, my dear."

He came lumbering from the trees, hatless and not very steady on his feet. Martha's heart began to race. She called herself a ninny. Surely she had nothing to fear from an Army officer.

"I thought I heard movement out here," he continued as he approached. "I'm glad to know it's someone friendly."

The false cordiality alarmed her. He smelled of whiskey mixed with sweat. With his back to the moon, he resembled a grotesque two-legged elephant. He moved closer.

"Lovely night, isn't it?"

"I don't know. I mean, yes. I must go back—"

"So soon? Please don't. Not yet."

How kind and gentle he sounded. His voice, pitched low, was that of a trustworthy uncle. And yet she heard something else in it. Something that confused her, made her momentarily indecisive.

He took her inaction for consent. "There, that's better. I only want to demonstrate my high regard for you."

Drunk, she thought. That's what it is. She had seen her poor dead father drunk many times and knew the signs.

"You're a charming girl. Exceptionally lovely for one so young." His big round head hid the moon. He took another step toward her. "I'd like for us to be friends."

His hand stretched toward her hair, picked up the strands that lay gleaming on her left shoulder. All at once she was immobilized, terrified.

He petted her hair, rubbed it between thumb and fingers. Slowly

601

he increased the tension until he was pulling it. Pulling *her*. His puffy breathing sounded like the noise of a steam engine.

"Let go of me. *Please.*"

He stiffened, no longer friendly. "Keep your voice down. You mustn't attract attention."

To emphasize that, he seized her forearm. She cried out softly.

"Damn you, don't do that," Bent exclaimed, panicking. "Don't, I tell you." This time her outcry was louder, and so was his. "Stop it! Stop it, do you hear?"

Shaking her, expostulating, he didn't know anyone else was there until he saw the sudden look of relief in her moonlit eyes. He pivoted like a man turning to face a firing squad. He stepped back when he saw Charles Main—

And beyond him, bursting from the trees, the older Lantzman boy followed by the mother. The moon flashed on the long barrel of the jaeger musket in her hands.

Together, Bent's face and that of the girl told Charles all he needed to know. Mrs. Lantzman rushed to her daughter's side. Voices began to overlap.

"Martha, did he hurt you?" The brother.

"I knew it wasn't safe for you to go walking." The mother.

Bent, hoarse and upset: "I did nothing to her. Nothing!"

And the girl: "Yes, he did. He put his hands on me and started playing with my hair. He wouldn't stop—"

"Quiet," Charles said. "Everyone keep quiet."

They obeyed. He saw a sentry hurrying toward them, several troopers not far behind. He stepped around Mrs. Lantzman, wigwagged his arm.

"Go back to camp. Everything's all right."

The sentry and the others turned and moved away again. Charles waited until they were out of sight beyond the cottonwoods, then gave Bent a fierce look. The captain was perspiring heavily, weaving on his feet. He avoided Charles's eye.

"Martha, are you hurt?" Charles asked.

"N-no."

"Take her back to your lean-to, Mrs. Lantzman. Keep her there the rest of the night."

Small fists clenched on the musket, the woman stood her ground. Her glance bayoneted the captain. "What kind of men do they send to serve in Texas? Men with no morals?"

"Mrs. Lantzman, this won't help," Charles interrupted. "Your daughter's all right. The incident is unfortunate, but we've all been under a lot of strain. I'm sure the captain regrets any accidental indiscretion—"

"Accidental?" The girl's brother snorted. "He's drunk. Smell him!"

Bent blurted, "Damn you for an impertinent—" Charles seized the captain's upraised arm and thrust it down. Bent gasped, opened his fist, let his arm fall to his side.

Charles grasped Martha's shoulder lightly and her brother's. He turned them both toward the trees. "Stay in the lean-to and try to forget about this. I'm sure Captain Bent will offer his apology to all of you."

"*Apology?* Under no circumstances will I—"

Again Bent stopped. He whispered, "Yes. Consider it tendered."

Mrs. Lantzman looked as if she wanted to shoot him. Charles spoke softly to her. "Go. Please."

The woman passed the musket to her son. She put her arm around Martha's waist and led her away. Bent pressed both palms against his face, kept them there for about ten seconds, then lowered them.

"Thank you," he said to Charles.

Charles didn't reply.

"I don't understand why you helped me, but I am—grateful."

"Nothing would be accomplished if she shot you. And she'd only regret it later. If there's to be any punishment for what just happened, it should come from the proper quarter."

"Punishment? What do you mean?"

Again Charles was silent. He turned and stalked away through the wind-tossed grass.

Five miles from Camp Cooper, Bent galloped to the head of the column where Charles was riding. They had been traveling in a drizzle since shortly after breakfast. Charles's spirits felt as bedraggled as his men looked.

Bent cleared his throat. Charles could predict what his superior was going to say.

"I appreciate your actions on my behalf last night. I attempted to convey my feelings then, but you were in no mood to listen. I thought I should try again."

Charles gazed at Bent from beneath the dripping brim of his hat.

He could barely contain his disgust. "Captain, believe me, I didn't do it to help you personally. I did it because of the uniform you're wearing. I did it for the sake of the regiment. Do you understand?"

"Yes, surely. I—I don't expect you to feel kindly toward me. What I want to ask—that is—since we'll soon be back in camp—what do you think Mrs. Lantzman will say?"

"Nothing."

"What?"

How sickeningly hopeful Bent looked then. Charles leaned over the other way and spat.

"She'll say nothing. I spoke to her at breakfast. She understands that an accusation would serve no purpose. Perhaps Martha even learned a valuable lesson. Mrs. Lantzman's point of view is simple and eminently decent. Since no real harm was done, why should she ruin you?"

Now came the insidious part. If his method was less than admirable, his purpose could hardly be faulted. He held Bent's eyes, continuing:

"But I know she'd be glad to come back to Camp Cooper or even travel to Fort Mason, if I asked. She would do it if I needed her at my court-martial. To testify to my character and the character of others."

Bent's brows flew up. He understood. He realized he had escaped one trap only to be forced into a more humiliating one. His face grew hostile again.

"Your tactics are worthy of a criminal."

"Bullshit, Captain. While I save my career, I'm handing you a chance to save yours. To do it is easy. Just keep your mouth shut. If you don't like that idea, however, we'll put the entire matter in front of Major Thomas. He's sat on plenty of courts-martial down here. I'm willing to trust his judgment."

"No, no—" Bent raised one of his fancy gauntlets; it was torn across the back. "I accept your terms. There will be no charges."

Charles couldn't help a sudden, cold smile.

"Thought that was what you'd decide."

He touched his hat brim, reined to the left, and went galloping back along the line, mud flying up behind him. A big gob struck the yellow cloth-and-gold embroidery of Bent's left shoulder strap.

49

The Lantzmans rested overnight at Camp Cooper, then left for their farm with an escort. Bent disappeared in his quarters, violently sick with dysentery again. Charles knew little about medicine, but he suspected the recent turmoil had precipitated the captain's illness.

In General Orders from Washington, Charles and the captain received commendations for the rescue of the Lantzman family. Lafayette O'Dell received his posthumously. His body was never found.

Bent requested and was granted medical leave in San Antonio. It fell to Charles to write letters to the families of O'Dell and the three other men lost in the action at the farm. He had no talent for the task, disliked it intensely, but got it out of the way in a single evening.

By the time he finished the last letter he was able silently to put words to a feeling that had been stirring in his mind for the past couple of days. He was not the same officer, not the same person, who had set out with the relief detachment.

Oh, things were just about the same on the surface. He was still flamboyant, and he smiled about as much as he had before. Yet all of that concealed a profound inner change, a change born of everything he had seen and been forced to do while on the rescue mission. The West Point cadet was a pleasant but not very real memory. The romantic amateur had become a hardened professional.

A boy had died and given rise, phoenixlike, to a man.

"I heard a mail sack arrived this morning," Charles said on the fourth day after his return.

"Yes, sir. These came for you." The noncom passed him a packet of three letters tied with string, adding, "The sack sat in a warehouse in San Antonio for a month and a half."

"Why?" Charles snapped, leafing through the packet. The letter on top was nearly a half inch thick. On all three he recognized Orry's handwriting.

"Can't say, sir. Reckon it's just the Army way."

"The Army way in Texas, at any rate."

Charles went outside and headed for his quarters, ripping the thick letter open as he walked. He noted the April date, then the first sentences:

> *Your inquiry about your commanding officer prompts my immediate and concerned reply. If he is the same Elkanah Bent I know from the Academy and Mexico, I warn you most urgently that you could be in great danger.*

Abruptly Charles broke stride, stopping to stand motionless in the center of the dusty parade. Though the morning was scorching, he was all at once cold.

> *Let me attempt to explain—although, as you have doubtless grasped from direct encounters with the gentleman in question, neither a complete nor a logical explanation of his behavior is possible. That was also the case when George Hazard and I were unfortunate enough to meet him for the first time—*

Hastily, Charles folded the letter and, with a sharp look around, strode on to his room. There he sat down to read the closely written pages that unfolded the bizarre tale of two West Point cadets who had incurred the undying enmity of a third. At the end he laid the pages in his lap and stared into the sunlit space created by the rectangle of the open window. Orry was right; it was impossible to comprehend a hatred so consuming or long-lasting that it would seek as victims other members of the Main and Hazard families. But the hatred was real; the past weeks had presented him with harrowing proof.

As the minutes stretched on, he read the letter twice more, paying special attention to Orry's account of some of the events in Mexico. Those rereadings did nothing to lessen his shock. If anything, they heightened it.

He was thankful his cousin had warned him. And yet, knowledge was, in some ways, worse than ignorance. Bent had nurtured his hatred for more than fifteen years, and that made Charles see the true enormity of the man's madness. The result was a feeling of mortal dread that was new to him, and shameful, and completely beyond his control.

*

In subsequent days, whenever he was forced to speak to Bent or appear with him in formations, he did so with extreme difficulty. Always he was conscious of the truth he knew to be hidden behind the captain's sly eyes.

For his part, Bent seemed considerably less antagonistic. Indeed, he seldom said a word to his second lieutenant except as duty required. That was a relief. Maybe the danger had lessened as a result of the threats of testimony from Mrs. Lantzman. In any case, as the weeks went by, Charles's apprehension began to diminish. He looked forward to the day when new orders for himself or Bent would separate them.

Until then, he had no choice but to be vigilant.

While the rescue expedition had been away at the Lantzmans', a known renegade had taken refuge on the Comanche reservation. Leeper, the agent, had subsequently allowed the Indian to leave. Believing Leeper was remiss in not locking up the renegade when he had the chance, farmers in the district were now petitioning Governor Houston to close the agency.

That was one of the subjects the men at Camp Cooper discussed and argued over during the autumn. There was also a good deal of joking about the experiment at Camp Verde, where Egyptian camels imported by Secretary Davis were being tested as beasts of burden. And the Second spoke proudly of Captain Van Dorn's successful foray against the Indians at Wichita Village.

The Ohioans in Company K talked a lot about events back East, too. Vying for reelection to the Senate, Stephen Douglas had debated the Black Republican, Lincoln, at various towns in Illinois. Experts seemed to feel that Douglas would be returned to Washington when the state legislature made its choice in January, but the victory might prove costly. During the meeting at Freeport, Lincoln had maneuvered his opponent into a damaging admission.

The admission had come during a complex debate about the Missouri Compromise of 1820 and the more recent Dred Scott case. In the Scott decision, the Supreme Court had upheld the inviolability of the property rights of slaveholders, had ruled that the Missouri Compromise banning slavery north of a demarcation line was unconstitutional, and had thus effectively negated the theory of popular sovereignty. Never mind, said Douglas in response to Lincoln's shrewd questioning; Supreme Court or no, there was still one simple, legal, and eminently practical way for any territory to bar slavery, and that was for the legislature to refuse to enact laws specifically protecting the slave owner's rights. No prudent man would risk valuable Negroes in territory where he might stand to lose them. "Slavery can't exist a day or an hour anywhere," the Little Giant said, "unless it is supported by local police regulations."

Douglas's view was christened the Freeport Doctrine. Commenting on it, a Southern officer from the First Infantry at Camp Cooper said to Charles:

"That man's done himself in. The Democrats down in our part of the country will never again support his candidacy for anything."

In October, Senator Seward gave an address in upstate New York that was widely reported. Seward said North and South were locked in what he termed an "irrepressible conflict" over slavery. The statement inflamed the South all over again, and even ardent Republicans on the post agreed that Seward's angry rhetoric had pushed the region closer to secession.

Still, few could imagine Americans ever taking up arms against other Americans. The conflict remained a war of words.

Occasionally Elkanah Bent injected a comment into the discussions. He had returned from his long leave having lost ten pounds but none of his peculiar opinions. He said a shooting war was entirely conceivable and left no doubt that he'd be happy to see it.

"War would permit us to put theory into practice. After all, why were we trained? What's the whole purpose of our profession? Not to keep the peace but to win it once the blood starts to flow. We have no other calling. It's a holy calling, gentlemen."

Several officers, including Charles, took note of Bent's exalted expression. Some shook their heads, but Charles did not. Nothing the man said surprised him any longer.

Over the winter he never spoke to Bent except in the course of duty. So he was astonished one evening the following April when he answered a knock at the door of his quarters and found the captain standing outside in the balmy darkness.

Bent smiled. "Good evening, Lieutenant. Are you prepared to receive visitors?"

"Certainly, sir. Come in."

He stepped back, the presence of the captain heightening his tension to a peak. Bent strutted into the room, and Charles closed the door. He smelled whiskey.

Bent's appearance was startling. For the call the captain had donned his dress uniform, complete with sash, saber, and plumed hat, which

608

he now removed. His hair was parted in the center and glistened with fragrant oil. He glanced at some large, brown-tinted daguerreotypes lying on a chair.

"Pictures from home?"

"Yes, sir. They were taken at a barbecue in honor of my cousin Ashton's wedding anniversary. Most of these people are from nearby plantations."

To test the visitor, he handed over one of the photographs. He pointed to a stern, bearded face and said carefully, "That's my cousin Orry Main. He encouraged me to go to the Academy. He went there himself. About the time you did, I think."

Bent pressed his lips together. He studied the bearded face, but Charles saw no flicker of response. The man was good at dissembling—something else that made him dangerous.

"I have a hazy recollection of a cadet named Orry," Bent remarked. "I hardly knew him. Even in those days, Yankees and Southern boys didn't mingle a great deal."

The captain started to return the picture, then gave it a second scrutiny. He tapped the image of a dark-haired woman standing at the edge of the group. She had a rigid look, a certain glazed quality in her wide eyes. Yet he found her breathtaking.

"What a beautiful creature. There's something exotic about her."

Why the devil was the captain interested in Madeline LaMotte? Charles asked himself. Why was he here at all?

"She's a Creole, from New Orleans."

"Ah, that explains it."

Bent wondered about the woman's connection with the Mains. Was she a relative by marriage or merely a neighbor? But he put a rein on his curiosity; if he questioned Charles further, he might somehow slip and reveal his true feelings about Orry. He stared at the lovely face a few seconds longer, then released the photograph.

Charles cleared the other daguerreotypes from the chair, and Bent sat down. His eyes fixed on the younger man. "I've wanted to call on you for some time, Lieutenant. To express my thanks for your discretion these past months."

Charles shrugged, as if to say the captain should have expected nothing else.

"But silence is essentially negative," Bent continued. "I've been anxious to put our relationship on a positive footing. In the future I would like to count on your friendship."

My silence, Charles thought. He's worried. He wants a promise that I'll continue to protect him. But Charles wondered if that was the whole explanation.

Bent peered at him in a curiously intense way. He licked his upper lip, then added: "Naturally, you can count on mine."

Charles didn't like the implications of the remark, the tone of which was far too friendly for comfort. Where beneath Bent's smarmy cordiality did the trap lie? He couldn't tell, and the uncertainty lent a slight nervousness to his reply:

"The past is gone, Captain. I have no intention of bringing it up again."

"Good. Good! Then we can truly be friends. I have influential contacts in the War Department. Throughout Washington, in fact. They've helped my career, and they could help yours."

Orry had explained fully how Bent succeeded in spite of a poor record. Influence. Charles resented the captain's thinking that he'd be willing to take the same route.

"Thank you, sir, but I really prefer to get ahead on my own."

Bent jumped up. Spots of color appeared in his cheeks. "A chap can always use help, Charles—" Quickly he checked himself. That had been too angry by half. But he couldn't help it. The tall, superbly built young officer repelled Bent because he was a Main and a Southerner. Yet at the same time Charles attracted him. So much so that, after weeks of indecision, he had finally drunk enough whiskey to generate the Dutch courage he needed to make this overture.

Had Charles caught a whiff of the spirits? Bent hoped not. He tried to smile.

"I will say you require less help than most. For one thing, you're the very picture of a soldier." Suddenly dizzy with excitement, he let his emotions carry him on; he touched Charles's forearm. "You are an exceptionally handsome young man."

Gently, but with firmness, Charles withdrew his arm.

"Sir, you'd better leave."

"Please don't take that tone. Brother officers should give one another aid and comfort, especially in a lonely, godforsaken place like thi—"

"Captain, get out before I pitch you through that window."

Livid, Bent jammed his hat on his head. He slammed the door behind him. His cheeks were burning.

A coyote barked as he hurried away through the spring dark, wanting to do murder. One day, by God, he would.

*

Charles had thought himself beyond shock where Bent was concerned. How wrong he had been.

What had just happened did more than confirm rumors about the captain's sexual predilections. It demonstrated that Bent's strange appetites lived side by side with his hatreds, and depending upon the mood of the moment—and how much he had imbibed—sometimes one aspect or the other dominated. The realization put a last daub of nastiness on the picture of madness that Charles carried in his imagination.

His lamp-lit room had suddenly grown confining. He flung on his best hickory shirt, stuffed it into his pants, and tramped to the stable to see to his horse. The camp's night sounds—sentries calling the hour and the ''all's well,'' an owl hooting above the murmur of the spring wind—soothed his nerves and settled him down.

Outside the stable he halted and gazed at the stars. He inhaled the yeasty odors of hay, dung, and horseflesh, and immediately felt better, cleansed. He would forever associate those smells with the Army and with Texas—both of which he had come to love.

Thinking of Bent again, he was unexpectedly touched with pity. What must it be like to inhabit that lumbering body, with little worms forever gnawing at sanity from the corners of the mind? The pity intensified—but then his own stern and silent warning cut through:

Better not feel too sorry for a man who'd like to kill you when he's sober.

That threw it back into proper perspective. Charles knew he must continue to be wary until the day when the inevitable Army transfer separated him from the captain. That *would* happen—and it was something to look forward to, wasn't it? He drew another deep breath, savoring the sweet smells of the Texas night. He was whistling as he strode into the stable.

50

Orry watched secession fever spread like an epidemic that summer and fall. Huntoon traveled all over South Carolina and into neighboring states, addressing crowds at churches, barbecues, meeting halls. He solicited memberships for the African Labor Supply Association, dedicated to reestablishment of the slave trade. He continued to advocate a separate Southern government, citing all sorts of reasons, from Seward's "irrepressible conflict" to the arguments culled from Hinton Helper's little book, which of course he never mentioned by name.

Orry admired his brother-in-law's energy, if not his views. He admired Ashton's energy, too; she went everywhere with her husband.

During the autumn, Orry took note of an interesting and perhaps significant contrast. Up in Columbia, State Senator Wade Hampton addressed the legislature and pleaded for preservation of the Union. He also argued against the resumption of the slave trade. His remarks were widely reported and almost universally scorned by the state's plantation aristocracy. Whatever personal popularity he possessed among his peers vanished overnight, while Huntoon's continued to increase.

Cooper was dividing his time between the affairs of the Democratic party and the shipyard on James Island. He said construction of the huge *Star of Carolina* would begin by the first of the year. Orry decided to carry that news to George in person. He missed his best friend and was eager to see him again.

When Brett learned of the proposed trip, she begged Orry to take her along. She wanted to go on from Pennsylvania to St. Louis, where her brother could chaperone her visit with Billy. Orry didn't relish such a long journey, but he recognized that Brett was lonesome for her young man. He gave in with only a little argument.

They hadn't gone far before he was regretting his decision to travel. In North Carolina, where they changed trains for the first time, he asked the depot agent for a timetable.

"Ain't got any," the agent said, in the nasal twang Orry associated with the hill folk of the state.

"Then can you at least tell me when our train is scheduled to arrive in—?" He didn't bother to finish. The agent had turned away behind the wicket.

Orry walked to the bench where Brett was seated. "They don't seem to like questions here. Or maybe it's South Carolinians they don't like." There were many anti-slavery men in North Carolina; the agent had probably identified Orry's accent.

On the next leg of their journey, a Negro porter—a freedman— contrived to drop one of Brett's portmanteaus, the one she had asked him to handle with special care. It contained some fragile gifts they were taking to Lehigh Station. The mishap occurred while the Negro was lifting the portmanteau from an overhead rack. Close to tears, Brett unwrapped a blown-glass pelican she had bought for Constance. The ornament was in three pieces.

"Sure am sorry, ma'am," the porter said. Orry thought he detected a malicious gleam in the man's eye.

At Petersburg, Virginia, a new conductor came on board. Orry showed his tickets, which were stamped with the seal of the issuing railroad in Charleston. The conductor's manner grew officious. "Change in Washington, then Baltimore," he said in a voice that suggested New England origins.

"Thank you," Orry said. "We have seven pieces of luggage. Will I be able to find a baggage man at the Washington depot?"

"Afraid I couldn't say. I have nothing to do with porters. Mebbe you should have brought one of your nigger slaves."

Orry uncoiled his long frame and stood. He had a good three inches on the conductor, whose attitude immediately became less truculent. "I resent your rudeness," Orry said. "I don't believe I've done anything to justify it"—he waved the ticket—"unless you consider coming from the South to be an offense."

"Please, Orry," Brett whispered. "Let's not have a scene."

The conductor took the opportunity to break away. "I'll send the car porter," he called as he disappeared through the door at the end of the first-class coach.

They never saw him again. Or the porter, either.

Rolling toward Richmond through the fall sunshine, the train lurched from side to side. Orry stared out the dirty window. "Why are we having so blasted much trouble? Am I doing something to invite it?"

Brett closed her copy of *A Tale of Two Cities*, the year's fastest-selling book. Giving her brother a melancholy look, she said, "No—unless it's speaking with a Carolina accent."

"You sure I haven't come down with some kind of persecution fixation?"

She shook her head. "I've noticed a definite change in the way we're treated. It's not at all like the treatment we used to get in Newport. Then, people were friendly. They aren't any longer."

"But Virginia and North Carolina are the South!"

"Not the deep South. The cotton South. There are a lot of men and women in both states who are more Yankee than Southern. That's the difference."

She resumed her reading. The antagonism was startling to him; he found himself resenting it strongly. His dark mood was still with him when they arrived in Baltimore.

From Camden Street they had to transfer to the depot of the Philadelphia, Wilmington and Baltimore line. Brett enjoyed the ride by horse car, but Orry was too hungry to be interested. Before their next train left he needed a meal.

Railroad officials kept predicting that dining cars would soon be found on every train, but at present few had them. The alternatives were unappealing. You could buy something to eat from one of the hawkers who roved up and down the trains, or you could harden your nerves and settle for the bad fare served in grimy depot restaurants. In Baltimore, Orry was driven to the latter.

He held the dining-room door for Brett. She lifted her skirts, prepared to step over the threshold, and glanced at the counter and the tables adjoining. All the customers were men. One or two cast bold, almost insulting looks her way. Orry bristled. She shook her head.

"I'm really not hungry, Orry. I'll sit out here on this bench and wait for you. I'll be perfectly all right."

He helped her get settled, then entered the restaurant. Boisterous conversation filled the place. He scanned the room, saw an empty table, walked to it, and seated himself.

He ordered smoked pork with mashed turnips and johnnycake on the side. Then he drew out the small Bible he carried almost everywhere these days; he liked to read the Song of Solomon because so many verses reminded him of Madeline. He hadn't spoken to her since Ashton's anniversary barbecue. Their conversation had been short, formal, and inconsequential; she seemed disconnected from reality, not herself. He had asked Justin whether she had been ill. Justin merely smiled.

615

Orry bent over the open Bible. A few minutes later the waiter slammed a plate down. He also managed to spill some of the coffee he was serving. Orry held his temper.

He tried to read while he ate. He couldn't concentrate; the voices at the next table were too loud. Finally he leaned back in his chair, listening.

"That's all the damn Southrons can talk about, a separate government." The speaker was the oldest of a trio, a skinny fellow with white chin whiskers. "I say let 'em have it. Let 'em launch their leaky boat and sink with it."

"Hell, no!" That was a man with a crooked nose, a loutish sort with the look of a commercial traveler. "Anyone who goes along with that or even suggests it should be hung high enough for everyone to see what a traitor looks like."

"That's right," said the third man, a middle-aged nonentity.

Orry knew the three men were boors reinforcing each other's opinions. He knew he should sit quietly, avoiding trouble. But the continuing irritations of the day moved him beyond the border of prudence. He put his coffee mug on the table with just enough of a thump to draw their attention.

"Come now, gentlemen," he said with a faint, chilly smile. "You sound as if the establishment of a peaceful Southern government would threaten you personally. I'm not in favor of the idea either, but I don't call it treason. Just foolishness. I must say it's an understandable foolishness. The South has suffered insults and calumnies for a generation."

If any others in the room agreed with him, they kept quiet. The fellow with the chin whiskers asked, "What state are you from, sir?"

"South Carolina."

The man leaned on the big silver knob of his cane, smiling smugly. "Might have known."

The man with the crooked nose blurted, "Read the Constitution—then you'll know that secession is treason. You cotton-states boys have been threatening it for years, swinging it like a damn club! Well, go ahead—pull out. But if you do, Buck Buchanan has every right to clap you in irons. Or string you up."

A man nearby said, "Amen."

Then Orry noticed hostile faces at the counter. They belonged to a pair of burly types in soiled overalls. Switchmen, to judge from the thick hickory clubs lying in their laps.

"Hell"—one of the switchmen snickered—"Old Buck wouldn't do that. He's a doughface."

The fellow who had said amen agreed. "Then get the Army to hang 'em," someone else suggested. Outside, a station man began calling passengers for the Philadelphia express.

"Won't work," declared Crooked Nose. "The West Point crowd runs the Army. Most of them are Southrons. Comes to a choice between their oath to defend the country and setting up a government to protect their niggers, you know which way those boys would go."

Orry's temples pulsed visibly. Under his coat his shirt felt sodden with sweat. He laid his hand on his Bible.

"Watch what you're saying, sir."

"What's that?" Crooked Nose jumped up, overturning his chair. The pair of switchmen, clubs in hand, moved behind him. Two patrons flung down money and rushed out.

Without hurrying, Orry stood up. When Crooked Nose saw Orry's height and his blazing eyes, he retreated.

"I said you'd do well to watch your remarks about the Military Academy. I'm a graduate of that institution, and I fought in Mexico." He inclined his head toward his empty left sleeve. "I fought for the whole country, Yankees included."

"Is that right?" Crooked Nose snorted. "Well, *sir*, I still say you West Point princelings have a secessionist streak a mile wide."

Shouts. Some applause. One of the switchmen peered over Crooked Nose's shoulder. "Maybe this Southron gentleman is gonna miss his train. Maybe he's gonna get a new coat in Baltimore. A coat of tar and feathers."

Crooked Nose broke into a grin. Orry's eyes flickered over the faces ringing him. Hostile, every one. His stomach hurt. The switchmen began to sidle toward him.

A sudden, ratchetlike sound from behind the counter brought them to a halt. By the door to the kitchen stood a nondescript man with a cocked shotgun.

"Anybody supplies any new coats around here, they'll have to fit me with one, too." He addressed Orry. "I'm a Baltimore man born and bred. I regret you've received this kind of reception in our city."

"Orry?"

The sound of Brett's voice turned him toward the door. She rushed to him. Outside, the station official called for Philadelphia passengers to board.

"Orry, I don't want to miss the train. Come on."

Crooked Nose guffawed. "Gonna let little missy fight your battles? How come you're hanging around with her, anyway? I thought you cotton-states boys fancied dark meat."

Orry struck then. A single, driving, clumsy blow, straight to Crooked Nose's stomach. One switchman kept him from falling, the other raised his club, but the man with the shotgun called a warning.

Crooked Nose, making choking sounds, sagged, shuffled backward, then tripped on his overturned chair. Orry's fist was clenched so hard it looked as white as a boll of cotton. He whipped his eyes across the crowd.

"Orry, come away." Brett tugged his arm.

"Philadelphia express—final call!" The stentorian voice echoed through the depot.

That broke the tension, set up a scramble for the door. After a nod of thanks to the man with the shotgun, Orry turned and reluctantly followed his sister to the platform.

The express was rattling toward Wilmington. Sadness mingled with anger when Orry spoke.

"I didn't know that kind of hostility existed. Men ready to fight one another in public places. Incredible."

His erstwhile naiveté dismayed him. The situation in the country had deteriorated far beyond anything he had imagined. If some people envisioned a peaceful separation of the states, they were imbeciles.

"I'm glad we left when we did," Brett said. "You could have been badly hurt, and for no purpose."

His hand still throbbed from punching the man in the checked suit. He peered at his knuckles. "Guess you're right. But I don't like running from a fight."

She tried to make light of it. "You ran to catch a train."

Unsmiling, he muttered, "Damn Yankee trash."

"Orry, when you talk that way, you're no better than those oafs in the restaurant."

"I know. Funny thing is, I don't much care about that." He drew a deep breath. "I resent having to behave like a gentleman. I hate turning tail. I'll never do it again."

Their welcome at Belvedere was warm, although Maude was not part of it; she had gone to Philadelphia for a few days. The visitors

618

presented their gifts—Brett promised to send Constance a duplicate of the broken pelican—marveled at how the children had grown, and after a fine meal of duckling went off gratefully to bed. Orry slept nine hours but didn't feel rested when he woke.

"I can't wait to show you the Bessemer converter," George said at breakfast. He was full of energy and enthusiasm, which had the curious effect of heightening Orry's sour feeling. George had done nothing to offend him. It was the whole North that offended him. He hoped the mood would pass; it threatened to spoil the reunion.

George put a match to his second cigar of the morning. "Soon as you're finished, we'll take a look. I'm paying a steep royalty, but in the long run I anticipate that it'll be worth it."

"You don't sound convinced," Orry said.

"Oh, I am—to a point. The time saving is enormous. But there's still a problem with the process. I'll show you."

Orry didn't want to ride all the way across the smoky, foul-smelling grounds of Hazard Iron, step into an iron-roofed shed, and there peer at an egg-shaped contraption that rotated on a pivot. But he did it to humor his friend.

The workmen had finished a blow and were tapping the converter into a floor trench. The steel flowed like a ribbon of light.

Proud as a parent watching a child, George said, "A chap in Wales solved Bessemer's worst problem. Did Cooper tell you about that?"

"Yes, but I didn't understand most of the explanation." His tone said he didn't care.

George's reaction veered from disappointment to annoyance, but only for an instant. "Bessemer was producing what the trade refers to as burnt iron. He purged out the carbon, which meant there was none to transform the iron to steel, and he had no idea of how to put some back in. The Welshman experimented with adding charcoal and manganese oxide. Next he tried a compound the Germans call *spiegeleisen*—iron, carbon, some manganese. That did the trick. While Bessemer and the Welshman wrangle over who owes what to whom, I'm experimenting with *spiegeleisen* and paying Bessemer his royalty at the same time—even though his American patents are still up in the air. I'm not yet convinced the process is practical, though."

"Why not?"

"It involves too much guesswork. The carbon content can be judged only by the color of the converter flame. That's no way to make steel reliably, batch after batch. Another fellow may have come up with a method better than Bessemer's, a German-born Englishman named Karl Siemens. I've written him—Orry, you aren't interested in a syllable of this, are you?''

"Of course I am."

George shook his head. "Let's go outside where it's cooler."

Once there, he looked with concern at his friend. "You haven't seemed yourself since you arrived. What's wrong?"

"I don't know."

He did know but could not say it aloud. He was angry with his friend simply for being a Yankee.

The Hazards dined at two that afternoon. Orry still felt tense and cross. While he dutifully brought George up to date on the status of his investment, he kept seeing him as a virtual stranger. Had they once called each other by ridiculous names like Stick and Stump? Inconceivable. The times had grown too grim for nicknames or laughter. Perhaps they were even too grim for friendship.

"That's excellent progress," George said when Orry concluded. "I'm happy to hear it." He lit a cigar.

Orry coughed and waved the smoke away. George frowned and muttered an apology. But he didn't extinguish the cigar, merely transferred it to his other hand.

After a moment of strained silence, Orry began, "You never told me your reaction to Elkanah Bent turning up in Texas."

"I was thunderstruck when you mentioned it in that letter. I'd completely forgotten him."

"The point is, George, he hasn't forgotten us. If Bent still hates me, and can transfer that hatred to my cousin, the same thing could happen to you."

His friend's laugh was curt, hard. "Let him come to Lehigh Station and try whatever he wants. I'll give him a reception he won't forget."

"I was thinking more of your brother, Billy. He's still in the Army."

George waved his cigar. "Oh, I said something to him right after I heard from you. But I advised him not to waste time worrying about some lunatic—at least not until his path crosses that of the infamous Captain Bent. You shouldn't worry either. God, I can't believe the Army's never caught up with him," he finished with a shake of his head.

George's cavalier dismissal only heightened Orry's annoyance. Fortunately there was a diversion. William, a handsome boy who bore a strong resemblance to his father, had been squirming with excitement for the past few minutes. Now he burst out:

"Tell me how Charles is fighting the Indians!"

"That was last year," Orry snapped. "Now he's off to the Rio Grande, chasing some Mexican bandit named Cortinas. I wrote your father all about it—ask him."

Young William caught the crossness of Orry's reply and he in turn recognized the lad's bewilderment. To make up for it, Orry began to tell him about the Second Cavalry's pursuit of the border bandit. Patricia, a year younger than her brother, wasn't interested. She and her mother and Brett fell to discussing fashions, and especially the gown from Charles Worth of Paris, which Constance had ordered for a gala charity ball. The ball, first of its kind in Lehigh Station, would raise money for the schoolhouse.

"The dress is much too grand for such an affair." Constance laughed. "But I do love it, and George insisted I buy it. I'm afraid the local ladies will point fingers, though."

"Jealously," George said. Orry was envious of the affectionate glance that passed between husband and wife.

"'Specially Aunt Isabel," Patricia said.

Orry asked, "How are Stanley and his wife?"

Patricia answered by sticking out her tongue and making a hideous face. Constance lightly tapped her daughter's wrist and shook her head. George said, "We don't see much of them. Stanley's thick with Boss Cameron, and Isabel has her own friends. Thank heaven. To contradict Scripture and that fellow Lincoln, our house is divided, but it manages to stand very nicely."

Constance smiled in a rueful way. "There is one difference, dear. Stanley and Isabel's separation from us isn't voluntary. You threw them out."

"True, but—" A noise at the dining-room door diverted George and the others. "Ah, Virgilia."

Hastily, Orry pushed his chair back and rose. "Good evening, Virgilia."

"Good evening, Orry," she replied as she swept to an empty chair. She might have been saying hello to a carrier of cholera.

"I didn't know you were visiting," Orry said, sitting again. He was shocked by Virgilia's appearance. She looked ten years older than when he had last seen her. Her skin had a sickly yellow cast; her dress needed laundering, her hair combing. Her sunken eyes held a wild glint.

"I arrived this morning." As always, she managed to turn a trivial remark into a pronouncement. Orry wondered about her Negro paramour, the runaway, Grady. Rumors of their liaison, more and more sensationalized with repeated tellings, had reached and scandalized Charleston. Was she still living with him? Orry didn't intend to ask.

"Tomorrow I'll be traveling down to Chambersburg," she went on. Irritably, she motioned to one of the servant girls standing by the wall. The girl rushed to serve Virgilia's soup.

Virgilia's eyes locked with those of the visitor. Don't let her goad you, he said to himself. But it was hard to heed the warning. Frequently Virgilia touched off a red rage within him; in his present mood that could easily happen.

Brett watched the two of them closely as Virgilia added, "I'm helping with the work being done by an abolitionist named Brown. John Brown of Osawatomie."

Orry had heard of Brown, of course. Who hadn't? He had seen engravings of the man's gaunt face and long white beard in *Harper's Weekly*. Born in Connecticut, Brown had been active as an abolitionist for a long time. But he had really become notorious in Kansas where he and five of his sons had fought several bloody battles on behalf of free soil. In 1856 men under Brown's command had slain five pro-slavery settlers in the so-called Pottawatomie Massacre.

Recently he had been lecturing in the Northeast to raise money for some mad scheme of his—a provisional government he had proclaimed up in Canada. Presumably it was connected with the underground railroad. Brown's tarnished history and Virgilia's challenging stare prompted Orry to a blunt reply:

"I can't imagine anyone wanting to help a murderer."

Anxious looks flew between Brett and Constance. Virgilia pursed her lips.

"It's to be expected that you would say something like that. Calling names is the chief means of discrediting anyone who speaks the truth about slavery or the South. Well, you and your kind should be warned. You won't be practicing your barbarities or running your secret breeding farms much longer."

"What the devil does that mean?"

"One day soon a messiah will lead your slaves in a great revolution. Every white man who doesn't support it will be destroyed."

Shocked silence. Even Brett was fuming. Orry's anger, smoldering for days, burst into flame. He thrust his chair away from the table. Stiffly, he said to George, "Please excuse me."

Constance gave her sister-in-law a stabbing look. Then she turned to Orry, "You shouldn't be the one to leave."

Virgilia smiled. "But of course he will. Southerners find the truth unbearable."

Orry closed his hand on the back of his chair. "What truth? I've heard none at this table. I'm bone-weary of being treated as if I'm personally responsible for every offense committed by the South—either those that are real or those you've conceived in your deranged mind."

Color rushed to George's face. "Orry, that's strong language."

Orry barely heard. "Breeding farms! How do you come by these fantasies? Do you find them in yellow-backed novels?" George stiffened again at the reference to pornography. Orry's voice rose. "Do they thrill you, arouse you? Is that why you constantly dwell on them?"

He was marginally aware of Constance herding the children from the room. Virgilia's smile grew angelic. "I would anticipate a denial of evil from those who perpetuate it."

The room seemed to tilt and blur. Orry could no longer tolerate the sound of her voice, impregnable in its smugness. Restraint departed, rage poured out.

"Woman, you're mad!"

"And you are finished, you and your kind."

"Shut up!" he shouted. "Shut up and go back to your nigger lover where you belong!"

As soon as the last word was out of his mouth, shame overwhelmed him. He felt as if the floor were sinking beneath his boots. Moments ago his vision had blurred. Now he saw faces with perfect clarity. Angry faces. The angriest belonged to George, who had torn the cigar out of his mouth and was squeezing it so hard the dark green wrapper cracked.

Virgilia struggled to maintain her false smile while Brett glared. Once more Constance attempted to restore peace:

"I think it's you who spoke intemperately, Virgilia."

Cold eyes fixed on George's wife. "Do you?"

"Would an apology be so difficult?"

"Not difficult but unnecessary."

Orry wanted to pick up his wineglass and hurl the contents in her

623

face. Despite his shame, his wounded pride dominated. These people challenged, judged, and passed sentence on an entire social system and damned the good along with the bad. It was not to be borne.

He noticed George scowling at him and snapped, "I should think you, at least, would take issue with her conduct."

George flung his broken cigar on the table. "I take issue with her choice of words, but she's on the right side."

George's hostility went through Orry like a sword. The rift, long a fearsome possibility, had become inevitable. He collected himself, squared his shoulders, and spoke with stinging intensity.

"I don't believe, sir, we have anything further to discuss."

"That," George said, "has become evident."

Orry looked at him. It was impossible to deny the fury he saw on George's face—or felt within himself. Never before had he and George Hazard been enemies, but they were enemies now.

"I must find my hat," he said to his sister. "We're leaving."

Brett was unprepared for the announcement, speechless. He strode to her side, gripped her elbow, and steered her to the front hall. "Kindly deliver our luggage to the local hotel," he said without looking back. A few seconds later, the front door closed with a click.

In the dining room the only person smiling was Virgilia.

George didn't return to the mill that afternoon. He roamed the house, a cigar in one hand, a tumbler of whiskey in the other. He was mad at Orry, mad at himself, and didn't know what to do next.

Virgilia vanished upstairs. Constance came down after seeing to the children. William ran outside, and Patricia went to the music room. It was here George found his daughter half an hour later. She was laboring through a minuet on the pianoforte.

Patricia saw her father standing in the doorway, looking glum.

"Papa, are you and Orry not friends anymore?"

That simple question jolted him, wrenched everything back into proper perspective.

"Of course we are. Orry will be back here before supper. I'll see to it."

In the library where he kept some writing materials he sat down, pushed the iron meteorite aside, and inked a pen. He wrote swiftly, commencing the note with the words: *Stick—will you accept my apology?*

"You want Mr. Main?" The clerk at the Station House consulted his ledger. "He took a room at the day rate for his sister, but I believe you can find him in the saloon bar."

The servant from Belvedere pushed through the slatted swinging doors and crossed the deserted barroom to a table by the window. There a gaunt, bearded man sat staring into an empty glass.

"Mr. Main? From Mr. Hazard, sir."

Orry read the note and briefly reconsidered his decision to leave on the evening train. Then he remembered the atmosphere at Belvedere and all the things that had been said. He couldn't accept George's apology or his invitation to return, as if nothing had happened. And if that scuttled the *Star of Carolina*, it was Cooper's problem.

The servant cleared his throat. "Is there a reply, sir?"

"Just this."

Orry tore the note and dropped the pieces into a brass spittoon.

"Goddamn him!" George exclaimed. "Can you believe what he did?"

"Yes," Constance said. "You've described it ten or twelve times already."

Teasing him did no good. Besides, she didn't feel amused, although under happier circumstances she might have said her husband was a comical sight as he paced barefoot up and down the bedroom with his dead cigar clamped in his teeth and his slight paunch showing at the waist of his linen underdrawers, the only garment he was wearing.

"Of course I have," George said. "I tender a perfectly sincere apology, and in return the son of a bitch insults me."

The windows of Belvedere stood open to catch the autumn breeze. In cool weather George loved to sleep curled around his wife, and she loved having him there. But she doubted either of them would sleep much tonight. He had been cursing and fulminating ever since the servant returned from the Station House.

"You were just as hard on Orry, darling." She sat against the headboard with her unbound hair spilling over the shoulders of her muslin gown. "There's guilt on both sides—and it was really Virgilia who caused the whole thing. I will not tolerate her disruptions of this household indefinitely."

He raked a hand through his hair. "Don't worry, she's already left for Chambersburg."

"Of her own choice?"

"No, I insisted she go."

"Well, that's something." Constance adjusted a bolster at the small of her back. The muslin gown stretched taut between her breasts. She began to brush her hair with slow, lazy strokes. She had reluctantly become convinced that Virgilia's abusive behavior was incorrigible, had passed the edge of toleration. She wanted to say that George hadn't solved the problem of his sister and wouldn't until he turned her out for good. But this was not the moment to raise that issue.

"And Orry—has he left Lehigh Station already?"

"I don't know, and I don't give a damn. I have a notion to write Cooper and call in my loan. I can find better things to do with two million dollars. Those bastards are probably building the flagship for a secessionist navy!"

"You'd accuse Cooper Main of that?" A gentle smile. "Now you're sounding as unreasonable as your sister."

George flung the dead cigar out the window. A whistle on the Lehigh line drifted up the hill, a mournful sound. "He didn't even have the decency to reply." Speaking to the dark outside, he sounded sad rather than angry.

"Darling, come here."

He turned, a helpless, almost boyish expression on his face. He walked to the bed and sat down with the small of his back against her hip. His legs dangled over the side, not quite touching the floor.

Hating to see him hurting, she began to stroke his temple. "All of us behaved wretchedly today. Let Orry calm down for a week or so. You calm down, too. Then you'll both feel like patching it up. You've been friends too long for it to go any other way."

"I know, but he—"

Her fingers on his lips silenced the protest. "This afternoon you let a political fight come between you and the best friend you have in all the world. Do you realize how foolish that is? How ominous? How can this country survive if friends can't rise above the quarrel? If men like you and Orry—decent, reasonable men—don't find a solution to the problems, can you imagine the alternative? The future will be in the hands of the Southern fire eaters and the John Browns."

The soft, soothing pressure of her fingers tamed his temper at last. "You're right. Up to a point. I'm not sure words like *fight* and *quarrel* are truly adequate to describe what's happening in this country."

"I'm not sure I understand."

"To me, words like *fight* and *quarrel* have a—well, almost a trivial sound. They suggest that people are falling out over"—a hand in the air helped him grope for the rest—"over hairstyles or the cut of a lapel. This argument runs much, much deeper. It goes all the way down to bedrock. Are you entitled to hold someone in bondage just because that person has black skin? Can you sunder the Union at will? I know my own answers to both of those questions. But not to this one: In the face of such issues, how can you stand up for what you believe and keep from losing a friend at the same time?"

Constance regarded him with loving eyes. "With patience," she said. "Patience, and reason, and goodwill."

He sighed. "I hope you're right. I'm not sure."

But he was grateful for her counsel and her help. To demonstrate that, he leaned against her bosom and gave her a long, tender kiss.

Soon the pressure of her lips increased. He slipped his hand between her back and the bolster. Arms around his neck, she kissed him with passion. Autumn wind blew the curtains as they made love, finding comfort in each other and temporary release from their confusion.

Afterward, lying pleasantly warm with their arms entwined, each was visited by the same unspoken thought: Patience, reason, and goodwill were fine, but were they sufficient? Perhaps the nation's affairs were already past the point of rational control. Perhaps destiny was already in the hands of the fire eaters and the John Browns.

Yes, and the Virgilias, too.

51

Simon Cameron's barouche creaked along Pennsylvania Avenue. Out for a bit of sightseeing with his mentor, Stanley basked in the pleasant sunshine.

The sound of Scala's Marine Band playing "Listen to the Mocking Bird" slowly faded behind them. The composer of that piece of music had dedicated it to Harriet Lane, President Buchanan's niece and hostess in the executive mansion. No doubt she and Old Buck—he was close to seventy now, an old-fashioned bachelor—were out on the lawn of President's Park this minute, shaking hands with the audience at the band concert. The President was highly visible around Washington. Only yesterday, following a lavish dinner of oysters, terrapin, and French wine, Stanley had gone for a walk on this same avenue and bumped into the President, who was out for his daily one-hour stroll.

Made bold by the wine, Stanley had stepped up and spoken to Old Buck. Of course the two had met before, in Pennsylvania. The President not only recognized Stanley, but if a slight frostiness was any indication, he was quite aware of Stanley's association with Boss Cameron. Thinking back to the encounter, Stanley remarked:

"I know the President's no friend of yours, Simon, but he does come from our state. And when I met him again yesterday, I was frankly impressed with him."

"Yes, but you have also told me you're impressed with Washington."

The sarcasm brought a flush to Stanley's cheeks. He had said the wrong thing.

"Surely you can't be impressed with that," Cameron continued with a contemptuous gesture at the Capitol; its unfinished dome was topped by a crane and ugly scaffolding. Cameron sighed, shook his head. "How can I possibly make you a trusted associate if you continue to commit these errors in judgment? When will you learn there is nothing in this town worth a penny except the power?"

Stanley's color deepened. He knew Cameron hadn't befriended him because of his brains but only because he possessed certain other assets. Still, he hated to have his limitations discussed so openly or in such a caustic way.

But he mustn't alienate his mentor. Momentous changes were in the wind, changes that could carry him and Isabel to this city and a position at the heart of the national government.

Cameron refused to let up. "Never let me hear you say you're impressed with Old Buck. We're Republicans now. The President is the enemy."

Stanley nodded and forced a toadying smile, then tried to steer the conversation to a different tack. "What about next year? Do you think the Democrats will run Steve Douglas?"

"Hard to say. The party is badly split. Douglas alienated the entire South with his Freeport Doctrine."

"Then we have a real chance to elect Seward."

That very evening Stanley and Cameron were to attend a private reception for the senator at Kirkwood's Hotel. The two men had traveled from Pennsylvania expressly to meet with Seward and with General Scott—gouty, opinionated, and, like the senator, smitten with presidential ambitions. Last night they had interviewed Scott for an hour; he had left his headquarters in New York just to see Cameron, another demonstration of the Pennsylvanian's importance in Republican affairs. All this mingling with notables had an intoxicating effect on Stanley. He wanted to get back to Washington at all costs—as an insider.

Cameron reacted negatively to the mention of Seward. "After that remark about an irrepressible conflict, he can't possibly win. Of course we mustn't tell him so tonight, but the fact is the party will have to pick a man much less bellicose. One who offends the fewest people."

Stanley blinked. "Who is that?"

"I don't know yet. But I'll tell you one thing"—a smile—"I'll be the first to know his name. He won't be nominated until I say so."

Stanley knew the Boss wasn't joking. Few Republican politicians could offer what he did—virtually absolute control of a large machine in an important state.

Cameron went on, "I intend to come out of the party convention with a job at Cabinet level. Any candidate who promises less won't get my support. And when I move to this wretched town, my friends will move with me."

Sunlight flashed in his eyes as he looked at Stanley. "I'm speaking of those friends who have proved their loyalty beyond all doubt."

The message was clear, if familiar. Stanley asked, "How much do you need this time?"

"Ten thousand would help. Twenty would be ideal."

"You have it."

Beaming, Cameron leaned back on the plush cushions. "I knew I could count on you, Stanley. I'm sure there's a job waiting here for a man of your intelligence."

Billy rowed toward Bloody Island as the light faded. Brett sat at the bow facing him, a parasol canted over her shoulder. He could hardly keep his eyes away from her or control a physical reaction to her presence.

He kept reminding himself that her brother expected him to behave like a gentleman. Not an easy task, given his months of loneliness out here and the heart-stopping beauty he saw in the tilt of her head and the curve of her bosom.

After nearly a week of traveling, Brett and Orry had arrived in St. Louis the day before yesterday. Almost at once, Brett told him about the quarrel at Lehigh Station. She said Virgilia had caused it, which disgusted Billy but didn't surprise him. He and his sister had never been close. He often found it hard to believe she was a blood relation.

So far, Orry had chaperoned the young people in a very relaxed manner. On two previous occasions he had left them alone for over an hour, permitting them to wander where they would in the raw riverside town. Today, pleading a stomach upset caused by catfish he'd eaten at noon, he had remained at the hotel while Billy took Brett across the Mississippi on the ferry, then rented the rowboat. He wanted her to see what had kept him busy all these months.

Orry was certainly treating him politely and with consideration, Billy thought as the boat nosed through shallow water to the long shoal. Did that mean he had changed his mind about the match? Billy hoped so.

The boat crunched on the graveled bottom. Billy jumped out. Standing ankle-deep in the river, he extended his arms.

"Jump. You won't get wet." But he hadn't beached the rowboat as firmly as he thought. When she stood up, the motion drove the boat away from him. "Wait, let me catch the bow line," he exclaimed.

Too late. She jumped. He tried to catch her, but he was off balance. Down they went, the huge splash scattering dozens of small silvery fish.

"Oh, Lord," she said in disgust. They sat on their rumps in five inches of water. Suddenly both of them started to laugh.

He helped her up. Her bodice clung to her body, revealing the tips of her breasts through layers of wet fabric. She shook a shower of droplets from her parasol and giggled.

"Your uniform's a sight. I suppose I don't look much better."

"Well," he replied in a grave way, "at least now you'll remember your visit to St. Louis."

"How could I forget St. Louis when you're here?"

Said lightly, it nevertheless carried an undertone of seriousness. Their eyes held. He pressed toward her through the shallows, circled her waist with both hands, and pulled her to him. Her wet, sweet mouth roused him all the more. Her lips parted. She pressed herself close.

Presently he whispered, "For a proper Southern girl, you don't worry much about appearances. Here we are kissing in broad daylight—"

"I don't care if the whole state of Illinois sees us. I love you, Billy. I'll never love anyone el—" Over his shoulder she noticed something that instantly banished romance. "The boat!"

He had to wade into deep water to retrieve it. He pulled it well up on shore and anchored the bow line under a heavy rock. He slapped his wet cap against his trousers as he rejoined her, glad for the distraction the boat had provided. It had helped him calm down a little.

He took her hand as they walked toward the cottonwoods. Immediately, he felt a renewed pressure in his groin. The enforced celibacy was just too damn much. He glanced at Brett, and her eyes seemed to be saying the same thing.

He showed her the two rows of pilings at the upper end of the wooded shoal. The forty-foot space between the rows had been refilled with sand and stone, the outer faces of the dike built up again with ramparts of brush.

It had been a hard, dirty job. Billy had labored at it all summer, positioning the barges, sinking new pilings, dumping stone, swatting insects, and dealing with the quirks and quarrels of his hired civilian crew. Most of the time he had worked without his shirt. His back had repeatedly reddened and blistered, but now his skin was a dark nut color, the repairs were done, and he could show them off with pride.

"Ice damaged the dike at the south end of the shoal, too. We've been repairing that. We'll be finished in another two or three weeks."

"Then what will happen?"

"I'll be transferred."

"Where?"

"Wherever they need engineers. One of my workmen asked why I had to spend four years at West Point to learn how to load rocks on a barge. I was hanged if I knew the answer. But it's good, useful work, and I've enjoyed it. I'll be glad to do the same kind of job somewhere else."

She nodded. They were strolling arm in arm through the rustling cottonwoods. The sky had turned a brilliant deep blue; Billy always thought of it as the color of October. Some cumulus clouds drifted overhead. The sinking sun tinted them hot orange. The contrast with the sky was striking and, to his way of thinking, romantic.

"I don't care where I go," he resumed, "so long as I'm near you." He stopped, turned her toward him, held her forearms. "I want to marry you, Brett. Soon."

"I feel the same way. It seems like we've been waiting a century. Do you know I'm twenty-one already?"

"I'd forgotten. Why, you're practically ancient."

Despite the joke, he too had been aware of his age lately. At twenty-four, a man was ready for responsibilities. "I can take care of you properly now. I've been saving half my pay every month, so—" He cleared his throat. "What would you think if I spoke to Orry while you're both here?"

She hugged him. "Oh, please do."

"I want to be sure I approach him at the right moment—"

She gave him a gentle smile. "You're always so cautious and careful. I don't think there will ever be a right moment anymore. The world's in such turmoil—"

"But I'm not certain Orry likes me. What if I speak to him and he's still angry with George?"

"He's all over that." Again she crushed against him, whispering, "I'll go out of my mind if we have to wait much longer."

"So will I."

"Talk to him tomorrow. Or tonight!"

"All right. I'll do it as soon as I can, I promise."

It had a firm, emphatic sound that concealed his inner doubt. He felt like a general who had finally committed his troops to battle.

They kissed again while the orange clouds floated above the Mississippi in a sky so lovely it seemed to deny even the possibility of trouble in the world.

Orry found St. Louis a lively and energetic place but ill-mannered, bumptious. Raw as the unpainted lumber of many of its buildings. He felt very much the elegant South Carolinian as he and Billy strolled along the riverfront on the morning following Billy's trip to Bloody Island.

Orry was carrying an expensive walnut cane he had just bought as a souvenir of his visit. He swung the cane forward in a little circle, then in a circle the other way. They passed a dozen noisy Negro stevedores loading crates on a barge. In mid-channel a huge sternwheeler churned northward toward Des Moines. Passengers lined the rails, waving. Orry watched the vessel with admiring eyes; he had fallen in love with steamboats, which seemed to him like elegant floating palaces.

Billy cleared his throat. His light blue trousers still bore signs of the soaking they had received. Orry knew what was coming and wished he could avoid it.

"Orry, I appreciate your willingness to talk to me."

The taller man twirled his cane and tried to joke. "Nothing novel in that. We've been talking to each other for years."

"Yes, sir, but this is important. It concerns Brett."

Grave again, Orry nodded. "So I assumed."

A wagon piled with cotton bales went by. The mule's shoes rang on the cobblestones. The men strolled another ten seconds without speaking. Sometimes Orry thought Billy too cautious—an ironic contrast to his older brother. He did regret that this interview was taking place just now, although anger with George had nothing to do with the feeling; in fact, he held himself responsible in large part for what had happened at Lehigh Station. At the proper moment he would dispatch a letter to George and try to patch things up.

From a café on the left drifted the delicious aroma of coffee; from a saloon came loud voices and the smell of sawdust. Out of the corner of his eye Orry noted Billy's apprehensive expression. To make it easier for him, Orry spoke first.

"You'd like permission to marry Brett."

Billy practically exploded with relief. "Yes! I can take care of her now. Not lavishly, but she'll never want, I promise you that. I think

634

my prospects in the Army are excellent. I'll be leaving St. Louis soon—''

''Do you know where you'll be transferred?''

''I've asked to be assigned to one of the Federal forts in the South. Fort Pulaski in Savannah. Fortress Monroe. The ideal post would be Charleston. I've heard about some plans to repair the harbor fortifications there.''

''Well, Brett would be happy to have you closer to Mont Royal.''

''Sir, we don't want to just visit any longer. We want to marry.''

The statements were more than a bit brusque. Pausing at the head of a busy passenger pier, Orry faced the younger man, frowning.

''I understand that, Billy, but I'm afraid I can't give my permission.''

Billy's eyes flickered with resentment. ''Why not? Do you think I'd be a poor husband for Brett?''

''I expect you'd be a fine one. It has nothing to do with your character.''

''What, then? Have you changed your mind about the Army? Do you think it's a bad career?''

''No, and I'm sure you'll do well. Or you would in ordinary times. Alas, these times aren't ordinary. The country's riven with trouble. The future's uncertain, if not downright grim.'' He let out a breath and told the rest of the truth. ''Especially for two young people who come from different sections.''

''You mean because I'm from Pennsylvania and Brett's a Southerner, you think we can't get along?'' With quiet strength, he added, ''Don't judge us by what happened between you and George.''

Orry held his temper; he was able to speak calmly. ''Brett told you?''

''She did.''

''Well, I can't say my decision is entirely unrelated to the quarrel, but not in the way you think. Your brother and I haven't fallen out permanently. He's still my best friend. At least I hope he is. However, there's no disputing one fact: George and I quarreled over issues that are all but unavoidable these days. The same issues could put immense pressure on you and my sister. Suppose this crazy secession talk led to some concrete act of hostility. How would it affect the Army? Specifically, how would it affect an officer with loyalties both to his government and to a Southern wife?''

''Seems to me you're searching pretty hard to find objections.'' Billy's voice had an edge on it now.

So did Orry's as he countered, "I am explaining my reason for saying no."

"Are you withholding your permission permanently or just temporarily?"

"Temporarily. Believe me, I'd be glad to have Brett marry a Hazard. But not until the future is a bit more clear."

Billy stared him down. "What if the two of us should decide to marry without your blessing?"

At that, Orry's expression chilled. "I don't think Brett would do such a thing. Of course you're free to ask her."

"Yes, sir," Billy said with a nod. "I believe I will. Excuse me? I have some business with my clerk."

His eyes unhappy, Orry watched the younger man's stiff back move away down the waterfront.

That night, in the parlor of their hotel suite, Brett said, "I was disappointed by the answer you gave Billy."

"When did you see him?"

"A little while ago, when I went downstairs. He's convinced you dislike him personally."

Orry slapped the arm of his chair. "That isn't true. Apparently I failed to make myself clear to him. I just want to think it over awhile longer. As you know so well, people are taking sides in this country. Your background and his would very likely force you onto opposite sides. I wouldn't want you involved in a marriage with that kind of pressure."

"Seems to me it will be my marriage." She stamped her foot. "Seems to me I should be the one to decide."

"Don't talk like Ashton," he snapped, striding to the window. There he turned. "If you're going to defy me, tell me straight out."

"I told Billy I couldn't do that. At least not while there's a chance you'll change your mind."

The threat was faint but unmistakable. Her decisiveness induced a sudden and unexpected melancholy—perhaps because he tended to forget that she was already an adult, in charge of her own destiny, and it took an incident like this one to remind him that his guidance was no longer needed or wanted. To remind him as well of how swiftly time went by, working its implacable changes.

Gazing from the window, he watched another paddle-wheeler churn south on the Mississippi. Sparks trailed upward from the smokestacks,

636

vivid in the dark but quickly gone. Like a man's ambitions. A man's dreams.

He didn't want to be guilty of denying happiness to others because it had been denied to him. That was a wretched and selfish way to behave. The possibility tempered his resolve somewhat, filled him with a desire to make peace. With her and with Billy.

He walked to Brett and clasped her hand.

"I like Billy. I know he'd care for you. But marriage is a commitment for a lifetime"—*ah, wouldn't Madeline be proud of you*, said an acid voice in the darkness of his thoughts—"so you ought to be very sure of your feelings."

"Orry, I am! I've known Billy for years. I've been waiting for him for years."

"Will it hurt to wait a little longer?"

All the light had left the parlor. They could no longer see each other clearly. She uttered a soft, weary sigh.

"Oh, I suppose not."

He'd won. Not a victory. Merely a reprieve.

The night was even more unhappy for Billy than for Brett. Sleep refused to come, and he was troubled by depressing thoughts about Orry's rejection; sectional animosities and the possibility of a war; even by memories of a nearly incomprehensible warning from George. A warning which he had just remembered. It involved some crazed Army officer who hated all the Hazards, God alone knew why. His brother had even suggested the officer might pose a threat to him, somehow.

Well, he had neither time nor inclination to take that kind of thing seriously—or even remember it on any occasion except a gloomy one like this. No, not when he had Brett to fret and dream about.

Three days later, on a Thursday, Billy saw the visitors aboard an eastbound train.

Orry had said little to the young officer after their near quarrel. Now, standing beside their coach, he realized this was his last opportunity to go beyond cool, empty pleasantries, to make Billy feel better.

He grabbed Billy's hand to shake it. That helped disarm him. Then Orry surprised him by smiling.

"I think you and Brett could weather almost any storm together. Just give me a month or so to convince myself, eh?"

"You mean we can—"

Orry raised his hand to interrupt. "No promises, Billy. I didn't close the door; I'm sorry if you thought I did. Like you, I've always been cautious. Ask your brother."

"Thank you, sir." Beaming, Billy took and pumped his hand. Then Brett hugged her brother.

Orry left the young people whispering, their foreheads close together. His conscience was salved, but he felt no better about the future as he climbed aboard the train.

52

Screaming wakened him, a woman's screaming, loud and shrill. Orry rubbed his eyes. The train was standing still. People were running along the aisle of the coach. One tall man bumped the dim coal-oil lantern hanging at the end of the car. The lantern swung wildly, throwing distorted shadows over the walls.

On the seat across the aisle, Brett was waking. Orry stood, trying to make sense out of the confusion. Outside, the woman continued to scream. A curt male voice silenced her. From the vestibule Orry heard the conductor:

"They want everyone off. I don't know what's wrong, but I'm sure no one will be harmed. Please hurry. Watch your step."

The conductor struggled against the tide of people pushing toward him. He called to Orry, Brett, and a few others who had been doing their best to sleep sitting up. "Please hurry. Everyone must go outside."

Still not fully awake, Orry wondered if all this commotion was necessary. Surely it was just some minor accident. He tugged his big silver watch from his waistcoat pocket. He thumbed it open while Brett crossed the aisle, stepped past him, and raised the window blind on a rectangle of darkness.

The watch showed half past one. That meant it was already Monday morning. Monday, October 17. Early Sunday, they had left Wheeling on this B&O express for Baltimore, where Orry was to purchase several thousand dollars' worth of shipyard equipment for Cooper. He had the long list of specifications in his luggage.

Brett leaned against the window and cupped her hands around her eyes. Suddenly she jerked back, her face white.

"I saw a man walk by outside. He had a musket."

"I don't believe it."

He leaned past her and looked out. Dim in the distance, a few lamps gleamed. He felt reassured by signs of civilization. Suddenly a hand closed on his shoulder from behind.

He whirled, ready to strike. It was only the conductor.

"Please, sir, get off the train." The man was in a panic, practically begging. "I am the representative of this railroad. My name's Phelps. All passengers are my responsibility. Please do what I ask until we get permission to proceed."

"Permission from whom?" Orry's voice was stronger now, his sleepiness gone.

"From the armed men outside. They have control of the station. They say they have also captured the Federal Arsenal and Hall's rifle works. They strike me as exceedingly determined."

Somewhere a gun exploded. Brett, startled, uttered a soft cry, then looked up and down the car. "Everyone else has gone. We'd better do as this gentleman asks."

Orry's mouth grew dry. He felt tense, instinctively alarmed as he often had in Mexico. He followed Phelps to the head of the car, only then thinking to ask the obvious question:

"Where are we?"

"Harpers Ferry. Last stop in Virginia before we cross the river to Maryland."

Preposterous. This was nickel-novel melodrama, being performed in the middle of the night for reasons that were as yet incomprehensible. Yet an undercurrent of fear persisted. Brett was behind him, clutching his hand as he followed Phelps into the cold, damp air.

He moved down the iron steps, his field of vision widening. Lamps hung from the roof beam of the platform. Their light revealed five armed men, four white, one black. Down to the right, other men with revolvers and carbines were herding passengers into a small, drab building next to the platform.

To the left Orry spied another figure. He was sprawled on his back near an empty cart. A baggage handler, Orry guessed. The front of his tunic was splotched with blood.

Orry helped his sister down the last step, then moved in front of her. Phelps confronted the armed men.

"I demand to know when you will permit this train to continue to its destination."

The conductor's words were stronger than his voice, which had a crack in it. The black man tucked his carbine under one arm, walked up to Phelps, and struck him in the face.

"You in no position to demand anything, mister."

The conductor rubbed his cheek. "Do you realize the penalty for interfering with the United States mail? When word of this atrocity is telegraphed to Baltimore—"

One of the white men interrupted. "The wires east and west of here are cut. You go put the lamps out in all the cars, then get inside with the rest. You have your choice of the depot or the hotel right next door." Evidently the hotel was the small, drab structure.

"What the devil's going on here?" Orry said. The man with the carbine gave him a sharp look.

"Southron, are you? Better keep your mouth shut, or I'll turn our nigra boys loose: I 'spect they'd like to settle some scores with you."

Orry put his arm around Brett and guided her down the platform to the hotel. A small sign identified it as the Wager House.

Brett's cheeks were drawn, her eyes huge. "What are they doing, Orry? Is this a robbery?"

"Must be." He could think of no other explanation.

A young man with a rifle stood guard at the hotel entrance. Inside, a woman sobbed while a man, his voice tense but controlled, urged her to loosen her corset and keep calm. Near the door, Brett stumbled. The startled guard pushed her, evidently fearing an attack.

Brett reeled against a window bay. Orry swore and started for the guard, who jumped back and leveled his rifle.

"One more step and you'll never see Baltimore."

Orry stopped, his fist tightly clenched.

"Put up your gun, Oliver. We have no quarrel with these people."

The deep, resonant voice belonged to a tall, middle-aged man who came striding from the dark at the end of the platform. He wore a farmer's shirt and old cord pants tucked into muddy boots. His white beard was trimmed to a length of about an inch. His craggy face had a familiar look, yet Orry couldn't place it.

The young man still had his rifle in firing position. "Oliver," said the bearded man.

"All right, Pa." He lowered the gun. The butt thumped the platform softly.

Orry glared at the bearded man. "Are you in charge of these ruffians?"

With exaggerated politeness, the man said, "Be careful with your language, sir. You are addressing the commander in chief of the Provisional Government of the United States, Captain Smith."

Not Smith. John Brown of Osawatomie. Orry recognized the face from engravings in illustrated weeklies, even though the beard had been much longer. Had he cropped it, hoping that would make identification more difficult?

Brown's blue eyes resembled bits of pond ice. "My son meant no harm to the young woman. He was merely protecting himself. Tempers run high in an enterprise of this importance."

"Enterprise?" Orry snorted. "Damn fancy term for train robbery."

"You insult me, sir. We are not thieves. I have come from Kansas to free all the Negroes in this state."

Despite Brown's calm tone, Orry sensed madness in the fierce glint in the man's eyes. He thought of Virgilia then. Was this her revolutionary messiah?

"You mean to lead a revolt?" he asked Brown.

"I do. I already have possession of the United States Armory. No more trains will be permitted through this station. You will go inside and keep silent until I decide on the disposition of this one. If I'm interfered with, I'll burn the town and have blood. Do I make myself clear?"

Grim-faced, Orry nodded. Then, supporting Brett with his arm under hers, he led her into the small lobby and to a horsehair settee.

A small boy began to cry; his mother drew him onto her lap. A husband chafed the hands of his sniffling wife. Orry counted eighteen passengers sitting or standing around the lobby.

Opposite the door they had entered was a second one, this leading to the street. Half open, it permitted a view of another of Brown's men, a Negro who paced slowly back and forth with a Navy Colt in his hand. Orry saw farmer's shoes and ragged pants several inches too short.

He sat down next to Brett, rubbed his palm back and forth over his knee. Obviously John Brown had recruited slaves or former slaves. Deep in Orry's gut old childhood fears were stirring.

At the station doorway, Phelps put his head in and said, "I am attempting to negotiate with Captain Smith for release of the train and its mail. Please be patient and remain calm." Then he was gone.

A clock with a brass pendulum tick-tocked behind the lobby counter. The boy's crying continued. Orry yawned. He thought of John Brown's eyes, and for the first time he believed in Senator Seward's irrepressible conflict.

He was jolted by Brett's whisper. "Orry, that man's been watching us."

"What man?"

"The guard outside."

"The captain's boy?"

642

"No, the other one. The nigra. There he is again."

Orry looked up and as if one nightmare were not enough, confronted another.

Just outside the door hovered a dark face, its good looks scoured away by care and hunger. Orry had seen that face at neighborhood gatherings along the Ashley, and would have recognized it anywhere.

"*Grady*," he whispered, and walked swiftly to the door.

Grady stepped back as Orry came outside and shut the door. A few misty lights glowed in homes on the mountainsides, but little could be seen of the town itself.

"Grady, don't you remember me?"

"'Course I do, Mr. Main." He cocked the Colt. "Better stand right there. Captain Smith says to shoot if anybody causes trouble." He sounded as if he hoped someone might.

"How many are you?" Orry's breath plumed in the night air as he spoke.

"Eighteen," Grady replied quickly. "Thirteen white men, the rest nigra."

"How on earth did you concoct a scheme like this?"

"Captain Smith, he's been planning it a long time. We been living across the river at a rented farmhouse quite a while now. We get supplies and guns shipped down from Chambersburg."

One more shock on top of the others: Virgilia had said she was bound for Chambersburg.

"Is your—" He couldn't bring himself to say *wife*. "Is George Hazard's sister with you?"

"Yes, she's at the farm with the other women."

"God," Orry whispered.

"Go back inside, Mr. Main. Sit quiet an' don't provoke us an' maybe the captain will let the train go on. With the guns and ammunition that's in the Armory, we're going to bring the jubilee. If anybody stands against us, blood will run."

"You can't win, Grady. The blood will be yours."

Grady's pride exploded in anger. He extended his right arm to full length. His hand trembled, but whether from excitement or uncertainty it was impossible to say.

The muzzle of the Navy Colt quivered an inch from Orry's nose. Orry stood motionless, rigid in fear. Five seconds passed.

Five more—

Suddenly the hotel door opened. "Orry?"

Grady jerked the Colt down, self-disgust evident on his face. "Get in there!" He pushed Orry toward his sister. Orry followed her inside. With his heavy plowman's shoe, Grady kicked the door shut behind them.

The lobby was still. The passengers dozed or simply stared at nothing. Hours had passed. All emotion had been spent. It had been a long time since anyone had cried or even spoken.

Brett slept with her head on her brother's shoulder. Orry watched the clock's brass pendulum sweep back and forth. Soon the pendulum slowed and seemed to float from side to side. Orry knuckled his eyes, tiredness and strain beginning to affect him.

Conductor Phelps entered, looking haggard. "Everyone please get aboard. They're going to let us go." He whispered that news, as if fearful that saying it any louder might cause Smith to change his mind.

Men and women gasped and rushed toward the door. Orry roused Brett, led her outside and down the platform past the guns of four guards. They climbed the steps to the darkened coach, and within minutes the train was chugging slowly through the covered bridge over the Shenandoah River.

Phelps walked ahead of the cowcatcher, searching for any signs that the structure had been deliberately weakened. One by one, the coaches rolled out from the shadows of the bridge. Dawn had reached the Blue Ridge. Orry sat with his forehead against the sunlit window, thinking that he should tell Brett who Captain Smith really was. The car passed Phelps, who jumped onto the rear steps.

In the aisle a man waltzed his weeping wife around and around. Phelps came into the car. Another woman rushed to him, clutching a scrap of paper. "I'm going to throw this off. We must warn everyone of what's happened."

"But we'll be in Baltimore in just—"

The woman paid no attention. As she hurried away, Phelps took off his cap and scratched his head.

Orry felt drained—and convinced for the first time that only armed force could meet the threat of Yankees such as John Brown. Suppose you granted that slavery ought to be ended—and in his most private thoughts he sometimes granted exactly that—even so, violent revolution wasn't the way. Revolution had to be resisted.

That was his conviction as he watched scraps of paper blow past the window. Messages thrown from the cars by the passengers who had survived the night.

Messages carrying the news of Harpers Ferry to the world.

Three evenings later, Orry bought a paper at their Baltimore hotel. In the lobby, in restaurants, and in the streets, people were talking of nothing but the raid, which had ended with only two of the insurrectionists left uninjured. Brown's men had killed four townsfolk. One was the Negro baggage handler Orry had seen lying on the platform. For a time a great-grandnephew of President Washington had been held hostage.

The insurrectionists had finally been overcome by a detachment of Marines rushed from Washington. The commander of the detachment was Lee, and he had been accompanied by Charles's old friend Stuart. Brown himself had been wounded defending an engine house in which he had taken refuge. He was now in jail at Charles Town, Virginia.

Orry took the paper up to the suite. "They list Brown's men who were killed," he said when Brett entered the sitting room. "One is a Grady Garrison, Negro."

"Garrison?" she repeated.

Orry shrugged. "He must have adopted the last name of that Boston rabble rouser."

Brett's face was nearly as melancholy as his. "Is there a mention of Virgilia?"

"No, not a word. It's presumed that any of the conspirators who didn't take part in the raid fled after the shooting started. The farm isn't so far from Harpers Ferry that they couldn't hear the gunfire."

"Well, much as I dislike Virgilia, I hope she got away."

"I do too. For George's sake."

Frightening as it had seemed when Orry was in the middle of it, the raid, it was now clear, had been a pathetic doomed affair. A conspiracy organized by madmen, executed by misfits. Even so, it was sending shock waves through the country and around the world. If the North and the South had not been irreparably split by the events of the last few years, they would be split now, he thought.

So it proved in the days that followed. Not even bleeding Kansas had divided the nation quite so completely. Late in October, Brown went on trial for conspiracy to incite a slave revolt and treason against the state of Virginia.

Influential Northerners praised him and spoke out in his defense.

Emerson called him a new saint. In the South, Huntoon's reaction was typical. He denounced Brown as a homicidal maniac and his scheme as "our homeland's deepest fears made manifest." With that Orry sadly agreed. Although Brown's raid didn't propel Orry into the camp of the fire eaters, he found himself a good deal closer to it.

Fear of further uprisings spread like a plague. Along the Ashley, planters and their wives spoke of little else. The LaMotte brothers formed a militia-style marching organization of like-minded men, the Ashley Guards. Huntoon was named an honorary captain.

George wrote Orry to apologize for his behavior at Lehigh Station. He made no reference to Virgilia or to her presence at the Maryland farm. George found it deplorable that some Southerners were blaming Brown's raid on the so-called Black Republicans. He said Brown was clearly in the wrong, except perhaps in the matter of his original motivation. The desire to see all slaves freed was, in George's opinion, laudable.

"Laudable!" Orry crushed the note and flung it into a corner.

On the night of December 1, church bells pealed across the North from Maine to Wisconsin. It was a night of mourning for John Brown. Next day he ascended a scaffold in Charles Town and gazed peacefully at the bleak and wintry sky as the hangman settled the noose around his neck.

That evening Cooper dined at Mont Royal. He expressed regret over the day's events. "They shouldn't have hung him. While he lived he was just a poor lunatic. Now they've turned him into a holy martyr."

A few days before Christmas, Orry had confirmation of that in another letter from George. The letter concluded:

> *People still speak passionately about the raid. Do you know Grady took part in it and died at Harpers Ferry? I have been told that Virgilia also spent some time at the farm, but this I cannot confirm. She has disappeared; I have neither seen nor heard from her since the night of our quarrel—for which I once more tender profound apologies. Will you not break your silence, old friend, and write and tell me that you accept them?*

*

646

Orry did so—grudgingly. An hour later, he tore up the letter.

The events at Harpers Ferry stayed with him in an obsessive way. They were responsible for the decision he reached about Brett in late December.

53

Clarissa had earlier indicated her delight with the candle-bedecked Christmas tree, so Orry had moved her drawing board downstairs to a corner close to it. She sat at the board now, alternately gazing at the flame of a candle for five or ten minutes at a time and cheerily nattering as she worked on the latest version of the family tree.

Clarissa's hair was pure white and her smile as ingenuous as a baby's. Orry sometimes envied his mother's separation from reality. He seldom liked anything in the world these days. He especially disliked the responsibility he was about to discharge.

Brett entered, sliding the doors shut behind her.

"One of the girls said you wanted to see me."

He nodded, standing wide-legged before the bright hearth. Brett frowned; she sensed tension. She tried to relieve it with banter.

"Your beard is showing some very becoming touches of white. In another year or so you'll be able to play Saint Nicholas."

He didn't smile. "At the moment I have another role, that of your guardian. I thought we should discuss the matter of you and Billy."

"His letter was the grandest present I could have hoped for!" Billy had written to say there was an excellent chance he'd be assigned to a group of engineers who were soon to start repairs on Fort Moultrie, located on Sullivan's Island near the entrance to Charleston harbor.

She studied her brother. "I hope you can make Christmas perfect and give me the other gift I want."

"I can't give you permission to marry him. Not now, anyway."

He said it so bluntly she wanted to cry. But she considered that kind of behavior unworthy of a lady and quickly got herself under control. In the corner, Clarissa hummed "Silent Night."

"Pray be kind enough to state your reasons."

Brett's arch tone antagonized him. "They are the same as before. We are on a collision course with the Yankees. Reasonable men discuss the need for compromise, but nothing is done. And if anyone has been responsible for pushing the South toward an independent government—"

"Are you saying you want that?"

"No. I am saying it's coming. Please let me finish. If anyone helped to promote secession, it was John Brown. Men on the other side share the feeling. In the *Mercury* last Saturday, Professor Longfellow was quoted on the subject of the hanging—which he of course opposed. Do you know what he said, this great poet, this humanitarian? 'This is sowing the wind to reap the whirlwind, which will come soon.' " Orry shook his finger like an evangelist. "Soon. That was his word."

"Orry, why can't you understand? Billy and I know the sad state of affairs in this country. It doesn't matter. We love each other. We can survive the worst."

"You think so, but I continue to believe the pressures on your marriage could be ruinous."

Secretly, he had been influenced not only by Brown's raid and its aftermath but by contemplation of Madeline's unhappy marriage and the terrible toll it had taken on her. He honestly thought his sister might be equally unhappy, though for completely different reasons. He wanted to end the discussion.

"I'm sorry, Brett. I can't allow you to do it. Please convey my regrets to Billy."

She answered quietly. "I'll do no such thing."

He blinked. "Explain that remark, if you please."

"It's very simple. If I don't have your blessing to marry, I'll marry without it."

His voice hardened. "The approval of your family no longer matters?"

"Of course it matters. I'd prefer to have it. I'd much rather keep peace between us. But if keeping peace means I can't have Billy, peace can go to the devil."

"Hold your tongue. You're not entitled to make pronouncements—to say what you will and won't do. You're just a girl. A foolish one at that!"

Orry's shout caused Clarissa to glance up with a slight frown. She stared at the bearded man and the young woman confronting each other, then shook her head, failing to recognize them.

Brett's voice shook as she whispered, "Better to be foolish than what you've become."

"What do you mean?"

"I mean you aren't fit to tell anyone how to behave. You never smile. You're angry with everything. I'm sorry you have to live alone. I'm sorry it makes you so miserable. But I refuse to live that way."

650

Orry was stunned by his desire to strike her. He managed to restrain himself, pointed toward the front hall.

"Go to your room."

With one last, venomous look, she picked up her skirts and fled.

In his bedroom an hour later, Orry lurched to the old pier glass he used for dressing. The empty sour-mash bottle dropped from his hand, thumped on the carpet, and rolled.

He peered into the glass, searching for something to disprove his sister's accusation. He couldn't find it. He seized the mirror with his hand and tipped it over. It fell not on the carpet but on the polished pegged floor beyond, shattering with a huge crash. He staggered toward the door, his waistcoat hanging open and his collar and the buttons of his right sleeve undone. His speech was a slurry mumble.

"It was many—and many—a year ago, in a kingdom by—in a kingdom—"

He couldn't go on. His drink-dulled memory had failed him. He picked up a fragile chair and swung it against the wall, reducing it to kindling. In the hall he spied a small gilt mirror, jerked it from its peg, and trampled on it. Then he staggered to the staircase.

Alarmed black faces peeped at him from doorways below. He clutched the banister with his hand and somehow stumbled all the way to the bottom without breaking his neck. Another mirror loomed on his left, an ornate one Ashton had purchased in Charleston long ago. He had never realized there were so many mirrors in the house. Mirrors to show him what he was: a failure as a man, a failure in everything he had ever tried to do.

He ripped the mirror off the wall, carried it outside into the frosty dark, and hurled it against the nearest tree. Shards of glass fell like a silvery rain.

He ran back into the house, found another full bottle of sour mash, and dragged himself up the stairs again, shouting gibberish in an angry voice.

At her drawing board, Clarissa listened with a look of puzzlement. After a moment she sighed and returned to her work.

"To Charleston? In the middle of the night?" Downstairs next morning, Orry slitted his eyes against the harsh daylight. "Where was she going, a hotel?"

"No, sir," the nervous house man responded. "To Mr. Cooper's. She had four trunks with her. Said she planned to be there awhile."

"Christ," he muttered.

His intestines churned, his head hammered. Brett had run away while he lay passed out in the wreckage of his bedroom. He had never behaved like that before, never in his entire life. His shame was worse than his physical misery, and his pride was shattered. His own sister had beaten him. It might have been possible to drag her back from the Mills House or some other hotel, but she had cleverly chosen Tradd Street. She knew, and so did he, that Cooper would give her sanctuary as long as she needed it.

He kicked tinkling bits of mirror with the toe of his boot. "Clean this up." Feeling sickness and defeat in every bone, he slowly climbed the stairs again.

On New Year's Day, 1860, Orry wrote a letter to his sister. It was couched in vaguely threatening language, employing words such as *defiance*, *duty*, and *authority*. It asked for her immediate return to Mont Royal.

He sent the letter to Charleston with a slave. But even as he was writing the pass, he felt a sense of futility. It turned out to be justified. He received no answer.

A couple of days later Cooper paid a visit. Orry accused him:

"You're abetting a family quarrel by permitting her to stay with you."

"Don't be an ass," his brother retorted. "It's better that she live with Judith and me than in some public lodging house. Brett's perfectly all right—which is what I came to tell you. As to the rest, I am abetting nothing, unless it might be her long-overdue effort to assert her independence. It is her life, after all. She's not some nigra girl to be married to whomever you think will produce the best offspring."

"You son of a bitch."

Cooper reached for his hat. "I had heard you were acting like a drunken boor. I'm sorry to discover it's true. Good-bye."

"Cooper, wait. I apologize. I haven't been feeling mysel—"

His brother had already left the room.

54

With every month that passed, the storm winds blew harder. Late in the spring the Democratic party convened its national nominating convention in Charleston. From the start the Douglas candidacy—Cooper's cause—was in trouble.

In the aisles of Institute Hall on Meeting Street, in caucus rooms and on curbstones, Cooper and others argued that unless the party chose a man who could appeal to voters in other regions, the South would suffer. The Black Republicans could be worse medicine than Douglas, he insisted. Few listened. Douglas men were a rapidly shrinking minority.

Then came a critical test of principle. Douglas's floor operatives refused to support a black code protecting slavery in the territories. Infuriated, delegates from six Southern states walked out of the hall to plan a rump convention. Huntoon proudly left with the others from South Carolina. In the joyous crowd in the gallery, Cooper spied Ashton, flushed and applauding wildly.

It was all over. After fifty-seven ballots, the convention adjourned without naming a candidate. The party was hopelessly sundered.

In early summer the regulars, or National Democrats, assembled in Baltimore and nominated Douglas. The dissidents, calling themselves Constitutional Democrats, gathered at Richmond to endorse unrestricted slavery in the territories and to nominate Kentucky's John Breckinridge. A third splinter group tried to rally concerned citizens behind unswerving support of the Constitution, but the effort was considered a straw in a windstorm.

At the Wigwam in Chicago, Lincoln's managers defeated Seward and won the nomination for their candidate. One statement in the platform adopted by the convention was explosive. It said Congress had no authority to condone or promote slavery by permitting its expansion into the territories. Slavery could be allowed to exist wherever it had in the past, but the Republicans stood squarely against its spread.

"Their platform is an abomination," Huntoon declared to Cooper. "It virtually guarantees the South will fight if that ape is elected."

653

"Since a fight is what you want, I'm surprised you don't campaign for Lincoln."

"Why, Cooper, I surely don't know what you mean," Huntoon said with a bland expression.

But there was a merry light in his bespectacled eyes.

In steady rain the Wide-Awakes marched in Lehigh Station.

George stood in front of the apothecary's, watching them. The cigar clenched in his teeth had been extinguished by the rain, and the torches of the marchers fared only a little better. It was a foul night, too damp and raw for August.

The young men passed, twenty in all, wearing oilcloth capes and kepis. On their shoulders they carried brooms, ax handles, or dummy muskets. As the head of the column vanished into darkness, a small band appeared, the drums pounding, the horns blaring "Dixie's Land," a minstrel song that had been adopted as the anthem of all the new Republican marching clubs. An Ohioan had written the song; George had first heard it when Bryant's Minstrels played Bethlehem last year.

Bobbing torches cast sullen light and flung long, sinister shadows. The drums woke memories of Mexico. George saw his son's face pass in the band. Even though William's cheeks were puffing in and out—he played a cornet—he somehow managed to smile.

All the Wide-Awakes were smiling. Why, then, did they remind him of soldiers off to war? Why did this parade, with its jaunty marchers confident of a Republican victory, fill him with thoughts of gunfire, and blood, and formless feelings of dread?

Ashton called at Tradd Street in mid-August.

"Land sakes, Brett, I thought your intended would surely be in Charleston by now!"

"I though so too," Brett replied. "It's taken months for them to prepare his orders."

"The Army always did move like an elephant," Cooper remarked. He looked thinner than usual these days. Fatigue circles showed under his eyes. The *Star of Carolina* project was going badly, and Cooper was not encouraged by the calamitous accident which had befallen Brunel's great Trincomalee freighter the preceding year. It had left the mouth of the Thames in September, only to be ripped apart by a huge explosion. The ship had survived, but Brunel never knew it; the

654

report of the disaster was the last news he heard before he died on the fifteenth of September.

Ashton, of course, never paid attention to such things. With her lower lip stuck out, she patted her sister's hand. "I surely do feel sorry for you. Is there any definite word about Billy's arrival?"

"Yes, fortunately," Judith put in. "It came the day before last."

Ashton's eyes flashed. "Tell me!"

Brett said, "Billy's to report to Captain Foster the first week in September. Foster is the engineer who just arrived in the city. The one sent to repair Fort Moultrie."

"Why, that's wonderful news. It'll be ever so convenient to have Billy here in Charleston."

Cooper puzzled over his sister's curious expression, her odd choice of words. Billy's presence might be enjoyable, but why should it be convenient for anyone except Brett? Ashton must have been speaking of Brett's situation.

Yet he wondered about that, recalling the strange glint in Ashton's eyes. What it meant he couldn't imagine. But then, he understood Ashton even less than he understood Orry these days.

From high in the gallery, Cooper listened to Huntoon speaking to an overflow crowd in Institute Hall. Ashton's husband was delivering the last of several addresses in support of Breckinridge for President. Actually, the half-hour oration was largely a harangue against Lincoln.

"A vulgar mobocrat!" Huntoon thumped the podium. The crowd roared. "An illiterate border ruffian pledged to promote hatred of the South and equality for the niggers!"

Groans. Cries of "No, no!" from every corner of the hall. Unable to take any more, Cooper rose, ignoring angry stares from those around him. As Cooper left, Huntoon once more invoked Lincoln's name, producing more booing and hissing, then a raw-throated yell:

"Kill the baboon!"

Tumultuous applause. They wanted a fight. They refused to heed what Lincoln said—that he would adhere to the platform of his party and not interfere with slavery where it already existed. They heard only their own voices prating of betrayal and the need for resistance. Cooper was more discouraged than he had been in years.

Billy got a shock when he arrived at Fort Moultrie. In fact, he got several.

He remembered Charleston as a friendly, hospitable place where the pace of life was leisurely. Now an air of suspicion and near hysteria prevailed. People talked warmly of secession, hatefully of Lincoln and the Little Giant. They eyed Billy's uniform in a distinctly unfriendly way.

The second shock came when he realized the nature of the work to be done at the fort on Sullivan's Island. Drifted sand was to be cleared away from the parapet because armed men could too easily climb those slopes and storm the ramparts. Some of the fort's fifty-five guns were to be repositioned to provide better protection for Castle Pinckney and Fort Sumter in the harbor. These were preparations for war.

Everyone, military or civilian, knew the Federal garrison probably could not withstand an organized military attack—or even that of a determined mob. Sullivan's Island was a long, sandy strip of land fronting the sea. Round about the old fort, which was actually the third structure to bear the name Fort Moultrie, stood any number of summer residences. The fort's interior was vulnerable to sniper fire from the nearby rooftops.

Furthermore, the Moultrie garrison was small: sixty-four men and eleven officers. The core of the fighting force consisted of two companies of the First Artillery—the total including eight regimental bandsmen—under the command of Colonel John Gardner, a relic of the War of 1812 who was ready for retirement. A brusque Yankee from Massachusetts, Gardner didn't hide his distrust of all Southerners—a poor practice for a commandant who had to deal with and employ local people.

The senior captain, Abner Doubleday, was a tough, capable officer who had graduated from West Point the summer George arrived. Doubleday was especially disliked in Charleston because he made no secret of being an abolitionist.

Four members of the engineers were stationed at Moultrie—Captain John Foster and Lieutenants Meade, Snyder, and Hazard. Also on the post during daylight hours were some civilian workmen Foster had hired in the city and a few artisans he had imported from the North.

During Billy's first week on duty, Captain Foster twice sent him into Charleston on business. There he again took note of the unconcealed hostility directed at any representative of the Federal government. He expressed his dismay to Doubleday as they stood in the evening wind near an eight-inch howitzer aimed at the Atlantic. Doubleday had just supervised the loading of the howitzer with double canister.

"What did you expect?" Doubleday snorted in response to Billy's comments. "The people of South Carolina are preparing for war. If you don't believe me, just wait till the election's decided."

Uneasily, he glanced along the parapet. All of Moultrie's artillery was mounted *en barbette*, in the open, unprotected by casemates. A hundred men on the roofs of the summer residences could make it impossible for the First Artillery to operate the guns.

"That's why we fire this lovely lady every day or so," Doubleday added. "So the local folk don't think we're defenseless—even though in some ways we certainly are."

He shouted the command to fire. The howitzer boomed and bucked, frightening summer guests strolling the beach and dappling the sea with deadly bits of iron.

One warm Saturday in late October, Captain Foster gave Billy permission to dine away from the post for the first time. Billy was thankful for the opportunity. He had already seen Brett on several occasions, and he knew about her quarrel with her brother. But whenever he pressed the subject of marriage, she immediately began to talk of something else. Was she changing her mind about him? He had to know.

That Saturday night they ate supper at the elegant Moultrie House. The hotel was located in Moultrieville, the village at the end of the island nearest the harbor. After the meal, Billy and Brett walked arm in arm along the beach. A trick of reflected light from low clouds gave the ocean a pure white sheen. Ten pelicans, one behind the other, flew past two feet above the water, which was breaking on the shore with an almost waveless murmur.

"Brett, why don't we get married?"

"Because you're so busy moving sand away from the walls of the fort, you don't have a spare minute."

"Be serious. You told Orry you didn't want his permission—"

"Not quite. I told him I didn't need it. But I'd like to have it. I was furious with Orry the night I left Mont Royal. I said some things I regret."

Gently she stroked the sleeve of his uniform. "Of course I love you. I'll marry you no matter what. But I hate to antagonize my family. I care for them as much as you care for yours. Don't you understand?''

"Yes, of course. But we've already waited so long—''

The sentence trailed off. Looking down the shore, he saw Captain Doubleday pacing the parapet with a woman. Even in conversation with his spouse, the captain had a stern air.

"I don't want us to lose this chance,'' he resumed. "Charleston is tense. Anything could happen.''

"Billy, you sound angry with me.''

"It's the delay I'm angry about. I appreciate that you don't want to alienate your brother, but will he ever see things our way? Maybe not.''

She didn't answer. The line of his mouth hardened.

"I love you, Brett, but I can't wait forever.''

"Neither can I, darling. Cooper promised to speak to Orry again. Just give them both a little more time.''

He gazed out to sea where the howitzer shot had fallen night before last. "Time seems to be the one thing we're rapidly running out of. Come on, let's go back to the hotel and see if your boatman has drunk himself senseless.''

He sounded so cross, Brett didn't say another word as they hurried toward Moultrieville in the gathering dark.

On election day Colonel Gardner sent Billy into Charleston. Reacting to the temper of the city, the colonel had drafted a message to Humphreys, the officer in charge of the four-acre government arsenal. Humphreys was to be ready to load a large quantity of small arms and ammunition onto a Fort Moultrie lighter next day; stored in Charleston, the ordnance was too easily available to a mob.

Billy rowed himself over to the Battery, a hard, time-consuming trip. Gardner had given him permission to eat supper at Tradd Street, so he didn't want an enlisted man standing around waiting for him. On the Battery he saw workmen erecting a liberty pole. Many houses displayed dark blue bunting carrying the state's palmetto emblem. Some loiterers surrounded the head of the steps Billy had to climb after he tied his boat. One, a tough-looking little fellow with a greasy leather eye patch, jerked a thumb at the boat.

"What d'you figure to take back to the fort in that, sir?''

Billy reached the top step and put his hand on his holstered Colt. "Myself. Do you object, sir?''

"Leave him be, Cam," another roughneck said to the man with the patch. "Nigger Abe won't be elected for hours yet. After he is, I expect we can find this peacock again."

Billy's heart thudded. His gut tensed as he walked forward toward the roughnecks. At the last moment they stepped aside and let him through. He quickened his stride. He had been bluffing when he reached for the revolver. He couldn't use it even to defend himself; such an incident might precipitate an attack on the fort.

He delivered Colonel Gardner's message to the nervous commander of the arsenal. "I'll have everything ready," Humphreys promised. "But I'll wager we never get it off the dock. The hotheads won't permit it."

Billy passed the Mills House on his way to Cooper's. He was walking on the opposite side of the street, but he had no trouble recognizing Huntoon and Ashton as they emerged from the hotel. Huntoon touched the brim of his fancy hat, but Ashton's greeting was no more than a faintly disdainful nod.

At Tradd Street the mood seemed melancholy. Cooper was not home yet. Judith tried to entertain her guest by gathering the children around her at the piano and encouraging them to sing while she played, but they soon stopped; enthusiasm was lacking, somehow. Finally Cooper arrived, apologizing for his tardiness. He had come from James Island, where there were more problems with laying the keel of *Star of Carolina*.

For supper Judith had prepared a delicious oyster pie with a crackling crust—the oysters came right from the beds in the harbor—but Billy wasn't hungry. Brett seemed distracted, fussy. Conversation flagged. Judith was serving silver goblets of strawberry ice when bells began to peal.

Cooper frowned. "Saint Michael's. The telegraph must have brought the first returns from the North."

"Is it true that tomorrow is an unofficial holiday?" Judith asked.

"It's true. On the way home I bumped into Bob Rhett. He was jubilant. He said today marked the start of the American revolution of 1860." Cooper grimaced.

They heard band music. "I'd like to see what's going on," Billy said. "Army blue may not be popular or even healthy in a week or two. Would you feel uneasy to be outside, Brett?"

She shook her head. Soon she and Billy were strolling down Meeting toward the Battery. Cooper and Judith had stayed home.

The street was exceptionally busy for early evening, the crowds turbulent though generally good-natured. Billy did notice several scowls, provoked, he assumed, by his uniform. Brett caught her breath in surprise.

"They're playing the 'Marseillaise'!"

"They're crazy," was his curt reply. A thudding report and a glare of light from the Battery brought him up short. Cannon fire?

Then he relaxed. It was only a salute, not a signal of hostilities. Lord, he was getting as jumpy as a frog on a hot stove.

As they crossed Water Street, Brett pointed. "Do you know those men? They're watching us."

"No," Billy replied, "I don't think I—wait. I recognize one of them. A loafer I ran into when I tied up at the Battery this afternoon."

That man, the runty fellow with the eye patch, waved to the others to follow him across Meeting Street. His voice carried as he said, "Let's talk to that young lady. I'd like to know why she's hanging around with a damn Yankee."

"We better tell her it's unpatriotic," said another.

"Persuade her," said a third, scooping a stone out of the street.

Billy counted seven in the group. Four or five had picked up rocks. "Stand behind me," he said quietly to Brett.

"But surely we're in no danger on a public thoroughfare—"

The band of men reached the sidewalk. People hurrying toward the Battery flowed past Billy and Brett, paying no attention to them. The man with the eye patch snatched off his filthy cap, hunched his shoulders, and made a great show of pretending to plead.

"Begging your pardon, miss, but the patriotic citizens of Charleston respectfully request that you don't soil yourself by associatin' with vermin from the fort."

Thud, another cannon salute went off. Red light flickered over the buildings along the street.

"You can go to the devil," Brett said. "I'll associate with whomever I please."

"Oh, yes? We'll see about that."

Eye Patch sidled forward. Billy pulled his Colt and cocked it. Once again it was a bluff; with so many people passing in carriages and on foot, he didn't dare fire. Behind him a woman spied the gun and let out a soft shriek. Several pedestrians rushed into the street to avoid trouble.

Eye Patch feinted for Billy's gun hand. Billy dodged away. Another man flung a rock. It flew past Billy and struck Brett's shoulder; she cried out. Billy swore, jumped forward, and laid the Colt barrel across the rock thrower's cheek. The man howled and danced backward, bleeding.

Billy looked around warily. The men were forming a semicircle, closing in. He didn't want to risk a brawl in which Brett might be seriously hurt. With reluctance, he shouted a word that ran counter to everything in his training and character:

"Run!"

Brett hesitated. He grabbed her arm and practically dragged her away toward Tradd Street. Like wolves after prey, Eye Patch and his friends pursued. Rocks flew. One hit Billy's neck and broke the skin.

At the corner of Meeting and Tradd, Eye Patch shouted for his gang to halt; Billy was already guiding Brett through the gate at Cooper's. Panting, they shut the gate and leaned against the wall of the entrance passage. *Thud* and *thud*, a second cannon on the Battery joined the first.

"I've never run from anyone or anything before," Billy gasped.

"It was"—like him, she was struggling for breath—"the only thing to do. I can't imagine people from South Carolina behaving that way."

He took her hand and led her to the stairs. He hadn't realized how far the hatred had spread or how deeply it ran. No wonder old Gardner disliked his post and Doubleday fired his howitzer as a warning. Charleston was out of control.

Next day, as Lincoln's victory in the popular voting became certain, the celebration intensified. When the lighter from Fort Moultrie arrived, an excited crowd refused to permit the small arms and ammunition to be loaded—exactly as the arsenal officer had predicted.

By evening there was jubilation throughout the city. Bands blared. Lamps and candles glowed in almost every house window. Groups of revelers, some sober, some not, roistered past Huntoon's home on East Battery.

He and Ashton were preparing to leave for the fireworks display on the Battery. Huntoon had found an old blue satin cockade, the symbol of resistance ever since Nullification days. He fastened it to his best beaver hat. Ashton stood before the glass and adjusted her bonnet with black and white feathers on it. Secession bonnets, the ladies called them. They were all the fashion.

"Are they really planning a special convention?" she asked.

"Absolutely. The legislature called it for the seventeenth of December, expressly to determine the state's future relationship with the North. It's coming, my darling." He took hold of her waist and whirled her around. "Independence. In Washington, Senator Chestnut resigned today. Senator Hammond, too."

Their impromptu celebration was interrupted by the appearance of a house boy.

"Gen'man to see you, Mist' Huntoon."

"Damn you, Rex, I can't see anyone now."

"He say it's important."

"What's his name?"

"Mist' Cam'ron Plummer."

"Oh." Huntoon's truculence faded immediately. "Send him to the side door."

The slave left. Huntoon and his wife exchanged sober looks. Then he slipped out of the room.

In the shadows at the side entrance, a man whispered, "I did the best I could, Mr. Huntoon. Did exactly what you asked. Kept watch till they showed up on the street, then went after 'em. But before we could roust 'em good, they turned tail and ran to the house on Tradd Street. I still got to pay my lads, though. We all done the best we could."

"I know, I know—keep your voice down."

Huntoon wasn't surprised that the scheme had come to nothing. The idea had been Ashton's, and he had opposed it. She had wept and raved until he relented. Her threat to sleep in a separate room for a month also had something to do with his decision.

But, after giving in, he had regretted it. A man with his ambitions couldn't afford foolish risks. In the future Ashton could indulge her vindictive nature if she wished, but he would refuse to become involved. To that he made up his mind as he began to count coins into the hand of the man with the eye patch.

55

Orry pushed his plate away. Cuffey stepped forward.

"Something wrong, Mist' Orry?"

"Tell the kitchen the beef is bad."

Cuffey brought the plate near his nose, sniffed, made a face. "Sure enough will. You want something else?"

He shook his head. "Is yours bad, Cooper?"

"Yes. I didn't want to say anything. I was just going to leave it."

Cuffey hurried out with the plates. Orry slouched in his chair. Autumn rain pelted the closed shutters of the dining room.

"Something's wrong in the smokehouse again," Orry said with a sigh. "Dampness getting in. I tell you, I never realized how much I depended on Brett until she left."

Cooper knew what his brother meant. The signs were small but they were unmistakable. Mont Royal's shutters were bleached pale as bone by the weather; they needed a fresh coat of oil and pigment. Expensive flocked wallpaper was peeling away in the guest bedroom. Clusters of dust gathered in corners. On his last visit he had been informed that Cuffey's Anne had delivered twin girls, but one of the infants had died because there were complications. No one had sent for Aunt Belle Nin.

Cooper tried to lighten the mood. "Well, you'll just have to marry one of those ladies of your acquaintance and give her a broom and a paintbrush for a wedding present."

"There isn't a one of them fit to set foot on this plantation."

The brusque reply startled Cooper and confirmed something Brett had told him. She said Orry no longer smiled, that his mind seemed to have taken a turn into somber regions familiar only to himself. Cooper believed it. He decided he had better get on to the purpose of his visit: "Well, I wish you were interested in someone. I don't believe Brett will be coming back."

"Because of Billy."

"That's right."

"Are you trying to tell me they're married?"

Cooper shook his head. "They're still delaying, although Billy is upset about that. Brett continues to wait out of consideration for you."

Orry uttered a scornful grunt and reached for the cut-glass decanter of whiskey. It had become a fixture on the table, Cooper noticed.

"She needn't wait on my account." Orry poured whiskey into the long-stemmed glass from which he had already drunk a large quantity of white Bordeaux. "I don't plan to change my mind in the foreseeable future."

Cooper leaned forward. "Don't you think you should?"

"Did she send you up from Charleston to say that?"

"She did not. Damn it, Orry"—he thumped the table—"despite the behavior of the LaMottes and some of our other neighbors, we are not living in the Middle Ages. Women are entitled to run their own lives. Please permit Brett to run hers—regardless of the risks you see or imagine. She's trying to keep peace in the family—which is more than I would do in her position."

"The answer is still no."

His resolution was wavering, though. He had thought about Brett's situation a lot lately. He knew Cooper was right and that he should grant the permission. Yet he wasn't quite able to do it. The news from Washington, Charleston, everywhere, was too threatening.

Cooper folded his napkin. He pinched the fold between thumb and forefinger. "Very well. Cuffey, would you kindly tell my driver to bring my carriage up immediately?"

"I thought you were spending the night," Orry said.

"What's the use? My view of the future is as dim as yours, but at that point we part company. Life is chiefly trouble and always has been. Brett deserves to live to the full while she can. You're standing in the way and apparently plan to continue. I regret that, but there seems to be nothing I can do about it. I'll look in on Mother and then go. Excuse me."

Stiff and unsmiling, he left the room.

Orry sat listening to the rain. Now Cooper had turned against him too. A moment ago he'd been wavering on the matter of Brett's marriage. But this latest rebuff stoked his anger and hardened his will.

He noticed there was no more whiskey in his glass. When had he drunk it? He couldn't remember. He stretched out his arm and closed his hand around the neck of the decanter.

*

"Look at that fog," Judith murmured. "I hope Cooper doesn't stay away half the night. I think he's getting sick."

Brett glanced up from the knitting needles whose operation she had been demonstrating to eight-year-old Marie-Louise. "Why did he go back to the yard? Is anyone working?"

"No. He went because he's upset. The ship's far behind schedule. His chief architect quit and returned to Brooklyn because he couldn't get along with the local workmen. Now the banks are hesitant about extending more credit in case commercial ties with the North are cut. Oh, it's such a dreadful mess."

She could have added that Cooper had also taken on the burden of Brett's problem. She didn't because it would only have produced guilt feelings, and Brett felt bad enough already.

Judith was desperately concerned about her husband. Last week he had come back from Mont Royal at four-thirty in the morning. Since then he had spent each day at the yard on James Island, and returned there every evening after supper. He kept a boatman on call at all hours. The man was beginning to complain.

But at least the boatman had his health. Cooper had lost eleven pounds—a substantial drop for someone of his slender build. Lately his face had a waxy look. While Brett laughed and murmured with Marie-Louise, Judith watched the fog coiling slowly past the moisture-speckled window. On a night like this what could Cooper possibly do at the yard?

She knew. He could destroy himself with worry.

The great keelson of the *Star of Carolina* bulked in the fog like the backbone of some prehistoric beast that had perished and rotted, leaving only this. Cooper turned away from it. The ship was a dying dream. He had at last admitted that to himself. But the dream had left tangible wreckage. What should he do now?

He plucked out a handkerchief, blew his dripping nose, and wiped it several times. He was getting sick. He didn't care.

Distantly, in the main ship channel, a steamer horn sounded at short intervals. The fog hung thick over James Island. Cooper would have been lost in it had it not been for the light of two lanterns hanging under the eaves of the shedlike office building. The lantern light diffused in great fan-shaped rays.

I might have pulled it off if Van Roon hadn't quit, he thought as he trudged through deep mud that seeped over his shoe tops and soaked his stockings. Van Roon, the architect, was the linchpin of the project. He had gotten into a fistfight with a poor clod hired to carry buckets of rivets.

A man of education and restraint, Van Roon had punched and cursed like a dockhand. Over what? The question of who would own the Federal property in Charleston—the armory, the forts—if the state declared its independence. Half a dozen of the workers had been taking turns at Van Roon before Cooper rushed in to break up the brawl.

Hopeless.

He reached the water's edge and peered toward the ship channel, imagining the pentagonal fort standing on its shoal out there. Sumter had been started during the winter of eighteen-twenty-eight—twenty-nine and never finished. To this day it remained unoccupied. But its proximity to the channel and the harbor mouth made it strategically important—perhaps more important than any other Charleston fort. What if old Gardner moved to fortify it? The sparks would fly then.

Fools were in control of the state Cooper loved so much. Fools and opportunists like Ashton's husband. They shouted their slogans, spouted their gaseous oratory, and forgot or ignored the manufactories of the North, the great industrial installations such as Hazard's. In all the South there was but a single ironworks of size, the Tredegar in Richmond. If war came, how would the South fight it? With gallant pronouncements and a barrage of cotton bolls?

What would happen in the next few months? Staring into the fog, Cooper felt he knew the answer.

"Apocalypse," he said half aloud, and then sneezed so hard his hat fell off.

The hat plopped into the water and floated out of reach. He waded in after it, but it kept bobbing away from him. He gave up the chase when the water rose to his thighs.

How marvelous, he thought with a chuckle. The Almighty pricks your pretensions by blowing your hat away.

Or was it a kind of warning? A warning that in the almost certain apocalypse, survival would be first and foremost a matter of small things? Practical things: Food. Shelter. A hat for the storm.

He sloshed back to shore and hurried to the office, caught by an inspiration: since no respectable naval architect could be lured to Charleston in these times, he would become the architect.

He pulled down engineering drawings hanging in wall racks. Flung the drawings on the big worktable. Turned the hanging lamp up to full.

He studied the drawings, then pulled down more, until the table was heaped with them. He scribbled calculations and questions. But he was finally forced to admit the truth. He knew a little about many aspects of the project, but not enough. His decision to do the architect's job represented the only means of saving the *Star of Carolina*. But it was, at the same time, hopeless.

At dawn the yawning boatman found Cooper slumped over the table unconscious and afire with fever.

"Bring that barrow over here. You people will have to step aside."

Billy's first command was directed to a civilian workman, his second to sightseers wandering on the dune near Fort Moultrie. The repair work was always hampered by local residents or vacationers who came to gawk. Billy frequently lost his temper with them.

Today was no exception. He ordered a family to pick up its picnic hampers and move off the dune his men were reducing so that snipers couldn't occupy it. The weather had turned hot again, unusual for November. Sweat ran so freely that he'd tied a red bandanna around his head to keep it out of his eyes.

He saw Captain Foster coming from the fort, motioning. He left the workmen and walked quickly toward his superior. Foster noticed that Billy was once again working barefoot. He disapproved but said nothing this morning; he had something else on his mind.

"Gardner's been relieved. We're getting a new commander."

"Who is it?"

"Major Robert Anderson."

"My brother knew a Robert Anderson in Mexico. An artillerist. He graduated from the Academy a few years ahead of Lee."

"That's the man. He's a Kentuckian. He's owned slaves. I suppose the secretary picked him to appease the local folk."

The decision was understandable. Gardner's attempt to transfer arms and ammunition from the arsenal had produced a statewide storm of criticism.

But a slave owner in charge of the Charleston forts? Billy didn't think it a very good omen.

He changed his mind when the major arrived.

Robert Anderson was fifty-five, tall, white-haired, impeccably polite.

He peppered his speech with references to God and professed complete loyalty to his flag and his uniform. He had fought bravely in Mexico and been wounded at Molino del Rey, which tended to enhance his reputation with his men. Billy found him austere but clearly conscientious and, he decided, worthy of trust.

A few days after reporting for duty, Anderson ordered a boat for a trip over to Sumter. Billy and Foster manned the oars, with Doubleday at the bow. Anderson said he didn't want enlisted men along to gossip and speculate about the significance of the inspection.

They made a complete circuit of the five-sided fort. Then Anderson directed them to rest their oars. His eyes roved over the brick and masonry of the left flank wall. Five feet thick, it rose fifty feet above the low-water line and looked toward the northwest. The fort had been designed with two tiers of gun rooms, but only the embrasures on the lower tier had been finished. On the tier above, the openings were six or eight feet square.

"Row around to the esplanade, please," Anderson said when he had completed his inspection.

The stone esplanade was situated at the foot of the gorge, the rear wall of the fortification. More than three hundred feet long and about twenty-five feet deep, the gorge faced the southwest. The rowers tied the boat near the sally port and scrambled up onto the esplanade, which Anderson paced from end to end before speaking.

"I've been reading some of the original engineering memoranda on this fort, gentlemen. She's solidly built. Ten thousand tons of granite in the foundations, plus sixty or seventy thousand tons of rock and seashells. If provisioned well enough, she could be held indefinitely. Even by a force as small as ours."

"But, sir," Captain Doubleday said, "if we fortified Sumter, it would undoubtedly be interpreted as a hostile act."

The captain was testing his Kentucky-born superior, Billy thought. For the first time there was sharpness in Anderson's voice.

"Indeed so, Captain. I have no plans to fortify Sumter immediately. But make no mistake. These forts belong to the duly constituted government in Washington and to none other. With divine help I will do whatever is necessary, consistent with my orders, to protect them. I have seen enough for the moment. Shall we go?"

"He sounds tougher than old Gardner," Billy whispered to Foster as they returned to the boat. Foster replied with an approving nod.

*

The next afternoon Brett was walking down Meeting Street carrying several parcels. Someone hailed her. Startled, she recognized Forbes LaMotte.

"Afternoon, Miss Brett." He tipped his hat. "May I walk with you? Take some of those packages for you, perhaps?"

"No, Forbes, I can't stop."

It was a lame excuse, but she didn't want to encourage him. His cheeks looked red as apples, and he was squinting. No doubt he had been whiling his time away in the saloon bar of the Mills House. He did a lot of that, she had heard.

Rebuffed, Forbes stepped aside. In a moment, all he saw of Brett was her back.

"Bitch," he muttered, retreating to the shade of the hotel entrance.

He didn't mean the angry word. Well, not completely. He hated Brett Main for preferring that Pennsylvania soldier, but he was still in love with her. She was the sort of girl you married, whereas Ashton—well, Ashton was solely for amusement. They saw each other every week or so, whenever they could arrange a safe rendezvous.

He recalled their most recent hour together. Afterward, he had bled and ruined a fine linen shirt because she had clawed his back so hard.

Badges of conquest, those marks. But he couldn't brag about them, and he'd have readily exchanged them and all the illicit meetings for just one word of encouragement from Ashton's sister.

Late in November a dispatch in the *Mercury* caught Orry's eye. Cadet Henry Farley of South Carolina had resigned and left the Military Academy on the nineteenth of the month. The paper crowed that Farley's action was a protest against Lincoln's election and preparation for service to the state.

Orry found the news depressing. He was certain other resignations would follow. Perhaps they would even spread from the Academy to the regular service.

That same day a letter from Judith arrived. She said Cooper had finally begun to recover from his influenza. He had been perilously ill for over a week. The tidings from his sister-in-law were welcome but did little to offset the gloom caused by the West Point story.

He blew out the library lamp and sat in the dark. Darkness seemed appropriate to the disintegration taking place all around him. Was there light in the land any longer?

He sat for hours, imagining the warlike sound of ghostly drums.

*

"Our boys are leaving the Academy right and left," Justin LaMotte exclaimed. "Capital!" He tossed the newspaper on a wicker table and ladled mint punch from a silver bowl. He passed the cup to Francis, then filled one for himself.

The brothers had just returned from a muster of the Ashley Guards. They resembled a pair of male birds in their cream-colored trousers and dark yellow coats with blue facings. Neither man was as yet equipped with a sword, but each had ordered one from a military armorer in New York City; fine Solingen blades were unobtainable in South Carolina.

"Do you think we'll be at war soon?" Francis asked, taking a chair. The veranda was pleasant in the December twilight.

Justin beamed. "Within a year, I'd guess. In the event of hostilities, I plan to raise a personal regiment and then offer it—"

He didn't finish the sentence. A frown creased his forehead as he watched the figure come gliding down the veranda.

"My dear, good evening. Would you care for punch?"

Madeline's gown was as black as her hair. Her skin was dead white. Her eyes showed extreme dilation. "No." She smiled in a tentative way. "Thank you." She passed into the house.

Francis clucked approvingly. "Handsome woman. She's looking a bit peaked, but she certainly has been calmer the past year or so. The change in her disposition never fails to astonish me. Remarkable."

"Yes, isn't it?" Justin sighed. "What a providential blessing. More punch?"

Madeline could no longer recall a time when her world had not had soft edges. She drifted through days that were little more than a series of blurs. She was unconcerned about people or events. Occasionally she remembered Orry with a vague sense of yearning, but she had long ago abandoned hope of encountering him again.

Once in a while, and with little or no warning, she enjoyed short periods of seeming normality. Her head was clearer, her senses sharper, her will stronger. At those times she was angry with herself because she no longer discussed public issues with her husband, nor did she dispute any of his statements, no matter how offensive or outrageous. She had surrendered. When she occasionally realized it, despair overwhelmed her.

She hadn't the energy to struggle against that despair or even wonder about its source. What good was struggle? What good was hope? The

670

world was dominated by cruel madmen. Two of them sat chuckling over mint punch in her own house this very moment.

After she left the veranda, one of her periods of lucidity came on. She wandered to and fro in her dusky sitting room, reciting snatches of poetry that came to mind from heaven knew where and recalling Orry's gentle dark eyes, the sound of his voice reading to her.

She must see him again. The moment she decided that, she smiled for the first time in days.

She uncovered the dishes on the tray brought to her room as usual. How delicious the thick, syrupy dressing on the plate of greens tasted. She loved it, now ordered it every day. She ate with relish, finishing everything, and hummed as she began to imagine her forthcoming reunion at the chapel called—

Called—

She couldn't remember its name. Gradually exhaustion claimed her again. Sinking back into cloudy indifference, she groped her way to the bed. Tears brimmed in her eyes—why, she didn't know. She murmured Orry's name once as she lowered herself to the bed. Fully clothed, she slept through the night.

In the morning she discovered that the tray had been cleared away and her sitting room brightened with a bouquet of hothouse flowers. She mused and fussed over them like a child with a toy, never once thinking of Orry.

56

"A visitor?" Orry said as he followed the house man to the head of the stairs. "I'm not expecting—God above, is it really you, George?"

"I think so," said the bedraggled traveler with the equally bedraggled smile. "Knock the cinders out of my hair and wash the dirt off my face, and we'll know for sure."

Orry rushed down the stairs. "Cuffey, take those carpetbags right up to the guest bedroom. George, have you had dinner? We'll be eating in half an hour. Why didn't you let us know you were coming?"

"I didn't know it myself until a few days ago. That's when I made up my mind. Besides"—with nervous movements he fished for a cigar—"I thought that if I wrote saying I wanted to come, you might not reply. You haven't answered any of my other letters."

Orry reddened. "I've been extremely busy. The harvest—and things are in turmoil in the state, as you know—"

"I can testify to that, all right. When I climbed off the train in Charleston, I almost believed I was on foreign soil."

"Any day now you could be right," Orry said after a humorless laugh. "Tell me, is that feeling widespread in the North?"

"I'd say it's nearly universal."

Orry shook his head, though he wasn't surprised by what his friend had said; the special convention called by Governor Pickens had already convened at the Baptist Church in Columbia. Everyone expected the delegates to vote for secession.

George cleared his throat to break the silence. "Will you pour me a drink? Then let's talk."

Orry brightened a little. "Certainly. This way."

He took George to the library. He was overjoyed to see his friend again, but the recent tension between them created a kind of emotional dam that kept him from saying so. He did break out his best whiskey. As he filled a glass for each of them, George remarked that he had visited with Cooper for a couple of hours.

"But I didn't come primarily to see him," George continued, sprawling in a chair. He pulled off one shoe and rubbed his stockinged foot.

Drink in hand, Orry stood with his back to the shuttered window. Pale winter light touched his shoulders and the back of his head. "Why, then?" he asked.

Can't he go at least halfway? George thought in a silent burst of frustration. He overcame it by remembering the unhappiness that had finally pushed him into the long journey to this room. He looked at the tall, forbidding man by the window and replied:

"For two purposes. The first is to try to save our friendship."

A crashing silence then. Taken aback, Orry couldn't find words. George leaned forward, the slope of his shoulders and the thrust of his chin reinforcing the intensity of his voice.

"That friendship is important to me, Orry. Next to Constance and my children, it's the thing I value most in this world. No, wait—hear me out. I offered my apology in writing, but I never felt it was adequate. I gather you didn't either. So I came here to speak to you face to face. Don't let the hotspurs down here, or radicals like my sister, wreck our good feelings for each other."

"Have you heard from Virgilia?"

George shook his head. "She's still in hiding. Frankly, I don't care. I shouldn't have taken her part that damnable day. I lost my temper."

Wanting to ease the moment, Orry murmured, "I would say there was bad temper on both sides."

"I didn't come to lay blame, just to ask your forgiveness. It's plain that South Carolina intends to leave the Union, though I'm afraid the act is a bad miscalculation. Some accommodation on slavery has always been possible, but if I read Washington's mood aright, none is possible when it comes to disunion. In any case, where this state leads, others are likely to follow, and that can only have dire consequences. The country's like a huge ship on a shoal, unable to free herself and slowly being ground to bits. The Hazards and the Mains have been close for years. I don't want that friendship ground to bits."

Once more Orry faced his visitor. The emotional dam crumbled. It was a relief to say what he felt:

"Nor I. I'm glad you came, George. It gives me a chance to apologize too. Let's wipe the slate clean."

George walked to his friend. "As clean as we can in these times."

Like brothers, they embraced in a great bear hug.

*

674

It wasn't long before they sat talking easily, as they had in earlier days. George grew reflective. "I really do fear a confrontation if South Carolina secedes. Not merely a political one, either."

Orry nodded. "Possession of the Federal forts has become a hot issue."

"I realized that when I came through Charleston. Someone's got to find a way out of this mess before the lunatics on both sides drag us into war."

"Is there a solution?"

"Lincoln and some others have proposed one. End slavery but compensate the South for the loss. Compensate the South if it takes every last ounce of gold in the treasury. It isn't ideal, perhaps, or morally clean, but at least it might avoid armed conflict."

Orry looked doubtful. "You haven't listened to Ashton's husband. He's typical of many leaders of this state. He doesn't want to avoid it."

"The son of a bitch would want to if he'd ever seen a battlefield."

"Granted. But he hasn't." Orry sighed. "Sometimes I believe you're right about slavery." His mouth quirked in a wry way. "Do you realize what a radical admission that is for a South Carolina boy? My attitude aside—I am well acquainted with the families who raise crops along this river. There isn't enough money in the whole Federal Treasury to persuade them to give up slavery, and that goes for those on the rice rivers and for the cotton planters up-country, too. No man except a saint would agree to dismantle the machine that creates his wealth. Why, my neighbors would let God strike them dead first."

"I rather expect He will," George said through a transparent blue cloud of cigar smoke. "The hotheads on both sides want blood. But there ought to be another way!"

Silence again. Neither man knew what that way might be.

Orry felt calmer and happier than he had in months. Tension that had built up for so long, the product of outside events as well as of the inner failings of each of them, had suddenly been relieved. He was in a receptive mood when George brought up the second purpose of his trip.

"I want to discuss my brother and your sister. They want to marry. Why won't you allow it?"

"Seems to me Brett is doing whatever she pleases these days."

"Blast it, Orry, don't go stubborn on me."

Guiltily, Orry reddened and glanced away. George pressed on. "She hasn't defied you to the point of marrying without your permission. And I can't fathom why you're withholding it."

"You can't? We discussed the reason. Trouble's coming, possibly war."

"All the more reason for them to have some happiness while they can."

"But you know where Billy's loyalty lies. With the Army and the government in Washington. And rightfully so. Brett, on the other hand—"

"Goddamn it," George exclaimed, "you're letting the hatreds of a bunch of fanatics and political trimmers ruin their lives. It isn't fair. What's more, it isn't necessary. Billy and Brett are young. That gives them strength—resilience. Of course there'll be pressure on them. But I know this, Orry. Together, my brother and your sister will weather the future a lot better than the rest of us. They're in love— and they happen to come from two families that care deeply about one another."

The words reverberated in the book-lined room. George walked to the cabinet containing the whiskey. His spirits plummeted, his hope evaporated. Orry was frowning.

For the third time stillness lay heavy in the room. Then, at last: "All right."

George pulled the cigar stub from his mouth. He was afraid his ears had tricked him.

"Did you say—?"

"All right," Orry repeated. "I always thought you were too reckless. But most of the time you were also right. I suppose Brett and Billy deserve a chance. Let's give it to them."

George whooped and did a little jig. Then he rushed to the door and tore it open. "Call one of your servants. Send him down to Charleston right away. Take the poor girl out of her misery."

Orry left. He wrote a pass for Cuffey. He was surprised at how good he felt: like a boy again, filled with an uncomplicated joy he hadn't experienced in years.

Back in the library, George adopted a mockingly serious attitude and congratulated his friend on his sagacity. They listened to the clop of Cuffey's horse departing, then fell to exchanging news. George talked of Constance and their children; Orry described Madeline's puzzling withdrawal, her apparent failing health. Then George raised the subject of the *Star of Carolina*.

"As I told you, I spoke to Cooper. I admit I'm having some difficulty adjusting to the possibility of a two-million-dollar loss."

"Cooper could repay every cent if everything was liquidated. I think he hates to do that because it's an admission of defeat."

"Even though he himself says the ship can't be finished? Well"— George shrugged—"I guess I admire that. Or I would if my investment was smaller. What a stinking mess we've all made of this world."

"That's always the complaint of old men," Orry murmured.

"Do you mean to say we're old men?"

"I don't know about you. I am."

"Guess I am too. Repulsive thought." George chewed on his cigar. "Stick, let's get drunk."

Orry glowed, hearing the nickname again. If things could never be just as they had been in those first, mint-bright years at the Academy, at least the two of them could pretend. Why shouldn't old men find comfort in games? The world was sinking into darkness.

"Stump, allow me," he said, first to reach the whiskey. "I have become an expert on drunkenness."

They both laughed, pretending it was a joke.

57

The afternoon George arrived at Mont Royal, the delegates to the secession convention traveled by train from Columbia to Charleston. The threat of smallpox in the capital had prompted the move. Thus Huntoon came home sooner than Ashton expected. But, like most other residents of the city, she was thrilled that the momentous deliberations would soon take place at Institute Hall. She was likewise overjoyed that her husband was personally involved in them. He would surely rise to power in the new nation, and she would rise with him.

Now she was hastily finishing her toilet so that she could go to the first session in the hall on Meeting Street. Suddenly, unannounced, Brett flew into her bedroom.

"Oh, Ashton—the most wonderful news. Cuffey rode down from home last night. George Hazard's there—"

"What does he want? A chance to snicker at our patriotic deliberations?"

"Don't be spiteful. He came to speak to Orry about Billy and me. And guess what."

Already a little worm of anger was gnawing away in Ashton, spoiling her excitement. "I can't imagine," she said, back at the mirror and patting a curl.

"Orry changed his mind. Billy and I can marry whenever we want."

Ashton had feared her sister was going to say that. It took all her will to keep from screaming in rage. Brett bubbled on.

"I sent Cuffey to the fort with the good news. I can't get over it! Things worked out right after all."

"I'm so happy for you."

Never in her life had Ashton found it this hard to smile. But smile she did. Then she embraced her sister, planted a kiss on her cheek. Brett was too flushed and breathless to catch the flash of fury in the eyes of the older girl. Otherwise Ashton's deception was perfect.

"We must talk about the wedding," Ashton said as she rushed to the door. "It'll be ever so nice to help you plan it. But we have to wait a day or so, until the convention concludes its business. I declare, I've never seen Charleston buzzing like this—"

And she was gone, overwhelmed with jealous hatred and a renewed conviction that she must strike against her sister and Billy Hazard at all costs.

Institute Hall was silent, the air electric. Spectators in the packed gallery strained forward to hear the report from the committee charged with the task of preparing an ordinance of secession.

Two days had gone by since the arrival of the delegates. Motions had been passed, amended, tabled. Special groups of observers sent by the states of Mississippi and Alabama had been received with great ceremony. But now, on the afternoon of the twentieth, the delegates had reached the revolutionary heart of the matter. The Honorable Mr. Inglis, committee chairman, took the floor to read the proposed draft.

Cooper sat in the first row of the gallery, his elbows on the rail in front of him. People pressed against him from either side. His eyes wandered over the floor below, moved from former Governor Gist to Senator Chestnut to Huntoon, who was sitting pink-faced and smiling like some cherubic assassin.

Women composed about half the gallery crowd. Most wore secession bonnets. Far to Cooper's right, Ashton watched the proceedings with a moist brow and parted lips. She looked as if she were experiencing something far earthier than the reading of a proclamation. Cooper found her expression not only surprising but also distasteful.

"We, the people of the State of South Carolina, in convention assembled—"

He listened, though he really didn't want to hear. The ramifications of this proceeding were enough to make a man's head burst. Would there be two national postal systems tomorrow? Two bank systems next week? People seemed blithely unconcerned. When he had posed such questions to a couple of local financial leaders, he had been treated to puzzled stares that quickly turned hostile. Poor old Main, said those looks. Mad as ever.

"—and it is hereby declared and ordained that the ordinance adopted by us in convention of the twenty-third day of May, in the year of our

Lord one thousand seven hundred and eighty-eight, whereby the Constitution of the United States was ratified—''

Slowly and sadly, Cooper's gaze again swept over those below him. Almost without exception, the men who had taken up this cause were prominent. They were men of intelligence and accomplishment. He could understand their anger, a generation old. But he would never understand the means they had chosen to vent that anger.

''—and also all acts, and parts of acts of the General Assembly of this State, ratifying amendments of the said Constitution, are hereby repealed.''

The spectators pressing against him on either side cheered and applauded. He recognized one as an employee of the U.S. Customs House; the other was a clergyman's wife. It was hard to say who howled the louder. Cooper leaned on the rail with his hands folded, thereby earning glares.

''—and that the union now subsisting between South Carolina and other states, under the name of the United States of America, is hereby dissolved.''

Pandemonium. The gallery surged up as if on signal. Cooper remained seated. The Customs House man grabbed his shoulder.

''Stand up, damn you.''

Cooper placed his fingers on top of the man's wrist, his thumb beneath, and removed the hand with apparent gentleness. But the man winced. Cooper gazed at him a moment longer, then returned his attention to those on the floor of the hall.

They were slapping backs, exchanging handshakes, boisterously congratulating one another. He would never understand their mass delusion. How in God's name could the state or the South go it alone? How could there be one continent, one people, and two governments?

After a lengthy demonstration of approval for the work of Mr. Inglis and his committee, the delegates and spectators settled down. Without debate, the ordinance was passed 169 to nothing. It would be signed—sealed—that night.

The moment that announcement was made, Institute Hall went wild again. Cooper sighed, rose, and fought his way up the packed aisle, seeing only a very few glum faces. One belonged to J. L. Petigru, a distinguished Charlestonian and old-time Whig lawyer much respected for his accomplishments and his family connections. Their eyes met briefly, like the eyes of mourners at a funeral.

Cooper rushed on out of the hall, his anger almost beyond containment.

*

Supper at Tradd Street was grim. Orry had brought George down from Mont Royal that morning to witness the deliberations at Institute Hall. They had been unable to get in. Orry seemed almost as downcast about secession as Cooper. George saw no point in repeating his prediction that the Federal government would respond without toleration.

Brett was depressed over the possible effects of the ordinance on her future. Fort Moultrie had been placed on alert in case the inevitable demonstrations degenerated into violence. She wouldn't see Billy tonight, and when she would see him next was uncertain.

Shouts and band music had been heard in the streets since afternoon. After supper the noise grew much louder. Soon bells were tolling all over the city. The melancholy within the house was virtually unbearable. Cooper reached for his hat.

"Well, gentlemen, they've signed it. This is an historic moment— shall we go out and watch Charleston celebrate her own ruin?"

"We're going too," Judith announced, bringing her shawl and Brett's. There was no arguing with them.

As the five of them left the house and turned toward Meeting, the cannon fire began.

The celebration of Lincoln's victory had been a mere rehearsal for this one. The narrow streets seethed with people. It was almost impossible to move rapidly on the wooden walks. Not three feet from George and the Mains, a string of firecrackers went off. Judith screeched, pressed a hand to her breast, then tried to smile.

They pushed on, up one side of Meeting and back down the other. Lights and transparencies decorated many windows. Among the subjects depicted were the palmetto flag, the Gamecock and the Swamp Fox, John Calhoun, and the facade of Institute Hall. Burning barrels of rosin bathed the street in gaudy red light. A fiery line traced its way into the sky behind Saint Michael's steeple, then burst into a bloom of pale stars. Continued explosions hurled other rockets aloft. Soon the sky twinkled with the fireworks.

Cannon on the Battery roared. Bands played. The crowd pushed back, crushing the revelers to permit the Ashley Guards to march by—one of many volunteer companies parading tonight.

A stout German blundered along, waving a placard,

682

HURRAH!
The Union
Is
DISSOLVED

"Wonderful, *ja?*" the placard bearer cried, blowing the odor of schnapps into Cooper's face. "But too long in coming. Too long!"

Livid, Cooper ripped the placard out of the man's hand. He broke the wooden slat to which it was tacked, then tore the card into pieces. Judith was pale.

Nearby spectators cursed Cooper. One or two began shoving. Orry moved beside his brother and shoved back. So did George, who jammed his face up to that of a man much taller.

"I'm a visitor to this city, but you'll have cause to remember me if you don't move along."

Orry laughed. For an instant the years had sloughed away and he had been watching and listening to young Cadet Hazard of West Point. The shovers moved on, and so did the German.

The air stank of powder, perfume, tobacco, overheated bodies. The sky shone with blue- and lemon-colored lights. No tune could be heard above the cannon fire, just occasional drumbeats and raucous horn notes.

"I don't think I've ever seen you this angry," Orry said to his older brother.

Cooper abruptly blocked the walk, confronting these four he loved; if any human beings would understand his piercing pain, they would.

"It's because I hate the position they've forced me into with their damned proclamation. All at once I don't know how I'm supposed to react. Where I'm supposed to place my loyalty. I hate feeling like a traitor to the state I've loved all my life. I hate being a traitor to the nation even more. The Union dissolved. For Christ's sake—"

"Cooper, your language," his wife whispered, unheard.

"—a Main *bled* to create the Union! If the rest of you don't feel like you're being torn apart—wait. These fucking madmen don't know what they've done. To themselves, their sons, all of us. They don't know!"

Ashen, he spun and pushed on, silhouetted against the firestreaked night. The others followed closely. Brett tried to console Judith, who didn't shock easily but was speechless now. Orry was already experiencing some of the confusion Cooper had described.

George's head hurt from the cannon fire. He seemed to hear only the thunderous reports, not the jubilant shouting and the laughter. He thought of Mexico. It was easy to half close his eyes, squint at the fire-washed buildings, and imagine that Charleston was a city already at war.

Faces floated past Orry, faces distorted by flame and by passion. The glaring eyes, the gaping mouths, grew less human every moment. Raw emotion distorted an ordinary countenance into that of a gargoyle, and the transformation was duplicated on almost every face he saw.

Brett pressed against Orry and clutched his arm, clearly afraid of the people buffeting them. Cooper and Judith walked close behind, followed by George, a wary rear guard. No one paid attention to them now.

Orry saw three young swaggerers of the town jabbing an old Negro with their canes. Then they doused him with the contents of big, bowllike beer glasses brought from the bar of a hotel behind them. He saw a respected member of the Methodist church with the neck of a bottle protruding from his side pocket; the man clung to a black iron hitching post, puking into the street. He saw the wife of a Meeting Street jeweler leaning back in a dark doorway while a stranger fondled her. Excess was everywhere.

So were the slogans, shouted in his ear or waved on placards or silk banners produced, seemingly, overnight. Three men with an unfurled banner swept down the sidewalk. Orry had to duck and urge the others to do the same as the banner's message loomed:

Southern Rights Shall Not Be Trampled!

The banner passed over them, and Orry straightened. Almost at once he saw Huntoon, who was hurrying in the wake of the banner carriers.

"Orry. Good evening." Ashton's husband tipped his hat, conspicuously adorned with a blue cockade, one of dozens Orry had seen tonight. Huntoon's cravat was undone, the tail of his shirt hung from beneath his waistcoat—unusual for a fastidious man.

But this was an unusual night, and that showed in Huntoon's uncharacteristically broad smile. "Is the celebration to your taste?"

The question was directed at all five of them and carried a malicious edge. Chiefly for Cooper's benefit, Orry imagined. "Not really," he answered. "I hate to see good South Carolinians making fools of themselves."

Huntoon wouldn't be baited. "I'd say revelry is quite in order and excess completely excusable. We've declared our freedom to the world." His glance touched Brett. "Of course our new independence focuses attention on the Federal property in Charleston. The Customs House, the arsenal, the forts. We're organizing a group of commissioners who will approach Buchanan on the matter. Surrender of the property to the sovereign state of South Carolina is now mandatory."

George moved to Brett's side. "What if Old Buck doesn't see it that way?"

Huntoon smiled. "Then, sir, we shall resolve the question by other means."

He tipped his hat a second time and moved on, blending into a crowd of a hundred or so that spilled through the street chanting, "Southern rights! Southern rights! *Southern rights!*"

Brett watched Huntoon until he disappeared. Orry felt her hand constrict on his arm. "He said that about the forts because of Billy, didn't he?"

Cooper overheard. "I wouldn't doubt it. The milk of human kindness flows sparingly, if at all, in Mr. Huntoon."

They glimpsed him again on the other side of Meeting, fighting his way up the steps of the Mills House, then turning to survey the turbulent street from the top step. The lenses of his spectacles reflected flames leaping from a barrel on the curb. The eyes of a smiling demon, Orry thought. It was one more disturbing image on top of many.

He thought of Major Anderson out at Fort Moultrie. In Mexico he had known Anderson by sight and by reputation. A fine officer, conscientious and able. What must he be feeling? Where would his loyalty lie in the coming months? With the slaveholders of his native Kentucky or with the Army?

So many Americans—so many West Pointers—would be tested now; forced to decide where they stood. Orry could almost believe some malevolent power had taken charge of the world.

"As you suggested, Cooper, an historic moment," he said. "Let's go home."

Demoralized and silent, they did.

On the Battery, surrounded and crushed by sweaty, screaming revelers, Ashton found herself unexpectedly stirred. It was as if the mob created currents of power that surged into the ground and then back up her legs, to the very center of her. The secret arousal left her light-headed and short of breath.

As always, it wasn't the outpouring of patriotism that excited her but the larger significance, the main chance. The oaths, the howled threats and slogans, were the birth cries of a new nation. James predicted that other cotton states would follow South Carolina's example, and that very soon a new government would be organized. He would play a preeminent role. In a matter of weeks, a long-held dream could become a reality. Power would be hers for the taking.

Another burst of fireworks splashed her face with scarlet light. Star shells whined skyward and exploded over Sullivan's Island, briefly illuminating the ramparts of the fort. Her face wrenched.

Then, superimposed on an imaginary picture of Billy Hazard, she saw someone equally familiar, standing a few yards away.

"Forbes." Clutching her secession bonnet, she fought toward him. "Forbes!"

"Mrs. Huntoon," he said with that exaggerated courtesy he displayed when they met in public. He bowed. She smelled the bourbon on him, mingled with his male odor. It increased her excitement, but tonight wasn't a suitable occasion for that kind of indulgence.

"Forbes, it's urgent that we speak," she whispered. "Tomorrow—as soon as possible. Orry has cleared the way for Billy and my sister to be married. I can't abide that. I won't permit it."

A moment earlier Forbes LaMotte had looked drunkenly genial. Now his mouth took on the appearance of a sword cut across his face. More skyrockets went off, bells and cannon created a din. He had to lean close to hear what she said next.

"South Carolina has taken action. I think it's time we did, too."

His relaxed, sleepy smile returned. "Indeed it is," he murmured. "I am at your disposal."

58

On the morning of January 25, 1861, Captain Elkanah Bent arrived in New Orleans. He was hastening to the only real home he knew, Washington. He had arranged a transfer just in time. The situation in the country was critical and deteriorating more each day. He was sure the War Department was preparing promotion lists and reorganizing for impending conflict. Or they would be as soon as that doughface Buchanan vacated the White House.

Today Bent wore a new and expensive civilian outfit. He had purchased the clothes in Texas right after making his decision to stop over in New Orleans for twenty-four hours. He felt it wouldn't be prudent to flaunt his Army uniform in such a pro-Southern city. By reliable report, Louisiana would soon secede, joining the five other cotton states that had already left the Union. People up North were referring to those states as the Gulf Squadron. It had a military sound, belligerent. That pleased him.

Strolling up Bienville, he savored the fragrance of bitter coffee from a café. Good coffee was just one of the city's worldly delights he intended to sample during this brief visit.

He counted himself lucky to get out of Texas when he did. There, too, secession was inevitable, and those in charge of the Department of Texas were clearly sympathetic to the South. Old Davey Twiggs, department commander, and Bob Lee, who had returned from Virginia last year to resume command of the Second Cavalry, were just two potential traitors in a command riddled with them.

He had been fortunate to get out of Texas for other reasons. He had admittedly botched the attempt to eliminate Charles Main, and he was lucky to have escaped a court-martial. With war likely, there could be new opportunities to strike at the Mains and the Hazards. He'd see what the records in Washington revealed. The prospect took some of the sting out of his failure.

Bent had never satisfied himself about one question: Did Charles know the real reason for his enmity? By now it seemed very unlikely that he did not; Charles and that damnable Orry Main must have exchanged letters on the subject. Letters in which Bent's relationship with Orry and George Hazard had been revealed. If by some remote chance there had been no such correspondence, the secret would certainly come out the moment Charles returned home on leave.

Once the Mains knew of Bent's continuing appetite for revenge, the Hazards would undoubtedly learn of it, too. But he still saw one advantage for himself. The members of both families would surely assume that his desire would fade or vanish in the turbulence of war. That mistaken assumption would be their undoing.

As Bent read the national situation, hostilities couldn't be avoided. Charleston was the flash point. The day after Christmas, Anderson's little garrison had made secret preparations and, when night fell, had transferred by boat to Fort Sumter, spiking the guns left behind at Moultrie and burning the carriages. As a result, the palmetto flag was now flying over all the Federal property in and around Charleston, except for the fort Anderson was occupying in the center of the harbor.

Anderson's garrison was still being permitted to buy fresh meat and vegetables from Charleston markets. But state militiamen were pouring into the city. They were being put to work realigning the guns at Moultrie, Castle Pinckney, and Fort Johnson.

In Washington during the past weeks Old Buck had purged his cabinet of Southern influence and adopted a harder line. He refused to meet with the South Carolina commissioners who came to the capital to argue for the surrender of Fort Sumter, and he sent their memoranda to the files unread.

On January 9 the opposing forces had reeled to the brink. Buchanan had dispatched a chartered side-wheeler, *Star of the West*, to Charleston. The relief vessel carried food, ammunition, and 250 soldiers. She had crossed the bar, and then the cadets from The Citadel who were manning the harbor guns had opened fire.

Anderson's batteries did not return fire to defend the incoming ship. Hulled once, *Star of the West* immediately put out to sea again, and the incident was over—except in Washington, where wrangling continued between the government and yet another South Carolina delegation.

Just a few days ago, Davis and other senators from the Gulf Squadron had left the Capitol after delivering farewell speeches whose contrived sentimentality was designed to mask their treason. This very morning on the city dock Bent had heard that Davis and others would soon convene in Montgomery, Alabama, to form a new government.

How could that government fail to come to blows with Washington? Old Buck wouldn't be President much longer, and the new man, that queer fellow Lincoln, though soft on slavery, was uncompromising about preservation of the Union. War was coming. The future looked splendid.

In this fine frame of mind, Bent ascended a beautiful black iron stair and knocked at the door of an establishment that had been recommended to him by a gentleman he had met while traveling. When the door opened, he used an assumed name to introduce himself.

Two hours later, half dressed, he was dragged to the rooms of the proprietress by a huge, ferocious-looking Negro who shoved him into a plush chair, then blocked the door, awaiting the settlement of the dispute.

"One hundred dollars is outrageous!" Bent declared as he tucked in his shirt and buttoned his sleeves. Here was one place where the authority of his uniform might have served him.

Seated behind her magnificent desk, Madam Conti appeared relaxed and comfortable in her indigo silk robe with its pattern of embroidered peacocks. She was a large, solid woman, about sixty. Her stunning white hair was exquisitely arranged. Near her beringed hand, incense smoldered inside a tiny brass temple; Oriental objects had been the rage ever since Perry's squadron had sailed into Yedo Bay, Japan.

"Nevertheless, Monsieur Benton, one hundred dollars is what you must pay. A girl as young as Otille commands a premium price." The woman consulted a scrap of paper. "You also requested several, ah, special services. I can enumerate them for you—if they have slipped your mind. Did she not inform you of the extra charge?"

"She most certainly did not."

Madame Conti shrugged. "An oversight. It has no effect upon the price."

"I refuse to pay, goddamn it. I absolutely refuse."

Madame Conti greeted the outburst not with anger but with a tolerant smile. Looking past Bent, she said, "Whatever shall we do with him, Pomp?"

"Keep on treating him like a gentleman," the black rumbled. "See if he might change his mind."

Bent's upper lip popped with sweat. He had heard the note of threat in the nigger's remarks. He struggled to maintain a courageous front. Madame Conti's smile didn't waver.

"Pour our visitor a little champagne. That might help."

"It will not," Bent said. She laughed and called for a second glass for herself.

Bent withheld another retort, attempting to plan his next move. Obviously he couldn't fight his way out of the bordello, nor did he intend to try. He let the situation drift a moment, accepting a glass of excellent French champagne from Pomp. He gulped it, then held the glass out to be refilled. Madame Conti gave the black man a nod of assent.

The champagne had a calming effect. Bent began to take notice of the elegant office. On walls of red-flocked wallpaper hung more than a dozen large paintings, all lit effectively by mantled gas jets. One huge canvas was a rollicking study of fur trappers on a river raft.

"That is my pride," the woman declared. "A Westerner named Bingham painted it."

Her pride was misplaced, Bent thought, downing more champagne. He eyed a portrait of a young woman hanging behind Madame Conti's left shoulder. The features of the beautiful, dark-haired creature were familiar somehow. But he couldn't place her.

Madame Conti noticed his interest. "Ah, you admire her? She worked here for a time many years ago. She was even more beautiful than my little Otille. And far more expensive."

Bitch, he thought. Wouldn't let him forget the bill, would she?

Then, abruptly, he knew where he had seen the exotic face in the painting. It was in one of Charles Main's family daguerreotypes.

No, just a moment. This woman, smiling her seductive painted smile, wasn't the same Creole beauty whose picture he had seen in Texas. The resemblance was strong but not exact. Sisters, perhaps?

"Who is she, Madame?"

Jeweled bracelets twinkled and clinked as the white-haired woman drank champagne. "I don't suppose it hurts to tell you. She was a poor girl who rose very high before she died. She left my employ to become the eminently respectable and respected wife of a rich New Orleans factor."

"The dusky cast of her skin is enchanting. The painter was inspired."

"Only by what he saw."

"You mean her skin was that way naturally?"

"Yes, Monsieur Benton."

"I'm fascinated. She creates a lovely romantic image—" He leaned forward slightly; a master schemer, he could be subtle when necessary. "How did her story end—if you know and wish to confide, Madame?"

She turned her chair, regarding the painted face with affection. "My dear girl had a daughter by her adoring husband after they married, but, alas, the beautiful mother died. In time, before he too succumbed, the loving father had to send the child far away to make a match. She looked as white as you or I, but some in this town knew her mother's background."

So that was the relationship; mother and daughter. Bent couldn't take his eyes from the painting.

"And they knew the child was not French or Spanish but octoroon. Years ago, attractive young women of mixed blood were favored creatures. No longer. The furor over slavery has seen to that. Today"— an expressive shrug, a melancholy smile—"being one-eighth Negro, however light the skin, is exactly the same as being all Negro— Monsieur Benton, what is wrong?"

Bent's hand had jerked, spilling champagne on her fine carpet. "An accident, Madame. My profound apologies."

He whipped out his kerchief, bending down to mop the rug, a difficult task because of his huge paunch.

The daughter of a nigger whore connected with that arrogant Main crowd? Obviously they didn't suspect; no woman with nigger blood would be permitted in a group portrait of plantation aristocrats. What a splendid piece of information! He didn't know how he'd use it, or when, but that he would use it he didn't doubt for a moment.

"Madame, you're quite right. The champagne has a soothing effect." His moist face beamed. "The services of the young lady were extremely satisfying, and I was wrong to quibble over the price. I'll pay in full. I'd even like to give her a handsome tip, if you'll permit it."

Madame Conti exchanged a look with the huge black man who for several minutes had been cleaning his nails with a long knife. At her faint signal, he slipped the knife out of sight.

"But of course," she said with a courteous nod.

A cold rain fell from the Texas sky. A dispirited Charles Main watched the last trunk being lifted and placed with others in the Army ambulance. The trunks belonged to Colonel Lee.

Five days ago, on February 8, Charles and two enlisted men had left Camp Cooper with urgent dispatches for the regimental commander. They had ridden 165 miles in foul weather and had arrived to find that Lee had been relieved and called back to Washington by direct order of General Scott. No doubt Scott wanted him to declare his intentions—and his loyalty.

Lee's departure was more evidence of the chaos spreading through the land. Although important border states such as Tennessee and Lee's own Virginia had not yet joined the secession movement, Texas had been out of the Union since the first of the month—against the pessimistic advice of Governor Houston.

During the hours Charles had been riding with the dispatches, a new Confederate government had been born in Alabama. Jefferson Davis was its provisional president, and its provisional constitution was already drafted.

President-elect Lincoln was traveling eastward from Illinois by train. He was forced to stop frequently along the way to make exhausting speeches to constituents. In Washington, Senator Crittenden had put forward desperate compromise proposals on slavery, but the effort had failed. With all the cotton-state members gone, it had been easy for the Senate to pass a measure admitting Kansas to the Union as a free state.

Meantime, Major Anderson's command remained huddled in Fort Sumter, ringed by strengthened batteries and South Carolina gunners itching for a scrap. Charles often wondered if Billy was still on duty at the fort. Anderson had sent several of his men to Washington with dispatches or requests for instructions. Perhaps Billy had been one of them. Charles hoped and prayed his friend would get out of the fort alive.

In Texas the frontier posts seethed with suspicion and rumors of impending takeovers by state military levies or the Texas Rangers. Although known to be a Southern sympathizer, General Twiggs had four times appealed to Washington for orders. Four times he had received vague and meaningless replies.

One story, authenticated by a San Antonio paper, seemed to typify the Army's state of turmoil. In January one of the Military Academy's most respected graduates, Pierre Beauregard, had been appointed superintendent. He had held the post less than a week and been removed because Louisiana's secession made him suspect. Men who had bled in Mexico, broken bread together, and shared hardships for years now regarded each other as potential enemies, capable of almost any treachery. It depressed Charles, who was still uncertain about his own decision and his own future.

Now he waited for Lee in the rain. Nine other officers were waiting with him. Finally the colonel appeared, wearing his talma and forage cap. One by one the officers stepped up to offer a salute and a word of good luck. The last to arrive, and the most junior, Charles was the last to speak.

"It has been an honor to serve with you, sir."

"Thank you, Lieutenant."

"I wish you a safe journey."

"I don't relish the circumstances that require me to undertake it. I do want to say this to you, however. You're a good officer. No matter what else changes, that won't."

"Thank you, sir."

Lee started away. Charles's inner confusion prompted him to disregard protocol. "Colonel?"

By the side of the ambulance, Lee turned about. "Yes?"

"Which way will you go, sir? North or South?"

Lee shook his head. "I could never bear arms against the United States. But what if it became necessary for me to carry a musket to defend my native Virginia? I had frankly hoped to avoid that kind of question. I thought President Buchanan might restore harmony between the sections by playing on love of country, but he failed. I thought the melting influence of Christianity might resolve the slave issue, but it hasn't. I've owned slaves, and my conscience has tried me because of it. The institution will wither. It should. As for secession, in my view it's nothing but revolution. Yet at this moment, men who are in most respects eminently decent have established a new government on the pillars of secession and slavery, and so I am unsure of the future and of my own reactions as well."

Lee's face looked haggard in the rain. "I'm certain of one thing only. No matter how each man or woman answers the question you asked, I think there will be but one result from what we've allowed the extremists to do to us. Heartbreak. Good-bye, Lieutenant."

He trudged to the front of the ambulance and climbed up beside the driver. The vehicle lurched forward through the mud and rapidly faded into the dreary distance.

Charles walked back to the stockade. Pondering his own confused state of mind, he could only conclude that Lee was right. North and South, both would suffer before this terrible business was done.

Two days later, in San Antonio, old Davey Twiggs surrendered all the Federal posts in Texas to state forces. Men loyal to the Union were urged to depart for the Gulf ports and given assurance of safe conduct, though for how long no one was prepared to say.

Charles completed his journey from Fort Mason and arrived at Camp Cooper just an hour before its Union contingent was to pull out. The men were under the command of Captain Carpenter, First Infantry. Some were on horseback, some on foot.

Dirty and exhausted from long hours in the saddle, Charles watched the Ohioans from Company K ride out in a column of twos. One was Corporal Tannen, who had been a private in the skirmish at Lantzman's farm; Charles had pushed for his promotion. Tannen took note of those remaining behind, leaned out to the left, and spat.

"Any man who stays is unfit to wear Army blue." He said it loud enough for all to hear.

"What's that, Corporal?" Charles called.

Tannen returned his stare. "I said if you stay, you're a yellow traitor."

"I seem to have been robbed of my rank," Charles said as he flung off his bear-claw necklace, then his filthy and sweat-blackened hide shirt. Before anyone could react, he cocked his revolver and passed it to an Alabama trooper standing next to him.

"So no one interferes."

The Alabama boy grinned, nodded, and got a better grip on the gun. Charles approached Tannen's horse.

"You helped me once. I was grateful. But your remark cancels that."

Tannen looked down at him. "Good. Fuck you."

Charles reached for him. Tannen tried to lash Charles's face with his rein. Charles caught the rein and whipped it round and round the corporal's left wrist. The horse began to buck.

Tannen drew his saber. Charles twisted it away and flung it out of reach. Then he dragged the Ohioan from his saddle and pounded him until his nose looked like pulped berries. Breathing hard, he spoke to the others who were leaving.

"Pick him up if you want him. I'll kill the next one who calls me a traitor."

He removed his foot from the middle of Tannen's back and stood with his hands at his sides until Tannen was thrown belly down over a horse. Soon the Union men were gone.

An hour later, Charles wrote his resignation. Then he packed.

Since there was no regular Army officer left to accept the resignation and report it to Washington, he hammered a nail into the door of his room in the barracks and impaled the paper on the nail. Within minutes he was bound for the Gulf.

Lee might ponder the philosophical subtleties, but his own future had been decided in a far simpler way. Ah, well. He had never been a deep man. Just a hell raiser and a horse soldier. The South might need someone like him as much as it needed philosophers.

He hated leaving Texas, which he had come to love. He thought slavery a foolish system and likely a dying one. But his blood called him home. He pushed his horse hard all the way to the coast.

BOOK FOUR

MARCH INTO DARKNESS

*I tell you there is a fire. They
have this day set a blazing torch
to the temple of constitutional
liberty, and, please God, we shall
have no more peace forever.*

LAWYER JAMES PETIGRU
OF CHARLESTON, *during the
celebration of secession*
DECEMBER 20, 1860

59

Sumter felt more like a prison every day.

Billy occupied a dank, brick-walled room in the officer's quarters along the gorge. The room was doubly dismal because it was dark most of the time. The garrison had almost used up the candles and matches Mrs. Doubleday had purchased in January, one day before she and the other garrison wives went North. Billy had one waxy stub left. He lit it for only a few minutes each day while he added a mark to his improvised calendar—vertical lines scraped into the wall with a fragment of brick. So far in February he had marked the wall twenty-one times.

He no longer saw Brett. He was not one of those detailed to travel over to the city every couple of days, there to purchase some salt pork and vegetables. This reprovisioning was carried out with the sufferance of Governor Pickens, at the urging of some prominent gentlemen of Charleston.

Some other gentlemen, equally prominent, hated the idea of the garrison's receiving food and mail, and said so frequently. One of Brett's letters informed Billy that Rhett of the *Mercury* was particularly strong about starving the garrison into surrender. Billy suspected the governor had the same objective and was merely pursuing it in a different way. Pickens had refused to permit the forty-three civilian masons and bricklayers to leave Fort Sumter. Presumably they would continue to devour provisions, thus hastening the day when Anderson would have to ask for terms. Several officers were outspoken in saying that the governor was bluffing, that he had no power to issue such an edict. Doubleday argued that the workmen could be dumped ashore in the dead of night if Anderson truly wanted to be rid of them. He didn't say it to Anderson's face, however, and the commandant, sensitive to the immense danger in any confrontation with local authorities, didn't push for a test of the question.

Brett reported that the provision detail marched to and from the Charleston market with loaded muskets. Crowds followed the soldiers, and now and again someone yelled Doubleday's name. He was the most hated man in the fort, a known Black Republican. If he ever set foot in the city, she predicted, he would be mobbed and hanged.

So, like Billy, Doubleday remained a prisoner in the harbor.

Billy kept as busy as he could. When the masons under his command finished bricking up the unused windows in the second-tier casemates, Foster put them all to work on the main gate. A thick wall of stone was mortared into place on the inside, with just a single, iron-covered bolt hole left in the center. As soon as wall and bolt hole were done, Anderson ordered a twenty-four-pound howitzer moved up to cover the new, smaller entrance.

Everyone in the fort had fallen into a kind of stupor. Working hours were long; tension heightened normal tiredness. The toll was particularly heavy on Captains Seymour and Doubleday. They alternated as officers of the day and spent every other night awake.

The seriousness of the situation made the soldiers more candid, less concerned with protocol. This was demonstrated one afternoon when Doubleday and Billy watched from the parapet as a small schooner warped in to a wharf on Morris Island. The schooner was carrying railroad plate that would be spiked to the slanted timber face of a battery under construction on Cummings Point, little more than twelve hundred yards away.

"Look at that," Doubleday exclaimed. "We're giving them all the time in the world to place their guns and bring up their ammunition."

It was true. From Moultrie, now heavily fortified with cotton bales and sandbags, all the way around to Cummings Point, cannon menaced the harbor fort. Their state artillery crews practiced regularly. Right this moment Billy could see men scurrying around a dozen guns while above them strange flags with palmetto or pelican devices fluttered in the sunshine.

Like most others in the garrison, Billy found Major Anderson a decent, conscientious man—if rather old and pious. He felt compelled to respond to the implied criticism.

"If the major tried to stop it, he might plunge this whole country into a shooting war. I wouldn't want that responsibility, sir."

"Nor I," Doubleday snapped. "Believe me, I appreciate the dilemma, but it doesn't change the fact that hesitation deepens our danger."

"Do you think that peace conference will help matters?" Billy asked. The state of Virginia had issued the call for the conference, and ex-President Tyler had convened it at Willard's Hotel in Washington.

But some important states, including Michigan and California, had refused to send delegates.

Doubleday's answer to the question was blunt: "No. In my opinion we can't save the Union and slavery too." He thumped the parapet with his fist. "I wish the major would forget his orders for an hour and let us reduce those batteries. If we don't, we'll soon be surrounded by a ring of fire."

A ring of fire. An apt term, Billy thought as he watched stevedores continuing to unload the schooner's cargo. South Carolina guns were trained on Sumter from every direction except seaward. Wasn't it inevitable that someone, impetuously if not on direct order, would discharge one of those pieces at the fort and start a war?

Brett's next note confirmed the impending danger. War fever was running high in Charleston. Doubleday and others in the garrison assumed this was why President Davis moved forcefully to take over the Charleston batteries in the name of the new government. Davis also dispatched official Confederate emissaries to Washington to sue for a surrender of the disputed property.

It was from Anderson himself, a few nights later, that Billy heard one more surprising piece of news. "Davis is sending his own officer to command the batteries." The major sighed. "Beauregard."

They stood by one of the ten-inch columbiads on the barbette. Half of Sumter's forty-eight usable guns were mounted in the open, the other half in the casemates below. About fifty yards off the fort, the *Nina* was passing. She was one of the pair of guard steamers the state kept on constant patrol in the harbor. Sharpshooters at her stern recognized Anderson, hailed him, and flung mock salutes. The tall, hollow-eyed commander remained motionless.

"Captain Beauregard of Louisiana?" Billy said.

"Brigadier General Beauregard now. Confederate States of America. When I taught artillery at the Academy in thirty-six and thirty-seven, he was one of my best pupils. He was so good, I retained him as an assistant instructor after he graduated." The major's gaze drifted to the iron battery rapidly nearing completion on Cummings Point. "I expect we'll soon see a more professional placement of many of the guns."

Then Anderson swung to face his subordinate. Sunset light falling over Charleston's rooftops and steeples emphasized the lined look of his face. "But I've been meaning to inquire about your young lady, Lieutenant. Is she still in the city?"

"Yes, sir. I get a letter every day or so."

"The two of you still want to marry?"

"Very much, sir. But that doesn't appear practicable right now."

"Don't be too sure. As you know, Captain Foster doesn't wish to see you gentlemen from the engineers do line service"—all the engineering lieutenants had volunteered as officers of the guard, but Foster had vetoed the idea—"so when your work is finished, I shall keep your situation in mind."

Billy's hope soared. Yet at the same time he felt another pull. "That's good of you, sir, but I wouldn't want to leave if there were to be hostilities."

"There will be no hostilities," Anderson whispered. "None of which we initiate in any case. Can you imagine the catastrophic results if Americans were to open fire on other Americans? That kind of collision will not take place because of any action of mine, and I'm not ashamed to say I fall on my knees every night and beg God to help me keep that vow."

The contrast with Doubleday's simmering pugnacity was clear. Billy watched the sun fading from the roof peaks and turned his mind to the hope Anderson had held out. He hardly dared think about it because of the great possibility of disappointment.

Slowly he gazed around the harbor, picking out the various batteries on the sand and mud flats. He identified each in terms of its armament: columbiads, mortars, twenty-four- and thirty-two- and even forty-two-pounders.

A ring of fire. Waiting to be ignited by order or mischance. As the sun sank, he felt a renewed, almost overwhelming pessimism.

That same evening Orry stepped off a river schooner at the Mont Royal landing. Twenty minutes later he joined Charles in the library.

"What's the situation in Charleston?" the younger man asked as he poured two glasses of whiskey.

"Bad. Business is stagnating. The merchants are starting to squeal."

"Are people leaving?"

"On the contrary. The city's never seen so many tourists. But they're spending only what they must. The same goes for the home folk."

"Can't say it surprises me. Who wants to throw money away when civil war may erupt any minute, and two weeks from now bread could cost twenty dollars a loaf?''

With a smile that was more of a grimace, Charles sank back into a chair and flung one leg over the side. His homecoming had been pleasant for a day or two, but very quickly that sense of enjoyment had left him. He and Orry had discussed Elkanah Bent at some length, and although few new facts were added to what Charles already knew, he was once again depressed by the magnitude of the man's hate. Surely it would burn itself out if war erupted. In any case, he was reasonably certain their paths would never cross again.

Bent wasn't the only cause of his malaise. He missed the West and, to his surprise, no longer felt entirely at home in his native state. He didn't dare admit that he could think of but one antidote for his uneasiness: fighting.

"The news gets worse," Orry remarked after sipping from his glass. "There is a considerable amount of bad feeling about the new government. When forming it, Davis appears to have ignored South Carolina."

Charles digested that, then put the subject aside. He asked, "How is everyone at Tradd Street holding up?"

"Cooper's doing as well as can be expected, considering that the cargo ship is now a lost cause and part of his land has been commandeered for another iron battery."

"I gather it was a choice between consenting or facing the possibility of a mob burning down the yard. Judith and Brett are looking after Cooper, but he's pretty despondent. His worst fears have been realized."

"Did you see Ashton?"

"No. I'm told James is thick with Governor Pickens, and despite Montgomery's evident disdain for South Carolinians, they say James is maneuvering for a post there. Oh, and one more thing—I have it on good authority that all these war preparations have left the state dead broke."

"What about that seven-hundred-thousand-dollar loan they're trying to place?"

"No takers."

"Well, maybe things'll veer back to normal somehow. Maybe the issue of the fort will be settled peaceably."

"President Davis has said he'll take Sumter by negotiation or he'll take it by force. Lincoln will be inaugurated in a couple of weeks—perhaps then we'll have some clue as to which it will be."

The two former soldiers stared at one another in the darkening library, neither in doubt about the outcome that was wanted by those who were in control of the state.

Some forty-eight hours later, Huntoon was standing at the rail of the guard steamer *Nina*. He held a plate of chicken salad in one hand, a glass of Tokay in the other.

A party of thirty gentlemen had come aboard for this sunset cruise to inspect the disputed fort. On the afterdeck a buffet had been spread beneath a striped awning. The food had been prepared by a select committee of ladies, of which Ashton had contrived to become a prominent member. Half a dozen slaves from as many households had been ordered out to staff the serving area.

The wind blew briskly from the northeast, promising a chilly February night. As Huntoon munched away, *Nina* completed a turn in the main ship channel and put in toward the city, white water purling off her paddles.

"You know, Governor," Huntoon remarked to the man standing next to him, "the lack of decisive action is becoming an irritant to many citizens."

"My hands are tied," Pickens retorted. "General Beauregard will be here soon, and as far as the interim is concerned, President Davis has let me know in unmistakable language that he is the one in charge, not I."

"Hmmm." Huntoon sipped his wine. "I thought the palmetto state seceded to preserve its sovereign rights. Have we already surrendered them to another central government?"

Pickens glanced over his shoulder, apprehensive about eavesdroppers. "I wouldn't speak so loudly—or so critically. Not if you still hope to earn yourself a place in Montgomery."

"I certainly do. It appears to me that men of principle and courage are sorely needed down there. We must force the issue."

"James, you're too precipitous," the governor began, but the younger man immediately interrupted.

"Nonsense, sir. If we don't act, others will. Yesterday I heard serious discussion of a new secession movement. Some influential planters in this state are talking of pulling away from the Davis government and petitioning Great Britain to make South Carolina a protectorate."

"That's preposterous," Pickens exclaimed, but his voice had a

704

nervous note in it. And with good reason. Lately, his friend and colleague in secession, Bob Rhett, had heard rumors of a reconstruction plan that Stephen Douglas was promoting in a last-ditch effort to save the Union. The governor wanted no part of lunatic schemes to establish a British colony, but neither did he want reconciliation.

"We must act with restraint for a while longer. The Davis emissaries will fail in Washington. By then Beauregard will be in place, and we'll have our war."

"I do hope so," Huntoon murmured.

His attention was abruptly caught by the sight of an officer watching from Fort Sumter's terreplein. He recognized Billy Hazard. He lifted his wineglass to salute him.

The Yankee upstart nodded with inattentive casualness. Huntoon found the response offensive. We'll have our war, and you will be among its first casualties, he thought as the guard steamer chugged on toward the city piers.

60

The hand on Brett's arm was bruising. The voice had the high, flat accent of the up-country.

"Here, my lass, all I asked was directions to—"

"Ask someone else." She hauled off and drove the point of her shoe into the man's shinbone.

He swore and called her a name. The odor of his whiskey breath fumed around her as she tore from his grip and fled down Meeting Street. The man, a burly young fellow in soiled clothes and a broad-brimmed wool hat, lurched after her.

Impelled by fear, she ran swiftly in the February dusk. She dashed to the right, into Tradd Street. Her pursuer yelled something about Charleston whores but came no farther than the corner.

A moment later she risked a look back. The man was moving across Meeting, a passing shadow among others. She shuddered.

Charleston was swarming with visitors from all parts of the South. They had come to sightsee, to watch the fuses of practice shells sketch red lines in the night sky, to listen to street-corner Ciceros denounce the awkward ape from Illinois, to marvel at the precise drill of the Citadel cadets, and to murmur over the gaudy colors and designs of the uniforms of the state military units.

Most of the visitors were still spending very little. And a lot were riffraff, like the young man from whom she had just fled. He had accosted her as she was hurrying home from the public market, where she had given a hamper of cheese, bread, candles, and matches to the shopping detail from Fort Sumter.

There, too, she had faced a measure of danger. She could still see the venomous faces and hear the epithets as she passed the hamper to a corporal. *Traitor* was the mildest name she had been called; most of the names were filthy.

"Mr. Rhett and his crowd are always railing against the Northern mobocracy," she said to Judith after she was once more safe in the house. "I'd say we have our own mobocracy right here in Charleston."

"Feeling seems to run higher every day," Judith agreed. She reached out to tap her sturdy son's wrist. "Judah, don't play in the oyster stew."

But the boy continued to trail his spoon back and forth through the bowl. On the other side of the table, Marie-Louise fidgeted. "Mama, is Papa going to be gone again tonight?"

"Yes, he's very busy these days."

The eyes of Judith and Brett met briefly; both understood the lie just uttered. No business reasons compelled Cooper to linger on James Island after dark. Construction on the *Star of Carolina* had come to a halt weeks ago. Yet he went back to the yard day after day and stayed until midnight or later. Haggard and emaciated, he was behaving like some ghoulish spectator at the scene of a railway disaster, sifting through the wreckage in search of an explanation—as if explanation could undo the damage. Brett worried about her brother almost as much as she worried about Billy.

"Oh, you must see the *New York Herald* that Cooper brought home day before yesterday," Judith exclaimed. "There's a new play being performed there. It's all about Fort Sumter. The paper gives the name of the actor who's personating Lieutenant William Hazard."

"You mean the characters are named for real people?"

"I do. Anderson, Doubleday—they're all in it."

"Is that art or greed?"

"More the latter, I suspect," Judith replied.

Brett sighed. How bizarre the city and the nation had become in only a matter of weeks. Little by little Americans had gotten mired in a kind of genteel madness in which very little was unthinkable. Worst of all, the madness threatened the young man she loved. Everyone said there would be war the moment Lincoln was inaugurated. Beauregard would give the command to the batteries, and the eighty men at Sumter would be killed by cannon fire or by the bayonets and musket balls of storming parties.

She had nightmares about that, nightmares about attending Billy's funeral. She feared those dark dreams so much that she could hardly go to sleep these nights. Since leaving Mont Royal she had lost twelve pounds, and great circles of shadow ringed her eyes.

In the parlor she used sewing scissors to clip the item about the play. Two loud thuds in quick succession made her jump.

Mortars, she realized. The Mount Pleasant battery. She had gotten so she could identify the source of every practice round. She was not the only Charlestonian with that newfound talent.

As the booming echoes faded, she gave a small exclamation, discovering that as the mortars went off, the scissors had slipped. The point had pricked the fleshy part of her left palm, and she hadn't even felt it. She watched a brilliant crimson drop ooze out and trickle toward her wrist. Another drop formed.

The sight of blood, coming hard upon the artillery fire and following the drunken manhandling on the street and the cursing at the market, shattered her emotional defenses. "Billy," she whispered. Tears filled her eyes. "Billy."

She pressed the bloodied hand to her mouth and fought to control her fear.

"You mean their damn President had to *sneak* into Washington?"

"Yessir. He was wearin' cast-off clothes and so was his detective hireling, Pinkerton. They arrived on a sleeper in the middle of the night like common travelers. Like criminals!"

"Why'd Lincoln get off the regular train?"

"Feared a plot to assassinate him, they say. If I'd been close by, I might have lent a hand with—oh, evening, Mr. Main."

"Gentlemen."

With an expression of distaste, Cooper nodded at the men but did not tip his hat. The two were corporals in some state artillery unit that reported to the commander of the James Island forces, Major Evans.

Cooper had overheard the gloating conversation as he approached from the back of the shed the state authorities had constructed at the edge of his shipyard, having advised him in writing that the structure would be put up with or without his permission. Inside the shed stood a special ordnance furnace, its coals banked now. During a bombardment, the furnace would heat shot intended to start fires within Fort Sumter.

Churlish louts, Cooper thought as he stomped past the men and the shed. He coughed hard in the night damp. Out on Sumter a blue signal light was glowing. Looking at that, he wasn't forced to look at the keelson of the unfinished vessel. It sat there in the thickening mist, a mockery of all his dreams for the South. Well, he was no different from Brunel in that respect. The little engineer had seen his dream demolished, too.

Cooper noticed lights in a mortar battery farther down the shore. He decided not to continue walking in that direction. He squatted and let handfuls of sandy loam slip through his fingers as he stared seaward into the mist.

He was faced with a decision. Secretary of the Navy Mallory had telegraphed from Montgomery to say he was sending two members of the Committee on Naval Affairs to call on Cooper. They would arrive in the morning. He knew what they wanted.

His warehouse. His yard. His ships.

He thought their new government misguided, its cause tragic. Why, then, did he agonize for even one instant over how he would answer the visitors? He knew the answer to that, too.

He agonized because loyalty to his state was tugging at him like an ocean tide, tugging with a power he had never thought possible. He hated that, but he was unable to stop it.

He rose and tramped back toward the shot furnace. His stomach growled. He recalled he hadn't eaten since morning, when he had wolfed a slice of Judith's fine dark bread. He was uninterested in eating, uninterested in anything except the decision that had him stretched on an emotional rack. What should he do?

No, that wasn't precisely the question. Any man who professed to be sane should get out of the South while there was still time. He must rephrase it. What *would* he do?

He had only until morning to decide.

"Rex, what were you whispering about?" Ashton had been passing the pantry and had overheard the boy and the senior house man, Homer, conversing in a furtive, excited way.

The boy cringed away from his mistress. "Wasn't whisperin' about nothin', Miz Huntoon."

"Damn your nigger hide, I heard you. I distinctly heard the word *Linkum*."

Rex gulped. "Linkum? No, ma'am, I swear I never—"

The pressure of Homer's dark brown hand on his arm stopped him in mid-sentence. Homer, in his forties and stooped from years of toil, gazed at the boy with resigned eyes. "Won't do no good to lie. Go harder with both of us if you keep on. Better just to swallow the medicine."

He turned to Ashton, signifying his readiness to do what he had recommended to the youngster. But Rex was rebellious.

"No, Homer, I won't—"

Homer's crushing grip on his wrist made him cry out. Ashton's breathing grew loud and raspy as she said, "Take down your breeches, both of you."

Her hickory rod lay in its accustomed place in the kitchen. The cook and two house girls exchanged glances of alarm as the mistress rushed in, snatched the rod from the high shelf, and hurried out again.

Ashton felt compelled to nip this fascination with Lincoln before it grew to dangerous proportions. All over Charleston—all over the state, in fact—the slaves were stirring, whispering that one word—*Linkum*. Some who could read understood him to be the North's new ruler. Few of the rest knew much of anything about him, beyond the fact that he was a Black Republican. But their masters hated Black Republicans so violently that Linkum clearly had to be the Negro's friend.

In the pantry, Homer and Rex had dropped their trousers and faced the wall. Ashton ordered them to pull down their torn underdrawers as well. They were reluctant, but they obeyed. At the sight of the boy's sleek, muscled flanks, Ashton felt a little internal spasm.

"Five apiece," she said. "And if I ever again hear either of you utter the name of that rascally ape, you'll get ten—or more. Who will take the punishment first?"

Homer, calmly: "I will, ma'am."

Ashton's breasts felt tight within her dress. She was breathing fast. She saw Rex cast a swift, fearful look over his shoulder. "No, I think not," she murmured, and swung the rod.

The whack was loud as a shot in the pantry. Rex hadn't braced his palms on the wall firmly enough. His chin shot forward, and he got quite a bang. He yelped, then threw another look backward. A wild, resentful look; murderous, almost.

"Keep your eyes on the wall, nigger," Ashton said. She struck him with all the force she could muster.

Homer clenched his right hand, leaned his head forward, and closed his eyes.

Afterward, she felt as if she had passed through a torrential storm into more tranquil air. She retired to her room and there lay dozing pleasurably on a chaise. Her limbs had a languorous heaviness.

In her imagination she reexperienced the punishment. At first she pictured it exactly as it had happened, feeling many of the accompanying sensations. Then she varied the images; it was no longer a black boy and a black man she whipped, but a cringing, whining Billy Hazard.

711

She and Forbes LaMotte were frustrated because Billy was bottled up at Sumter, never allowed to come into the city. But with General Beauregard due to arrive at any moment, there might be a change. The earlier attempt to have Billy mauled and injured had been foolish, she realized now. Of course she would prefer to squash Billy personally but she and Forbes would be content if he died in the fort.

Unconsciously, her hands slipped down below her waist. Sweat stippled her upper lip and forehead. She shut her eyes and watched the screen of her imagination display a new picture: Billy amid fire and crumbling stone. The South Carolina batteries blew Sumter to pieces around him. Slowly he sank from sight. Breathing hard, she pressed herself.

Let it come, she thought. O Lord, let it come soon.

She moaned softly. A sudden movement of her body jerked the chaise two inches to one side.

The Georgian toppled over. Forbes LaMotte sidestepped to permit his victim to fall past his legs. The man landed face down in the sand of the alley. Overhead, thunder drummed in the dark clouds of a March afternoon.

Forbes flexed his bruised right hand, then adjusted his cravat. Behind him stood a slender, sallow young man wearing elegant clothes. He had let Forbes do most of the fighting.

Using his elbows, the Georgian attempted to rise. Forbes had knocked out three of his teeth. Blood and saliva coated his lips and chin. Gently Forbes lowered the sole of his shoe onto the man's head, then pushed. The man's face buried in the sand again.

Forbes reached inside his coat for a slim silver flask. He shook it. Half full. He uncorked it, put his head back, and gulped the rest. He tucked the flask into a roomy side pocket and glowered at the fourth man in the alley—another well-dressed Georgian who hunched against the wall of a shed, obviously frightened. The man had watched while Forbes kicked and pounded his companion into unconsciousness.

"Now, sir," Forbes said in a slurred voice. "Shall we resume the discussion that necessitated this little disciplinary action? Let's see. When Mr. Smith and I ran into you and your fellow visitor on the Battery, you were loudly criticizing those of us who reside in Charleston. You said we presumed to speak for all the South."

The sallow young man, Preston Smith, stepped forward. "Presumed arrogantly. Those were his exact words."

Forbes blinked. "I remember."

Preston Smith's malicious eyes flicked to the terrified Georgian. Preston enjoyed a good muss, especially when others did the fighting. He hoped he could keep this one going.

"He also said we act as if being born in South Carolina confers a patent of nobility."

"Patent of nobility," Forbes repeated with a bleary nod. "That was the remark that riled me the worst." With the toe of his boot he nudged the fallen man. "I should say we proved there's something to it. You two gentlemen met your betters today."

Preston snickered. "I'm not sure he believes you, old friend."

Forbes gave an exaggerated sigh. "Why, no, I don't believe he does. We shall just have to impress the lesson upon him too."

He stepped over the fallen man and moved toward the other Georgian, who would have melted into the shed wall if that had been possible. The man glanced one way, then the other, and, just as Forbes reached for him, bolted.

At the sight of the man's flying coattails, Preston burst out laughing. "You'd better not stop till you get to Savannah, you ignorant cracker."

"Tell them your friend is missing in action," Forbes shouted.

The running Georgian cast one wild look backward, then disappeared. Forbes laughed so hard, tears came to his eyes.

Preston fastidiously dusted his knees and sleeves with his kerchief. "Damn me, I hate all these tourists," he declared as Forbes picked up his hat. The friends started down the alley in the other direction. "They think they can come here and say whatever they please."

"It's our duty to teach 'em otherwise. Blasted dry work, though. Join me in another drink?"

"But Forbes, it's barely two in the afternoon."

Forbes didn't like the implication of the remark. "What the hell does that mean?"

Preston withheld his answer. How could he tell his friend that he was imbibing too heavily? Of late, Forbes did almost nothing but celebrate South Carolina's independence in various barrooms around town. And drinking did little to improve Forbes's disposition. When he lacked a target such as the two Georgians, he sometimes turned on his friends. Preston saw the warning signals that this might be about to happen again and hastily invented an excuse.

"Why, it only means I'd be glad to but I can't—I'm supposed to be at Doll Fancher's salon at two. Come, let's find your carriage again. Then I'll go on.''

"Don't need the carriage," Forbes snarled. "All I want is another drink.''

The two walked on in silence while the rain clouds muttered and darkened above them. When Preston inadvertently stumbled and bumped his friend, Forbes pushed him away, hard.

Their route took them from the alley to Gibbes Street, then down Legare to the Battery, where they came upon a company of elderly men drilling with equally ancient muskets.

The home guard had been visible in Charleston for several weeks. It was an unofficial police force designed to intimidate the slaves and keep them docile in the event all young and able-bodied men were suddenly called to military service. Preston hailed one of the guardsmen, a gray-bearded relative of his, Uncle Nab Smith.

Forbes felt raindrops on his forehead. The first splashes quickly became a drizzle. The rain hid the dark hulk of Sumter out in the harbor.

Forbes's carriage and driver were waiting by the seawall. Preston helped his friend inside. Attempting to negotiate the small step, Forbes fell twice. Once he was seated on the wine-colored plush upholstery, he crooked a finger at Preston.

"Climb in and I'll drop you at Doll Fancher's.''

"No, thank you, it's only a block. I'll be there by the time your boy turns this rig around.''

Forbes's smile grew stiff. "Goddamn it, Preston, I said get in and—''

"I'll see you in a day or two," Preston interrupted, knowing better than to linger. In such a mood Forbes had once broken a seaman's back in a brawl in a waterfront saloon. Although Preston had provoked that particular altercation with several sarcastic remarks, he had been horrified by his friend's capacity for violence.

Preston left quickly. Forbes leaned back against the cushions as the rain intensified. He struggled to remember the date. Oh, yes. March third. Tomorrow in Washington that damned ape would be inaugurated.

"Where you want to go, Mist' LaMotte?'' the driver called.

"I don't know. Drive up Meeting and I'll decide.''

He was weary and bored. That was why he drank so heavily and started fights with tourists. His occasional assignations with Ashton

714

no longer provided much satisfaction. Various local artillery units, eager to add the prestige of the LaMotte name to their roster, were begging him to accept a commission, but he had no interest in the offers. He hated discipline.

He was sufficiently lucid to realize that a peculiar simmering rage was loose within him. He knew his acquaintances recognized that fact. Even Preston, a vicious fighter when the odds were safely in his favor, stayed away from him a good part of the time. Clinging to the hand strap of the swaying carriage, Forbes wondered why he felt so angry and why brawling did little to relieve that anger.

Staring into the rain, he was driven to confront the answer. The one woman he had desired most had rejected him. He had never stopped hating Brett Main for favoring someone else. Paradoxically, he had never stopped wanting her, either.

He sat up suddenly, releasing the strap. Was the hurrying figure real or a figment of his imagination?

No, he wasn't that drunk. He thumped the roof and shouted over the chatter of the rain. "James, pull to the side." Then he leaned out the window and waved.

"Brett? Brett, over here!"

The moment she heard the voice, she recognized it. She turned to see Forbes stumble down from the carriage. He swept off his hat.

"Please permit me to drive you wherever you're going. A lady shouldn't walk in this weather."

That was obvious. But when setting out for the home of a seamstress several blocks away, Brett had assumed she could reach her destination before the shower started. Now the shower had become a downpour. She was getting soaked.

Surely it couldn't hurt to accept his assistance; he was, after all, a gentleman. Impulsively, she closed her dripping parasol and stepped toward the carriage.

She sank onto the plush cushions with a grateful sigh. Forbes closed the door behind her, took a seat opposite, and relayed the address of the seamstress to the Negro driver. The carriage lurched forward.

Forbes settled his hat on his knees. His smile had a sullen, almost angry quality, she realized with a sudden tight feeling in her stomach. His eyes were glassy. She began to regret her decision.

"Haven't seen you for an age, Brett. You look fetching, as always."

"You look fine yourself, Forbes." The words came with difficulty.

He pinched his waistcoat between thumb and forefinger. "Putting on weight, I'm afraid. I reckon that's what comes of spending so many hours in barrooms. Don't have much else to do. Nor much to think of besides you."

"Really, Forbes"—her laugh was uncomfortable, nervous—"we settled that a long time ago."

She glanced out the window on her side. They had gone only a block; the carriage was moving slowly. Good. She'd jump out if he grew boorish.

He watched her silently for a few seconds, his odd, sly smile heightening her tension. Abruptly, he dropped his hat on the cushion and heaved himself over next to her. The carriage springs creaked. His sudden movement somehow transmuted her fright to determination.

"I thought you were being courteous when you made your offer. Don't disillusion me."

"I can't be courteous. I care for you too damn much." He took hold of her wrist. "Brett—"

"Stop it," she said, not in a prudish way, but firmly.

"Afraid I can't do that, sweet." His thumb began to stroke back and forth over the inside of her wrist, just above the ruching on her muslin glove. "I can't keep you out of my mind five minutes, seems like. I would think you'd favor a man who cares for you that deeply."

With her left hand she reached for the handle of the door. "I have to get out."

He seized her shoulders, flinging her back against the wine-colored cushions. "Hell you do," he growled as he brought his mouth down on hers, hurting her.

Through his parted lips poured the smell of his breath, rancid as the fumes from a distillery. His right hand dropped to her bodice. Pinning her with his left side, he mauled her breast and breathed against her chin and throat.

"Jesus, I love you, Brett. Always have—"

"Let go of me!"

"No, damn it." He twisted onto his left hip, flung his right knee over her to pin her to the seat. The pressure of his fingers grew rougher. Through layers of cloth he hurt her nipple. Although she was terrified, she started to work her left hand out of the muslin glove.

"Brett, you don't belong with that sawed-off Yankee soldier. You need a man who's big enough in every respect to give you what a woman—"

716

With a shriek he jerked away. She had reached across and clawed his cheek. Three nail tracks bled.

It took him a moment to react. He touched his face, drew his hand away, and saw scarlet stains on the frilly cuff of his shirt. That sight focused his rage. Cursing, he again groped for her with both hands. She unfastened the door. It flapped open. Before she could leap out, he seized her right arm. She exclaimed softly, thinking he meant to do her injury. She leaned down, grasped her parasol from the floor, slashed at his head. Once, twice, three times—

"Mist' Forbes, what's wrong down there?"

The old driver guided the vehicle nearer the curb and reined to a halt. On the other side of Meeting, pedestrians gaped at the sight of a respectably dressed white woman struggling with a gentleman in his carriage. Brett was too frightened to worry about appearances. She hit Forbes again, then tore away from him and hurled herself out the door. She missed the step and sprawled in the muddy street.

"Ho, look out!" shouted a drayman, pulling his team aside at the last moment. Passing her with only inches to spare, the heavy wheels flung mud over her face and clothing.

She staggered to her feet, her hat falling off. The rain drenched her again. Forbes hung in the carriage doorway, looking like some demented goblin as he yelled:

"You goddamn bitch—"

She heard no more; she turned and ran.

Shaking, Forbes came to his senses. He realized men and women on the sidewalk were watching him. Someone mentioned his name. He flung himself back inside the carriage and jerked the door shut.

He leaned back, patted his cheek with his handkerchief. The sight of blood infuriated him all over again. He nearly punched a hole in the ceiling with his fist.

"Drive on!"

Fleeing the scene of his humiliation didn't help. He pulled out his flask, remembered it was empty, and hurled it out the window. He hated Brett more than ever. He wished he could throttle her to death, then row out to Sumter and shoot that Yankee son of a bitch she fancied.

Gradually, the sound of the rain and the motion of the carriage soothed him a little. He thought of Ashton, clung to her name and her image like a man clinging to a life preserver.

Ashton was on his side. Ashton would help him get revenge.

*

That night, hundreds of miles away, Stanley Hazard and Simon Cameron attended a reception for the President-elect.

Three railroad detectives provided by Mr. Pinkerton stood guard outside the doors of the private parlor at Willard's. Inside, cabinet members and guests mingled and talked softly. Lincoln had come down from his rooms a few minutes ago. Stanley had spoken with him. He was not impressed.

He left Lincoln cracking another joke and searched for his patron. He found Cameron in earnest conversation with Chase, the stiff, priggish secretary of the treasury. Of all the cabinet members, Chase was the most outspoken and perhaps the most unswerving on the need to free the Negroes. Stanley found the man's idealism offensive.

At last Cameron broke away and joined Stanley at the champagne bar. The boss looked powerful and important, Stanley thought. And well he might. Exactly as he had planned, Cameron had bargained his convention votes for the post of secretary of war in the new administration.

Cameron drank a little champagne, then tapped a bulge beneath his coat. "A friend passed me a summary of the inaugural address."

"What are the salient points?"

"About what you'd expect, given his past pronouncements." Cameron's voice was pitched low. His eyes kept moving, darting, to make certain no one wandered close enough to overhear. "He refuses to yield on disunion. Says it's unconstitutional and, ultimately, impossible. He'll continue to hold Sumter, but if there's to be war, the Confederacy will have to initiate it. Altogether"—again his eyes shifted, watching— "an undistinguished speech from an undistinguished man, not to say an inadequate one." Cameron murmured the last few words while bending his head to sip champagne.

Inadequate hardly described it, Stanley thought. Tomorrow General Scott would be stationing riflemen on the curbstones and rooftops along Pennsylvania Avenue, to guard against possible insurrection. A shameful beginning for what promised to be an inept administration. With a few exceptions, of course.

Cameron extended his glass for a refill. When he had it, he moved away from the bar, continuing, "But what do you think of the new President?"

Stanley glanced through the crowd to the ugly, angular profile. "A prairie buffoon. Any fellow who pokes you in the ribs and tells stories

718

as coarse as his certainly can't amount to much.''

''Precisely. In my opinion, that is the weakest man ever sent to the White House. But that's to our benefit. The power will then devolve to us.'' Suddenly animated, he signaled with his glass. ''Seward, old friend! Just the man I want to see.''

The boss rushed away. Soon he was arm in arm with the new secretary of state, whispering to him. Stanley consumed more champagne and basked in the reflected limelight. He was happy to be here, almost deliriously so.

He would have a post in Cameron's department. Isabel would be thrilled with Washington. For his part, Stanley was savoring the thought of power and of the chance to increase his wealth. Insiders always gained from their positions, the boss said. Stanley secretly hoped the rebels would go ahead and provoke war down at Charleston. If they did, the opportunities to make money would increase just that much more.

61

Early the next afternoon, Billy paced outside Major Anderson's office with his forage cap under his arm. He had to wait while the commandant finished a letter apologizing for a practice round that had slammed into the cotton bales at Fort Moultrie. With both the Sumter and South Carolina batteries being tested frequently, accidents were common. After each mishap, the offenders rushed an explanation to the other side. Most of the explanations were elaborately formal, but with accidental war a distinct possibility, Billy supposed too much apology was preferable to too little.

Hart, Anderson's orderly sergeant, appeared with the finished letter. "He'll see you now, sir," the noncom said as he hurried off down the dim, echoing passage.

Billy stepped into the commandant's office, another dingy brick cubicle lit by the stub of a candle. Anderson returned the younger officer's crisp salute with a slow, weary one. Then he pointed to a stool. "Rest yourself, Lieutenant. You won't be resting much during the next few days."

Anderson's fingers showed a tremor as he touched a fat pouch of oiled cloth. "I've written some new advices for General Scott. I'd like you to carry them."

"To Washington, sir?"

"Yes. I want the general to know that in my estimation penetrating the harbor defenses and reinforcing this garrison would now require a force of at least twenty thousand men. There are some other confidential communications in the pouch as well. Pack your kit and be ready in three hours."

Billy's mind reeled. To be released from this dark, oppressive place was what every man in the garrison wanted, though few admitted it. Would he have a chance to spend a little time with Brett before he left Charleston?

"I can be prepared sooner than that, sir."

Anderson shook his head. "Not necessary. Hart will be departing shortly to row over with my letter of apology to Captain Calhoun.

He will also call on Pickens at the Charleston Hotel, to obtain your clearance. Even with the governor's consent, a departure is a touchy business. I'm told that each time a boat puts out from our dock, bands of men swarm to the Battery. They hope it will be Doubleday coming over." After a curt, humorless laugh, Anderson added, "In any case, Hart won't be back for a while. You'll go at dusk or a little later."

"Yes, sir."

"And, Lieutenant—pack everything. Unlike some of the couriers I've dispatched to Washington, you won't be returning."

"*Sir?*"

Pale, Billy stared at his commanding officer. This was crushing news; he would be leaving Brett in a city that might be ravaged by war at any hour. Knowing that, why did the major have a queer half smile on his haggard face? Was Anderson losing his grip?

The major quickly explained. "You are on leave until tomorrow evening, at which time I shall expect you to board a northbound train. Hart has prepared your orders to that effect. You could use the intervening hours to call on your young lady. If you can get a message to her promptly, you might even have sufficient time to marry her. Hart's willing to deliver such a message if you can write it in the next ten minutes."

Billy was speechless. He could hardly believe his good fortune, Anderson noticed.

"Don't look so stunned, Lieutenant. Someone must go. Why not you? I sent Lieutenant Meade home to see his ailing mother in Virginia— this is a much happier set of orders. I do realize I'm treading in the province of your superior, the chief of engineers, but I expect he'll forgive me when I explain the circumstances."

Anderson's gaze grew somber again. "Even with clearance from the governor, you may have trouble getting through the city. That's why I'm keeping you here till it's almost dark."

Billy decided it was time to stop questioning his luck and start capitalizing on it. "Sir, if the schooner could take me to the C.S.C. pier above the Customs House, I could have Cooper Main meet me with a closed carriage. He could drive me to Tradd Street, and Brett and I could slip out of Charleston before daylight."

"You don't want to be married at Main's house?"

"I think it would be safer to travel up to Mont Royal. There's a railway flag stop not far from the plantation."

"Well, whatever you decide, getting through the city will be the hard part. I urge you to keep your revolver fully loaded at all times."

Billy saluted and pivoted, leaving the commandant staring at the candle with melancholy eyes.

At the boat landing, Anderson shook his hand. "You're an excellent officer, Lieutenant Hazard. With a few more years of experience, you'll be an outstanding one. Give my regards to your bride."

"Sir, I will. I can't thank you enough—"

"Yes, you can. Get that pouch to Scott. I want him to understand the hazards if he should attempt to storm the bar with a few hundred men in longboats." Anderson's voice grew husky with strain. "I repeat what I have said before. If this country's to be plunged into a bloodbath, the responsibility will be Washington's, not ours."

He stepped back, fading into darkness. "Please get aboard, sir," a voice called from the deck of the little schooner. Billy could just glimpse a face above the binnacle light.

He hurried down the steps while the slack sails flapped in the night wind. An ominous sound, somehow.

"Thank the Lord I was home when Anderson's orderly arrived," Cooper said as Billy jumped to the C.S.C. pier. "Judith's waiting in the carriage."

"Where's Brett?"

"At the house. She wanted to come along, but Judith urged her to stay and pack. She doesn't have all that much time to assemble her trousseau—we'll be on the road well before sunrise. I have already sent a man to Mont Royal. Orry's to have the rector present tomorrow afternoon at one sharp."

"When does the train leave?"

"A little over three hours later. Half past four."

They carried on the conversation as they strode rapidly toward the head of the pier where the carriage was waiting. The fast pace matched Billy's heartbeat. In spite of his tension, he felt exhilarated, happy for the first time in months.

"Thank you, Gerd," Cooper said to a stout man who handed him the reins. "I'll drive, Billy. Stay well back from the window. There's always a small crowd loitering at the Customs House, and those buttons on your uniform shine like lanterns."

He was straining to keep his tone light, but Billy could hear an anxious note. Cooper slipped as he mounted the spokes of the front wheel. He grimaced, then completed his climb, saying, "Sometimes not owning slaves is damned inconvenient. You must do everything for yourself. No wonder the institution's lasted."

Billy managed a chuckle as he opened the door on the left side. Judith was seated on the right. He greeted her, at the same time touching the leather dispatch case slung over his left shoulder. The catch was still secure.

Cooper hawed and started the carriage. By the light of a lantern on the warehouse gable, Billy saw tears on Judith's cheek. "What's the matter?" he exclaimed.

"Nothing, nothing." She smiled and cried at the same time. "I'm a ninny to carry on so, but I can't help it. In these times there are so few reasons to be joyful, but this is one." A sniff, a firm shake of her head. "I do apologize."

"Don't. I feel the same way."

"Look sharp," Cooper called. "Larger crowd than usual tonight."

Billy shifted his saber so that he could move more easily. Then he eased his revolver partway out of the holster. Ahead, on the right, men were laughing and talking boisterously. Suddenly one of them shouted, "You, there. Hold up."

Billy's stomach knotted as he felt the carriage slow down. Cooper swore an exasperated oath.

The voices of the men grew louder. Billy hitched over to the center of the seat, the darkest part of the carriage. Obliquely through the right-hand window he could glimpse the front of the Customs House, once Federal property.

The carriage swayed to a stop. Judith held her breath. "State your name and business," said a rough voice.

"My name is Main, I'm a citizen of Charleston, and my business is my own. I'll thank you to release my horse and stand aside."

"He looks all right, Sam," another man said. The first speaker grumbled something. Billy heard movement outside.

Judith clutched his arm. "Get down! They're coming to look in."

Just as she whispered, Cooper applied the whip. But the carriage didn't move. "Let go of the horse," Cooper demanded. At the same time a coarse face appeared in the right window. The man jumped on the step. The lanterns on the Customs House lit up the carriage interior. The man clung to the window frame, eyes rounding.

"Sojer in here!"

A loud outcry followed. "Is it Doubleday?" Pushing and shoving, others appeared at the window. Billy pulled his revolver.

Simultaneously, someone ordered Cooper to climb down. The reply was the whack of a whip against flesh. An unseen man let out a shriek. Cooper yelled like a teamster and lashed the horse.

The carriage lurched into motion. Meantime the man on the step had levered the door open and was struggling to work himself around it and thus inside. The man's right hand still gripped the bottom of the open window. Billy leaned across Judith and rapped the man's knuckles with the gun barrel.

The man's fingers spasmed, but he held on. Billy shoved his left boot against the door and pushed. The door swung outward. The man dropped from sight.

Upraised fists and glaring eyes went by in a blur. Then Cooper raced the carriage into the darkness beyond the Customs House. He turned right, recklessly fast. Billy was struggling to catch the door and close it. He almost fell out headfirst before he was successful.

A moment later he leaned back and rested his revolver on his leg, gasping for breath.

"You were very quick," Judith said by way of a compliment.

"Had to be. Didn't want to miss my own wedding."

But his smile was forced. His heart was still hammering, and he'd be a long while forgetting the bloodthirsty look of the faces outside the carriage. They told him again how deep and dark the schism had become.

The sight of Brett drove away all his grim thoughts. Left alone in the parlor—Cooper had quietly shut the doors—the two young people hugged and kissed for five minutes.

He had almost forgotten how fragrant her hair could be, how sweet her mouth tasted, how firm and strong her bosom felt when she pressed against him. Finally, gasping and laughing, they sank to a settee, holding hands.

"I wish we could be married tonight," she said. "I know I won't sleep a wink just anticipating tomorrow."

Reluctantly, he said, "I won't be coming back to Charleston. Are you certain you're willing to go north?"

The enormous significance of his question registered on her for the first time. Uncertainty came, then fear. It would be hard to live in the midst of Yankees, away from her family.

But she loved him. Nothing else mattered.

"I'd go anywhere with you," she said, murmuring against his cheek. "Anywhere."

Shortly after ten that night, Cooper paid a short visit to the house on East Battery. As Ashton listened to him speak, she maintained her composure only with great effort. After Cooper left, she hurried to the study to relay the news to Huntoon.

He flung down the brief he had been studying. "I really don't fancy attending the wedding of a damn Yankee."

"James, she's my sister. We're going."

Before he could argue, she picked up her skirts and rushed out. She stopped in the hall, pressed her palms to her cheeks, and struggled to organize her thoughts. By this time tomorrow, if no one interfered, Billy and her sister would be gone for good. She had only this one chance.

But one was all she needed.

Smiling faintly, she moved on. At the desk where she kept the household accounts, she wrote a note to Forbes, telling him to ride upriver early in the morning. She said he could take a helper if he wished, but it had to be someone trustworthy. He was to wait at Resolute for further word.

She added a few more lines of explanation, closed and waxed the sheet, then ran to the kitchen with the note and a pass.

"Rex, take this to Mr. Forbes LaMotte. Try his room on Gibbes. If he isn't there, go to the saloon bar of the Mills House. The barman often knows Mr. LaMotte's whereabouts. Don't give up, and don't come back until this is safely in his hands."

Cowed by the whipping he had received, Rex nodded and kept nodding until she finished her instructions. But as the boy slipped down the stairs to the back door, his eyes shone with a dull rage that expressed his hunger to pay her back.

Cooper's crowded carriage reached Mont Royal late in the morning. The March sun was mild, the cloudless sky that soft, pure shade of blue that Brett believed to be unique to Carolina. Would she ever see it again?

The children scrambled out the moment the carriage stopped. Cousin Charles ruffled Judah's hair affectionately, then took Marie-Louise by her waist, lifting her and whirling her around. She clung to his neck, squealing delightedly.

Judith followed Brett out of the carriage. Billy came next, feeling hot and awkward in the new broadcloth suit obtained from a German tailor Cooper had awakened at midnight. Billy was startled to see Charles in full uniform, buttons polished, saber hanging from his sash.

The friends embraced. "Why in the world are you all dressed up?" Billy wanted to know.

Charles grinned. "I'm dressed up in your honor, Bunk. I figured that if one officer asked another to be his best man, the best man should look the part. Truth is, I miss the uniform. The Army, too."

Orry emerged from the house, his somber appearance enhanced by the long, dark coat he wore. To the noisy group on the piazza he announced, "The Reverend Saxton will be here at half past twelve. I told him to come early. He's such a toper, I figured he'd want a stiff drink to see him through the ceremony."

Laughter. Cooper hauled down a small leather trunk in which Billy had packed his revolver, his uniform, and the leather dispatch case. Cooper thumped the trunk on the ground beside Brett's and wiped his forehead with his sleeve. Brett said to Orry, "How's Mother?"

"About the same. I explained three times that you were being married. Each time she professed to understand, but I know she didn't."

Judah jumped up and down, pointing. "Someone's coming."

Sure enough, rolling up the lane between the great trees, a carriage could be seen in a dust cloud. "That's Ashton," Brett said—without great enthusiasm, Billy observed.

With a jingle of traces and another billow of dust, the carriage braked behind Cooper's. From the driver's seat, Homer regarded the white people impassively, while Rex sprang down to open the door for Ashton and her husband.

Huntoon's congratulations were clearly perfunctory. Ashton darted from Brett to Billy, hugging each in turn and treating them to blazingly sweet smiles.

"Oh, I'm so happy for you and Brett. I can say that with complete sincerity, being married myself."

Her eyes flashed like polished gems. Billy couldn't tell how she really felt, but remembering past intimacies, he reddened as she pressed her cheek to his. Then she puckered her lips and gave him a loud, smacking kiss. Cooper noticed Homer gazing down at his mistress with sullen eyes. He wondered at the reason.

Charles scraped a match on one of the white pillars. It left a mark, to Orry's visible displeasure. Billy pointed to the long green cigar Charles held between clenched teeth.

"When did you take up my brother's habit?"

"Since I came home. Have to fill the time somehow. I'd rather be fighting, but I reckon you can't have everything."

It was a clumsy attempt at humor, ill timed and inappropriate, both to the occasion and to the background of essentially tragic events in Charleston. The remark was greeted by complete silence. Charles blushed and busied himself with generating smoke from the ten-inch-long Havana.

"Come on, you two," Ashton trilled. She took Billy's arm with her right hand, Brett's with her left. "Aren't you simply famished? I am. Surely there's something in the house—" Orry nodded. "Oh, isn't this an exciting day? Such memorable things are going to happen to both of you!"

And with that she swept them inside.

Charles lingered after the others had gone. He was embarrassed by his gaffe and curious about the high color in Ashton's face. She seemed genuinely happy about her sister's marriage. Why, then, did he have a troubling feeling?

A feeling that she was giving a performance.

62

The heat of the day bathed Madeline with drowsy warmth. She had just come from the kitchen, where she had seen to the preparation of spiced ham for dinner. The kitchen girls said the weather was fine and rather cool. If that was true, why was she sweltering?

Justin chided her for complaining of being hot. In the last few years heat bothered her as it never had before. She wondered whether some internal change was responsible. But she felt too lazy, too sleepy, to think about the question for very long.

Drifting along Resolute's downstairs piazza with no particular destination in mind, she tried to recall her husband's whereabouts. Oh, yes. He had tramped into the fields with his old musketoon for some target practice. Justin took his service with the Ashley Guards very seriously. He predicted with great glee that in a matter of weeks he'd be shooting in earnest.

"—time is it?"

"Almost one. She should be sending another message in an hour or so."

Three feet away from one of the open windows of the study, Madeline stopped to listen. It took her several seconds to recall the identities of the speakers: Justin's nephew Forbes and his unpleasant, rail-thin friend Preston Smith. Both had arrived unexpectedly on horseback at mid-morning. Why Forbes had not ridden another ten miles up the Ashley to his father's plantation he had failed to explain. Madeline received few explanations for anything anymore. She was treated as an object, a fixture. She was usually too spent and indifferent to care.

Now, however, a raw note of urgency in the voices pricked through the dull mental state in which she seemed to drift perpetually. Forbes had used the word *she*. Why would a woman be sending him a message at Resolute? To arrange an assignation, perhaps?

She rejected that possibility as soon as she heard him ask, "The pistols ready?"

"Yes."

"You filled the powder flask?"

"I did. We'll have to be mighty careful with the powder. Wouldn't want to pour too much in one of those guns."

"Damn right."

Both young men laughed, a cheerless sound, almost brutal. Like a tiny ticking clock, fear began to pulse in Madeline's mind.

She deliberately blinked several times. This needed her attention. Her *full* attention. She shifted her weight to her left foot. The boards beneath her creaked.

"Forbes, I heard something."

"Where?"

"Not sure. Might have been outside."

"I didn't hear a thing."

"You weren't paying attention."

"All right, go look if you're scared," Forbes said with a sneer. Dizzy, Madeline pressed sweating palms against the white siding. Sunlight through festoons of Spanish moss laid a shifting pattern of shadow on her pale, wasted face.

"Oh, never mind," Preston grumbled, shamed. "Probably just one of the niggers."

Madeline almost swooned with relief. She pushed away from the wall. Gathering her skirts as quietly as she could, she hurried toward the end of the piazza—away from the open windows. The conspiratorial voices speaking of messages and loaded guns had succeeded in piercing her lethargy. She must try to stay alert to learn more. It was no easy task. Languorous indifference was lapping at her mind again.

She fought it as she slipped into the house by a side entrance. She must not let down. Something was afoot at Resolute. Something peculiar and—if she could believe what she heard in those voices—something sinister as well.

Charles gave Billy an envelope.

"Train tickets to the—to Washington. I almost said capital. But it's only your capital now. Old habits break mighty hard."

Billy tucked the envelope into his pocket. Charles held out a small velvet box. "You'll need this, too."

Billy pressed the catch, then reddened. "My Lord, I completely forgot about a ring."

"Orry figured you might, with everything so rushed." Charles prepared to light another mammoth cigar. "Wish I had a few of these

730

to send to George. Don't know if he's man enough to smoke 'em, though.''

Billy laughed. Orry opened the library door and looked in. "If the groom and best man are ready, we'd better start. The rector's already consumed three glasses of sherry. One more and he won't be able to read the prayer book.''

"Oh, you look just lovely,'' Ashton said with a clap of her hands.

Brett was fussing in front of a pier glass. She plumped up one of the dolman sleeves of her new dress of dark orange silk. "I'm so glad I could be here to stand up with you,'' Ashton went on. "I'm so grateful you asked me.''

Brett hurried to the older girl, took her hands, and felt affection flowing between them. "You're my sister. I wouldn't want anyone else. But I'm the one who should say thank you. I know how you felt about Billy once upon a time.''

"That was just a silly infatuation.'' Ashton pulled away, then turned her back. Her voice rose slightly. "I have the man I want. James is a wonderful, considerate husband. He—''

Orry's impatient call drifted up the stairs. Brett rushed to the bed for her bouquet of dried flowers. "We'd better go.''

"What time does your train leave the flag stop?''

"I think Billy said four-thirty. Why?''

"I want Homer to drive the two of you there in our carriage.''

"Ashton, that isn't neces—''

"Hush,'' Ashton interrupted, composed again. "I'll have it no other way. Our carriage is ever so much more comfortable than Cooper's old rattletrap. Besides, Cooper doesn't have a coachman. It's disgraceful to see a member of the Main family doing nigger work—''

Bombarding her sister with words, Ashton urged her out of the door. "You run downstairs, and I'll be there in a jiffy. I just want to find Homer, so everything will be ready.''

It was Rex, not Homer, whom Ashton sought after she slipped down the back stairs. She ordered the boy to race to Resolute on foot, with instructions to deliver her message to no one but Forbes LaMotte. She reinforced the order by digging her nails into Rex's thin brown forearm until she saw pain in his eyes. The nigger had been uppity ever since the whipping. She knew he was just itching to get even. If she kept him scared, he wouldn't dare.

She wrote a pass and shooed Rex out through the pantry. Then she patted her carefully done hair, fixed a sweet smile on her face, and glided to the front of the house to participate in the last happy moment of Billy Hazard's life.

"And now, you may kiss the bride."

After this pronouncement, the Reverend Mr. Saxton exhaled in a way that carried sherry fumes to those seated nearby. Clarissa pressed her palms together like a delighted child. She had watched the ceremony with great interest, even though it involved strangers.

Behind her, Marie-Louise uttered a dreamy sigh, then murmured, "Oh, wasn't it lovely?"

"It's as close as you'll ever get to the altar," her brother Judah said with a leer. "You're ugly as a fence post."

The girl kicked his shin. "And you're mean as a snake."

From behind, Cooper flicked each on the ear with the tip of his index finger, then induced silence with a fatherly scowl.

Brett had heard scarcely a word of the reading from the prayer book. When they had to kneel, it had been necessary for Billy to give her a gentle nudge. She knew the ceremony was sacred and important, but her heart was beating too fast for concentration. In a couple of hours she would be leaving the land of her childhood to be a wife in a strange, even hostile country. The prospect was terrifying—until the moment she gazed into her husband's eyes, so full of love and reassurance.

He put his arms around her. She felt his strength flood into her. With Billy beside her, she could suffer through the worst the North could offer. She would hide whatever longing or fear she felt and build a fine future for both of them.

Kissing him, she made that silent vow.

Orry had chosen to sit in the third and last row of chairs, fearful of how he might react during the ceremony. Fortunately, he remained dry-eyed, although he felt the churn of powerful emotions.

He thought of Madeline. Of old age and the days passing in lonely procession. He thought of the crisis at Sumter. Even a year ago it would have been inconceivable to imagine that an American family like the Mains would be living under a new flag.

Perhaps he was prey to so much turmoil because any wedding was a watershed. A joyous occasion, yet a marking of profound change from the way things had been. He was determined to emphasize the happy aspect. He kissed his sister's cheek and congratulated her warmly after the ceremony.

"I hope you mean that," she said, nestling against Billy, who held her protectively, one arm around her waist. "I'd like to think this marriage will help keep our families close, no matter what happens."

Orry looked at the bridegroom. A handsome, competent young man, brother of his best friend. Yet this same young man with the broad, almost bemused smile normally wore not a fine broadcloth wedding suit but a uniform. "I'd like to think so, too," Orry declared, trying to conceal the doubt suddenly engulfing him. "Come on, now—into the dining room while the wine is still cold."

He shepherded them out. They passed Ashton, who clung to the arm of her bored, fretful husband. Ashton stared at the newlyweds with an intense gaze that fortunately went unnoticed.

In the foyer at Resolute, Forbes listened to Rex's message, then sent him to the kitchen to claim a reward of some hot cornbread. Justin strolled out of the study with Preston Smith. The sleeves of Justin's silk shirt bore signs of his tramp through the fields—bits of leaf and twig. Preston had a large saddlebag slung over one shoulder.

Both men glanced at Forbes, who nodded and said, "Four-thirty."

Preston looked past his friend to an ormolu clock standing on a fine fruitwood chest, just below the old saber on the wall. "Then we have plenty of time."

"But I'd just as soon saddle up and leave now. I don't want to risk missing them."

"Nor I," Preston agreed with a sly smile.

Justin smiled too. He swaggered to the wall, moistened the ball of this thumb, and wiped away some speck only he could see on the nicked blade. The sun through the fanlight flooded the wall around the weapon, setting it afire.

"Boys, I wish you well," Justin said as he drew his thumb back and forth along the blade. "You'll be performing a public service by killing young Mr. Hazard. There'll be one less officer in the Yankee army. It'll be a fine comeuppance for that Mont Royal crowd, too."

"My sentiments exactly." Forbes grinned, but his eyes were hard.

"I'll be waiting for news of your success," Justin called as they tramped out. Giving a pleased sigh, he started back to the study. After he had taken only a few steps, he was distracted by a faint noise

733

at the head of the staircase. When he spoke, his voice was unexpectedly hoarse.

"What the devil are you doing up there, Madeline?"

It was obvious what she was doing. She was listening.

Standing in the deep afternoon shadow, she clutched the stair rail tightly. Then she descended two steps with more than her usual animation, he thought. Sudden anxiety touched him. Had the recent doses of laudanum through some mischance been too weak?

She clung to the banister with white hands, coming down another step, and another. The black silk of her bodice rose and fell in a way that suggested great effort. Her shadow-circled eyes brimmed with disgust.

The situation called for a firm stand. He marched to the center of the foyer, planted his boots wide apart, and hooked his thumbs over his belt. "Eavesdropping on our guests, were you?" The question carried an unmistakable threat.

"Not intentionally. I"—her voice strengthened—"I was on my way to the sewing room. What were you talking about, Justin? Who are they going to kill?"

"No one."

"I heard the name Hazard."

"Just your imagination. Get back to your room."

"No."

She came down two more steps, then closed her eyes and caught her breath. Her pale forehead glistened with little sparkles of perspiration. He realized she was still struggling against the effects of the drug.

"No," she repeated. "Not until you explain. Surely I misunderstood. You can't be sending your own nephew out to murder someone."

Panic engulfed him then. He blurted, "You stupid slut, get back to your room. Now!"

Again Madeline shook her head, gathering her strength to continue her slow, labored descent of the stairs. "I'm leaving," she said.

It took her the better part of ten seconds to negotiate the next two risers. He knew then that he had been foolish to panic. She was too weak to do anything about what she had overheard. He managed to relax a little and let his amusement show.

"Oh? To go where?"

"That"—she rubbed her forehead with a handkerchief crushed in her left hand—"is my affair."

Her mind had grasped the sense of desperate urgency a moment after Justin had spoken the name Hazard. Now she heard hoofbeats

734

echoing down the lane as she reached the bottom of the stairs. Fear renewed her strength, helping to overcome the terrifying lethargy. She stumbled toward the front door. Justin sidestepped, blocking her.

"Please let me pass."

"I forbid you to leave this house."

At the end of the sentence his voice cracked and grew strident. That was the final proof that the plotting was altogether real. Someone at Mont Royal was to be slain. She didn't know the reason, but she knew she must prevent it—if she could.

She started around her husband. He fisted his hand, moved deliberately to her left, and smashed her in the side of the head. With a cry, she sprawled on the floor.

Lying there, she stared dazedly up at him for a time that, to her, seemed endless. Then, gasping, she put her hands beneath her, regained her feet, and once more moved on across the foyer.

Justin struck her again. This time the back of her head hit a corner of the fruitwood chest, a sharp, hurting blow. Her outcry was loud. She rose on one knee, desperately striving to move.

A door opened. Two black faces peered from the rear hall as Justin loomed over her. "If you insist on behaving like a stubborn animal, you'll be treated like one." He kicked her hard under her left breast.

Madeline recoiled back against the chest again. The chest hit the wall and rattled the saber. The ormolu clock tipped over, rolled off, and shattered. She lay gasping, fighting for breath, while her eyes watered and everything blurred.

Justin swung around and strode across the foyer. "Goddamn you, what are you staring at? Close that door or I'll flay you."

The terrified slaves disappeared. Madeline's vision cleared a little. She fumbled for a grip on the edge of the chest and then, by force of will, dragged herself up.

Justin turned, saw her on her feet, and swore. She heard the staccato drumming of his foot heels behind her as he charged, spewing filthy curses. With an agonizing effort, she snatched the saber from its pegs, whirled, and slashed.

The nicked edge opened his face from his left brow to the midpoint of his jaw. For a second, pink meat showed beneath the separated skin. Then blood began to leak, spilling down his cheek and spattering his silk shirt.

He pressed his hand to the wound. "You fucking whore!" With his other hand outstretched, he lunged toward her.

She flung the saber away and instinctively swayed out of his way.

735

His momentum carried him on. He struck the wall headfirst, like some actor in a low farce, and slowly sank to his knees. He rested his bleeding face on the chest and moaned.

Two other slaves hovered outside, attracted by the noise. Madeline recognized one of them. "Ezekiel, come with me. I need the buggy." She gestured to the second black. "See to Mr. LaMotte."

Two minutes later she was whipping the buggy down the lane toward the river road.

"Young. He said *young*."

The buggy's left rear wheel slammed into a deep hole, almost throwing her off the seat. She fought to keep the vehicle from careening into the ditch as it flashed by the Six Oaks. The open air had sharpened her senses and cleared her head somewhat. She had just remembered her husband's reference to *young* Mr. Hazard. She took that to mean George's brother was the intended victim. He must have left the fort in Charleston harbor, but where was he now?

Light-dappled trees streamed by in a blur. Wind beat at her face. What a prize fool she had been to stay with Justin for so long. For months and months, her will to resist had been sapped by a puzzling exhaustion. Before that, it was her misguided sense of horror that had kept her at Resolute.

But there was no honor in the man to whom she had been brokered in marriage, nor in most of his family. Until this afternoon, however, she hadn't realized how degraded they were.

She had paused at the head of the staircase, looked down, and discovered Forbes receiving a whispered message from the young slave. The boy didn't live at Resolute, so obviously he had been sent from somewhere else. Sent with a message Forbes was anxious to receive.

Then Justin had strolled into sight with young Smith. She had at first believed she was listening to the planning of some prank. In a few moments the cruel words and facial expressions told her the reference to killing was meant literally.

Now she hoped she might find young Mr. Hazard at Mont Royal. Failing that, she prayed he could be located, warned in time. Orry would know what to do. Oh, God, she should have left Justin and married Orry long ago.

The cooling rush of air continued to invigorate her body and her mind. The pins and shell combs that fastened her hair had all worked oose, and the long, black strands began to trail out behind her. Lather was already showing on the wild-eyed gelding that propelled the buggy at breakneck speed.

She felt an immense, exultant sense of release. She would never go back to Resolute. Never go back to Justin—

And damn the consequences.

63

Shortly before three, the family gathered to wave good-bye to the newlyweds. Billy wanted to leave early enough for a leisurely ride to the little woodland way station.

It was a perfect afternoon for a wedding trip, Charles thought as he lit another cigar. Mild March sunshine slanted through the mossy oak trees, and the air was rich with the smell of wet earth. The low-country spring was coming on. Damn if he didn't feel like riding down to Charleston and finding a girl.

He helped Homer lift and tie trunks and portmanteaus on top of Huntoon's carriage. During this, Brett and Billy said their farewells to the family members, Ashton standing aside to be last. "Oh, I do wish you both Godspeed and much happiness. A long life, too," she added. Sunshine flashed in her dark eyes as she hugged her sister.

"Thank you, Ashton," Billy said. He shook her hand in an awkward way. In fact, Charles thought awkward the perfect word to describe Billy's behavior with Ashton all afternoon. Well, no wonder; Billy had been infatuated with her for a good long time. In Charles's opinion, his friend had wound up with the better girl. Ashton had drive and brains, but a mean streak, too.

"Bison"—Billy stepped up to Charles and extended his hand—"take care of yourself especially if things heat up at Sumter."

"Sure will try." Their clasp was firm and long. "You keep in touch. 'Course, I know you won't be able to do it right away. Other things occupy a man who's just married."

"I'm sure counting on that."

They both laughed. Brett had just finished embracing her mother one final time. She wiped away a tear and said teasingly, "That sounds wicked."

Charles grinned. "You're right, but we need a smidgen of smut in these festivities. The bridegroom didn't get a proper bachelor dinner."

"Lucky to get a proper wedding trip in times like these," Orry said in his dour way.

Clarissa continued to smile and blink like a child who was bewildered but determined to be pleasant in spite of it. Some of the house servants had slipped outside to join the leave-taking, so there was a crowd applauding and calling encouragement as Billy helped his new wife into the carriage.

He leaned out and waved. So did Brett. Sunshine glowed on her tears. Homer shook the reins over the back of the team. As the carriage pulled away, everyone waved and shouted more farewells. Charles drew his saber and gave the newlyweds a formal salute just for the devil of it.

Peering past the blade in front of his nose, he noticed Ashton dabbing her eyes with a hanky in one hand while she waved with the other. Just as he lowered his sword to sheathe it, he caught one full view of her face—a smug smile, lasting no more than a few seconds and unnoticed by the others, all of them watching the carriage rattling down the lane through slanting rays of light.

Charles's neck prickled. He stepped back so that a pillar hid him from Ashton. No matter what she had told the newlyweds a moment ago, she surely did not look as if she wished them well. What in the world was going on?

Something odd, for certain. Perhaps he'd get a clue if he kept his eyes open and didn't drink too much.

He asked Cuffey to bring him a glass of champagne. Then he unfastened the collar of his uniform and sprawled in a rocker in a cool patch of shadow. He rocked slowly, alone and content to be. Sipping and rocking, he finished the champagne before his patience was rewarded. A black boy appeared at the corner of the house, dusty and out of breath. "Homer be here, sir?"

"No, he left with the carriage. He'll be back presently."

It took Charles a moment to place the youngster. Rex, that was his name; Ashton's other servant. Where had he been? His faded blue flannel shirt was dark with sweat, as if he had run a long way.

Avoiding Charles's eyes, the boy hunkered down on the far side of a pillar. Charles distinctly recalled saying a few words to Homer during the eating and drinking after the ceremony. Rex had been nowhere in sight. Puzzling.

Charles raised his head in response to noise and a dust cloud in the lane. The sound of racing hooves and buggy wheels quickly grew louder. He jumped to his feet when he spied the vehicle's haggard, frightened-looking driver.

"Madeline," he called, tossing aside his cigar as he ran into the drive. A moment later he seized the bridle of her exhausted horse, then helped her down. He started to release her waist, but she clung to him.

"Madeline, you look scared to death. What's wrong?"

She gazed up at the tall young officer, her expression confused. She struggled to collect herself. All at once she noticed Rex sitting tensely against the pillar. Observations began to connect.

"I saw that boy at Resolute just a little while ago. I'm sure of it."

By then Rex had raced down the piazza and out of sight.

The motion of the carriage was soothing, the mood it created euphoric. Shadows of pines and water oaks flickered on the cushions opposite them, projected there by the light falling through roadside groves. Billy held Brett in the curve of his left arm.

"Happy?" he asked.

She sighed. "Blissfully. I never thought we'd reach this moment."

"I never thought Orry would allow us to reach it."

"It was your brother who melted him, you know."

Billy chuckled. "The old grads say that if you get through West Point, the place will influence your life forever—in ways you can't imagine when you're a cadet. I finally believe it."

Brett thought a moment. "How long do you expect you'll be detained in Washington?"

"No way of telling. It could be days, weeks, or even—"

"Horsemen coming, Lieutenant Hazard."

Homer's voice turned Billy toward the open window. The slave didn't sound alarmed. Yet the mere fact that he had alerted his passengers suggested something unusual about the riders. Billy could hear them off the left rear quarter of the carriage. The hoofs thudded on woodland earth. They were approaching through the trees. Peculiar.

"Who is it?" Brett asked.

Billy leaned out the window. Dust clouds speared with sunlight spread behind the carriage. Two dim figures, centaurlike, loomed in that dust, but he could discern no details until the horses stretched into a gallop. Out of the dust came the riders. Billy's hand clenched on the sill of the window.

"An old friend of yours. That LaMotte fellow."

Even then Brett acted more puzzled than worried. Forbes spurred ahead. His companion, a skinny fellow, finely dressed and about his own age, was close behind. Brett leaned from the other window.

"Why, that's old Preston Smith. What in the world are the two of them doing on this twopenny road?"

Billy had a suspicion they weren't riding for the sport of it. And they weren't out here in search of company; the carriage hadn't passed a human habitation for several miles. A rider appeared on either side of the carriage.

"Homer, pull up," Forbes yelled. He had a big smile on his face, but it struck Billy as false. Forbes gestured in a commanding way. "I said pull up!"

Looking worried, the driver tugged on the reins and shifted his foot to the brake lever. The carriage swayed as it stopped. All around it dust rose slowly, like a curtain. The branches of overhanging trees reached down to brush the luggage lashed on top. At this point the road narrowed to little more than parallel dirt tracks with a high crown of weeds between.

Preston Smith coughed, then put away the kerchief he had been holding to nose and mouth. Forbes rode around the back of the coach to Billy's side. He kicked his left leg up onto his saddle and rested his elbow on the inside of his knee. Brett leaned across her husband.

"It's quite a surprise to see you way out here, Forbes."

Dust lay all over Forbes's hair, lightening it several shades. He appeared relaxed and friendly. Yet Billy distrusted that impression; there was an odd glint in his eyes. Billy thought of his service revolver. It was packed away up on top. Damnation.

"Had to pay my respects," Forbes replied. "You know my friend Preston Smith, I believe."

With a cool nod, Brett said, "Yes, we've met."

"No, sir," Forbes went on. "I couldn't let the bride and bridegroom leave without offering a word of congratulations." His smile glowed. "I know you'll forgive me if I don't say the best man won."

Below the window, out of his line of sight, Brett clutched her husband's knee. Billy's heart beat faster. He voiced the thought that had occurred to both of them.

"LaMotte, how did you know we were married?"

Smith patted his skittish horse. "Oh, we just heard it somewhere. I don't believe I've had the honor, sir. You are Lieutenant Hazard?"

His tone said meeting Billy was anything but an honor. Billy stared him down. "That's right."

"Preston Smith. Your servant."

Smith's smile was contemptuous. All at once Billy didn't believe

742

this encounter had happened by accident. He glimpsed the jaws of a trap.

Homer cleared his throat. "We'd best not tarry or we'll miss the train, Lieutenant."

Forbes looked at the black man. "Bound for the passenger stop, are you?"

Homer didn't blink. "Yes, sir, and I believe we'll mosey along."

"Nigger, you aren't going anywhere till I give you leave."

Angry, Billy said, "Drive on, Homer." From the corner of his eye he saw Smith lean backward, reach down to a saddlebag, and bring up a huge brass-chased flintlock dueling pistol. It was swiftly, almost effortlessly, done. Smith smiled as he pointed the gun at Homer.

"You touch those reins and there'll be nigger blood all over this road."

"We don't mean to be quarrelsome," Forbes said, his grin bigger than ever. "But we rode a piece to pay our respects, and we mean to do it. Now, Mr. Yankee Soldier, you climb down from that coach and out from behind your wife's skirts so I can congratulate you proper."

Brett's hand tightened again. "Billy, don't."

But anger was running high in him. He pushed her hand away, kicked the door open, and stepped to the ground.

Forbes sighed. "No, sir, I just can't say the best man won. Although it does appear you'll be on top for a while, if you catch my meaning."

Billy reddened. Smith laughed, a kind of whinnying. As a great snowy egret went sailing over the tops of the pines, Billy took a step toward Forbes's horse.

"Watch what you say in front of my wife."

Forbes and his friend exchanged quick, pleased looks. "Why, Mr. Hazard, that sounds suspiciously like a threat. I consider a threat to be a personal insult. Or did I perchance misinterpret you?"

"Billy, come on," Brett called. "Don't waste your time on these bloody-minded fools."

Forbes turned his smile on her. "You know, sweet, I still confess a fondness for you—even though that tongue of yours sometimes transforms you into a first-class fishwife. Bet you even hump like one."

"*LaMotte, you son of a bitch, get off that horse!*"

Tossing his head and laughing, Forbes maneuvered his mount out of the path of Billy's lunge. Then he slid to the ground, smoothed his palms over the hair at his temples, and strolled forward.

"I don't believe I misinterpreted that remark, sir. You insulted me."

With a grave nod, Smith said, "He surely did."

Forbes stood gazing down at Billy, who was almost a full head shorter. "I ask for satisfaction, sir."

Homer watched in consternation as Brett leaped from the carriage. "Walk away from him, Billy. Don't you see he came here to bait you? I don't know how he found out we were leaving, but don't play his game."

Eyes warily fixed on his adversary, Billy responded with a small shake of his head. "Stay out of this, Brett. LaMotte—"

"I said," Forbes interrupted, "I demand satisfaction." His hand swept up, then whipsawed across Billy's face. The open-palm slap resounded loudly. "Right here and right now," Forbes finished, his charming smile settling in place again.

"Damn you," Brett burst out. "I knew you were jealous, but I didn't know it had driven you crazy. How long have you been planning this?"

"A long time, I won't deny that. But it's the fairest and most honorable way for me to settle my differences with Mr. Hazard. Preston is carrying a spare pistol in his saddlebag. He'll act as my second. For yours"—his glance jumped from Billy to the carriage— "reckon you'll have to serve, Homer. I'd say it's fitting for a Yankee to have a nigger second."

Brett's voice was cracking from strain. "You mustn't do this, Billy."

"Please be quiet," he cut in. He took her shoulders, then led her around the coach to the other side. Bending close, he whispered, "I've got to fight him. Can't you see he came chasing after us so he could kill me? If we try to leave, he'll find some pretext to shoot me outright. This way—"

He swallowed. Perspiration had gathered on his chin. A drop fell suddenly, darkening his lapel like a bloodstain.

"At least I have a chance."

She shook her head, gently at first, then harder. Tears welled in her eyes. Billy squeezed her arm and walked back to the far side of the carriage. She heard him say:

"All right, LaMotte. Let's use that field over there, by the marsh."

"Your servant, sir," Forbes said, and bowed.

Billy stripped off his coat, cravat, and waistcoat. He flung them over the spines of a yucca plant growing near the drooping fronds of a wild palm. Homer approached, but Billy waved him back.

"Stay with Brett. I can do this by myself."

"Why, certainly, it's simple enough," Smith agreed as he summoned the duelists into the sunshine at the center of an open stretch of bermuda grass that was seething softly in the wind.

Smith held out his hands. In each lay a dueling pistol. A matched pair, Billy noted, further proof the roadside meeting was not accidental. Men simply didn't go for an afternoon's gallop packing such pistols in their saddlebags.

"I will load these with powder and ball in plain view of both you gentlemen. Then, starting back to back, you will take ten paces at my command. After the tenth you may turn and fire at will. Any questions?"

"No," Forbes said, rolling up one sleeve, then the other.

"Get on with it," Billy said.

Mocking him with another bow, Smith knelt in the grass, opened his saddlebag, and drew out two powder flasks, one about a third the size of the other. From the larger flask he poured propellant powder down the muzzle of the first pistol. After he seated the ball and a cloth patch, he primed the frizzen with the finer-grained powder from the small flask.

He handed the gun to Forbes, who gave it a cursory inspection and nodded. Forbes seemed more interested in watching his friend steady the second pistol between his legs, muzzle uppermost.

Billy saw Smith reach for the large flask again. Forbes cleared his throat. Billy turned toward him.

"You don't object to a man pissing before he fights, do you?" Billy shook his head. "Then perhaps you'll be kind enough to hold this till I come back."

He was already extending his pistol. Billy had to take it, and as a consequence he didn't see Smith shift the position of the flask over the muzzle of the gun he was loading. Most of the propellant powder spilled into the thick grass.

It had been well planned and accomplished in a twinkling. Forbes's distracting query had drawn Billy's attention at the proper moment; the maneuver with the powder had gone unnoticed. All anyone saw was Smith crouching, the pistol partially obscured by his knee and the waving grass.

Smith finished seating the second ball, primed the pistol, and said,

"There." He rose and held the heavy gun, which now contained too little powder to propel the ball with anything like its designed muzzle velocity. It was in no way a lethal weapon.

At the spot where Smith had crouched down, Billy noticed a few powder grains speckling the grass. He thought of asking that the pistols be exchanged but quickly squashed his suspicion. Not even a jealous suitor would stoop so low as to tamper with weapons used in an affair of honor.

Forbes returned. Billy handed him the first pistol. Smith extended the second gun. "Thank you," Billy said, and took it.

Smith cleared his throat. "Gentlemen, shall we commence?"

64

"Is Billy Hazard here?" Madeline asked. About five minutes had passed since her arrival at Mont Royal. Charles had helped her inside to the library and sent for Orry, who stood with his back against the closed doors, a stricken expression on his face.

"He left," Charles told her. "With Brett. They're going to catch a northbound train at the flag stop. They were married two hours ago."

"Married," Madeline repeated in a dazed way. "That must have something to do with it."

"With what?" Orry said.

His voice was sharper than he intended, but he was being battered by emotion: joy that sprang from her unexpected arrival, grief that wrenched him when he looked at her poor, wasted face. She had lost even more weight, but something far worse had happened to her, although he didn't know what it was.

"Forbes," she whispered. "Forbes and his friend Preston Smith. They left Resolute just before I did. I overheard them speaking to Justin about—about killing Billy. Someone from here must have brought word that he and Brett were leaving."

Charles bit down on the stub of the cigar, which had gone out. "Could it be the boy you saw outside?"

"I don't know." Madeline's eyes had acquired a queer, glassy fix. "It must be."

"Which boy are you talking about?" Orry wanted to know.

Charles's expression was bleak now, forbidding. "Ashton's boy, Rex. I'll find him."

He crossed to the door. Orry passed him, striding to Madeline. "You're certain they were talking about harming Billy?" Charles stopped at the door, awaiting her answer.

"The word I heard was killing." She fought an impulse to weep; she couldn't seem to control herself. "*Killing.*"

Orry scowled. "By Christ, I'll speak to Justin about—"

"There's no time," Madeline cried. "And Justin doesn't matter anymore. I've left him."

Orry stared, not understanding.

"Left him," she said again. "I'm never going back to—" Before she could finish, she pitched forward in a faint.

She fell against Orry's chest and drove him a step backward, but he managed to catch her and hold her up. "Send someone to help me with her," he exclaimed to Charles.

Charles nodded, a thunderous look on his face as he left.

"Ashton, where's your boy?"

His cousin glanced from the silver tea service. She had been about to pour cups for herself and Clarissa in the parlor.

"Do you mean Rex?"

"I do. Where is he?"

Charles's stark eyes drove the smile from her face. "Outside, I reckon. Whatever is making you so cross?"

She was dissembling desperately; she had heard the buggy arrive just as she and her mother sat down. From the window she had observed Madeline, dirty and ugly as a witch, being helped inside. She hadn't dared poke her nose out of the parlor for fear something had gone wrong.

Charles didn't answer her question. As he stalked out, his boots slammed the floor so hard it shook.

With a bright, interested smile, Clarissa said, "I didn't recognize that young man. Is he a visitor?"

"He's your nephew, Mama!"

Her tone brought tears to Clarissa's eyes. Ashton rubbed her cheek with quick little motions. "I'm sorry I burst out like that. I've developed the most violent headache all at once—"

"Perhaps the tea will help."

"Yes. Yes, perhaps."

Her hand shook as she attempted to pour. She missed the cup and nearly dropped the pot. "Oh, damn."

The profanity brought a gasp from Clarissa. Ashton slammed the pot back on the tray. Then she leaped up and paced back and forth. Charles was onto something. Definitely onto something. If she appeared too curious, she might incriminate herself—yet did she dare leave him alone with Rex? The boy was just itching to do her ill.

For a minute or so she was wracked by indecision. Finally she dashed out of the room without a word of explanation. Clarissa folded a napkin and began to wipe up the tea the young woman had spilled.

So nervous, that girl. Clarissa tried hard to recall her name but could not.

On the kitchen porch, Charles crouched over Rex, one palm resting against the gray cypress siding next to the boy's ear. He had found Rex gnawing a chunk of salt pork, and before the boy could scramble away, Charles had squatted down and cowed him with that forbidding hand against the wall.

"Rex, I won't stand for lies, do you understand?"

Desperate dark eyes swept the lawn beyond Charles's shoulder. The boy knew he was caught. In a small voice he said, "Yessir."

"You ran all the way to Resolute and back, didn't you?"

Rex bit his lower lip. Scowling, Charles leaned closer.

"Rex—"

Faintly: "Yes."

"Who did you speak to over there?"

Another hesitation. "Mist' LaMotte."

"Justin LaMotte?"

Rex scratched his head. "No. Mist' Forbes. I was tole—"

He stopped. Charles prodded:

"Who told you? I want you to say the name of the person who sent you to Resolute." He already knew it, of course; once he had gotten past his initial surprise and disgust, the plot was all too transparent and believable. He took his hand away from the wall and touched Rex's arm gently.

"I promise that if you tell me, no harm will come to you."

The boy struggled with that, studied Charles, and was at last persuaded. Abruptly, a peculiar smile jerked his mouth. But Charles was losing patience.

"Damn it, boy, we haven't time for this. I want to hear you say—"

"Rex? There you are. I've been searching everywhere."

Charles stood up and turned to see Ashton running toward them.

Breathless, she reached the kitchen porch. "Come along, you imp. I need you this instant."

"I need an answer from him first," Charles said.

"But Charles"—a pretty pout, but he thought he detected fear behind it—"I must get ready to drive home."

"You can't go until Homer comes back with the carriage." Heavy irony then. "If we can believe Madeline, that may take a while."

749

"Madeline LaMotte? You mean to say she's here?"

"You watched me help her across the veranda. I saw you trying to hide behind the window curtain."

Scarlet rose in Ashton's cheeks. She stammered in uncharacteristic confusion. Charles seized the moment to turn to the boy.

"I'm waiting, Rex. Who sent you to Resolute with the message that Billy and his new wife had left for the train?"

Ashton saw the trap closing. Pretense was useless, but her instinct for self-preservation was strong. She thrust by Cousin Charles, raising her right fist upward. "Rex, you keep your mouth shut if you know what's good for you—*oh.*"

The boy stared at the fist trembling near his face. Charles had blocked its descent by seizing Ashton's wrist. The boy's eyes grew large, and Ashton felt sick. She knew what Rex was thinking about: the whipping.

"She did."

His words had a spitting, stinging sound. Charles sighed and let go of his cousin. She rubbed her wrist.

"What on earth's he talking about? I don't have the slightest—"

"Stop it," Charles broke in. "Madeline told Orry and me everything she overheard at Resolute. Lying won't help you anymore. Or threatening this boy, either." He squeezed Rex's shoulder. "Better get out of here."

Rex ran.

Charles watched a transformation take place on Ashton's face then. Her cheeks grew livid, and her smiling pretension disappeared. He could hardly believe what he saw. In a soft, wrathful voice, he said:

"My God—it's true. You want your own brother-in-law hurt or killed."

Her silence and her defiant eyes affirmed it. He wasted no time on recriminations. Clutching his saber, he ran like a madman for the stable.

Ashton took a step after him and screamed at the disappearing figure: "It won't do any good. You're already too late. *Too late.*"

"One," Smith called in a loud voice. The duelists started to walk in opposite directions, eyes straight ahead, pistols at their sides.

"Two."

The wind tossed the grass and ruffled shining water in the marsh.

750

Sweat ran down Billy's neck, soaking the collar of his fine wedding shirt.

To clear his mind of distractions, he fixed his gaze on a low branch of live oak directly in front of him. He examined the feel of the dueling pistol in his hand, thought of how he must raise and fire it.

"Three."

Brett's hands were clenched so tightly her forearms ached. She stood by the carriage, wondering how this terrible moment had come to them. Who had told Forbes where they were? It was nearly impossible for him to have come to this particular road by accident.

"Four."

Homer was standing about six feet to the right of Brett. As the duelists separated, he saw a glance of understanding flash between young LaMotte and his second. Homer had picked up a gray stone about three inches in diameter and now began to drop it nervously from one hand to the other, thinking, Something sure isn't right about this business.

"Five."

To Brett's left, Preston Smith stood by the horses he and Forbes had ridden. He wanted to stay close to his saddlebag in case things didn't go precisely as planned. He glanced down at his right boot, reassured by the bulge of the special pocket sewn on the outside. Then his eye flicked past Brett to Homer, who was perspiring and passing a rock from hand to hand. They had nothing to fear from a frightened nigger. A feeling of satisfaction flooded over Smith, a feeling so intense he nearly missed the next count.

"Six."

Billy's vision blurred. A panicky feeling tightened his gut and dried his throat. He wanted a last look at Brett. Thoughts went screaming through his brain at incredible speed:

Why should you look at her?

You'll see her again.

Maybe you won't.

How did they find us?

A noise intruded at the edge of his awareness, a pounding, soft and steady. He had never known his heart to sound that way.

"Seven."

Homer knew what he had seen in the sly look that flickered between the friends. He knew what he smelled here in the sunshine. They had plotted young Hazard's murder, those two. He didn't know how or why, but he was positive it was true. The thought of what was coming sickened him so badly that he turned to the coach and leaned on the front wheel, his hand closing tight around the stone.

"Eight."

Brett, too, misinterpreted the drumming sound for a moment. Then she realized she was hearing a horse coming swiftly along the road from Mont Royal. Over the noise of hoofs, a man was shouting.

Smith heard it also. One of the horses he was holding shied and whinnied. That obscured part of the shout:

"—Billy, watch—"

Brett's eyes flew wide. "That's Charles."

"Nine," Smith called.

Forbes turned around, his confidence melting. He didn't need to look at sallow, frightened Smith to know the horseman signaled the undoing of their plan. Billy had stopped responding to the count. He stood watching the road in an expectant way. Rage and desperation took possession of Forbes. He had a clear shot at the back of Billy's head—

Smith had forgotten to call ten. No matter. Forbes raised his arm shoulder-high and leveled the gun.

Homer was aware of the penalty for attacking a white man, but he couldn't stand by and see murder done. He flung his right arm back, then forward.

Smith didn't exactly understand what the black man was doing, but he recognized it as threatening. He yelled and bowled past Brett. As he ran, he reached toward his right boot.

The stone went sailing toward Forbes as he squeezed the trigger. Brett saw that the stone would miss by a yard or more. But it did its work anyway, arcing into Forbes's field of vision and causing him to jerk his head to the left. His pistol arm jerked too. An explosion— a puff of smoke—

The stone thumped into the wind-whipped grass. Forbes's jaw dropped. Billy turned around, staring at his adversary.

Smith had knocked Brett against the carriage as he passed. She straightened; Billy was unhurt. The mounted man was in sight. "Charles!" she cried. The word was muffled by a guttural scream.

She spun around, flung a hand to her lips. Smith's face was a grimacing mask as he grunted and pulled his right hand back. Out of

752

Homer's stomach came the blade of the bowie knife Smith had snatched from his boot.

"Oh." Homer stared at the torn and bloodied front of his shirt. "Oh," he said again in surprise and pain as he started to topple sideways. Smith shoved with his free hand to help him along. Homer died as he fell.

Belatedly, Billy realized a ball had buzzed past his ear. Except for the distraction of the rock Homer had thrown, the ball would probably have hit him.

Charles reined his sweat-covered horse. He was still in uniform. His saber sheath banged his leg as he started to dismount. Billy wrenched his eyes back to Forbes—Forbes who had fired before the final count. Tried to shoot him in the back. Shaking with anger, Billy lifted the dueling pistol and took aim. He touched the hair trigger. There was a flash at the frizzen—a crack that seemed somehow small and flat.

Forbes hadn't changed position by so much as one inch. Billy had aimed for the center of his breastbone. How could the ball have missed such a large, stationary target?

Then, some ten paces away on a patch of bare earth, something dark caught his eye. He stalked toward it, watched it define itself to lead-colored metal. The ball. *The ball from his pistol, lying there spent—*

He recalled Smith's crouching while he loaded the weapons, recalled spotting spilled powder. They had carefully planned to short the charge in his pistol. He swore an oath and flung his gun into the grass.

"Forbes!"

Forbes spun in response to the shout from Smith, who threw his bowie knife by the tip, flipping it end over end. Forbes let the knife land in the grass near his feet, then snatched it up. He shifted the knife to his left hand. Then, out of his right boot, he snaked a second one, identical in design but unbloodied and two inches longer.

The sun struck silver flashes from his hands as he sidestepped toward Billy. "Sorry your shot missed." Forbes uttered a crazy kind of laugh. "Bet you're a whole lot sorrier."

"I didn't miss. The ball never came close to you. It's lying right over there in that bare place. There wasn't a full charge of powder in my gun."

"Smart fucking Yankee, aren't you?"

Wind lifted Forbes's hair, then pasted it against his sweaty forehead.

Empty-handed, Billy backed away. One step, then another. Forbes came on, scuttling sideways like a crab.

"You shouldn't have messed with Brett. Shouldn't have set foot in South Carolina. Reckon they'll send you home in a sack, but I guarantee your kin won't want to open it and look at you."

He moved the right-hand knife in a small circle, then started the same kind of motion with the left one. "Not after I fix up your face."

Billy retreated again. He decided to make a dash to the nearest tree, try to tear off a limb before one of those knives—

"Billy."

The voice wrenched his attention toward the carriage. Smith had disappeared. Charles had reached Brett; his collar was unfastened, his light blue trousers dirty. His face was wrathful as he pitched his saber into the field.

Billy stepped to the right so that the sword would land between him and Forbes. As the saber tumbled, Smith jumped into sight at the rear of the carriage. He had sneaked past Homer's corpse and around behind the vehicle. He dashed for the saddlebag on his horse. The saber landed much nearer Billy than Forbes. Billy ran to get it.

Smith pulled a four-barrel derringer out of the saddlebag. Charles saw him, cursed, and lunged. Smith took four running steps into the field. He emptied all four barrels at Billy. After the last popping explosion, Billy felt a ball hit him. He groaned in pain and staggered forward.

Charles caught Smith from behind, spun him around, ripped the empty derringer out of his hand, and smashed him with a right fist, then a crossing left. Clumsy blows but powerful ones. Smith grunted; red mucus fountained from his nose.

Billy had fallen. Blood stained the left sleeve of his shirt above his elbow. On his stomach, he pushed up with both hands. Pain flashed through his left arm. His hand refused to support him.

Silver stars of light twinkled a couple of feet in front of him. He groped for the hilt of the saber, then nearly dropped the weapon as he lurched to his feet. A shadow lengthened in the grass. Billy flung himself to one side. Forbes's right-hand knife missed him by no more than two inches.

Pain drained his energy and muddled his mind. All he could do was retreat, parry, try to collect himself. Forbes's sweating, grinning face loomed huge, his eyes blazing with an obsession to kill.

Billy defended himself by instinct. All of the fine, planned moves he had learned at West Point slipped away in a haze of fright and throbbing pain. Forbes slashed with his left-hand knife. Billy blocked it with the saber, then tried to push Forbes away. He lacked the strength.

Forbes chuckled deep in his throat. "Got you now, Yankee." He bored in, knives slashing, turning, confusing Billy with their glittering motion. Billy parried air. Forbes laughed and came on, confident again.

Once more Billy retreated, trying to organize an attack. He was too weak from the loss of blood he could feel streaming hot beneath his shirt. It had reached his wrist, dripped from his cuff.

Brett called something, but he didn't dare turn. He stumbled over heavy, exposed roots and was suddenly backed tight against the huge trunk of a tree. Forbes's eyes widened with delight. He stabbed for Billy's face with the right-hand bowie knife.

Billy wrenched his left shoulder forward. The knife throbbed in the tree. Rather than trying to free it, Forbes struck with the second one. Billy wrenched the other way. The knife ripped his shirt, raked his ribs, and buried itself two inches in the trunk.

Forbes was standing very close now, realizing each stab had missed. With a desperate look he reached past Billy with both hands and started to pull the knives loose. Billy knew it was his last chance. He lifted his knee, drove it into Forbes's stomach. Forbes gasped and staggered back two steps. With a little maneuvering room, Billy rammed the saber into Forbes and thrust until he felt the point scrape against the backbone.

Forbes collapsed face down. The impact drove the hilt against his chest. The point of the saber suddenly tore through the back of his shirt and jutted into the light.

Shaking, Billy turned away. The pain in his arm wasn't half so bad as the spasm of sickness that emptied his stomach while he leaned against the tree.

Brett gave a ragged little cry and rushed toward her husband. Charles called, "Bring him back here so I can look at that wound." Then he turned his attention to Smith. He dragged Forbes's crony up by the collar and pushed him against the carriage. Smith held his crotch, tears on his cheeks. Charles shook him.

"Stop caterwauling and listen! Once upon a time I fixed your kinsman Whitney, and I can do the same for you. Fact is, I'd like

755

to. But I reckon we've spilled enough blood. So you get out of here before I change my mind."

Whimpering, Smith staggered toward his horse.

"On foot," Charles said. "I'll keep the animals."

Without a backward look, Smith lurched into the road. An impulse seized Charles; he shied a pebble at the hobbling man. Smith yelped, grabbed his neck, and broke into a run.

Charles's smile faded as he looked at Ashton's dead slave, then toward the spot where Forbes's body lay hidden by the long grass, its place marked by the saber sticking into the sunshine. Flies swarmed on the bloody point.

Billy staggered to the carriage with his right arm around Brett and his left hanging limp and bloody at his side. "They trumped up a duel," he gasped, and then in a couple of sentences described the treachery with the pistol and how he had discovered it.

"Bastards," Charles growled. He tore Billy's sleeve and examined the wound. "Passed right through the fleshy part, looks like. Lot more blood than damage. Brett, give me some long pieces of petticoat. I'll tie it off."

She turned her back and raised her skirt. Charles tilted his head to study the angle of the sun. "We'll have to skedaddle to make that train. Are you up to it?"

"You're damn right we are," Billy said. "I want to get out of this benighted place."

"Can't say I blame you," Charles murmured.

"I never realized Forbes was so crazy and vicious," Brett said over her shoulder as more cloth tore. "How did you find us in time?"

"Madeline LaMotte overheard Forbes and Preston talking at Resolute. Talking about you. After they left, she drove to Mont Royal to warn us. I saddled up and took the road I knew you'd taken."

"But—how did Forbes know we were leaving just now? Or that we were going to the train?"

Charles accepted the lacy strips Brett handed him. He began to wrap them around the upper part of Billy's arm. Billy clenched his teeth. His color was improving.

"Not certain about that," Charles hedged, concentrating on what he was doing so as to avoid his cousin's eyes. "I'll ask some questions when I take Homer's body back to the plantation. Meantime, you two climb in the carriage. And hang on tight to each other. I'm going to go like hell the rest of the way."

*

Charles was as good as his word, driving to the flag stop at reckless speed. The train was heard whistling in the south as the carriage swayed to a stop. Charles dashed across the track to the cypress shed, flung back the lid of the box, and ran the flag up the pine pole. By the time he finished, the cowcatcher was in sight.

Over the hiss of steam and the clang of the bell, Billy tried to speak. "I don't know how to say—"

"Don't bother. All in the line of duty. One Academy man looking out for another."

"But you let go of your commission."

"That doesn't mean West Point will let go of me." Charles was surprised, even irked, to find himself so close to tears. All the shocks of the afternoon had probably conspired to cause that.

He hid his feelings as best he could, rushing to unload the luggage and place it on the platform. As the train slowed, the freight and mail cars passed. Then came faces behind dusty windows, faces whose bland passivity disappeared the instant they saw the bedraggled threesome—the soldier, the girl, and the young man with his coat draped over his shoulders and traces of blood showing on his bandaged arm.

Brett threw her arms around Charles's neck. "Oh, Cousin—thank you. Explain to all of them."

"I will. You climb aboard," he added with a glance at the impatient conductor.

Billy followed her. Standing on the second step from the bottom, he gazed down at his friend. They clasped right hands.

"Don't have any idea when we'll see each other, Bison."

The realization hit hard. "No, I don't either."

"You take care."

"You do the same. A safe journey to you and your wife."

"Thank you. We'll meet again."

"I know."

Charles harbored doubts. With all the trouble in the country, their only future meeting place might be a battlefield. With each of them on a different side.

Damnation, don't think that way and spoil everything. It's been a rough enough day already. He managed the old reckless smile, lifted his hand, and stood waving as the train chugged off.

Some passengers had come out to the platform of the last coach. As the coach went by, Charles heard an obscenity. Something flew

757

past his face. He looked down to find a gob of spittle on the front of his uniform. "Shit," he said.

He didn't stay angry for long. His smile came back, and from the shadows at trackside he called out mockingly to whoever had spat on his Federal uniform.

"Done like a true Southerner."

Rubbing his eyes, he trudged across the track toward the carriage. The train disappeared down a natural tunnel in the pines. He felt its last vibrations as he stepped off the rail.

He wished he could drink himself insensible. But he was summoned back to the red field, and to Mont Royal, by unfinished business.

65

> *"I know moon-rise,*
> *I know star-rise,*
> *Lay this body down—"*

The words of the old Gullah hymn came clearly through the windows of the dark library. The slaves were singing for Homer, whom Charles had brought back in the carriage. He had left Forbes for the cormorants to pick. Compassion had its limits.

"That's how it happened, nearly as I can piece it together," Charles was saying. "They meant to murder Billy."

He put his cigar back in his mouth and stretched his long legs in front of his chair. Orry lingered in the corner, his shadow falling on the old uniform. "Couple your account with what Madeline told us, and it becomes conclusive. God above, Charles, I had no idea they hated him that much."

"Brett said almost the same thing before she left. Jealousy played a big part, I reckon. How is Madeline?"

"She was fine when I spoke to her an hour ago. I trust she went back to sleep."

"LaMotte is probably searching for her."

Orry nodded. "That's something else I must attend to this evening. But first things first." He sounded stern. "Have you seen Ashton since you returned?"

"Saw her right as I drove up. She wanted to take charge of Homer's remains. I said no and she disappeared."

Orry strode to the candle-lit foyer. Cuffey jumped up from the stool where he had been dozing. "Find Mrs. Huntoon and her husband," Orry said. "Tell them I want them in the library. At once."

Cuffey hurried away. Charles turned so that he could observe his cousin. By the glow of the foyer candles, he saw the set look of Orry's expression.

"Help me light some lamps, Charles. When I tell them, I want to see their miserable faces."

Ashton's color was high as she entered the room. She was instantly on the attack.

"I resent being ordered about like a common servant. If you think I'll dignify the accusations of niggers and troublemaking wastrels"— Charles laughed—"by responding to them, you're badly mistaken."

Orry's hostility was conveyed in an icy-calm tone. "No one plans to accuse you of anything. There's no need. The facts speak eloquently."

Huntoon had been hovering behind his wife. Now he moved to the left. The flames of the lamps reflected on the circles of his spectacles. "See here—"

"Save your oratory for Montgomery," Orry interrupted. "I have one or two things to say, and I prefer to get them said as quickly as possible. The first matter concerns your slave, Homer. Did he—does he have a family?"

Ashton answered. "James bought Homer from a gentleman in Savannah. I believe he had a wife and children there."

"From which you separated him without a thought. Christ Almighty. It's no wonder the Yankees despise us."

Again she went on the offensive with a mixture of bluster and arrogance. "Orry, whatever is wrong with you? I refuse to be subjected to this kind of treatment."

Huntoon's outrage matched hers. "She speaks for both of us. We're leaving."

Orry nodded. "Indeed you are."

"We'll take Homer's body back to Charleston."

"No. He'll stay here with our people. I'll try to locate his family."

Huntoon pulled off his glasses, puffed out his chest, and stepped in front of his wife. "I insist. The nigger may be dead, but he's still my property."

Orry looked at him steadily. "He stays here. You aren't fit to touch him."

Huntoon lowered his head and rushed his brother-in-law. He tried to hit Orry's jaw with his right fist. Orry stepped back, reached across and batted Huntoon's forearm aside, as if he were driving off an insect.

Huntoon stumbled, gasped, and fell sideways, managing to catch himself on both hands and one knee. His spectacles were still in his left hand as it struck the floor. There was a crunch. When Huntoon staggered up, pieces of glass fell from the bent wire ovals. He was livid.

Orry ignored him, turning to Ashton. "Today you divorced yourself from this family. From Brett, Charles—all of us. Once you and James leave this plantation, never come back."

"Gladly!" she screamed.

Huntoon protested. "Ashton, he hasn't the right—"

"Shut your mouth and come on!" She gave his arm a yank and swept to the doors, fighting to control herself. From the entrance she looked back. Orry hardly recognized her as his sister, so thick and foul was the hatred clotting her eyes.

"You just remember this," she whispered. "James will soon have an important post with the new government. The government will be keeping its eye on people who make disloyal utterances, like the one you made about Yankees despising us. The government will punish traitors."

She marched into the foyer. Huntoon trotted after her like an obedient pet. As he disappeared, a last fragment of glass fell from his spectacles and struck the floor with a tinkling sound.

"My God," Orry said with sadness and disgust. "I don't know what's happened to her."

Charles struck a match on the sole of his boot and relit his cigar. "I do. The same thing's happened to a lot of people I've run into since I came home. One taste of power and all their common sense flies out the window."

Shaking his head, Orry sat at his desk to collect himself. Charles announced his intention to stroll down to the river landing.

Orry pulled a sheet of writing paper from a drawer. "Before you go, would you ask Cuffey to step in? I should send a note over to Resolute."

"All right. I'd like to put some of our people on watch. When Francis LaMotte learns what Billy did to his son, we may have visitors. Do you object to some of the nigras carrying muskets for a few days?"

"No."

"Then I'll see to it." A smoke trail floated behind him as he left.

Orry stared at the blank paper. Even a year ago he would have considered a permanent falling out with his own sister unthinkable.

What had just happened was new evidence of how far down a dark road the family had traveled.

When he was honest with himself, he would admit he had never liked Ashton much. He also recognized that she possessed a certain ruthless strength that better suited a man. Thus he did not casually dismiss her threats. God only knew what devious plots she and her husband would concoct in Montgomery.

His speculations soon induced anger, an anger directed against the Huntoons, the LaMottes, and all the other reckless men who had plunged the South into turmoil and crisis. Some of that anger poured into his quick, slashing pen strokes.

In five minutes he was done writing. He dispatched Cuffey on muleback with the note and a pass. The slave rode off through a light rain that had started to fall. When Cuffey was out of sight, Orry stepped inside from the damp darkness.

He caught his breath. Lit by windblown lights at the head of the staircase, Madeline gazed down at him.

Justin held tight to both arms of the chair as he put his left foot into the boot. The slave crouching over his leg with the boot hooks was justifiably nervous. All evening the master of Resolute had been drinking, shouting, and generally keeping the house in an uproar as he awaited the arrival of his brother.

A long gauze pad was wrapped around Justin's head. It covered his ears and the top of his skull and was tied underneath his chin. The gauze concealed the sutures put in by Dr. Sapp. Whiskey helped dull the pain, which the doctor had assured him would pass in a day or two. But he'd carry a scar, perhaps a bad one, the rest of his life.

He heard horses in the drive. He screwed up his face for one last effort, grunted, and got his foot all the way into the boot, though he knocked the slave on his rear doing it. With no apology, Justin stomped to the foyer.

The fanlight glowed with the light of pine torches held by the riders. As the door crashed open, the torches began to smoke. Francis strode in. Justin could see the rain slanting down more heavily behind his brother.

"Took me a little while to pick out three niggers I could trust with muskets, but we're here."

"Good," Justin said. "We'll bring that slut back before daybreak."

762

Francis dabbed his wet face with a handkerchief. "I didn't think she meant that much to you."

"She doesn't. But my honor does. My reputation—what the devil's that?"

Both ran outside as Cuffey's mule came clopping up the drive into the circle of smoky light. The slave wore his pass on a string around his neck; the downpour made the ink run down the sheet in little blue waterfalls. Cuffey dismounted and respectfully pulled off his hand-me-down beaver hat. He produced a piece of writing paper that was folded and closed with a letter seal.

"This for you, Mist' LaMotte."

Justin snatched it. Cuffey suspected the message would not produce a pleasant response, so he scurried back to his mule, mounted, and rapidly rode away.

"The son of a bitch," Justin whispered. He was unable to read past the first couple of lines. His face turned the color of a ripe plum. "The insufferable, presumptuous son of a bitch."

He saw Francis's blacks watching, whirled, and stalked back inside to hide his consternation. His brother followed. He plucked the note from Justin's hand, carried it over to a lamp on the wall where the pegs had not long ago held a sword. Francis read the brief note to the end, then shook his head. "Why would Main give your wife sanctuary?"

"Are you a complete idiot, Francis? The bastard hates me! He always has. He'd like nothing better than to see me humiliated in front of the whole neighborhood."

"He says that if you set foot on his property, he'll shoot you." Francis folded the note. "Do you believe him?"

"No."

"I do." Anxiously, Francis continued, "Let her go. No woman's worth your life. Women are like interchangeable parts of a gin. You can get the same service from one that you get from any other."

The coarse sophism had great appeal. True enough, Justin wanted to inflict harsh revenge on Madeline for slashing him, on Orry for this latest insult. Yet he hated to traipse around the countryside and further advertise his loss. More important, he really didn't care to face a gun with Orry behind it.

Relieved, Francis saw that he might be able to talk his brother out of a vendetta. He laughed and clapped Justin's shoulder.

"Look here. If repaying her means so much—"

763

"I want to repay both of them."

"All right, both. I'll ask Forbes to think of a way. I assume Forbes is here—"

"No."

"He hasn't come back?"

"Not yet."

"That's peculiar."

"Oh, I suspect he and Preston went off to celebrate."

The explanation satisfied Francis. "I wouldn't mind a nip myself."

Justin was pouring two whiskeys when the slaves waiting in the rain raised a commotion. The brothers rushed outside to see Preston Smith arriving. He was wild-eyed and as mud-spattered as his horse. He jumped down and staggered to Francis.

"I ran all the way to your plantation. They told me you were here."

"Preston, what's the trouble?"

"That Yankee soldier killed Forbes."

Little Francis LaMotte seemed to wither and shrink even more. Preston glossed some of the details, but he couldn't distort the story too much, not and make it comprehensible. It was evident that Forbes and Preston had botched their plan for revenge and that Forbes had earned what he got.

Strangely, Francis could find little anger within himself. He felt tired, old, beaten. Later he might want Charles Main's head, but at the moment he experienced only a grieved lethargy.

"Francis?" Justin touched his sleeve. "I'll go with you to Mont Royal." He hated the thought.

Dry-eyed and stooped, Francis shook his head. "I must go home. I have to tell his mother."

He mounted and, with his slaves in single file behind him, slowly rode away in the rain.

"Should you be up?" Orry asked from the foot of the staircase.

"I feel fine," Madeline said. "Better than I have in a long, long time."

He believed her. Although she was exceedingly pale, her eyes were clearer than they were when he had spoken to her earlier. He waited as she came down the stairs, pushing at her unbound hair with an embarrassed expression.

"I must look frightful."

"You look splendid."

"My dress is a ruin—"

"Madeline, it doesn't matter. It only matters that you're here."

He longed to put his arm around her, hold her close, and kiss her. He ached for that. Images of their meetings at Salvation Chapel swept through his mind. He remembered the struggle to contain or deny his feelings. All at once he was in the midst of that struggle again.

"I'd like to walk outside," she said.

"It's raining."

"Yes, I heard it when I woke. But the air's so sweet and invigorating. I've been tired for months—constantly."

And inexplicably withdrawn, unapproachable, Orry added to himself. Another thought occurred to him. "Have you been taking any medicine?"

"What?"

"Medicine. Certain kinds might make you feel worn out most of the time. Lonzo Sapp is Justin's physician, isn't he?"

"That's right."

"Has he prescribed anything?"

"A celery tonic, but that was—oh, months and months ago. So far back, I hardly remember, though I do recall I only took it for a few weeks."

"And there's been nothing else since?"

"Nothing."

"Well, I'm glad you're feeling better, whatever the reason. It's been a grim day, a grim time, but it's over."

When he had spoken with her upstairs, he had briefly described the events involving Billy and Charles. She had expressed dismay over Forbes's behavior but little surprise. Orry had yet to tell her he had banished Ashton and her husband. As for the letter to Justin, he'd keep that to himself, at least until he learned whether it was effective.

Medicine. The word set off a new and startling sequence in Madeline's mind. She tried to recall all the occasions when her food had seemed to have an odd taste. It had happened many, many times. But never once had she been clever enough or devious enough to guess that her husband might be responsible. Could some drug have been introduced to pacify her? That Justin would do such a thing was likewise a startling idea, but not an unthinkable one. She would never have proof, she supposed. Still, such a scheme on his part would certainly explain her months of lethargy and indifference.

"Madeline?"

His soft, anxious voice interrupted her reflection. She turned to him.

"You had a fearful look on your face. What were you thinking?"

"I was thinking about Justin. What do you suppose he'll do about my leaving?"

"I trust he'll do nothing."

She crossed the foyer. "I'm never going back."

He followed, opened the door for her. "That makes me very happy." He released the knob and faced her. Longing put a catch in his voice. "I'd be happier still if you'd stay with me."

She stood gazing at the rain, her arms folded across her breasts and her hands clasping her forearms. "I love you for saying that, my darling. But are you quite certain you'd be willing to risk the scandal?"

Standing behind her, he laughed. "What's a bit of scandal in a world losing its mind?" His right hand closed on her shoulder. "I'd risk the pit of hell for you, Madeline. Don't you know that?"

She pressed her left hand over his. "Gossip about adultery isn't what I'm talking about."

"What, then?"

She turned, drew a long breath. "Something no one knows, except perhaps a few people in New Orleans who are very old now."

She gazed at his bleak, tired face. In view of all that had happened today, she could no longer conceal it.

"My great-grandmother came from Africa to New Orleans on a slave ship. I'm one-eighth Negro. You know very well what that means in this part of the world." She showed him the back of her white, veined hand. "In the eyes of most people, my skin might as well be black as a lump of coal."

The revelation left him thunderstruck for a moment. And yet, compared to the other shocks of the day, this had no power to affect him. Brushing his palm over her cheek, he said in a gentle voice:

"Is that all there is to tell?"

"Not quite. My mother's origins meant she was unfit to associate with white men except in one capacity. Unable to better herself except in one way. She was a prostitute. My father found her in a house in New Orleans, but he loved her enough to take her out of there and marry her—despite what he knew about her."

"I love you the same way, Madeline."

"I wouldn't want you to feel you had to say—"

"The same way," he repeated, bending to her mouth.

Her first kiss was shy. After so many months apart, they were very nearly strangers; tired strangers, at that. But he soon felt the emotional tides rising, the tides so long dammed.

She leaned back, her hands locking behind his neck. Rain blew in from the darkness to spatter her forehead and glitter in his beard. "Of course"—hope was shining in her eyes now—"there's little chance of the secret's ever coming to light. Those few who know are very old and far away."

Again he kissed her. "I don't care. Understand? *I don't care.*"

With a little cry, she pulled herself against him. "Oh, my God, how long I've loved you."

He felt her body tight to his, her breasts and her billowing hip. Her windblown hair tossed against his cheek. "I love you too."

"Take me upstairs."

"Madeline, are you sure—?"

She stopped his words with a kiss. "We've both waited too long, Orry." She kissed him again, fervently. "Far too long."

"Yes," he said, moving with her toward the stairs. "So we have."

In the dark of his bachelor's room, she bared herself without shame. With her gentle, compassionate hands to help him, so did he.

Orry feared she'd be repelled by the sight of his stump. He was grateful for the dark that hid it. She kissed him and touched him everywhere, including that ruined part of him. She shared his flaw as he had shared hers earlier, with no qualm. She brought her nakedness to him, and their emotions surged like floodwaters let loose. Their relief was immense and complete. They drowned in each other, rose to float in lassitude awhile, then drowned again as new tides seized and hurled them on.

Presently they lay drowsing, her arms around his chest, her murmurs a counterpoint to the comforting sound of the rain and to a halloo from Charles down in the drive; he was evidently calling to one of the sentries he had posted.

Well, he could handle the guarding of Mont Royal for an hour or two. Orry wouldn't have disturbed the moment for anything. He had never known such joy.

During Madeline's first days at Mont Royal, she suffered an assortment of symptoms. She complained of itching skin and a thirst no amount of water could quench. During the daylight hours, chills alternated with periods of sweating. Asleep, she often raved and mumbled. The doctor Orry summoned could diagnose nothing more specific than female complaint, and he issued that pronouncement with noticeable uncertainty. He prescribed three tonics, none of which Madeline would take.

She flew into unprovoked rages, although about the tenth day these began to occur less frequently. At the same time her symptoms moderated, then disappeared altogether.

Marked improvement followed at once. She lost her pallor. Her flesh was once more pink with life. Soap and hard brushing restored a glow to her black hair. She regained ten pounds, which rid her of the haggard look that had been her lot for more than a year.

Charles had kept the armed slaves on watch for two weeks. There were no visitations by either of the LaMotte brothers, no threats in any form. Yet it was clear that events in the dueling field had come to light. Cuffey had visited the field and found Forbes's body gone.

One afternoon Charles encountered Francis while riding on the river road. Charles reined in, his heart beating hard. The older man's accusation was brief and blunt:

"Your friend murdered my son."

"Killed," Charles corrected. "He killed Forbes after accepting a challenge. Nor was the fight a fair one. Preston Smith tampered with my friend's pistol. I'm sorry Forbes is dead, Francis, but I'm willing to testify to the circumstances at any time. In front of a magistrate or on the dueling ground. Your choice."

Francis gave him a long, bitter look and rode on.

That was the end of it.

Gradually Charles relaxed the vigilance at Mont Royal. Orry studied a medical book from his father's extensive library and discovered that Madeline's recent symptoms matched those of a person whose regular dosage of laudanum had been abruptly withdrawn. Why had the doctor pretended ignorance? Orry supposed it was because, being a local man, the physician was acquainted with Madeline's husband and didn't want to involve himself in an unsavory domestic matter. Better to appear incompetent than to antagonize the LaMottes.

Madeline and Orry speculated that Justin for months had secretly been administering tincture of opium to dull her senses. Certainly it would have been possible with the connivance of the house slaves. The circumstantial evidence, as well as her new energy and restored

768

clarity of mind, lent further credence to the theory. But they would never be sure.

In the evenings, after Charles had taken supper with them and left, Orry and Madeline liked to discuss the day's news from Charleston. There was precious little of it that could be termed reliable. One day the *Mercury* would proclaim that Anderson's garrison was about to be withdrawn; the next, the story would be characterized as just another rumor. It went on that way until mid-March, while Beauregard diligently rearranged the batteries, the better to bombard Sumter if bombardment became necessary.

Other rumors warned of relief flotillas steaming from the North. But the only representatives of the Yankee government who showed up were three men sent to assess Anderson's situation. One of the three was a Colonel Lamon, known to be a crony of Lincoln's.

Presumably the new President was making up his mind about the fort. Governor Pickens continued to insist that any attempt to provision or reinforce Sumter would be repulsed. President Davis also repeated his promise to take Sumter by force if it could not be won by negotiation.

Such pronouncements deepened Orry's gloom. He felt that the entire South was being led down a dark road toward an even more stygian darkness. His dreams were filled with drumming, screaming, gunfire; the fools who prated of glorious war on behalf of injured honor had never whiffed a day-old battlefield corpse.

The national situation turned his thoughts to the money George had put into the *Star of Carolina*. Guilt about the investment weighed more heavily on him with each day that passed. Early April brought a fresh spate of rumors, including a persistent one that a relief force had put out to sea from New York. Huntoon and the other fire eaters repeatedly called for action against the fort in the harbor. All this pushed Orry to a decision.

Charles tried to argue him out of it, saying that if war erupted, he was absolved of responsibility. Orry countered that war absolved him of nothing, since George wouldn't have risked a penny in such a chancy enterprise were it not for personal friendship.

He took the train to Atlanta and remained there seventy-two hours. When he boarded another train to go home, he was carrying a small satchel.

He arrived in Charleston on the night of April 11. He trudged through milling crowds to Tradd Street. Cooper was astonished to see him.

"I went to Atlanta," Orry explained. "I mortgaged Mont Royal."

"What?" Cooper looked almost witless with surprise.

"We owe George part or all of his investment. We owe it now, before the firing starts. I raised six hundred and fifty thousand dollars." He nudged the satchel with his boot. "Cash."

"For the entire plantation? That's a fraction of what it's worth."

"I was lucky to get anything. I want as much from you as you can come up with, and I want it immediately."

"How do you propose I get that kind of money?"

"You have collateral. The shipping company and the James Island property are still valuable."

"Orry, the local banks won't give loans now."

"Try."

Cooper looked at his brother's worn face and saw no ground for argument. "All right." He sighed. "In the morning. I'll see to your room. You need some sleep."

Orry wakened in the dark, hearing thunderclaps. Red light glared through the shutters he had closed against the spring breeze. He thrust the shutters open. A shell arched high over the rooftops, then dropped.

He rushed downstairs. Cooper, Judith, and the children were at the windows. "What time is it?"

"Four, four-thirty, something like that," Judith answered in a sleepy voice.

"That sounds like the harbor batteries."

Another boom, another flush of red beyond the roofs and steeples. The floor shook. Cooper nodded and put his arms around his children in a protective way. Orry had never seen his brother so sad.

"It's all over. We're at war," Cooper said. After a moment he added, "I don't think the banks will be doing business this morning."

66

Major Anderson continued to return the vastly superior fire of Beauregard's guns until late on the afternoon of the twelfth, Friday. But the situation of the garrison was hopeless, and he and every other man in the fort knew it.

By some miracle, no one had died during the thirteen-hour bombardment. Anderson reckoned it was only a matter of time, however. He was thinking of asking for terms, particularly the right to give a formal military salute to the flag flying over the fort, the Stars and Stripes, before he ordered it lowered for the last time.

Up at Mont Royal, Orry was packing a small carpetbag with a razor, strop, soap, some shirts, and underdrawers. He threw the carpetbag into the carriage along with the satchel of money. The satchel was closed by a small, cheap lock, the key for which reposed in his watch pocket. The lock could be easily forced, but he figured he would attract less notice with two ordinary valises—one held in his hand, the other gripped between body and arm—than he would with one bag and a bulging money belt.

Madeline kissed him and tried to hide tears of anxiety. She knew the risk he was taking, traveling north just now, but she said nothing.

Not so Charles, who had reluctantly agreed to take him to the flag stop in the carriage.

"You shouldn't go, Orry. You owe him nothing."

"I owe him my life. Drive." He slammed the carriage door behind him.

Clarissa slipped up beside Madeline, whom she didn't recognize, and waved cheerfully to the departing stranger. Madeline wondered if she would ever see him again.

On Sunday a freight derailment in North Carolina blocked the northbound line and delayed Orry's train six hours. Passengers in the first-class coach talked of little besides the Sumter crisis. From the accents and the sentiments he heard, Orry judged most of the speakers to be Southern. A few hundred miles north that situation would reverse. He would need to be very careful about what he said, and to whom.

At twilight the track was cleared and the train chugged on. Soon they stopped at a station in a small piedmont town. The ticket agent was gesturing and shouting in the dusk.

"Sumter's fallen. Anderson pulled out. Word just flashed over the telegraph."

Cheering filled the coach. The vendor hawking day-old newspapers in the aisle gave Orry a suspicious stare when he didn't join in. Orry stared right back and the vendor moved on. It seemed there was no escape from the suspicion and enmity swirling through the land.

Next morning, in Petersburg, he left the train for a meal in the depot. He took the money satchel with him and placed it carefully between his feet under the table. The flyblown dining room raised echoes of a similar stop in Baltimore two years ago. This time, however, Orry encountered no hostility; people were too busy discussing yesterday's events in South Carolina. Several times he heard the word *victory*. Most of the customers agreed that Virginia's departure from the Union was inevitable now that a blow had been struck.

Shaking his head, he quickly finished his beef hash and corn grits. Then he bought a paper. When the train left Petersburg, a paunchy, well-dressed man sat down next to him. Orry paid no attention. He was immersed in the telegraphic dispatches on the front page. The day before, Sunday, Anderson had formally surrendered the fort in Charleston harbor. Ironically, it was during preparations for the ceremony that the first life had been lost.

According to estimates in the paper, four to five thousand rounds had been exchanged during the bombardment. There had been no casualties, but the shelling had started fires throughout the fort. Some had still been smoldering yesterday. Flying sparks had ignited a pile of cannon cartridges. The explosion had instantly killed one of Anderson's artillerists and wounded five others.

First blood, Orry said to himself. He was convinced there would be more, much more.

The Federal commander had been allowed to salute his flag before striking it and leading his men to waiting longboats. The boats carried the soldiers out past the bar to a Federal relief flotilla that had proved to be something more than a rumor—the ships had arrived offshore during the bombardment. Soon the chartered liner *Baltic* and her accompanying warships were steaming northward, in defeat. Orry doubted it would be long before the Lincoln government reacted.

When he finished reading, he fell into conversation with the fat man, who intoduced himself as Mr. Cobb of Petersburg, a commercial traveler.

"British needles and the finest sewing threads," Cobb explained in his soft Virginia voice. "Distributed only to the best mercantile establishments. Heaven knows what will become of my trade with all this trouble. I take it you are also a Southerner?"

Orry nodded. "From South Carolina."

"How far are you going?"

"Into Pennsylvania."

"Permit me to offer a word of advice. I was in Philadelphia last week, and I had a difficult time. I might go so far as to say it was extremely difficult. Southerners are too easily identified by their speech. At one point I felt my life might be in jeopardy. I am not traveling beyond Washington on this trip, but even so I have taken precautions."

His plump finger ticked against his lapel, where Orry saw a rosette of red, white, and blue ribbon.

"I suggest you do the same, sir. Any store carrying notions can supply you with the materials for a Union rosette."

"Thanks for the suggestion," Orry said, although he had already rejected it. He did not believe wholeheartedly in the cause of the South. But neither would he wear the colors of the other side.

The only part of Washington he saw was a railway terminal. Army officers and civilian families thronged the platforms and waiting rooms. Most of the officers were arriving; most of the families were leaving. Southerners, he presumed, homeward-bound after resignation from a post with the government or the military.

That Monday evening, by the smoky light of depot lamps, he watched the country take its next lurching step toward widespread war. A sweating man in shirt-sleeves chalked news bulletins on a blackboard. One said President Lincoln had declared the existence of an insurrection and called for seventy-five thousand volunteers to bear arms for three months.

Applause swept the small crowd standing in front of the board. Orry turned to go to his train. The crowd pressed forward, shouting approval of the President and cursing the South. He found he couldn't move.

"Excuse me."

No one budged. Three men close by gave him hard scrutiny. He wished he'd brought a pistol on the trip.

"What did you say, mister?" one man asked.

Orry knew he should speak as few words as possible. But he resented that restriction, and so ignored it.

"I said I'd like to get through, if you have no objection."

"Why, this here's a Southron gent," a second man growled. Immediately, onlookers pressed Orry from all sides; most, it seemed to him, were sweaty men with stubbled faces and hostile eyes. They blocked him in front and on both flanks. Beside his back, he could hear ugly-sounding whispers spreading. His mouth went dry.

The crowd jostled him. There was barely room for him to slip the money satchel up beneath his right arm and clamp it there. Hands plucked at the satchel. Voices overlapped.

"What you got in that bag, reb?"

"Val'ables, I bet."

"Let's see."

Immediately the cry was taken up. "Let's see. Let's see!"

Panic started a ringing in his ears. He felt the satchel start to slip. He deliberately reached across the front of his coat. The man whose hand was on the satchel gasped at the sudden move.

"If simple courtesy won't persuade you to let me through, gentlemen, I'll have to resort to other means."

Orry slid his fingers under his left lapel. The man holding the satchel let go. "Watch it, lads. He's armed."

Those close by abruptly lost their enthusiasm for baiting him. He kept his hand beneath his lapel as one man, then others, shuffled backward to open an aisle. It wasn't easy to carry the bag with only the pressure of his upper arm, but he managed. He walked quickly along the aisle, feeling his furious heartbeat against the palm of his hand.

Free of the crowd, he hurried away. A couple of men shouted obscenities. He didn't look back.

He tried to sleep on the train but he was too shaken. He sat with the money satchel clamped between his feet. Next morning in Philadelphia, he located a large dry-goods store and purchased a small pair of scissors, needle, thread, and pieces of ribbon in three colors. From the ribbon, with patience and the aid of a ruddy woman behind the serving counter of a restaurant, he fashioned a rosette.

The woman seemed happy, even proud to help him. "You from Virginia?" she asked in recognition of his accent. "Lot of anti-slavery feeling in certain parts of the state, they say."

He merely smiled. Any suspicion she felt disappeared as she fastened the rosette to his lapel.

Orry reached Lehigh Station late on Tuesday, April 16. The town had grown larger; a new borough, consisting of a few dozen hovels and cheap houses, South Station, sprawled along the opposite bank of the river. In the depot, a man with a paste brush was posting a bill on the wall by the yellow light of a lantern. Orry saw that it was a recruiting notice, urging men to join a volunteer regiment being organized in response to President Lincoln's call.

He passed out of the light, but not before he was noticed by several loungers in front of the Station House. How could they help but notice a tall, bony man with dusty clothes, two bags, and only one hand to take care of them? Orry hoped the rosette was visible.

As he walked by the hotel, he heard one lounger say, "Queer duck. Anybody know him?"

The others said no. One remarked, "Looks a little like old Abe, don't he?"

"Could be his brother." The speaker left the hotel porch and ran after Orry. "Want a hack, mister? Only ten cents to any point in town."

Orry raised his eyebrows in a questioning way, at the same time nodding at the lights of Belvedere on the hilltop.

"The Hazard place?" The townsman fingered his chin; anyone visiting the only millionaire in Lehigh Station must be well off himself. "That's a nickel more."

Orry agreed with a nod. The open buggy ascended the steep hill. Suddenly a thin, fiery-white line appeared in the black sky above Belvedere. The streak of light fell toward the earth at an angle close to perpendicular. It vanished a moment after Orry realized it was a shooting star.

Scents of the warm springtime were quickly diluted by the fumes of the mill. Hazard Iron's three furnaces cast a deep red light over nearby hillsides. Smoke billowed from each furnace, and the breeze bore the pounding rhythm of steam engines. A menacing sound, somehow.

Panic seized Orry as the driver deposited him in front of the mansion. He hadn't thought to telegraph ahead. What if George had gone off somewhere?

An eager boy, breathless from running, answered the door. He was

775

taller than his father and less stocky, but the resemblance was unmistakable.

"William, don't you recognize me?" Orry removed his hat and smiled. The appearance of that smile in the middle of his tangled beard gave him a less forbidding look. William's wariness vanished. He whirled around.

"Pa? Pa, come here. Wait'll you see who's at the door." He stepped aside. "Come in, Mr. Main."

"Thank you, William." Orry entered and William took his bags. "You're tall as a tree. How old are you now?"

"Thirteen." Then he added, "Almost."

Orry shook his head and walked into the dazzle of the lower hall. He heard a door open, then close on the second-floor landing. He didn't bother to look up there because George was striding out of the dining room, his shirt-sleeves rolled above his elbows and his ever-present cigar in hand.

"Stick? Godamighty, I don't believe this."

He rushed forward. Constance came from the kitchen, equally astonished. George bobbed up and down on his toes, delighted as a little boy. "What the devil are you doing in Pennsylvania? And what's that?"

Orry glanced down at his lapel. "I had to wear it to get through the enemy lines."

George and Constance smiled at the little joke, but memories of larger events soon returned with crushing force. That showed when Constance hugged him and said:

"It's so wonderful to see you. Isn't the news from Sumter simply terrible?"

"Terrible," he agreed. "George, I came about a matter of business."

Once more George looked surprised. "I shouldn't think there's much business being done anywhere right now. I keep wondering how secession will affect mundane things: Bank transactions. Postal deliveries—ah, but we needn't stand here discussing that. Are you hungry? We just finished supper. A couple of fine roast ducklings. There's plenty left."

"A little food would be welcome."

"Then come along. My God, I can't believe you're here. It's like old times."

Constance put her arm around her tall son. She smiled again as the men walked toward the dining room. Orry did wish it could be like old times, but all he had seen on his journey told him the wish was an idle one. Never again would there be a day like that in 1842 when the two of them had stood at the rail of the Hudson River steamer with their hopes and illusions still intact.

They were old men now. Gray men. George's hair was streaked generously with it. And they had somehow let their world be pushed into the chasm of war. The knowledge robbed the reunion of joy. Grim-faced, he followed George and his cigar to the dining room.

While Orry ate, they exchanged items of news. Billy had reached Washington safely with his new wife. "And with a slight wound," George added. "Billy didn't go into details, but I gather there was an altercation with a former suitor of Brett's."

"Yes." Orry said no more.

"He's been promised a few days' leave. I'm expecting the two of them here at any time."

"I'd like to see them, but I can't wait. Things are chaotic at home."

"Chaotic everywhere," Constance said with a sigh.

George nodded glumly. "They say Virginia will secede tomorrow or the next day. She'll pull most of the fence-sitters with her. All the border states may go. Feelings are running high"—he pointed his cigar at the rosette—"as you must have discovered."

Orry finished his coffee, less weary now. But he had experienced no lifting of his spirits. He was glad to be with his old friend, yet he continued to feel this might be their last meeting for a long time.

After a silence, Constance spoke with obvious reluctance:

"Virgilia has come home."

Orry almost dropped his cup. "From where?"

"That," George growled, "we do not ask."

"Is she here this evening?"

George nodded, and Orry recalled the sound of a door's opening and closing upstairs as he arrived. Had Virgilia seen him?

Well, it didn't matter. Even though he had taken some elementary precautions down in the town, he really hadn't planned to make this visit a secret one.

"The poor creature's destitute—" Constance began.

"It's her own doing," George snapped. "I don't want to talk about it." His wife looked away. To Orry he said, "Now, what kind of business could be important enough to bring you all the way up here? Don't tell me Cooper's ready to launch the big ship."

"I wish that were the case. I don't think she'll ever leave the ways. That's why I came and why I brought the satchel I left in the hall. It contains six hundred and fifty thousand dollars. I'm sorry there isn't more, but I could only raise that much."

"Raise? Raise how?"

"Never mind. I didn't want your investment capital tied up in the South and subject to confiscation. You didn't loan it to us for that purpose."

George frowned, glanced at his wife and then back to his friend. "Perhaps we should discuss this in the library."

"Come, Billy," Constance said, patting her son as she rose.

"Billy." Orry smiled. "You call him that?"

She nodded. "When George's brother is home, he's Big Billy and this is Little Billy. It's confusing sometimes, but we like it."

William pulled a face. "Not all of us like it."

"He's right," Constance said, teasing her son by keeping a straight face. "Stanley claims it's undignified."

"That is why we like it," George said as he stood up. Orry laughed, spontaneously and hard. For a moment he could almost imagine the old times had returned.

"You say Billy's wound is healing satisfactorily?" Orry asked as George shut the doors and turned up the light.

"So I'm informed. He and Brett are happy even if the country isn't." He rummaged for glasses and a decanter. "I think we need some whiskey."

He poured two stiff drinks without asking whether Orry cared for one. Same old Stump, Orry thought. In charge of every situation.

"No, it isn't at all happy," Orry agreed as he took the whiskey. He drank half of it in three gulps. The warmth exploded in his stomach, soothing him a little. He fished for the key and unlocked the satchel he had brought from the hall. He opened it to show the large-denomination bills. "As I told you—that's the reason I brought this."

George picked up one banded bundle, struck speechless for a moment. Then he said softly:

"It's a very honorable act, Orry."

"The money's yours. I think you deserve it more than the Montgomery government. Which, by the way, has been established with men of solid and conservative bent in charge."

"So I noticed. Jeff Davis. Alec Stephens of Georgia—"

"The South Carolina crowd, including our mutual friend Young Hotspur"—at Orry's reference to Huntoon, George grimaced—"was virtually ignored. They aren't pleased."

"Why were they left out?"

"I'm not sure. I would suspect the conservatives thought them too extreme. Feared they'd detract from the respectability of the new government. In any case, I didn't think you'd want your money confiscated by men whose principles aren't exactly compatible with yours."

George threw him a quizzical look. "Are they compatible with yours?"

"I'm goddamned if I know anymore, Stump."

He slumped into a chair. His friend snapped the satchel shut, then seated himself next to the library table where the meteorite still rested. Almost without thought, George picked up the dark brown cone as he said, "Well, my assertion stands. You did an exceptionally honorable thing."

Embarrassed, Orry saluted his friend with his glass. Then his melancholy smile faded, and he pointed to the rough-textured object in George's hand.

"Is that the same one you found in the hills above the Academy?"

"Yes."

"I thought so. I remember some of what you said about it. Something about star iron having the power to destroy families, wealth, governments—the whole established order of things. I do believe we're about to see that opinion tested. You spoke of honor. There's damned little of it among individuals and even less"—his voice was low now, sardonic—"a flash or two every century?—among nations and political parties and groups crusading for their holy causes. But if war gets started soon, factories like yours will be responsible for eradicating even the little bit of honor that's left. Cooper's known it for a long time. He tried to make us listen. We refused. If there's to be a war, and it appears there is, it'll be the kind of new, total war Mahan predicted. Annihilating not just troops of the line but everything."

He shook his head. His exhaustion, and the whiskey consumed so quickly, produced an odd, light-headed state in which thoughts flowed freely, as did the words to express them. "And what are the South's resources for that kind of struggle? A vision of the future which is beginning to look pathetically outdated. Our rhetoric. Our slogans. And our soldiers."

"Southern officers are the cream of the Army, don't forget."

"Aye," Orry said, nodding. "And carrying out their orders will be a lot of tough farmers who can fight like the very devil, even though they never heard of Mahan or Jomini or, ironically, owned a single slave. But what are they up against? Your numbers. Your millions and millions of clerks and mechanics. Your infernal factories." The next was barely audible. "A new kind of war—"

Orry was silent a moment. Finally he went on, "Regardless of how it comes out—regardless of which side dictates the terms and which side accepts them—we'll all be the losers. We abdicated, George. We let the lunatics reign."

He flung his head back and poured the rest of the whiskey down his throat with a single gesture. After a moment he closed his eyes and shuddered. Slowly and with great care, George replaced the meteorite on the table and stared at it.

Orry opened his eyes. He thought he heard a distant tumult. George stirred. "Yes, the lunatics reign. But what could we have done?"

"I'm not sure. Cooper was always cautioning us with Burke." He struggled to remember and quote correctly. " 'When bad men combine, the good must associate, else they will fall one by one—' "

On his feet suddenly, he reached for the whiskey. "I don't know what the hell we could have done, but I know we didn't ask the question soon enough or forcefully enough. Or often enough."

He poured, drank two-thirds of a glass. George pondered what his friend had said. Then he too shook his head. "That's such a simple answer. Maybe too simple. The problem's incomprehensibly tangled. Sometimes I think one man is such a puny thing. How can he change anything when there are great forces stirring? Forces he doesn't understand or even recognize?"

Orry's reply was the same depressing truth he had admitted a few moments earlier. "I'm not sure. But if great forces and events aren't entirely accidental, they must be created and shaped by men. Created and shaped by positive action and by lack of it, too. I think we had a chance. I think we threw it away."

Inexplicably, his voice broke on the last words. He felt tears in his eyes. Tears of pain, of failure, frustration, and despair—he was damned if he knew all their wellsprings. For one blinding moment the friends stared at each other, stripped of every emotion save their realization of culpability and the fear it generated now that the slogan-chanting mobs were abroad in the North and the South. Abroad and marching steadfastly toward Mahan's new apocalypse—

Mob. The word, and certain noises, shattered Orry's dark reverie. He turned toward a window. He heard voices outside. Not a large crowd, but a ferocious one.

George frowned. "Sounds like a bunch of town roughnecks. What do you suppose they want?"

He reached for the velvet curtains. The sudden crash of the door spun him around.

"Virgilia!"

The moment Orry saw her, he knew why the mob had come.

67

Outside, the tumult increased. George pointed to the window, his voice mingling shock and rage. "Are you responsible for that, Virgilia?"

Her smile was sufficient answer.

"How the hell did they get here?" he demanded.

A rock smashed one of the windows. The heavy drapes kept the glass from flying, though it tinkled loudly on the floor beneath the curtain's gold fringe. Orry thought he heard someone shout the word *traitor*. He brushed his hand across his mouth.

"I sent one of the servants to the hotel." Virgilia looked at Orry. "Right after I saw him step through the front door."

"In the name of God—*why?*"

Orry could have answered George's question. And he was barely able to contain the revulsion the sight of Virgilia produced. She was only a few years his senior, but she looked twenty years older than that. Her print dress, faded from many washings, fit too tightly; she had gained at least fifteen pounds. But the weight was only one sign of a continuing deterioration. Her complexion was pasty, her eyes sunken. Wisps of hair straggled to her shoulders, and when she turned to answer her brother, Orry saw dirt on her neck.

"Because he's a traitor," she whispered. "A Southerner and a traitor. He murdered Grady."

"He had nothing to do with Grady's death. You've taken leave of your—"

"Murdered him," she repeated, her eyes on Orry again. Those eyes glowed with a hatred so intense, it was almost a physical force. "You did it, you and your kind."

George shouted at her. "The Federal troops killed Grady!" But she was beyond the reach of reason, and it was then Orry knew what it was that she had brought into the room. It was more than the odor of stale clothes or unclean flesh. It was the stink of death.

"I sent for those men," she said to him. "I hope they kill you."

Suddenly, like a bolting animal, she ran at the draperies hiding the broken window. "He's in here!" she screamed. George leaped after her, grabbed her arm, and flung her backward.

She fell, landing hard on hands and knees. Without warning, she began to sob, great, mindless bellows of pain. Her unpinned hair hung like a curtain on both sides of her drooping head. Mercifully, it hid her madwoman's face.

George eyed the drapes she had almost reached and opened. He pitched his voice low. "There is a local freight eastbound at eleven o'clock. I think it would be advisable for your own safety—"

"I agree," Orry cut in. "I'll go now. I don't want to endanger your family. I'll slip out the back way."

"The hell you will. They probably have someone watching there. You leave this to me."

George started toward the hall. Virgilia struggled to her feet. George turned back to look at her. "Virgilia—"

He was too overcome to continue. But he didn't need words. His eyes and his reddening face conveyed his feelings. She backed away from him, and he strode on to the front hall.

There, Constance, the two children, and half a dozen servants were anxiously watching the main door. Firelight shimmered on the fanlight above. The men outside had torches. Orry saw the door handle shake, but someone inside had been alert enough to shoot the bolt when the mob arrived.

"Who are those men?" Constance asked her husband. "What are they doing here?"

"They want Orry. It's Virgilia's doing. Take the children upstairs."

"*Virgilia?* Oh, dear God, George—"

"Take them upstairs! The rest of you, clear the hall." To Orry: "Wait here a moment." As the servants scattered and Constance hurried the youngsters away, George disappeared into a wardrobe closet beneath the staircase.

He reappeared, struggling into his coat. On the lapel Orry noticed a patriotic rosette, smaller and much neater than his own. Over George's arm hung a military-issue gun belt. From the holster he plucked an 1847-model Colt repeater.

He flung the belt on a chair and quickly examined the gun. "I keep it loaded and handy in that closet because I've had a few surprise callers—employees I've discharged, that sort of thing—"

He twirled the cylinder, then turned toward the front door. A stone crashed through the fanlight, spilling glass over a wide area. "Dishonorable sons of bitches," George growled. "Follow me."

His short, stocky legs carried him straight toward the door, which

784

he unlocked with no hesitation. Orry was right behind, frightened yet oddly delighted, too. The years had rolled away, and they were in battle again—George in the lead, as usual.

George flung the door open with what Orry thought was calculated bravado. It had no effect on the mob that surged up the steps of Belvedere, shouting and cursing. Orry counted twelve to fifteen men armed with rocks and cudgels. "There's the damned Southerner," one screamed as Orry followed George onto the porch. "There's the traitor."

Another man shook a smoking torch. "We want him."

George's shoulders were thrown back. He looked pugnacious and powerful as he raised the Colt repeater and extended his arm. With the muzzle pointed at the forehead of the man who had just spoken, he thumb-cocked the gun.

"Take him. I guarantee you and a few others won't survive the attempt."

Orry stepped to the left of his friend, within a couple of feet of the men crowding the steps. He thought he recognized two of the loungers from the hotel.

"Let's rush him," someone else yelled.

George pointed the Colt at the shouter. "Come on. It's an old military axiom. The one who gives the order leads the charge."

"Damn it, Hazard," another man exclaimed, "he's a Southron. A palmetto-state man. All we want to do is show him what we think of disunionists—traitors."

"This gentleman's no traitor. We graduated in the same West Point class, then went all the way to Mexico City with General Scott. My friend fought for this country just as hard as I did, and that empty sleeve shows you the reward he got. I know most of you. I don't want the death of a single one of you on my hands. But if you mean to harm an honorable man like this, you'll have to remove me first."

The noise level dropped. Orry saw eyes shift from George's gun to other parts of the porch. Some in the crowd were estimating how they might flank the pair and thus overcome them. A couple of men slipped away from the back of the mob, but George quickly covered them.

"The first to move will be the first to fall."

The two men held still. Five seconds became ten. Fifteen—

"We can take them" a voice growled. But there was no response. Orry's heart was pounding. It could go either way—

"Hell," someone said. "It ain't worth gettin' killed."

"That shows good sense," George said, still with a feisty tone. "If that's the attitude of the rest of you, you're free to move. Just make sure you move away from the porch, down the hill and off my property." He paused, then stunned them by shouting in his best West Point voice, "Get going!"

They responded to the command and the threat of the Colt. By ones and twos they shuffled away, leaving only a few oaths in their wake.

A minute went by. Another. Orry and George stayed on the porch, alert in case the mob's mood changed again. Finally George lowered the Colt and slumped against a pillar.

"Close," he said softly. "But we're not out of the woods yet. Fetch your valise while I send someone for the buggy. The sooner we get you on a train, the better."

Orry didn't argue.

One servant drove, another rode astride the buggy horse. Each man carried a gun, as did George. He had already started a search for the servant who had taken Virgilia's message to the mob. The man would be sent packing.

George and Orry were still shaken by the confrontation. George sat in preoccupied silence as the buggy bumped its way down the hill. Presently Orry said, "What are you thinking about?"

"These foul times. We might have prevented all this if we'd responded with the best that's in us. Instead, we seem to have responded with the worst. I wonder if we're capable of anything else."

Silence again. Orry tried to lighten the moment by telling his friend what he'd had no chance to tell him before—that Madeline was with him at last and would remain. When the future was a little less cloudy, they planned to consult a lawyer and obtain a divorce for her.

"That's fine, splendid," George murmured as the buggy passed some outlying houses. His eyes, ceaselessly moving, swept shadowed stoops, yellow-lit windows, then the street. Abruptly he leaned forward. Ahead, silhouetted against the lamps of the hotel and depot, four men had stepped into the street to await the buggy.

"Look sharp, you two," George called to his men.

Panting, Virgilia ran along the path that led over the hill behind Belvedere. She didn't dare flee into town; George had gone in that direction.

Brambles snagged her skirt and slashed her hands, which were clasped tightly around the handle of a huge, bulging carpetbag. She was a strong woman, but even so she could barely carry the bag, which gave off clanking sounds each time it bumped her leg.

She had returned to the mansion once too often. She knew that now. Never again would she set foot in Lehigh Station.

And why should she? She hated the whole family. Pompous little George and priggish Stanley, their wives, their precious white-skinned children. They understood nothing of the struggle taking place in the world. They pretended to be in sympathy with it, but they had no real appreciation of its hardships and cruelties. They were pampered hypocrites, the lot of them.

Her loud, rapid breathing sounded like sobbing. Suddenly she stumbled, fell. But she never once let go of the carpetbag.

She regained her feet and hurried on. No one was pursuing her, but she labored up the steep hillside as if the opposite was true. When George had looked at her, too overcome to speak, she had known she must run.

Her shoulders and upper arms already ached horribly. She had stuffed too many things into the carpetbag before leaving the house: candlesticks, silver, garments from Constance's wardrobe, and several of her most valuable pieces of jewelry—items Virgilia could readily sell to obtain money to live.

She didn't consider it stealing, only payment of what was rightfully hers. George and Stanley had always demeaned her because she was a woman. Their scorn had grown worse when she took a black lover. One day, she vowed as she panted her way to the hilltop, she'd pay them. She'd pay them all.

The buggy rolled on toward the waiting men. They remained in the middle of the street. George touched the driver's arm.

"Don't stop, and don't go around them. Hand me your gun."

The driver gave George his Colt. The only sounds for about half a minute were the clopping of hooves and the faint squeak of a rear axle. George held his breath and raised the two guns so that they could be clearly seen.

When the muzzle of the horse was within a yard of the silent men, they stepped aside.

In the dim light, Orry recognized two who had been in the mob at Belvedere. One of them spat on the street while staring straight at him. But Orry was past all anger, too spent to react. The buggy rolled on.

"Made it!" George exclaimed with a tense smile.

They waited almost an hour inside the depot, with the two servants on watch outside. Nothing further was seen of the troublemakers.

George now seemed as exhausted as his friend. Their conversation was fitful. Orry brought up Elkanah Bent, but George immediately dismissed the subject with a weary wave. Now that war had come, he said, there were far worse things to fear than one deranged officer. Billy had been warned, George intended to put Bent out of mind permanently, and that was that.

Silence ensued. Like George, Orry too wondered how they had come to such a point of crisis in the country. Where had they failed? What had they left undone? Some solutions had been proposed but never seriously considered. The plan of compensated emancipation put forth by Emerson and others. Resettlement of freed slaves in Liberia so as not to flood the industrial North with cheap labor. Had there been even a faint hope of those ideas being implemented? Would Garrison and Virgilia have consented? Or Calhoun and Ashton's husband? He didn't know. He never would.

The rails lit up as the locomotive loomed. The station agent had flagged the freight. George accompanied Orry to the spot on the platform where the caboose was likely to stop.

"Special passenger," George explained to a pair of puzzled brakemen. He pressed money into their hands. He was about to bid his friend good-bye when his eye lit on Orry's crudely made rosette. "Just a minute."

He unfastened the rosette and tossed it away. Then he took off his own and pinned it on Orry's lapel.

"You might as well wear one that looks genuine. I'll be damned if I want to be responsible for them lynching you in Maryland."

They embraced. Orry boarded the train.

68

Orry reached Philadelphia the next morning. He left for Washington at four in the afternoon. A hard rain was falling. He sat with his forehead against the wet window, almost like a man in a trance. One memory, one image, sustained him now: Madeline.

Presently, after darkness fell, the train jerked to a halt. Lamps burned on a rickety platform. By their light he saw a northbound train standing on the other track. Passengers were crowding the platform, taking the opportunity to escape the smoky cars for a little while. Those around Orry got up to do the same. He felt no inclination to move.

"Where are we?" he asked a conductor.

"Relay House."

"Why are both trains stopped?"

"To pick up passengers from a local from the east shore. There'll be some people going north, some going south."

"That's fitting," Orry said. The conductor looked at him as if he were unbalanced.

Staring into the rain, Orry suddenly spied familiar faces. He jumped up, took three long strides down the aisle. Then, abruptly, he halted.

Bending to peer through another window, he studied his sister and her husband. Would he compromise the young couple or create danger for them if he spoke to them? Billy was in uniform.

He let out an oath. For a second he had started to think like the mob: *If you're a Southerner, you're a traitor.* He walked quickly to the head of the car.

Rain struck his face as he worked his way across the platform. "Brett? Billy?"

Surprise and confusion registered on the faces of the young couple when they recognized him. A few people gave him suspicious looks, but his rosette reassured them.

"What in the world are you doing here?" Brett exclaimed.

"Going home. I paid a visit to Lehigh Station. George said he was expecting you any time."

"I'm on leave," Billy said. "After that, everything's pretty uncertain."

"How's your arm?"

"Fine. No permanent damage." He circled Brett's waist and held her. "Those two or three hours after the wedding seem more like a bad dream than anything else. To this day I'm not sure why all of it happened."

"Nor I," Brett added. Orry still didn't know whether he'd ever be able to tell her of Ashton's involvement.

She noticed his rosette. "Where did you get that? You haven't undergone some miraculous conversion, have you?"

"Not quite. George gave it to me. To get me through enemy lines, you might say."

The east-shore local was chugging in. Passengers got off and rushed for the other trains with their luggage. "How is George?" Brett asked.

"Good as ever."

She touched him gently. "How are you?"

"Better than I ever expected to be. I reckon you don't know Madeline LaMotte left her husband. She's staying at Mont Royal. We've been friends for years."

Brett showed no surprise. Instead, she smiled. "I suspected something like that. Oh, there's so much to ask you, Orry—I can't think of a quarter of it."

A conductor from the northbound train called impatiently, "All aboard, please. We're half an hour late as it is."

Brett flung her arms around her brother's neck. "When will we see you again?"

"Not for a while, I expect. I don't think even Mr. Lincoln or Mr. Davis knows what's going to happen next. Whatever it is—even if there's fighting—I want the Hazards and the Mains to keep their ties unbroken. There are few things in the world that matter as much as friendship and love. They're both very fragile. We must preserve them till these times pass."

"I promise we will," she said, all at once crying.

"Here's the strongest bond yet." Billy lifted her left hand to display her wedding ring.

Orry nodded. "I finally realized that. It's the reason I changed my mind about the marriage."

"I'm glad you did," Billy said, smiling.

"*Boooard!*" the conductor cried. His colleague on Orry's train

790

repeated the cry. The northbound conductor jumped to the steps of a coach and waved to the engineer. The noise—steam, bells, voices—instantly increased.

Billy and his brother-in-law shook hands. Orry hurried back to his car. Steam billowed up, hiding the platform that had become deserted within a space of seconds. The engine on the northbound track lurched, and soon both trains were pulling away in opposite directions, leaving the little island of light behind as they gathered speed in the vast dark.

In Washington, Orry again changed trains, this time to an express. Just before it departed, four men got aboard, young men in civilian clothes struggling with a great assortment of valises and parcels. From their posture and the way they moved, Orry knew they were soldiers, Southern soldiers going home.

They took seats two rows behind him. He listened to their conversation. Would Lincoln and Jeff Davis send armies into the field? Would the trains soon stop running? Would new currency be printed in Montgomery? Their questions were innumerable, answers nonexistent.

The rain slacked to a drizzle. Chugging slowly through the seedy capital district, the train crossed some of the sloughs and vacant lots so common there. In one weed-grown field Orry saw a military unit drilling. There were a few lanterns scattered here and there, but the dark figures were discernible chiefly because of a faraway light source, indefinable except as a bright, ghostly glow. He saw rows of bayonets on musket barrels; for an instant while he watched, one bayonet glittered like a star.

The militia was marching and counter-marching in the rain because Washington was vulnerable now. Just across the river was Virginia, the country of the enemy.

Where was Lee? Where were some of Orry's old comrades from Mexico? Little Mac McClellan, whom he had envied but never liked. Jackson, who had gone off to teach cadets at the Virginia Military Institute. Breezy George Pickett, such a good soldier and so seldom serious. How he'd love to see some of them again.

But not on a red field. Not if opposing generals arranged the reunion. Men who had been almost as close as brothers at the Academy might at this very moment be planning campaigns to annihilate one another. It was unthinkable, and it had happened.

He saw it all summed up in the blind marching of that nameless unit, a vision of gaunt shapes, sharp shiny steel, dim lamps flaring in the rain. The war machine was rolling.

God help us all, he thought.

A light rain was falling on Tradd Street that night. Cooper wrote a letter he had been thinking about for some time. When he finished, he went searching for his wife. He found Judith just coming down from settling the children in bed. With war fever sweeping the state, Judah and Marie-Louise tended to become overly excited and stay up too late.

Without preamble, Cooper announced his decision. Judith's response was a moment of stunned silence. Then:

"Do you mean it?"

"I've already signed the letter to the gentlemen who called on me. I'll send it to Montgomery tomorrow. After the first of May, all the assets of the Carolina Shipping Company, including our vessels, belong to the Navy Department."

She shook her head as she sat down. "How can you make that decision, believing as you do?"

"Neutrality is the coward's way out. We either support the war or move north. I think secession's wrong, and the institution that brought it about is even worse. I think we'll be punished. Crushed. And yet"— a troubled look, a gesture—"I feel a loyalty, Judith."

She looked skeptical. He drew a breath. "There's one other part of my discussion with the committee members that I didn't tell you about. They asked me to go to London as an agent for the department."

"*London?* Why?"

"Because they know the Confederacy can't survive without food and manufactured goods supplied by others. Mr. Lincoln knows it too. Blockade is a weapon the Yankees will surely use against us. When it happens, there must be counter-strokes. A ship like the *Star of Carolina*—"

"What are you talking about?" Judith exclaimed, angered and upset. "She'll never get off the ways!"

"I said one like her. Designed to carry heavy armament. Designed for war. A commerce raider. She would roam the earth and do inestimable damage to Yankee shipping." He glanced at his wife from under his eyebrows. "Because of my experience here in Charleston, the department wants me to investigate the possibility of constructing such a vessel in Britain."

"That means we'd have to take the children."

"And be prepared to stay a year, perhaps more."

"Oh, Cooper, how can we? The cause is wrong!"

"If not already lost," he said with a nod. A flaming vision of Hazard Iron floated in his thoughts. "Still, even though I can't explain my reasons fully or adequately, I feel I must go. No, let me be completely truthful. I want to go."

Again she searched his face. "All right. I detest the idea, and I fail to understand your logic—if there is any. But you know I'd never desert you. I suggest you book steamer passage."

"I already have. We leave from Savannah a week from Friday."

He took her in his arms and held her while she cried.

Next morning, at the yard on James Island, he saw to the erection of a tall iron pole. When the pulleys and halyards were in place, he watched two of his men unfold a huge flag. It consisted of three broad bars running horizontally; the top and bottom ones were red, the center one white. A field of deep blue in the upper left held a circle of seven white stars.

He was struck by the resemblance between the new flag and that of the nation the seceding states had left. Even while we trumpet our independence, we can't bring ourselves to cut all the cords, he thought as the Stars and Bars rode up the pole, caught the wind, and spread against the sky.

69

Early next day, on a primitive road in south-central Alabama, a closed carriage bumped toward Montgomery. A dozen trunks and valises crowded the boot and the top. Rex was driving. Inside, Huntoon labored at a polished-oak lap desk. He had finally been summoned to take a minor governmental post, which satisfied him for the moment. Both his post and his influence would not remain minor for long. At that he had been more fortunate than many of the other leaders of South Carolina. Bob Rhett, for example, had been rejected as a candidate for president of the Confederate States because he was perceived as too extreme.

Huntoon was willing to take certain risks to establish himself. All during the final tiresome leg of their journey, from Columbus, Georgia, to Montgomery, he had been writing a memorial to the Confederate Congress. The thrust of it was an attack on the conservatism of the Confederacy's provisional constitution. In language and scope, it was remarkably close to the old Constitution, except that slavery was protected. But, rather remarkably, the new constitution prohibited the African slave trade. That provision definitely had to be changed.

Huntoon's memorial also called for the new confederation to name itself the United States of America, thus demonstrating to the world that it represented the one true constitutional government on the continent. He argued that the Yankees were the ones who had perverted the principles of the Founding Fathers.

At the moment he was stuck on the conclusion. He had written, "We must prove that an aristocracy can govern better than a mob," but he could go no further. Perhaps it was the sight of his wife that distracted him and barred the smooth flow of words.

Ashton was leaning against the interior wall, gazing out the window at the pleasant cotton fields through which the road twisted and dipped. Despite dust and the general disarray produced by travel, she looked extremely fetching, Huntoon thought. He felt a physical response and recalled that it had been more than a month since he had been permitted to enjoy intimate relations. She didn't seem to need that from their marriage any longer.

He cleared his throat. "My dear? I've run aground. Perhaps you can help me frame a felicitous conclusion."

He held out the last of several closely written sheets. Pouting, she batted it away.

"I'm not interested in all that silly jibber-jabber, Jamie."

Under the desk his rigidity wilted. From his expression, she decided she had stung him a little too hard. She leaned over to allow him to feel her tightly bound breast against his sleeve.

"Montgomery will be a wonderful experience for us. What matters isn't the verbiage, the philosophy, but the power we—you can accumulate and use. We waited a long time for this opportunity. We mustn't fritter it away on useless exercises."

She had grown excited; the thought of power always had that effect. If her husband didn't climb as high or as swiftly as she thought he should, there would certainly be others in Montgomery worthy of her consideration. In Montgomery or Richmond, she amended silently; there was already widespread talk about the capital soon being moved out of the cotton belt to Virginia.

The conversation, as well as a long period of self-denial following Forbes's untimely death, had built tension within Ashton. Even if she didn't like her husband very much, he could be used to relieve it.

"Jamie, Jamie—put that silly paper away. Can't you see I've been missing your company terribly?"

"You have? I hardly noticed."

His cynicism was only a momentary pose. With a touch of her hand, she brought him to impatient tumidity. Ashton was a little surprised at the suddenness and intensity of her own desire.

He forced her over against the opposite seat, one hand constricting on her breasts, one groping up her leg beneath her skirts. Dreadful, crude man, she thought. But he would serve. She closed her eyes and imagined a gala ball at which she was presented to President Davis, who was utterly charmed by her intelligence and beauty.

As the coach labored on, Rex scratched his head and leaned out to one side. He was intensely curious about the cause of so many loud creaks and cries from within. But, alas, the angle was wrong; he couldn't see a thing.

That same night, Elkanah Bent stood at the bar in Willard's Hotel. He was sipping whiskey while he totted up figures on a scrap of paper.

He was pleased by the final sum. After paying the tailor's bill for his new uniforms, he would have just enough left to lease the small flat he had found. Many good houses and apartments had become available in Washington recently; scores of traitorous officers and bureaucrats were fleeing home to the South.

It behooved him to occupy better quarters than a hotel room. His influential friends had secured him a brevet to full colonel, a promotion not at all unusual for a career officer in these days of frenzied preparation for war. Bent only hoped the war would last longer than a few months. Some predicted it would not. General Scott made frequent reference to "the fatal incapacity of the Southerners for agreeing or working together." He said it would adversely affect military performance.

Well, time enough to worry about that. Tonight he wanted to celebrate. A fine meal, then an hour's companionship. He would need to make credit arrangements for the latter, however. He knew one sordid black brothel where it was possible.

He was exalted by thoughts of the coming conflict. Blood would run. Thousands and thousands would die. He rejoiced at this long-overdue chance to display his skills and earn the reputation—the glory—he knew to be his just portion.

And along the way he might be able to settle some old scores.

He would never get over botching the attempt in Texas. And now that damned Charles Main had defected to the South like so many other dishonorable soldiers whose actions made them deserving of a firing squad. But war had a curious way of twisting fates and fortunes. Who knew but what this one might bring him an opportunity to strike directly at the Mains. He mustn't forget they were somehow connected with a woman attempting to pass herself off as white, a woman who was not only a nigger but the offspring of a New Orleans whore.

As for Billy Hazard, surely he would be able to keep track of him. The young engineering officer was remaining on active duty. Bent had already ascertained that at the adjutant general's office. He'd get the lot of them, both families. He believed that because of another conviction he held—neither the Mains nor the Hazards would suspect that his desire for revenge could survive in the chaos that was surely ahead. Their stupidity was his trump card.

He finished his whiskey and called for another. He admired his uniform in the mirror behind the bar. He became aware of two men next to him who were engaged in loud conversation. One was arguing that a reconstruction plan should be prepared and publicized immediately, to encourage the South to return to the fold.

797

Bent slammed his glass on the bar. "If you believe that, sir, you belong on the other side of the Potomac."

The man was eager to debate. "I take issue, sir. The Lord Jesus Christ Himself stated that mercy—"

"No mercy," Bent interrupted. "No quarter. Never."

A few listeners cheered. The argumentative man took note of the unpopularity of his view and said no more.

Bent preened in front of the mirror. What a splendid day this had been. A man was lucky to live in a time of war.

War. Was there a sweeter, more delicious word in all of the English language? He felt so fine that he left a whole twenty-five cents for the barman.

He strutted out of the hotel, enjoying one of his favorite thoughts. Bent and Bonaparte began with the same letter. It was not a trivial coincidence. By God, no. It had immense historical significance. Before long the world would appreciate that.

A few days later, in the Blue Ridge foothills near Harpers Ferry, Virgilia visited Grady's unmarked grave.

It was a sweet, warm April afternoon. She had driven from the railway station in a hired buggy, which she had pulled to the side of the dirt road at the foot of a low hill covered with maples. She had tied the horse to a branch, walked halfway up, and dropped to her knees beside a mound surrounded by trees.

"Oh, Grady. Grady."

She fell forward on the new grass covering the mound. She had dug the grave, filled it, and piled up the earth with her own hands. In the confusion just prior to Brown's capture, she had crept into Harpers Ferry, located Grady's body, and hidden it. Not long afterward, one of the other conspirators, a Negro woman, had helped her move it here, where no one would dig it up and desecrate it.

Brown was gone now, his dream of a glorious revolt dying with him on the gallows. Grady was gone too. But their blood-price had bought a great gift: the war. Fighting had not yet started, but she was convinced it soon would. She reveled in the thought as she lay with her thighs and breasts crushed against the mound, as if it were Grady's living flesh.

She imagined rows and rows of Southern corpses with heads gone, stumps of arms gushing blood, holes where the genitals had been. She moaned and trembled as she thought of the coming epiphany of her cause. There would be work for her, bloody work others were too scrupulous or fainthearted to perform.

But she would perform it. She would answer the call of her own hatred of those who enslaved others, those who enslaved beautiful black men. She had left her family, insufferable moralizing prigs, forever. She had cut herself off from humanity and now lived solely for her memories and one companion:

Death, who was her friend and God's righteous instrument.

At Mont Royal, shadows seemed longer, the spring nights darker, than ever before. Orry had no interest in planting and husbanding a rice crop, nor had he any confidence in Jeff Davis's announced plan to use cotton to win European recognition of the Confederacy. In his opinion, Davis was a damn fool. The European market was glutted with cotton. Who would care if the South withheld its crop?

A strange impulse for change was stirring in Orry these days. He was restless in the familiar rooms, the old grooves. Only Madeline's presence and the easy way she fitted herself into his life made existence bearable.

Confusion and doubt seemed to be his lot. One night, sleepless, he went browsing in the library. He pulled out a volume he hadn't looked at in years. It was *Notes on the State of Virginia*, the only book ever written by Thomas Jefferson.

He hitched up his nightshirt and sat down to read awhile. Presently he reached a line that leaped out because it had been underscored with a pen. Three words, *Amen and amen*, had been inked on the margin beside it. The line read:

"Indeed I tremble for my country when I reflect that God is just; that his justice cannot sleep forever."

Jefferson, a Southerner and a slave owner, had been writing about slavery. What confounded Orry was the marginal notation. He had studied enough old plantation ledgers to recognize the handwriting. It was his father's.

The three words suggested that Tillet, so staunch a defender of slavery in public, had actually harbored doubts about it. Doubts he had kept hidden all his life. The old sinner, Orry thought with a surge of sympathy. Well, what decent man wouldn't harbor doubts—especially now that the consequences were so cruelly apparent?

Encountering Tillet's doubts only enhanced his own, which were profound. They embraced both the history of the Mains and that of every man who lived by, and therefore tolerated, the peculiar institution. Ever after, Orry regretted that he had given in to the impulse to take that particular book off the shelf.

A few minutes after sunrise one misty morning, Orry and Charles went riding on the plantation. Pale clouds stirred around them as they galloped, phantom men on phantom horses in a landscape of gray shot through with smoky orange. Beneath the layers of mist, the flooded fields shone like polished metal.

A file of slaves trudging along a check bank loomed on the right. The driver turned to offer a laconic salute to the master. But even at a distance, Orry detected a certain mockery in the black man's bearing, a certain resentment on his face.

Soon a swirl of mist hid the spectral column of men. But other parties of workmen were out that morning, and Orry realized he had been riding among them without taking note of their presence. They simply existed, like trunk gates or the kitchen building. They were items of property.

He thought again of Jefferson's book. Items of property. That was it, wasn't it? The reason the North, the world, perhaps even the Lord Himself, was calling the South to judgment—

"Wade Hampton's raising a mounted legion," Charles called suddenly. "I'm reporting for duty in two weeks."

"I didn't know."

"I was only notified yesterday. I'm tired of waiting and fretting. I want to do what I was trained to do." He leaped his horse over a ditch. His hair, badly in need of barbering, bobbed and danced at the nape of his neck. "It should be a glorious fight."

The remark made Orry realize how great a gulf separated them. It was caused by more than a difference in their ages. Even after seeing action in Texas, Charles hadn't lost his love of brawling.

Orry didn't want his silence interpreted as agreement. "Glorious?" he called back. "I think not. Not this time."

But Charles was already cropping his horse for greater speed, and he was laughing with such joy of life he never heard the dour voice behind him. Hair streaming, he went galloping toward the misty sunrise, the perfect picture of a cavalier.

Next day Orry received a letter from the state government. He hid it until evening, when he could discuss it with Madeline in the warmth of their bed.

"They asked me to consider a commission. Possibly a brigadier's. Apparently the lack of an arm is no handicap at that rank, and they claim my former service makes me invaluable. Invaluable—imagine that."

He laughed, but there was scant humor in it. Then: "Do you know, Madeline, years ago John Calhoun said West Point men would lead great armies? I don't suppose he imagined they would lead them against each other."

After a moment she said, "How do you feel about the proposal?"

He lay back and stroked her hair. "It's tempting, but I'd hate to leave you here alone."

"I'm not afraid of Justin."

"It isn't Justin who worries me. Have you noticed how some of the plantation people are behaving? They've gotten lazy. A few have an almost arrogant glint in their eye. This very afternoon I caught Cuffey whispering with another house man. I heard the name 'Linkum.'"

She assured him she would be fine if he chose to leave. He thanked her, but he knew his decision would spring from something far more elemental. His land, Main land, was threatened now. Would he or would he not defend it?

"I'll show you the letter in the morning," he said. "I do believe I'll have to give them a favorable answer."

"I almost knew you'd do that when the call came."

The call. The words touched off bursts of memory, the strongest of them aural. The old, nearly forgotten drums were beating again, summoning him, demanding that he answer.

"How would you feel if I accepted a commission?"

She kissed his mouth. "I'd regret it." Another kiss. "And be proud." A third, still longer and sweeter. "And wait for you to come back to me at the first possible moment."

Her arms clasped him tightly. He didn't think he'd ever been so happy. She whispered to him:

"I love you too much to lose you, my darling. If you go away, I'll pray such prayers God can't help but send you back safe and sound."

Stanley's crony, Boss Cameron, had secured a post for him in the capital. Washington was already showing signs of turning into a warren of profiteers, influence peddlers, and political hacks. But old, plodding Stanley was invigorated by the new challenge, and Isabel looked forward to an exciting social adventure. Stanley and his wife had already closed their house and enrolled their boys in a fashionable Washington school. At fourteen, the twins were undisciplined ruffians. Their absence would be welcomed by the entire town of Lehigh Station.

Up in Rhode Island, a violent storm destroyed a large section of roof at Fairlawn. George received the news by telegraph and decided to leave by train the next day to assess the damage. Constance said she wanted to go with him. She needed a holiday; she was peeved at the world and inexcusably short-tempered with William and Patricia. Brett and Billy promised to look after the children, since Billy hoped to be at Belvedere a few more days before returning to duty.

That night, after a lengthy meeting he had called in his office at Hazard's, George found himself unable to sleep. By eleven-thirty he was in the library, a full tumbler of whiskey before him on the polished table, six inches to the right of the rough brown object he had treasured for so many years.

He stared at the meteorite a long time, finding himself less proud of his trade, less certain of its worth, than in the past. He saw all the destructive uses to which star iron had been put throughout the centuries, and to which it would soon be put again. He finally drank the whiskey around three in the morning, and extinguished the lamp and climbed to his bedroom and the warmth of his wife's slumbering form, but even then he failed to find rest.

Newport had a dead, abandoned look under gray skies. George and Constance felt strange staying in the great house all by themselves. Yet at the same time they relished their unfamiliar privacy.

On the afternoon of their first full day at Fairlawn, George met for an hour with the building contractor who would repair the roof. Then he and Constance went for a walk along the deserted beach. White combers were breaking. The sky had a vast, wintry look unsuited to springtime. She kept her arm in his, eager for the sense of contact.

"You never told me the reason for the night meeting, George."

"Nothing secret about it. I called in all the foremen and told them we were placing the factory on a twenty-four-hour production schedule. We're already receiving orders from the War Department. No doubt Stanley will see that we get many more. We're liable to come out of this richer than ever."

"At the price of a certain number of dead bodies."

He frowned. "Yes, I suppose that's true."

He stopped and turned toward her. He had to get something into the open. "Stanley says Washington wants all the Academy men it can find."

"For the Army?"

"Or government posts."

She looked at him steadily. "Do you want to serve?"

"Want isn't quite the right word. Somewhere, in some fashion"—he took a breath; it was far from the happiest admission he had ever made, yet there was relief in saying it—"I feel I must."

She started to cry, but immediately fought back the tears and squared her shoulders. "It's your decision, darling." She took his arm again. "Could we go back to the house now? I feel a sudden and quite uncontrollable urge to make love."

Despite her smile, he still saw a glint of tears. He cast an eye at the scraggly underbrush visible behind large boulders up at the edge of the beach.

"What's the matter with right there?" He managed an impish smile, then kissed the tip of her nose. "Unless, of course, you deem yourself too conservative, Mrs. Hazard."

"George"—a pause, a teasing look—"did you ever do this sort of thing before we were married? At West Point, for instance? You seem to fall into it quite naturally."

"I have no comment."

She thought again. "What if we're seen?"

"By whom? There isn't another soul for miles."

"It's rather chilly."

"I'll keep you warm."

"Do you really think we dare?"

"Of course. Wartime has a disastrous effect on convention. People know they might not get a second chance."

She saw that his jest hid something somber. There was no humor in his eyes. She clasped his hand tightly. They turned their backs on the lifeless sky and ran toward the rocks.

70

At Belvedere, Billy and Brett went in to supper together. Billy suggested they go walking afterward because the spring night was so fine. They both understood that there was a second, unstated reason; the passing hours had released an increasing poignancy. Late that afternoon he had received a telegraph message: orders to return to Washington the following morning. The thought of his imminent departure depressed Brett and ruined her appetite.

Toward the end of the meal, there was a commotion. A sudden light suffused the twilight sky beyond the dining-room windows. As Billy, Brett, and two serving girls rushed to look outside, a distant shudder shook the house to its foundation. One of the girls gasped. A groom came running excitedly into the room, exclaiming that a shooting star had blazed bright as noon, then disappeared in the next valley.

The meteor striking the earth would account for the concussion they had all felt. The unnerved man spoke of the many shooting stars seen above the valley of late. He trembled and whispered something about God's fury coming to the land.

Brett took those remarks with outward calm, yet the strange light and the tremor heightened her uneasy state as she and Billy set out for the hilltop overlooking the three brick furnaces of Hazard Iron. It was a splendid evening, cloudless and warm. Thousands of stars were visible, breathtakingly bright from horizon to zenith, except where their glow was muted by phosphorescent light veils.

A peculiar acrid odor came drifting over the top of the hill they were climbing. The smell was borne on a thin, nearly invisible smoke. "What's burning?" she asked as they reached the summit, both slightly out of breath. They stood surrounded by thick clumps of laurel, the blooms white in the darkness.

Billy sniffed. "Don't know but it doesn't seem far away. Just down there. Wait here; I'll go see."

He scrambled down through more of the laurel. The blowing smoke thickened somewhat, and the strange, scorched odor increased. He felt the crater before he saw it; the heat washed against his face. Finally, with the help of the starlight, he perceived it—a pit nearly twelve feet across, black in the side of the hill. He could not see the meteorite itself, but he knew it was there.

"Nothing to fret about," he said when he returned to the crest. "The shooting star, or a piece of it, struck the hill."

She sheltered in his arms, trying to conceal her anxiety and her sense of isolation. Of course George and Constance always did their best to make her feel at home. She enjoyed the company of their children, and caring for them gave her something to do. Yet she had not really adapted to life in Pennsylvania, to the valley, its people, or their ways. The psalmist said the Lord protected the stranger, but she wasn't sure about that.

And now she could no longer contain her feelings.

"Billy, I'm frightened."

"Of the war?"

"Yes, and frightened of your leaving. I'm frightened of not knowing where you are or whether you're safe. I'm frightened of the townspeople and the way some of them look at me accusingly because I'm a Southerner. I'm frightened of everything. I'm so ashamed to admit that, but I can't help it!"

Her voice sounded faint, lacking the strength he always expected from her. Well, he was just as scared as she was. He had no idea where the Army would post him.

He did have a fair idea of what sort of duty lay in store, though. Engineers tore down the trees, prepared the roads, and built the pontoon bridges on which great armies advanced. Engineers went ahead of all the regular troops and were usually first within range of enemy guns.

"Everything's so uncertain," she was murmuring. "There's so much hate, so much joy at the prospect of killing. Sometimes I hardly see how any of us can survive."

"If we love each other enough, we can survive anything. So can our families. So can the country."

"Do you honestly believe that?"

"Yes, I do. Once when I was feeling low, George helped me by doing this." He broke off a sprig of laurel and put it in her hand. "The laurel thrives where other plants die. Mother always believed our family's like the laurel, and I expect yours is too. Strong enough, because there are a lot of us who love each other to live through anything."

She looked at the sprig with its small white flower, then tucked it into a pocket of her dress. "Thank you."

When he bent to kiss her face, he tasted her tears; but her voice did sound stronger.

"As soon as I know where I'll be stationed, and if it's possible to send for you, I will. We'll get through this all right."

She turned, kissed him again. "Oh, I love you, Billy Hazard."

"I love you, Brett. That's why we'll get through."

After another long kiss, she turned once more and rested comfortably with her back against his chest. They watched the stars while the spring wind gusted across the summit of the hill. The laurel tossed and murmured. Billy had spoken his hope, not his certainty. He knew full well the hope was fragile.

The darkness proved fragile, too. They faced away from the sprawl of Hazard Iron, but even so they soon grew conscious of its light all around them, a strengthening red glow that seemed to tinge the whole river valley. The lamps of the town grew dim behind it; some faded altogether.

Billy didn't want to look around or even acknowledge the existence of the factory, but it was unavoidable. The sanguinary glare from the three furnaces washed out the stars. He heard men shouting, working through the night in the smoke and the fire, to the earsplitting sound of steam engines strained to the limit.

He shut his eyes a moment. It didn't help. Scarlet light flowed over his wife's hair and shoulders. The vagaries of the wind surrounded them with smoke and fumes from the mill. The valley and the world seemed to fill with the noise of the great machinery hammering on, turning out the first of tons of iron for armor, for the Union, for war. The wind blended the smoke from Hazard's with that from the hillside where the meteorite had fallen, burning away the laurel as if it had never been.

Slavery brings the judgment of
heaven upon a country. As nations
cannot be rewarded or punished in
the next world, they must be in this.

GEORGE MASON OF VIRGINIA
1787

AFTERWORD

North and South is the first of three projected novels about a group of Americans caught up in the storm of events before, during, and after the Civil War.

Some would argue that the Old West is the essential American experience. It is probably the most romanticized. But for many others, the central experience of the still-unfolding story of our republic remains the War Between the States.

As Richard Pindell of the State University of New York wrote in an article on *Gone with the Wind*, it is, first and foremost, "entirely *our* war." Its causes reach back beyond Jefferson to the first white speculators who trod our shores. Its effects reverberate onward to the nineteen-fifties, sixties, seventies, and eighties like a storm that refuses to surrender its fury.

Out of the primary issues of slavery and secession there came glory, misery, and myth. Robert Penn Warren has said the war gave the North its treasury of righteousness and the South its great alibi. It also gave American blacks, if not freedom in fact, then at least the legal basis for freedom. To American families on both sides of the Mason-Dixon Line it gave an estimated 600,000 dead.

Historians say the war marks our national coming of age. A brief period of two decades taught us more about ourselves and American society than we had learned in all the years since the arrival of the first colonists. More, perhaps, than we cared to know.

And yet we remain fascinated with the period. We refight its great battles in books and articles, classrooms and discussion groups. We ponder its cautionary lessons or ignore them, and see its central issues still spilling blood in our streets. It is this power, this sometimes tragic outreach of past events, that attracted me to the subject, as it has attracted so many other writers and scholars.

Some interesting reactions have attended the preparation of this book. At a party not long after the subject was announced, a woman asked—and rather testily, I must say—"How can a Yankee presume to come down South and write about *us?*"

The last word bothered me. I wanted to reply that I thought of myself as an American, not a tub thumper for a particular region or cause. But I tried to give her a better answer: "The same way any professional writes about any period he didn't directly experience. By studying, walking the ground, trying to extend a storyteller's imagination into the minds and hearts of characters." So this may be a good place to comment on the book's historical content.

The primary purpose of *North and South* is to entertain. Still, I wanted the story to be an accurate reflection of the period; not so much a retelling of every last incident that contributed to the outbreak of war in Charleston harbor, but a fair presentation of prevailing attitudes and tensions on both sides.

There were, for example, voices like Cooper Main's here and there in the South. And when the cavalryman O'Dell speaks of the need to resettle new freedmen in Liberia, he is only saying what quite a few Northerners said—including, on occasion, Lincoln. Many who were strongly in favor of abolition did not believe blacks worthy or capable of full participation in American democracy; regrettable as that view may seem today, to distort it in a historical novel, or omit it altogether, would be a disservice to accuracy and to all those who have struggled so hard to change such attitudes.

Although I have tried to make the book historically correct, there have been minor alterations of the record in a few places. There has always been a reason for such alteration. A couple of examples should demonstrate.

Company K of the Second Cavalry Regiment served with distinction in Texas in the late 1850s. The officers and men of my Company K are, of necessity, fictitious, and so is the incident at Lantzman's—although it is not unlike those that actually took place during the period. Details of life and activity of this famous regiment are faithful to the record.

Sometimes I have made a change for reasons other than the requirements of the story. In memoirs of West Point life written in the last century, for instance, the plural form of demerit is spelled the same way—demerit. I added an *s* because in a contemporary book, the correct spelling looks like an error.

Another question I heard during the writing—this one, too, occasionally put forth with a distinct edge—was this: "And which side do *you* take?"

I never answered because I always found it the wrong question. I see only one worthy "side"—the side of those who suffered. The side of those who lost their lives in battle, and those who lost their lives more slowly, but no less surely, in bondage.

Here we confront another great lure of the subject: its fascinating and tragic paradox. The schism should not have happened, and it had to happen. But that is my interpretation; as one historian has said, "Every man creates his own Civil War." The statement helps explain the fascination of the conflict, not only for Americans but for millions of others around the world.

It is time to pay some debts. A great many people played a part in the preparation of this book. Foremost among them are two editors— Carol Hill, who helped shape the plan, and Julian Muller, who did the same for the manuscript. The work of each was invaluable.

For assistance with research I must especially cite the Library of the United States Military Academy, West Point, and particularly the map and manuscript librarian, Mrs. Marie Capps.

The reigning expert on the Academy in the mid-nineteenth century is, I think, Professor James Morrison of the history department at York College of Pennsylvania. Professor Morrison is also a former Army officer and West Point faculty member. He answered many questions he doubtless found naive and spent precious time providing me with a copy of the Tidball Manuscript—a memoir of life at the Academy by Cadet John C. Tidball, class of 1848.

Tidball's narrative deserves publication and widespread attention. If professional historians wrote with a fraction of the color, humor, and humanity of this nineteenth-century soldier, history would be a more attractive study to many more people. At the end of the handwritten Tidball papers, I found myself wishing I had known the man. I know I would have liked him.

The Beaufort County, South Carolina, Library and its branch on Hilton Head Island were once again of inestimable help in locating scores of obscure source materials. I owe special thanks to Ms. Marf Shopmyer, who kept faithful track of my seemingly endless requests for books, documents, periodicals, and newspapers of, and dealing with, the period of the story. Appreciation is also due to the cooperative staff of the South Carolina State Library, Columbia; I have seen few research libraries to equal it.

My thanks to Rose Ann Ferrick, who once again brought not only superior typing ability to a heavily marked manuscript, but sharp-eyed and frequently witty editorial judgment, too.

Having acknowledged the assistance I received, I must now stress that no person or institution cited should be held accountable for anything in the book. The story, and any errors of fact or opinion, are solely my responsibility.

The late Bruce Catton gave us writing about the Civil War that is without equal. Since first reading Catton, I have never forgotten his metaphor "the undigestible lump of slavery." So much said in just five words. I have made free use of the metaphor in the book and here acknowledge that fact.

The good counsel and good humor of my attorney, Frank Curtis, have been a source of strength and cheer. I also owe a special debt to Mike and Judi, whose friendship I prize and whose kindness helped me through dark days that inevitably accompany any long stretch of creative work. I don't expect they know how much they buoyed me, which is why I thank them now.

Lastly, I thank Bill Jovanovich for his continuing interest in the project, and my wife, Rachel, for her never-ending support and affection.

JOHN JAKES

Hilton Head Island
August 24, 1981